Companions

Peter Darman

I would like to thank the following people whose assistance has been integral to the creation of this work:
Julia, for her invaluable help and guidance with the text.
'Big John', for designing the cover.
Alamy Limited for the cover image.

List of principal characters

Those marked with an asterisk * are Companions – individuals who fought with Spartacus in Italy and who travelled back to Parthia with Pacorus.

Those marked with a dagger † are known to history.

The Kingdom of Dura

*Alcaeus: Greek physician and chief of the medical corps in the army of Dura

*Arminius: German, former gladiator and now a centurion in the army of Dura

*Byrd: Cappodocian scout in the army of Dura

Dobbai: Scythian mystic, formerly the sorceress of King of Kings Sinatruces, now resident at Dura

*Drenis: Thracian, former gladiator in Italy and now a centurion in the army of Dura

*Gallia: Gaul, Queen of Dura

* Godarz: Parthian governor of Dura

*Lucius Domitus: Roman soldier, former slave and now the commander of the army of Dura

*Pacorus: Parthian King of Dura

Rsan: Parthian governor of Dura

†Surena: a native of the Ma'adan and an officer in the army of Dura

*Vagharsh: Parthian soldier who carries the banner of Pacorus in the army of Dura

The Kingdom of Hatra

*Diana: former Roman slave, now the wife of Gafarn and princess of Hatra

*Gafarn: former Bedouin slave of Pacorus, now a prince of Hatra

Other Parthians

*Nergal: Hatran soldier and formerly commander of Dura's horse archers, now the King of Mesene

†Orodes: Prince of Susiana, now an exile at Dura

*Praxima: Spaniard, former Roman slave and now the wife of Nergal and Queen of Mesene

Non-Parthians
†Akrosas: Thracian, king of the Getea tribe
Athineos: Cretan sea captain
†*Burebista: Dacian gladiator
Cleon: Greek patriot
Decebal: Dacian king
Draco: Thracian, king of the Maedi tribe
Hippo: High Priestess at the Temple of Artemis, Ephesus
Kallias: High Priest at the Temple of Artemis, Ephesus
Malik: Agraci prince, son of Haytham
Marcus Aristius: Roman tribune
†Quintus Caecilius Metellus: Roman governor of Ephesus
Radu: Thracian, king of the Bastarnae tribe
Timini Ceukianus: senior *editor* of the games at Ephesus

Introduction

'Halt!'

Asher pulled on the reins to stop the mule as it walked past the open gates into the Citadel. He smiled politely at the burly centurion who had been standing to one side outside the guard room, two more mail-clad guards armed with spears walking in front of his beast to prevent it going any further. One grabbed its reins and looked with disinterest as the centurion halted a few paces from him.

'Get down and state your business.'

Asher smiled politely and alighted from the driver's seat. He unconsciously fidgeted with one of his long side curls as he did so.

'You are a Jew?' said the centurion, a note of condescension in his voice.

Asher smiled politely again. 'Indeed, sir.'

He pointed to a beautiful cedar box positioned in the rear of his cart.

'I have an appointment with the queen, regarding some documents of her father's.'

The centurion's ears pricked up. 'King Pacorus?'

Asher placed his hands together and nodded solemnly. 'Indeed, God rest his soul.'

The centurion must have been at least six inches taller than Asher, and was twice as wide as the lean Jew standing before him. Dura's army may not have been the force it once was but its soldiers were still a credit to the kingdom, their weapons and armour the finest that money could buy and their discipline legendary. The spirit of the old king lived on, Asher thought. The centurion's helmet was burnished and sported a magnificent white transverse crest that indicated his rank, as did the silver greaves that covered his shins. He carried a short sword at his left hip and a dagger in a sheath on his right hip, though Asher noticed that the ordinary soldiers by his mule carried swords in scabbards that hung on their right sides. No doubt one of the many idiosyncrasies associated with military life.

The centurion tapped the vine cane he was holding against his right thigh. He turned and shouted towards the office.

'There's a Jew here says he has business with the queen.'

He turned back to Asher.

'Name?'

'Asher, sir.'

'Says his name is Asher.'

A clerk dressed in a plain grey tunic came from the office.

'Asher, grandson of Aaron, is listed as having an appointment with the queen, centurion.'

The centurion waved the clerk back to his office and pointed his cane at the box in the back of the cart.

'Open it.'

'It is for the queen,' protested Asher.

The centurion casually rested his left hand on the top of his sword but said nothing. Asher understood the implied threat well enough.

'It might be full of snakes or scorpions,' said the centurion. 'You might be an assassin sent by one of the queen's enemies to murder her. Can't have that. Now open it.'

'Does the queen have any enemies?' said Asher, trying to lighten the mood.

The centurion's dark eyes narrowed as he moved menacingly closer. Asher smiled once more and scurried to the rear of the cart, pulling the box towards him and opening the lid. Inside were rolls of papyrus, half a dozen of them arranged side by side.

'As you can see, sir, no snakes.'

'Take them out,' ordered the centurion.

Asher was going to protest but thought better of it. So he took each roll out of the box and laid them beside it. The centurion placed his cane on the cart and picked up the box, holding it aloft and shaking it a few times. Satisfied, he placed it back on the cart and walked off.

'Let him pass,' he ordered the guards who retook their positions at the gates. They rested their oblong shields on the ground as Asher replaced the rolls in the box, secured the lid and climbed into the driver's seat. He ordered the mule to walk forward and nodded his head at the guards as he passed. They ignored him as he entered the courtyard of Dura's Citadel. On his right was a large barracks block that occupied almost the whole southern wall, and beyond it the great stables where the warhorses of the cataphracts were housed. He felt strange to be back in this place, where once he had been a frequent visitor when his grandfather had been the kingdom's treasurer. That seemed like another life.

He halted the cart at the foot of the stone steps leading to the entrance porch of the palace. Guards standing sentry by the stone columns ignored him as he walked up the steps carrying the cedar box. How much history had been made on these steps? He stopped and turned to look at the open gates. Once kings rode from those gates to decide the fate of empires.

'The queen awaits.'

He snapped out of his musings to see a short, elderly man with thinning hair dressed in a long white robe with red leather sandals on his feet standing at the top of the steps. He had an imperious air and waved Asher forward with his right hand. He turned and walked into the porch, Asher hastening up the steps to follow. They passed more guards in the reception hall that led to the throne room, the doors to which were closed. The steward turned and pointed at the box Asher was holding.

'I will take that.'

Slightly taken aback by his brusque manner, Asher frowned but handed over the box. He was beginning to regret his visit to the palace. It was well known that the queen could be testy and short-tempered but it appeared that her staff shared the same attributes. It was most tiresome. More pleasing was the agreeable aroma of myrrh that filled the hall, the incense being burned in the stands either side of the doors to the throne room. The steward turned and ordered him to follow as one of the guards opened a door and they both entered Dura's centre of power.

Light lanced into the chamber through small windows set high in the walls, their footsteps on the stone tiles the only sound as they made their way to the far end where Queen Claudia sat on her high-backed throne. Once there had been two thrones on the stone dais when King Pacorus and Queen Gallia had ruled Dura but the latter had been dead for many years and the old king had renounced his powers long before his recent demise. Those powers had been inherited by the middle-aged woman sitting before him, who observed him like a spider watches its prey. He bowed his head to her.

'Hail, Queen Claudia.'

Her lip curled lightly in acknowledgement as her dark eyes watched the fussy steward place the cedar box on the floor in front of the dais. Once he had done so she waved him away with a curt swipe of her hand. He walked backwards across the tiles, bowing his head as he did so, being careful not to fall over as he withdrew from the queen's presence. There was a time when Princess Claudia was reckoned a great beauty, having inherited her mother's lithe frame, thick locks and high cheekbones. But that was long ago. Now those locks, though still thick, were as dark as night and her once beautiful face had taken on a severe countenance. Her mother had dressed in white and blue and had worn dazzling gold jewellery that complemented her great beauty and blonde hair. But her eldest daughter wore no adornments and dressed entirely in black, thus increasing her intimidating appearance.

Her black eyes continued to study him as the steward left the chamber and the door was closed. To avert her uncomfortable gaze he looked up at the standard hanging on the wall above the dais behind her. The large square banner was white with gold edging and sported a red griffin. It had accompanied Dura's army on many campaigns down the years but looked as though it had been made yesterday. Asher blinked and took a closer look. It appeared pristine though he knew this could not be. Perhaps his eyes were failing him.

'Asher, grandson of Aaron.'

The queen's words made him jump. He smiled and bowed to her.

'Your servant, majesty.'

She pointed a bony finger at the cedar box.

'You said you had something that concerned my father. Is that it?'

Asher nodded. 'We all grieve for you, majesty. It is hard to believe that the king is dead.'

Her face remained an emotionless mask. 'He was lonely in his autumn years. He is with my mother now.'

The notion that the queen might now be lonely flashed through his mind, but he remembered that she had always refused any suitors. And so rumour had it she had her mystics and sorcerers that always surrounded her. Today though, only her Amazon guards surrounded her. As a boy he had remembered them as long-haired beauties attired in mail and white tunics. But today, though they still wore mail armour, their black tunics and leggings gave them the appearance of demons of the underworld. Perhaps that was the idea. Those closest to the queen rested the tips of their swords, made of the magical Ukku steel, on the floor. The others lining the walls had their swords in their scabbards.

There was a time when the Amazons rode into battle beside Queen Gallia but now they did little fighting. Their task was to protect their queen who rarely left the confines of the Citadel, let alone the city. Of course they still practised with their bows on the shooting ranges outside the city, but unkind rumours circulated that the queen used them as assassins on occasion and had trained them to use magic against her enemies.

'What is in the box?' asked the queen.

Asher smiled, bent down and lifted the lid to reveal the papyrus rolls.

'Before he died my grandfather suggested to your father, the king, that he record his experiences for posterity. At first the king was reluctant, afraid perhaps that his memory would fail him, which would lead him to omit important details. But my grandfather persisted; employing scribes to write down what your father told them. After a while the king became accustomed to dictating his experiences and took to the task with relish.'

Asher held out a hand towards the box. 'These are the result. Or at least what we have discovered so far.'

The queen rose from her throne and stepped off the dais, stooping to pick up one of the scrolls.

'So far?'

'Yes, majesty,' replied Asher. 'My grandfather left a mountain of documents that my family have yet to go through. I myself have had little time to catalogue them, being swamped by business matters.'

The queen carefully placed the scroll back in the box and returned to her throne. She waved over one of her guards.

'Take it to the terrace.'

The Amazon bowed, replaced the lid and took the box from the chamber, disappearing through a door that led to the palace's private quarters.

'And what business would that be, Asher, grandson of Aaron?'

'Papyrus, majesty,' replied Asher. 'My family owns a plantation to the north of the city.'

The papyrus plant is a reed that grows in marshy areas around rivers, and whereas it was forbidden to create marshes near the city, further upstream the crown gave licences to businessmen that allowed them to create artificial marshes where papyrus could be grown. Such areas attracted mosquitoes and disease and the workers who harvested the reed often succumbed to illnesses. But the trade was lucrative for papyrus was in great demand throughout the Parthian Empire and beyond.

'And business is good?' enquired the queen.

Asher smiled. 'Very good, majesty.'

'Tishtrya has smiled on you, has she not?'

'Tishtrya, majesty?'

'The Goddess of Rainfall and Fertility who fills the Euphrates with water and provides you with the marshes where you grow your papyrus.'

The queen stared at his curly side hair.

'You follow the same religion as your grandfather, grandson of Aaron?'

Asher nodded. 'Yes, majesty.'

'You believe that there is only one god?'

'That is what my religion teaches, majesty,' answered a now sweating Asher. He knew all too well that the queen was the protégé of Dobbai, the sorceress who had befriended King Pacorus and Queen Gallia and who had hated his grandfather. Many of his faith had feared persecution when the old king had died, but thus far it had mercifully failed to materialise.

The queen nodded. 'Well, my father always believed that Dura should be a kingdom where men and women were free to worship what gods they chose to follow.'

10

'He was a great man, majesty,' said Asher.

'Thank you. You may go.'

A relieved Asher bowed deeply to her, turned on his heels and quickly made his exit. Halfway across the tiles the queen called after him.

'You will of course send any further documents pertaining to my father to the palace.'

He stopped, turned and bowed again.

'You can count on it, majesty.'

He breathed a deep sigh of relief when he left the Citadel. Normally a hard-headed businessman, he had been unnerved meeting the queen. Perhaps it was her remoteness, the aggressiveness of her guards or the air of foreboding bordering on malevolence that hung over the entire Citadel. Or perhaps it had been nothing more than a figment of his imagination. After all, Dura had been good to him and his family. He lived with his wife and children in a mansion inside the city. He and his relatives were free to follow their religion and the kingdom's soldiers ensured that his business and its workers were unmolested. The bureaucracy put in place by his grandfather and his friend Rsan, who had been the governor of the city, ensured that taxes were collected with the minimum of corruption. And for her part the queen ensured that the defences of the kingdom were maintained. Trade flourished, taxes were well spent – if such a thing was not a contradiction in terms – and the kingdom prospered.

He pulled up his mule and looked back up at the Citadel atop the rock escarpment where it stood like an eagle guarding its nest, or griffin for that matter. Around him the main street that led from the Citadel to the Palmyrene Gate was heaving with people, camels, carts and people. He prayed to God that Dura would continue to prosper now that King Pacorus was dead.

Behind the palace's throne room, reached via a corridor in the private quarters, was a large terrace that sat atop the high rock escarpment upon which the Citadel was built. It overlooked the blue waters of the River Euphrates below and the lands east of the river. Across the waterway was Hatran territory, which was formerly ruled by King Gafarn before his death. It was now the realm of his son, King Pacorus, named in

11

honour of the man who had made the Kingdom of Dura such a force in the empire.

Claudia settled herself down in the large wicker chair on the terrace, the same chair that had belonged to Dobbai, the mystic who had been the sorceress of King of Kings Sinatruces, to date the greatest supreme ruler that the Parthian Empire had ever known. Claudia smiled as she recounted the tales that Dobbai had told her of Sinatruces when she had been a small girl. How he had coveted her mother, Gallia, but had been outwitted by Dobbai into giving Pacorus a kingdom all of his own and keeping her mother out of the amorous embrace of the king of kings. As a male servant placed the box of scrolls on the table nearby and bowed, Claudia remembered the days of her childhood. Of the frequent gatherings on this very terrace that were held to decide the fate of Dura and the empire. She remembered the fierce black-robed Haytham, king of the Agraci, his son Malik and his daughter Rasha. The stern and uncompromising Lucius Domitus, commander of Dura's army. The lanky, smiling Nergal and his red-headed wife Praxima, the dear friends of his parents who went on to become living gods at Uruk. But it was Dobbai she remembered the most, the one who had helped to bring her into the world and who instructed her in the ancient knowledge of spells and charms and how to catch glimpses of the workings of the gods.

She picked up one of the scrolls and looked up to see the land bathed in sunlight. Across the river the road to the two pontoon bridges that spanned the Euphrates, giving access to the city, was full of camels, mules and carts. An endless stream of commerce that coursed both east and west to satisfy Rome's and Egypt's insatiable desire for silk, the luxurious material produced far to the east in China. The latter sent other products west, of course – ironware, medicines, bronze mirrors, and farming and metallurgical techniques – but it was the demand for silk that gave the great trading route its name. The commerce was not just one-way: camel trains transported alfalfa, grape, flax, pomegranate, walnut and cucumber to China. The rulers of the latter also had a taste for more exotic goods from the west: peacocks, elephants and lions. So every day camel trains criss-crossed Parthia loaded with goods, every one paying small dues for safe conduct along the Silk Road.

The latter was the lifeblood of the empire just as it was for Dura's prosperity.

Claudia glanced at another wicker chair a few paces away, the one her father had sat in every day as the sun began its descent in the western sky and the temperature on the terrace became bearable. She smiled at the memory of him laying his aching left leg on a padded foot rest as he told her that his greatest achievement was not on the battlefield but securing peace with the Agraci that meant the trade caravans could travel west from Dura to the oasis city of Palmyra and on to Syria and Egypt. Prior to this historic agreement the Kingdom of Dura and its wild lords had been at war with the Agraci but her father's peace with Haytham had changed everything. She smiled as she remembered Haytham himself sitting on this terrace, a thing once thought impossible. They were good times, even though her memory of them was as a young girl.

She unfolded the papyrus roll on the table. Because it had been used for a long work the text was written horizontally along the roll and divided into columns. She began to read the neatly written words, keeping a segment of the roll flat in front of her, the ends on the left and right rolled up for convenience. The writing was not her father's but as she began reading the words she soon heard his voice in her head, recording an episode from the early years of his reign as the King of Dura.

As the gods have decreed that I will have to wait a while longer before I can join my dear, beloved wife in the afterlife, and to put an end to the incessant nagging of Aaron, my aged treasurer, I have decided to record a number of my experiences so that posterity will remember me. Or at least that is what Aaron has told me. I actually think that my miserable attempts at being a scribe will be quickly forgotten, notwithstanding that Aaron has provided me with enthusiastic, attentive scribes to write down my words. They will write in Greek because Aaron has told me that all the great books of history are written in that language and therefore stand more chance of being read by future generations. I am not confident that the next generation of Dura's citizens will be interested in my ramblings, let alone future generations. But for the sake of putting an end to Aaron's hounding I have decided to become a scribbler.

When I first suggested the topic of this work Aaron began his pestering again, insisting that it was not a suitable subject for the reminiscences of a king. But I politely informed him that after having finally surrendered to his demands to write about my life, I should at least be free to choose the subjects. I suggested that perhaps it would be better if I acted as his scribe and committed to papyrus the experiences of his long life. Whereupon he became irritable and said that sarcasm did not suit me. But he said no more on the matter and so I began this tale of an episode that took place many years ago and even after this great passage of time still seems remarkable. Because it has been so long and because so much has happened in the intervening years, I hope I have remembered the sequence of events accurately. Those who took part deserve that at the very least.

Chapter 1

Phraates was dead.

My father had arrived at Dura with this sad news just before the army had arrived back from its campaign in Mesene that had seen King Chosroes deposed and Nergal and Praxima installed in his place. Chosroes had joined the faction of Narses and Mithridates and had attempted to capture Dura itself, but not before he had endeavoured to have me executed. His plans had come to nothing, however, and his army had been defeated before the walls of my city. He had scurried back to his capital at Uruk and I had followed him. The army's machines had breached Uruk's ancient walls and we had stormed the city. Chosroes had taken his own life rather than be captured and so a new era had begun in Mesene.

I had been in high spirits on the march back to Dura but the news of Phraates' death had saddened me greatly. In truth he had not been a great high king; indeed, some might say that he had been a weak and vacillating one who had been responsible for the outbreak of civil war in the empire. But he had always been generous to Dura and its king, making me lord high general of the empire after the great victory over Narses at Surkh and giving me a large amount of gold as a reward after the battle. The treasure had allowed me to speed up the strengthening of Dura's army, which had been fortuitous as I was able to use it to destroy a Roman army that had invaded my kingdom. I was thus indebted to Phraates and even though he had, as a result of the machinations of his poisonous son Mithridates and his scheming wife Aruna, subsequently stripped me of the rank of lord high general, I would always regard Phraates with affection and respect.

'Really? Even though he made you look like a fool at Ctesiphon, sent you off on a fool's errand into Mesene that nearly resulted in your death, and sat idly by while Chosroes and the soldiers of Persis tried to reduce your city to rubble?'

Dobbai was rubbing her hands with relish as she recounted the slights that Phraates had dealt me, or so she believed. I was standing at the foot of the palace steps and was about to hand a note I had written the day before to a courier who waited beside his horse.

'This is not the time nor place to discuss matters of high strategy,' I told her.

She cackled as she descended the steps and pointed a bony finger at the leather tube that held the note.

'What's that?'

'Nothing.'

'For the king himself to be busying himself with handing a document to a courier would suggest that it is far from nothing.'

I cast her a sideways glance. 'It is a letter to the one who masquerades as the king of kings, if you must know.'

She raised an eyebrow. 'An invitation to a feast, perhaps?'

I chuckled. 'Hardly.'

'May I see it?'

I was tempted to hand the message to the courier so he could be on his way. However, I had to admit that I was rather pleased with myself concerning what I had written, believing it most erudite. I shrugged and passed it instead to Dobbai. She opened the case and extracted the letter, her hawk-like eyes darting over the text:

To King Mithridates

Word has recently reached me that your father, King Phraates, has died of a broken heart. It indeed breaks my heart to think that such a good man has departed this world, and sickens me greatly that the one who was the cause of his death has stolen his crown and now dares to call himself the King of Kings.

I have also heard that you hold me responsible for your father's death, and have used this lie to deceive numerous other kings of the empire into electing you to your present high office. And now you seek to make yourself master of all the Parthian Empire, but I have to tell you that while I still live you will never know peace. For you are a poison at the very heart of the empire, and every day that you sit upon the throne Parthia dies a little.

The only cure for the empire is to remove this ulcer, this rottenness, and that includes your lackey Narses, another traitor who fouls the empire by his mere existence. I will not rest until you and he have suffered the same fate as those other traitors Porus and Chosroes. This I swear by all that is sacred.

I remain, your implacable enemy.

16

Dobbai said nothing as she rolled up the letter, carefully inserted it into the tubular case and handed it to the courier.

'It is to get to Ctesiphon as speedily as possible,' I told him.

He placed the case in a leather pouch slung over his shoulder. 'Yes, majesty.'

He vaulted into the saddle, turned his horse and trotted from the courtyard, the iron shoes on his horse's hooves clattering on the flagstones. I watched him exit the gates and smiled to myself. He would ride over the pontoon bridge across the Euphrates and head southeast towards the great sprawling palace complex at Ctesiphon, the political heart of the empire, located on the eastern bank of the River Tigris. The courier would probably reach the court of Mithridates in around five or six days, making use of the post stations that could be found throughout the empire. Simple mud-brick buildings surrounded by a wall with stables attached, they held fresh horses where couriers could pick up a new mount before proceeding to the next station. Established along all the main roads in the empire, usually thirty miles or so apart, they greatly facilitated communications within Parthia.

'And now we wait,' I said.

'Wait for what?' asked Dobbai.

I walked back up the steps towards the palace, Dobbai trailing after me.

'For Mithridates and Narses to march against me, of course. They will not be able to ignore such a challenge.'

Dobbai cackled as we walked through the colonnaded porch into the palace's reception hall, guards snapping to attention as we passed and court officials bowing their heads.

'You think that they will risk their lives fighting you, son of Hatra?'

We walked into the empty throne room, my griffin banner hanging on the wall behind the two thrones on the dais.

'I have issued a challenge and they will not be able to ignore me.'

Our footsteps echoed on the stone tiles as we walked to the door at the far end that led to the palace's private quarters. I opened it and went through into the corridor that led to the bedrooms where we slept. There was a small guardroom at the corridor's entrance and another door opposite that led to the palace terrace. Servants on their knees were scrubbing the floor and two guards stood sentry outside the guardroom. They brought their spears to their chests in salute as I passed and the servants stood up and bowed their heads as I walked on to the balcony.

'You are wrong, son of Hatra,' said Dobbai as she walked over to her wicker chair and sat in it.

It was going to be another blisteringly hot day, the sun already roasting the Citadel from a clear blue sky. More servants arranged a sunshade over Dobbai and offered her cool fruit juice as I too took a seat and stretched out my legs. The terrace faced east so the Citadel could welcome the rising of the sun each morning and the journey of Shamash, Lord of the Sun who blessed the earth with warmth and life each day.

A nursemaid brought Claudia, my young daughter, from the nursery, holding her hand as the infant gingerly placed one foot in front of the other. Her eyes lit up when she saw me and I swept her up in my arms, kissing her on the cheek.

'You are the one who is wrong,' I told her as Claudia saw Dobbai and held out her arms imploringly to the old woman. Even at this tender age there was a strong bond between the two. I took Claudia over to the old witch and placed her in her lap. She may have had a haggard, fearsome visage but Dobbai was remarkably tender and affectionate with Claudia, who soon began to close her eyes. I dismissed the nursemaid.

'Narses and Mithridates will not be able to resist raising an army and marching against me,' I announced. 'And just like I did with Chosroes I will defeat them both before the walls of this city and send their heads back to Ctesiphon as a present for Queen Aruna.'

Dobbai took a sip of her juice.

'You have it all worked out, don't you? You will kill Narses and Mithridates just like you did Porus and Chosroes, peace will return to the empire and you will be instrumental in choosing a new king of kings, one more to your liking.'

I emptied a cup of juice. 'Why not? We all want peace in the empire and there can be none while Mithridates and his pet dog rule at Ctesiphon.'

Gallia appeared on the terrace after her early morning training session with the Amazons. Every morning it was the same. She would rise early and ride from the city with her guards to the training grounds south of the city to practise shooting from the saddle at different sized targets. The training also involved riding fast at melons placed on top of posts and slicing them open with sword strikes. Despite having changed into baggy leggings and a new white tunic her cheeks were still flushed and she was wiping her neck with a towel. Her blonde hair was arranged in a single plait down her back to make wearing a helmet more comfortable. She gladly accepted a cup of juice from a servant before kissing Claudia and flopping down in a chair.

'I swear it gets hotter each day,' she complained.

She looked at me. 'I did not see you at the training fields earlier.'

As well as the Amazons the training fields were also used by Dura's horse archers and cataphracts, and the early morning hours were very busy as officers endeavoured to put their men through their paces before the fierce midday heat arrived.

'I had no time today. Affairs of state.'

Dobbai chortled. 'What he means is that he is endeavouring to provoke Mithridates.'

Gallia emptied her cup and looked at me. 'Provoke Mithridates?'

'Your husband has written a letter to the high king informing him that he is a malignant poison that should be removed from the empire,' stated Dobbai before I could reply. 'By doing so he hopes that Mithridates, filled with wrath, will raise a multitude and march against Dura, thereby granting the King of Dura another opportunity to employ his fearsome army on the battlefield. Have I summed up your intentions succinctly, son of Hatra?'

'We all know that Mithridates and Narses are thieves and murderers,' I said. 'The world would be a better place without them.'

Gallia appeared underwhelmed. 'Why should they dance to your tune?'

Dobbai chuckled. 'The crux of the matter.'

I looked at my wife. 'Why? Because I have insulted the office of high king, that is why. Once Mithridates has received my insult the eyes of the empire will be upon Ctesiphon, watching to see what actions he takes.'

'Or he could ignore you,' said Gallia.

'A more preferable option for our devious high king, I think,' added Dobbai.

I tapped my nose with a finger. 'He cannot do that. The office of high king will mean he has to answer my provocation if the holder wishes to maintain credibility in the eyes of the empire.'

Dobbai looked at Gallia and rolled her eyes.

'What a ridiculously romantic fool you are, son of Hatra. I doubt that Mithridates has even considered what the office of high king entails, aside from the prospect of great wealth and power. You think your insult will provoke a response? It will, though not the one you expect. But if you think that Mithridates will march against you then you will be disappointed.'

'He is a coward,' I sneered.

'And worse,' agreed Dobbai. 'But consider this. The other kings of the empire may despise and ridicule Mithridates but he has achieved something that they all crave.'

I looked at Gallia whose face wore a confused expression. Dobbai stroked the forehead of the sleeping Claudia.

'He has brought peace to the empire, admittedly of a sorts. But from the Indus to the Euphrates there is now a general peace.'

'Peace?' I scoffed. 'What sort of peace is it where the Romans occupy the Kingdom of Gordyene, once the domain of King Balas? Where the traitor Narses helps himself to the Kingdom of Sakastan and the high king tries to barter away my own kingdom to Rome?'

'The one where there is no war,' replied Dobbai casually. 'Your experiences with the kings of the empire must have made you realise that only you among them have a relish for war.

Phraates, poor fool that he was, recognised it straight away. That is why he made you lord high general.'

'I do not relish war,' I insisted.

'But war relishes you, son of Hatra. Have you ever wondered why it has been relatively easy for you to turn the backwater of Dura into one of the most feared kingdoms of the Parthian Empire?'

I had to admit that I had given the subject no thought. I shrugged indifferently.

'It is because you are beloved of the gods, son of Hatra. Your path was determined long before took your first steps. The immortals have made things easier for you.'

'Everything I have achieved I have done so by my own efforts,' I snapped.

Dobbai continued to stroke my daughter's head. 'Let us for the moment leave to one side the fact that you were born into the Hatran royal family, rulers of one of the empire's richest cities that has one of Parthia's most formidable armies.'

Gallia laughed but I saw nothing amusing in Dobbai's comments.

'Many men who are born into wealth and power end up as fat, licentious tyrants,' I said.

'Then consider this,' continued Dobbai. 'Do you not think it strange that in your first battle you managed to capture a Roman eagle, which the commander of your army informs me is a wondrous thing? And then you get yourself captured by the Romans and shipped to their homeland. But instead of ending your days as one of their slaves you are rescued and become a great warlord in an army of slaves. Now Lucius Domitus has also informed me that when the slave army was crushed the survivors were nailed to crosses as an example of what happens when slaves rebel. But you miraculously manage to escape the Romans and return to Parthia. Do you think all these things are mere coincidences or just an endless stream of luck?'

'If the gods truly love me as you say,' I replied, 'then they would have given Spartacus victory over the Romans.'

'Don't be petulant, son of Hatra. It is not proper that slaves should be running around slitting their masters' throats. It is against the natural order of things. Would you wish to see

21

the slaves in your own parents' palace rise up and slaughter Hatra's royalty?'

I said nothing.

'I thought not,' said Dobbai smugly.

'Mithridates will not march against you, Pacorus,' said Gallia. 'You defeated him and Narses at Surkh, you destroyed the army of Porus before that and your army still has blood on its swords after defeating the Romans and Chosroes. Only a fool would lead an army against you.'

'You are wise, child,' said Dobbai. She gave me a sly glance.

'Of course you could always take your army to Ctesiphon if you are at a loose end.'

I was appalled by the idea. 'I will not instigate hostilities. Besides, to do so would entail marching through Hatran and Babylonian territory and I will not violate the territorial integrity of those two kingdoms.'

'Well, then,' said Dobbai. 'You had better find something else to amuse yourself with for I tell you now that the sun will fall from the heavens before Mithridates marches against you.'

The city council was underwhelmed by my announcement that I had written to the high king, challenging his rule in the hope that he would take the field against me. As usual we met in the headquarters building that was opposite the palace in the Citadel. It was the official office of Lucius Domitus, the commander of the army, who liked to reside in the command tent in the legionary camp immediately west of the Palmyrene Gate. But the headquarters building was never empty, being the location of the army's records where clerks worked administering its business. Now he was sitting in a chair in the spacious room looking out onto the courtyard that we used for the meetings of the city council, as usual toying with his dagger, occasionally staring out of one of the open windows when a detail of soldiers marched or rode by.

Lucius Domitus looked as though he had been carved out of a block of granite, there being not an ounce of fat on his stocky frame. He was as fighting fit as the army he led and I could tell that he would rather be leading a twenty-mile route march than be sitting in this room.

'And so I expect our new high king to march against Dura as soon as he receives my letter.'

I was expecting a reaction but there was silence. Domitus was trying to balance the point of his dagger on the end of a finger and Rsan, the city treasurer, had clasped his hands together and was staring at the smooth surface on the table we were sitting round. The lean, cropped-haired city governor, Godarz, wore a confused expression while Orodes, Prince of Susiana and step-brother of Mithridates, who had been banished by the new high king, stared blankly out of the window.

Eventually the prince looked at me and shook his head.

'He will not come, Pacorus. He will regard your insults and provocations as small prices to pay if it means Dura's army stays on the western bank of the Euphrates and leaves him and Narses free to rule the empire.'

Domitus frowned as the dagger fell and clattered on the floor.

'I hope I have your attention, Domitus,' I said.

He picked up the blade and slipped it back into its sheath.

'You want to kill Mithridates? Then let us take the army across the Euphrates to Ctesiphon and storm the place. Simple.'

Orodes' mouth opened in horror. 'Whatever we think of Mithridates, he has been elected high king by a majority of the kings in the empire. To march against him would plunge the empire into civil strife once more.'

'I will not be marching against Ctesiphon,' I reassured him. 'I have no wish to incite another civil war.'

Domitus grunted. 'Orodes' brother is a coward. You will have a long wait.'

'My *step-brother*,' Orodes reminded the army's commander. He was always keen to emphasise that though they shared the same father they had two different mothers.

I pointed at Rsan. 'We will be withholding the annual tribute to Ctesiphon until further notice. Let us see how the king of kings likes that.'

The tribute was a yearly payment of gold that every Parthian kingdom sent to the treasury at Ctesiphon, based on the number of horse archers every king could raise.

23

Rsan appeared alarmed. 'Is that wise, majesty?'

'Very wise,' I replied. 'I would rather use the gold to raise and maintain my own soldiers than see Dura's money being spent by Mithridates.'

Domitus laughed. 'First sensible thing you have said all day. But it still won't provoke Mithridates or Narses. What is the King of Persis doing, anyway?'

Godarz ran a hand over his crown. 'The reports garnered from the trade caravans is that he has returned to Persepolis, prior to marching east to consolidate his new kingdom.'

I had won a great victory over Porus of Sakastan and his elephants prior to the even greater victory at Surkh. But it continually irked me that so complete had been my victory over Porus that his kingdom, Sakastan, had a vacant throne, his sons also being killed in the battle near the Euphrates. Sakastan was located immediately east of Persis and following Narses' intrigues he had been given the crown of Sakastan by Mithridates. Thus did Narses become the king of both kingdoms thanks to my actions.

Dobbai opened her eyes. 'Narses plays the great king and will amuse himself in his new domain for a while. He is no fool and knows that to offer battle to you, son of Hatra, will result in his defeat and possible death. As such the prospect offers little attraction. However, that does not mean he will not try to strike at you.'

'Or those closest to you,' said Gallia.

Everyone looked at her.

'You fear an attempt on your life?' said Godarz with concern.

Gallia shook her head. 'Not me, or indeed anyone here, but there are others who are vulnerable.'

I wracked my brains. 'Who?'

'Nergal and Praxima,' she replied.

Before I had stormed Uruk I had made plans to install an ally on Mesene's throne, and in the aftermath of my victory had asked Nergal, the former commander of my horsemen, to become King of Mesene. I had promised that Dura would always support him until he was able to rebuild his kingdom's army. Gallia had vehemently opposed the idea, believing that

Nergal and Praxima would be too isolated and vulnerable at Uruk.

I pointed at the hide map of the empire on the wall behind me.

'You are right, my love, that Mithridates could strike at Mesene from Susiana, but if he did then we would receive intelligence from Babylon and Elymais, which would give us time to reinforce Nergal.'

Gallia stood and walked over to the map, pulling her dagger from her right boot. She rested the point at Susa and then pointed it at Uruk.

'Mithridates is closer to Uruk than we are and could reach our friends' city before we can.'

'You are right, Gallia,' agreed Domitus, 'but such an eventuality would be welcomed by Pacorus.'

He looked at me. 'Am I right?'

Gallia spun round to look at me as I felt my cheeks flush. She then eyed Domitus.

'What do you mean?'

The chiselled features of Domitus' face broke into a broad grin.

'Let's say, for the sake of argument, that Mithridates and Narses send an army to attack Nergal. We've all seen Uruk's high walls. Which means that an army will have to lay siege to the city to capture it. Only one kingdom in Parthia has siege engines to batter down defences and that is Dura. So an army lays siege to Uruk to starve it into surrender.'

Domitus rose and laid a hand on my shoulder. 'And that gives Pacorus time to march his army south, cross the Euphrates and destroy the besieging army before the walls of Uruk.'

'Is this true, Pacorus?' asked Gallia.

'If Mithridates or Narses attack Uruk then I will march to its aid,' I answered.

'That is not an answer, son of Hatra,' smirked Dobbai. 'What your wife wishes to know is are you using Mesene as a bait to entice your enemies to walk into your trap?'

'There is no trap,' I protested. 'Dura is Mesene's ally and will stand by Nergal. Mithridates knows this and so does Narses.'

Gallia returned to her chair. 'You should write to Nergal warning him that his kingdom faces an attack.'

'He already knows that, my sweet,' I said. 'Besides he is no fool. He has the city garrison, eight hundred Margianans to stiffen his forces, plus whatever Surena can raise among the Ma'adan.'

Domitus chuckled. 'The marsh dwellers? About as useful as a paper sword.'

I wagged a finger at him. 'You underestimate them, Domitus. They will prove useful allies to Nergal.'

For years Chosroes had waged a war of annihilation against the Ma'adan, the people who inhabited the great marshes through which the Tigris and Euphrates meandered before they emptied their waters into the Persian Gulf. Surena, my former squire and now an officer in Dura's cataphracts, was one of those people and was currently helping Nergal enlist recruits from among the Ma'adan.

'You should recall the marsh boy,' Dobbai said suddenly. 'His destiny does not lie among the swamps and reeds of his people.'

'I'm sure Nergal will send him back to us presently,' I replied.

Orodes leaned forward to look at Dobbai. 'Have the gods revealed his true purpose to you?'

Dobbai flicked a hand at him, rose and walked towards the door.

'The gods have better things to do than whisper in my ear, prince. But I will say this: Mithridates will never set foot on the western bank of the Euphrates and neither will Narses. If you wish to kill them you will have to go and get them.'

With that she opened the door and departed, mumbling to herself as she did so. Gallia was still studying the map as Dobbai closed the door behind her.

'What is this place?' she said, turning to Rsan who had spent his whole life at Dura. She was pointing to a settlement at the spot where the Tigris and Euphrates entered the Persian Gulf.

'That is Charax, majesty,' answered Rsan. 'A port that was formerly under the control of the King of Mesene, but no longer.'

26

'No longer? Why?'

'It was established by Alexander of Macedon nearly three hundred years ago, majesty,' said Rsan. 'Since then its fortunes have declined sharply. It has been destroyed by floods at least twice.'

'It is part of Mesene?' queried Gallia.

'Technically, yes,' said Rsan. 'But it has been many decades since Uruk has exercised control over Charax. Today the port exists as a sort of independent city, though only because it is out of the way and no one has the inclination to subdue it. But it too pays dues to the empire.'

Gallia was intrigued. 'In what way?'

'Boats dock at Charax and then sail up the Tigris or Euphrates to trade their goods in either Babylon or Seleucia where they are taxed.'

'Who rules Charax?' I asked Rsan.

He stroked his beard. 'Let me see. Ah, yes, a man named Tiraios if my memory serves me correctly. The port was prosperous many years ago but the Silk Road has reduced it to a backwater in every sense of the word. Alas for Tiraios.'

After the meeting I wrote letters to King Vardan at Babylon and King Gotarzes at Elymais, both allies, alerting them of my missive to Mithridates and asking them to keep watch for any troop movements in Susiana and Persis. But with the news that Narses was travelling east to Sakastan I thought it improbable that Mithridates would attempt anything on his own. And so I waited. After two weeks nothing had happened, and after a month it became obvious that my letter had been ignored. Frequent messages came from Nergal reporting no activity on his eastern border, and from Vardan stating that nothing was happening at Seleucia. Even Gotarzes bewailed the torpor. He hated Mithridates and Narses more than I did and would have liked nothing more than a war against them. But Ctesiphon sent envoys to Elymais to maintain cordial relations with its king and pointedly ignored the Kingdom of Dura and its ruler. The army trained, the trade caravans travelled through the kingdom on their way to Palmyra and I paced the palace terrace waiting for an invasion that would never happen. I received a letter from my father, admonishing me for insulting the high king and reporting that the Romans in Gordyene were quiet. Zeugma sent protestations of peace and my mother wondered when we would be visiting Hatra again. The whole empire appeared to have been gripped by an outbreak of peace that was as infuriating as it was welcome.

The only bright spot was the gathering of the Companions.

This annual assembly was a feast for all those who had travelled with me from Italy in the aftermath of Spartacus' defeat. As well as the survivors of the force of Parthians that I had led into Cappadocia they included Greeks, Gauls, Italians, Germans, Dacians and Thracians. After the night of revelry, when I sat on the palace terrace nursing a hangover, Byrd paid me a visit. Though he was not the most sociable of individuals he always made the effort to attend the gathering, usually ending up sitting on his own at the end of a table in the banqueting hall, alone with his thoughts.

He looked more like an Agraci in his flowing black robes, black headdress and dark, unkempt features. But then he had made his home among the desert people, residing at Palmyra with Noora who never left the settlement.

'I trust she is well, Byrd,' I said, pressing a damp towel to my forehead.

He nodded. 'She well, lord.'

'Gallia is always on at me to convince you and Noora to come and live in Dura. She has even earmarked a mansion in the city that could be your residence, should you so desire.'

He shook his head. 'I like Palmyra.'

I eased myself back into the chair and placed my feet on the stuffed stool. The throbbing in my head was at least beginning to subside.

'Gallia believes that living in a mansion is preferable to sleeping in a tent, Byrd.'

'I like simple life, lord.'

I opened my eyes and looked at him.

'You are a Companion, Byrd. You don't have to call me "lord". What news do you have of the Romans?'

'Romani quiet. We hear stories of great rivalries in Rome.'

'That's good. If the Romans are fighting among themselves then they won't be bothering Dura, or Palmyra for that matter.'

28

I immersed the towel in the bowel of fresh water on the table beside me, wrung it out and replaced it on my forehead.

'My scouts report no activity east or west of the Euphrates,' said Byrd.

I smiled to myself. He commanded fifty hand-picked scouts that were the eyes and ears of Dura's army. Mostly ragged-looking Agraci, they were a law unto themselves, riding hither and thither at their own beck and call. Their refusal to obey anyone save Byrd and me drove Domitus to distraction and he was forever complaining about their appearance or non-appearance when they decided to take themselves off at a moment's notice. But for all their shortcomings I reckoned them to be the finest group of scouts in the Parthian Empire. And to date they had always provided me with accurate information regarding an enemy's whereabouts and strength, and the army had never been surprised on campaign. This made Byrd and his fifty scouts priceless and that is why I never interfered with their peculiar ways. Every month a payment of gold was sent from Dura's treasury to Byrd at Palmyra to pay him and his scouts. The amount was generous, which was a bone of contention with Rsan, but I reckoned it money well spent for it provided me with information concerning what was happening beyond Dura's borders.

'I'm glad that your men are collecting intelligence, Byrd,' I told him, 'but the caravans also convey gossip concerning what is going on east of the Euphrates.'

He reached into his robes and held out his hand to me, a gold coin between his fingers.

'What's this?'

'From Gerrha,' he replied.

'Gerrha?'

The name was vaguely familiar but I could not place it. I took the coin. It was newly minted and on one side bore the head of Simurgel, the bird-god symbol of Persis. I placed the towel on the table and sat up as I turned the coin in my hand.

'This is the currency of the Kingdom of Persis,' I said.

Byrd nodded. 'Lord Yasser recently escorted a caravan carrying incense from Gerrha.'

Yasser was one of Haytham's warlords who commanded a large stretch of territory in the southern Agraci lands. Byrd told me that Gerrha was the capital of the Kingdom of Dilmun, a domain in eastern Arabia, and Gerrha itself was a large port that traded in goods coming from east of the Indus. Its boats transported incense and spices throughout the Persian Gulf and also into Parthia via the Tigris and Euphrates.

'Yasser imposed a tax on the caravan and then escorted it north toward Petra,' said Byrd.

I laughed. 'He is a merchant now rather than a warlord.'

Byrd nodded.

'Yasser must be getting soft,' I remarked.

'Haytham himself visited Kingdom of Dilmun and proposed trade treaty based on the one he has with Dura. You have changed him, Pacorus.'

I felt immensely proud and smug at that moment. Perhaps future generations would view me as the Parthian who tamed the Agraci, not with bows but with words.

'Thing is,' continued Byrd, 'Yasser talked to the camel drivers and they told him that many of Narses' agents in Gerrha hiring boats with gold.'

'Boats?'

Byrd nodded.

'Perhaps Narses wishes Persis to become a great trading kingdom,' I suggested. 'Why else does he need boats?'

Byrd had no answer to my question but I was secretly pleased that Narses was occupying himself with affairs within his own kingdom, and presumably his newly acquired kingdom of Sakastan.

The next few days were a happy time as I hunted with Gafarn, Diana, Nergal and Praxima, taking with me the saker falcon named Najya that had been a present from Haytham. Gafarn, my former slave, now my adopted brother and a prince of Hatra, was in high spirits as he basked in the love of his wife, the former kitchen slave from Capua who had escaped from the gladiatorial school with Spartacus. I had hope that they would bring the young son of Spartacus with them to Dura but he had been left behind at Hatra.

'Your mother dotes on him,' Gafarn said to me as we rode back to the city after a day hunting desert quail. The sun was dipping on the western horizon – a golden molten ball of fire resembling Praxima's wild red mane hanging around her shoulders.

'I remember the night he was born,' said Nergal.

'The night Claudia died,' lamented Praxima.

'I have often wondered what would have happened if she had lived,' said Gafarn. 'Perhaps Spartacus would not have thrown his life away in battle the next day and we would all still be in Italy.'

'Being chased around the country by Crassus,' I said.

'Or perhaps we would have defeated Crassus and ended up as rulers of Rome,' offered Nergal.

'I prefer our new home,' said Praxima.

'What is it like, being a god I mean?' asked a smiling Diana.

'Tiresome,' replied her friend. 'Total obedience gets on my nerves and no one looks you in the eye.'

'How is Surena getting along?' I asked.

'Very well,' said Nergal. 'He has raised a good number of Ma'adan recruits who are being trained in the ways of war by Kuban and his officers. They are enthusiastic recruits.'

'What is the view of those men who used to serve Chosroes?' I asked.

'They are soldiers,' replied Nergal. 'Those who survived our storm of the city now serve me.'

Praxima giggled. 'Besides, we have High Priest Rahim on our side and no one dare challenge him.'

'It was a stroke of luck you two resembling the old gods of Uruk,' said Gafarn.

'Dobbai would say that luck played no part in it,' I said. 'She would say that it was the will of the gods that led Nergal and Praxima to Uruk. That I was merely an agent of their desires.'

'She doesn't like me,' said Gafarn.

'She is very wise,' I agreed.

'Just as the people of Uruk believe that Nergal and Praxima were sent by the gods,' said Gallia, 'so do the inhabitants of Dura believe that Dobbai was sent to protect the city. She was the one who gave Dura's army its banner, the golden griffin of the Durans and the statue that guards the city.'

31

'It is always best to have the gods on your side,' said Nergal. 'It makes things much easier.'

'Let us hope that the gods speedily do away with Mithridates and Narses,' I said.

'Mithridates writes honey-coated letters to our father, Pacorus,' said Gafarn, 'pledging eternal friendship and peace between Ctesiphon and Hatra.'

'He ignores Dura,' I stated.

'And Uruk,' added Nergal.

'He seeks to isolate us from the rest of the empire,' I said. 'To let our two kingdoms wither and die like vines deprived of water.'

'Like Charax,' said Nergal.

Gallia's ears pricked up. 'What do you know of Charax? Its name was raised at a council meeting recently.'

Nergal shrugged. 'A poor city built where the Tigris and Euphrates flow into the Persian Gulf. Boats from the port frequently visit Uruk to unload their cargoes for sale in the city. It is rumoured that its ruler, Tiraios, is a tyrant but he has no army to speak of, or so the Ma'adan inform me.'

'They fight this Tiraios?' asked Gafarn.

Nergal laughed. 'The Ma'adan will fight anyone who encroaches on their territory.'

'But not you, my friend,' I said.

Nergal nodded. 'No, they are our allies.'

That night the kitchens cooked the quail we had caught and we ate them in the banqueting hall, which seemed eerily quiet after the raucous feast of the Companions. We mostly ate in silence, Gallia, Diana and Praxima exchanging the occasional word. Though we all loved these annual gatherings the eve of journeys home was always a sad affair. Part of me wished that I still lived in Hatra with my parents and Gafarn and Diana, with Nergal and Praxima living in one of the great mansions in the city. But we all had our own destinies to fulfil and it was a futile exercise to wish for what would never be. And so we sat in silence, each mulling over their thoughts.

'You know that you will always have a home at Dura should you so wish,' I said suddenly to Nergal and Praxima.

They both looked at me in confusion, as did the others.

'We have our own home now, Pacorus,' said Nergal, 'but I thank you for the offer.'

'A strange thing to say,' remarked Gafarn, his lean features illuminated by the torches that flickered on the wall behind us.

'I don't trust Mithridates, that is all,' I answered.

'Who does?' said Gafarn.

'Pacorus is worried that Mithridates will attack Uruk instead of Dura. Is it not so?' Gallia stated bluntly.

Nergal seemed unconcerned, shovelling some spiced rice into his mouth.

'If he does then Uruk's walls are high and strong and he possesses no siege engines. The city is well stocked with provisions to withstand a siege until our allies arrive.'

'I can be at Uruk in two weeks,' I reassured him.

Gafarn took a sip of his wine. 'Pacorus, have you ever considered that Mithridates may not even give your existence a passing thought?'

I looked at him. 'I don't understand.'

'It's quite simple. He has achieved his lifelong ambition of becoming king of kings and has the allegiance of most of the kings in the empire.'

'Half,' I corrected him.

He held up a hand to me. 'Have it your own way. But the fact remains that he is high king, the other kings of the empire either support him or tolerate him but all wish to avoid any further bloodshed.'

'Except Pacorus,' said Gallia.

'Except Pacorus,' agreed Gafarn. 'If you ignore him then I can assure you that he will ignore you.'

Gafarn looked at Nergal. 'And you, my friend. I do not wish to offend your new kingdom but Mesene has always been regarded as a poor relation among the empire's family of kings.'

'Not all that glitters is gold, my love,' said Diana.

'Wise words,' I said.

'We would not swap Uruk for all the gold in Ctesiphon,' said Praxima defiantly.

I smiled. Same old Praxima – wild and fierce. No wonder Gallia had chosen her to be second-in-command of the Amazons.

'My point is,' continued Gafarn, 'that Mithridates has no interest in raising an army to try and subdue Dura or Mesene. He would rather sit on his throne and receive slavish homage from his army of courtiers, concubines and eunuchs at Ctesiphon. I am sure he is mindful of the fate of other kings who have challenged you in battle, such as Porus and Chosroes.'

'He's right, Pacorus,' said Nergal.

Gafarn wore a smug smile. 'I usually am.'

Nergal and Praxima left early the next morning, their escort of a hundred horse archers drawn up in the courtyard as we said our goodbyes on the palace steps.

I embraced Praxima and Nergal.

'If you need me just send word,' I told him.

He smiled and shook his head. 'You worry too much. But do not leave it too long before you and Gallia visit us.'

The Mesenian camp had been pitched outside the city where the rest of Nergal's horse archers and the camels loaded with tents and supplies were waiting. They would cross the pontoon bridge and travel back to Uruk along the eastern bank of the Euphrates. At a leisurely pace of around twenty miles a day it would take them fifteen days.

Domitus and Godarz were also present to bid farewell to their friends, a colour party of the Durans arrayed in front of the treasury and headquarters building in the courtyard. Its golden griffin shone in the early morning sunlight as Nergal and Praxima rode from the Citadel.

Gafarn and Diana left an hour later, Gallia sharing a tearful farewell with her friend on the palace steps. Diana kissed Claudia and then embraced me as their escort rode into the courtyard. My father had given them two companies of Hatra's cataphracts: two hundred men and horses encased in gleaming scale armour, burnished helmets glinting in the sun and every one sporting a red plume. Each rider carried a long lance called a *kontus* that had a vicious point and a steel butt spike. There was no wind and so the red pennants bearing a white horse's head hung limply on the thick shafts. Nevertheless Hatra's professional armoured horsemen looked magnificent in their scale armour comprising overlapping steel scales shimmering in the sun. Hugely expensive to raise and maintain, cataphracts were a visible symbol of a king's wealth and power and Hatra was blessed that it could field fifteen hundred of them. The Hatran camp had been established across the river, in Hatran territory, where the four hundred squires and servants waited with the camel train loaded with armour, weapons, tents, food and fodder for the journey back to my father's capital.

Trumpets sounded, the colour party stood to attention and my friends led their escort from the Citadel. We stood on the palace steps until the last of the cataphracts had left, piles of horse dung in the courtyard the only reminder of their presence. Domitus dismissed the Durans, stable hands came into the courtyard to clean up the mess and Gallia took Claudia back to her nursery. Godarz made his excuses and walked over to the treasury where Rsan waited for him to discuss new farming tenancy agreements. The royal estates extended south from the city for a distance of a hundred miles and the peace with the Agraci meant that there was a lot of land adjacent to the Euphrates waiting to be irrigated and farmed.

I walked to the stables, saddled Remus and rode him from the Citadel to the Palmyrene Gate. I left him in the care of a guard and ascended the stone steps in the gatehouse to reach the stone griffin that stood sentry over the city. Already the entrance to the city was filling with travellers, traders bringing their wares to Dura to sell in the markets, and citizens walking from the city to work in the fields or in the sprawling legionary camp half a mile to the west. Across the deep wadi beyond the city's northern walls was the vast caravan park where hundreds of camels spat and grunted as they were led to water troughs fed by water from the nearby Euphrates. The ill-tempered, stinking beasts were Dura's lifeblood for they transported the precious silk from China to Egypt and Rome where it was worn by fine ladies and men. As I stood beside the stone statue I subconsciously turned the gold coin Byrd had given me in my right hand.

'So, the feast of drunkenness and gluttony is over for another year.'

I stopped playing with the coin and turned to see Dobbai approaching.

'The stable hands told me that you had left the Citadel,' she said. 'I thought I would find you here.'

35

'Really? Been using your magic again? I could have been visiting Domitus or practising shooting on the ranges.'

She stood next to me, saying nothing as she stared at the legionary camp where hundreds of men were going about their daily duties.

'You always come here when you are brooding,' she said at last.

I turned the coin between my fingers. 'Who said I was brooding?'

'It's written all over your face. What's that?'

She was looking at the coin I was toying with.

'Nothing. Just a coin.'

She suddenly looked very serious. 'May I see it?'

I shrugged and passed it to her. She held it up and examined it closely, holding it up to the sun.

'Byrd gave it to me,' I said as she grunted and scratched at its surface with her hawk-like nails.

'One of Haytham's lords collected it when a trade caravan paid him to cross the desert from Gerrha to Palmyra. It is…'

'The currency of Persis,' she said. 'It is a message from the gods, son of Hatra. The spectre of Narses rises up.'

'I have scouts on the other side of the Euphrates,' I told her. 'Nothing stirs on the borders of Persis.'

'What else did Haytham's lord tell your Cappodocian?'

'That the agents of Narses are hiring boats at Gerrha,' I said. 'Perhaps he intends to sail his army up the Euphrates,' I joked.

She said nothing, fixing me with her black eyes. She held up the coin to me.

'The gods warn you of great danger, son of Hatra. You must act quickly.'

'The army is liked a coiled cobra, ready to strike,' I reassured her. 'If Narses dares show his face it and I will be ready and waiting.'

She clenched the coin in her fist. 'He will not come here but he will strike at you, son of Hatra.'

She turned and walked back to the stone steps.

'I will dispose of this coin. It is evil and should not be allowed to remain inside this city.'

'Give it to Rsan,' I told her.

She stopped and turned to face me. 'No. It must be taken to the river and cast into the water so it will travel south and return to the lair of its master.'

The voyage of Dobbai down the Euphrates on a small fishing vessel was one of the few highlights of that week. There is a small harbour at the base of the rock escarpment upon which the Citadel sits and mostly it is occupied by a handful of fishing boats. Those who worked on the river usually hauled their vessels onto the riverbank at the end of the day. But on the day Dobbai took Narses' gold coin downriver the harbour was packed with boats, all filled with people who had paid to accompany Dura's famous sorceress on her mysterious journey. I did not know how they had found out about the coin or Dobbai's intentions, though palaces are notorious places for gossip, but whatever the reason dozens of boats followed the one that contained her as it cut through the calm, blue waters. Gallia was on the same boat along with the half a dozen legionaries that Domitus insisted should guard the queen. I did not go, preferring to stay in the palace. I thought the whole thing nonsense and merely designed to increase Dobbai's reputation as a weaver of magic.

When she returned she insisted that she see me. I had been visiting Domitus in the legionary camp when a courier on horseback arrived from the Citadel with a message that war was upon us.

'Who sent this message?' I asked the man, one of Dura's horse archers dressed in a loose white tunic, baggy brown leggings and boots.

'Your sorceress, majesty.'

Domitus groaned. 'Best ignore her, Pacorus. She probably wants to tell you about a fish she caught during her trip on the river.'

We were in his large command tent in the centre of the camp, which was modelled on the Roman equivalent. The only difference being that there were no granaries in Dura's camp. They were located in the city. But there were workshops and a hospital where Alcaeus, the wiry haired Greek physician who headed the army's medical corps, could usually be found.

I picked up my helmet. 'The one thing I have learned since coming to Dura, Domitus, is that it is unwise to ignore Dobbai's prophecies. Surely you have not forgotten the sandstorm that she foretold?'

When the army had been preparing to march north to intercept a Roman army commanded by Pompey, Dobbai had ridden to the legionary camp and ordered that everyone should seek refuge in the city. Domitus had been enraged and had threatened to kill her, but changed his mind when a fearsome sandstorm descended on Dura and battered the city for days.

The commander of the army now appeared disinterested.

'Just humour her. I'm sure that will do the trick.'

I nodded at him and walked to the tent's entrance. The courier stood where he was, looking sheepishly at me.

'There is something else, majesty.'

'Well spit it out, then,' commanded Domitus.

The courier stared directly ahead. 'Your sorceress said that General Domitus should also attend her in the palace.'

'Looks like you are coming with me,' I grinned.

Domitus sighed and stood, picking up his helmet. He ambled up to the courier.

'The old witch called me general?'

The courier swallowed. 'Not exactly, lord.'

'So what did she say, exactly?'

The man squirmed and swallowed again. 'That the king should bring the Roman with him.'

Domitus laughed. 'Well, then, let's go and see what the old hag is babbling about.'

When we arrived at the palace we found Dobbai, Gallia and Orodes in the throne room, my wife sitting in her high-back seat and Dobbai pacing up and down in front of the dais. A bemused Orodes was standing beside Gallia with arms folded when we walked into the chamber.

'Please close the doors behind you,' said Dobbai when she saw us.

I nodded to the guards who shut the doors and retook their positions flanking the entrance. I walked with Domitus to my throne, the general curling his lip at Dobbai as he passed her.

38

'You received a summons too?' I remarked to Orodes as I sat down beside a worried Gallia.

'Are you all right?' I said to her.

'Fine,' she snapped as Domitus took his place beside me, acknowledging Orodes with a nod.

Dobbai turned to face us all.

'I understand now. The son of Hatra gave me a coin that came from the south.' She glared at me. 'That he should have given me as soon as it came into his possession. But what is done is done. I realised that the coin the Cappadocian pot seller gave to the son of Hatra was a sign from the gods. Today I gave the coin to Enki so that he could return it to its corrupt master.'

'Who's Enki?' said Domitus.

'The God of Water,' replied a serious Orodes.

'Indeed, prince,' said Dobbai. 'At least you are acquainted with this land's deities.'

She looked down her nose at Domitus. 'Though the son of Hatra has shown some wisdom regarding forging alliances, and has achieved renown for his battlefield exploits, I have often thought it a weakness that he brought to Dura a ragtag collection of different races who have no knowledge of or respect for Parthia's gods.'

Domitus was unconcerned. 'If your gods are so offended by Dura's ragtag collection of different races, as you call them, how is it that the kingdom has prospered since we arrived?'

Dobbai pointed at me. 'Because he is beloved of the gods, Roman, whereas you are not. So thank your gods that you have the king you do, for as they smile on him so they also smile on you, albeit indirectly.'

'They are too generous,' Domitus said in mockery.

'Can we get back to the reason why we have all been summoned here,' I said.

'Patience, son of Hatra,' said Dobbai. 'When I travelled down the Euphrates I told the captain of the boat to stop when I saw two horned vipers wrapped round an old log.'

She scowled at Domitus. 'For those who are ignorant of such things, Enki's symbol is two serpents entwined on a staff. I thanked Enki for his divine sign and tossed the coin into the water. After a few moments the water began to foam and the captain of the vessel and his men began to wail like small children. I told them to be quiet else Enki would send a giant turtle to devour them.

'After a few minutes the water became calm and crystal clear. I could see all the way to the bottom of the river and saw shoals of fish and great eels moving across the riverbed. The fish disappeared and I saw the vision of a beautiful fair-haired woman in a white dress with a green sash around her waist. She had a golden wreath around her head and had the wings of a swan. It was the Goddess Nike.'

'Nike is a Greek god,' said Domitus.

'Very good, Roman,' remarked Dobbai. 'I am glad to see that you are not totally ignorant of the gods of other races.'

'What has a Greek goddess to do with Parthia?' asked Orodes.

Dobbai smiled. 'Because, prince, Enki reveals to me that the followers of Nike are marching against the son of Hatra.'

Domitus laughed. 'The Greeks are marching against Dura. Well I reckon that by the time they have marched all the way across Asia and Syria they will be in no fit state to fight.'

'Sometimes, Roman,' spat Dobbai, 'you display the intellect of a bullock. I did not say that the Greeks were marching against us but the followers of Nike.'

I looked at Domitus who rolled his eyes. Orodes looked thoughtful but appeared none the wiser. It was Gallia who spoke first.

'The city of Charax.'

Dobbai clapped her hands. 'Well done, child. You alone are perceptive enough to see the blindingly obvious.'

'The city of Charax is at least six hundred miles from Dura,' I said. 'Even if Tiraios had a mind to strike against me, I doubt that his army is up to marching such a distance, let alone fighting a battle at the end of it.'

'It would take the legions a month to march that distance,' added Domitus, 'and they are the fittest soldiers in the world.'

'It does seem unlikely,' Orodes said to Dobbai, 'that King Tiraios would march against Dura, lady.'

Dobbai did not immediately reply as she regarded first me and then Domitus and Orodes. She eventually shook her head and sighed.

'Men really are like bullocks with their thick heads, muscles and small brains. The gods grant you the miracle of seeing the future and all you can do is scoff.

'I did not say that the Charax would march against Dura but against you, son of Hatra. You should wash out your ears and pay close attention to what people say to you. I would have thought that careful consideration is a prerequisite of kingship.'

'You speak in riddles, old woman,' said Domitus irritably. 'Pacorus is the King of Dura so any enemy that marches against him marches against the city.'

She pointed a bony finger at the commander of my army.

'The son of Hatra chose well when he appointed you the chief of his army, for what are you but a blunt instrument that he uses to batter his enemies into submission. As you are incapable of divining the nature of what Enki has revealed I will explain in simple words.'

She looked at Orodes and me.

'And you two pay attention as well.

'The enemies of the king may strike at him without the need to approach this city, which even the most simple-minded fool knows is to invite destruction.'

Domitus grinned and winked at Orodes.

'Notwithstanding the lack of imagination among the senior officers of its army, I told you, son of Hatra, that the gold coin given to you by the Cappadocian was a sign and so it was. It indicated that Narses is planning a strike against you. But where? He knows, as does the whole empire, that two armies have been destroyed before Dura's walls. He has no intention of coming to this place and adding his name to the list of those kings you have killed.'

'I did not kill them,' I protested. 'I defeated them in battle.'

Dobbai chuckled evilly. 'I am sure that is a great comfort to Porus and Chosroes. But to continue.

'If Narses marches west he will have to invade Babylonian and Hatran territory, which will in turn cause Media and Atropaiene to declare war on him, perhaps even Margiana and Hyrcania.'

'And don't forget Elymais,' said Domitus.

'The empire would once again be plunged into civil war,' remarked Orodes glumly.

'Well done, prince,' said Dobbai. 'And that is the last thing Narses and Mithridates want. So Narses desires to strike at the son of Hatra without the risk of embroiling the empire in war. How does he do this?'

I had no idea where this was leading and neither did Orodes or Domitus. We looked at each other with blank faces as Dobbai shook her head in despair.

'Bullocks!'

She smiled at Gallia. 'Let me tell you all a story. Enki is the creator and protector of humanity who watches over us. When the world was young Enlil, the god who grants kingship, attempted to destroy humans with a great flood.'

She looked at Domitus. 'Because their never-ending noise prevented Enlil from sleeping. But Enki foresaw Enlil's plan and instructed people to build a great ark so that humanity could escape the flood. He now foresees Narses' plan and warns of an enemy approach by water.'

'How long would it take a fleet of boats to travel up the Euphrates, sailing against the flow of the river?' asked Domitus.

'Not as long if they were to attack Uruk instead,' said Gallia.

Dobbai nodded in admiration. 'You alone are the one who understands the vision Enki sent me, child. Narses intends to attack Uruk, or at least he has bribed or flattered Tiraios to do it for him.'

Now I was worried. 'Uruk? Are you sure?'

'You said yourself that Narses was hiring boats in Gerrha,' said Dobbai. 'What does he want with boats if not to transport an army?'

'You think that Narses has joined with Tiraios?' asked Orodes.

'Of course not,' snapped Dobbai. 'The King of Persis has better things to do than befriend the ruler of some impoverished backwater. However, he is more than capable of convincing said ruler to attack Uruk by providing him with boats, soldiers and the promise of riches and titles after Uruk has been taken, promises that he has no intention of keeping, I might add.'

'Even if what you say is true,' said Domitus. 'What purpose does an attack on Uruk serve?'

'Narses knows that the son of Hatra is ridiculously sentimental,' replied Dobbai. 'As such he knows that the deaths of the new rulers of Uruk would hurt him greatly.'

She looked at Gallia. 'And others among his family. Narses also knows that such an act would place him in high favour with Mithridates and Queen Aruna, who also desire vengeance upon the son of Hatra.'

'You are really cheering me,' I said.

Domitus was sceptical. 'Uruk's walls are high and strong and Nergal is no fool. Besides, the people who live in the marshes to the south...'

'The Ma'adan,' I said.

Domitus nodded his head. 'They will warn Nergal of the approach of any hostile forces through their territory.'

Orodes wore a concerned look. 'All the same, we should send a courier to Nergal immediately to warn him of the impending threat.'

'A sensible precaution,' agreed Dobbai.

I began tapping my finger on the top of my spatha's walnut grip, ideas running through my mind. The gods had been kind by revealing the future to Dobbai and we would be able to warn Nergal of the threat to his city. And yet the thought of Narses threatening my friends rankled.

'The son of Hatra believes that not only a letter should be sent south,' remarked Dobbai casually.

'What are you thinking?' Gallia asked me.

'Narses thinks I am a helpless lamb that he can bully and frighten,' I replied. 'But Narses needs to believe that Dura is a cobra that can strike hard and fast when required.'

I turned to Orodes and Domitus. 'I intend to honour the gods by acting on the valuable information they have provided. It is time to give King Tiraios a lesson in humility.'

Chapter 2

I told Domitus and Orodes not to mention the forthcoming expedition to Mesene to their officers or to anyone else. Gossip is like leprosy and spreads more rapidly. I did not want the knowledge that we were marching south to become common currency. That afternoon I wrote a letter to Nergal warning him that he might be attacked from the south and should increase the number of guards on Uruk's walls and the number of patrols in the south of his kingdom. As the courier trotted from the Citadel Marcus Sutonius walked through the gates, as usual dressed in his grey tunic, sandals and floppy hat. He could have been mistaken for a poor gardener, were it not for the fact that the guards snapped to attention when he passed them. He was, after all, the army's chief engineer. He bowed his head when he saw me, then again to Domitus when he caught sight of the army's commander. The sun was now burning down from a clear sky and the temperature in the courtyard was rising fast.

'Come inside,' I told him as I turned and walked into the headquarters building.

Marcus and Domitus followed as I entered the meeting room and flopped into a chair, sweat running down my neck. I pointed at a jug on the table next to the wall.

'Help yourselves.'

Marcus Sutonius filled a cup with water and handed it to Domitus, then filled another and placed it on the table in front of me before serving himself. He was the most unmilitary looking individual I had ever come across, with his thinning brown hair and slight paunch. Now in his forties he had a wiry frame, which made his paunch look larger than it was, and was shorter than both Domitus and myself. But he had a keen mind and his engines were worth five thousand men on the battlefield.

'I hope I have not torn you away from something important, Marcus,' I said.

'I had to postpone a meeting with the head of the guild of farmers. That is all, majesty.'

Domitus took off his helmet and placed it and his vine cane on the table.

'Guild of farmers? Jupiter save us.'

44

'On behalf of the members of the guild he will be petitioning the king for the use of the army's soldiers to assist in dredging the kingdom's canals.'

'He can forget that,' snorted Domitus dismissively.

'Actually, general,' said Marcus, 'dredging is a growing problem. At the time of the spring floods the Euphrates rises and fills the canals with water, which is then used to irrigate the land.'

Domitus frowned as Marcus gave him a lesson in farming techniques.

'The spring meltwater ensures excellent farming but also silts up the canals, which have to be constantly dredged.'

'So the farmers can dig them out,' said Domitus.

'The head of the guild suggests that as his members pay taxes for the supply of water from the canals, general, then it is the crown's responsibility to maintain said canals.'

'He has a point,' I remarked. 'However, I have a more pressing problem, Marcus.'

I pointed at the large hide map of the Parthian Empire on the wall opposite.

'What is the quickest way to get two thousand legionaries from Dura to Uruk?'

'On rafts,' replied Marcus without hesitation.

'Would they be able to keep up with an equal number of horse archers?' I probed him further.

'I would suggest, majesty,' said Marcus, 'that it is the other way round. Will your horsemen be able to keep up with the rafts?'

'A column of horse archers can travel up to thirty-five miles a day,' I told him.

'Even in this heat?' queried Domitus.

'Even in this heat.'

Marcus took a sip of water and stood, walking over to take a closer look at the map. At length he turned to face us.

'The Euphrates is no longer in spate but the current is still substantial, though in two months it will drop to a crawl. I believe that a force of soldiers on rafts could cover around fifty miles a day, perhaps more.'

'Are you sure?' I asked.

'Quite sure, majesty.'

'Then it would be better to put the horsemen on rafts as well,' I said.

'Are you going to get your sorceress to conjure up dozens of rafts?' said Domitus. 'Because it may have escaped your notice, Pacorus, you have none.'

He was right. Even if I commandeered all the fishing vessels that the kingdom possessed I doubted that we would be able to ferry even a thousand soldiers downriver. I sat back in my chair.

'Then I will ride south with horse archers only,' I said.

'We do, however,' said Marcus, 'have thousands of date palms.'

Domitus screwed up his mouth. 'Date palms?'

'Yes, general,' replied Marcus, 'the Euphrates Valley is littered with them. A very interesting tree. Did you know, for example, that every part of it has a useful purpose? The palm sprout can be eaten, as can the dates themselves, of course.'

I held up a hand to him. 'That is all very interesting, Marcus, but hardly helps me.'

'The thing is, majesty,' continued Marcus, 'is that the wood of the date palm is very buoyant, making it ideal for constructing rafts.'

Domitus remained unconvinced. 'It would take a lot of rafts to transport two thousand horse archers, two thousand legionaries and their supplies to Uruk.'

Marcus closed his eyes for a few seconds, mumbling to himself as he did so.

'I would estimate around a hundred a fifty rafts,' he said.

'How long will it take to construct such a number?' I asked.

Marcus looked at Domitus. 'If I was provided with all the manpower required then less than a week.'

'It is an ambitious plan,' said Domitus.

'But it is better for men and horses to arrive at their destination fresh as opposed to exhausted after a forced march,' I said. 'Build your rafts, Marcus.'

The kingdom of Dura comprises two parts: the hundred miles of territory to the north of the city and the same length of ground to the south of the capital. The northern lands were heavily cultivated, being the realm of Dura's score of lords, a group of hardened men who had fought the searing heat, scorpions, snakes and Agraci to establish their domains. Before I had come to Dura they had also been at war with Dura's ruler, Mithridates. He had been a prince then but had already showed himself to be unfit for high office. The city had been established over two hundred years ago and had prospered greatly in the years that followed due to its location on the trade route between east and west. The royal estates to the south of the city had been cultivated and the earth had been turned green, with unending date palm groves running parallel to the Euphrates. But then the Agraci arrived like a plague of locusts and the estates had withered. But the date palms had remained.

Now the Agraci were my allies and the lands to the south of Dura were slowly being restored to their former glory, but it would take many years, perhaps decades.

The day after my meeting with Marcus and Domitus a new plague of locusts descended on the estates to the south of the city: thousands of sweating legionaries armed with axes and saws who began felling thousands of date palms so Marcus could build his rafts. The trees can grow up to a hundred feet in height and have trunks that are nearly two feet thick. Marcus and his engineers went among the trees and selected only the tallest for felling, marking each one with white chalk so Domitus' men would know which ones were to be cut down. Not all the legionaries were allocated to felling trees. Half were detailed to haul the logs to the riverbank where the rafts would be assembled in the water.

The logistics were simple if daunting: each raft would measure approximately ten thousand square feet, with two layers of logs laid on top of each other. The top layer would be at right angles to the timbers underneath, both layers lashed together with ropes, wooden wedges and nails. Each raft required one hundred and twenty separate logs – eighteen thousand to build one hundred and fifty rafts. And that did not include the steering arms that were mounted fore and aft. Nor did the amount of timber required take into account the planks that had to be fitted to the decks of the rafts that would transport the horse archers – twenty men and horses on each raft – so the animals would not suffer any leg injuries in the depressions between the separate logs.

It took less than two days to fell eighteen thousand trees.

'What about my boys?' said Domitus as he stood with me on the riverbank observing the hive of activity that spread along the side of the Euphrates. 'They might twist their ankles.'

'They can watch where they put their feet,' I replied. 'Horses have a tendency to panic when they board rafts or boats and lose their footing.'

'And elephants,' said Domitus.

'Elephants?'

'Many years ago Rome was fighting a people called the Carthaginians.'

Domitus stopped and pointed his cane at the nearest raft in the water, on which stood a party of legionaries who were being directed by one of Marcus' engineers to lash the logs together. Though one had been forgotten and was drifting away from the bank.

'Look lively,' he shouted. 'If that log escapes one of you will have to swim and get it.'

The legionaries looked up and two leapt off the raft into the water to catch hold of the log before the current took it.

'You were saying,' I prompted him.

'Mm?'

'About the Carthaginians.'

'Ah, yes. Well they had a general named Hannibal who was a bit of a genius by all accounts. Won just about every battle. Anyway he marched an army from Africa, through Spain and into Gaul so he could invade Italy. He had elephants in his army, dozens of them. But when he got to a river called the Rhone he had great difficulty in getting them across. They don't like water, you see. So Hannibal had big rafts constructed.'

He pointed his cane at the long line of half-built rafts disappearing into the distance.

'Like these ones. And he covered their decks with soil and bushes to fool the elephants into thinking that they were stepping on to earth.'

'Did it work?' I asked.

'Mostly. A few panicked and fell into the water and drowned or swam across.'

'Can elephants swim?' I asked.

He shrugged. 'Apparently. They stick their trunks out of the water.'

I thought it unlikely that such a large beast could swim.

'What happened to this Hannibal?' I asked.

'He won every battle except the most important one,' replied Domitus.

'Which was?'

He gave me a wicked smile. 'The last one.'

He slapped me on the arm. 'When I was a centurion, all those years ago, it was methodically drilled into me that the reason that Rome always emerges victorious is that it always wins the last battle in a war. You know that.'

'Do I?'

He gave me a wry look. 'How many victories did Spartacus win? How many eagles did he take? How many Romans did you and your horsemen kill? But it all ended in the Silarus Valley and Rome was victorious. Won the last battle, you see. Just like you intend to win the last battle with Narses and Mithridates. You are very Roman in that.'

'I am not at all like the Romans,' I protested loudly, causing the men on the nearest raft to turn their heads towards us.

Domitus emitted a gruff laugh. 'Not in the way you look, perhaps, with your long hair, but your determination to exact vengeance on your enemies, no matter how long it takes, is very much the Roman way of doing things. After all, what does Dura's army exist for if not to be the instrument of its king's will?'

I held up a finger to him. 'The army exists to safeguard the city and kingdom of Dura Europos, Domitus.'

'If that is true,' he said. 'Then why are all these rafts being built?'

I ordered earth to be spread on top of the rafts that would transport horse archers. Marcus also suggested building wooden rails around their edges so the beasts would feel more secure on the rafts, akin to being corralled in a small field. I also decided that a thousand men would be drawn from the Durans and a thousand from the Exiles to prevent the accusation of favouritism. Though both legions were part of the army a fierce competition had grown up between them, which Domitus

49

encouraged but also controlled. A healthy rivalry was good for morale and fighting spirit, but if unrestrained could lead to feuds and animosity. That is why I decided to take an equal number of men from each legion.

'Sensible,' remarked Domitus.

At the end of the week, as promised by Marcus, the rafts were ready to travel, each one being equipped with rudders fore and aft to manoeuvre them on the water. I had convened the meeting of the council on the palace terrace and ordered the doors to be shut to preserve secrecy. Rsan had brought two clerks who sat and recorded all proceedings, having been warned beforehand that they were not to reveal to anyone what had been discussed, on pain of death. To make the meeting as comfortable as possible it was held in the late afternoon when the sun was dropping in the west and the heat had abated somewhat. Dobbai sat in her chair with her eyes closed, ignoring us all.

'You are still maintaining the fantasy that it is an exercise, Pacorus?' asked Godarz.

I nodded.

'I doubt anyone believes that,' said my governor. 'In any case a hundred and fifty sizeable rafts are difficult to conceal from prying eyes. No doubt their construction is already the talk of the trade caravans.'

'People will have things to talk about soon enough when they are no longer there,' I said. 'Regarding more practical matters. Orodes, I would like you to take charge of the army in our absence.'

He looked most unhappy. 'I would prefer to come with you.'

'If you come and we are all killed then who will lead Dura's army?' I said. 'Only you have the authority and experience to command it. And in the event of my death Godarz will become king. I have written a note that says as much and have deposited it with Rsan.'

My treasurer nodded solemnly to Godarz.

The governor was confused. 'But surely Gallia will rule if you are killed.'

'I am going to Uruk with Pacorus,' said Gallia. 'As are the Amazons.'

50

I had tried to convince her to stay but it had been futile. She had never been wholly convinced that making Nergal and Praxima the rulers of Mesene had been wise, the more so now that they were in imminent danger. She told me that the thought of them in danger was like a knife being twisted in her guts. So that was that.

'Let us hope we arrive in time,' she said.

Rsan cleared his throat loudly.

'Have you something to say, Rsan?' I asked.

He leaned forward. 'Forgive me, majesty, but,' he lowered his voice as he glanced at Dobbai, 'correct me if I am wrong but we have had no reports from Mesene that Uruk is being attacked. Surely King Nergal would have sent word if his city was in danger. It would appear that you travel south on the flimsiest of pretexts.'

Domitus raised an eyebrow but said nothing while Godarz grinned at his friend.

'Have a care, tallyman.'

The venom-laced words of Dobbai made Rsan blanch. She opened her eyes and looked at him.

'It would be a foolish man indeed who ignores the warnings of the gods. Uruk is in grave danger, that much is certain, and if it falls then Narses and Mithridates will be emboldened to strike against Dura.'

'That is why I going south,' I said. 'We leave in two days.'

The waters of the Euphrates were now blue as the level and current dropped following the surge of the early spring meltwaters, which turned the river brown. Though it was still spring the temperature was rising and I was concerned that men and horses on rafts would suffer under cloudless skies and with no shade. Therefore Marcus had shades constructed on each raft, comprising canvas sheets strung between poles fitted to the edges of each deck. This delayed our journey by a day but was time well spent. Dobbai gave instructions that each raft was to be daubed with red, blue and black paint, the favourite colours of Enki. This would please the god and ensure that no vessels would be lost during the journey.

On the morning we left Gallia and I kissed a sleeping Claudia and ate a breakfast of dates, bread and cheese on the palace terrace. According to protocol we should have taken our meals in the banqueting hall but I thought it slightly ridiculous that two people should eat in a hall designed to feast dozens. Gallia was dressed in her white tunic, mail shirt, leggings and boots, her sword in its scabbard resting against her chair.

'Do you regret making Nergal and Praxima the rulers of Mesene, Pacorus?' she probed.

'Not at all. Nergal is a good commander and can hold his kingdom without my help, especially now he has the Ma'adan as allies.'

She smiled and shook her head.

'What?' I asked.

'The Ma'adan are marsh dwellers, Pacorus. Poor people who eke out a miserable existence among reeds and mud banks. Do you really think they can aid Nergal?'

'They are good fighters,' I insisted. 'And I am sure that Surena has been busy raising a force to secure Nergal's southern flank.'

'Surena, I had forgotten about him,' she said. 'I hope he repays the faith you have placed in him. I remain far from convinced. Still, at least Viper will be pleased to see him.'

We said our farewells to Orodes, Rsan and Godarz on the palace steps. The courtyard was filled with mounted Amazons in their full war gear. In front of them Vagharsh, my Parthian standard bearer, sat on his horse, the griffin banner wrapped in a waxed canvas sleeve to keep it safe from the elements. Already the thousand Durans and thousand Exiles would be marching to the river where the rafts waited. Rsan was as punctilious as ever, bowing his head to me first and then to Gallia. Godarz embraced me and kissed Gallia on the cheek, while Orodes clasped my forearm.

'If Dobbai is right then while we are fighting the soldiers of Charax Narses might try a strike against Dura,' I said.

'Do not worry, my friend,' said Orodes, 'I will deal with any threat to your city. Though I doubt that there will be any attack. As far as my dear step-brother and Narses are concerned, you are still at Dura.'

He leaned in closer. 'I do not wish to poor cold water on the visions of your sorceress, but what will you do if no threat to Uruk materialises?'

I slapped him on the arm. 'Then we will have a great feast in Nergal's palace and afterwards return home.'

A stable hand brought Remus to the foot of the steps, another holding the reins of Epona, Gallia's mare. I walked down the steps and slipped my bow into the leather case attached to the four-horned padded saddle, my quiver holding thirty arrows slung over my shoulder, another two attached to my saddle. I took the reins of my white stallion and vaulted into the saddle. It was early but already warm, the sky blue and cloudless. It would be a hot day. Remus flicked his tail impatiently as I adjusted my helmet and Gallia mounted Epona behind me. I might have fooled the citizens of Dura into believing that I was going on exercise but Remus sensed otherwise. He was a veteran of many campaigns and knew the difference between exercises and the real thing. I patted his neck.

'Easy boy.'

He snorted and scraped at the stone flagstones, eager to be away.

'Your horse appreciates the urgency of the situation.'

I recognised the voice of Dobbai who walked from behind Remus.

'I leave my daughter in your care,' I said to her.

'Your daughter is in the care of the gods, son of Hatra, but rest assured that she is perfectly safe in this stronghold.'

I nodded at her and tugged on Remus' reins, wheeling him to the left. Gallia rode Epona to my side and together we trotted from the Citadel, a guard of honour from the Durans standing to attention as we passed them and rode through the gates. Immediately behind us came Vagharsh and then a hundred Amazons riding two abreast. We rode down the city's main street towards the Palmyrene Gate. Already the streets were beginning to fill with citizens going about their business as well as those who crewed the trade caravans wishing to visit the markets, eating and drinking places or the city's brothels. Everyone on the road parted as our column of riders approached, many raising their arms to cheer as we passed.

Even with my Roman officer's helmet covering my face everyone recognised Remus, the white stallion who had travelled back with me from Italy. Some said that he flew across the ocean with wings given to him by the gods, which were invisible to mortal eyes. I drew my *spatha*, the Roman two-edged sword that was a gift from Spartacus, and saluted the stone griffin as I passed beneath it and exited the city. Gallia did the same, as did the Amazons, for everyone knew that no army would take Dura Europos while the griffin remained above the gates of the city. I slid the sword back in its scabbard and regarded my armour. It too was Roman, a gift from an old friend I had fought beside it Italy, a gruff German named Castus who sadly was no longer with me. Dura's army wore white to symbolise the purity of its cause but my armour was black. It was a two-piece leather cuirass that was muscled and embossed on the upper front with a golden sun motif, with two golden winged lions immediately beneath. Over the thighs and shoulders were fringed strips of black leather adorned with golden bees. Though the Amazons and cataphracts wore armour the nineteen hundred horse archers that waited outside the city wore no metal protection on their heads or bodies.

It always filled me with pride and awe when I saw large formations of Parthian horsemen, the physical manifestation of the empire's strength. Of all the things that Parthia possessed it was its herds of horses that were the most precious. Without the horse there would be no cataphracts to shatter enemy formations or horse archers to rain down volleys of arrows on opponents. And not just any horse. The hundreds of horses that now stood in line in their companies were Akhal-Tekes, or Turkomans, horses descended from the animals ridden by the Turkmen tribe hundreds of years ago. Raised in the inhospitable terrain of the deserts in the east, they had long backs, shallow ribcages and long croups. Their coat is exceptionally fine and their tails silky. With their fine and elegant heads and long legs they had a regal appearance, which was entirely apt as they were treated like kings.

Just like Remus the Teke has a high opinion of himself as well as being vigorous and restless in nature. He responds to gentle training but becomes stubborn and resentful if treated rudely. Parthians soon discovered this and found that if they lavished care and attention on them, they would be rewarded with having the finest warhorses in the world. So, just as in other kingdoms in the empire, Dura had a small army of

54

farriers, veterinaries, stable hands and *seises* – trainers skilled in raising Tekes. The horses even had a specialised diet comprising dry alfalfa, pellets of mutton fat, eggs, barley and *quatlame*, a fried dough cake.

And what was the result of all this expensive care and attention? A horse that had extraordinary speed and stamina, and which could tolerate heat and hunger and do without water longer than any other breed. Truly a gift from the gods.

The company commanders saluted then followed the Amazons as we continued our journey to the rafts. I had originally commanded that two dragons – two thousand – of horse archers would travel south, but this had been reduced by one hundred when Gallia had decided that she and the Amazons would be accompanying me. Marcus had worked out the exact number of men and horses, plus supplies together with the fifty horsemen still due to arrive, that could be transported on the rafts. When we arrived at the river he was busy organising their loading. They looked like a long line of pagodas in the morning sunlight, each one covered with canvas awnings. When we dismounted the company commanders came forward to receive instructions from Marcus' men regarding which rafts their men would board.

'All have been marked with a number, in addition to the colours that your sorceress insisted be painted on each one, majesty,' Marcus told me.

I looked at the line of rafts disappearing south along the river.

'You have done an excellent job, Marcus. My congratulations.'

He looked at the first group of horses was being led towards a raft.

'We have also scattered earth over the decking to facilitate the smooth loading of the horses, as you ordered.'

He frowned and shook his head as one of the horses started snorting as its owner tried to lead it on to a raft.

'It would have been better, majesty, to have taken foot soldiers only.'

'Then I would have no missile support, Marcus,' I told him. 'And I am without your ballista, don't forget.'

55

A column of wagons pulled by mules trundles past, each one loaded with supplies: spare canvas, tents, weapons, quivers full of arrows, javelins, swords, armour and helmets. I was suddenly worried that a hundred and fifty rafts would not be enough.

'I hope we have enough room for the men, horses and supplies, Marcus.'

He looked at me aghast. 'I can assure you that my calculations are correct, majesty, down to the last spare mail shirt.'

The thundering of hooves interrupted our conversation as Byrd, Malik and the scouts arrived: fifty black-clad men with unshaven faces riding sleek Arabian horses. Malik jumped from his horse and handed the reins to a startled clerk. He walked up and embraced me as Byrd also dismounted and scanned what appeared to be the apparent chaos of carts, men, horses and rafts.

'I was wondering when you would arrive,' I said to him.

Byrd ambled over and nodded.

'You nearly missed the trip, Byrd,' I said.

'You not leave for hours yet,' he sniffed.

I had sent a message to Byrd and Malik requesting their presence. I had informed them of the true purpose of the journey because I needed Malik to send a message to Haytham's lords that Duran troops would be making camp on their territory as we headed to Uruk. Halting on the western side of the Euphrates would save having to land on Babylonian territory and would thus keep King Vardan ignorant of the whole expedition. Vardan was an ally and friend of my father and if he found out about my aiding Mesene then so would my father. There would then follow a stern Hatran lecture about not embroiling the empire in another civil war and that I could do without.

'My father approves of your actions,' Malik told me, 'but rebukes you for not inviting him along. He is finding the transition from warlord to merchant difficult.'

I laughed. 'You mean rich merchant, Malik.'

The peace agreed between myself and Haytham had made Palmyra the destination of the trade caravans taking silk to Egypt, which was making the Agraci king extremely wealthy.

'If it is any consolation to your father, Malik, I am sure that he will still have to use his sword when the Romans decide that Palmyra is a prize worth fighting for.'

Byrd was right about the commencement of our journey. It took three hours to load the rafts with men, horses and supplies and it was hot and airless when we finally pushed off from the riverbank. Each raft was crewed by four men who were used to travelling on the Euphrates. They stood fore and aft on each raft, using their rudders to steer. In the upper reaches of the Euphrates there are many rapids where the water flows quickly through steep canyons and gorges, making travel by boat extremely hazardous. But in the Euphrates Valley the river is wide – between five hundred and sixteen hundred feet – and the current slower. The flow took us now as we drifted downstream. It appeared that we were hardly moving, the surface of the river calm and seemingly undisturbed by our passage. Only by studying features on the shore was I able to discern that we were indeed not stationary.

Ahead were the rafts carrying the legionaries and supplies, behind the vessels transporting the horse archers. I was in the company of Gallia, Vagharsh and seventeen Amazons. The horses had been tethered to the rails and were in the shade of the awnings, the sleep-inducing movement of the raft having a calming effect on them, for which I thanked Shamash. I smiled when I saw Vagharsh asleep with his head resting against his saddle, snoring loudly. As soon as the horses had been loaded and tethered they were relieved of their saddles and saddlecloths, and the Amazons had also taken off their mail shirts and helmets. They stacked their bows, quivers and sword belts by their saddles and either followed Vagharsh's example or sat in groups talking. Two, however, were always on guard, one watching the eastern shore, one scanning the western riverbank. For what I did not know, since to the west was Duran territory and the east was Hatran lands. But they had been taught never to let their guards down, even in friendly territory.

I took off my armour and dumped it beside my saddle, then placed my helmet beside it. There would be little to do until we landed to make camp for the night, and that was still six hours away. Gallia was deep in conversation with two of her

Amazons so I decided to take the opportunity to grab some sleep. But first I wanted to ensure that Remus was fine. I walked over to him and noticed that his tail was raised high, as was his head. His ears were also pointing forward. He was more than fine: he was extremely happy. I soon discovered why.

Standing beside him, stroking his neck and speaking softly to him, was Viper, the child-like wife of Surena. She saw me and stopped stroking my horse.

'Apologies, majesty,' she said in her girlish voice.

'Please do not stop on my account. He likes it.'

She smiled and continued to stroke Remus' neck.

'He likes you,' I said.

'We all love Remus, majesty.'

'I am sorry that Surena had to be sent to Mesene. I did not intend to separate you from your husband but only he can act as a liaison officer between King Nergal and the Ma'adan.'

'I understand, majesty. We are both soldiers and know that duty comes before personal pleasure.'

I stifled a smile as I looked at her girlish figure. It was hard to believe that she was a woman let alone an expert killer. With her small breasts and short-cut brown hair she could have easily been mistaken for a novice of a religious order. Her large brown eyes opened wide as she smiled and whispered to Remus, who was basking in her attention. Like most of the Amazons I knew almost nothing about her, except that Gallia was very fond of her and Surena adored her. As I had plenty of time on my hands I decided to increase my knowledge of this child-like assassin.

'Do you have any family, Viper?'

'No, majesty. I was told that I was captured as a baby when the High King Sinatruces raided my parents' village, somewhere in the east. I was taken to Ctesiphon and raised to be a slave in the palace. In truth it was not an arduous life. I was raised in the family of a kindly steward until I was thirteen summers. Then I had to leave his village and live in the palace. I worked in the kitchens where one of the cooks decided that I should share his bed after I had served the high king his meals.'

'It is often the case,' I lamented.

'Well, I killed him with a cooking spit and fled the palace. I reached the Zagros Mountains and for a while lived in the wild, catching animals and eating berries and roots. But the winters in the mountains are cruel and I was forced to beg for shelter in one of the villages on the edge of the mountains.'

'That was fortunate,' I said.

She shook her head. 'Not really, majesty, because after the village headman had raped me he sold me as a slave to the commander of a passing caravan. He raped me too, as did his men.'

I was horrified and possessed of a seething anger against the wretches who had committed these acts. But Viper told her story in a matter-of-fact fashion. The experience had obviously hardened her.

'But the gods smiled on me,' she continued, 'because the caravan was carrying silk and was heading for Egypt. In between abusing me and forcing me to cook their meals the men told stories of the King of Dura, his warrior wife and her band of fighters called Amazons. And I made myself a promise that I would become an Amazon. So when the caravan reached Dura I disappeared among the throng in the caravan park and fled to the Citadel. My luck changed that day because as I reached the Citadel's gates Praxima, that is Queen Praxima, was riding out leading a party of Amazons. I did not know who she was but I threw myself to the ground in front of her horse and begged her to take pity on me and let me join the Amazons.'

She looked at me and smiled.

'Praxima must have recognised a kindred spirit because she jumped down from her horse, lifted me up and embraced me. I have been in the embrace of the Amazons ever since.'

'It comforts me that you are a member of my wife's bodyguard, Viper,' I said. 'But tell me, what is your given name, for surely you cannot have been named Viper at birth?'

I thought I detected sadness in her eyes.

'I do not know the name my parents gave me, majesty, because they were killed when I was a baby. But I was told later that there was a horned viper near me when the soldiers found me. They were amazed that it had not killed me but the commander of the raiding party said that it showed that I had the favour of the gods and so they took me to Ctesiphon. The high king's sorceress thought it very auspicious that I was a slave in the palace.'

59

She shrugged. 'That is what I was told.'

'You knew Dobbai?'

'No, majesty. She was the high king's confidante and counsellor and I was just a lowly slave. I cannot even remember seeing her at Ctesiphon.'

Remus turned his head and grunted, indicating that she should continue stroking his neck. She giggled girlishly.

'Remus is like a high king among horses, majesty.'

I smiled as she stroked his neck once more.

'Don't tire yourself out, Viper,' I told her. 'He will let you do that all day long.'

I returned to where Gallia was now sitting alone on the deck, her back resting against her saddle, and a floppy hat over her face.

I squatted down beside her.

'Are you asleep?'

She lifted up the brim of her hat. 'Apparently not.'

'I have just been talking to Viper. Did you know that she was a slave at Ctesiphon during the time that Dobbai was the sorceress of Sinatruces?'

She sighed. 'Of course.'

'And she is named thus because she was found as a baby with a coiled horned viper nearby, seemingly guarding her?'

Gallia let the brim of the hat fall over her face. 'I know.'

I was perturbed. 'Why did you not tell me?'

'To what end?'

'Does Dobbai know Viper's history?'

She lifted the brim of her hat once more and gave me a sly smile. 'Oh, yes. She is very pleased that Viper is an Amazon, as am I. She was very aware of Viper's history and believes her coming to Dura is a favourable omen. Now please let me get some rest. This heat is intolerable.'

By now most of the Amazons were either resting or asleep but I was restless, eager to get to Uruk. I walked to the rear of the raft where two men with skin turned dark brown by the Mesopotamian sun were holding the long rudders. They bowed their heads when they saw me.

'It seems as though we are hardly moving,' I said.

The nearest individual, a tall man with sinewy arms and gold rings on his bony fingers, turned and looked at the river.

60

'It may appear so, majesty, but the current is strong.'

'You are a fisherman?'

He nodded. 'As was my father and his father before him. The gods bless the Euphrates and fill it with fish.'

'You will be away from your nets for many days,' I said.

There would be no way to get the rafts back to Dura, aside from hitching them to horses on the riverbank and towing them back upstream. But that would be time consuming and in any case even if they were taken back to Dura they would most likely be left to rot on the riverbanks. Far better to burn them after we had finished with them. The crews would have to walk back to Dura with the army.

'How will your family survive without the money from the sale of the fish you sell in the markets?'

He looked at his companion and they both smiled. He flashed a set of white teeth at me.

'Lord Marcus has paid us well for our services, majesty.'

'War is much more profitable than fishing, majesty,' added his shorter companion.

How wrong he was. War was not only ruinously expensive but also damaging to the empire, which relied on the Silk Road for its wealth. Without trade there would be no revenues for the various royal treasuries, and thus no standing armies of horse archers and cataphracts. Even Mithridates recognised the importance of trade, which is why he did not interfere with the trade caravans travelling to Dura on their way to Palmyra and Egypt. To do so would incur the wrath of the Chinese emperor whose merchants transported silk from the east, and not even a king of kings would dare to do that.

We travelled forty miles the first day.

There were still three hours of daylight left when the lead raft, on which Domitus was travelling, drifted to the western bank, having signalled by means of the sun's rays reflecting off hand-held pieces of shiny steel plates that those following should do the same. Steel spikes hammered into the bank provided moorings for the rafts as the horse archers led their mounts off the vessels to exercise them, leading them on foot at first before riding them a short distance inland. The legionaries, meanwhile, began constructing the camp in which everyone would shelter for the night.

The sword of every legionary, as in the Roman Army, was a *gladius*: a two-foot length of the finest steel with a double edge and sharp point. In battle the Durans and Exiles armed with these short swords turned into two irresistible saws, reducing anything in front of them into mangled flesh and bone. But the *gladius* was not the item most used in a legionary's arsenal. That honour lay with the entrenching tool. The Romans called it *dolabra* – a wooden handle with an iron head that had a broad cutting edge at one end and a sharp point at the other. It saw more action than the *gladius*, javelin and shield combined, being used every day when on campaign to erect the ditch and rampart that surrounded a camp.

When the horse archers had finished exercising their mounts they were issued with entrenching tools and joined the legionaries in digging the ditch that would surround the camp. The earth removed from the ditch was used to erect a rampart behind it, upon which wooden stakes were planted to form a palisade. It took around three hours to erect the camp's defences and the tents inside, all arranged in neat rows and blocks with the command tent in the centre. While the camp was being established the Amazons and Byrd's scouts reconnoitred the surrounding terrain, which was actually still Duran territory. Curious villagers stood and stared at the mail-clad warriors that trotted into their settlements, then cheered and gathered round Gallia as she announced her presence to the headman. Most of these villages were newly established after the peace treaty with Haytham and my wife reported back to me that they appeared to be prospering.

Of course the building of the earth defences around the camp and the scouting patrols were unnecessary as we were still in friendly territory, but when on campaign the army followed protocol irrespective of its location.

The next day the army struck camp before dawn, legionaries packing up their eight-man tents and horse archers grooming and feeding their horses before exercising them briefly so they could empty their bowels and bladders before they were loaded on the rafts. Each day had up to fourteen hours of daylight and under a blazing sun and little wind the last thing the riders wanted were rafts awash with horse urine and dung.

We covered over fifty miles on the second day and nearly sixty on the third. The threat of war seemed far away as we passed fishermen on the river casting their nets into the calm blue water. We shouted to them that we were allies of King Vardan for now the eastern bank of the Euphrates was Babylonian territory. The appearance of a hundred and fifty rafts loaded with soldiers and horses would have been reported to Babylon and Hatra, of that I had no doubt, but my father and Vardan could only guess at our intentions. For all they knew we could have been travelling south to take part in exercises with the Agraci.

'You haven't got a hope in Hades of your father and Vardan thinking that,' remarked Domitus, shielding his eyes from the sun as he peered at the riverbank lined with curious Babylonian villagers. 'They are not stupid.'

It was the seventh day and we were nearing the northern extent of Mesene territory. The eastern side of the river did not change in appearance, being covered with date palm groves. Well-tended irrigated fields and fishing boats littered the riverbank. But on the western side there was only scrub and desert. That was Agraci territory and they were herders and raiders, not farmers.

'It was clever of you to think of using rafts to transport your men, Pacorus,' said Malik.

I had asked him, Domitus and Byrd to join me on my raft, mainly because I wanted someone to speak to during the journey. We put into shore for two hours at midday to water the horses and let them and everyone else stretch their legs and relieve themselves. And also give the crews an opportunity to rest. But the days were still long and tedious.

'He didn't think of it,' scoffed Domitus. 'It was Marcus Sutonius who came up with the idea. You can't beat a Roman mind when it comes to practical matters.'

'Do I detect a wistful tone in your voice, Domitus?' I teased him. 'A longing for the homeland?'

'I would rather be the slave of Mithridates than go back to Rome,' he spat. 'Being condemned to the mines banished any affection for the homeland I might have had.'

'You do not mind killing your own kind?' Malik asked him.

Domitus shrugged. 'Why should I? Pacorus pays my wages and I kill anyone who threatens his kingdom.'

'You see, Malik,' I said, 'Romans are practical in all things.'

'I like to think that part of your heart belongs to Dura, Domitus,' said Gallia.

He winked at her. 'I've lived in worse places. The people are agreeable enough and you and Orodes are good company.' He jerked his head at me. 'He can be a bit naive at times but all in all Dura is a tidy little city.'

'You forgot to mention being the commander of Dura's army,' I said, 'with all the attendant glories, honours and wealth that the position brings with it.'

'I thought Domitus lives in a tent outside the city,' remarked Malik.

'He does,' I answered, 'but only because he chooses to. He could have a mansion in the city if he so desired.'

Domitus screwed up his face. 'Living in mansions and palaces makes you soft. I prefer to live an uncomplicated life. Just like fighting: keep it simple.'

'Just like the Roman worldview,' I remarked. 'Everything belongs to Rome and if anyone disagrees, kill them.'

'Such an outlook has its merits,' offered Domitus. 'Pacorus has yet to learn that it is better to kill your enemies rather than let them live.'

'You speak of Narses and Mithridates?' said Byrd.

Domitus nodded.

'Perhaps one of them will be at Uruk,' said Malik.

Domitus scratched his nose. 'I doubt it. They will send others to do their dirty work.'

'Like Tiraios,' said Gallia.

Malik turned his tattooed face towards her. 'Who?'

'The King of Charax, a city near where the Tigris and Euphrates enter the Persian Gulf,' I told him. 'Dobbai believes that he and his army are the ones who will attack Uruk.'

'I remain to be convinced,' sniffed Domitus. 'When we get to Uruk I suspect we will find Nergal and Praxima residing in their palace, untroubled by this Tiraios.'

The following day was as uneventful as the preceding ones as the current took the rafts further downstream. The

64

Euphrates narrows to around five hundred feet as it approaches Uruk and the flow increases. This meant that we had would reach the city by midday, which meant spending only a few more hours on this accursed raft. I had come to realise what a caged animal must feel like: pacing up and down for hours in an attempt to relieve the boredom. Our line of rafts covered a distance of three miles on the river but the individuals on every one would have seen the thin pillars of black smoke in the sky that appeared to be many miles away.

There was a flurry of signals between the rafts as one by one the crews were instructed to head for the eastern riverbank. I looked at Gallia and we both knew that Dobbai's prophecy appeared to have become a terrifying reality. She barked an order to the Amazons to saddle their horses and ready themselves. There was no panic, just an ordered haste as they put on their mail shirts and helmets, fitted the bowstrings to their recurve bows, strapped on their sword belts and checked their quivers.

I placed the white saddlecloth on Remus' back and then threw the saddle on top. As I began securing the saddle's leather strap under his belly the tall fisherman with the gold rings came to me.

'You ride to war, majesty?'

I slipped Remus' bridle over his head. 'It appears so. If you see any enemy soldiers or anything that makes you suspicious, get yourselves across the river and wait there.'

He looked over at the opposite riverbank. 'To Agraci territory?'

'Do not worry,' I told him. 'They are our allies not our enemies now.'

He gave me an unconvincing half-smile and wandered off. He and his companions probably feared the Agraci more than they did Parthian enemies but I had no time to worry about their welfare.

I heard trumpet blasts ahead and knew that the legionaries had left the rafts and were now forming up in their cohorts. The raft's crew placed a row of planks from the deck to the bank so we could walk our horses ashore where Amazons began vaulting into saddles to await their queen's orders. Like the horse archers each one carried three full quivers, one slung over their shoulders, the other two fastened to their saddle horns.

I vaulted into the saddle at the moment Malik and Byrd appeared, behind them their black-attired scouts riding black horses. Their faces and heads were covered by loose-fitting black *shemaghs* – square pieces of black cloth that protected the face, head and neck from the sun. They also added to the overall forbidding appearance of Byrd's scouts.

'Find out what is happening,' I told him, 'but don't get yourself killed.'

Byrd turned to stare at the columns of black smoke on the horizon.

'Uruk under attack.'

'It would appear so,' I said.

He grunted, tugged on his reins to turn his horse and cantered away, his men following. Malik raised a hand to me and followed his friend.

The horse archer company commanders were marshalling their men into formation as I rode Remus down the line of rafts to where Domitus was organising his cohorts. We were less than ten miles from the city, I estimated, about three hours' march from Nergal's capital. A forced march would get us there faster but I was conscious of the fact that each legionary was hauling at least sixty pounds in weight on his back – food, water bottle, cloak, spare clothing, armour and weapons, entrenching tool and eating utensils – all strapped to what the Romans called a *furca*. This was a wooden pole with a crossbar at the top, to which the pack that contained his equipment is strapped. As with many things Roman it was extremely practical and in an emergency could simply be dumped on the ground. But because we had brought no carts or mules the men were also burdened with the wooden stakes that surrounded the camp at night, plus spare javelins and shields.

Domitus stood in the middle of a knot of his officers, pointing his vine cane to the cohorts and then towards the smoke to the south. He dismissed them when he saw Gallia and me approach. His men were facing south with the river on their right flank and the fields of Mesene's farmers on their left. Ominously, there was no one working the land, which suggested that the nearest villagers had fled. To where I did not know.

Domitus held his helmet with its white transverse crest in the crook of his arm. He squinted up at me.

'Looks like the old witch was right, then?'

'It would appear so,' I replied sadly. 'I have sent Byrd and Malik ahead to find out more.'

'We had best get started,' said Domitus. 'You had better keep your horsemen close in case we run into the enemy. First I will move the cohorts inland.'

'That will delay our advance,' said Gallia.

Domitus pointed his cane at the next field. 'It will take an age marching across these fields and through date palm groves and will tire out the boys unnecessarily.'

Before Gallia had a chance to reply he pointed his cane at one of his officers who turned and barked an order to his trumpeters. There was a blast of the instruments and then as one the legionaries turned left and began marching away from the river.

'He's right,' I said to Gallia who closed the cheekguards on her helmet and wheeled Epona about to trot away.

'The Amazons will form the vanguard,' she called to me as she led her warriors towards the east where the legionaries were marching.

Vagharsh began coughing behind me as the horses of the Amazons kicked up a small dust cloud. The legionaries, meanwhile, had broken into song as they tramped across the baked earth, a mournful ballad about my victory over Narses at Surkh. I smiled as I heard them sing about Narses disguising himself as a woman to escape the slaughter and their hopes of meeting the men of Persis again in battle.

'Brotherly business, isn't it, killing each other?' said Vagharsh.

I dug my knees into Remus' sides and he cantered forward. I rode to where the score of company commanders of the horse archers sat on their horses waiting for instructions. Like the Amazons they each carried three full quivers of arrows, their bows in the leather cases hanging from their saddles. They also carried swords and daggers but only in the event of an enemy rout would the horse archers be unleashed to use their close-quarter weapons. Their strength was in their mobility and ability to unleash devastating volleys of arrows. But being unarmoured they were very vulnerable if they engaged in a mêlée. I ordered two companies to provide flank cover and another to cover the rear of our army. The remaining companies would dismount and walk their horses in the rear of the cohorts, rotating with the mounted companies every hour.

After twenty minutes we had left the fields and swung south to march across the iron-hard ground as we headed for Uruk. Domitus had been right about leaving the fields. In every kingdom that bordered either the Tigris or Euphrates villagers positioned their fields next to small irrigations ditches or reservoirs that channelled water from the rivers. As a result, complex irrigation systems sprang up everywhere. To march through those fields and accompanying irrigation ditches would have been extremely taxing for foot soldiers and horses alike. Much better to march across hard, even ground.

The nearest village, a collection of small mud-brick homes with reed roofs, was deserted. The animal pens were also empty, which suggested that the residents had fled with their animals. To where we had no idea. Hopefully Byrd would be able to cast some light on the mystery.

The legionaries were still singing as they tramped south, though they must have been sweltering under the sun and from the loads they had to shoulder. But they had been trained hard by Domitus and were well used to route marches under a merciless desert sun. After two hours Byrd and Malik returned with the news that I had dreaded.

Domitus called a halt so they men could rest and drink from their water bottles as I called for an impromptu war council. Byrd, his robes covered with a fine layer of light brown dirt, slid off his horse and unwrapped his *shemagh*. The area around his eyes was covered with dust.

'Uruk under attack,' he stated matter-of-factly.

Malik was more informative.

'We rode to where villages to the west and north of the city have been burned, Pacorus. We saw parties of foot soldiers in the settlements but they are merely patrols.'

'Many boats on the river,' said Byrd.

Domitus looked confused. 'Boats?'

68

'Carrying soldiers,' continued Malik. 'They are rowing up the main canal that leads to the city.'

Uruk was sited five miles to the east of the Euphrates and was connected to the river by a series of canals that provided water for the inhabitants. Most were small, narrow channels that fed reservoirs inside the city. A man could step over them with ease. But there was a large canal — at least fifty feet wide, its sides faced with stone — that ran directly east from the river and which bisected the city. It brought water from the river to irrigate the great gardens inside the city that had been created by its kings for their recreation. It also divided the city in two. To the south of the great canal were the homes of the citizens and the city's businesses, while to the north lay the great White Temple of Anu, the Sky God, and the spacious royal quarter that contained the verdant gardens.

'The soldiers carried round, red shields, Pacorus,' said Malik.

'Did they carry any insignia?' enquired Domitus.

'White wings,' answered Byrd.

'The symbol of Nike,' said Gallia, 'the goddess worshipped by the people of Charax.'

'So Tiraios has become our enemy,' I remarked bitterly. 'We must draw away the enemy soldiers in those boats from the city, otherwise they will sweep into Uruk and burn it.'

I looked at Byrd. 'Did your men see what was happening where the canal passes the walls?'

He shook his head. 'But archers still in towers either side of canal. They are still shooting at the enemy.'

'That would suggest Nergal still holds the city walls,' I said. 'Very well. Domitus, you will lead the foot south towards the canal. I will take a dragon of horse archers and gain the attention of the enemy to force them to array themselves to the north of the canal. Hopefully this will relieve the pressure against Nergal's soldiers. Gallia, you will stay with Domitus to guard the flanks of the foot.'

Malik coughed. 'The dust of Mesene gets in my nostrils.'

Domitus looked up at the angry white sun. 'Let's hope we can destroy the enemy quickly. Fighting in this heat will test even my boys.'

'Then let us not tarry,' I said. 'Shamash be with you all.'

Domitus raised his cane in acknowledgement and sauntered back to his waiting officers. Gallia nodded and wheeled Epona away to ride back to the Amazons, while I cantered over to the company commanders of the horse archers. As the trumpets and whistles of the Durans and Exiles sounded I ordered half to report to Gallia and the rest to gather their men and follow me. Half left us in a cloud of dust to receive their orders from my wife as the others rode away to their waiting companies. I turned Remus to face south and then nudged him forward. Malik was right, this land was parched and even small movements kicked up clouds of dust. What would be the effect of two thousand iron-shod horses and two thousand hobnailed sandals on this baked surface?

'This standard is going to be reduced to tatters soon,' remarked Vagharsh behind me as he slipped off the waxed sleeve that protected my griffin banner.

I turned and looked at the red griffin and the gold edges of the standard.

'It looks as pristine as the day I first saw it in my father's palace.'

Vagharsh gripped it with his right hand and straightened his arm, but there was no wind and so it just hung limply on the pole.

'The rumour is that it is bewitched and cannot be damaged,' said Vagharsh confidently. 'Let's hope the same applies to the man who carries it.'

I laughed and urged Remus on, a thousand horse archers behind us as we broke into a canter and headed south. We were about four miles from the Euphrates and there were no fields or irrigation canals to impede our progress, just a hard-baked dirt surface made of gravel and pebbles that the horses' hooves kicked up to disturb the soft soil underneath. To our left was an endless expanse of sun-scorched desert that ended at the Tigris some fifty miles to the east, to our front the high walls and towers of Uruk. I prayed we were not too late.

It took us twenty minutes to near the canal; the muffled sounds of battle coming from the left where boats filled with enemy soldiers were trying to force an entry into Uruk. We were perhaps a quarter of a mile away from the watercourse and I could see the two towers that flanked the canal, though it was impossible to ascertain whether archers were still shooting down from their ramparts. Byrd and Malik galloped up, their horses covered in sweat and their black robes turned light brown by dust. Byrd unwrapped his *shemagh* as his scouts galloped through my companies and halted behind them.

'City still holds out,' he said, 'but canal full of boats loaded with soldiers.'

I cursed.

'How many soldiers?'

Byrd looked at Malik.

'Thousands,' replied the Agraci prince. 'It is only a matter of time before they storm the city.'

'Byrd, I would ask you to take your men to request that Domitus speeds up his march.'

'What are you going to do?' Malik asked me.

'To pick a fight, lord prince,' I answered.

Byrd replaced the cloth around the lower half of his face and dug his knees into his tired horse, galloping away. Malik reached behind him and pulled a recurve bow from a leather case. I also saw he had three quivers attached to his saddle, their contents protected by leather covers.

'I would assist you, Pacorus,' he said.

'That looks like a Parthian bow,' said Vagharsh. 'I hope you didn't steal it.'

'I found it,' answered Malik.

I was intrigued. 'Found it?'

'Before you were Dura's king, Pacorus,' replied Malik, 'the high king of your empire sent Mithridates to rule your city. He believed himself to be a great warlord but my father destroyed his army. I took this bow as a trophy of our victory.'

Vagharsh laughed.

'Let us hope you have more luck with it than its former owner,' I said. 'Keep yourself safe, Malik.'

I turned and signalled for the company commanders to come forward. The sounds of battle were getting louder and they were straining at the leash to get to grips with the enemy but I counselled caution.

'I will take one company forward to reconnoitre,' I told them. 'You must impress on your men the importance of conserving their arrows. We have no supply train to draw on so when they empty their quivers there will no replacements. Aimed shots only. Now go.'

Each archer carried ninety arrows but they could be expended in around fifteen minutes of continuous shooting. Byrd had told me that the enemy army was large. Horse archers without any arrows were useless.

There was a succession of horn blasts followed by the companies deploying into line, each one of two widely spaced ranks. I reached down and uncorked the water bottle and took a swig. The liquid was warm and barely alleviated the dryness in my mouth. I replaced the cork. It was going to be a long, hot day and I would need its contents in the hours ahead. The lead company came forward and halted a few paces behind me. Each man took an arrow from his quiver and nocked it in his bowstring. I gave the signal to move forward. Malik was beside me and Vagharsh directly behind as our horses broke into a walk and then a canter, the low rumble to the rear indicating that the company was following.

We were now less than four hundred paces from the canal, the walls of Uruk perhaps a quarter of a mile on our left. Though I could clearly hear the noise of men fighting coming from the city walls the ground to our front was empty. It was most odd. Then I saw a few figures ahead, shimmering individuals on foot that appeared as if by magic. Then more and more until suddenly there were hundreds of warriors flooding the ground directly ahead. They were leaving their boats on the canal to face the horsemen that had suddenly appeared immediately north of the canal. Good. That is what I had intended.

I raised my hand to signal a halt as more and more warriors appeared like devils from the underworld as they clambered from their boats. I recognised them. These were not the soldiers of King Tiraios. They wore baggy yellow leggings, loose fitting red tunics and leather caps on their heads. They carried round ox-hide shields and were armed with a variety of sword and spears. These men came from Sakastan.

'So Narses has not been quelling insurrections in Sakastan but gathering an army,' I said aloud.

Malik looked at me quizzically.

'Nothing,' I said.

72

To add to the sounds of battle the noise of horns and drums suddenly erupted within the ranks of the warriors of Sakastan. The latter had now gathered into a brightly coloured block with a wide frontage. There were perhaps two thousand but scanning their ranks I saw no slingers or archers. The din of drums and horns increased as I called forward the company commander and gave him his orders.

'Raking attack, left to right, half volleys only.'

He saluted and trotted back to his men, relaying my orders as the red and yellow horde ahead began shouting war cries and banging their weapons against their shields in an attempt to intimidate us. A few left the ranks to run forward to open their arms to reveal their torsos to taunt us.

What is war but a series of training exercises interspersed with death and gore? Dura's army had been forged by Lucius Domitus, ex-Roman centurion and later commander in the army of Spartacus, a man who was as hard as the *gladius* he wore at his hip. There was nothing remarkable about Dura's army. It was smaller than most armies fielded by the other kingdoms of the empire, but it was staffed by professionals, men who did nothing from dawn till dusk but train. Endless drills that made them as efficient as Marcus Sutonius' machines. Every legionary knew his role and place in the century, cohort and legion, knew the meaning of every call made by the trumpets and every whistle blast that came from a centurion. It was the same among the horsemen: every horse archer practised drills and shooting on the training fields every day and the cataphracts trained to be the mailed fist of the army. And Domitus had integrated the horse and foot so they could work together on the battlefield, an apparently seamless amalgamation of legionaries fighting on foot and highly mobile horsemen. Dura's army had a simple motto: train hard, fight easy.

In most Parthian armies the horse archers would be unleashed against an enemy in a wild, disorganised charge: thousands of horsemen swarming around an enemy shooting so many volleys of arrows that they would black out the sun. Behind the armies would be dozens, sometimes hundreds, of camels loaded with spare quivers that the horsemen would ride to in order to replenish their ammunition. But eventually even camel trains ran out of ammunition.

But we had no camel train and so we had to adapt our tactics accordingly. Raking attack, left to right, half-volleys only. Every man of the company understood the drill well enough: they had practised it many times on the training field. There was no need for a signal as the first rank wheeled their horses left and the company commander galloped to the head of the line to lead the attack. The enemy, seeing us seemingly immobile and intimidated, became louder in their war cries and taunts, walking forward and spitting in our direction.

The commander directed his horse forward a few yards and then wheeled it right to advance towards the enemy warriors, several of whom had dropped their leggings to take a piss in our direction, to the great amusement of their comrades. The commander cantered forward and then broke into a gallop as he swung his mount to the right again so he could ride from left to right across the front of the enemy formation. His and his men's arrival was greeted with jeers and whistles from the enemy. Until he and they swung left in the saddle, pulled back their bowstrings and shot their arrows.

A Parthian recurve bow is so called because the central part of the limbs curve towards the archer while the tips of the limbs curve away from him. This shape gives more power to the arrow when it was released. And had the enemy been more attentive they would have noted that the bows equipping the horsemen riding across their front at a distance of just over fifty paces were short, had a setback centre section and had limbs that were thick in proportion to their width. The Sakastanis must have thought that we too were engaging in insults and taunting, until the archers released their bowstrings.

The whoosh of the arrows as they were shot was drowned out by the jeers of the enemy. But the high-pitched screams of men being struck by three-winged bronze arrowheads were clear enough above the din. The riders took their time shooting to conserve ammunition, letting loose only three arrows each before they wheeled right to take them back to their starting positions. But every arrow found its mark, some going through shields to strike unarmoured torsos and necks. Half the company had killed or wounded a hundred and fifty men by the time its second rank began its assault. Like their comrades the riders galloped across the enemy's front, shooting arrows as they did so and keeping out of range of any spears that were hurled at them. The Sakastanis' bravado had evaporated as they huddled together to present a wall of shields and levelled spears to my horsemen. But all this did was to make it easier for the archers to kill more of them, closely packed as they were and having useless headgear and no armour protection. The second rank likewise killed at least a hundred and fifty more of the enemy.

Three hundred Sakastanis had been killed or wounded for no losses.

The company made another attack, again raking the enemy formation with arrows that felled over two hundred more of the enemy. Each horse archer had now shot six arrows and I was considering letting them make a third assault when suddenly hundreds more soldiers appeared from the canal, and more importantly from near the city walls. This indicated that I had managed to draw the enemy away from where the fighting was taking place with the defenders. Perhaps the entire enemy army had been diverted to deal with my presence. I was feeling very happy with myself and was pondering whether to commit the whole dragon when the officer of the company that had been attacking the Sakastanis galloped up.

'Enemy archers massing, majesty.'

I peered into the haze that was thickening as a result of the dust kicked up by our horses.

'Where?'

He turned and pointed to the left of the Sakastanis where I could make out groups of individuals in the dusty dimness.

'They are also from Sakastan, majesty. I recognise them from when we defeated Porus.'

I remembered too. Porus' archers were equipped with long bamboo bows the height of a man, which required one end to be anchored on firm ground before they could be shot. But if they managed to release a volley their missiles would hit my horsemen easily. We had but moments to act.

'Sound retreat,' I ordered.

The officer saluted and galloped back to his men, his signaller blowing his horn to indicate an immediate withdrawal.

I turned to the officers of the other company commanders behind me. 'You will also withdraw your companies immediately.'

They too saluted and rode back to their men.

'Time to go, Vagharsh,' I said, wheeling Remus around and digging my knees into his sides. He grunted and raced forward, his hooves churning up the dry surface as he did so. I turned and looked at the rapidly fading mass of archers grouping in front of the canal, my heart pounding in my chest as I waited for the arrow storm to engulf us.

If the enemy loosed a volley I did not see it as Vagharsh and I brought up the rear of the fleeing horse archers. They reined their horses to a halt when they ran into Gallia and her Amazons, the advance guard of the rest of the army. Her face was streaked with sweat when she removed her helmet to speak to me a few moments later.

'Running away, Pacorus?' she grinned.

'A tactical withdrawal, my sweet.'

I looked past her to see a long line of white shields sporting red wings.

'I hope we have enough men,' I said.

'And women,' she added.

We rode to where Domitus was marching alone before his front rank of legionaries, vine cane in hand and appearing as nonchalant as he would be on a morning stroll in Dura. He raised his cane to signal a halt as we approached. I jumped down from the saddle.

'The garrison is still fighting and I have managed to draw the enemy from their boats onto land to the north of the canal. That's the good news.'

He took off his helmet, pulled a cloth that was tucked in his belt and used it to wipe his sweat-covered brow.

'And the bad news?'

'It would appear that we are heavily outnumbered.'

He gave Gallia a crooked smile. 'We are always outnumbered.'

'They have archers,' I informed him, 'so when you advance make sure your men are in *testudo* formation.'

I looked at the two thousand legionaries and the horse archers that were deploying on their flanks. I was concerned by our lack of numbers.

'I hope our numbers are enough.'

'We have enough,' growled Domitus. 'You should remember that the steel that runs through the veins of my boys is far more important that the steel they hold in their fists. And like a fist we will smash straight through them.'

Chapter 3

The dust haze still hung in the air as the cohorts made their way towards the canal, which was around five hundred yards away. The legionaries dumped their *furcas* and went into all-round defence mode, those in the front ranks forming a shield wall and those behind lifting their shields above their heads to create a roof of wood and leather. Domitus had grabbed a spare shield and stood in the centre of the battle line, which was composed of twenty-five centuries in a single line. Each century was composed of eighty men in eight ranks, each rank containing ten men. It was a thin line that had a frontage of around three hundred yards. But there was a substantial reserve − two thousand horse archers − because I could not commit the horsemen until the location and strength of the enemy's bowmen had been determined.

Byrd and Malik wanted to take the scouts forward but I forbade it.

'I do not wish to lose two friends and all my scouts,' I told them, 'so you and they will remain with me.'

We were advancing at a slow walking pace, which at least gave the horses some respite, the legionaries shuffling forward under the cover of their shields. An unnerving quiet had descended over the battlefield, which at least indicated that the fighting where the canal entered the city had halted. The archers on the towers would be able to see our presence by now, which would hopefully raise the garrison's morale. I stared ahead and realised that at least the haze was diminishing now that the horses were no longer kicking up dust. The view was not reassuring.

The enemy mass had lengthened to not only match the frontage of Domitus' men but also outflank them substantially. In the centre was a line of helmets, spear points and large round shields − the soldiers of Charax.

'Stay here,' I said to Gallia, Byrd and Malik as I urged Remus forward.

Vagharsh followed but I turned and shouted to him.

'You too, I need to talk to Domitus.'

I galloped forward to the rear of the giant *testudo* as it inched its way towards the enemy. I jumped from the saddle and handed the reins to a startled legionary in the rearmost rank.

'Hold these,' I said and then pushed my way through the century.

'Mind where your tread, bloody idiot and get out of my way' were but a few of the insults I had to endure from burly, gruff soldiers whose minds were focused on the coming fight and had no time for their king at this time. I stooped low and shoved my way through the ranks. I recognised a transverse crest in front of me.

'Domitus,' I hissed.

'What in the name of Mars are you doing here?'

I stood immediately behind him. 'Those soldiers in front are from Charax. You remember us talking about them? They probably fight in the old Greek style. You remember the tactics from the Sons of the Citadel?'

'Of course,' he snapped. 'Now get back to your horse boys and make sure no one turns our flanks.'

'Shamash be with you,' I said to him as I turned and endured more insults as I made my way to the rear of the century. As I took Remus' reins and vaulted into the saddle I heard Domitus shouting to his centurions, alerting them to the tactics of the enemy and to spread the word to the other centuries.

I galloped back to my queen and scouts as a loud whooshing sound erupted behind me. Gallia gave the order to stop as I brought Remus to a halt in a cloud of dust and turned him to face south. Just in time to see the sky filled with thousands of black arrows arching into the blue sky. The legionaries halted as the missiles fell out of the sky and struck their shields.

There followed a second volley and once again the Durans and Exiles sheltered beneath their shields – three layers of wood glued together with the grain of the wood at right angles to the preceding layer, faced with thick leather. The shields were locked tight above and facing the enemy because arrows had a nasty habit of finding any gaps to strike bodies. And so the centuries stood, immobile, as the soldiers of King Tiraios marched across the bone-hard surface towards them.

Know your enemy was a phrase that was heard often enough in the classrooms where the Sons of the Citadel were instructed. These were the best and brightest officers of Dura's army, men earmarked for future high command. I had hired Parthian, Greek and Egyptian scholars, Chinese philosophers and Roman engineers. I had originally envisaged the school as a place where boys would be tutored to become Dura's future military leaders. But once established it became apparent that the army's best serving officers would also benefit from the school's pool of hired wisdom. And so it was.

The best commanders among the legions, horse archers and cataphracts soon learned of the tactics, composition and capabilities of every kingdom in the Parthian Empire, as well as those of our greatest foe: Rome. This meant that no matter what adversary Dura's army faced its leaders would be well acquainted with the enemy it was about to fight. And today was no different.

Alexander of Macedon, the demi-god who had conquered the world, had founded Charax. But that had been two hundred and sixty years ago and since that time the city had been destroyed by floods, rebuilt and seen its status greatly reduced. Today it was a trading centre and something of a backwater. Its kings were more concerned with commerce and the price of precious metals from the east than with wars and conquest. How easy it must have been for Narses to bribe and flatter Tiraios to make him a pawn in his plans. Just as the King of Persis had dangled the prospect of glory and riches in front of Chosroes, so he had no doubt convinced the King of Charax that Mesene would be easy to conquer, the more so with thousands of warriors from Sakastan to reinforce Charax's army.

That army now marched confidently towards Domitus' men. Curiously, though Alexander of Macedon had founded Charax, its army was equipped and organised in an older Greek style. Not only had Charax not waged a war in decades but also its location made huge phalanxes equipped with the eighteen foot-long sarissa unworkable. Where could such a formation deploy outside a city surrounded by fields, palm groves and marshland? Instead the primary weapon of the Charaxian soldier was an eight-foot stabbing spear with a leaf-shaped blade at one end and a vicious counter-balance spike at the other end called a 'lizard sticker'. Tiraios' men fought in a phalanx, eight ranks deep instead of sixteen favoured by Alexander and his father, the first three of which held their spears overhead to strike downwards. The following five ranks held their spears at an angle of forty-five degrees. The city had adapted the tactics of its army to suit the terrain it was expected to fight in. But we knew how it fought.

As the enemy phalanx approached I heard melodious music coming from its ranks. Like Greek armies of old the Charaxian advance was accompanied by flutes, drums and horns, the music designed to both inspire their own men and strike fear into their enemies.

It was an impressive sight: a great phalanx nearly equal to the frontage of Domitus' centuries advancing as one, each phalangist protect by hardened leather greaves, leather cuirass and bronze helmets. The latter covered the head and most of the neck and had cheek pieces and nose guards that swept forward to such a degree that they nearly met in the centre of the face. The eyes, nose and mouth of its wearer were virtually enclosed. Charaxian helmets also had white crests on top, which not only provided defence against falling spears and blows to the top of the head, but also made the wearer taller and more fearsome. But such a helmet was uncomfortable and impaired the vision and hearing of its wearer.

As well as protecting an individual from the neck to above the knees, a Charaxian shield also facilitated mutual protection in the phalanx. Around three feet in diameter, they were made of wood and faced with leather, both inside and out. Bowl shaped, they were held with the left arm placed through a central band gripped via a leather strap attached to the shield's rim. Every shield was painted red and emblazoned with two white wings in honour of the Goddess Nike.

The enemy phalanx walked forward accompanied by its musicians as whistles and trumpets blew among the legionaries and the *testudo* dissolved. Those who had been wounded by arrows were assisted to the rear to be treated by physicians. I thanked Shamash that there appeared to be few casualties. Then the centuries advanced. Tiraios had subjected Domitus' men to volleys of arrows to soften them up and now he intended to smash them to pieces using his heavy foot. It was a sensible if predictable tactic but he entirely misunderstood the enemy he was facing. His men fought in a relatively loose formation whereas Dura's foot fought in more compact bodies, but as both sides closed on each other the Charaxians encountered a nasty surprise.

As both sides broke into a run when they charged each other a volley of javelins came from the ranks of the legionaries. The Romans called a javelin a *pilum* and it was nothing more than a four-foot shaft of ash topped by a solid triangle of wood, onto which was riveted a thin iron shaft around two and half feet in length that ended in a tiny triangular tip. On impact the iron usually bends, which makes pulling it out of a shield much harder. In fact a javelin stuck in an enemy shield renders the latter useless. But more than this; a volley of javelins destroys the impetus of an enemy charge.

It was so now as the first two ranks in every century hurled their javelins as the two sides closed on each other. Five hundred javelins lanced through the air to land among the front ranks of the enemy phalanx. The first two ranks in each century then pulled their swords from their scabbards as the third and fourth ranks also launched their javelins over their heads towards the now disorganised front ranks of the phalangists – another five hundred iron-tipped missiles embedded themselves in Charaxian shields. And then each legionary went to work with his *gladius*.

Actually that was incorrect. Each first rank legionary barged into the enemy with his body weight behind his shield. This either knocked a phalangist to the ground where he could be finished off by the second-rank legionaries, or shoved him rearwards into his comrades behind. Either way the phalanx was stopped dead in its tracks and its discomfited members had no time to reorganise themselves after the javelin storm before the legionaries were among them.

I gave a shout of triumph. 'Now we will see the mettle of these Charaxians.'

'What about them?' asked Byrd, pointing at the soldiers of Sakastan standing motionless in two huge blocks, a great gap between them where the Charaxian phalanx had been before it advanced. Towards the rear were the archers, redundant now that the phalanx and the legionaries were locked in combat.

'They will attack soon, Pacorus,' Malik warned me.

He was right but I was worried about what the enemy archers would do. If they advanced then I would not be able to deploy my horse archers against the Sakastanis without incurring heavy losses. I was desperately trying to decide what to do when the two formations of enemy spearmen and swordsmen from Sakastan made up my mind for me.

There was a great blast of horns that temporarily drowned out the clatter of combat coming from the centre of the battlefield as the two enemy flanks charged. They moved quickly, breaking into a run almost immediately, fracturing their ragged formation as groups of warriors raced forward. This Tiraios was clever. He knew that his own soldiers were the best troops he had and had committed them against my foot soldiers. But he also knew that if the less disciplined, armed and equipped Sakastanis could sweep around the flanks of my foot soldiers then they could tip the battle's balance in his favour. The dragon of horse archers that Gallia had led south was positioned to the right rear of Domitus' men, the dragon that I commanded being positioned on the left, parallel to the one on the right.

'Gallia,' I said, 'take your dragon and stop those enemy warriors threatening Domitus' right flank. I will do the same on the left.'

She nodded and shouted at Epona to move forward. Seconds later she and Amazons were galloping over to the waiting companies of horse archers.

'I would ask you to safeguard my wife, lord prince,' I said to Malik.

His face broke into a grin. 'Have no fear, my friend, I will see to it.'

'I too,' said Byrd, who raised a hand to me and then followed Malik in the wake of the Amazons.

I dug my knees into Remus and he shot forward towards the waiting companies on the left flank. They were already nocking arrows in their bowstrings in anticipation of combat, for they knew that the horde of warriors charging towards them had to be stopped. I thanked Shamash that the speed of their advance would negate the enemy's archers from delivering any supporting volleys.

The commanders of the companies came forward as a red and yellow tide surged towards us from the south.

'First five companies will assault them head-on,' I ordered. 'The second-line companies will strike their flank. Shamash be with you.'

They saluted and galloped back to their men. I urged Remus forward as the signallers behind me blew their horns and a thousand horsemen moved forward. The first-line companies, each one in two ranks as before, broke into a canter and then a slow gallop as they advanced towards the oncoming warriors. As the middle company caught up with me I could see that the enemy numbered thousands. I nocked an arrow in my bowstring and aimed the arrow up at the sky. I released the bowstring and plucked another arrow from my quiver as those beside and behind me did the same. The company, like the others, was widely spaced for we had no intention of charging into the oncoming mob. The distance between it and us was around four hundred paces and diminishing fast as we shot two more volleys. Just as they had done on the training field as soon as the horns sounded we turned our horses left and left again, to take us away from the oncoming mass. We twisted in the saddle to shoot a volley over the hindquarters of our horses as we retreated before the Sakastanis.

The enemy's charge had been slowed but not stopped by our volleys but its impetus was greatly curtailed when the other companies of horse archers struck it in the flank.

The five companies that had been in the second line turned left and rode away from the army before swinging right to head towards the canal. They galloped hard and then turned completely around so they were riding parallel to the right flank of the charging enemy warriors. They then proceeded to rake them with arrows from a distance of around two hundred paces. Close enough to ensure that their arrows found their targets; far enough away to safeguard against being hit by the missiles being shot by their comrades in the first-line companies.

In a matter of minutes each horse archer had emptied one of his quivers – nearly thirty thousand arrows shot at the enemy. Not all of them had hit an enemy warrior, especially as the horses had once again kicked up a prodigious amount of dust that reduced visibility. But it destroyed the momentum of the enemy's charge.

After retreating three or four hundred paces we turned our horses and rode back south once again, this time at a canter. The dust was everywhere, stinging our eyes and getting into our noses.

'Halt!' I shouted.

The last thing we needed was to blunder into the enemy unawares. Spears and swords could inflict terrible injuries on horse bellies and legs. The sounds of battle could still be heard to the right where the centuries were locked in a ferocious battle with the phalanx but ahead there were only muffled sounds of shouts, screams and shrieks. Suddenly figures on foot appeared ahead, two hundred paces away perhaps. One, two, a dozen, fifty.

'Shoot them down,' I shouted.

Seconds later there was a succession of whooshes as my archers began shooting. Sitting stationary in the saddle they were not only able to shoot up to six arrows a minute, they could also do so with deadly accuracy. The companies deployed in one long line of two ranks, the first ranks shooting their bows as they emptied a second quiver. The enemy's leaders desperately tried to rally their men and several led them forward in an attempt to disperse us. But we emptied our third quivers and littered the ground with heaps of the dead and dying.

'Second rank to move forward,' I ordered.

The signallers blew their horns and the second rank walked their horses forward through the first rank, now out of ammunition. The haze once again subsided as the five companies that had been raking the right flank of the enemy returned and deployed behind the five companies I commanded, which were still walking their horses forward. The officers came to me and reported that they and their men had empty quivers.

'Your men have no arrow left?' I queried.

They shook their heads.

'There were many enemy soldiers, majesty,' said one.

'We reaped a rich harvest,' added another.

I dismissed them and rode forward to where those horse archers still possessing ammunition were busy felling enemy warriors. I gave the order for them to halt their shooting immediately. As the dust settled I could see the enemy falling back, many tripping over the bodies of their dead comrades that had been felled by our arrows. On the right the chant of 'Dura, Dura,' could now be heard and I smiled. Domitus had broken the enemy's resistance. But what was happening on the right flank?

The arrival of an agitated horse archers pushed that subject temporarily to the back of my mind.

'My commander sends his greetings, majesty,' he babbled hurriedly, 'but begs to report that soldiers of Chosroes are approaching from the left.'

He turned and began pointing frantically towards the city walls.

'Calm down,' I told him. 'Your commander is obviously wrong. Chosroes is dead.'

He began shaking his head liked a demented person.

'No, majesty,' he insisted, 'the enemy have black vipers painted on their shields.'

'Perhaps Chosroes has returned from the underworld to haunt you,' suggested Vagharsh, 'bringing with him an army of demons.'

'If he has,' I replied, 'then you will join me in facing them, Vagharsh. Follow me.'

I shoved my bow back in its case and drew my sword.

'Keep pressing the enemy,' I told the company commanders. 'Above all guard General Domitus' left flank.'

The legionaries were now moving forward inexorably, hacking the Charaxians to pieces and pushing their rear ranks back towards the canal. I rode over to where the company on the extreme left of my horse archers was apparently keeping watch on King Chosroes, newly returned from the dead. The excitable archer accompanied me and Vagharsh as I saw with my own eyes what appeared to be a small phalanx of spearmen marching across the company's front, perhaps three hundred paces away. I brought Remus to a halt in front of the company commander, a thin man with dark-brown skin and a black beard. He bowed his head.

'I was at Uruk when we stormed the city, majesty,' he told me in a low voice, 'and I remember what Chosroes' palace guards looked like.'

He pointed at the newly arrived phalanx of spearmen. 'They looked like them.'

I nudged Remus forward so I could take a closer look at these devils from hell.

'Careful, Pacorus,' said Vagharsh.

'It may have escaped your notice Vagharsh,' I called back to him, 'but they appear to be marching across our front and are ignoring us.'

The battle appeared to be going in our favour, notwithstanding that most of my ten companies of horse archers had used up all their ammunition. The warriors of Sakastan had been cut to pieces by volleys of arrows and were falling back, pursued by those horse archers that did have missiles. And in the centre Domitus' men were pushing back the Charaxians, albeit slowly in a vicious battle of attrition. Only two questions remained unanswered: where were the enemy archers and how was Gallia faring on the right wing?

I rode to within two hundred paces of the ghost phalanx that was still marching across our front. I slowed Remus and saw that its men were indeed attired and armed in the fashion of Chosroes' palace guards. They wore bronze helmets, red tunics under cuirasses of overlapping bronze scales and carried large round shields faced with bronze and sporting a black viper motif. They were armed with spears that had leaf-shaped blades, the front rank holding their lances levelled, the ranks behind carrying theirs at an angle of forty-five degrees. I counted ten ranks but could not ascertain the number of files. At a guess I estimated their numbers at three hundred.

Vagharsh pulled up his horse beside me as the soldiers wearing the colours of an enemy pointed their spears towards us and began cheering.

'Well,' said Vagharsh, 'either Chosroes has returned from the dead a changed man or they are not demons from the underworld.'

The phalanx continued to march until it was a hundred paces from the remnants of Tiraios' right wing – perhaps five hundred exhausted and demoralised men – and then it increased its speed to a trot. Like the five companies of horse archers that had been shooting at the Sakastanis as they stumbled backward but which were now out of ammunition, I watched like a spectator as the men in the phalanx gave a great cheer and charged at the enemy. There was a long crunching sound and then a series of screams and cries as the phalanx drove into the enemy, its front rank thrusting spears into the unarmoured torsos of the enemy. The Sakastanis stood and fought for perhaps a minute before fleeing in every direction, some towards the canal, most towards the waiting companies of horse archers. They dumped their shields and weapons and scattered, running for their lives. What followed was highly unusual as the horse archers replaced their bows in their saddle cases, drew their swords and then charged the fleeing warriors. It was one of the few times that I saw horse archers engage foot soldiers, albeit ones that were largely defenceless and demoralised. It quickly degenerated into a slaughter as the horsemen went to work with their swords.

The phalanx of bronze and iron, meanwhile, had halted among the dead and dying Sakastanis. A figure left the front rank and began running towards us.

'What now?' said Vagharsh.

'Perhaps he holds a grudge against you, Vagharsh.'

The figure slowed some fifty paces from us and raised his spear in salute.

'This gets stranger by the minute,' mused Vagharsh.

The figure rammed his lizard sticker into the ground and took off his helmet, to reveal black shoulder-length hair and a square, clean-shaven face with a thin nose. Surena grinned at me.

'Hail, majesty.'

I slid my sword back into its scabbard. 'The mystery is solved.'

I nudged Remus forward.

'Greetings, Surena. Your appearance is most fortuitous. Where is King Nergal?'

'He left the city several days ago, along with the queen, majesty.'

I leaned forward. 'Then who has been defending Uruk?'

Surena's dark brown eyes flashed with pride. 'Me and Rahim, majesty.'

He pointed at the phalanx he had been leading. 'Plus a few hardy Ma'adan warriors.'

'Stranger and stranger,' grunted Vagharsh.

The horse archers had finished butchering the hapless Sakastanis by now and were regrouping in their companies. My thoughts turned to Gallia.

'Report to General Domitus,' I said to Surena. 'I must go to secure my right flank.'

Surena saluted and grinned at Vagharsh, who shook his head and followed me as I rode back to the companies of horsemen. I left five to support Domitus' men and took the remainder across the rear of the still steadily advancing centuries towards the right wing. The ground where the Durans and Exiles had been fighting was a ghastly sight: dead and dying everywhere, many crying out pitifully for water or assistance. I felt no pity, only relief that most appeared to be enemy soldiers.

Remus was tired now, his breathing heavy as he thundered across the baked earth, he and hundreds of other horses kicking up clouds of dust to add to the agonies of injured men. My silk vest and tunic were soaked with sweat and my head felt as though it was on fire under my helmet. Sweat stung my eyes. My mouth tasted foul.

Our pace was agonisingly slow because even though our mounts would run themselves into the ground if we demanded it of them, no true Parthian would willingly cause the death of his horse.

At last we passed the last centuries on the right of the line and came upon our right wing, or at least four companies of it. Fear rose within me as I frantically looked around for my wife. She was nowhere to be seen and neither were the Amazons. I halted the column as an officer from one of the companies rode over to report. He and his horse looked remarkably fresh.

'Report,' I ordered.

He bowed his head. 'When the enemy charged the queen formed all the companies into a wedge formation, majesty, and charged straight at them, the queen and the Amazons at the tip of the wedge. The enemy was halted and then scattered by our volleys of arrows.'

89

'Where is the queen?' I snapped, looking past him to where bodies lay scattered on the ground. He pointed towards the Euphrates.

'Pursuing the enemy, majesty,' he replied. 'She left those whose ammunition had been exhausted behind.'

I gave the order for all but a hundred men to remain with Gallia's four companies and support Domitus' men, taking the remainder with me towards the Euphrates. There were hardly any sounds of battle now, just a dust haze that hung over the carrion field. I took a swig from my water bottle and then urged Remus forward. Vagharsh and the company followed as we cantered west towards the river. Dead men in baggy yellow leggings and red tunics indicated the path my wife had taken.

We rode for around four miles until we came across dismounted horse archers standing near where the canal meets the Euphrates, their horses standing in groups back from the canal's edge. When they saw my banner the men began to cheer and raise their bows in salute.

'Dismount,' I ordered when we reached the companies.

I slowly descended to the ground and handed Remus' reins to Vagharsh who had also dismounted.

'Wait here,' I told him.

I walked towards the canal bank, which was lined with archers. Others were standing behind them, cheering as the ones in front shot their bows. There were calls of 'the king' as I made my way forward. The throng parted and I saw Gallia standing, helmet by her feet, with bow in hand at the canal's edge. She turned and gave me a beautiful smile as I took off my helmet and ran to embrace her. More cheering.

'I thank Shamash that you are safe,' I whispered into her ear.

'And you, my love,' she purred. She pulled away and gave me a mischievous grin.

I glanced at the canal and was surprised to see it was filled with a plethora of boats, most of them simple rowing vessels no more than twenty feet in length.

'Keep shooting,' barked Gallia.

The archers lining the bank recommenced their shooting, aiming at boats that were filled with enemy soldiers desperately trying to reach the Euphrates and safety.

Gallia plucked an arrow from the nearly empty quiver slung over her shoulder and nocked it in her bowstring.

'After we had scattered the enemy's wing,' she said, drawing back the string to nearly her right ear, 'many enemy soldiers fled on foot towards the Euphrates.'

She released the bowstring and her missile shot through the air to hit a rower in a boat on the far side of the canal. He made no noise as he slumped over his oar.

'The enemy's archers fled to their boats and have escaped, I regret to say,' she continued, pulling another arrow from her quiver. 'But these soldiers, whom I recognise from when we fought King Porus, were not so lucky.'

She released her arrow and killed another oarsman in the same boat, the girlish Viper a few feet away slaying the man behind him. All along the canal bank archers were releasing arrows at the dozens of boats on the waterway, many of which contained only dead men.

I looked at Viper. 'Surena led a force from the city to aid us,' I said to Gallia, 'but Nergal and Praxima are not in Uruk.'

She stopped shooting and looked at me, surprised. 'Oh? Where are they?'

I shrugged. 'I know as much as you.'

'We are running out of arrows, majesty,' a senior officer of horse archers reported to Gallia. She looked at her own quiver.

'Two arrows left.'

She looked back at the canal where seemingly dozens of boats lay stationary in the water, their crews dead. Other boats were still running the gauntlet between the archers lining the bank and the safety of the Euphrates but a short distance away.

'We must return to the city,' I said to Gallia, 'satisfying though this may be.'

She turned to the officer. 'Give the order to mount up and ride to the city.'

'Viper,' she called.

Surena's wife walked over, bowing her head to both of us.

'Your husband has marched from the city, my husband tells me. You have been apart for too long, so go to him.'

91

She turned to the officer. 'Give Viper an escort so she can be reunited with her husband.'

Viper smiled, bowed and ran to her horse.

'It would appear that Surena has saved Uruk,' I said as Viper and a company of horsemen galloped away.

'But where are Nergal and Praxima?' asked a concerned Gallia.

We left the remnants of the enemy army on the canal to ride back to the battlefield. As ever with the field of honour after an engagement it presented a dreadful sight. We sought out Domitus and found him standing among his legionaries, most of whom were either sitting or lying on the ground. Guards had been posted and medical staff were attending to the wounded as hundreds of Durans and Exiles took a well-earned rest. He raised his cane when he saw us approach, the men around him looking up as I slid off Remus' back and walked over to him. I held out my arm and he gripped my forearm.

'Good to see you, my friend,' I said, 'Uruk has been saved.'

He looked tired and exhausted.

'That was a hard fight and it was close for a while.'

He nodded towards where a line of Charaxian dead lay heaped at the canal's edge.

'If there had been any more of them we would not have been able to break them.'

Gallia walked up and embraced him. 'Praise the gods that you are safe, Domitus.'

He gave her a weak smile and turned when he heard giggling, to see Surena, resplendent in his bronze scale armour and red tunic, embracing Viper. Normally such a display of affection would attract whistles and whoops from the soldiers, but they just stared at the couple with listless expressions.

'He always comes up smelling of roses,' was the only comment Domitus made.

As far as I could tell he was unhurt, though several of the metal discs that adorned his mail armour had been knocked off and his helmet's crest was all but gone. I also noticed that the leather facing on his shield was badly torn. For a while he said nothing as he looked up and down at his spent legionaries resting, some drinking from water bottles, others apparently asleep. At length he straightened his back and gave a loud sigh.

'Those soldiers from Charax were well armoured and trained,' he told me. 'Each man wore a bronze helmet that covered his head, carried a shield that protected the area from the shoulders down to the thigh and wore greaves that shielded the area from the knees to the feet.'

He raised his cane and pointed the tip at my neck. 'But they had a weak spot, the exposed neck area, which we could stab at. I thank Mars for our javelins, though, for without them we would have been hard pressed.'

'We had an easier time on the flanks against the warriors of Sakastan,' I said.

Domitus let his cane drop. 'Surena,' he bellowed. 'Get your arse over here.'

Surena kissed Viper once more and ran over, his bronze armoured cuirass shimmering in the sunlight that was roasting horses and men and adding to the thirst that gripped our soldiers.

Surena grinned. 'Yes, general?'

'Where is Nergal?'

'Out of the city,' said Surena, who grinned triumphantly at Gallia.

'Why?' snapped Domitus.

'Because he heard that an enemy army had sailed up the Tigris,' said Surena. 'He got that news from the Ma'adan. It was obviously a ruse to lure him and the army away from the city.'

'Obviously,' said Domitus irritably. 'So who is in charge until he returns?'

Surena drew himself up and stood rigidly to attention. 'I am, general.'

I was surprised. 'You, Surena?'

He grinned again, which did nothing to improve Domitus' mood. 'Yes, lord. The garrison commander was killed when the enemy first attacked so I took over.'

He pointed at his phalanx of Ma'adan. 'We held the enemy at the canal with the help of the garrison.'

'Well, then, *commander*,' said Domitus firmly, 'my men need water and carts to transport the wounded inside the city so they can be treated.'

93

Surena pointed towards the canal. 'There is plenty of water in the canal, general.'

Domitus glared at him. 'It's full of dead, bleeding bodies, boy.'

'General Domitus is right, Surena,' I interrupted, keen to prevent any potential violence between the two. 'We badly need medicines, water and transport.'

Surena saluted and ran back to his men.

'If it wasn't for Viper I would banish that arrogant young puppy,' sneered Gallia.

Like Domitus she had never taken to Surena, my former squire who was now a member of Dura's cataphracts. But he was a brave, resourceful young man who had a quick mind. And he was a born leader, a man others followed because he had absolute faith in his own abilities and overflowed with confidence. My wife and the commander of my army believed it was arrogance, nothing more, but I knew Surena had the potential to be a great warlord.

He was also a good officer. He despatched runners to the city to order that Uruk's northern gates be opened and supplies and carts be sent to the army that had saved the city. A grateful populace also arrived with the transports carrying water and beer for the victors, though Domitus prohibited his men drinking any alcohol. To fill a dehydrated and exhausted body with beer would invite delirium and unconsciousness. I stayed on the field of battle until the last of the wounded had been evacuated on carts and the sun at last began to drop on the western horizon. It was a huge, blood-red ball that provided a fitting epitaph to this costly day. Domitus handed me a full water skin and I drank from it greedily. My arms and legs ached and I had a headache but at least the fearsome heat was abating.

'I shan't be sorry to see the end of this day,' remarked Domitus, looking at the many dead bodies that were being collected for cremation after soldiers of the garrison and impressed labourers had stripped them of anything useful. Our own dead – a hundred legionaries and a hundred and fifty horse archers – had been loaded on carts for cremation inside the city in the presence of the populace in a religious ceremony that would take place at midnight. The wounded amounted to over a hundred legionaries and eighty horse archers, all of whom I hoped would see the new dawn.

'We should get some food in our bellies,' I said, 'otherwise we will be fainting by the time the ceremony begins.'

'We should burn our dead here, where they fell,' growled Domitus. 'And observed by their comrades, not by ogling civilians.'

'They will not be ogling, they will be paying their respects and praying for their souls,' sounded a deep voice behind us.

We both turned to see Rahim, High Priest to Anu, standing with his hands folded across his broad chest. Completely bald, he towered over Domitus by at least six inches. Dressed in a long-sleeved white robe edged with gold, his dark brown eyes stared at my general, unblinking, daring him to challenge the chief representative of the Sky God on earth.

Domitus nodded at the corpses of the enemy. 'What about them? Are you going to pay homage to them as well, priest?'

Rahim raised an eyebrow, or at least the skin above his left eye moved because his eyebrows had been shaved.

'Their souls are doomed. We will burn their bodies to prevent the spread of pestilence.'

His demeanour suddenly changed as he looked at me and let his arms drop to his sides.

'Hail, King Pacorus. You answered Anu's call and I thank you.'

'You have his sorceress to thank for him being here, priest,' sniffed Domitus.

Rahim regarded Domitus for a moment. 'Lucius Domitus. The king and queen have told me much about you. About how you were a condemned criminal that King Pacorus rescued from a living death, of how you fought for the slave general and then travelled back to Parthia to become the sword of Dura.'

Domitus smiled, the first time he had done so this dreadful day.

'You honour me.'

The rays of the descending sun glinted off Rahim's gold earrings as he nodded thoughtfully.

95

'It is said in many of the empire's palaces and temples, Roman, that you are Namtar, the demon of death, sent by the gods to do the bidding of King Pacorus. Looking around I can see that the gossip has credence.'

Domitus tilted his head at the priest. 'You honour me again.'

'But you are wrong about the king's sorceress, Roman. Who do you think was responsible for sending the message to her? It was Anu, father of all the gods.'

He raised his shaved eyebrow again. 'And of evil spirits and demons, including you, Roman.'

Domitus slapped me hard on the shoulder. 'This is my lord on earth, and Mars is my lord above.'

Rahim frowned. 'Mars?'

'The Roman god of war,' replied Domitus.

'Your gods have no power in this land,' said Rahim loudly.

'Well I am not a god,' I said, 'and urgently require refreshment and a wash if I am to attend tonight's ceremony.'

I led Domitus away by the arm as Rahim strode off to supervise the cremation of the enemy dead.

'There is no point in annoying him, Domitus. He holds great sway in the city.'

'Priests,' spat Domitus disparagingly. 'They're all the same. Arrogant, sanctimonious and a waste of a good skin. Still, I like the name they have given me.'

'It is not a compliment, Domitus.'

He winked at me. 'Course it is.'

Domitus may have had a low opinion of priests but even he appreciated the cremation ceremony that evening. He stood with Gallia and me in the compound of the White Temple, the great ziggurat that was the earthly home of Anu. The city's population had been recruited to build the funeral pyres before the night came, thousands of people bringing felled trees from the huge Royal Orchard that was adjacent to the palace to create a great mound of wood. The ziggurat was built of mud-bricks but was faced with white stone illuminated by dozens of torches positioned along the ramps leading to its summit – the residence of Anu. As such only the high priest, his senior priests and the king and queen were allowed access to its sacred interior.

The legionaries and horse archers stood to attention around the funeral pyre, the latter without their horses, which were resting in the royal stables. Also in the compound were arrayed Surena's Ma'adan, resplendent in their bronze armour and helmets. Members of the garrison ringed the massive stone platform of the White Temple, like the Ma'adan wearing bronze armour and helmets and carrying shields sporting a black viper motif. Clearly Nergal had not had time to choose his own insignia to replace that of Chosroes.

Byrd and Malik were also standing with us at the foot of the stone steps that led to the first of the ziggurat's five receding tiers. Byrd's scouts, though, had absented themselves with their commander's permission. The Amazons stood with the horse archers, five of their number wrapped in white sheets on the pyre after being slain in the battle. Some of the populace had been allowed into the White Temple's compound, which was surrounded by a white stone wall, mostly the most influential and prosperous merchants and officials and their wives. The rest were kept outside. Nevertheless, thousands of citizens ringed the temple's compound, grateful that their city had been saved from being plundered and that they had been saved from slavery or death.

Gallia looked tired and upset at having lost five of her bodyguard, the price of charging headlong into the enemy, though I did not tell her that. As midnight approached Rahim's white-robed, shaven-headed priests began chanting, a tedious dirge that only added to my headache that was stubbornly refusing to ease. A dozen of them led bulls by their ring noses to the funeral pyre, though only so they could watch the cremation and not for sacrificial reasons.

'I hope they are docile,' Domitus whispered to me, 'otherwise they will stampede when the fire is lit.'

'They are probably drugged,' I told him.

'Might as well slit their throats, then,' said the general loudly, causing a priest holding a bull nearest to us to turn and glare at him.

'Bulls are the symbol of Nanna, the Moon God, Domitus,' I informed him. 'As such these beasts are sacred and may not be harmed.'

He was going to say something in reply but was stopped from doing so by the booming voice of Rahim, standing at the top of the steps.

'Great Nanna, brother of Nergal and father of Shamash, deliver the souls of these brave men to heaven that Anu may welcome them into His domain.'

'He forgets that Amazons also lost their lives,' hissed Gallia. I held her hand to comfort her.

Rahim nodded to half a dozen of his priests who walked forward carrying torches and set light to the pyre. The latter had been liberally doused with oil to ensure the newly cut wood burned quickly. Within minutes yellow flames were flaring, illuminating the faces of hundreds of legionaries and horse archers drawn up in their ranks, each one no doubt thinking that but for the grace of the gods it could be their bodies being consumed by fire.

Rahim's voice boomed again, though this time it had competition from the roaring flames.

'Great Anu, master of men, founder of dynasties, the drop of rain on the branch, the king of all things, we give thanks that You are our security.

Hail Anu!'

The citizens and priests answered with their own acclamation of the Sky God and then Rahim raised his arms to still them as the flames began to consume the bodies of the fallen and the heat warmed our faces.

'Anu maketh fear in all things,' shouted Rahim. 'He is the clay which is the flesh of all existence. He is the pointing hand and the hand outstretched for mercy. He is the teacher of all. From Him all the oceans of the world gain their power. From Him all is both growth and decay. He is the eye that perceives and the mouth that names. He is the cause of all, the beginning of creation. By Him all things reproduce themselves. He is the cycle of all and the signs therein. He is one; there is no other beside Him.

'Great Anu, we thank you for sending King Pacorus and his army to Your city in its hour of need.'

Rahim halted his speech to allow polite applause to ripple through the crowd, while the Durans and Exiles rapped the shafts of their javelins against the backs of their shields. When the commotion had died down Rahim spoke again as the pyre became an angry fireball.

'Great Anu, we also give thanks for Your wisdom in sending us Surena, a man of the Ma'adan.'

Great applause and cheering came from the crowd at the mention of Surena's name. I looked at Gallia and smiled but she just rolled her eyes.

'Such is Your wisdom, Anu,' continued Rahim, 'that you fashioned a saviour from a people that were once Uruk's enemies, and in doing so have united the people of Mesene and the Ma'adan of the marshlands into one tribe, united behind King Nergal and Queen Allatu. Hail Anu!'

The crowd began chanting 'hail Anu' as Domitus leaned towards me.

'I told you Surena always comes up smelling of roses.'

The next day, as the wounded were treated, horses groomed and examined for any wounds, Domitus sat with his officers in one of the palace's offices and made a list of those who had been killed, wounded or had distinguished themselves in battle. The latter was always of intense interest among the different branches of the army, not least because of the rivalry between the Durans and Exiles and horse archers and cataphracts. However, though Domitus always reported to me with pride the names of those who had displayed heroism above and beyond the call of duty, he was even prouder when he reported that there were no instances of cowardice.

'It proves that hard training pays dividends in battle,' he always used to tell me. 'If every drill and trumpet call is second nature to a soldier, so familiar that he can do it in his sleep, and he has faith in his commanders and equipment, then the battle is already half won. But do you know what is the cement that holds men together in the furnace of combat?'

I shook my head.

'Loyalty.'

'To me?' I enquired.

'Don't be stupid,' he scoffed. 'Loyalty to the men standing next to him and behind him. Men fight and die for their friends, not for kings or consuls.'

The death of the garrison commander during the siege had de facto made Rahim the governor of the city in Nergal's absence. It was a role he slipped into easily enough. He was, after all, the spiritual leader of the kingdom and so assuming secular power was a natural step. But it was only for a day because Nergal and Praxima returned to Uruk with a small escort on the second morning following the cremation of the fallen.

The first we knew of their arrival was when a panting soldier arrived at the palace from the city's eastern gates with news that the king and queen were approaching. Surena ordered the garrison to immediately stand to arms and parade on the square in front of the palace, and issued the same order to his Ma'adan. Gallia left us to assemble the Amazons while Domitus suggested that an honour guard from the Durans and Exiles should also greet their arrival. I agreed and walked with him to the barracks where my men were quartered. It was fortunate that because Chosroes was a tyrant he had recruited many guards to ensure his safety, which were housed in barracks in the expansive palace compound in the northeast of the city, adjacent to the Royal Orchard where Chosroes had hunted. The soldiers that Nergal had left behind to guard the city had comprised four hundred of Surena's Ma'adan and five hundred spearmen and archers of the garrison.

Rahim and fifty of his priests arrived sweating and panting at the palace moments before Nergal and Praxima rode through its entrance. They rushed to the top of the steps where I waited with Domitus, Gallia, Byrd and Malik. On one side of the square stood two centuries of Durans and the same number of Exiles, alongside them fifty of my horse soldiers and the Amazons. Opposite stood Surena in front of his Ma'adan and two hundred men of the garrison. There was absolute silence when the returning rulers trotted through the gates of their palace. The garrison's signallers blew their horns and the Durans and Exiles their trumpets as Nergal and Praxima vaulted from their saddles and bounded up the steps. Ignoring all protocol they embraced Gallia and me and then Domitus, Byrd and Malik.

Rahim's eyes widened in shock as he beheld me and my friends touching the king and queen's semi-divine bodies. Rahim knew that Nergal and Praxima were not gods but he and everyone else who lived in the kingdom believed that they had been sent by Anu to rule over them. The ancient tablets held in the shrine at the summit of the ziggurat told of the arrival of Nergal and Allatu at Uruk, showing the former to be a man with the legs of a cock and the latter having the head of a lion. The fact that Nergal had long, gangly legs and Praxima red hair was confirmation that they were indeed sent by Anu. That and the fact that the tablets also foretold Nergal arriving at the city at the head of an army, which he had done as the commander of my horsemen.

Rahim's priests fell to their knees and placed their foreheads on the stone tiles as the high priest bowed his head.

Gallia had tears in her eyes she held Praxima. It had been my idea to make her and Nergal rulers of Uruk but I often had pangs of guilt about doing so. Gallia and Praxima had forged a close friendship in Italy and both had survived the slave revolt to make their home at Dura. When I had stormed Uruk and installed her and Nergal on its throne I had also deprived my wife the company of one of her closest friends, the other being Diana. Now both lived far from Dura.

'Get up, all of you,' Nergal commanded the priests. 'This is a great day.'

The holy men rose as one but kept their heads bowed in the presence of their king and queen.

After he had embraced us all Nergal gestured to Surena to attend him. He left his Ma'adan and bounded up the steps, bowing to Nergal and Praxima when he reached them.

'I received your message, Surena,' said Nergal, 'it greatly cheered us. I thank you for assuming command of the garrison in the hour of the city's need.'

'It was Surena who saved Uruk, Nergal,' I said.

'What King Pacorus says is true, divinity,' added Rahim. 'Commander Surena led the garrison and his detachment of Ma'adan with great valour, guided as he was by Anu.'

'We are in your debt, Surena,' said Nergal. 'Take off that helmet so we can see your face. What reward would you have me grant you, saviour of my city? Name it and it shall be yours.'

Surena took off his bronze helm and bowed his head to Nergal and Praxima, then at me. He turned his head to glance at the Amazons drawn up in their helmets and mail armour.

'Great king, I would ask that I be allowed to go back to Dura with my wife.'

Domitus laughed. 'Ha, bet you didn't expect that, did you Nergal? You thought to give him a high command and big house in the city but all he wants is to go home holding his wife's hand.'

He pointed a finger at Surena. 'I hope you're not going soft, boy.'

Anger flashed in Surena's eyes but he held his ire in check.

'If the general wishes to pitch his sword skills against my own he will find me more than accommodating.'

'I think we have all had our fair share of fighting these past few days,' I said firmly.

Praxima, always intoxicated by the thought of impending violence, laughed.

'I would like to see which one would triumph. Domitus the master, or Surena the rising star.'

'There will be none of that,' commanded Nergal. He looked at Surena.

'Your wish is granted, Surena, for it would be cruel to separate you from Viper any longer. Go back to Dura with the gratitude of the people of the Kingdom of Mesene.'

Wearing a wide grin Surena returned to his soldiers as Nergal and Praxima declared that they were retiring to the palace to rest and satisfy their hungers. The parade was dismissed and the soldiers returned to barracks. Nergal and Praxima asked us to take breakfast with them even though we had already eaten.

'You will eat with us too, Rahim,' said Nergal.

So we again sat at the breakfast table in the company of our newly returned friends. The largest chamber in the white-walled palace was the great vaulted main hall that led to the throne room. But the domed dining hall, though still substantial, was smaller and more intimate, with a white marble dais at one end, upon which the table of the king and queen was set. As at Dura a corridor linked the dining hall to the kitchens. After they had washed and changed their clothes Nergal and Praxima invited us all to sit with them at the top table. Rahim found eating in close proximity to the son and daughter of the gods and the informality between them and us most uncomfortable.

Servants brought figs, fruit, bread, cheese, boiled eggs and yoghurt from the kitchens and laid the platters on the table. They served fruit juice from silver jugs as Nergal told us what had happened before we arrived.

Before he did I heard Praxima tell Gallia that the palace's servants were all free men and women who had been hired by the chief steward. She may have been a merciless killer on the battlefield but she never forgot that she had once been a slave and, like me, had no desire to see others reduced to such a miserable existence.

Nergal tore off a great chunk of bread as Domitus nibbled on a piece of cheese.

'Surena has proved he is worth his weight in gold to Mesene. When he came here he and I visited the Ma'adan to speak to their elders.'

'That must have been interesting,' said Gallia.

Domitus finished his cheese and picked up a date. 'I hope you didn't get raped by a water buffalo.'

Malik smiled but Rahim's face wore a deep frown.

'Having Surena with me eased communications considerably,' continued Nergal. 'I told the elders that they would be free to graze their beasts on dry land and go about their daily lives unmolested, while Surena said that he would be raising a contingent of warriors from among the Ma'adan to serve me.'

'That must have gone down well,' said Domitus.

'Afterwards I sent a hundred water buffalo and a thousand fishing nets to the Ma'adan as a sign of my good faith,' said Nergal.

'A most wise decision, divinity,' smiled Rahim, nibbling on a grape.

'Soon after that groups of Ma'adan young men came to the city saying that they had come to fight for Surena,' said Praxima.

'Bare foot, dressed in rags and half starving, a most unprepossessing sight,' murmured Rahim.

'So what did you do with them?' asked Domitus.

Nergal drained his cup of fruit juice. 'We fed them, gave them new clothes and trained them to be soldiers. Train hard, fight easy, Domitus, just as we did at Dura.'

I was surprised. 'And the garrison's soldiers and the city's citizens accepted the Ma'adan among them?'

Rahim answered for his king. 'The people of Mesene are loyal to Anu and His chosen ones. The coming of their divinities was foretold many centuries ago. It is not for us to question their decisions.'

At that moment I realised what the source of Nergal's authority and power was. It wasn't his army, which in truth was a poor relation of the fighting forces that could be mustered by the other kingdoms of the empire. It was Uruk's priests. Rahim and his subordinates told the citizens that Nergal and Praxima had been sent by Anu and no one questioned the holy men of the White Temple. And if Mesene was suddenly welcoming the Ma'adan instead of hunting them like animals, then who were mere mortals to question the will of the gods?

'It was the Ma'adan who alerted us to a great fleet of boats carrying soldiers heading towards Mesene,' said Praxima, tossing back her long red locks.

Nergal dipped a piece of bread in a pot of honey. 'On the Tigris. So we took Kuban and three thousand horse archers raised by the lords of the kingdom east to intercept them.'

Kuban was a squat, hardy warrior from the Kingdom of Margiana, which was ruled by King Khosrou. He and a thousand others had originally been sent by Khosrou to fight for Gallia, so taken had the king been with my wife when he had met her at the Council of Kings at Esfahan. After fighting with distinction at Dura Gallia had gifted Kuban and his men, now numbering eight hundred, to Nergal and Praxima to stiffen their army. They rode hardy horses of the northern steppes and were armed with bows, swords, daggers and long spears – and were ruthless.

'We intercepted and slaughtered the invaders,' stated Nergal, 'cut them down when they left their boats.'

'It was easy,' said Praxima.

Nergal shoved the honey covered bread into his mouth. 'Too easy. In fact we had been deceived for the force on the Tigris was nothing more than a decoy to allow the main invading force to travel up the Euphrates and attack Uruk.'

'Those we killed at the Tigris were warriors from Sakastan,' said Praxima contemptuously. 'I recognised them from when we fought Porus.'

'Narses' soldiers now,' I spat.

'We will pay him back for despoiling our lands,' promised Praxima.

'What about this King Tiraios?' said Malik. 'He might be tempted to attack Uruk again.'

Nergal turned to his high priest. 'Rahim, what do you know of Charax?'

'Only that it is poor, divinity, poorer than even...'

He stopped himself and blushed, obviously thinking twice about what he was about to say.

Nergal smiled. 'Poorer than Mesene, you were going to say. It is all right. I am fully aware that my kingdom is not a rich land.'

'The point is,' said Domitus, emptying a platter of figs, 'that poor or not most of Charax's army has been butchered before the walls of this city. Does anyone know how many enemy soldiers were slain?'

'Upwards of five thousand,' said Rahim with relish, 'including nearly two thousand from Charax.'

Domitus puffed out his cheeks. 'That's a lot of men to lose, especially for a poor kingdom. I don't think you will have to worry about Tiraios for a long time.'

'It is he who will have to worry,' promised Praxima.

We stayed for a week at Uruk, the wounded being treated and the rest enjoying the hospitality of a grateful populace. Surena and Viper took long walks among the remaining date palms, doum palms, sycamores and fig trees of the Royal Orchard. Gallia and Praxima organised picnics by the side of the artificial lakes in the orchard and we spent hours reminiscing about our time in Italy. Gallia even persuaded Byrd and Malik to join us on one occasion, though my chief scout hardly said anything, just staring at the pure white swans as they swam gracefully across the water. He had not changed one bit since the time I had first met him in Cappadocia all those years ago.

Domitus had scorned the idea of a picnic and instead had asked that Surena's Ma'adan be allowed to accompany him as he took a thousand legionaries into the desert on a route march. Nergal had agreed and suggested that Kuban, who had returned to the city, play the role of enemy with his mounted warriors. Domitus had agreed. Three men died in the subsequent mock battle ten miles north of Uruk, but my army's commander thought the exercise well worth it.

When he returned, after he had washed the dust of Mesopotamia from his body, I talked with him. He was dressed in a simple grey tunic, sandals and leather belt as I walked with him through the palace on his way to speak with Surena. As usual he carried his cane and had his *gladius* and dagger hanging from his belt.

'I hope you two are not going to fight each other,' I said.

He rolled his eyes. 'I have better things to do than teach your cocky young protégé a lesson in sword fighting.'

'Mm. Well good. Anyway, I have been thinking.'

'My congratulations,' he said flatly.

'Try to be serious. What is your opinion of Kuban and his men?'

Domitus twisted his cane in his hand. 'Narrow-eyed killers, the lot of them. But good horsemen and Nergal is lucky to have them.'

'You think they are capable of working in conjunction with foot soldiers?'

He shrugged. 'With enough training, I don't see why not. What are you thinking?'

'That the legionaries should stay here for six months to stiffen Uruk's defences, just in case Narses tries another venture.'

We passed through the main hall and exited the palace, arriving at the top of the steps that led down to the paved square where Surena's Ma'adan were drawn up on parade. They looked a fine body of men, the late afternoon sun glinting off whetted spear points, bronze armour and helmets.

'Not a bad idea,' mused Domitus, 'but you realise that if you leave nearly two thousand legionaries here and Nergal trains them to work with those flat-faced northern devils of Khosrou's, Praxima will be bending his ear to raid Mithridates' kingdom just across the Tigris.'

I smiled at him. 'Precisely.'

Surena saw us approaching and shouted an order to his men, who snapped their spears to their sides as they came to attention. Domitus walked up to him, the younger man looking down at Domitus from behind the nose guard of his helmet.

'Your men did well on the exercise,' said Domitus. 'I had my doubts about them but credit where credit's due. Well done.'

'Thank you, general.'

'Please stand at ease, Surena,' I said, 'and take that helmet off. It's like talking to a statue.'

He removed his bronze helm and smiled proudly.

'Stand easy!' he bellowed.

His men relaxed and stood at ease.

'Where is he, then?' asked Domitus.

Surena turned and waved forward a soldier in the front rank behind him. Attired like him in a cuirass of overlapping bronze scales, he sprinted forward and snapped to attention before Surena.

'This is Jasham, general,' said Surena, 'whom I have selected to assume command of my soldiers when I leave for Dura. Take off your helmet, Jasham.'

The soldier did so to reveal a round face with a hard expression and shoulder-length black hair. He was the same height as Domitus but had broader shoulders.

'I recognise you,' I said. 'You were one of the youths that sprang the ambush against Chosroes' soldiers when I was their captive.'

'That is correct, lord,' Jasham replied without emotion.

'You have come a long way,' I told him. 'Well done.'

I now understood why Nergal had been so unconcerned about Surena leaving Uruk. He knew that the command of the

Ma'adan would be in the hands of one of Surena's childhood friends who came from the same village as Viper's husband.

'How many of the men I see before me were part of that gang of young raiders who preyed on Chosroes' soldiers?' I asked Surena.

His face wore a wide grin. 'A score, lord, all raised to commanders.'

'Disciplined cut-throats,' opined Domitus. 'I like it.'

The Ma'adan were again drawn up in their ranks the next day when we left Uruk. The previous evening, at the feast given in our honour in the palace, I told Nergal and Praxima that I would leave all the legionaries with them for six months as a precaution against any further enemy incursions. I saw Praxima's eyes light up with excitement and heard Domitus' words in my head. But I knew that Nergal had a wise head on his shoulders and would not start any unnecessary wars. Or at least I hoped he would not.

Gallia embraced her friend and then led the Amazons from the palace, Byrd's scouts leading the way with the horse archers following. I had decided that I would cross the Euphrates and ride back to Dura on the western side of the river. As Malik was with us this would not be a problem and would save us having to ride through Babylonian and Hatran territory, and save me having to explain my movements to King Vardan and my father.

On a crystal clear day, with the sun high in a blue sky and the waters of the Euphrates calm and clear, we trotted across the temporary bridge that had been constructed by lashing the rafts that had transported us to Uruk together and entered Agraci territory. We were sad to leave our friends but were in high spirits at having destroyed Narses' plan and the army he had sent to implement it. As the sun shone on my back I was content in the knowledge that the gods were smiling on Dura and its king.

Chapter 4

Byrd and Malik rode ahead to announce our presence to Yasser, whose land we were entering. The other scouts went with them, more out of something to do than to ensure the security of their commander or the Agraci prince. The region to the west of the Euphrates was a desolate landscape of rocky outcrops, smooth sandy plains and sparse vegetation. It was a sun-blasted land that was avoided by Parthians, not least because it was the domain of the feared Agraci, in addition to many snakes and scorpions. So the land adjacent to the Euphrates lay abandoned, despite the fact that it flooded every spring and burst forth with plant life, before once more becoming arid and inhospitable in the summer. But to us it was a land of tranquillity and peace, home to our Agraci allies. We knew that the journey home would be uneventful, though we had reckoned without the complaining of Lucius Domitus.

He may have been a general but he was used to marching on foot and found riding in the saddle strange and alien. Nergal had given him a beautiful five-year-old light brown mare to ride back to Dura, an animal with a calm temperament and a relaxed gait. It should have been an ideal mount for Dura's general but instead he did nothing but complain about it and the saddle.

Each day we rose at dawn and groomed and fed the horses, checking them over for any loose shoes and sores. Then we ate our breakfast before saddling our mounts and riding for two hours before walking the horses for a further hour to conserve their energy. We usually rested during the two hours either side of midday, taking the horses to the Euphrates to quench their thirst and wade in the water, before riding them for a further three hours in the afternoon. Without the impediment of wagons or soldiers on foot we were able to cover up to forty miles a day. On the third day it all became too much for Domitus, who had forgotten the lessons he had learned about riding on the trip to Esfahan for the Council of Kings.

'This wretched beast hates me,' he whined, shifting in his saddle. 'And I've got blisters on my arse as big as camel spiders.'

Gallia laughed. 'My sympathies.'

'I don't want sympathy,' snapped Domitus, 'I want to be off this bloody horse.'

'You are uncomfortable because you are sitting all wrong,' I told him. 'Look at how we sit in the saddle. You are positioned too far forward. Relax and sit back.'

Our saddles had four padded horns, two at the front and two at the back, which held the rider in place. However, novice riders had a tendency to sit forward because initially it felt as though the rear horns did not offer enough support and they feared tumbling from the saddle.

'You must trust the saddle, Domitus,' said Gallia, 'just as you trust the sword that hangs by your side.'

Domitus squirmed in the saddle again. 'Trust? It's not natural, sitting on a mangy beast with your legs dangling in mid-air.'

'You should not insult your horse, general,' said Surena behind us. 'It will take offence. Try to use your legs to grip the front horns of the saddle, and keep them bent.'

Domitus was unimpressed. 'When I want your advice I will ask for it.'

'He's right Domitus,' I said, 'you should not upset the beast you are riding on. After all, in battle your life might depend on it.'

Domitus smiled bitterly at me. 'Not my life. I prefer to fight on foot like I was trained to do.'

'But Romans have horsemen, general,' said Viper riding next to Surena, her girlish voice causing him to smile.

'They have horsemen,' he agreed, 'but they are only used after the legions have broken the enemy, that and for scouting.'

He pulled his cane from his belt and was about to beat his mare on the hip.

'Don't use your cane on your horse,' I ordered him. 'A horse is directed by weight distribution, leg pressure, verbal commands and the bit in his mouth, or her mouth in your horse's case.'

'I'm amazed you can remember all that in battle,' he said.

'It comes naturally after a while,' I said. 'If you spent more time in the saddle you would soon get used to riding.'

'You can forget that,' he insisted. 'As soon as we get back to Dura my feet will be moving me around.'

110

To spare our bodies from the worst of the heat we wore large white cotton cloaks from our shoulders that also covered the hips of our horses. Our helmets dangled from our saddle horns and we wore broad-brimmed floppy hats on our heads. The horses also wore 'hats' to shield their heads from the sun.

When Byrd and Malik returned in the company of Yasser, Domitus' 'wounds' were treated by an aged healer who smeared myrrh on the general's rump to treat his blisters. That night Yasser entertained us in his large goatskin tent. We sat cross-legged in a circle on the floor as his men brought thin metal platters heaped with rice and roast goat. We ate with our fingers, the hulking figure of Yasser sitting next to Gallia, milk dripping on his thick black beard as he drank and laughed with my wife.

'I will ride to Uruk and lend King Nergal some of my warriors,' Yasser promised me. 'Your wife has been telling me about your recent victory. Your fellow king will be wishing to exact revenge for the invasion of his kingdom.'

Yasser was not concerned about the politics of the empire or the safety of Mesene, but as an Agraci raiding and plunder was in his blood and he sniffed an opportunity to lead his warriors on an expedition of slaughter. I often thought that the peace between Dura and Haytham brought nothing for the Agraci to do save provide protection for the trade caravans that criss-crossed their land.

'I'm sure King Nergal will welcome any reinforcements,' I replied.

He pushed a mouthful of rice into his mouth. 'And you, lion of Parthia, will you take your army east to kill Mithridates?'

How I would have liked to answer yes to that question but I had no appetite to plunge the empire into another civil war.

'Mithridates will answer for his crimes,' I answered evasively.

We left Yasser to his thoughts of rape and plunder and continued our journey north, finally reaching the southern boundary of my kingdom on the fifth day. There were no settlements this far south of Dura but the mass of date palms growing near the river was testimony to a time before the Agraci when the city's rulers had cultivated the land dozens of miles south of the city. There still stood the remains of villages, mostly derelict mud-brick walls that had once been villagers' huts. We stayed in one such abandoned settlement on the evening of the fifth day, dozens of flickering campfires ringing the mud-brick remains where the horse archers were cooking their evening meals. Nergal had given us a hundred camels that carried our tents, food, supplies and fodder. We had also half-emptied his armouries of arrows, which I had promised to replace as soon as I reached Dura.

'It's good to be home,' remarked Domitus, sitting with his back against the remains of a wall, the flames illuminating his chiselled features.

I looked around at the miserable remains of the village.

'Hardly the most luxurious of Dura's settlements.'

'In time the farmers will return,' said Byrd.

'That is my aim, Byrd,' I replied. I nodded at Malik. 'Now we have peace on Dura's southern and western borders my intention is to bring the people back to these parts.'

'Pacorus the farmer. I can't see it,' opined Domitus. He nodded at the meat cooking on thin spikes over the fire.

'I hope you are not trying to poison us, Malik.'

The Agraci prince flashed a smile. 'The problem with you, Domitus, is that you see the desert as your enemy.'

'That's because it's full of poisonous snakes, scorpions and spiders,' he replied. 'Like those you are cooking. Make sure you don't give me any meat with poison in it. I've suffered enough on this trip.'

Gallia shook her head. 'I wouldn't have thought a few blisters would bother a man who has fought in so many battles.'

Domitus watched Malik turning the bits of meat over the fire. 'Battles are easy affairs and don't last that long, not like the hours of misery my backside has had to endure over the past few days.'

'The myrrh did not help?' grinned Malik.

'It helped,' conceded Domitus, 'though I will probably have a scar. What is it?'

Malik held up one of the spits. 'This? Lebetine viper. Very tasty.'

He replaced the sizzling meat over the fire.

'As I said, Domitus, you see the desert as your enemy but the Agraci view it as their friend. Take these snakes, for example. If one bites you then you will most likely die.'

He removed one of the spits and passed it to me.

'But if you catch one, skin it and cook it over a fire then it will feed you. And the venom is in their fangs, which are in the head, which we cut off. So you see, Domitus, it is quite safe to eat.'

He also handed spits to Gallia and Byrd before holding one out to my general. The meat was chewy but had a pleasant taste and was very filling.

'Not bad,' conceded Domitus.

The next day Malik, Byrd and the scouts rode north ahead of the main column to alert the soldiers of the nearest garrison of our approach. This would be a small mud-brick fort, one of fifty that I had established north and south of Dura – twenty-five to the north and the same number to the south – positioned a short distance from the Euphrates. Each one was enclosed by walls, ringed by a wide ditch and had a small barracks for forty men – half a century – plus stables for four horses. They were positioned at five-mile intervals to give Dura ample warning of the approach of any enemy threat.

When we arrived at the fort we found that the garrison arrayed on parade in front of the stronghold. Domitus' mood improved enormously as he inspected the two score of legionaries and their commander. He found nothing out of order. Following the inspection the commander, a fresh-faced man in his early twenties, invited Domitus, Gallia and myself to take refreshments in his headquarters, in truth nothing more than an office containing a desk, pigeon holes along one wall that contained scrolls, wooden shutters either side of the door that opened out on to the courtyard and half a dozen stools arranged along one wall.

Gallia preferred to stay with the Amazons but I wanted to send a message to Godarz via courier pigeon that we would be arriving back at Dura in two days. So while I sat at the table and scribbled a note to my governor, Domitus shared a cup of wine with the youthful commander.

'Do you see anything down here?' he asked.

The commander shook his head. 'Occasionally a group of Agraci will visit us, but otherwise no, general. Very quiet.'

Domitus took a swig of the wine. 'Good, long may it continue to be so.'

He told his subordinate about the battle at Uruk, the defeat of the enemy and about the two thousand legionaries that had been left with Nergal in case there was another attack against Mesene.

'When are we marching against Mithridates, general?' he asked. 'Or are we going to let him march against us so we can defeat him on our own soil.'

I stopped writing and looked up at him.

'What do your men say of Mithridates?'

He was slightly taken aback. 'Forgive me, majesty, I did not mean to speak out of turn.'

'You didn't,' I told him. 'But answer the question.'

He glanced at Domitus who nodded.

'The men say that Mithridates and Narses are cowards who deserve to die and that Dura's army is the instrument to carry out the sentence.'

'And what do you say?' I probed.

He looked my directly in the eye. 'I agree with my men.'

I handed him the small note. 'See that this is sent on to Dura's governor.'

He took it, saluted and barked to a guard outside to enter. He held out the note.

'This is to be sent to Dura, see to it.'

The legionary took the note, saluted and left. It would be rolled up, placed in a small container that would be fixed to the leg of a courier pigeon, which would fly to the next fort where it would be read and sent on to the next fort and so on until it reached Dura. It would be on Godarz's desk before the end of the day. I rose, walked over to the earthenware jug and poured myself a cup of wine. It had a bitter taste.

'Where are you from?' I asked him.

'Gordyene, majesty.'

'King Balas' kingdom,' I said. 'You are a long way from home.'

'Dura is my home,' he said firmly. Domitus smiled approvingly.

'When did you leave Gordyene?' I asked.

'After my father was killed at Tigranocerta, majesty.'

Balas had allied himself with the king of Armenia, Tigranes, a great warlord, when the Romans had invaded Armenia. But a Roman general named Licinius Lucullus had fought their combined army at a place called Tigranocerta. It was said that the army of Tigranes and Balas numbered over one hundred thousand men, but it had been no match for Roman tactics or discipline and at the end of the battle Balas was dead and Tigranes defeated.

'Does your family still live in Gordyene?'

'No, majesty,' he answered. 'My mother and sister live in Dura. We crossed the border and went to the city of Nisibus where Lord Vata is governor. After resting there a few days, where Lord Vata provided food and tents for all the refugees from Gordyene, I heard that the Kingdom of Dura was recruiting soldiers for its army. So we continued on south to Hatra and then Dura.'

'You and your mother and sister walked all the way from Gordyene?' I asked.

I knew that many men had made the long journey south following the occupation of Gordyene by the Romans but I had heard of no women making the journey on foot.

'Yes, majesty,' he declared proudly.

I finished the wine and placed the empty cup on the table.

'The next time you are in Dura, commander, please convey my gratitude and compliments to the womenfolk of your family.'

The rest of the stay involved myself and Domitus inspecting the fort's barracks, small hospital, granary, workshop and stables. We ended the tour by scaling the ladder that led to the top of the watchtower where a lookout could observe the surrounding terrain for miles around. I told him he was relieved until we came down. He saluted and left us.

We stood in silence for a few minutes, taking in the view: the blue waters of the Euphrates to the east, groves of date palms adjacent to the river to the north and unending desert to the west.

'Imagine that,' I said at length. 'Walking for hundreds of miles to get here, and with two women in tow.'

'It's like I told you. This army contains soldiers who have steel in their veins. That's why it is so respected and feared.'

I turned my face away from the harsh land of sand and rock.

'Which is more preferable, Domitus, to be respected or feared?'

'To be feared,' he replied instantly. 'If an enemy fears you then the battle is already half won.'

'Do you think Mithridates and Narses fear us?'

He scratched his close-cropped scalp. 'Definitely. That's why they attempt to conquer the kingdoms of your friends instead of attacking Dura, and use others to do it. They are like those snakes that Malik killed and roasted. They will only strike when the time is right. Unless you march against them, that is.'

'It is too risky.'

He gave me a sly glance. 'We could cross the Euphrates, march across your father's and Vardan's territory and strike at Ctesiphon before Mithridates has time to muster an army. Kill him and that devil of a mother of his and half of your troubles will be over. You know how dilapidated Ctesiphon's defences are.'

'You want me to violate the territorial integrity of Hatra and Babylon, attack Ctesiphon and kill the high king?' I said.

He grinned wickedly. 'Glad to see all that royal education you had as a boy wasn't wasted.'

'I'm Parthian, Domitus, not Roman.'

But I knew that he was right about one thing: Mithridates and Narses would continue to attack my family and allies. His idea was tempting and I had openly declared my hatred and contempt for Mithridates for killing his own father. I had no proof except the assurances of Dobbai that it was so. But if I too killed a high king then I would be no better than Mithridates. And that I could not live with.

The rest of the journey consisted of visiting each fort along our route with Domitus inspecting its garrison. It was a pleasant enough pastime and each commander took great pride in showing off his men and their pristine quarters. Gallia dazzled them with her smile and gracious attitude and as we

116

neared Dura itself we began to come across newly established villages whose farmers were working the land. The garrisons of the forts had assisted in digging the canals that fed the farmers' fields, with the result that between every village and the Euphrates there sprang up intricate irrigation systems. The villagers worked long hours in the fields under a merciless sun that turned their arms and legs dark brown. Their main crops were barley and millet, but they also grew onions, radishes, garlic, leeks, turnips, flax and lettuce. The treasury had supplied each new village with seeds for the crops as well as a small number of sheep, goats and cows, which had been assigned to the headman. In return each settlement was expected to submit a yearly quota of flax, wool and grain. The trade caravans paid for the army's horses, weapons and armour but it was the farmers who filled the bellies of my soldiers and provide them with the material for their uniforms. They and the kingdom were prospering and it was a happy state of affairs.

But the next day a very unhappy Orodes presented himself.

He arrived at the head of a hundred of his bodyguard: cataphracts attired in scale armour and helmets, though minus tubular steel armour on their arms or legs. Their horses were not wearing scale armour but instead beautiful large red saddlecloths and on their heads had burnished steel armour that glinted in the sun. Each horseman carried a *kontus* and was also armed with a sword, mace, dagger and axe. Behind Orodes a standard bearer carried the banner of the prince's native land, Susiana: a great red flag showing an eagle with a snake in its talons. His men wore bright red tunics beneath their armour, white leggings and brown leather boots. The overlapping scales fixed to the thick hide they wore over their tunics were steel and shimmered in the sun like fish scales. They were a magnificent sight.

Orodes was in the company of Malik and Byrd, who as usual had ridden ahead of our column with the scouts, though only to relieve their boredom as we were now close to Dura and there was no danger of being surprised by an enemy.

I halted the column as Orodes rode up and raised his hand to me.

117

'Hail, Pacorus. My congratulations on your victory.' He bowed his head formally to Gallia.

'Lady.'

I looked at Domitus, both of us realising that there was something wrong with the usually affable prince of Susiana.

'What is troubling you, Orodes?' I asked.

He said nothing for a few seconds as Gallia smiled kindly at him. But then he took a deep breath and exhaled.

'I was left in command of Dura's army, Pacorus, a matter of great responsibility when war may break out in the empire at any time.'

'I would trust no other man to safeguard my city and kingdom, my friend,' I said.

His eyes still blazed with anger. 'I know that. And you know that I would gladly lay down my life for you and your family without a moment's hesitation.'

Domitus shifted uncomfortably in his saddle. 'Is there any point to this?'

I held up a hand to him. 'What is troubling you, Orodes?' I asked again.

'I cannot have my authority undermined, Pacorus,' said Orodes firmly. 'I may be an exiled prince with no lands or money but I still have my honour.'

'You have more than that, lord prince,' said Gallia softly, who was concerned that Orodes was in a state of distress. 'You have the love and loyalty of your friends who will never abandon you.'

Orodes smiled at her but then fixed me with a determined stare as I racked my brain trying to think who had undermined him. Godarz? I dismissed the idea. For one thing they were friends and my governor would never interfere in the day-to-day running of the army. Rsan? It was inconceivable. My treasurer was loyal and conscientious but would never challenge a prince of the empire, even less the son of the late High King Phraates.

'Your sorceress,' said Orodes.

'Dobbai?'

'She has sent two companies of horse archers to the Syrian border,' said Orodes through gritted teeth. 'Two hundred horsemen despatched without my knowledge or authority. It makes me a laughing stock, Pacorus. It is intolerable.'

He was right and I was angry. But why would she do such a thing? Domitus was also not amused.

'She risks starting a war with the Romans,' he said. 'In which direction did the horse archers go?'

'West to Palmyra,' said Orodes.

'Malik,' I said, 'I would ask you to ride to your father's capital immediately and try to find out what has happened to two hundred of my men.'

Malik raised his hand and wheeled his horse away.

'I go to,' stated Byrd as he tugged on his horse's reins and followed his friend.

The calm, relaxed atmosphere that had hung over the column changed to anxiety and haste as we rode hard for Dura. Orodes was on my left and my wife on my right as the scouts followed Byrd west into the desert and Orodes' bodyguard rode in column formation beside the Amazons.

'When did the horse archers leave Dura?' I asked.

'First thing yesterday morning,' said Orodes. 'I was carrying out an inspection of the forts north of the city when a courier arrived from Godarz informing me that they had left the city. By the time I had returned to the Citadel it was late afternoon. I sent a messenger to recall them but they had not returned by this morning.'

'You should burn the old witch for this,' spat Domitus, who was finding the speedy journey very uncomfortable. Orodes noticed his discomfort.

'Are you wounded, Domitus?'

Gallia laughed. 'He has blisters the size of camel spiders.'

'Glad you find it funny,' said Domitus.

Orodes looked concerned. 'My sympathies, general.'

We arrived at Dura two hours later, our horses panting and sweating and our bodies soaked in sweat. We cantered through the Palmyrene Gate and up the city's main road to the Citadel, the trumpets of an honour guard celebrating our arrival. The horse archers left us to ride to their barracks in the west of the city, just beyond the walls of the Citadel. I jumped from the saddle as a stable hand came forward, took Remus' reins and led him away. Epona was likewise removed as the

119

Amazons and Orodes' cataphracts dismounted and led their mounts to the stables. Domitus eased himself out of the saddle and dismounted gingerly, saying a silent prayer of thanks and raising his cane threateningly to his mare.

'Domitus,' I barked, 'leave her alone.'

The chief steward scuttled down the steps and bowed his head.

'Where's Dobbai?'

'On the palace terrace, majesty. Will you and the queen be requiring refreshments?'

I walked past him up the steps with Gallia, Orodes and Domitus following.

'No.'

Servants cleaning the throne room's floor got off their knees and bowed as we raced by them towards the door in the far corner giving access to our private quarters. A guard standing sentry by it opened it to allow us to enter. We walked into the corridor leading to the palace's sleeping quarters and continued through another door that led on to the terrace.

It was another blisteringly hot day but Dobbai was seated in her wicker chair, her legs resting on a footstool and a large shade positioned over her to offer protection from the sun's rays. We walked over to find her eyes closed. I cleared my throat.

She opened one eye. 'Ah, so you have returned, son of Hatra, and with another victory under your belt, I hear.'

'We are not here to discuss that.'

She sighed, opened both eyes and sat up.

'I see, then what other reason can you have for disturbing an old woman's mid-morning rest?'

She held out her arms to Gallia who walked forward and embraced her.

'Sit, child. You look tired and thirsty.'

Dobbai waved over one of the servants standing near the door which had a large awning over it to provide them with shade.

'Bring water and fruit for our returned heroes.'

I held up a hand to stop them. 'I am king here.'

'As you wish,' remarked Dobbai unconcerned.

120

The servants stood and looked at each other, unsure what to do as the chief steward came on to the terrace.

'Very well,' I said, 'bring refreshments.'

The servants bowed and left for the kitchens as the steward organised others to arrange chairs and sunshades for us.

'Very kingly,' Dobbai said to me.

'I have heard,' I said in a stern voice, 'that you commanded two companies of horse archers to be sent to Syria without Prince Orodes' authority.'

Dobbai sighed and rose to her feet. 'So now we come to the real reason that you are acting like a precocious child, son of Hatra.'

'You risk war with Syria,' I said loudly.

'I was left in charge of the army,' added Orodes, 'and only I had the authority to send soldiers outside the kingdom.'

'If this was Rome your head would already be decorating the gates of the Citadel,' said Domitus with relish.

'How short your memories are,' she retorted. 'The gods send me a vision that allows you to save the Kingdom of Mesene and yet you threaten my life. That's gratitude for you.'

'No one threatens your life,' stated Gallia firmly, daring Domitus to contradict her.

Dobbai walked to where I, Orodes and Domitus were standing in line.

'Like small boys you think that because you wear swords and bellow commands at other boys you are like gods.'

'Not gods,' I said, 'just men eager to avoid war with Roman Syria while we face the possibility of further conflict with Mithridates.'

Dobbai shook her head and returned to her chair.

'Do you really think that I would initiate any actions that would endanger your kingdom, son of Hatra?'

'By sending horse archers to Syria you do just that,' said Orodes, becoming increasingly frustrated with Dobbai's nonchalant attitude.

Dobbai eased herself back in her chair. 'First of all, prince, I did not send the horsemen to Syria. I sent then to the Syrian border, there to await the arrival of a sister who is coming to Dura.'

I took a seat under a shade and indicated to Orodes and Domitus that they should do likewise. The heat was oppressive.

'Sister? You have a sister?'

'One is bad enough,' whispered Domitus.

'I did not say I had a sister,' snapped Dobbai. 'I use the word in the context of a feminine associate, who like me is a member of an ancient sisterhood.'

Gallia's ears pricked up at this. 'Sisterhood?'

Dobbai nodded. 'The Scythian sisterhood, child. Now more than eight hundred years old, and during that time our order has seen empires fall and kings rise.'

The chief steward retreated towards the entrance as servants brought refreshments to the terrace and served us cool drinks and slices of melon and apple.

'You have said nothing of this order before,' I said.

'Do I enquire about the workings of your army or the topics of the conversations you hold with your commanders?' she asked. 'I do not.'

'You still have not explained why you sent two companies of horse archers to the Syrian border without my permission,' said Orodes.

'To provide an escort for my sister, of course,' replied Dobbai matter-of-factly. 'As a man of honour, lord prince, I would have thought that you more than most would appreciate that a solitary woman travelling through Agraci territory is risking her honour at the very least, if not her life.'

Orodes looked at me and shook his head in exasperation.

'Well,' I said, 'at least they aren't invading Syria. We have that to be thankful for at least. But you must apologise to Prince Orodes, Dobbai.'

'You would have me apologise for carrying out the wishes of the gods, son of Hatra?'

'Wishes of the gods?' said Domitus derisively. 'You send horsemen to escort one of your fellow witches here and you say it is the work of the gods.'

'What do you know of the thoughts of the gods, Roman?' she shot back.

'What message from the gods does your sister carry?' I asked her.

122

She looked at me as though I was deranged. 'How should I know?'

Domitus started nibbling a large piece of melon, the juices dripping down his chin as he spoke. 'She has been sitting on this terrace in the sun too long, Pacorus. It has obviously roasted her brain.'

'Are you certain that the gods are at work?' Gallia asked Dobbai.

'Quite sure, child. Consider this. A member of our order suddenly writes to me saying that she is coming to Dura to visit me. We do not gather every year like your ridiculous Companions, so why else would she suddenly declare her interest in me and Dura?'

We all looked at her in expectation of an answer. But she merely settled back into her chair and closed her eyes.

'All will be revealed.'

Orodes rose, bowed to Gallia and then me and strode towards the door, stopping only when he heard Dobbai's deep voice.

'Prince Orodes.'

He turned.

'If I caused you offence I apologise. It was not my intention.'

He nodded. 'I accept your apology.'

'Like small boys,' said Dobbai under her breath as Orodes left us.

Samahe was her name.

It meant 'dark haired girl' and was an accurate reflection of her appearance, though she was certainly no girl. Like Dobbai it was difficult to place an age on her but she was certainly advanced in years. Her arrival had become the main topic of palace gossip. So when word came from the Palmyrene Gate that a column of horse archers and camels was approaching the city from the west, servants, stable hands, legionaries and horse archers not on duty gathered in the courtyard to catch a glimpse of Dobbai's 'sister'. Indeed, the route from the Palmyrene Gate to the Citadel was soon lined with curious spectators when word spread that Dura was to be graced by a second sorceress.

123

I stood at the top of the palace steps with Gallia, Godarz and Rsan as the horse archers trotted into the courtyard. Directly opposite curious scribes stood in the open windows of the headquarters' building and treasury. Burly, squat blacksmiths drifted from the armoury to look as well. I had never seen the courtyard so crowded.

'Even kings do not receive this kind of reception,' I said to Gallia.

'People are curious, Pacorus. They believe that Dura is doubly blessed by one of Dobbai's sisters visiting us.'

I looked around. 'And where is Dobbai?'

Gallia shrugged as Domitus and Orodes walked from the headquarters building and strode across the courtyard. Both were dressed in full war gear, Domitus wearing his helmet that had a magnificent white crest and Orodes carrying his helmet in the crook of his arm. The horse archers saluted as they passed and walked up the steps to us.

'I thought you said you had better to things to do,' I said to Domitus.

He nodded to Gallia as Orodes bowed deeply to her. 'I wanted to see what all the fuss is about. Where is the old witch?'

'Careful, Roman,' I heard the voice of Dobbai behind us. 'Samahe is regarded as a powerful sorceress who can bend men's minds to her will.'

'Not this man,' he growled.

As the horse archers deployed into line facing the palace a camel sauntered into the courtyard accompanied by the horsemen's commander. All eyes were on the black-clothed figure riding on the camel as the commander escorted it to the foot of the steps and signalled for the companies' horns to be sounded. The camel grunted in disapproval as the Citadel was filled with the sound of horn blasts, followed by the rasping sound of two hundred swords being pulled from their scabbards as the horsemen saluted me. The commander jumped down from his horse and tugged on the camel's reins. The beast spat at him before bending its front legs and then its rear legs to sit on the stone slabs. The commander stepped forward to assist our visitor off its back.

124

She was shorter than Dobbai, being no taller than five foot, and though she was also wearing a black *abaya*, a long black robe, it was obvious that she was plumper. She was wearing a *tarha*, a black shawl, over her head but I could see that she had a round face. Gallia made to walk down the steps but I stopped her.

'I think not, my sweet. We are, after all, monarchs and not her servants.'

Dobbai brushed past us. 'You are so pompous sometimes, son of Hatra.'

She walked down the steps as the commander stepped back and bowed to me. The two black-clad women exchanged formalities and then walked together up the steps. Samahe ascended two of them before stopping and turning to the commander.

'Come here, boy.'

He looked at her and then me, unsure what to do. I nodded to him and he walked to her. She reached into her *abaya*, pulled out a small rolled parchment and handed it to him.

'At the next full moon read the words on this document and then burn it. The woman you desire will be yours.'

He blushed but attempted bravado. 'I know not what you mean, lady.'

'Don't be a fool,' she said loudly. 'It is written all over your face for the world to see that you are in love with one who does not return your affections. Now take it and be thankful.'

He took the parchment.

Samahe turned and walked towards us. 'Young men in love are so predictable.'

'All men are predictable, sister,' said Dobbai.

Our portly guest reach the top of the steps, smiled at me and bowed deeply, then did the same to Gallia.

'Hail, King Pacorus of Dura and his beautiful queen, Gallia of the Gauls. Slayer of Lucius Furius, Porus of Sakastan and Chosroes of Mesene, victor of Surkh and saviour of Uruk. I salute you for your courage and choice of queen, for though I, like many, have heard of the beauty of Queen Gallia only now do I fully appreciate her grace. The gods smile on you, King Pacorus, and on this fair city of Dura.'

I had to admit that her words were gracious but before I could reply a delighted Gallia stepped forward and took Samahe's hands.

'You are most welcome, Samahe, and tonight we will hold a feast to honour your arrival.'

'We will?' I said.

Gallia turned and fixed me with her blue eyes.

I smiled at Samahe. 'A feast sounds a most excellent idea. Please enter our home. Quarters have been prepared for you. You must be tired after your journey.'

'That's you out-manoeuvred,' Domitus said to me.

Samahe linked her arm in Gallia's and Dobbai did the same on my wife's other side as all three walked into the palace's reception porch, Samahe's voice filling the chamber.

'Wherever I went all I heard were the names King Pacorus of Dura and his blonde-haired wife Gallia. You two have been the talk of Apamea for months.'

Apamea was a city in Syria on the right bank of the Orontes River. The site of a settlement since ancient times, it had been greatly expanded by Seleucus Nicator, one of Alexander of Macedon's commanders and the founder of the Seleucid Empire. That had been over two hundred years ago and now the city boasted a population of over one hundred thousand people. Like every other settlement in Syria, however, it was now under Roman control.

'I was wondering, King Pacorus,' said Samahe as we all walked into the reception hall, 'if you could spare a morsel to eat for a poor traveller whose throat has been turned into dry tinder from all the dust inhaled during the journey.'

'Of course,' I told her, 'you are free to avail yourself of Dura's hospitality.'

'You are most generous,' announced Samahe as we left the reception hall and entered the throne room.

'Now, where was I? Oh yes, Apamea. Of course the man responsible for making your highnesses the chief topic of city gossip was Pompey, of course.'

'Pompey?' I said.

'Yes,' said Samahe, whose voice seemed to be getting louder by the minute. 'He was most taken by you. Told the governor that you dressed, acted and spoke like a Roman. He believes that you will become a client king of Rome. He told me that you are halfway there already.'

'You spoke to Pompey?' I said.

'Of course. Nice enough man but I fear he will end badly. He's honest, you see, and honest men always end up disappointed and with a dagger in their hearts, that or their throats slit.'

'How many soldiers do the Romans have in Syria?' asked Domitus bluntly.

Samahe stopped and turned her head to take a long look at the army's commander. He met her gaze with cold, brown eyes.

'This is the Roman you told me about, sister?' she said to Dobbai.

'It is,' replied Dobbai.

'It doesn't matter how many soldiers they have, Roman,' replied Samahe, 'because they pose no threat to Dura. The Jews are proving rebellious and so the might of Rome is turned towards them.'

'It was ever so,' remarked Dobbai caustically.

Samahe continued to walk towards the dais. 'But if you really wish to know how many soldiers there are in Syria,' she called to Domitus, 'then I will ask the governor of Apamea. He is a nervous wreck, convinced that he will be poisoned. He calls me to his palace every week, insisting I prescribe him healing potions and antidotes. He is so bland and uninteresting that no one really notices him, so the idea that anyone would poison him is preposterous. A combination of nerves and rich food is responsible for his stomach cramps.'

'He might not be so keen to employ you when he learns that you are here,' I said.

She laughed. 'I told him I was coming here. He asked me to give you a message.'

'What message?'

'That he hopes you will visit Apamea soon. He says that any friend of Pompey is his friend also.'

Domitus laughed and Rsan looked alarmed.

'I am *not* Pompey's friend,' I stated. 'I am Parthian.'

'Is he always like this?' Samahe asked Dobbai.

127

'Always, sister. Everything is always black or white to the son of Hatra. You are either his enemy or his friend. There is no middle course.'

'That is a shame, lord king,' said Samahe. 'You dress like a Roman and should act more like them. Diplomacy can sometimes achieve more than the sword.'

'You mean duplicity and betrayal,' I answered.

'You see, sister,' said Dobbai, 'he is a hopeless romantic.'

After Samahe had examined and expressed her admiration for my griffin banner that hung on the wall behind our thrones, we walked to the banqueting hall where I ordered food to be brought for our guest. She sat on the top table as bread, fruit, cheese, sweet meats and pastries were brought from the kitchens. Out of courtesy we sat with her as servants filled our plain cups with wine and water.

Samahe's appetite was amazing and I soon appreciated why she was overweight. She devoured great quantities of bread, cheese, yogurt and honey before servants brought slices of freshly roasted chicken, camel and grouse. Meat juices dripped from the corners of her lips as she shoved one piece after another into her mouth, all washed down by liberal quantities of wine. And all the while she never stopped talking.

She picked up a chicken wing and looked at Orodes. 'My sister has told me of your predicament, prince. But you must not despair for you will reclaim your inheritance and more.'

'More?' said a curious Orodes.

Samahe began pushing the chicken into her mouth 'All will be revealed in time.'

She chewed the meat and looked at her greasy hands. She turned to a servant, a young girl holding a bowl of water in her hands, a towel draped over her lithesome right arm.

'Slave,' she called, 'come here.'

The girl blanched with alarm and made to hurry to Samahe's side but I held up a hand to stop her.

'There are no slaves here,' I said to our guest.

Samahe's mouth opened in surprise. 'No slaves?'

'All who work in the palace are free and are paid for their services.'

Samahe's eyes widened as she looked at Dobbai.

'It's true, sister. The son of Hatra fights not only to rid the empire of Mithridates but also to make the world a better place.'

'So you see, Samahe,' I said, 'as a friend of slaves I would not be welcome in Apamea, or any part of Syria, I think.'

The servant looked at me, unsure at what to do. I nodded so she could offer the bowl to Samahe. The old woman washed her hands and dried them on the towel, all the time keeping her black eyes on the girl's, who looked terrified.

'What is your name?' Samahe's voice was soft and kind.

'Farimah, lady,' she answered in a tremulous voice.

'Glorious moon,' said Samahe. She reached into her robe and held out her hand to the girl. It contained some sort of silver charm.

'Take it child, by way of an apology. Keep it close at all times and you will see your children grow into adulthood.'

The girl's eyes lit up. 'Thank you, lady. But I have no children.'

Samahe smiled, though her fat lips created more of a smirk.

'You will.'

The girl bowed and retreated to the kitchens. Samahe sat between Gallia and Dobbai, opposite me, and she now leaned across the table. Her breath reeked of wine.

'Pretty girl, if a little timid.'

'Did you see her destiny in her face?' I asked.

She belched, the distasteful aroma blasting my face.

'All I saw was an attractive young girl who most likely will succumb to the charms of a lustful young man. They will marry, she will fall pregnant and her first child will kill her.'

'You can predict the destiny of something that is not yet born?' said Godarz, his forehead creased with disbelief.

'You are an old man,' Samahe said to him, 'and you probably did not see her thin hips. A child could split her in two with ease, poor girl.'

'So you gave her something to widen her hips? Are you a god?' asked Domitus derisively.

'They say that you can take a Roman out of Rome but never Rome out of a Roman,' remarked Samahe. 'The charm will save her life when she gives birth, Roman, that is all I am

129

prepared to say on the matter. I did not come here to give charms to young virgins.'

'And why did you come?' I asked.

'Not that we are not glad to have you here,' added Gallia, who seemed fascinated by everything about Samahe.

Samahe rested a hand on my wife's arm. 'My sister said that you were gracious and wise and I can see that it is so.'

She turned to me with a slightly haughty demeanour.

'I have no idea why I am here, only that the gods gave me a clear sign that I had business in Dura.'

'What business?' sneered Domitus, who seemed to have taken a dislike to her.

'It will be made plain at the appropriate time.'

'Did you not hear my sister tell you, son of Hatra,' said Dobbai sternly, 'that you and Gallia are the talk of Apamea.'

'What of it?' I answered.

Dobbai looked at Samahe and shook her head.

'What of it? You must know that the gods use people to convey their messages. What clearer message can there be when thousands of voices are speaking your name? Where Dura and its king are heard on every corner, in every home and marketplace? Even a dullard would know that the gods were telling my sister to come here.'

It was all very ambiguous and frankly ridiculous, but out of politeness I did not press the point further. So Samahe consumed more meat before progressing on to slices of watermelon and grapes. She then declared that she would like to retire and rest before the evening's feast. Gallia and Dobbai escorted her to the room that had been set aside for her, leaving the menfolk at the table.

'She is obviously mad,' declared Domitus.

'Eccentric, certainly,' said Orodes.

Rsan was concerned about more practical matters.

'I hope the kitchens have enough food for this evening, majesty.'

We refilled our cups and laughed at the thought of this fat old woman from Apamea consuming Dura's entire food stocks.

We left the banqueting hall as the first preparations for the evening feast began, servants arranging the tables that were usually stacked against the walls in rows at right angles to the top table and benches alongside them. The hall could seat five hundred people and at least half that number was in attendance by the time I took my seat alongside Gallia, Dobbai and Samahe, who declared to being ravenous after her nap.

Domitus sat down at a table with his senior officers and a select number of centurions. The former were technically tribunes as the Durans and Exiles were organised along Roman lines. However, it was common knowledge that Domitus despised the rank of tribune due to his experience of them during his time with the Roman army, and so they were simply referred to as officers. Orodes sat at another table with the senior horse archer and cataphract commanders. And at a further table were the Amazons. Everyone stood as four trumpeters blew their instruments to signal our arrival, taking their seats after we had done so.

The hall was soon filled with a frenetic din as drink flowed, amplified by the chamber's relatively low ceiling. Samahe recommenced her assault on the palace's food supplies as she greedily consumed sizzling strips of goat on beds of rice, the white flesh of fish caught earlier in the Euphrates and ribs of pigs smeared in a spicy sauce.

These events always raised my spirits when I saw a sea of young, eager faces before me, the cream of Dura's army. An army though newly created that had enjoyed a string of victories. And morale was high following the relief of Uruk and the defeat of the soldiers sent by Narses. I knew all talk among the officers and men concerned when they would be marching east against Mithridates. I did nothing to deter such talk, as I knew that it was transmitted to the merchants of the trade caravans that travelled through Dura. They in turn would report it to the towns and cities they visited, and word would reach Ctesiphon that Dura's army would be paying it a visit. It was untrue but anything that gave Mithridates sleepless nights cheered me.

So I drank, ate and listened to Samahe regale us with tales of the governor of Apamea and her dealings with other high-ranking Roman officials. She was a wily old goat as I noticed that she treated the servants with respect and never let an opportunity slip to flatter Gallia. Dobbai seemed quiet and withdrawn, however, as though something was troubling her. She picked at her food.

'Chicken not to your liking, Dobbai?'

'I saw a bat today, the first time I have ever seen one during daylight.'

I put down my cup. 'A bad omen?'

She picked up a piece of chicken and nibbled it half-heartedly. 'It predicts a long journey.'

I picked up my cup and drained it. 'If it is an omen then all it signifies is Samahe's trip from Syria.'

She looked at me. 'Perhaps.'

The next day began as every other: rise at dawn, a sparse breakfast and then a ride to the training fields outside the city where horse archers, cataphracts and legionaries drilled and trained with their weapons. Rsan was always complaining at the weekly meeting of the council about the high number of arrows, lances and javelins that were damaged beyond repair during these training sessions. As a civilian he failed to realise that realistic training paid dividends on the battlefield, but all he saw was a long list of expensive items that needed to be replaced.

I always enjoyed morning training, when the temperature was still bearable and the air fresh. Gallia always attended with her Amazons and for a few hours it was like we were back in Italy. Domitus drilled his legionaries and afterwards we all assembled in his command tent to rest our aching limbs and share tales about the old days with Spartacus. Orodes attended as well, though when he had first arrived at Dura he had felt somewhat of an outsider. He had not shared in our experiences in Italy. But he too had fought by our side on our return to Parthia so now everyone considered him an honorary Companion.

The afternoons, when the sun roasted the earth and the wind created great clouds of dust that seeped into clothing and buildings, were given over to administration. It was mundane and tedious but integral to the smooth running of a kingdom. Once a week I sat in the throne room listening to petitioners who came to the Citadel to either air a grievance, convince me to invest in a money making scheme or offer a bribe so their son could join the cataphracts. Army recruitment was dealt with by the officers of Domitus and Orodes in the headquarters building and so before a father had offered his money to ease his son into Dura's famed heavy horsemen, I told him to walk across the courtyard and speak to the relevant individuals.

I found these gatherings tedious in the extreme but my father had taught me that a people should have access to their king, even if at times he ignored their words.

'Smile, show an interest in what they are saying and treat them with courtesy,' he had told me. 'Simple acts can win you life-long allegiances, something that no amount of gold can buy.'

And so I sat, smiled and took an interest. Gallia rarely attended these meetings, though she made a point of sitting next to me if she learned that a slave trader was going to petition me to allow the sale of people in Dura. They always got short shrift from my queen. Rsan, who always attended, would stand by the dais and look forlorn as the slaver made a rapid exit from the throne room, and with him any taxes that the treasury would have earned from his lucrative business.

The petitioners waited in the reception hall where they were searched for any weapons they might have on them, after which guards escorted them into the throne room. Any that appeared to be deranged or religious fanatics were quietly ejected from the Citadel. It was unfortunate that an opportunity to meet Dura's king attracted the least savoury elements of the kingdom as well as the more worthy.

The guards flanking the dais stepped forward to prevent a man from jumping on to it to embrace me after I had told him that he had my permission to sell replicas of the griffin statue above the Palmyrene Gate on his market stall. He looked alarmed as four legionaries with drawn swords bore down on him, before Rsan told him that no one was allowed to touch the body of the king.

The man, whose slightly threadbare appearance suggested his stall barely made a profit, clasped his hands together and retreated a few paces.

'Forgive me, highness,' he said, 'but it is the first good news that I have had in an age.'

'Trade is poor?' I asked.

He shook his head and smiled. 'Trade is good, majesty, but a wife and five children are many mouths to feed.'

'Five children?'

He grinned. 'Shamash has been kind to me.'

No wonder he looked tired. 'Well, hopefully your idea will make you lots of money to enable you to feed and clothe your family. Actually, I am surprised that no one has thought of the idea before. Present yourself at the treasury tomorrow and Lord Rsan's clerks will issue you with the relevant licence.'

I waved the guards back. 'Shamash be with you.'

The trader bowed his head. 'And may He smile upon you and your family, highness. And may the griffin always stand as guardian of your city. And may your fame strike terror into the hearts of your enemies.'

I smiled and indicated to the commander of the guards to escort him from the chamber, flattering though his words were. He was still wishing me good fortune when the doors were closed.

'Another satisfied citizen, Rsan.'

'I have to confess that his idea was a most unique one.'

'And profitable, no doubt.'

His eyes lit up. 'Let us hope so, majesty. Your treasury always requires re-nourishing.'

The doors opened, the officer of the guard entered and marched across the stone tiles. He bowed his head to me.

'There is a man outside, majesty, requesting an audience. He says that he is an old friend.'

'What is his name?'

The officer frowned. 'He said he is an old sea dog, majesty.'

'Search him for weapons,' commanded Rsan.

'We have already done that, sir.'

'Then show him in,' I ordered.

The figure momentarily framed in the doorway was broad shouldered, and as he and the two guards walked into the throne room I smiled when I heard his voice, a voice I thought I would never hear again.

'They took my sword and dagger. Thought I was some sort of assassin. But I told them, Pacorus and I go back a long

134

way. Of course you weren't a king then, just a poor renegade. Times change, it seems.'

I jumped up as he approached, a burly man with a huge ragged beard and long, untidy hair, a grizzled face and massive tattooed forearms.

'Athineos, is it really you?'

He gave me a wicked grin. 'None other.'

He held out his right hand and I clasped his forearm and he locked me in an iron embrace.

'It has been too long, my friend,' I said.

He slapped me on the shoulders and stepped back. 'You know how it is. A week turns into a month that turns into a year and before you know it five years have passed.'

He looked around the throne room.

'Still, looks like you've done all right for yourself.'

His expensive leather boots, gold rings on his fingers and gold earrings suggested that the gods had also smiled upon him.

'Smuggling is paying handsomely, judging by your appearance,' I teased him.

He feigned hurt. 'Smuggling? I'm a legitimate captain of commerce, I'll have you know. Working for the People and Senate of Rome.'

'Rome?'

He scratched his nose. 'No choice, young king, seeing as the Romans control the Mediterranean after the Cilician pirates were destroyed. My ships are moored at Tripolis waiting for a shipment of animals and I kept hearing about a young Parthian king who rides a white horse and defeats all his enemies and has a blonde-haired queen. Very unusual in these parts.

'So I said to myself, Athineos, it has to be that young fool I shipped from Italy, along with a few dozen more who had elected to follow him. Looks like they made the right decision.'

I ordered the guards to find Domitus and Godarz and bring them to the palace as I invited Athineos to take refreshments with me on the palace terrace. I told Rsan to inform the waiting petitioners that the king had been called away on urgent business and to come back next week as I walked with the Cretan sea dog from the throne room.

On the terrace a servant informed me that Dobbai was showing Samahe the griffin statue at the Palmyrene Gate with

135

Gallia in tow. I sent a rider to urgently request their presence at the Citadel. I would have shown Claudia off to Athineos but a nursemaid informed me that she was taking her afternoon nap.

'So, I see you have not been spending all your time killing your enemies,' said Athineos as a servant offered him a goblet of wine.

Fortunately the sun had passed its highest point and was now slowly descending towards the west, resulting in the terrace being covered in welcome shade. I told Athineos of my return to Hatra, of being given the crown of Dura and the subsequent civil strife in the empire, ending with a summary of the current stand-off with Mithridates.

'No one talks about him in Syria,' said Athineos. 'In Syria the name on everyone's lips is Pacorus of Dura.'

'The Romans tried to capture my kingdom,' I said.

He nodded. 'I know, an army sent by Crassus. But you managed to charm Pompey and that has worked to your advantage because those two are bitter enemies. Very clever.'

He began turning one of his rings on his fingers. He was going to say something when Domitus and Godarz appeared, both of them delighted to see the man who had made our escape from Italy possible. Athineos embraced them both and began regaling them with stories of his piracy and bedding women, no doubt most if not all of them invented. He drank more wine and soon his cheeks were flushed as the alcohol made him louder and more gregarious.

He shouted and cheered when Gallia, all blonde hair and long legs, glided onto the terrace. Before she had time to say anything he had scooped her off her feet and planted a host of kisses on her cheeks.

'You're still as lovely as the first day I clapped eyes on you,' he told her. 'Why don't you come back to Tyrus with me? I've got three ships and enough work to retire a wealthy man, albeit not a king.'

'A tempting offer,' said Gallia, giggling and flirting with him. 'But alas I have a daughter.'

His face registered shock, even though he already knew this. 'I don't believe it. You haven't got on ounce of fat on you.'

She waved a hand at him and took a cup of water offered by a servant. As everyone laughed and joked no one saw

Dobbai and Samahe shuffle into our presence. Both were attired in black but the colour of Dobbai's robes looked positively bright compared to the expression on her face.

'Dobbai,' I said, 'this is Athineos on whose ship we travelled back to Parthia after fighting by the side of Spartacus.'

'Why is he here?' she snapped.

The chatter died down as everyone looked at her. Dobbai's curt manners and cutting tongue were well known but we were at a loss regarding her instant hostility to Athineos.

'Is this your mother?' grinned the Cretan.

'Pacorus' mother is charming and attractive,' said Domitus, 'so the answer to your question is no. This is Pacorus' sorceress.'

Unconcerned by Domitus' insult, Dobbai walked over to Athineos.

'Your coming is an ill omen.'

'That's enough,' I said. 'Athineos is an old friend and deserves some respect.'

Dobbai continued to fix Athineos with her eyes. 'Very well. With respect I ask you again. Why are you here?'

'I have heard about you, lady,' smiled Athineos, trying to win Dobbai over with his charm. 'Your reputation has spread far and wide.'

'Honeyed words have no effect on me, servant of the Romans,' spat Dobbai. 'I am not an innocent maiden easily deceived by flattering words.'

'Whatever the reason he is here,' I insisted, 'he is very welcome.'

Dobbai sneered at Athineos and walked over to her chair, inviting Samahe to sit in the one next to hers.

'Tell him the reason you are here, captain,' she said as she settled her back against the cushions.

Athineos smiled awkwardly at me and again began fiddling with his rings.

'I have to confess that I do bring some news that might interest you,' he said. 'Not that I wouldn't have come to see you anyway.'

'Of course not,' remarked Dobbai dryly.

'Spit it out, then,' I told him.

He looked at Gallia and me and then at Domitus and Godarz before taking a great gulp of wine.

'Burebista is alive.'

Chapter 5

I stared at him, stunned and disbelieving.

'Impossible,' hissed Gallia. 'I was there the night he fell. Just outside Rhegium.'

'She's right,' I said. 'Burebista fell the night we helped Spartacus escape from Crassus' trap outside Rhegium.'

Athineos held up his hands. 'I do not know of the episode you talk about. But I do know this. There are to be gladiatorial games at Ephesus this summer. I was one of the captains commissioned to collect wild animals to transport to the city. Anyway, I got talking to the agent who commissioned me and he told me that these games are going to be spectacular, with all the top gladiatorial schools sending their fighters to take part. He operates out of Capua, you see.'

Gallia's expression hardened. 'Capua?'

Athineos smiled at her but received an icy stare in return.

'Anyway,' he continued, 'he told me that the school of Lentulus Vatia was sending its top gladiators to take part, including Burebista the Dacian.'

Gallia suddenly looked miserable and went to the stone balustrade, staring out across the waters of the Euphrates. I walked over to her and slipped my arm around her waist.

'Are you ill?'

She gave me a smile but her eyes were full of sadness.

'I never thought I would hear that name again.'

'What, Burebista?'

'No, Lentulus Vatia. *Lanista* of Capua's *ludus*, the man I was sold to by my dear father.'

Godarz was angry. 'This is all nonsense. Burebista died years ago in Italy. We were all there, captain, and saw him fall.'

'I am just reporting what I have heard, that is all,' pleaded Athineos. 'I thought it unlikely too until he told me that after he was found on the battlefield this Burebista was nursed back to health on the orders of Crassus himself. He was then sold to the *lanista* at Capua to be trained as a gladiator. He is an *Eques*.'

'A horseman?' I said.

'A gladiator trained to fight on horseback in the arena,' said Domitus.

'Except the agent told me that this horseman did not need any training to ride a horse,' continued Athineos, 'on account of him being part of the mounted slaves who fought beside Spartacus.'

'Many horsemen fought beside Spartacus,' said Godarz. 'This is ridiculous, Pacorus. There are many men called Burebista. It is a common enough Dacian name.'

'Well,' added Athineos, 'the agent told me that this Burebista fought with the Parthian, meaning you Pacorus, that is King Pacorus. And in celebration of this, or mockery depending on your point of view, in the arena he rides a white horse.'

My blood ran cold. I wanted to laugh and tell Athineos that he had been spun a fairy tale, hoodwinked, deceived. I could not because a voice inside my head told me that his words must be true. But after all these years?

'Your story has one major flaw, captain,' said Godarz. 'We saw Burebista fall outside Rhegium.'

'Except that you did not.' I turned to see Dobbai resting her chin on her thumbs, staring at Godarz.

My governor curled his lip dismissively at her. 'We were there; you were not.'

Then she looked at me. 'The doubt etched on your face, son of Hatra, tells me that you believe the words of this pirate. So, did you see this Burebista fall?'

'Burebista is dead,' I insisted. 'He was killed at Rhegium.'

Dobbai gave me a knowing look.

'Then the matter is closed.' She looked at Athineos. 'The man you have been told about, pirate, is obviously a different individual from the one who fought with the son of Hatra in the slave general's army.'

'It is as Dobbai says,' I said, avoiding the old witch's eyes.

'I just thought you should know, that is all,' remarked Athineos quietly.

He stayed with us for two days, during which time he said nothing more about Burebista or the games at Ephesus. I escorted him on a tour of the city, the caravan park where we talked with the merchants of the Silk Road and the legionary camp. Dobbai and Samahe made themselves scarce during this time and I noticed that Godarz took himself away on a visit to

140

some of Dura's lords who lived in their great mud-brick strongholds to the north of the city. Athineos was impressed by what he saw, particularly when Gallia put the Amazons through their paces on the shooting range, though I think the old sea dog was ogling the shapely bodies of the women of my wife's bodyguard rather than admiring their archery skills.

I had asked him to stay in the palace but he told me he had rented a room in one of the city's brothels. He said the combination of good food, wine and attractive, available women made even a palace pale in comparison. On the morning of his departure he rode to the Citadel after I had finished on the training fields. He found me brushing down Remus outside the stable block where he was housed. Around me dozens of stable hands, farriers and veterinaries were mucking out stalls, fitting new shoes to horses and listening to cataphracts pointing out possible health problems with their mounts. The scene resembled one of the city's squares on market day.

Two legionaries escorted Athineos to where I stood among a hundred horse archers who I had trained with earlier.

'I see you still have your horse, then,' Athineos grinned.

I waved the guards back.

'Remus is one of the most famous horses in Parthia,' I told him.

He walked up and stroked Remus' neck. 'Not only in Parthia but Syria too. You have made quite an impression, King Pacorus.

'I came to say farewell. Time for me to get back to my ships.'

'And wild animals.'

'You do not approve?' he said.

I stopped brushing Remus' flank and stretched my back. 'We all have to earn a living.'

'Even kings?'

I nodded. 'Even kings. The taxes levied on the trade caravans that pass through Dura help to pay for all of this.'

I held out an arm to the stables. 'War is an expensive business.'

'Good job you are good at it, then.'

He offered me his hand. 'Thank you for your hospitality.'

I took his hand and laughed. 'Shouldn't you be saying that to the mistress of the brothel you have been staying at?'

He winked. 'Already have, don't you worry.'

His expression suddenly changed to one of deadly earnestness. 'I will be at Tripolis for three months should you wish to partake of my hospitality. After that I will be sailing to Ephesus to deliver the animals for the games.'

He patted Remus on the neck, gave me a wry smile, turned and walked away, the guards escorting him back to the courtyard where his own horse waited. I finished brushing my horse and took him back to his stall. The stables were filled with the pleasing aroma of freshly laid straw and clean horses. The air vents in the ceiling were open to prevent it getting too hot inside the stalls, fifty of which were in this particular block. Epona was housed in another, larger block where the horses of the Amazons were quartered. I placed my saddle on a hook on the wall opposite Remus' stall and draped his saddlecloth over a wooden rail underneath. Each stall was large enough to allow a horse to turn around, lie down and get up without bumping into the walls. And like the other horses Remus had his own hay manger, water trough and window vents that allowed air to circulate.

I leaned on the top of the door to his stall. In each side wall were metal grilles to allow him to see into the next stall. Horses are social animals and like to know they are in the company of other horses. In this way they are happier and not stressed.

'Well, Remus, life is never simple. Just when you think you have solved one problem another takes its place.'

Around me stable hands and horse archers had been busy leading their horses to their stalls, sweeping the floor or refilling hay mangers and water troughs. The building had echoed to the sound of their activity but now it fell silent. I felt a pair of eyes on me and turned to see the figure of Dobbai. This was highly unusual as she rarely if ever visited the stables.

'Remus needs rest after his morning exertion,' I said, 'but I can find you a fresh horse if you so desire.'

She gave me a disdainful look. 'Do not try to be clever, son of Hatra, it does not suit you. The pirate has gone?'

'He has.'

142

She walked over to stand beside me. 'And what will you do now?'

'Well, after I have finished here I have a meeting with Rsan to discuss tenancy agreements for farmers wishing to work the land that belongs to the royal estates.'

'Don't be a fool!' she snapped. 'I was not talking about your tallyman's piles of useless parchments, as you well know.'

I said nothing.

'You think he is still alive, don't you? And like a seed planted in the earth the pirate's words will grow louder in your mind until they are like a pair of kettledrums being constantly banged inside your skull.'

I walked away. 'Have you ever thought that it is perhaps your words that torture me, Dobbai?'

But she was right. Over the following days the only thing I could think about was Burebista. I racked my brains trying to remember what had happened that night outside Rhegium. I remembered the snow, the burning towers and ramparts and the breakthrough of Spartacus' army. But I knew that I had not seen Burebista fall.

'You're thinking of going, aren't you?'

I was standing on the balcony of our bedroom, the light fading from the earth as another day drew to a close. Another day of normality in Dura but a period of torment for me. I sighed and went back into the bedroom. Gallia was dressed in an alluring cotton robe, very sheer and very thin. I could see her breasts and the shape of her thighs clearly. Normally such a vision would stir my loins but I felt nothing. I was detached, as though I was watching the scene rather than being a part of it. I sat on the edge of the bed and sighed.

'Sorry, what did you say?'

'Orodes and Domitus took the army east today. They intend to burn Ctesiphon, kill Mithridates and then march on Persepolis.'

I jumped up. 'What?'

She laid back on the bed, her locks cascading over her neck and breasts.

'Now that I have your intention perhaps you could answer my question.'

'Which was?'

'When are you leaving for Tripolis?'

I looked at her and thought I might deceive her with bluff but her eyes told me that she already knew the answer.

'What if it is true?' was all I could say.

'What if it is? What can you do about it? Take ship with Athineos and rescue Burebista from the arena? It is not your concern, Pacorus. Your concern is here, with me and your daughter, in Dura.'

That night, as she lay asleep in my arms, a slight wind rippling the net curtain at the balcony's entrance, I lay awake and thought of Burebista. I remembered the big, courageous Dacian who had risen to be the commander of a dragon – a thousand horsemen – in Italy. Brave Burebista, always smiling and never downcast. Now condemned to the living hell of the arena. Dobbai was always telling me that the gods sent men signs, omens and warnings. What else could Athineos' visit be but a sign? And why had Samahe suddenly appeared at Dura? It was not a coincidence, of that I was now certain, though the exact purpose of her visit was yet to be revealed.

I sat up. 'No.'

The next day I was treated by Alcaeus. The chief of the army's medical corps rarely visited the Citadel, being content to restrict himself to the hospital in the legionary camp. There he could practise his medical skills and supervise his fellow physicians. Occasionally he would walk to the Citadel to see Claudia but we saw him almost every day after training sessions when we took refreshments in Domitus' command tent. Tall with wiry hair and a black beard, like his fellow medics he wore a simple white tunic with a leather bag holding his medicines over his shoulder and a pair of sandals on his feet. He looked more like a philosopher than a healer but he was probably more intelligent than any of us and had a great thirst for knowledge. It was his analytical mind that led him to dislike Dobbai, whom he regarded as a charlatan and troublemaker. But he knew that Gallia was immensely fond of her and so he avoided the old woman.

Alcaeus gently lifted my left arm above my shoulder and observed my facial expression.

144

'Well, you will be pleased to know that nothing is broken, otherwise you would be screaming by now. Best to avoid your morning routine for a couple of days.'

Domitus placed a towel in a bowl of water and then applied it on the back of his neck.

'That must be the first time that Pacorus has fallen off his horse. I thought Parthians are born in the saddle.'

I had been shooting at targets on the ranges but my mind had been elsewhere. After I had turned in the saddle to shoot an arrow at a target over Remus' hindquarters my mind was thinking about the games at Ephesus when Remus pulled up as we neared the end of the course and I had toppled from the saddle. It had caused great mirth among the horse archers I had been training with.

'My mind was elsewhere,' I said.

'Thinking about Burebista,' said Gallia, accepting a drink of water from Domitus. It had been a hot morning and threatened to be an even hotter afternoon.

Domitus rolled his eyes. 'Mother of Jupiter, you're not still going on about that, surely?'

I ignored him. 'Alcaeus, tell me about Ephesus.'

The doctor filled a cup with water and sat on a stool.

'Ephesus? A rich trading port in the eastern Aegean and the site of the sanctuary of the Goddess Artemis. Why do you ask?'

'I have heard that there are annual games held there,' I said evasively.

'Roman gladiatorial games,' he sneered. 'Yes, I have heard. There are no levels to which the Romans will not sink to, no offence Domitus.'

Domitus smiled. 'None taken.'

Alcaeus stood and began pacing, much like I imagined a Greek philosopher would do when delivering a lesson.

'The Great Theatre at Ephesus is one of the wonders of the world, I have heard, being able to seat over twenty thousand people. It was built during the reign of Lysimachus over two hundred years ago. He was one of the *Diodochi*, of course.'

'What's that?' asked Domitus.

Alcaeus stopped and stared in amazement at him. 'Do you know nothing of Greek history, Domitus?'

'Not much,' sniffed Domitus. 'There wasn't much call for it when I was fighting for Rome, and even less now I'm at Dura.'

Alcaeus shook his head gravely. 'I suppose you have heard of Alexander of Macedon?'

'Naturally,' replied Domitus. 'One of the few Greeks who was good with a sword.'

'The *Diodochi* were the successors of Alexander,' continued Alcaeus, 'men who served under him during his conquests. I believe Lysimachus was one of his bodyguards. Anyway, after Alexander's death he became the ruler of Thrace and Asia Minor and founded Ephesus.'

'It is now under Roman rule,' said Gallia.

'Like many cities and regions, lady,' replied Alcaeus sadly. 'Laying that aside, you may be interested to know that legend has it that Ephesus was founded by the Amazons, the warrior women of myth made real by Dura's queen.'

Domitus laughed but Alcaeus ignored him.

'Having fought a bruising battle with Heracles, the demi-god who was the last mortal son of Zeus, the Amazons regrouped at a spot that later became Ephesus. I have heard that there are four statues of Amazon women in the temple itself.'

'Was Artemis an Amazon?' I asked as I stretched my shoulder.

Alcaeus shook his head. 'No. Artemis is the daughter of Zeus, the king of the gods, and one of the three maiden goddesses of Olympus. She is also the daughter of the Goddess Leto. Artemis is the Goddess of the Moon, Goddess of the Hunt and the twin sister of Apollo.'

I looked at Gallia and saw that she was enthralled by his words.

Alcaeus looked at Domitus. 'The Romans also worship Artemis, though for some unexplained reason they call her Diana.'

He smiled at Gallia. 'In civilised places Artemis is known as the Maiden of the Silver Bow because she is typically shown carrying a silver bow and arrows, the latter representing the rays

146

of the moon. She also wears silver sandals and rides in a silver chariot.'

'And people worship Artemis at Ephesus?' asked Gallia.

'They travel from far and wide to say prayers at the Temple of Artemis,' said Alcaeus. 'It is the largest place of worship in the world.'

I was sceptical. 'Bigger than the Great Temple at Hatra, Alcaeus?'

He nodded his head. 'Yes.'

'Even though you've never seen it,' said Domitus.

'The dimensions of the temple are common knowledge; a hundred and fifty yards in length, seventy-five yards in width and sixty feet in height.'

'That is one large temple,' I agreed.

'Why such an interest in Ephesus?' Alcaeus asked me.

'Athineos mentioned it, that's all,' I said.

Alcaeus sat down and finished his water. 'Strange him turning up after so long.'

'Stranger than you think,' said Domitus, who looked at me. 'Tell him.'

Alcaeus looked extremely interested in what I was about to say and Gallia was nodding. They were right, of course, as Alcaeus himself was a Companion.

'Athineos told me that Burebista lives and is a gladiator at the same school where Spartacus was forced to fight before he escaped.'

Alcaeus' eyes opened wide in amazement. 'The Dacian? And you believed him?'

I shrugged, which hurt my shoulder. 'He had nothing to gain by lying. The point is, he told me that Burebista would be taking part in the games at Ephesus this summer.'

'Alas for Burebista,' was Alcaeus' only comment.

'Pacorus has a mind to go and rescue him,' said Gallia casually.

Domitus spat out the water he was drinking and Alcaeus' eyes opened wide a second time.

'Tell me that was a joke,' said Domitus.

'You do realise that Ephesus is under Roman control?' stated Alcaeus.

I nodded. 'I know that.'

'And that such an important city will have a large garrison,' added Domitus.

I nodded once more.

'You waste your words,' Gallia told them. 'Ever since Athineos left us my husband's mind has been elsewhere, I suspect mostly on that snow-swept night at Rhegium, the last time he or any of us saw Burebista alive.'

'Gallia is right,' I told them, 'I have been distracted, I will not lie.'

'Did Athineos say that he had actually seen Burebista?' asked Alcaeus.

I shook my head. 'He had been told by one of the games' organisers that the gladiatorial school in Capua was sending its fighters to Ephesus, one of which was named Burebista the Dacian.'

'I am sure it is a common name among Dacians,' said Alcaeus. 'And anyway, aside from the fact that he died at Rhegium, Athineos did not actually see him with his own eyes.'

'Even if he had,' I said, 'he would not have recognised him as he never knew him.'

'A man tells another man of a man called Burebista who might be the same Burebista that served with you in Italy,' remarked Domitus. 'You have to admit, Pacorus, that it is all very vague.'

'And not worth risking your life over,' said Alcaeus firmly.

As Alcaeus had advised me not to haul myself into a saddle until my shoulder had healed, I walked back to the Citadel in the company of Gallia. Her Amazons likewise walked behind us, the sun roasting our horses and us as we approached the Palmyrene Gate. I glanced up at the griffin statue, drew my sword and raised it in salute as I neared the open gates. I had done so ever since it had been put in place above the gate and I believed it to be a gesture that would bring me luck on the battlefield. Alcaeus thought me foolish no doubt but I was not alone as Gallia and the Amazons also drew their swords and saluted the statue. I caught site of two black figures standing by the griffin. Gallia saw them too.

We left Remus and Epona in the care of the Amazons, who mounted their horses and rode to the Citadel as we climbed the steps inside the gatehouse. I was rubbing my now aching shoulder as we walked onto the battements above the gates.

'It looks far bigger up close,' observed Samahe, staring up at the statue. 'Most impressive.'

'Have you hurt yourself playing war games, son of Hatra?' said Dobbai.

'He fell off his horse,' Gallia told her.

'You have a fine city, King Pacorus,' remarked Samahe as she turned to me. 'I now know why I was brought here.'

'I thought you came of your own free will,' I said.

She smiled at me and brought her hands together, entwining her fingers.

'All things are connected, young king. Just as our lives are mapped out by the gods, so do the immortals send signs to ensure that we follow the right path.'

'Portents, son of Hatra,' said Dobbai grimly.

'The gods have brought me here to help you in your quest, King Pacorus,' continued Samahe, 'to which end I have sent a letter to another of our sisters who will provide you with advice and aid. She will be expecting you.'

I was confused. 'Quest? What quest?'

'To rescue your friend,' answered Dobbai. 'That is why you have been moping around like a love-sick shepherd following the pirate's departure.'

I opened my mouth to speak but Dobbai held up a hand to me. 'You are above all loyal, son of Hatra. Loyal to your friends and loyal to your ridiculous sense of honour, and an even more ridiculous notion of right and wrong.'

'They are the cornerstones of civilisation,' I said tersely.

Dobbai looked at Samahe and rolled her eyes.

'That is debateable, son of Hatra, but what I believe is not important. It is what you hold dear that will decide your actions.'

'You are intent on travelling to Ephesus?' asked Samahe.

I looked at her and then Dobbai and Gallia. Their expressions told me they already knew the answer. I could have denied it, told them not to be absurd. But the truth was that I felt nothing but relief.

'You think I am mad?' I said to Gallia.

She kissed me gently on the cheek. 'I think that loyalty is perhaps the greatest virtue, behind love of course.'

'It might get me killed,' I told her.

Gallia looked at Dobbai and Samahe. 'Not with their help, I think. Besides, I am coming with you.'

I walked back to the Citadel in the company of all three, a score of legionaries ringing us to provide security. A crowd quickly gathered around us as we slowly ambled up the main thoroughfare, the two old women with us finding the walk taxing in the afternoon heat.

'Are you mad?' I said through gritted teeth to Gallia.

'No,' she replied calmly. 'Are you?'

'You heard what Samahe and Dobbai said, Gallia. The coming to Dura of the former and Athineos were portents. I'm convinced that Burebista is still alive and that I should be the one to rescue him.'

'And did you not hear Alcaeus?' said Gallia. 'Ephesus was founded by the Amazons. I think that is a sign that I should accompany you in your adventure.'

I stopped and faced her. 'Adventure! To travel to a Roman stronghold alone is hardly an adventure.'

My voice had been raised and not only had the legionaries heard my outburst but so had the citizens nearest to them. There was a murmur among the crowd and many anxious faces peered at us.

'It is unseemly for the king and queen to argue in public,' said Dobbai. 'If you want to shout at each other you should do so behind closed doors.'

I looked around and saw the quizzical and confused expressions. I smiled and raised my hand to the crowd and began walking.

'This is not over,' I whispered to Gallia.

But when we reached the palace, and following a full-blooded argument behind closed doors in the throne room, Gallia's position remained the same. She was determined to accompany me to Ephesus where we would rescue Burebista and bring him back to Dura.

'And how precisely will you do this?' asked Dobbai as we sat in the banqueting hall eating our evening meal.

As usual Samahe was consuming great quantities of rice, roast chicken, fish, bread, fruit and beer. I had little appetite.

'I was hoping that you, or your "sister", might be able to assist me.'

'Assist *us*,' added Gallia.

Samahe stopped eating and looked at Dobbai.

'To the north of the great Caspian inland sea,' said the sorceress from Syria, 'is a herd of winged horses that I have the power to summon. They will be able to transport you to Ephesus. I can also weave a cloak of invisibility so the Romans will be unaware of your presence.'

'Really?' I said.

'No, not really,' replied Samahe, who dipped a biscuit in honey and pushed it into her mouth.

'Do you really think we can summon up armies of demons from the underworld to assist you, son of Hatra?' said Dobbai. 'The gods may send signs but it is you alone who must rescue your friend.'

'We could pack a ship with soldiers, wait until dark and then assault the place where Burebista is kept,' I said, thinking out loud.

Dobbai shook her head. 'No, no, no.'

'You are thinking like a warrior king, majesty,' said Samahe with a mouth full of pork.

'That is because that is what I am,' I replied.

'Then you must learn to think like the Romans so your entry into Ephesus goes unrecognised,' she continued.

I was at a loss as to the meaning of her words. 'I do not understand.'

Samahe gulped down a cup of beer. 'Consider this, King Pacorus. If I wished to pass through your kingdom unnoticed, what would be the best method, considering that your soldiers have eyes on all directions and places as they look out for would-be assassins?'

'Be a member of a trade caravan,' said Gallia before I could answer.

Dobbai pointed at her. 'Exactly, child, the secret is to blend in, become one of the crowd.'

'You are suggesting that we masquerade as followers of Artemis?' I suggested.

151

'How will that get you close to your friend?' said Samahe. 'No, King Pacorus. If you go to Ephesus only your brains and your sword will save you, not the worship of a foreign goddess. Just as you have embraced Roman ways at Dura so you must do the same at Ephesus.'

There followed another sleepless night as I lay beside Gallia staring at the ceiling, trying to fathom the meaning of Samahe's words. Was she suggesting I impersonate a Roman officer? But how would that help my plan? What was my plan, aside from taking ship to Ephesus? My head was aching so I rose and drank a cup of tepid water. It was warm. The net curtain at the open balcony doors was absolutely still with no wind to disturb it. I lay back down and closed my eyes as thoughts swirled in my mind. Eventually I slipped into an uneasy sleep and dreamt of a great battle between Parthians and Romans. I saw a figure on a horse, cloak billowing behind him as he charged into the dense Roman ranks, spear in his right hand. The enemy fled before him and I followed. He glanced over his shoulder and smiled at me. He had a helmet on that covered most of his face so I could not identify him. But at the same time I knew of him. I remembered a friend telling me of him, a friend now dead. He was the Thracian horseman and I had my answer.

The next morning I told Gallia of the vision and she wrapped her arms around me. There were tears in her eyes as I told her my plan to free Burebista from slavery.

'Please tell me that this is some kind of joke, though I fail to see the humour in any of it.' Godarz was not amused.

Rsan squirmed uncomfortably in his chair and Domitus stopped toying with his dagger and let it fall to the floor as I finished talking. I had convened a special meeting of the council but had ordered that there be no scribes present to record proceedings and kept the door shut. Fortunately it was still early morning so the temperature in the room was still bearable, though there were beads of sweat on Rsan's forehead.

'It is a sensible plan,' said Dobbai.

Godarz slammed a fist on the table, causing Rsan to jump.

'Sensible? Then my ears must have deceived me as I thought I just heard that Pacorus was intending to travel to

Ephesus. In addition, his wife intends to go with him and all to rescue a person that she had little time for, if my memory serves me right.'

'He is a Companion, Godarz,' stated Gallia firmly.

Godarz held his shaven head in his hands. 'In case you had not noticed, majesties, you have a kingdom to rule, a kingdom that is currently under threat of invasion.'

'Mithridates will not march against Dura, governor,' Dobbai assured him.

'It is folly, Pacorus,' said Orodes, 'sheer folly.'

'No, lord prince,' fumed Godarz, 'it is idiocy.'

'It is no different from every time I have led the army from Dura,' I said. 'In every campaign there is the possibility that I will not come back. That is the nature of war.'

'Except that you are not going to war,' stated Domitus. 'You are embarking on a fool's errand that will probably get you killed.'

He picked up his dagger and looked at Gallia. 'Why would you risk your life and perhaps make your daughter an orphan for a man you detested?'

'It is the will of the gods,' was Gallia's reply.

Godarz pointed at Dobbai. 'I blame you for this. Ever since your arrival at Dura you have filled the king's head with nonsense and now we see the result. If you really cared for Pacorus you would tell him that he should forget this ridiculous idea.'

Dobbai sneered at him. 'It is not my place to issue orders to the king.'

Domitus guffawed. 'Really? You are usually very eager to voice your opinions in these meetings.'

'It is my decision and mine alone,' I said. 'I will not stand by while Burebista is enslaved by the Romans, forced to fight for his life in the arena.'

'If you fail, Pacorus,' said Domitus, 'there is no way that we will be able to assist you. You will be on your own.'

'I know that,' I replied.

Godarz threw up his arms. 'I have never heard such lunacy. Let us suppose for a moment, just suppose, that you do embark on this absurd mission. When Mithridates and Narses learn that the King of Dura is no longer in his kingdom; indeed, has gone overseas, they will invade your realm.'

I nodded. 'Which is why our leaving must remain a secret. I estimate that we will be away no longer than two or three months, during which time we will officially be visiting my parents at Hatra.'

'And what if your parents desire to visit you here, at Dura?' asked Orodes.

'Then you will inform them that we have travelled to Uruk to visit Nergal and Praxima,' I answered. 'In addition, I do not want any knowledge of the visit to Ephesus to leave this room. Servants and guards may appear to be statues but they are notorious gossips.'

'Very wise, son of Hatra,' agreed Dobbai. 'Though you two will not be the only ones going to Ephesus.'

'You intend to take a bodyguard?' queries Orodes. 'In which case I insist that I accompany you both.'

Dobbai shook her head. 'It is not your destiny to accompany the son of Hatra, valiant prince, on this occasion.'

'I should go,' said Domitus.

'An excellent idea, Roman,' agreed Dobbai. 'It is, after all, a nest of your people that the son of Hatra is visiting.'

She looked at me. 'Take the Greek physician, too.'

'Alcaeus?'

'Yes. He is a Greek and will prove useful if you suffer injuries in the arena.'

Godarz looked most alarmed. 'Arena?'

Dobbai cackled. 'Of course you will not know. The son of Hatra has decided to become what the slave general was before he incited the lowborn to rise up. A gladiator.'

Godarz stormed out of the meeting as Domitus fell about laughing and Orodes looked mortified. I said nothing about the vision of Spartacus I had had in a dream but remained convinced that I was supposed to enter the arena.

'Why else would the revelation that Burebista still lives be disclosed to me at this time?' I asked Dobbai and Samahe that evening as we relaxed on the palace terrace. 'I followed Spartacus once. Why not a second time, and in the arena where he made his reputation?'

'It is ambitious, I agree,' said Dobbai.

'And would please the gods, I have no doubt,' added Samahe.

'Spartacus revealed himself to Pacorus in a dream,' said Gallia. 'It cannot be a coincidence.'

'As you stated, Samahe,' I said, 'all things are linked. In a city filled with gladiators who will notice one more? And masquerading as one will give me access to Burebista.'

'And then, son of Hatra?'

'And then we will formulate a plan to get him and us out of Ephesus,' I said.

Godarz purposely avoided me over the succeeding days, Rsan explaining that his friend was upset and angry that I would not change my mind. I told him that his temper would subside before I left. I knew that Godarz considered Gallia to be like a daughter and she viewed him as a father figure, and as such the thought of her being placed in danger caused him substantial grief. But she visited him in his mansion and told him that she was in danger every time she rode to war with the Amazons. She left him on good terms but Godarz's stubbornness resulted in him keeping his distance from me. I prayed his anger would dissipate before we left.

'You waste your time on such frivolities,' Dobbai told me the next day as she and Samahe stood before me in the throne room. 'You are a king and he is your governor. It is not his place to dispute your decisions, only obey.'

'He is a Companion,' I told her, 'and is entitled to speak his mind.'

On her advice I dismissed all the guards and had the doors to the chamber closed so that only four of us remained, Gallia sitting beside me on her throne. I had suggested that we could speak in private on the terrace but Dobbai told me that the servants had a habit of listening at the door, either that or decided to clean the bedroom closest to the terrace, the balcony of which was next to the latter, separated by a thin wall.

'Servants are notorious gossips, I learnt that at Ctesiphon,' she told me.

'The servants at Ctesiphon are all slaves,' said Gallia, 'not free men and women as they are in this palace.'

Dobbai looked at her kindly. 'Just because you pay them instead of flogging them does not mean they refrain from

155

indulging in idle chatter. If you wish to mask your journey to Ephesus you must be more careful.'

'You are right,' I agreed. 'Still, it should be relatively easy for the four of us to leave the city under the pretence that we are visiting Hatra.'

Dobbai looked at Samahe, the latter pursing her lips.

'Unfortunately it cannot be just the four of you.'

'There must be seven,' insisted Dobbai.

'Why?' asked Gallia.

'Because, child,' answered Samahe, 'that number is auspicious and is beloved of the gods. There are seven moving objects in the sky: the sun, moon and five planets. They are called "wandering stars" and act as the messengers of the gods.'

'It is particularly significant to the Goddess Inanna,' added Dobbai, 'and since the queen has decided that she will be accompanying you, son of Hatra, you both need to enlist the goddesses' support.'

'I thought Inanna is the Queen of Heaven,' said Gallia.

'She is also the Goddess of Warfare,' replied Samahe, 'and like you, majesty, is equally fond of making war as She is of making love.'

Gallia blushed at this but I smiled.

'I believe that the Babylonians knew Inanna as Ishtar,' I said.

Samahe smiled and Dobbai seemed surprised.

'Very good, son of Hatra, perhaps we will make a thinker out of you yet. When Inanna descended into hell she was forced to pass through seven gates, at each of which She was required to remove one of Her garments, until She stood before Her sister Erishkigal, the Queen of the Underworld. Naked and defenceless, Inanna was struck dead by seven plagues. Resurrected, upon her return from hell She passed through the seven gates once more, this time putting on one of Her garments that She had left at each gate. So you see that the number seven holds a very personal meaning to the goddess.'

'It is no coincidence that Her symbol is the seven-pointed star,' added Samahe.

'The goddess also has power over rains and storms,' said Dobbai, 'so you would do well to enlist Her aid to prevent you being drowned in heavy seas before you reach Ephesus.'

156

I was convinced. 'And who shall be the other members of our party.'

Dobbai shrugged. 'How should we know? It is for you to choose them, son of Hatra. My only advice would be to take the marsh boy.'

Gallia was appalled. 'Surena?'

'He is tedious,' agreed Dobbai, 'but it is no coincidence that your husband met him when he did. His star rises and his arrogance may be of use.'

'That is all the help we can give you,' said Samahe, 'but I have written to one of our sisterhood who will aid you during your journey. I will explain more when your departure approaches.'

'And in the meantime,' said Dobbai sternly, 'be careful what you say at all times. And if you do decide to take Surena make sure the young idiot does not blab his mouth off.'

Gallia smiled cruelly. 'You have no need to worry about that.'

Life went on at Dura as usual: the caravans arrived at the city carrying silk and other precious commodities to satisfy rich Egyptians and the army trained and recruited. Messages arrived from Uruk that the eastern and southern borders of Mesene were quiet. My father sent me a terse note congratulating me on the relief of Uruk, though he urged me not to provoke either Mithridates or Narses. I received a similar missive from Vardan at Babylon, though his language was much more polite and diplomatic. I paid visits to newly arrived caravans and talked with their chiefs, asking them what they had seen and heard on their travels to Dura. They told me that the roads were full of caravans and travellers but no armies. I already knew that because any hint of conflict and the roads emptied as if by magic. What I was more interested in was any plans and schemes they might have heard of. But they all reported that they had heard nothing. It all amounted to a quiet Parthia, for which I gave thanks to Shamash.

Gallia kept pestering me as to who else, aside from Surena, Alcaeus and Domitus, would be accompanying us to Ephesus. I told her I had no idea and asked her for suggestions. She shrugged and said that as it had been my idea in the first place I should be the one to select those who would go. Two

157

more to complete our band of seven. I had not yet asked Surena but I knew he would not refuse. Our lucky escape from Roman horsemen in Hyrcania had convinced him that he was invincible, and such faith would serve him well at Ephesus. I considered asking Viper but dismissed the idea. If she came Surena's mind would be focused on her rather than more important things. In the end it was Domitus who provided the answer, though it was not his intention.

I received an invitation to his command tent on the following afternoon. In the morning I had taken part in a joint training exercise with a thousand of Hatra's horse archers that had been sent to Babylon following my relief of Uruk. My father had been worried that the attack on Mesene was the prelude to a general offensive that would be launched by Mithridates and Narses and had wanted to stiffen Babylon's defences. Hatra, meanwhile, mobilised its entire army but then stood it down when it became apparent that Mithridates was content to remain idle at Ctesiphon. So when the horse archers returned to Hatran territory the commander sent his compliments to me when his force camped for the night just across the Euphrates. I sent a message back inviting him to take part in a joint exercise the next morning. The sight of three thousand horse archers and five hundred cataphracts thundering across the desert was most impressive. Afterwards I invited the Hatran commander and his officers to dine in the palace that night.

Domitus' invitation arrived when I was relaxing on the terrace playing with Claudia. Dobbai was sleeping in her chair in the shade and Samahe was conspicuous by her absence. Gallia had no idea where she was. Claudia fell asleep in my arms as the messenger walked onto the terrace and gave me a crisp salute.

'General Domitus sends his compliments, majesty, and requests your presence in his command tent.'

'On what business?' I asked.

'I do not know, majesty.'

'Very well, you may go.'

He gave another salute and departed. I stood with Claudia in my arms and handed her to Gallia.

'She's getting bigger,' I said, kissing her forehead as I passed her to my wife. 'Where is Samahe? I hope she is not wandering around the city causing trouble.'

'She is in her room preparing for her journey, son of Hatra,' said Dobbai, 'as you should be instead of showing off to your father's soldiers.'

I rolled my eyes at Gallia, kissed her on the head and left the terrace. As Remus had already been ridden hard that morning I took another horse, a young mare, from the stables and rode her from the Citadel escorted by a dozen horse archers. There was much traffic on the city's main thoroughfare and at the Palmyrene Gate there was a great congestion of carts, camels and donkeys, all loaded with wares for sale in the markets. The temperature was high and so were tempers as the guards at the gate tried to establish some order. Our presence only added to the chaos.

'Make way for the king,' shouted the commander of the horse archers.

His order was greeted with pleas and shouts as traders and their families threw up their arms and berated those in front of them. The centurion on duty at the gates blew his whistle and ordered his men to use their shields to clear a path for us. But moving a line of carts and camels loaded with goods is not an easy thing, and soon men and women were screaming and hurling abuse at the legionaries as they and their animals were shunted aside. I gave the order to dismount and lead our horses through the press as camels spat and grunted and legionaries cursed.

The centurion was trying hard to keep his temper in check as a small, rotund man in brown robes berated him, oblivious to the fact that he was facing a man nearly a foot taller and twice as broad.

'Your soldiers dare to threaten me and my goods. I have to pay the city's officials for the hire of my stall, for the collection of my rubbish and have a tax levied on the sale of my goods. And for what? So I can be abused in the street like a common criminal?'

'Move your camels immediately,' ordered the centurion, 'they are blocking the street.'

'They will not move while your soldiers are threatening them, son of a thousand desert warthogs. They are sensitive and do not respond to threats.'

The centurion's grip tightened on his cane. 'What did you call me?'

'Centurion,' I shouted.

I handed the reins of my horse to the commander of my escort and walked over to him. He saluted.

'Majesty.'

The trader squinted up at me and then realised who I was. He placed his right hand on his chest and bowed to me.

'Majesty, forgive me, I did not realise you were here.'

'Your camels seem to be causing some congestion,' I said.

'They do not respond to threats, majesty,' he said, his head still bowed. 'I am just an honest trader trying to earn a living.'

The centurion eyed him suspiciously and placed the end of his cane on the man's shoulder.

'Move your camels or I will have you arrested.'

The trader looked at him with alarm and then at me, a pleading expression in his eyes.

'I'm sure we can settle this without the need to arrest anyone,' I told the centurion, 'and can get this man's camels moving without the recourse to violence.'

The trader smiled. 'Darius, majesty, named after the Persian king.'

'And what is on your camels, Darius?'

'Pots, majesty,' he replied, 'all shapes and sizes and very popular with the women of the house.'

He saw a legionary jab the blunt end of his spear into the rump of one of his camels.

'Don't do that to my babies, you stupid heathen.' He bowed his head to me and scuttled off to console the camel.

'Try to get this mess sorted out,' I told the centurion, 'and do not beat or arrest anyone. That's an order.'

'Yes, majesty.' He looked at Darius and shook his head. 'A good flogging often works wonders, majesty.'

'Men like Darius are the lifeblood of this kingdom, centurion. Their taxes pay for the army's wages, weapons and equipment. We are all connected, you see, like a giant spider's web.'

He looked at me in confusion. 'Majesty?'

'It doesn't matter. Just do not flog or arrest anyone.'

We threaded our way through the press of people and animals and mounted our horses outside the Palmyrene Gate. I saluted the griffin and then we rode to the legionary camp, the vast complex of neatly arranged lines and rows of eight-man tents that could house up to ten thousand soldiers. In the centre of the camp stood the imposing structure of Domitus' command tent, behind it the smaller tents that housed the golden griffin standard of the Durans and the silver lion standard of the Exiles. Sentries guarded them night and day for the totems were semi-religious icons, revered and loved by the soldiers.

The escort took my and their horses to the stabling area as I took off my helmet and went inside the command tent. I found Domitus in the main reception area in the company of Drenis and Arminius. All three stood as I placed my helmet on one of the side tables.

'Here he is,' said Domitus, 'the champion of the arena.

I gave him a disapproving look but he raised his hands submissively.

'Calm yourself. They both know of your new trade and have offered their services.'

'Please be seated,' I said, helping myself to a cup of water. Even though the ventilation flaps in the roof were open it was still hot inside the tent. Domitus walked to the flaps and tied them together to ensure our privacy. Soon it would become even hotter. Sweat was already running down the face of Arminius, the strapping German ex-gladiator who was one of those who had escaped from the *ludus* in Capua with Spartacus. One of those beside him had been Drenis, smaller in stature and his body covered in scars collected in the arena and on the battlefield. Like Spartacus he was a Thracian, his swarthy features indicating his race. And like Spartacus he had short-cropped hair whereas Arminius kept his light brown hair shoulder length.

'You are making a mistake, Pacorus,' said Drenis bluntly. 'Burebista is dead.'

161

I went to one of the chairs placed opposite Domitus' desk and sat in it.

'You are wrong, Drenis. Burebista lives.'

'What he meant, Pacorus,' said Arminius, 'is that though he might be alive at the moment Burebista is certain to die sooner rather than later.'

'He is a Companion,' I said, 'and as such I will not abandon him.'

Drenis sighed. 'So you plan to impersonate a gladiator and then what?'

'And then I will gain access to him and we can work out a plan to free him.'

'Not if you are fighting him,' said Arminius.

'I do not intend to fight him, Arminius,' I replied.

'So you have decided on what type of gladiator you shall be?' queried Drenis.

This was turning into an interrogation. 'What type?'

'If you choose to be an *Eques* then you will be fighting Burebista,' said Arminius.

'What types of gladiator are there?' I asked. 'As I have no wish to fight my former subordinate I will not be an *Eques*.'

'Then you have a choice between Thracian, *Provocator*, Samnite, *Murmillo*, *Retiarius*, *Secutor* or *Hoplomachus*,' said Drenis.

I was totally perplexed but he and Arminius spent the next few moments explaining to me the difference between the categories of gladiator. There was the Thracian who fought with a short sword and small rectangular shield; the *Secutor* whose shield was larger, as was that of the *Provocator*; the *Murmillo*, the 'fish man', who usually fought a *Retiarius*, the 'net man' who was armed with a trident and net.

'What about this *Hoplomachus*, the "hoplite fighter"?' I asked.

'He is based on the old Greek hoplite warriors,' said Drenis. 'Armed with a thrusting spear, short sword, dagger and carries a small, round bronze shield. He fights a *Murmillo* or Thracian.'

'This is madness,' Arminius said suddenly. 'You may be a great warlord and king, Pacorus, but you have no knowledge of the arena and what is involved to be a part of it. I commend your loyalty to Burebista but I have to tell you that your scheme will end badly.'

'You waste your words, Arminius,' said Domitus, 'because he is determined to go. Is that not correct, Pacorus?'

I nodded gravely.

Domitus leaned back in his chair. 'You see. Hopeless.'

'Do you believe in destiny, Arminius?' I said. 'Do you believe that a man's life is mapped out by the gods?'

'Not really,' replied Arminius. 'I don't believe in the gods.'

I ignored his blasphemy. 'Consider this. Fate took me to Italy where I fought beside Spartacus. The gods decreed that I should live when thousands of others died, not only live but escape back to Parthia where I became King of Dura. I believe that it was no accident that I met Spartacus.'

'We can all say that,' said Domitus.

'You have been spending too much time with your witch,' stated Arminius bluntly.

'I believe that it is my destiny to go to Ephesus,' I said firmly, 'where I will free Burebista from slavery. I do not think it was an accident that Athineos came here to tell me that Burebista is still alive and inform me of the forthcoming gladiatorial games.'

'Which brings me neatly to another matter,' interrupted Drenis. 'Athineos.'

I was at a loss as to what he was implying. 'What about him?'

'You say that it was divine intervention that brought him here, which may or may not be true. But I suggest another, more human, reason: greed. Have you considered that it might be a ruse to lure you away from Parthia where you can be captured?'

'Captured, by whom?' I asked.

'The Romans,' said Arminius. 'I am sure that your head commands a high price in Rome, not least because you are a living survivor of the slave uprising and also defeated and killed one of Crassus' protégés not so long ago.'

'It would be a way to make a lot of money,' added Drenis.

163

I discounted the notion. 'Any assassin can attempt to kill me, be it one sent by Crassus or Mithridates. In addition, I could have been killed recently at Uruk or in any battle. I do not suspect Athineos of treachery and neither did Dobbai and she has a nose for such things.'

I looked at them. 'All I ask is that you assist me in preparing for the games at Ephesus. I do not ask any of you to come with me.'

'It's too late for that,' said Drenis. 'We are all coming with you, whether you like it or not.'

Domitus informed me that as a number of gladiatorial schools would be sending their fighters to Ephesus, he had come up with the idea that we would be masquerading as representatives of the *Ludus* Palmyra.

'Palmyra is not under Roman rule,' I told him.

Domitus tapped his nose with a finger. 'Neither is Egypt, at least not directly, but the Egyptians will be sending fighters to Ephesus.'

'Why don't we call ourselves the *Ludus* Dura?' I queried.

'Because we don't want to draw attention to Dura or its king,' answered Drenis.

It all seemed unnecessary but as they had given the matter some thought and I had not I went along with their plan. At least they had a plan. I left the tent feeling confident that I could snatch Burebista from the Romans and now had seven members of our little band. As I intended to speak to Surena about him accompanying us that left only one more to speak to. I was certain that my former squire would wish to be a part of the venture.

Chapter 6

Surena's eyes lit up. 'Yes, lord.'

I held up a hand. 'Wait, before you say yes you should hear what it entails.'

The day after the gathering in Domitus' tent I had visited my former squire in his quarters just beyond the Citadel's walls. As he was married to Viper they had rented two small rooms a short walk from the gates, though as both of them were on duty most of the time and had very little spare time they were rarely used. However, I insisted that they spend at least one evening each week alone in each other's company. I knew that as the Amazons were quartered permanently in the Citadel they saw each other often, but fleeting moments and embraces were no substitute for periods of privacy that every newly married couple should enjoy.

Viper was the only Amazon who was married thus far, aside from Gallia of course, and at first she was reluctant to leave her martial sisters. However, I persuaded Gallia to order her to spend one night out of every seven in the company of her husband. I did not wish to intrude on their privacy but wanted to speak to them both alone, so I walked from the Citadel in the company of Orodes. The prince had insisted that I should have an escort for the five-minute walk from the main gates. So half a dozen legionaries ringed us as we strolled through the gates and took a right turn to amble along the dirt track that ran along the outside of the western wall of the Citadel. I stopped and told the legionaries to return to their posts.

Orodes frowned as he watched them re-enter the gates. 'You should not walk around outside the Citadel alone, Pacorus.'

I smiled at him. 'I am not alone. You are with me and I think our two swords will be enough to frighten off any beggars or prostitutes that may assail us.'

'You still intend to go to Ephesus?'

I nodded.

'I would like to accompany you.'

I stopped and laid a hand on his shoulder.

'My friend, much as I would like your sword at my service I need you here to command the army. Godarz is a trustworthy governor but he is no general. Only you have the trust of the army.'

He appeared resigned to me leaving.

'I envy you, Pacorus.'

'A renegade king outlawed from the empire by the high king.' I laughed. 'There is not much to envy.'

'Not that. I envy your membership of the Companions. I have never known such a closely knit group of individuals who are relaxed in each other's company and would lay down their lives for each other without hesitation. They are like a sword blade that has been forged from many different metals.'

It was a good analogy.

'I understand now why you must go, even though I wish that you would not.'

'Let us hope that Godarz also comes round,' I said.

Orodes shrugged. 'He is older and views the world differently. He knows that life is precious, the more so when you are approaching its end. But perhaps his anger is also borne of frustration that he cannot go.'

'Orodes the philosopher,' I teased him. 'I like it.'

We arrived at Surena and Viper's lodgings, which were positioned above one of the businesses that supplied boots to the army. The aroma of freshly cut leather filled the air as we ascended the outside flight of wooden steps that led to the rooms above the workshop. It was early evening and most of the shutters on the rows of businesses and shops along the street were closed. A few individuals were going about their business and a mangy stray dog eyed us from the opposite side of the street as I knocked on the door.

A relaxed Surena had answered, a look of surprise on his face when he saw us.

'Lord? Prince Orodes?'

'May we come in, Surena?' I asked.

He grinned. 'Of course, come in. Viper, it is the king and Prince Orodes.'

We walked into a main room that smelt of cinnamon, a red curtain hanging at the entrance to the second room, the bedroom. Viper's eyes opened in amazement as she turned and

166

saw us. She was dressed in a simple blue blouse, tan leggings and the leather boots worn by the Amazons. She fell to her knees and bowed her head.

I walked over to her and lifted her up. 'Please get up. This is your house and we obey your rules here.'

Surena pulled out two rather aged and chipped chairs from the table. 'Please sit.'

Viper placed two wooden cups on the table and poured us some wine as we eased ourselves into the chairs. As they were the only two chairs in the room Surena stood next to Viper as I explained the purpose of my visit, which was to ask him to accompany us to Ephesus. After he had said yes I explained to him about Burebista, the games and the risks involved. He was more eager than ever.

He had his arm around a concerned Viper as I told him that we would be leaving in less than two months.

'I must ask you not to reveal any of this to anyone,' I said to them both.

'Yes, lord,' said Surena excitedly. He had a grin as wide as the Euphrates and was clearly delighted.

Viper was less happy. 'May I ask you a question, majesty?'

'Of course.'

'Why is Surena going with you? He is, after all, not a Companion.'

She may have had the appearance of a girl but she was no fool. Her brown eyes did not blink as she waited for an answer.

'What does it matter, my love?' said Surena before I opened my lips. 'This is a great honour.'

But Viper was still waiting for my answer.

'Well, Dobbai herself said that I should ask Surena to accompany me.'

Surena's eyes sparkled with excitement as he kissed his wife on the cheek.

'You see, everyone knows that the gods speak through the king's sorceress. I will be on a divine mission. What part will I play in this holy mission, lord?'

I had no idea. I had only sought to enlist him because Dobbai had advised it. But as to his role I was as ignorant as he was.

'All those taking part will be assembling on the palace terrace this time tomorrow,' I told him, 'where everything will be revealed.'

As we left I told Viper that I would do everything possible to ensure that her husband would return safely to Dura. She thanked me but her eyes were full of sadness, in stark contrast to the enthusiasm and excitement that filled those of her husband.

'It's all a game to Surena, isn't it?' remarked Orodes as we walked back to the palace, the temperature still warm as the city was bathed in the red glow of twilight. 'He thinks war and battle are contests to win fame and glory and does not consider the possibility of death or injury.'

'He has been the same since the first time I met him,' I said.

'When he rescued you from death at the hands of Narses?'

I nodded. 'His men, though boys would be a more accurate description, sprang a superb ambush that killed the guards before they had a chance to reply. Surena has a keen mind that makes him a good soldier and future commander. I have plans for him.'

'He is capable,' agreed Orodes, 'if a little hot-headed. So what role will he fulfil at Ephesus.'

'I have no idea.'

Dobbai had agitated for the meeting of those travelling to Ephesus to gather on the palace terrace the next day, despite me informing her that even if Surena agreed to make the journey, we still lacked a seventh person.

'The marsh boy will bite your hand off at the opportunity to add further lustre to his name,' she had told me.

She also told me that she had sent a message to another individual, requesting his presence at the meeting.

'What individual?'

'You will see, son of Hatra.'

I discovered it was Alcaeus, who was the last to arrive after Domitus, Drenis and Arminius. Surena had been the first to arrive and began pacing up and down the terrace until Gallia ordered him to either sit down or go into the courtyard. Dobbai and Samahe shuffled into our presence and dismissed the

168

servants and guards when everyone had arrived, ordering Alcaeus to close the door behind him.

'Well,' he said tersely to Dobbai, 'what do you want? I assume it is not any medication as you have your own potions to heal your ailments.'

She waved a hand at him. 'All will be revealed, Greek.'

'Welcome, Alcaeus,' I said, 'thank you for coming.'

He eyed everyone present, raising an eyebrow when he noted Surena's presence.

'I assume that this is not a social function.'

Domitus slapped him on the back.

'Welcome to the *Ludus* Palmyra, doctor.'

Arminius and Drenis laughed and Surena grinned, though he did not know what a *ludus* was. Alcaeus' expression darkened.

'What?'

I nodded at Domitus who proceeded to give Alcaeus a summary of what had been decided in his command tent. To say that he was underwhelmed would be an understatement.

'I have heard of this but before now have never actually witnessed it,' he remarked.

His words were met by a row of blank faces.

'Collective madness,' he said loudly. 'A kind of hysteria that takes hold of groups of people, probably prompted by a central figure of authority.'

He looked hard at me. 'Who the other individuals foolishly follow blindly.'

Dobbai chuckled. 'Whether or not the son of Hatra is mad or not is not yours to decide, Greek. He has set his heart on searching for his lost Companion and you have been selected to go with him.'

Alcaeus folded his arms defiantly. 'Have I?'

'I only wish to take those who are willing to accompany me,' I said.

'We need a good doctor, Alcaeus,' added Drenis.

'Besides,' added Domitus, 'the prospect of a nice trip to Greece must fill your heart with joy.'

Alcaeus glared at him. 'First of all, Ephesus is not in Greece. It is on the other side of the Aegean.'

'But it is a former Greek colony,' I said.

169

Gallia spoke for the first time. 'I apologise if you have been brought here under false pretences, Alcaeus, but it would comfort me greatly if I knew you were coming with us.'

'She's right,' said Domitus.

'We'll need someone to patch us up,' said Arminius.

Drenis grinned. 'Wounds suffered in the arena are different from battlefield injuries. Should be a nice new challenge for you.'

'You know they speak the truth, Greek,' added Dobbai.

Alcaeus looked at Gallia, who smiled warmly at him, then at me. He sighed and shook his head.

'I must be mad, too.'

Drenis, Arminius and Domitus cheered and Gallia walked over and kissed him on the cheek.

'Do not worry, sir,' said Surena, caught up in the moment, 'you won't have to treat me as I do not intend to get wounded.'

'No foreign blade will touch you, marsh boy,' said Dobbai. 'That is one of the reasons I chose you to accompany your king.'

'What are the others?' grinned Surena.

'That is not for you to know,' snapped Dobbai.

'So the party of seven is finalised,' announced Samahe. 'Good. Now you must prepare for your time of trial ahead. When the time comes for you to depart I will inform you of further measures you must take to aid you in your quest.'

'Now you may go,' commanded Dobbai.

'Just a minute,' said Domitus sternly. He pointed at Surena and looked at me. 'What did he mean when he said that he would not get wounded? You are not thinking of him stepping into the arena, are you?'

I had given no further thought to Surena's role. 'Well, I...'

'Of course he will enter the arena,' said Dobbai. 'The marsh boy attracts fame to him like a flame draws moths. Why else do you think I selected him? To clean the son of Hatra's boots?'

The days after were filled with preparations for Ephesus, in addition to the normal administrative duties that came with ruling a kingdom. The weekly council meetings were held as usual, I took part in training in the mornings and in the afternoons met with members of the party who would be going to the games. Like Godarz, Alcaeus was unhappy with the whole venture but although he grumbled I think a part of him was excited that he would be visiting a Greek city. As usual he undertook his preparations with thoroughness, interrogating Drenis and Arminius regarding the types of wounds gladiators suffered in the arena.

The armouries had originally occupied a campsite two miles north of the city where dozens of men and women had laboured night and day to produce weapons and armour for the legions, cataphracts and horse archers. After the Roman invasion of Dura the armouries had been relocated inside the city itself, both for security and because the army, now fully armed and equipped, no longer required the production capacity required of the earlier tented facility. So now the armouries were located to the north of the Citadel where, among the workshops, smiths and leather workers, a small circular patch of sand was quietly laid. Domitus requested that the sand was to be surrounded by a wooden wall just over the height of a man, with a single gate for an entrance.

Domitus had asked me to attend him at the makeshift arena and to bring Surena along, the young cataphract's eyes full of eagerness as we walked the short distance from the Citadel to the armouries. Stonemasons were working on a wall that would eventually surround the place where Dura's weapons were made, but for the moment it resembled a building site as a host of labourers brought mud from the Euphrates and mixed it with straw and sand to create mud-bricks to build the wall. Escorted by a dozen guards we walked between the buildings where the tools of war were being manufactured, the sound of metal being beaten on anvils filling the air. Eventually we reached the circular wooden wall that surrounded the patch of sand that had a diameter of no more than thirty paces. The single gate was open as I dismissed the guards and stepped inside with Surena.

'Welcome to the arena of Dura Europos,' said Domitus as he spotted us. He was standing in the centre of the enclosed space with Drenis and Arminius, all of them wearing just a tunic and their belts, attached to which were their swords and

171

daggers. I noticed that both Drenis and Arminius were barefoot. The former pointed at us.

'Take off your boots.'

Surena was taken aback. 'Why?'

'Why, *sir*,' snarled Domitus, 'remember whose company you are in, boy.'

Surena bristled at his words but I pointed at his boots and he reluctantly pulled off his footwear, as did I. The sand felt warm and soft underfoot.

Drenis stepped forward. 'You need to forget everything you have been taught about fighting. In the arena you fight barefoot.'

He pointed at Surena. 'Just like a legionary you have been instructed to fight as part of a unit. You now have to learn to fight as a single gladiator, alone and facing a multitude of threats.'

Arminius walked forward. 'But it is not just about fighting; it is also about putting on a show in front of thousands of people. You both have an advantage in that you have been fighting and training for years, at least you have Pacorus.'

He pointed at Surena. 'Tell me more about yourself, boy.'

'I'm not your boy,' replied Surena. 'I am an officer of cataphracts in the army of Dura.'

He held Arminius' gaze with a steely intent.

'It is important that we all work as a team,' I said, 'if we are to survive the festivities at Ephesus. Surena, you will give an account of your life before you came to Dura.'

I pointed at the three hard-faced veterans before me. 'And you three will desist from provoking my former squire.'

Surena twisted his right foot in the sand as he told us of his time among his people in the marshlands, first as a boy fishing and helping his parents, later as a fighter killing the soldiers of Chosroes. He finished with an account of the ambush where I first met him. Drenis looked at Arminius and nodded.

'That's enough to work on. And you, Pacorus, you still desire to step into the arena?'

I nodded.

'And have you given any thought of what type of gladiator you should be?' asked Arminius.

'There seems to be a wide variety to choose from,' I said.

'Naturally,' replied Drenis. 'Variety is an integral part of the games. No point in having gladiators dressed and armed in the same way fighting each other. Now young Surena, here, is obviously suited to the role of *Retiarius*.'

'What's that?' enquired Surena.

'A net man,' answered Arminius. 'You grew up wielding spears and nets to catch fish so wielding similar equipment in the arena should be easy enough.'

'Of course your face will be uncovered,' warned Drenis.

Surena was confused. 'What does that matter?'

Drenis smiled. 'Gladiators are considered among the lowest orders of Roman society, infamous if you like. A gladiator is a misfit and outcast from respectable society. For such an individual anonymity is often welcome.'

'I do not wish to hide my face,' announced Surena. 'I wish the crowd to recognise me.'

'*Retiarius*, definitely,' said Domitus.

'And you, Pacorus?' asked Drenis.

'What Spartacus was,' I answered immediately.

'Then it is settled,' he said.

'And you two, what were you?' I asked Drenis and Arminius.

'A Thracian, like Spartacus,' answered the former.

'A *Provocator*,' said the latter.

Drenis told us that he would supervise the construction of our armour and weapons, drawing on his experience in Capua where he had first met Spartacus. I asked Arminius about the *Provocator* and he informed me that this type of fighter was heavily armed and armoured, with a helmet, chest protector, protective sleeve covering his sword arm and a greave on his forward leg. He gave Surena an evil smile.

'No armour for the *Retiarius*, though, they are as naked as a new-born.'

'The net men rely on speed to surprise and stay alive in the arena,' said Drenis.

'Suits me,' shrugged Surena.

'And what about you, Domitus?' I said. 'What role will you be assuming in our little drama?'

173

He rubbed his hands and smiled. 'Your owner, of course. You are looking at the *lanista* of the *Ludus* Palmyra. Being successful I naturally have a beautiful wife, who happens to be a blonde-haired vision that I acquired in Gaul.'

'What?'

'I'm sure Gallia won't mind,' he informed me. 'After all, you want our deception to be convincing.'

Drenis raised an eyebrow at Domitus. 'In what world would a woman such as Gallia be interested in a wizened sack of leather like you, Domitus?'

Domitus held up his hands. 'Just remember that out of us all only I am a Roman. So it makes sense that I should be the *lanista.*'

'But why do you have to have a wife' I asked.

Domitus raised his eyebrows. 'What other role would you have her assume? A female gladiator, a slave? At least as my pretend wife she will be safe.'

'I will see if she is agreeable,' I said, not wholly convinced.

Drenis nodded. 'Good. Training begins tomorrow. Don't be late.'

Gallia laughed and thought the idea was most excellent when I informed her of Domitus' scheme. I still did not understand why she wanted to go to Ephesus but she said that it was her destiny to go there.

'Why?' I asked.

She did not know. 'All I do know is that Dobbai told me that Ephesus would give me the opportunity to bring matters to a close.'

'What matters?'

'I do not know.'

The next afternoon, under a blazing sun, I again walked to the armouries where my instructors waited to introduce me to the weapons and equipment I would be using at the games. Surena was already there when I dismissed my escort and walked to Dura's makeshift arena. Outside the open entrance was a table, upon which was laid a variety of weapons, shields and helmets. Arminius waved me over and told me to take off my boots, leggings, tunic and vest. Surena was already barefoot and half-naked.

Soon I was in the same state as I put on the loincloth made of wool, the purpose of which was to cover my genitals, and the large, thick leather belt that covered the lower belly.

'The Romans call it a *balteus*,' Drenis told me. 'It will stop an opponent slitting open your guts and littering the sand with your intestines.'

He passed me what looked like a leather windsock, which was actually overlapping leather segments attached to each other and fastened with straps.

'It's called a *manica* and protects your sword arm.'

I slipped it on and found that it covered the whole arm from the shoulder to the hand. My legs were also protected, by thick padding that wrapped around them, over which I put on a pair of highly polished bronze greaves called *ocreae*.

'I feel like a gaudily dressed actor,' I complained as I fastened the leather straps on the greaves that ended above my knee.

'The games are above all a spectacle of slaughter,' said Arminius.

Drenis picked up a helmet. He held it out to me.

'Your helmet, Thracian. The armourers worked all night to fashion it but I think they have done a good job.'

It was a heavy bronze piece with a horizontal brim like a hat and had a full visor that closed in the middle and opened out sideways. The lower parts of the visor halves had outward-projecting rims to guard the throat, and their hinges had metal guards over them as a defence against weapon strikes. Like the scale armour worn by the horses that carried Dura's cataphracts, the eyes were protected by the helmet's thick bronze circular visor gratings. On the forehead was an embossed palm of victory and it had a distinctive griffin crest.

I pointed at the crest. 'Dura's griffin. An auspicious omen.'

'You will see a lot of those at Ephesus,' Domitus told me, 'because in Roman culture the griffin is the guardian of the dead.'

'It is heavy,' I said.

'Fights in the arena are mostly short,' said Drenis as I placed it on my head and he assisted me in fitting the visor

175

halves together and securing the hinges. 'So unlike in the army you are not required to wear it for hours on end each day.'

He then handed me a small shield no more than two feet square. It was made of wood and faced with leather, being convex shaped and adorned with a red griffin motif. It was called a *parmula* and had no central boss. I thought it quite ridiculous. As I did the sword that Drenis handed me, a weapon that had a blade around fifteen inches long. Curiously, towards the point it had a bend of around twenty degrees.

'Did the armourer have a bad day?' I asked.

'It is called a *sica*,' said Drenis, 'and is designed to get around an opponent's shield and stab him in the arm, side or back.'

'What about my chest?' I asked. 'It is completely exposed.'

'It's meant to be,' said Arminius. 'A gladiator exposes his torso to demonstrate his willingness to die if necessary, and a means by which his opponent can bring his end about.'

'How reassuring.'

I was almost jealous of Surena. Almost. Compared to my absurd appearance he presented a much more modest display. Bare headed, he too wore a *manica*, though on his left arm, and a strange heavy bronze plate also fastened on the top of his left arm secured by means of a leather strap across his chest. It was called a *galerus* and projected some five inches above the shoulder, thus protecting the neck and most of the head from lateral blows. The upper edge was bent slightly outwards, thus retarding sliding blows and allowing the wearer's head more freedom of movement.

'This is not like any fishing spear I've ever used,' complained Surena as he held the trident in his hand. 'The prongs are too short and they are not barbed.'

Arminius snatched the weapon from his grip. 'Of course they aren't. You won't be hunting fish in the arena. The last thing you want is to have your main weapon stuck in someone's guts and be unable to retrieve it.'

He pointed at the net Surena held in his left hand. 'And barbed prongs can get caught in your net.'

Surena grinned and cast the net before him. 'Not in mine. I have fished with nets since I was a small boy.'

His net was made of strong hemp-rope with small lead weights attached to its sides for balance. It had a stronger thread around the outside so the *Retiarius* could tighten it around an opponent. The net was also fastened to Surena's wrist with a cord to make retrieval easier.

To be fair Surena was a model pupil, wielding the net and trident with ease as he sparred with Arminius and Drenis. Though I had worked with weapons since I had been a small boy I initially found training difficult.

As the days passed Arminius and Drenis screamed and shouted at me to move more quickly. They were equipped with the swords and shields carried by Dura's legionaries, though after a week Arminius attended a training session wearing a full-face bronze helmet with a large metal crest that resembled a fish's fin. Like me he too wore padded armour on his sword arm but only wore one greave. He told me that he was armed and equipped as a *Murmillo*, the 'fish man', whose opponent in the arena was the Thracian.

'Keep moving, Pacorus,' Drenis shouted at me as Arminius tried to pin me against the wooden wall.

'Use your mobility to dart in and out of range of his strikes. Look for a gap in his defences. If he traps you against the wall you are finished.'

I advanced a couple of steps but he charged and rammed his shield into me, throwing me back against the wall. Winded, I could not prevent him pinning me against the wood with his shield and holding the point of his sword against my chest.

'That's a kill,' shouted Drenis.

Arminius backed off and removed his helmet as I coughed and spluttered. I too removed my helmet. Drenis ran over.

'You are fighting like royalty, all honour and meeting the enemy head-on.'

'How else should I fight?' I pleaded.

'Like a gladiator,' replied Arminius. 'Forget your upbringing and the battles you have fought. A Thracian gladiator is lightly armed and therein is his advantage.'

I looked at him blankly. He pointed his sword at my bare feet.

'Quick footwork, Pacorus. Weave around your opponent, run away if necessary.'

'Run away?'

Drenis laughed. 'There is no honour in the arena, just death, shit, piss and blood. Use your mobility so your opponent strikes air with his weapons. Tire him out. If you are tired then kneel before springing into action.'

'Above all,' said Arminius, 'avoid the wall like the plague. You have great stamina, Pacorus, so use it.'

While I got back my breath Drenis put Surena through his paces. Already experienced in the use of a net and spear, albeit ones that had not been adapted for the arena, he had little difficulty in wielding his weapons. Domitus strolled over to where we were standing as Surena danced around Drenis, trying to entangle the latter in his net by either throwing it forward of deliberately leaving it on the ground so Drenis would step on it.

'He's a natural,' said Arminius admiringly. 'See how he takes advantage of the trident's reach to keep Drenis at bay, while at the same time keeping his net at the ready.'

'Looks like that old witch of yours was right, Pacorus,' said Domitus, 'in persuading you to take him along. And he has the advantage of already being well acquainted with his chief adversary.'

'Who's that?' I queried.

'Not who but what,' replied Domitus. 'His cockiness.'

We spent every day for nearly a month in that sandpit. Drenis and Arminius deliberately chose the hottest part of the day for training so the sand would become hot and uncomfortable to stand on. But it kept us moving as we sought the shade in the western side as the sun passed its highest point in the sky. I soon got used to the *manica* and leg protectors and learned to use my toes to aid my grip on the sand. And above all I learned to avoid the walls, aided by an enthusiastic Domitus who hovered around me, striking me with his vine cane if I got too close to the boards. We trained hour after hour, day after day.

Drenis and Arminius wanted Surena and me in the arena from the early hours but I insisted that for the sake of normality the usual routines should be adhered to. That meant early morning exercises on the training fields with the horse archers and cataphracts, though Domitus cancelled all full-scale exercises in the desert, which would have meant camping for two nights or more. As far as the army and kingdom were concerned their king was preparing for a war with Mithridates. Though that appeared a remote possibility. We received happy news that Narses was suffering from some sort of illness and had taken to his bed. Dobbai and Samahe told me that the illness was minor and would not kill him, but that they had both called on Irra, the God of Plagues, to visit him to increase his suffering. But I comforted myself with the knowledge that with Narses incapacitated, Mithridates was even less likely to make a move against me.

Domitus told me that he had written a letter to the organiser of the games at Ephesus as soon as I had decided that I would attend. Called an *editor*, he was responsible for arranging the games and ensuring that each event was a worthy spectacle. I was worried that giving prior warning of our arrival would jeopardise our mission, but Domitus reassured me that the opposite was the case.

'We can't just pitch up unannounced,' he told me. 'That would raise suspicions. In any case, we have to get authorisation from the *editor* to attend.'

'How do we do that?' I asked.

He grinned. 'I have told him that the *Ludus* Palmyra will be bringing four gladiators trained in eastern ways of fighting that will spice up the games.'

'You think it will work?'

'Oh yes. Any whiff of anything exotic or out of the ordinary is enough to arouse the interest of any *editor*. As long as he can put on a good show to satisfy the authorities and crowd he will send his authorisation.'

He rubbed his hands together. 'And if you get killed I will be a rich man.'

'How so?'

'Any fighter from a gladiator school killed in the arena receives compensation, or at least his *lanista* does. The fighter receives a decent funeral.'

'Your words are always a great comfort to me, Domitus.'

The words of abuse and encouragement I received from Drenis and Arminius helped me prepare for Ephesus as I got used to the heavy bronze helmet, peculiar curved sword and inadequate shield. After a while it felt strange to be wearing boots and I found my own sword, the *spatha* that Spartacus had given me, cumbersome and heavy.

'That's good,' Drenis told me, 'ideally you should not be using it at all so wielding the *sica* becomes second nature.'

At times Surena and I were pitted against three adversaries — Domitus, Drenis and Arminius — to prepare us for the more exotic bouts we might face.

'I thought you told me that gladiator fights are carefully arranged,' I said after being unceremoniously battered and dumped on my back after a gruelling ten minutes' duelling against the trio.

'So they are,' said Arminius, 'but an *editor* is always looking to spice things up if the crowd starts to get bored.'

The next day Arminius was attired in the armour and equipment he had worn when he had fought in the arena. They were the tools of a *Provocator*, 'The Challenger'. On his head he wore a heavy bronze helmet that covered his entire skull, two round grilled eyeholes allowing him to see his opponent. He carried a legionary shield and wore a *manica* on his sword arm. On his left leg was a greave that ended just above the knee and protecting his chest was a bronze *cardiophylax*, a buckled breastplate. Like me he wore a broad belt above his loincloth. He brought up his *gladius* and assumed an attacking posture. I leapt back and felt my feet sinking into liquid. I looked down and saw blood oozing from the sand. Horrified, I momentarily forgot where I was and then I was struck with the full force of Arminius' shield and placed flat on my back. He placed a foot on my chest and raised his sword.

'That's a kill,' shouted Drenis.

Arminius took his foot off my chest and I sat up. I pulled off my helmet.

'There's blood on the sand.'

'I know,' said Drenis, 'I put it there and scattered some sand over it. Caught you out, didn't it?'

Arminius called Surena over and hauled me to my feet.

'They have animal hunts and executions in the arena before the gladiator bouts,' said Drenis, 'and that means there could be lots of blood on or under the sand.'

180

Surena was disgusted. 'Don't they have slaves to clear it up?'

'It's far easier to sprinkle fresh sand over it,' said a now bare headed Arminius. 'Just remember that blood underfoot is just one unexpected thing you might encounter.'

'What are the other things?' I asked.

'Women gladiators for one,' said Drenis, 'though I doubt you will see any at Ephesus.'

'I will kill anyone they put in front of me,' stated Surena.

Drenis slapped him on the shoulder. 'That's the spirit.'

Three weeks before our departure date a letter arrived for Domitus from the office of the chief priest of the Temple of Artemis at Ephesus. It extended a warm welcome to *Lanista* Lucius Domitus of the *Ludus* Palmyra and stated that High Priest Kallias looked forward to seeing the school's four gladiators in the forthcoming games. Kallias explained that though he was not the actual *editor* of the games, who was away on important business, he was fully authorised by said official to decide who participated in the forthcoming games.

'We're in,' grinned Domitus.

We were sitting outside one of the armoury's workshops in the shade. Apart from Domitus we were covered in sweat and had stripped down to our loincloths. Surena, his shoulder-length hair matted to his skull and neck, stood and poured a bucket of water over himself. A guard had brought Domitus the letter as soon as a courier had delivered it to the palace.

'Why would it be delivered here?' queried Drenis, wiping his sweaty brow with a cloth.

'Because I sent another letter to Byrd at Palmyra,' replied Domitus, 'asking him to keep an eye out for a letter addressed to me that would be arriving at his tent, and when it arrived to have it sent on to me.'

'Such is the world of subterfuge,' I remarked.

'Talking of which,' said Domitus. 'We have not addressed the matter of your name during the coming games.'

'My name?'

'Well you can't use your own name,' stated Domitus. 'Plenty of Romans in the east of the empire will have heard of King Pacorus of Dura by now. And it won't take a genius to connect a man named Pacorus arriving from the east with the

181

same individual, especially when they clap eyes on Gallia, who has probably become as famous as you in Roman eyes.'

'If not more so,' said Arminius.

Drenis nodded. 'He's right, Pacorus, you should assume a different name.'

'What about Maximus?' suggested Drenis.

It was Latin for 'the greatest'.

'I think that would be tempting fate,' I said. 'What sort of gladiator calls himself "Maximus"?'

'A confident one,' said Arminius.

'I remember one man, a Greek who called himself "Nikephorus", a gladiator from Capua,' said Drenis.

Arminius' eyes lit up. 'I remember him, too. A great fighter.'

'What happened to him?' I asked.

'He retired a rich man,' answered Drenis. 'Bought a brothel in Paestum, I heard.'

Nikephorus meant 'bearer of victory' and had a nice feel to it. And the fact the owner of the name had finished his career as a gladiator alive was a lucky omen.

'Very well,' I said, 'Nikephorus it is.'

'What name should I use?' asked Surena.

We looked at him and each other. Domitus shook his head.

'You're not famous, boy, so you don't need another name.'

'I will be,' said Surena, 'One day I will be famous throughout all Parthia.'

Domitus rolled his eyes. 'If you survive Ephesus.'

He looked at me. 'It's not too late to back out, Pacorus. No one would think any less of you.'

'I will not abandon Burebista,' I said, 'for it would be the basest thing to do.'

I looked at them, three men I had known for years and who had followed me through thick and thin. And one individual who had just become a man and who dreamed of nothing but victory and glory.

'You know that I do not compel any of you to come with me. I know that the risks are great and the chances of all of us

182

returning slim. So if any of you are having second thoughts then…'

My words were interrupted as Domitus threw a bucket of water over me.

'You talk too much.'

Our days of training on the sand were now over. The preparations for our journey began with a message to Byrd and Malik at Palmyra, requesting their presence at Dura. When they arrived I asked them to join me on the palace terrace where the other members of the party destined for Ephesus were gathered. Orodes, Godarz, Dobbai and Samahe were also in attendance as once more the servants and guards were dismissed and the entrance was closed. My governor was terse with me but warm towards Gallia, embracing her and standing beside her. He looked genuinely distressed at the prospect of her leaving and probably blamed me. It was late afternoon and the light was slowly fading, the surface of the Euphrates below as smooth as a slab of blue marble. The terrace was in shadow and there was a light breeze that took the edge off the stifling heat.

I began by informing Byrd and Malik of the forthcoming journey to Ephesus and asked them to keep it to themselves. They immediately offered to come with us but I told them that there were already seven members of the party.

'What's so special about seven?' asked Malik.

'Dobbai thinks it an auspicious number that will win us the favour of the gods,' I told him.

He looked at her. 'And this will guarantee that they will all return alive?'

Dobbai shrugged. 'If I could guarantee that, desert lord, then I would be a god myself.'

'Then what is point of only seven travelling?' said Byrd curtly.

Dobbai twisted her ugly face into a frown. 'Because, pot seller, by choosing to take seven the son of Hatra pays his respects to the gods, and in so doing may win their favour.'

I could tell that Malik thought the whole scheme mad. 'You risk much, Pacorus.'

'You trust Athineos?' asked Byrd.

'He did not betray us when we left Italy,' I said.

183

'That is because we gave him a large amount of gold to buy his silence,' sneered Godarz. 'He is a mercenary and would sell his own mother if the price was right.'

'Which brings me neatly to my next point,' I said. 'Byrd and Malik, should Godarz's fears turn out to be well founded and we are indeed going to our deaths, I would like you two to track down Athineos and kill him.'

'I'll do that,' hissed Godarz as he appeared even more distraught.

'As will I,' stated Orodes.

I held my hands to them. 'My friends, if the worst happens you will have your hands full holding this kingdom from the pack of wolves that will gather once news of my death spreads.'

'Your opinion of yourself is very high, son of Hatra,' remarked Dobbai. 'Perhaps with you gone Mithridates will welcome Dura back into the family of Parthian kingdoms.'

'Not if I am king,' promised Godarz.

'Amusing though this speculation is,' I interrupted, 'I would like to travel to Ephesus knowing that if we are betrayed then vengeance will be visited upon our betrayer.'

Byrd gave a nod. 'It will be so.'

Malik placed a hand on his chest. 'I will not rest until this Athineos is carrion for vultures.'

'Good,' I said. 'We will be leaving tomorrow.'

The meeting over, everyone drifted away from the terrace. I noticed that Surena appeared to be very pleased with himself. He had good reason: he had excelled in training and Arminius and Drenis had told me in private that he had all the attributes to be an excellent gladiator. Gallia walked from the terrace with Dobbai and Samahe, all three deep in conversation. I was alone; at least I thought I was.

Godarz had stayed behind and now he came over to me. Despite being the city governor he wore his usual plain white tunic, sandals and red leather belt. His many years as a Roman slave had left its mark on him and though he was Parthian he dressed like a Roman, and also thought like one. He grabbed both my arms.

'It is not too late, Pacorus. You can still call off this mad venture.'

I looked down at his hands. He released his grip.

'I will not abandon Burebista, Godarz. You know this.'

'Are you going to rescue Burebista or find Spartacus?'

I walked to the stone balustrade and looked out across the Euphrates, now barely visible as the light faded.

'I do not know what you mean.'

Godarz followed me. 'Do you not? He is dead, Pacorus. You will not find him, or Claudia for that matter, at Ephesus. You chase ghosts, and in the process may become one yourself.'

I turned to face him. 'I will not abandon a Companion, Godarz. I did not ask anyone to accompany me. They have chosen to do so of their own volition.'

He laughed derisively. 'You are their king so of course they will follow you. But you risk everything that you have built here on a fool's errand. And, more importantly, you risk your wife's life.'

Now we came to it.

'I may be king but that is one person who follows her own mind.'

He threw up his arms. 'She follows you, Pacorus. Or are you so blind that you cannot see it?'

He pointed a finger at me. 'I will never forgive you if anything happens to that girl.'

His tone should have angered me but I respected him too much to be offended.

'I love Gallia more than life itself,' I said meekly. 'But the thought of Burebista being alive and a Roman slave tortures me, Godarz. It fills my every waking second.'

His eyes filled with concern. 'If you, Shamash forbid, fail to return I will not be able to hold Dura if the empire mobilises against me. I am not a great warlord like you.'

I placed a hand on his shoulder. 'My fights are not yours, my friend. If the worst happens get the best terms you can. Save the people rather than the kingdom. Get the army to Hatra. It will be welcome there. But I suspect that with me gone Mithridates will leave Dura alone.'

'And Claudia?'

'If you feel Dura will fall then get her to either Hatra or Palmyra.'

185

His eyes narrowed. 'Haytham?'

'She will be safe among the Agraci,' I said.

He placed his hands on the balustrade. 'As you wish.'

Silence descended between us as night slowly came. He continued to peer into the gloom as the servants came on to the terrace to light the oil lamps. The breeze had disappeared now and the chirping of crickets began to fill the air.

'I would have your blessing, Godarz,' I said.

He drummed his fingers on the polished stone, turned and embraced me.

'May Shamash protect you, Pacorus.'

I left the terrace a man at peace, knowing that any ill will that Godarz harboured had been banished. There was but one more thing to do.

After Godarz had departed I walked to the throne room where lamps flickered along the walls and from metal brackets suspended from the ceiling. Despite the abundance of lights the hall was still cast in a subdued illumination. The halls of Ctesiphon and Hatra had white marble floors, white marble pillars inlaid with gold leaf and white-painted walls, but Dura's Citadel had been built as a fortress not a palace, and so its buildings were entirely functional. They projected austere strength rather than gaudy opulence. I walked over to the dais, the guards snapping to attention as I stepped onto the stone and stood before the griffin standard that hung on the wall behind the thrones. There was a respectful calm in the chamber and I could hear my heart beat as I reached up and gently grasped the material. I closed my eyes and said a silent prayer to Shamash, asking that He would watch over us during the coming trial.

I left the palace and walked to the stables. The Citadel was still a bustle of activity, with the changing of the guard taking place at the gates, workers vacating the armoury and clerks leaving the headquarters building and treasury before the gates were shut. But the stables were quiet now, most of the staff having departed for their homes, leaving only a bare minimum of stable hands and veterinaries to oversee the night watch.

I walked into Remus' block and went to his stall, the two stable hands that would sit with the horses throughout the night rising from their stools and bowing as I passed them.

'He is quiet?' I enquired.

The older hand, a man who had worked at the Citadel for over forty years, smiled at me.

'Settled in for the night majesty. You thinking of taking him out?'

I shook my head. 'No. I just wanted to see him before...'

I nodded and walked past them to Remus' stall. He had heard my voice and his head was poking out over the gate when I arrived there. He grunted and nuzzled his head into me. I stroked his neck.

I spoke softly to him so the stable hands would not hear. I had told the commander of the stables that I was going on a long journey and that only Prince Orodes was to ride Remus, though he was to be exercised each day. There was no need to tell him this because any Parthian worth his salt knew how to take care of a horse. Remus began nipping my neck affectionately.

'Yes, yes, and I love you too. Now listen. I am going to be away for a while and you will be staying here. So no kicking or biting anyone and don't throw Orodes if he rides you from time to time.'

He looked at me with his blue eyes.

'No more sea journeys for you, old friend. If the worst happens then I will wait for you in the next life.'

I stroked his neck one last time and left the stables.

If the parting from Remus was hard then saying goodbye to Claudia was heart wrenching. As I stood with Gallia staring down at our sleeping daughter I was tempted to abandon the whole venture. To stay at Dura with my daughter and my wife. I looked at my wife and I could tell that she was thinking the same. But what would men think of me; what would Spartacus think of me?

'I have to go,' I whispered to Gallia.

'I know.'

I bent down and kissed Claudia's forehead. Gallia did the same and then we walked in silence from her bedroom. In the courtyard fourteen camels were being loaded with supplies –

among them the weapons and armour we would use at Ephesus – and others were equipped with saddles so we could ride them. Like Malik and Byrd we wore flowing black Agraci robes with *shemaghs* covering our heads and faces. Under these I wore my boots, leggings and white tunic, beneath which I wore my white silk vest. I also wore my *spatha* and dagger under my robes and carried my bow in its case attached to my saddle, Gallia and Surena also taking their bows. Three full quivers dangled from my saddle. In addition to the weapons packed on the camels Domitus, Drenis and Arminius each carried a *gladius* about their person, plus a dagger. Domitus wanted to bring his vine cane along but I convinced him to leave it at Dura. I had consulted Drenis and Arminius and they told me that a rich *lanista* would not carry a centurion's cane.

Malik, Byrd and four of his scouts, all mounted on horses, would provide an escort for our journey to Tripolis, and would bring the camels back to Dura after we had boarded ship at the port. They waited on their mounts near the Citadel's gates as we said our goodbyes. A teary Viper stood with her arms around her husband as I embraced Orodes and then Godarz. Rsan dutifully bowed his head and remained at a courteous distance. I turned to Dobbai.

'Look after Claudia.'

She flicked a hand at me. 'I have looked over her since before she was born. Your daughter's safety is assured. You should concentrate on your own fate, son of Hatra. And be sure to safeguard your wife. She will be a target.'

My blood ran cold. 'The target of enemy missiles?'

She rolled her eyes. 'Of male desire. More dangerous than any weapon forged on an anvil.'

Gallia embraced her and then Samahe called us to her.

'My time here is done. But I want you both to listen carefully. You must visit the city of Paphos on the island of Cyprus. Once there ask for the whereabouts of the seer Julia. She will be expecting you and will provide assistance.'

'What assistance?' I asked.

'That will be for Julia to decide,' answered Samahe.

'She is one of our order,' said Dobbai, 'so accept her offer of aid, son of Hatra. And do not annoy her.'

'Annoy her?'

188

'With infantile questions. Now go and rescue this slave you are so fond of.'

Surena was the first in the saddle, eager to be away on a new adventure that promised fame and glory. I had been assured that the camels we would be riding would be the most amenable that Dura had to offer. And as I eased myself into the wooden saddle bound together by rawhide and covered with leather, my camel dutifully waited until I was firmly in position until it rose to its feet. Byrd and Malik trotted from the Citadel as we sat cross-legged on the front of our camels' humps, over their strong shoulders, our feet on the beasts' neck. This gave each rider greater control over his animal as he could use not only the short reins but also employ pressure from his feet on the camel's neck. Just as well because each rider also held the reins of another camel carrying supplies. The latter included Agraci goatskin tents that we would use to sleep in during our journey.

With our faces and bodies covered no one gave the column of camels and their Agraci guides a second thought as we rode down Dura's main street and through the Palmyrene Gate, the duty centurion raising his cane as he recognised Byrd and Malik trotting past him. He frowned and waved his cane at us in an effort to expedite our exit from the city before the camels deposited piles of dung in front of his guardroom. I looked up at the stone griffin and bowed my head as we passed through the gates and began our journey to Tripolis.

Chapter 7

A camel can easily travel up to thirty miles a day, even in the merciless heat of a Mesopotamian summer. We joined the great press of caravans, carts and donkeys that filled the road from Dura to Palmyra on the first two days, Malik leading us south afterwards to keep away from his father's capital. We did not wish to avoid Haytham but for reasons of security we avoided the settlement. The fewer people who knew of our mission the greater our chances of success. So Malik and Byrd led us along little-used tracks, heading for small oases hidden beneath rocky outcrops where the camels and horses could be watered. After six days we travelled through passes between snow-capped mountains and arrived at the port of Tripolis.

We made camp outside the city among the tents and animals of the traders who had travelled from Parthia and other parts of Syria. They were either halting on their way to Egypt or would be selling their wares in the city for onward shipment to Rome. Our small party with its camels and goatskin tents blended in perfectly so as to arouse no suspicion. After the tents had been pitched Byrd's scouts lit a fire and began preparing our meal. Gallia, her hair and face covered with a *shemagh*, nudged me in the ribs when she saw two soldiers approaching.

'Romans,' she hissed.

'Calm down,' I told her, 'we are in Syria and this is a Roman city.'

The two legionaries, similar to the ones in my own army except from their red tunics instead of Dura's white, ambled past without giving us a second glance.

'I only like Romans that close when I am fighting them in battle,' snarled Gallia as she watched them pass by.

'We are going to see a lot of Romans over the next few weeks, so I hope you are not going to provoke any trouble.'

A pair of blue eyes looked at me. 'I know why we are here, Pacorus. You need not worry about me.'

When we sat down to eat, a cool but not unpleasant northerly breeze freshening the air, I spoke to Surena concerning not drawing attention to us.

'Do not cause any trouble while we are here,' I ordered him. 'I do not wish to jeopardise the mission before it has begun.'

'Yes, majesty,' he said.

'And don't call him "majesty",' said Domitus.

Surena frowned. 'Then what should I call you, lord?'

Arminius pointed a finger at Domitus. 'As your *lanista*, he's the one you should be calling "lord".'

'This is most confusing,' observed Malik.

'It is only temporary,' I said. 'Tomorrow we will go into the city to search out Athineos and finalise our departure, and also request that he stop off at Cyprus.'

Alcaeus chewed on his roasted goat. 'He will be stopping off at Cyprus anyway. It is on the way to Ephesus and he will wish to pick up fresh water and fruit for the rest of the journey.'

'Have you been to Cyprus, Alcaeus?' asked Drenis.

The doctor shook his head. 'No, but I have heard it is a wondrous island. It is where Aphrodite came from the ocean.'

'Who's Aphrodite?' said Surena, stuffing a chunk of meat into his mouth.

Alcaeus rolled his eyes. 'The Goddess of Love, Desire and Beauty. What do they teach you in the Sons of the Citadel?'

Surena grinned. 'How to defeat enemies and become a great warlord. Like the king.'

'Tell us more about Aphrodite,' I said.

'She was born when Cronus, the ruling titan, castrated Uranus, the Sky God, and tossed his genitals into the sea,' stated Alcaeus. 'Whereupon Aphrodite arose from the sea foam in a giant scallop and then walked ashore on the island of Cyprus.'

'What's a titan?' asked Surena.

Alcaeus sighed. 'Titans are elder gods who ruled the world before the Olympians overthrew them. Their ruler was Cronus, who was overthrown by his son Zeus.'

Surena was fascinated. 'Where are they now, these titans?'

'In tartarus,' answered Alcaeus, 'the underworld.'

Surena gazed into the flickering flames of the fire. 'I will be a titan of the arena.'

'Well just save any fighting for Ephesus,' I told him.

191

Alcaeus looked at Gallia, who had uncovered her face but kept her hair covered.

'You are right to cover your hair, Gallia. I'll warrant there are few women in the eastern Mediterranean with blue eyes and blonde hair.'

He looked at me. 'And even fewer with a husband who has a scar on his face. You must both take care.'

'We will,' I assured him.

The next day I rode into the city in the company of Malik and Byrd. I took them because I wanted them to be familiar with the appearance of Athineos, just in case he betrayed us. They would be no use as agents of revenge if they could not recognise their target. I thought it improbable that the Cretan would betray us. Then again, he was something of a mercenary and would indeed probably sell his own mother if the price was right.

Tripolis was over seven hundred years old, a great walled city that had been founded by the Phoenicians, a seafaring people whose ships had once sailed the Mediterranean. Roman soldiers stood sentry outside the northern gates and on the battlements as our beasts ambled through the ancient entrance, trade caravans filling the road in front and behind us. People on foot carrying bundles of wood, sacks of wheat and baskets of bread and fruit walked beside us as a sweating centurion stood outside the guardhouse wishing he was somewhere else. The air was filled with the sounds of chattering and complaining people, camels grunting as we moved through the entrance.

'Which way to the docks?' I shouted at the centurion in Latin.

'Just keep going until the air becomes less rancid,' he answered gruffly.

We carried on, passing markets selling fruit, fish and meat and heaving with people dressed in a variety of black, white, yellow and brown robes. The sun occasionally reflected off a bronze helmet or spear point, indicating that Roman legionaries patrolled the streets. But the atmosphere was of frenzied commercial activity rather than military occupation.

The city had originally been called Athar and had been ruled over by a king, who at times served as high priest in the temple of the city's patron god, thus ensuring that he ruled over the people both physically and spiritually. But now it was ruled by Rome, which had already begun to stamp its mark on Tripolis. The majority of the city comprised single-story mud-brick abodes, with old stone buildings in the administrative and religious districts. But outside the city, on the lower slopes of the mountains that rose up behind the city, among the cypress and cedar trees that blanketed the region, were newly built villas. And as we neared the docks area we passed newly constructed tenements to house Roman clerks, officials and their families.

'That soldier was right,' said Byrd, sniffing the air, 'it smells fresher here.'

The docks area was large and impressive, the jetties on the seafront comprising wooden platforms sitting on piles of stone blocks. At least a dozen merchant ships were moored alongside these quays, sailors and dockers loading two with goods, the others lying idle, a few sailors on board keeping watch. Two long breakwaters that curved first outwards and then inwards, resembling the front claws of a giant lobster, enclosed the harbour. These breakwaters had a sloping mound on the seaward side and a quay made of stone blocks on the leeward side. Docked stern first along these breakwaters were Roman warships: mainly triremes and biremes but also two huge quinqueremes with five banks of oars. Detachments of marines dressed in blue tunics, blue-faced shields and bronze helmets with blue plumes stood guard over each ship. We dismounted and looked around at the line of ships along the quay.

'Which ship belongs to the Cretan?' asked Byrd.

'I have no idea,' I said.

I accosted a flustered official who was walking towards us after appearing to remonstrate with a sailor who towered over him menacingly.

'Excuse me, friend,' I called to him.

He stopped and eyed us suspiciously, three figures wrapped in black robes, one of whose faces was adorned with black tattoos. He stopped but kept his distance.

'I am looking for the Cretan Captain Athineos,' I said.

He turned and pointed to a gap between two warehouses.

'Ask at the Cretan traders' office. They will know,' he said before scuttling away.

We led our animals between the warehouses into a square where the whitewashed offices of the ship owners and traders were located. Each building was a two-storey structure with wooden shutters covering the windows. Each office had a plaque outside its entrance, with names in Greek and Latin. I pointed to one that had an elephant symbol above its plaque.

'The office of African traders.'

'That doesn't help us,' remarked Byrd.

'There is the Cretan office,' said Malik, pointing to a building with a bull's head symbol above the door. The sign did indeed say it was the Cretan traders' association. I left them with my camel as I strode over to it and walked through the open doorway. A gaunt man with thinning brown hair looked up from the papyrus document he was reading.

'I am seeking the Cretan Captain Athineos,' I said. 'I was told that you would know his whereabouts.'

Behind him clerks were filing documents in pigeonholes, two of their number sitting at tables writing.

'You have business with him?'

I nodded. 'A cargo being shipped to Ephesus.'

'Ah, well you find him at the *Golden Anchor*, an inn around five minutes from here. He usually spends his days there between voyages.'

The inn was tucked away in a narrow street near the harbour, opposite a brothel whose pockmarked whores stood outside inviting passers by to sample their wares. I told Malik and Byrd to guard the animals while I went inside, various unsavoury characters loitering in the street casting us disapproving glances.

'Where is a Roman patrol when you want one,' I said.

Malik was armed with a sword and dagger but I was satisfied that his size and tattooed face would deter any aggression, though I was not so sure about the whores. They were calling to us to go over and enjoy their bodies.

'Try to ignore the temptation,' I grinned.

The interior of the inn was less inviting than the exterior, groups of sinister-looking individuals huddled at tables drinking and speaking in hushed tones. They turned their heads when I entered, scrutinising me before going back to their business. I scanned the dimly lit interior and saw a thick arm rise into the air.

'More wine over here.'

I recognised the voice and then saw the tattoos on the arm. I walked over to stand behind him.

'A bit early to be drinking, isn't it?'

He jumped up and turned to face me, a hand on the hilt of his sword. His two companions likewise rose menacingly to their feet. But Athineos threw back his head and roared with laughter.

'So, you came. I had to admit I had my doubts.' He slapped me hard on the arm. 'But here you are. Bring that wine, and quickly,' he ordered the innkeeper.

He pulled up a chair for me and indicated to his companions that I was a friend.

'Sit yourself down, lord.'

I looked around. 'My name is Nikephorus, Athineos.'

He tapped his nose with a finger. 'Say no more. Are you alone?'

'There are six others with me. You can accommodate them?'

He smiled. 'Of course, the price will be higher, though.'

The innkeeper brought a fresh jug of wine, though it tasted so bitter that I could have sworn it was vinegar.

'We can pay our passage, Athineos, and that includes the return journey.'

Athineos leaned forward. 'I'll have to take all the money for both journeys up front. Just in case you don't make the return journey, you understand.'

I raised my cup but then thought twice about taking another sip of the wine. I put it down. 'Very well.'

'We leave in two days,' he told me.

'Could you spare me a few moments, Athineos?' I said. 'There are two people I would like you to meet.'

His companions looked at me suspiciously but Athineos waved away their concern.

'Of course, any friend of Pacorus, that is Nikephorus, is a friend of mine.'

We walked outside to where Malik and Byrd were waiting. I introduced them to the sea captain, who blew a kiss at one of the whores standing on the brothel balcony opposite. She leered and pulled down her top to reveal one of her sagging breasts.

'They are waiting for you, Athineos,' she shouted.

'And I'll be over to sample your goods later,' he beamed.

Malik turned, looked up at the scabby woman and shuddered. 'You will lie with her?'

Athineos winked at him. 'I won't be lying. Still, a harbour is a harbour for my warship.'

He examined Malik's facial tattoos. 'You are Agraci, aren't you?'

'You know my people?' enquired Malik coolly.

'Everyone in these parts knows your people, though many without any affection.'

Athineos looked at Byrd. 'Are you coming as well?'

'We not coming,' answered Byrd. 'We just look after interests of Pacorus.'

'Well,' I said, 'I look forward to seeing you at the docks in two days, Athineos. Now we must be away. I have no wish to keep you from your wine and women any longer.'

'In two days, then.'

He turned and disappeared into the murky interior of the inn, leaving the three of us in the street. I took the reins of my camel from Byrd and led him out of the street and back into the square before getting him to kneel to allow me to sit in the saddle. I rode back to camp in the company of an unhappy Malik.

'You should not trust that man, Pacorus. He will betray you.'

'He might,' I agreed, 'and we might be killed in a storm at sea or I might get killed at Ephesus. But if I do not satisfy my curiosity then the doubt will eat away at me and drive me insane.'

'You should not be taking Gallia,' said Byrd.

'She believes it is her destiny to go to Ephesus,' I replied. 'But if you feel so strongly about it, Byrd, you are welcome to try to convince her to stay.'

But he did not say anything to Gallia and so, two days later, we all stood on the quay of Tripolis' docks, our clothes, gold, weapons, armour and Alcaeus' medicines in wooden chests that had been unloaded from the camels by the side of Athineos' vessel. We said our farewells to Malik and Byrd as their scouts began leading the camels away from the dockside. The Agraci prince took one long, last look at the Cretan captain before vaulting into his saddle and riding away with his friend.

Athineos stood on one of the overhanging side balconies of his ship and began shouting orders at his sailors.

'Now that the camels and horses have gone, get the beasts out of the warehouses. And hurry up. I want to be away before noon.'

The docks were busier than when we had first visited them, the quays heaving with dockers, sailors, officials and pallets and crates filled with goods to be loaded onto ships. Sacks of wheat were being hauled aboard one vessel, while dozens of amphorae filled with wine, olive oil and spices were being loaded onto another. But Athineos' vessels would be carrying more volatile cargoes: lions.

Athineos bellowed at his sailors to get our chests aboard before the animals arrived, and so we gave them a hand to load them on the ship. Gallia went to assist me carry one of the chests, which had rope handles on each end to facilitate lifting.

'It is heavy,' I told her.

She dismissed my concern. 'Just because I am a woman does not mean I am incapable of work.'

But it was filled with spare swords, armour, shields and tridents and she found it hard going hauling it up the gangplank. A grinning Athineos left his place on the side balcony and came over.

'She's not much use,' he said to me, pointing at Gallia, who like me was dressed in black Agraci robes.

'I can match you or any of your men, Cretan,' she snarled.

His eyes opened with surprise as he realised who she was. He hurried over to her side and grasped the rope with his huge hands.

'Forgive me, lady, I had no idea you were journeying with us.'

197

We hauled the chest aboard and placed it beside the others in front of the single cabin at the stern of the vessel.

'We'll put them in the cabin after we've loaded the beasts,' said Athineos.

He looked at Gallia. 'I think it might be best if you sleep in my cabin, lady. I'll bed down in the hold.'

As we stood in front of the cabin I noticed that the crew were bringing baskets filled with cured meat aboard.

'At least we won't starve,' grinned Surena.

'They're not for you, boy, they're for the lions,' said Athineos.

'I'm not your boy,' snapped Surena but I glared at him to hold his tongue.

The crowd on the docks parted as clerks shouted at slaves to pull the wheeled carts that held the lions: a score of snarling, angry beasts that looked in remarkably good health considering they had been transported from far away Gordyene or Atropaiene. I said as much to Athineos.

'If I don't get twenty fit and healthy lions to Ephesus then I won't get paid. So they have been treated like little princes on their way here.'

'To be butchered in the arena,' said a disapproving Gallia.

Athineos nodded at me. 'In the wild Parthian princes and nobles hunt lions. Don't see much difference between dying in the arena or dying in the wild.'

The cages, each one measuring around nine feet in length and width and four foot in height, were moved alongside Athineos' vessel and his other two ships. Dockers operating cranes lowered hooks on the end of ropes and then slaves nervously jumped on the carts to secure the hooks to ropes fixed to the tops of the wooden cages so they could be hoisted aboard. The animals began to get agitated and tried to maul the slaves. But the tops of the cages were tightly meshed to make this impossible; only the bars on the sides were more widely separated to allow air to circulate more freely.

One slave, standing on top of a cage with a snarling male lion with a huge mane beneath him, tried to catch the hook but missed as it dropped lower. I watched, horrified, as he crouched on the cage and reached down in an effort to retrieve the hook, only to have his hand that strayed near the bars ripped open as the lion's claws moved in a blur. The beast leapt at the bars and grabbed the poor wretch's arm in its mouth and began pulling it into the cage.

As the slave let out a series of high-pitched screams Gallia bent down and pulled her bow from its case and nocked an arrow in the bowstring.

'No,' implored Athineos, who jumped in front of her. 'Don't kill it. Please don't kill it.'

As horrified onlookers stood, transfixed, staring at the lion tearing at the slave's flesh, Athineos ran down the gangplank and rushed over to the cage. He stood on the opposite side to where the slave was screaming, reached in and grabbed the lion's tail. The beast, enraged, let go of the slave and spun round, launching itself at Athineos. It shook the cage as its bulk crashed into the bars that fortunately held.

A centurion, drawn sword in his hand, walked up to him with four marines in tow.

'Is this your animal?'

'Yes, sir,' replied Athineos. 'He's going to Ephesus to entertain the fine citizens of that city in the upcoming games.'

He pointed to his ship. 'We are trying to load it on my ship, sir.'

'Well get it loaded,' ordered the centurion, 'otherwise I'll have it killed. It's causing an obstruction.'

While this was going on Alcaeus had descended the gangplank with his medical bag and was attempting to treat the slave, who was now shaking as shock took hold of him. Blood was spurting on to the quay from the wound that Alcaeus was attempting to bind. Athineos bellowed at the crane operator to raise the hook as he jumped on the cart and then on top of the cage to secure the hook to lift it. The lion, now wanting more human blood, began clawing at the top of the cage as it and Athineos were hoisted up and over the side of the ship.

The centurion walked over to where Alcaeus was treating the slave.

'Leave him.'

'He's badly wounded, you imbecile,' replied Alcaeus.

I nudged Domitus. 'Trouble.'

I walked down the gangplank with him following as the marines circled Alcaeus menacingly.

199

'Offer to buy the slave,' I said to Domitus.

'What?'

'Just do it.'

Drenis and Arminius held Surena back as we walked over to the centurion, an irate Alcaeus and a trembling slave.

'*Salve*, citizen,' said Domitus to the centurion.

The centurion, about the same height as Domitus, looked at the general of Dura's army.

'Who are you?'

'Lucius Domitus, *lanista* of the *Ludus* Palmyra.'

The centurion grunted and pointed his cane at me. 'And him?'

'One of my gladiators, centurion.'

The slave groaned as Alcaeus tightened the tourniquet. The centurion pointed at the doctor.

'I told you to leave him. Now move, otherwise you will be arrested.'

Alcaeus ignored him.

'I wish to buy this slave,' said Domitus.

The centurion frowned. 'This slave?'

'I collect one-armed slaves,' replied Domitus, 'my wife likes to staff our villa with them. She says that one-armed slaves steal less because they are, by definition, less light fingered.'

The marines sniggered and the centurion was confused.

'He belongs to the port authority,' he announced, 'you will have to clear it with them. By the look of him he will be dead by tonight.'

I assisted Alcaeus in lifting the slave up and helping him towards the gangplank. He looked pale and half-dead but at least Alcaeus was no longer in danger of being arrested. While Domitus sauntered off to the office of the port authority with a representative of the organisation, the centurion and the marines, the rest of the lions were loaded on the ships. There were six cages on our vessel, each one holding a lion.

We placed the slave on the single bed in the cabin and I left Alcaeus to treat him and went back outside.

'That was dangerous,' Athineos rebuked me. 'They could have arrested you. And all for a slave? You're a strange one, Parthian.'

I paid Athineos for our passage while the sailors loaded food and water for the voyage to Cyprus. He told me that he would have visited the island anyway, but since I had paid him handsomely he was more than happy to call at the port of Paphos.

'Why Paphos?'

'I have an appointment with someone there.'

Domitus returned with the ownership papers for the slave, a Syrian named Adad. He tossed me the documents.

'He didn't come cheap. Let's hope he lives to thank you.'

An hour later we finally got under way. Small rowing boats towed Athineos' three ships from the dockside towards the open sea. The sailors unfurled the main sail and manned the steering oars at the rear of the overhanging side balconies. The vessel we were on was called a *corbita*, a ship that Athineos told me was the common merchant vessel of the Roman Republic. Ours, named *The Cretan*, was at least ninety feet long and twenty-five feet wide. There was a main mast positioned in the centre of the rounded hull, which had two smaller sails above it. On the bow was another sail called an *artemon* that aided navigation. Immediately behind the cabin was a small kitchen with a red-tiled roof, and behind that a white swan's head.

There was a stiff wind blowing when we exited the breakwaters and although the sea was choppy the vessel hardly swayed at all. I gave thanks to Shamash that its hull, constructed of planks secured by mortice and tenon, was very sturdy. Behind us the other two ships followed in line as we headed west to Cyprus.

Athineos told us that with a fair wind and nothing unforeseen we would make Paphos in three days. The crew went about their business and generally ignored us, no doubt the chief reason being that Surena, Drenis and Arminius practised their weapon skills on the deck in their gladiator equipment. I too spent most of the daylight hours practising with Domitus, though because of the lack of space it was impossible to replicate the sand of the arena. Still, it proved a useful exercise in getting used to my heavy full-face bronze helmet. Gallia spent her time sharpening her knife and giving any sailor who leered at her an icy stare.

Surena was in an ebullient mood; Arminius and Drenis more thoughtful and reserved. I watched Athineos bellowing at his sailors as they erected awnings over the cages holding the lions to keep them out of the sun. And then shouting some more when they spilt the beasts' food as they attempted to feed them without losing an arm or some fingers. Athineos treated each animal as though it was a prized pet, fussing over their welfare. He also commanded that the other two ships came alongside at regular intervals so he could enquire as to the wellbeing of the lions on their decks.

'I've been a sailor for over thirty years,' he told me on the afternoon of the second day, 'but this trip promises to be my most lucrative. So you can understand that I don't want to lose any of my cargo this close to completing the voyage.'

We were both leaning on the ship's starboard gunwale, staring at the calm blue waters of the Mediterranean below. The sun shone down from an almost cloudless sky, the pleasing breeze filling the ships' sails.

'The gods favour your enterprise, Athineos.'

'Mm. You think they will be as kind to you, young king, when you reach Ephesus?'

'I hope they will see my venture as worthy of their support.'

He shook his head. 'Foolhardy more like. Why would a man, much less a king, risk all for a man he has not seen in years, who is a Roman slave most likely and who stands a good chance of being killed in the forthcoming games? It makes no sense.'

'On the contrary, Athineos, it makes perfect sense. I am meant to go to Ephesus. It is my destiny. Indeed, you were the vessel sent by the gods that showed what course of action I should take.'

He looked surprised. 'Me?'

'Why did you travel to Dura to inform me that Burebista would be at Ephesus?'

He considered for a moment. 'I just thought you should know, that's all. But, on reflection, perhaps you are right. Then again, you always were a bit of a dreamer.'

'In what way?'

202

'I remember when you escaped from Italy. Instead of saving yourself and your pretty wife you brought half the slave army with you.'

'Hardly,' I said.

He looked at my gladiator attire and shook his head. 'You are a dreamer, young king, just like Spartacus.'

'You knew him?'

'I met him a couple of times, business matters, you understand. I liked him.'

'So did I,' I added.

He chuckled. 'Of course you did. You were kindred spirits, fighting for honour and freedom and basking in glory. I have no doubt that in different circumstances and if he had lived, you and he would still be in Italy, terrorising Romans and covering yourselves in glory.'

I had to admit the vision had a certain appeal.

'But,' he continued, 'life isn't about glory; it's about survival and making cold, calculating decisions. That's why the Romans always win, Pacorus, and why men like you end up dead.'

'You talk too much,' I told him.

He turned away from the sea and looked at his cabin.

'How's that slave you purchased?'

'Alcaeus says he will live, though his arm will be useless.'

'When we get to Cyprus,' he said, 'you must leave him on the island. The crew aren't happy he's aboard. They says it's bad luck.'

'Who is going to be interested in a one-armed injured slave?' I asked.

'Who indeed?'

He turned to walk away but then stopped and looked back at me.

'One thing you should know. The Roman governor of Ephesus is a man named Quintus Caecilius Metellus.'

The name meant nothing to me. He saw my indifferent expression.

'He's the bastard who conquered Crete, butchering many thousands of my countrymen as he did so.'

'You had family on Crete, Athineos?'

203

He looked around at his ship. 'This is my home, young king. My point is that Metellus regards anyone that lives east of Italy as being members of inferior races. If he finds out who you are you can expect no mercy.'

I smiled. 'I never expect mercy from the Romans, Athineos.'

He walked away shaking his head in despair. He said no more to me about my reasons for being on his ship but did tell my companions and me much about the island of Cyprus before we docked there. It was an Egyptian colony ruled by a governor sent from Alexandria, the capital of Egypt. But the fact that Egypt's pharaohs were descended from one of Alexander of Macedon's generals – Ptolemy Lagides – meant that the Hellenised island of Cyprus enjoyed a high degree of autonomy. Paphos was the capital of the island due to its proximity to Alexandria and also because it was a large port. It was not only a naval base but was also used for trade and export to Egypt of the island's raw materials, chiefly copper and timber.

On the third morning, with the sun at our backs and the sea resembling an endless shimmering blue carpet, we saw Paphos for the first time. To the sound of snarling lions *The Cretan* edged its way towards the long breakwaters that enclosed the harbour. As at Tripolis the anchorage was filled with *corbitas*, triremes, biremes, coasters and small fishing vessels. Ships were entering and exiting the harbour, sails being furled and unfurled depending on their destination. I stood with Gallia and the others at the prow as Athineos barked orders at his crew and the other two ships followed us into the harbour. Outside the port, on the white sand beaches that flanked the city, were shipyards and stone slipways positioned side by side for hauling vessels out of the water. At other stations ships were being constructed, surrounded by wooden scaffolding.

The port of Paphos was around twice the size of Tripolis and three times as busy. Athineos had told me that the eastern breakwater was six hundred and fifty yards long and fifteen yards wide, and like the western breakwater was made of stone blocks. The western breakwater was three hundred yards long and the opening between the two measured sixty yards. The result was a large anchorage that had two long wharfs inside it, in addition to the berths along the docks.

Because we already had our cargoes *The Cretan* and Athineos' other two ships were able to dock stern first at one of the wharfs, after which he sent his captains to report to the port authorities and fetch fresh food and water for the crews and animals. Two soldiers wearing red tunics, bronze helmets with red plumes, mail shirts, sandals and carrying white oval shields and short spears, ambled past our vessel.

Gallia curled her lip at them. 'Romans.'

'They're not Romans, lady,' said Athineos behind her. 'They are Egyptians. This is the pharaoh's island.'

A portion of the gold I had given Athineos for our passage was paid to the port authority for docking fees, with more going to purchase supplies for our onward journey to Ephesus. Though we had thus far enjoyed a pleasant voyage it was nice to feel earth instead of wood beneath my feet as we walked into the city that afternoon.

Paphos was a noisy, sprawling place that extended inland from the harbour, most of its teeming population living inside the high sandstone walls that surrounded the city. Like Dura Paphos had been constructed according to Greek doctrine, with a grid system of streets surrounding square blocks of buildings. And like the blocks the individual buildings were square, most white walled with red tile roofs. The city itself was divided into well-defined zones: public, residential and commercial areas, the latter being concentrated around the port. Beyond the city, to the north, were hills covered with cedar and pine trees, which had been used by Philip of Macedon and the Ptolemies to build their great fleets of warships. The hills were also dotted with white-walled villas – the country residences of the city's wealthiest citizens.

Arminius had stayed on the ship to tend to Adad and to allow Alcaeus to walk among his countrymen, as had Drenis who said he had no interest in wandering around a crowded, stinking city. But in truth the air of Paphos was mostly fresh, the breeze that either blew in from the sea or from the tree-lined hills blowing away the smells of crowded humanity. The people appeared to be well fed and healthy, though most walked around barefoot and were dressed in simple linen tunics called *chitons*.

As we walked among market stalls selling food, clothes, ceramics and jewellery, Alcaeus explained to us why Cyprus was such a prize for empires.

'The soil on the island is very fertile. This means that you can grow not only an abundance of tree crops such as vines, olives, citrus fruits, figs and pomegranate, but also barley and graze cattle and sheep. Cyprus is famous for its wines.'

'The buildings of the city resemble those of Dura,' observed Surena.

'That is because both Paphos and Dura were designed by Greek architects,' said Alcaeus, 'the best in the world.'

'You obviously haven't seen Rome, Alcaeus,' said Domitus. 'Its architecture is far grander.'

'Grander, yes,' I agreed, 'but perhaps not as functional. There is a beauty in simplicity, I think.'

Domitus looked at me with narrow eyes and pursed lips. 'I hope you are not turning into a poet or some sort of Greek boy-lover.'

Gallia laughed but Alcaeus stared at him with a look of mild disgust.

'I would remind you, Domitus, that it was Greece that gifted civilisation to the world and Greek is the language of choice among even Rome's ruling classes.'

Domitus was not convinced. 'The Romans have a phrase, "the Greek custom", which sums up Greek civilisation perfectly.'

'What is this custom?' enquired Surena.

'Sodomy,' replied Domitus bluntly. 'Too much exercising naked has resulted in most Greek males preferring young boys instead of women. That's why their armies are always defeated. Greek soldiers are more interested in molesting the man next to them in the battle line instead of sticking a sword in the man facing him.'

Alcaeus rolled his eyes and waved a dismissive hand at him. 'It may come as a shock to you, Domitus, but not everything in the world revolves around battles and fighting.'

'Only the most important things,' retorted Domitus.

'How are we going to find Julia?' asked Gallia, clearly bored over this trivial boys' talk.

'A good question,' I said.

'An enquiry at the office of the port authority would be a good starting point,' offered Alcaeus, 'and if that fails then perhaps we could ask in the temple district.'

'I would start at the squares where the beggars gather,' said Domitus. 'If Pacorus' witch is anything to go by I have no doubt that this Julia will be some foul-looking old hag without a pot to piss in. Jupiter knows what use she will be.'

'You must learn to trust Dobbai, Domitus,' said Gallia. 'She is beloved of the gods.'

'Unlike you, Domitus,' said Alcaeus.

'Beloved of the gods or not,' I said, 'finding her among this multitude might prove difficult.'

But when we returned to the docks we found a man waiting for us aboard Athineos' ship, a tall Greek with thick black hair and a heavy beard. He was dressed in a white silk *chiton* with red edging on the sleeves, a leather belt round his waist and expensive leather sandals on his feet. He was talking to Drenis when I stepped off the gangplank on to the deck, the Thracian pointing at me. The Greek turned and bowed his head.

'Greetings, majesty. My name is Talaos and I am here on the orders of the Lady Julia, who invites you to her house tomorrow.'

Gallia came to my side and removed her *shemagh*, shaking her long locks free. Talaos bowed his head to her.

'Welcome to Cyprus, Queen Gallia, my mistress looks forward to meeting you tomorrow.'

'You are well informed, Talaos,' I said. 'I hope our arrival is not common knowledge among the citizens of Paphos.'

'Your arrival is known only to my mistress and those whom she trusts, majesty,' Talaos replied.

I wondered about the relationship between this handsome young man and the seer. But he did not proffer any information regarding his position and I decided not to ask. But I did enquire about the location of his mistress' home.

He turned and pointed at the green-covered slopes beyond the city walls.

'She lives in the hills, majesty.'

'And how do we get there?' I asked.

'I will bring horses for you tomorrow morning, majesty.' He looked at Gallia. 'My mistress assumed that Queen Gallia would prefer to ride to her house.'

'Your mistress is correct,' smiled Gallia.

He bowed his head to us once more and then took his leave. Athineos sauntered over as Talaos walked down the gangplank and strode along the wharf.

'This seer must be a person of some importance, Pacorus, if she has a house in the hills.'

'She is probably the sorceress of some rich lord,' I said.

'Just like Dobbai is at Dura,' remarked Drenis.

'You should not go alone,' growled Domitus. 'You will be vulnerable.'

'We will be fine,' Gallia assured him.

'This is Cyprus, Domitus,' said Alcaeus, 'not a den of assassins like Rome.'

The next morning Talaos presented himself at *The Cretan* holding the reins of three horses, all of them well-groomed mares. Gallia and I still wore our *shemaghs* to hide our faces but had discarded our Agraci robes and wore loose leggings and our white tunics instead. We both wore our sword belts and Gallia had her dagger tucked into her right boot, but we left our bows on the ship. Talaos was bemused by Gallia's manlike appearance but was all courtesy and bows as we walked the horses along the wharf before mounting them when we had passed through the mass of sailors and dockers who were working on the main quay where cargo ships were being loaded and unloaded. I also saw slaves toiling under the watchful eyes of overseers with whips. Gallia saw them too but said nothing.

It was good to be back in the saddle and even better when we had ridden through the city's northern gates and travelled through copses of well-tended olive, carob and almond trees. Talaos was an accomplished rider and on the journey provided information regarding the island's commerce.

'Because it is an Egyptian colony, majesty, the majority of the island's trade is with Alexandria.'

We had left the main road to ride along a track that wound its way up a great tree-lined hill, giving us excellent views of Paphos and the glittering Mediterranean beyond.

'And what does the island supply Alexandria with?' asked Gallia.

'Timber and copper mostly, majesty,' said Talaos.

We continued on and came across a great vineyard that had been planted on terraces cut into the hillside. It covered many acres and dozens of slaves were working among the vines.

'Vineyards on the southern slopes mean good exposure to the sun and thus a greater yield,' Talaos told us. 'We are nearing the end of our journey, majesties.'

'Your mistress lives on the estate of the lord who owns this vineyard?' I asked him.

'This is my mistress' vineyard, majesty,' he informed me.

We ended our ride at a large two-storey white villa surrounded by neat rows of date palms, the cedars and pines extending up the hill behind the house. Barefoot slaves in immaculate white *chitons* came forward with heads bowed to take our horses as Talaos dismounted and ordered the slaves to take them to the stables. He invited us to accompany him inside the villa, the entrance to which was guarded by two soldiers who were armed and equipped similar to the ones we had seen patrolling the port.

'This Julia is either a shrewd businesswoman or has the patronage of a rich lord,' I said to Gallia. 'These slaves are better dressed than the servants in our palace at Dura.'

'But they are still slaves, Pacorus.'

Our entrance into the villa only confirmed to me that the seer enjoyed an opulent lifestyle. The house had been built according to the peristyle school, with a large central courtyard enclosed by a colonnaded porch on all four sides. The walls of the entrance hall were covered with frescoes depicting scenes from Greek myths, or so Talaos told me. I initially thought that we had walked into a brothel with depictions of naked men and women being chased by half-humans and half-animals in various states of arousal. The floor was a mosaic showing the Greek god Dionysus, the deity of wine, which I thought was more apt.

Talaos spoke quietly to an older man in a red *chiton* and then invited us to walk with him into the garden, taking us through a library that occupied both storeys and was dedicated to Athena, the Goddess of the Arts and Literature. The air was filled with the aroma of rose incense as we walked into the spacious courtyard. My first impression was the sound of running water coming from four large fountains standing among statues and flanked by immaculate flowerbeds containing irises, daffodils and Abyssinian roses. Even though the courtyard was large there were paintings of landscapes on the walls to create the illusion of even more space. The atmosphere imparted a sense of order and calm. Gallia took off her *shemagh* and smelt the air, closing her eyes and taking in the pleasing aroma.

'I too have often found this courtyard a haven from the bustle of the world.'

We turned to see a woman no more than five feet in height standing next to one of the fountains. She was dressed in a blue silk gown adorned with gold brooches, her dark brown hair arranged on top of her head and held in place with scented wax. She wore gold rings on her fingers and long, thin strips of gold dangled from her ears. Surrounding her dark brown eyes was shadow made from olive oil mixed with ground charcoal. Her bare arms were tanned and shiny, probably due to having olive oil rubbed on them. I detected a whiff of myrrh perfume coming from her. She clearly had very expensive tastes.

She smiled, her teeth white and complete. 'Welcome King Pacorus and Queen Gallia. I have been expecting you. Talaos, bring wine for our guests.'

She took Gallia's arm and led her towards the banqueting room that contained daybeds woven in leather standing at the same height as the tables to allow guests to recline as they took refreshments.

'So this is the famous Queen Gallia that Samahe has told me so much about. I am indeed pleased to meet you.'

'And you, lady,' said Gallia.

'Please,' insisted the seer, 'call me Julia. We are all friends here.'

Talaos reappeared with slaves holding beautiful silver drinking cups. He poured wine into them and served us after we had reclined on the daybeds. I sipped at the wine. It was one of the best I had tasted.

'So, lord king,' Julia said to me, 'you go to Ephesus on an heroic quest to rescue your friend from Roman slavery.'

'I do, Julia.'

She smiled at Gallia. 'And you have come here seeking my help in this noble venture.'

'Samahe said that you might be able to offer me aid,' I said.

She smiled and looked at Gallia. 'It is most auspicious that you, Queen Gallia, are to visit Ephesus, the site of the sanctuary of Artemis and a city that was founded by the Amazons.'

She turned her head and snapped her fingers at Talaos standing near the entrance.

'Bring the gift.'

He bowed his head and left the room as a slave came forward to refresh my cup.

'How is it that a member of the Scythian sisterhood came to live on Cyprus?' I asked.

'The members of our order go where they will, King Pacorus,' she answered evasively. 'You are indeed fortunate that one of the highest of our order has made your palace her home.'

Gallia looked at her. 'One of the highest?'

'It is no coincidence that Dobbai was the adviser of King of King Sinatruces. And now she lives at Dura.'

She looked at me, examining me closely and not speaking. I found her gaze uncomfortable and felt awkward.

'I have found princes to be mostly boorish and stupid,' she said at length. 'They usually destroy what their fathers have built. I have had many of them visit me here, fawning over me like desperate slaves.'

'They ask you to reveal their futures?' I asked.

She nodded. 'Mostly I tell them what they want to hear. That they will achieve fame and glory and make their father's achievements look pitiful. They pay me my fee and leave happy.'

'Is that not dishonest?' I said.

211

She raised a well-manicured eyebrow at me. 'Dobbai wrote that you are an incurable romantic. There are many futures, Parthian king, of which the gods reveal but a few. But I do not need the assistance of the gods to know what the future holds for some hapless individuals.'

She rose from her daybed. 'If a fat, idle prince of some meaningless minor kingdom under the heel of the Romans asks me what his future holds, then I tell him that he will live a long, happy life filled with riches and glory. It is not a lie but neither is it the whole truth. The fact that he will die in middle age of heart failure after sodomising one of his male slaves, or choking on a bone at a feast, is largely irrelevant.'

'Not to him,' I remarked.

She waved over a slave who refilled her cup. 'To be able to see the future is a precious gift from the gods. I would be abusing their benevolence if I indulged the whims of every idiot who presents himself to me. Only the deserving should benefit from divine knowledge.'

I did not know what to make of this woman who dressed and lived like a queen, but Gallia was clearly fascinated by her.

'What of princesses who visit you?' she asked.

Julia regained her daybed. 'I try to help them as much as I can, as I do with the other women who ask for my assistance. Women have a hard enough time in this life. I see no reason to add to their misery.'

'Are princesses miserable?' I asked, thinking of my own sisters, Adeleh and Aliyeh, both pampered princesses at Hatra.

'Inevitably,' said Julia, looking at Gallia as she spoke. 'Given by their fathers to foreign princes to secure alliances, they invariably either die in childbirth or live lonely lives in their dotage far from their homelands.'

Talaos returned carrying something wrapped in a red cloth. I stood in anticipation of receiving it. He bowed to Julia and handed the parcel to her. The seer stood and passed it to Gallia.

'For you, Queen Gallia.'

Somewhat surprised, Gallia stood and took it. She unwrapped the cloth to reveal a leather quiver filled with silver flight arrows. She pulled one of the arrows from the quiver and

I saw that its shaft was painted silver and its three-winged point was also burnished to resemble silver. It was most striking.

'The head looks like it is made of silver,' I said.

'That is because it is silver,' replied Julia as Gallia slipped it back into the quiver.

She laid a hand on Gallia's arm. 'You must listen closely, young Amazon. You must keep this quiver close at all times. The fate of you and your husband rests on you using these arrows when the time comes.'

'My wife is not fighting in the arena,' I stated.

Julia turned, frowning at me. 'I did not say she was. But her bow and these arrows will have an influence on what happens at Ephesus.'

She looked back at Gallia. 'Keep your bow and these missiles with you at all times. Artemis will ensure that each one will find its mark.'

Gallia seemed pleased with her gift and all that remained was for me to receive mine. I looked at Talaos who had returned to his station by the door. I then looked at Julia in expectation. She returned to her daybed and ignored me.

'What about me?' I enquired.

'What about you?' said Julia.

'Am I to receive any assistance?'

'No.'

I was not amused. 'I have come all the way here for nothing.'

'I thought you came here because Cyprus is on the route to your destination of Ephesus,' remarked Julia. 'However, as I can see that you are disappointed that your wife has received a gift and you have not, I offer this advice. When you have done with Ephesus seek the lions at the island of Lemnos. And afterwards strike when the silver man glitters.'

I was now totally confused. 'I do not understand.'

'You will at the time. What did I just say?'

I repeated her words.

'Good,' she said, 'remember them. They will save your life.'

'I have one thing to request of you,' I said.

Julia looked at me in anticipation. 'Speak, King Pacorus.'

I placed my hands behind my back. 'There is aboard the ship we are travelling on a slave named Adad who was injured most grievously at the start of our voyage. As a result his arm is withered and he requires rest and recuperation. I would ask that you give him refuge here as the sailors believe his presence on their ship is an ill omen and it may lead to difficulties.'

'What use is a one-armed slave?' said Julia.

'We will pay you of course,' I emphasised.

Julia smiled at Gallia. 'I have no wish to offend the king and queen of Dura, the latter especially as Dobbai speaks most highly of you. Therefore I will take the slave. Talaos will collect him this afternoon. I will add him to my fee.'

I relaxed and sat on the daybed. 'If you write to my treasurer at Dura he will see that the funds are sent forthwith.'

'The fee is five thousand drachmas.'

I nearly dropped my cup. 'Five thousand drachmas?'

'You hearing is impeccable,' remarked Julia.

An unskilled worker could perhaps earn half a drachma a day and even though I did not trade in slaves I knew that even the most highly prized rarely cost more than three hundred drachmas each.

'Much as I find your company interesting, King Pacorus,' said Julia, 'I am a businesswoman with large overheads.'

I looked around at her rich furniture and fittings. 'I can imagine.'

'So you will appreciate that my services do not come cheaply.'

'We will be happy to pay the fee,' said Gallia firmly.

Talaos escorted us back to the docks with another slave riding on a horse-drawn cart to enable Adad to be taken back to Julia's villa. Gallia was delighted with her gift but I felt duped. And to compound my sense of being cheated I had no idea where Lemnos was. The only positive result of our visit to Julia was that Adad would have a place of sanctuary where he could regain his strength.

His eyes were filled with tears of gratitude as he thanked me for saving his life. Alcaeus helped him down the gangplank to the waiting cart as I said farewell to Talaos. I raised my hand to Adad, whose salvation was included in the king's ransom I had paid for a miserable quiver of silver arrows.

Chapter 8

It took four days to reach Ephesus, the ships hugging the coast of Cyprus before heading northwest into open waters. I thanked Dobbai that she had insisted that our party numbered seven to appease the gods of the oceans because the Mediterranean was peaceful like a sleeping blue giant. The crew was happy that we were rid of Adad and the lions seemed content and well fed in their cages, Athineos fussing over them like a mother hen. We saw other ships during the passage to the coastline of Asia Minor, mostly *corbitas* like our own but sometimes a Roman trireme on patrol, its oars dipping into the water in perfect unison.

Athineos joined me one morning as one of these vessels passed our starboard side, around five hundred yards away, sailing towards the southeast.

I leaned on the gunwale to watch it pass. 'No more Cilician pirates in the Mediterranean now, then?'

'That's right,' said Athineos, 'Pompey cleared them from the sea so the Mediterranean is now a Roman lake.'

'It must have been a bloody business sinking all those Cilician ships.'

Athineos laughed. 'Pompey is a wily old fox. It is true that he had a lot of ships and men and did take the main pirate stronghold at Corecesium, but when he had captured most of the Cilician coast he bribed the pirates with promises of land outside of towns far away from the sea.'

'And did he keep his word?' I asked.

'Of course. The Cilician pirates are now farmers, though no doubt they indulge in cattle thieving from time to time.'

He stretched out an arm. 'But there are no Cilician pirates sailing the seas any more.'

He pointed at the trireme disappearing on the horizon. 'If the Romans capture you when you and your companions walk ashore at Ephesus you can expect to be crucified and your pretty wife similarly condemned, either that or sold into slavery. You want that?'

'Of course not, Athineos, but we have come too far to turn back. Anyway, perhaps we might be condemned to be galley slaves.'

He shook his head. 'Not much chance of that. Roman warships use only volunteers to row their oars.'

I was shocked. 'Surely not?'

'In a naval battle you want skilled oarsmen to power your ship not surly, half-dead slaves. So no being a galley slave for you, King Pacorus.'

'In any case we have the help of sorceresses.'

He looked at to sea. 'So you visited the old witch at Paphos. I was speaking to a few of the port officials and they said that she is a charlatan, a very rich charlatan.'

'She provided us with valuable aid,' I replied, not wishing to reveal the price of a quiver full of arrows.

He eyes me. 'Did she give you cloaks of invincibility, perhaps?'

I shook my head.

'Or the ability to summon giant birds to swoop down and rescue you from the clutches of the Romans?'

'No.'

He breathed in the sea air, turned and slapped me on the shoulder before walking off. 'Then you should pray for a speedy death, Pacorus.'

As we hugged the coast we passed many coves, inlets and tree-covered peninsulas but saw few people on the land and none on the plethora of small islands that dotted the sea just off the coast of Asia. Athineos informed me that the inhabitants had been seized and sold in the slave markets by the Cilician pirates many years before. Even though the Romans had cleared the seas of pirates, locals were still fearful of living too near the coast.

The islands and coast may have been deserted but as we got nearer to Ephesus the sea began to fill with vessels. They were mostly *corbitas* filled with food and supplies to sell in the city's markets but we also saw Roman warships and small fishing boats operating from Ephesus itself. As we neared the city Domitus appeared from the hold, having changed into the clothes of a *lanista*, or what he considered the owner of a gladiator school should wear: red boots, white tunic and a blue cloak secured to his left shoulder by means of a gold brooch. Around his waist he wore his sword belt, his *gladius* at his left hip and his dagger on the opposite side.

Drenis and Arminius burst into laughter when they saw him and Gallia frowned but Domitus was having none of it.

'You may mock but we are about to enter Roman territory and so all of you need to have a care. Henceforth you will all address me as *dominus*.'

Surena smiled in mockery. Domitus was facing him, their faces inches apart in seconds.

'You think this is a joke, boy. A loose word and we could all end up nailed to crosses. You want that for your king, your queen?'

Surena's smile disappeared. 'No, sir, that is *dominus*.'

Domitus turned to face all of us. 'And that goes for all of you. Watch what you say and keep your heads down. And Gallia, keep your head covered. You are already one of the most famous women in the East so we don't want people to see your blonde hair. Hopefully we can get hold of Burebista and leave Ephesus before the cat's out of the bag.'

To which end I pulled Athineos aside and requested a quiet word with him in his cabin. He knew the purpose of our mission but I told him that I wanted to be away from Ephesus as soon as we had secured Burebista.

'Shouldn't be a problem. I will be paid as soon as the lions are offloaded and after that there will be nothing to keep me here.'

'Good.'

'How are you going to rescue your friend, bearing in mind that there are a lot of Roman soldiers in Ephesus?'

'I will decide that when we get there.'

He scratched his head and went over to the small table at the bottom of the single cot in the cabin. He bent down to pick up a small chest and placed it on the table, the legs of which were fastened to the floor. He opened the lid, took out a roll of papyrus and held it out to me.

'Do you want to make a will before we reach Ephesus?'

'A will. Why?'

He gave me a rueful smile. 'Because you have as much chance of succeeding as those lions out there have of dying of old age.'

I declined his generous offer.

The next day we entered the harbour of Ephesus. The Romans called the city *Lumen Asia*, the 'Light of Asia', whereas the locals termed it the 'Market of Asia'. Both were right for Ephesus was a wonder to behold. We all stood on the deck with awe in our eyes as the sailors furled the sails and Athineos guided his vessel towards one of the great stone wharfs that projected out from the dockside, one of four in the spacious harbour that was enclosed by two long breakwaters. Alcaeus had told me that the harbour at Ephesus was the largest in Asia, perhaps the world, and looking at it now I considered it to be the latter.

Either side of the wharfs were docked merchant vessels of various sizes and a row of warships moored stern first. The aroma of spices and animals came from the great wooden warehouses lining the docks and which were filled with goods for shipment to Italy and Greece.

'I had heard of the great prosperity of Ephesus,' said Alcaeus as sailors jumped from the ship to secure the vessel to wooden posts on the wharf with ropes, 'but it has exceeded my expectations. You may be interested to know, Pacorus, that it is a great trading city not only because its hinterland is extremely fertile, but also because it forms the end of one leg of the Silk Road.'

'His name is Nikephorus,' hissed Domitus.

'Well, Nikephorus,' continued Alcaeus, frowning at Domitus, 'the soil around the city, irrigated by the River Cayster that flows into the sea here at Ephesus, supports huge numbers of vineyards and olive trees, plus fine grazing lands. The wines and olive oil from Ephesus are known throughout the civilised world.'

He looked at Domitus. 'Though I doubt they have heard of them in Rome itself.'

'Not just wine and olive oil, doctor,' said Athineos who placed his large hands on top of the gunwale, 'but also marble that is quarried a short distance from the city. It makes the city a lot of money. As do the markets where grain, pottery and metals such as iron, copper, lead, gold and tin are traded.'

'The city levies taxes on the markets just as we do at Dura?' I asked.

Athineos wiped his nose on the back of his hand. 'But Dura misses out on taxing the most lucrative trade of all. Slavery.'

'There will be no slave markets at Dura, ever,' insisted Gallia.

'That's a pity,' said Athineos, nodding at me, 'because it would make him a rich king.'

'He's already a rich king, pirate,' said Domitus.

Athineos looked confused. Alcaeus enlightened him.

'The Silk Road, captain, which runs through Nikephorus' kingdom.'

Athineos' expression changed to one of contempt as he spotted two individuals walking towards his ship.

'Look sharp,' he said to us, 'Roman tax collectors. Blood-sucking maggots.'

The two men, each dressed in a simple beige tunic, sandals and carrying leather bags over their shoulders, stopped at the bow of *The Cretan* as Athineos' two other vessels were secured alongside the wharf behind ours. One opened his bag and took out a waxed tablet and used a stylus to note the name of the ship on it. Both were thin, glum-faced individuals with thinning hair and sunken eyes.

'They look like they haven't eaten for a month,' observed Surena.

'Don't say anything,' a worried Domitus told us. 'They may look stupid but they miss nothing.'

The tax collectors walked up the gangplank, their eyes darting left and right as they examined the vessel. We retreated towards the cabin as they walked on to the deck.

'You are the captain of this vessel?' the older official asked Athineos.

Athineos explained who has was and what he and his other two ships were carrying, whereupon the younger official was told to examine the cargoes of the other two vessels. The official walked up to the first cage containing a lounging lion. Athineos followed him.

'Nice and tame, they are,' said the captain. 'Why don't you give him a stroke?'

The official turned up his lip at the prospect. 'It will be the port authority's business to transport your beasts to the holding pens near the arena. But they cannot be moved until they have the approval of the senior *editor*.'

'Senior *editor*?' said Athineos.

'The organiser of the games,' replied the official tersely. 'He likes to inspect all the animals and gladiators who will take part in the games personally.'

The official looked at our little group attired in black Agraci robes, all except Domitus. 'Are they pilgrims?'

'Pilgrims?'

'Visitors to the Temple of Artemis,' replied the official tersely.

'No, they are gladiators.'

The official seemed surprised but said nothing as he took out a tablet from his bag and made a note on it with his stylus. He walked over to Domitus who was obviously the only Roman among us. Athineos introduced him.

'This is Lucius Domitus, *lanista* of the *Ludus* Palmyra.'

'Here at the invitation of High Priest Kallias and the *editor*,' added Domitus.

The official's tone changed as he spoke to a fellow Roman. 'Welcome to Ephesus. I would be most grateful if you stayed aboard until the senior *editor* has greeted you. Can I ask how many fighters you have brought to the city?'

'Four fighters,' answered Domitus.

The official raised an eyebrow as he counted six individuals behind Domitus.

'Plus my wife and the school's doctor,' added Domitus.

'Ah, I see. Thank you for your time.'

He replaced the tablet back in his bag, nodded curtly at Athineos and walked to the gangplank, turning to the captain.

'I will send a slave to collect the mooring fee and levy on the goods you are carrying captain, to be paid immediately.'

'I look forward to paying them,' replied Athineos caustically. 'Parasite,' he uttered under his breath.

The slave arrived an hour later and Athineos came close to striking him when he unfolded the note and read the figure on it. He stomped off to his cabin and returned with a pouch full of drachmas, which the slave counted most officiously. This caused Athineos' blood to boil some more, though he managed to restrain himself as the slave thanked him and hastily departed. The captain bellowed in rage at a sailor who was goading one of the lions.

'Leave it alone or I'll feed you to him myself. You think I can afford to lose one of these beasts after what I have just paid to the port authority?'

He stalked the deck like an ill-tempered hyena and everyone avoided him, but his mood changed when the senior *editor* arrived. We spotted his carriage first, a *lectica* carried by eight tall slaves and surrounded by more slaves and four legionaries who shoved aside anyone in their way to clear the wharf of traffic. The *lectica* was a type of mobile bed, made of wood that had four poles at each corner to support an overhead canopy. From the canopy hung curtains to provide shade and privacy for the occupant. Two other poles were fastened to the sides of the *lectica* and these were the means by which the eight strong slaves carried their master on their shoulders. Inside the *lectica* the occupant lay on a soft mattress, with a bolster and pillows to allow him to sleep or read.

Athineos paced the deck nervously as the slaves placed the *lectica* carefully down beside the gangplank. All his efforts in transporting the lions to Ephesus and keeping them healthy came down to these few moments, when the *editor* would decide if they were suitable for the arena.

Once again we stood near the cabin as a slave pulled aside one of the lectica's curtains to allow the occupant to exit. Gallia stifled a laughed as a balding, fat Roman in an off-white toga was helped to his feet by the slave. Another slave carrying a sunshade immediately came to the Roman's side to prevent the sun's rays caressing his pink crown.

'A magistrate,' said Domitus, observing the broad purple border on the Roman's toga. 'A man of some importance.'

'And size,' said Gallia, prompting Surena to laugh.

'Quiet, boy,' snapped Domitus.

One of the Roman's slaves stopped at the top of the gangplank and announced his master.

'The magistrate Timini Ceukianus, Senior *Editor* of the games at Ephesus and nephew of Quintus Caecilius Metellus, Governor of Ephesus, conqueror of Crete and lord of all Asia.'

The magistrate waddled up the gangplank with two legionaries in front of him and the slave with the sunshade behind. Athineos stepped forward and tilted his head as Ceukianus stepped on to the deck.

'Welcome aboard, sir, I am Captain Athineos.'

Ceukianus waved a hand at him and walked past him when he spotted the cages.

'And these are the lions, captain?'

'Some of them, magistrate, the rest being on my other vessels.'

Ceukianus' piggy eyes opened wide as he peered at the beasts.

'They appear to be in excellent condition. My congratulations.'

Athineos stood beside him as Surena engaged in a staring match with one of the legionaries, until Domitus jabbed him in the ribs and told him to keep his eyes down.

'This one near tore off a slave's arm at Tripolis.'

Ceukianus clapped his puffy white hands together. 'I would have liked to have seen that.'

He turned to give the slave holding the sunshade a murderous look, pointing up at the sun. 'Keep the shade on me, wretch, otherwise I will feed you to this lion.'

He waved forward another slave who had come on deck. 'Arrange to have these animals and the others taken to the holding pens immediately.'

The slave bowed. 'Yes, *dominus.*'

'You will be paid the full fee for your lions, captain.'

A wide grin spread across Athineos' face. 'Thank you, magistrate.'

Ceukianus focused his attention on us. 'These are the gladiators from Palmyra?'

Athineos held out a hand to Domitus. 'The *lanista* Lucius Domitus, magistrate.'

Ceukianus' top lip lifted into a sneer as he regarded Domitus. In Roman society owning gladiators was a patrician pastime and was seen as glamorous, but managing them was regarded as beyond the pale of respectable society. Even to be seen in public in the company of a *lanista* was to risk scandal.

Ceukianus ignored Domitus as his eyes rested on the handsome face of Surena. He walked over to my former squire, the pungent smell of his sweating body entering my nostrils. He

223

was perspiring profusely despite being kept in the shade, the great amount of fat that encased every part of his body producing copious amounts of sweat. He licked his lips as he halted before Surena.

'You are a fighter?'

Surena, slightly perturbed by the obvious attention of this fat Roman, just nodded.

'And what is your speciality.'

'*Retiarius.*'

'Ephesus is lucky indeed to have such a handsome gladiator grace its arena,' drooled Ceukianus. 'And the *Retiarius* fights bare chested. How marvellous. I will keep an eye out for you.'

Surena's expression was hardening and I knew that if the Roman boy lover carried on he would probably strike him. I stared at Domitus to get his attention and nodded at Surena. Fortunately he too was aware of the danger.

'Would you like to be introduced to my other fighters, magistrate?'

Ceukianus' rising lust was rudely interrupted. He moved his plump face towards Domitus, his massive double chin wobbling as he did so.

He looked at me with barely disguised disgust.

'This one has a scar on his face. Most unattractive.'

'He's a good fighter, sir,' said Domitus. 'A Thracian.'

'I prefer the *Retiarius*. How much do you charge for a private display?'

Surena's nostrils flared with anger as the *editor* licked his lips.

'We can have a display here, sir, now,' said Domitus.

Ceukianus waved forward a slave holding a towel who used it to dab his porcine face with it.

'No, I am finished here. I would prefer a more intimate setting. Besides, this heat is intolerable. An official from High Priest Kallias will assign you quarters for your stay here during the games.'

He gave Surena a lusting glance. 'There is plenty of time for private amusements.'

With that he waddled across the deck and descended the gangplank to his *lectica*. He broke wind loudly as he bent down to sit on his overstuffed mattress, the slaves remaining stony faced as he disappeared behind a curtain and the litter bearers hoisted his bulk above their shoulders. As he and his entourage disappeared Drenis and Arminius doubled up with laughter.

'The only Romans I have seen of late have been legionaries wanting to kill me,' said Drenis. 'I had forgotten that Italy is also filled with fat, lecherous homosexuals with a penchant for handsome boys.'

Arminius placed an arm around Surena's shoulders. 'If you are a bit more polite you could be going to Rome as a magistrate's plaything.'

Surena was far from amused, though, shaking off Arminius' arm.

'I should have thrown him overboard.'

Drenis feigned horror. 'It is not the magistrate's fault that you are young and pretty.'

'That's right,' said Drenis, 'you should not have enticed him.'

'I did not entice him,' said Surena loudly.

Alcaeus rolled his eyes. 'It is amazing what amuses the minds of children.'

As the morning gave way to afternoon and the sun rose in the sky we were paid a visit from a representative of High Priest Kallias. In stark contrast to the attitude of the Roman officials this man was both friendly and informative. He came in the company of a score of slaves who were to transport our clothes and equipment on two-wheeled handcarts to our quarters.

He asked to speak to the *lanista* of the *Ludus* Palmyra, saying his name was Lysander and that he had been sent by High Priest Kallias to convey the *lanista* and his fighters to the accommodation that had been set aside for them for the duration of the games. Everything about Lysander was big: his round face, full head of curly black hair but most of all his personality. He never stopped smiling and laughing, welcoming Domitus and Gallia and shaking the hand of Athineos. He smiled when he saw the lions and congratulated the captain on bringing them to Ephesus in such a healthy state. He extended a warm welcome to myself, Surena, Drenis and Arminius and wished us good fortune in the days ahead. We took an instant liking to Lysander and felt at ease in his company.

After the slaves had loaded our chests onto the carts Lysander invited us to accompany him to our new home.

'A nice terrace house on the hill near the theatre,' he informed Domitus. He looked at us gladiators. 'I have been informed that your fighters are not what the Romans call "condemned to the games", *lanista?*'

Damnatio ad ludos meant 'condemned to the games' and denoted a criminal who had been given a life sentence in the arena, though usually the sentence would be a short one unless the individual was an accomplished fighter. Those who were under this sentence were not allowed beyond the confines of the *ludus*, as they were often violent criminals who would abscond at the first opportunity, whereas other categories of gladiators, especially those who had volunteered to fight in the arena, were allowed a certain amount of freedom.

'Don't you worry about them,' Domitus told Lysander, 'my boys are all volunteers, freemen who wanted to experience life inside the arena.'

'That's not how I remember my time at Capua,' said Drenis in a hushed tone to Arminius.

'Me neither,' said Arminius, 'I was captured by the Romans after a battle then hauled off to Italy in chains.'

'I'm a free man,' said Surena, 'no one has ever put me in chains.'

'That's because the marshlands where you grew up are too inhospitable for armies to campaign in,' I said.

'Right, then,' announced Domitus, 'let us go to our new home.'

Lysander smiled and Domitus took Gallia's hand as he led her down the gangplank. I was the last to leave the ship, Athineos pulling me aside before I went down the gangplank.

'Now listen, I still think you are engaged in a mad scheme that has no hope of success. I will be staying here for the duration of the games but no longer. But I can leave at any time before that if you come to your senses.'

I offered my hand to him. 'Thank you but no. You should have more faith, Athineos.'

'That is what your slave general, Spartacus, said to me once. And look what happened to him.'

'Hurry up, Nikephorus,' shouted Domitus, 'don't dawdle.'

I hurried down the gangplank and joined the other three 'gladiators'. Behind us the slaves pushed the carts containing our possessions. It took a while to exit the port, which was filled with wagons, dockers loading and unloading goods, slaves on their way to be sold, port officials, sailors and Roman marines. There was also the unusual sight of pilgrims leaving two ships that had just docked, long lines of white-clad men and women either singing prayers or mumbling chants as they shuffled down gangplanks.

'Pilgrims from the mainland,' Lysander informed us, 'visiting the Temple of Artemis.'

'Is it in the city?' asked Gallia.

'No, lady. It is situated just beyond the city walls. It was built on the spot where an ancient temple devoted to the Goddess Cybele was sited.'

'The mother of the gods,' said Alcaeus.

Lysander nodded. 'Yes, sir.'

The great warehouses were filled with wine, olive oil and grain for shipment to Greece and Rome, while pallets stood along the dockside stacked with slabs of marble for shipment to Athens. I had never seen the harbour that supplied Rome with its everyday needs but it cannot have been bigger than the one at Ephesus. Moving through the crush of people and goods we eventually reached Harbour Street, which was the main entrance to the city from the docks. It had obviously been designed to impress visitors because the slabs under our feet were marble and there were marble colonnades on either side of the thoroughfare.

Lysander told us that the street was six hundred yards long and twelve yards wide, with monumental arches along its course and shops on either side along its whole length. He informed us with pride that beneath the marble flagstones were water and sewage channels, the latter carrying the city's waste to the river where it would be carried out to sea. But his moment of supreme pleasure came when he pointed out the street lights positioned along the whole length of Harbour Street.

'At night watchmen light the oil lamps so the street is illuminated for pedestrians and charioteers alike,' said Lysander who was revelling in his position of tour guide. 'This street is but one of the twenty-six others that are paved with marble, though the others are lined with statues rather than street lights.'

'Street lights,' I said in wonderment to Drenis. 'I have never seen such a thing.'

'This place is dripping in wealth. No wonder the Romans wanted it.'

'The same reason they want Parthia,' I said bitterly, 'they would love to control the Silk Road.'

'Why isn't the city called Artemis if the temple was the first building here?' asked Gallia.

'A good question, lady,' replied Lysander. 'But according to myth the city itself was established by the queen of the Amazons, Ephos Hippo, hence the name Ephesus.'

He looked at my wife, her head covered by a *shemagh*. 'Have you heard of the Amazons, lady?'

All eyes turned to Gallia, which was noted by Lysander.

'Vaguely,' she replied.

'They were fearsome women warriors,' said Lysander, 'famed for their courage and mercilessness in battle.'

'They sound most interesting,' remarked Gallia casually.

We continued along Harbour Street, Lysander offering Gallia and Domitus litters to take them to their quarters but they declined. He made no offer to us; clearly the notion that gladiators were at the bottom of the social order had reached Asia. We passed shops selling food, clothes, pottery, gold and silver jewellery, wine and olive oil. Many of the buildings were two-storeyed, the ground floor being a shop and the first floor containing living quarters.

We saw few Roman soldiers, Lysander informing Domitus when pressed that for the most part the governor restricted his men to manning the walls and four gates into the city.

'Of course High Priest Kallias has his own temple guards,' said Lysander, 'who maintain security at the Temple of Artemis and the other temples in the city.'

'How many Roman soldiers are there in Ephesus?' probed Domitus.

'I have heard that there are two cohorts, *lanista*,' replied Lysander, 'plus the marines who when they are not at sea provide harbour security.'

When we reached our accommodation – a large house just below the houses of the rich on the slopes of Korressos Hill – we found a detachment of Roman legionaries waiting for us. The house had been built according to the peristyle school, with a gated entrance in the surrounding wall leading to a two-storey building with a central courtyard, around which were rooms for dining, relaxing and entertaining guests. There were also secure storerooms where the gladiators were expected to sleep under lock and key. The bedrooms were on the second storey. Happily there were no outward-facing windows, which would give us a degree of privacy, though I had reckoned without any guards.

A sour-faced centurion with a red transverse crest spoke first to Lysander and then to Domitus. He pointed his vine cane at us four gladiators.

'All those condemned to the games are to be confined to barracks during the games.'

Domitus smiled at him. 'They are all free men, centurion, and as I have lavished a considerable amount of money on them I would prefer that they stay where I can keep an eye on them. Don't want them getting a knife in the back before the games.'

The centurion examined each of us in turn. 'As you wish. But in that case I am ordered to allocate guards to stand sentry outside your accommodation at all times. And I would advise keeping them locked up at night.'

Domitus jerked a hand at us. 'They are professionals. You won't get any trouble from them.'

The centurion's hard visage cracked a smile. 'It's not them I'm worried about. Many of the locals don't like the idea of the games, reckons it offends their dainty Greek heritage.'

He placed the end of his cane under Lysander's chin. 'Isn't that right, Greek?'

'As you say, sir,' smiled Lysander.

The centurion kept his cane in place. 'That bearded bastard Kallias is itching to incite a riot to prove he's the ruler of Ephesus rather than the governor.'

'I would not know of such things, sir,' said a still smiling Lysander.

'I appreciate the offer of sentries, centurion,' said Domitus. 'I don't want to interrupt you but my wife is tired and eager to rest after her journey.'

The centurion took his cane away from Lysander's chin. 'Of course. Well, I hope your stay here is a profitable one. The papers we received from the Greek priests said you are from Palmyra.'

'That's right,' smiled Domitus.

The centurion stared at him. 'You don't look eastern.'

Domitus removed his *shemagh*. 'Me? No, I'm Roman through and through.'

The centurion relaxed instantly. 'Thank Jupiter for that. I've had a gutful of these eastern types. I spent three years in Syria marching across never-ending deserts.'

'Yes,' said Domitus, 'the area can be taxing.'

The centurion tucked his cane under his arm. 'I remember once we got caught in a sandstorm that lasted for days. Gave us a right battering. And then immediately after we came face-to-face with a Parthian king and his army.'

Domitus looked earnestly at him. 'Really, what king?'

The centurion thought for a moment. 'He's the ruler of a city on the Euphrates. King Pacorus, that's it. Palmyra is near Dura, isn't it?'

'It is.'

'Then you must know this Pacorus,' said the centurion

Domitus nodded. 'I have heard of him, yes.'

'Well, him and Pompey came to an agreement so there was no fighting. Strangest thing was, this Pacorus has soldiers armed and equipped like our own, that and thousands of horsemen. Rumour has it that he will soon be a client king of Rome.'

'He must be a formidable opponent,' said Domitus.

The centurion looked disparagingly at Lysander. 'Not really. You know what these eastern types are like, all piss and wind.'

He raised his cane to the side of his helmet in salute.

'I wish you good day, *lanista*.'

He marched away with six of his men, leaving another half dozen behind to guard the house. Lysander barked at the slaves to get our possessions into the house. When they had deposited the clothes in the rooms on the second storey and our weapons and armour in the storerooms and departed we took off our outer robes and relaxed on the daybeds. Lysander stayed and organised the serving of drinks and refreshments, slaves bringing jugs of wine and water from the kitchens and others serving us bread, honey, cheese, figs and peaches.

'You may leave us,' Domitus said to Lysander.

Lysander bowed, 'Yes, *lanista*. As the games are in two days' time perhaps you would like to visit the Temple of Artemis tomorrow.'

Domitus looked at Gallia, who nodded. 'That would be most agreeable.'

'The slaves of the household will attend to your needs, *lanista*,' said Lysander. 'If anything is remiss please send one to find me at the *agora*.'

He bowed once more and left leaving four slaves standing around the painted walls like statues, staring ahead. Domitus dismissed them all. Gallia took off her *shemagh* and shook her hair free and then removed her black robe. She removed her bow and the quiver of silver arrows which had been slung across her shoulders. We helped ourselves to food and wine. Ephesus had impressed us all, especially Alcaeus who was proud that a Greek city should inspire such awe. As we filled our bellies he told us that the Temple of Artemis would add to our wonderment, being one of the wonders of the known world.

'The garrison is not large for a city this size,' said Domitus. 'Two cohorts plus marines to control tens of thousands of potential trouble makers.'

'As long as the Romans do not commit sacrilegious acts against the Goddess Artemis and Her servants they risk no uprising,' said Alcaeus. 'In any case the city was not conquered but bequeathed to Rome by King Pergamon many years ago.'

'This high priest, Kallias,' I said, 'appears to wield great power.'

Alcaeus cut a slice of apricot. 'He is a king in all but name, wielding great spiritual and financial power. The bank of the Temple of Artemis is extremely rich.'

'What's a bank?' asked Surena, heaping a great chunk of cheese into his mouth.

'Where people can store their money safely,' answered Alcaeus, 'in addition to asking for loans to finance their business ventures. But it is rumoured that the temple treasury is also full of donations given by pilgrims.'

'Religion is very profitable,' remarked Domitus.

'Well,' I said, 'tomorrow we will visit this temple ourselves and see if what Alcaeus has been telling us these past few weeks has been an exaggeration.'

It was not.

Located a mile to the west of the city, we decided to walk from our quarters and thence to the temple, despite Lysander's' pleadings for Domitus and Gallia to be carried on litters. He gave the rest of us little attention as we followed the *lanista*, his wife and Alcaeus, not only answering questions but also asking them. He enquired about Palmyra, the gladiator school and Roman Syria. Domitus answered vaguely and Gallia, her body and face once more covered, said nothing.

'He asks a lot of questions,' Drenis said to me as we walked through the city's western gates in the company of hundreds of pilgrims.

I shrugged. 'He's friendly, that's all.'

'Too friendly for a slave,' said Arminius. 'Anyone who smiles as much as he does is up to something.'

I was having none of it. 'You two are too suspicious. Remember he's a Greek, not a Roman.'

As we neared the temple the throng of pilgrims swelled. Most were dressed in simple tunics and robes, many had flowers in their hair and others were chanting prayers or singing to the heavens with arms raised.

'It can get very boisterous,' said a smiling Lysander as we nearer the temple.

We all stopped and stood in awe when we first clapped eyes on the sanctuary, for if anything Alcaeus had understated its magnificence. It stood on a huge stone platform that had steps on all four sides. Every one of its columns was fashioned from white marble, the lower portions of which were carved with mythical figures in high relief.

'I never knew there was so much marble in the world,' uttered an awed Drenis.

As we shuffled forward among the crowd Lysander informed us that the temple measured one hundred and fifty yards long and seventy-five yards wide. Two great marble statues of the Goddess Artemis kneeling shooting a bow were mounted on stone plinths immediately in front of the temple. The arched roof, sixty feet above us, comprised marble pediments with carved figurines and carved marble roof tiles.

Inside the temple light was provided by fires that burned on the top of white stone bases. There were temple guards standing at the entrance and in front of the columns. Like most of Ephesus they presented an image of wealth, their bronze helmets adorned with white plumes and their torsos protected by bronze scale armour cuirasses. Their round shields were painted white and carried a silver arrow and bow motif – the symbol of Artemis. Like my own foot soldiers they wore white tunics and sandals on their feet, their weapons comprising a short spear with a leaf-shaped blade and a short sword in a scabbard. The latter was the *xiphos*, a Greek sword with a double-edged blade around two feet in length.

'They certainly look pretty,' Domitus said to me as he looked at a pair of guards. 'No expense spared with regards to their weapons and armour.'

'This city is overflowing with wealth,' I replied.

Lysander ushered us towards the centre of the temple where a huge statue of the goddess stood. It was ringed by guards to prevent anyone getting too close, and white-robed young women with oiled hair, bare arms and nothing on their feet were burning incense at stations around the goddess. There was a huge press of people around it and so we stayed at the rear of the crowd as others shuffled past to get nearer the statue. The pungent smell of burning frankincense and myrrh drifted into my nostrils as the beautiful women burnt more incense at the foot of the statue. It was a tall marble structure decorated with gold, silver and ebony. The goddess was depicted wearing a long dress carved with images of animals and a shawl made of bees. Her arms were outstretched and around her body were rows of breasts to symbolise her role as the goddess of fertility. On her head was a tall headdress that made the statue appear huge. But then everything about this temple was huge, from its tall columns to the great doors made of cypress and the never-ending ceiling made of cedar. Beyond the statue were lines of worshippers filing into another chamber. I nudged Domitus and pointed to them. He asked Lysander what they were doing.

'They are worshippers donating gifts to the goddess, *lanista*.'

'Quiet,' hissed a guard behind us, 'Hippo comes.'

There was a blast of trumpets and then a low, melodious beating of drums to herald the arrival of. Of whom?

'The high priestess,' whispered Lysander, bowing his head.

The hall grew silent as two guards preceded a line of young priestesses, all beautiful and bare foot like the ones feeding the incense burners. At their head was a striking woman with painted black eyebrows, full lips and piercing brown eyes. Slim, of medium height, she glided across the marble tiles, a silver necklace around her slender neck that nestled between her shapely breasts, silver hanging from her ears and more silver on her fingers, the metal a sharp contrast to her dark olive skin. She seemed very young for a high priestess.

I felt a blow on my left arm and turned to see a temple guard holding his spear shaft out towards me. 'I said head down. Show some respect.'

Hippo and her entourage passed and headed towards the main entrance. Muted voices returned to the chamber with her departure and the crowd relaxed. I turned to the guard.

'Touch me again and I will break that spear over your head.'

He levelled the spear. 'Have a care, pilgrim, I would not wish to spill your blood in the goddess' presence.'

Domitus was suddenly between us, holding his hands up to the guard.

'Apologies. He's a heathen from the East who knows no manners. He's here to fight in the games.'

The guard eyed me for a few seconds before returning his spear to the vertical position. 'Hopefully he will be killed on the first day, Artemis willing.'

Domitus laughed. 'He probably will be.'

He turned to me. 'Avert your eyes, Nikephorus. Show some respect.'

He bundled me away. 'Not a good idea provoking a fight in one of the most famous temples in the world that is full of worshippers.'

'I object to being prodded by a temple guard.'

'Stop thinking like a king and more like a gladiator,' he told me.

I caught Lysander's eye and he smiled at me. We moved past the statue towards the rear of the temple where more guards stood sentry outside the offices of the high priest and his lesser priests. Gallia stopped at one of the four bronze statues of Amazons mounted on stone plinths, each one showing a fierce female warrior, their right breasts missing, either shooting a bow or wielding a spear or sword. The removal of the breast facilitated the shooting of a bow, or so Lysander informed us. I stood on the opposite side of the plinth to Domitus and Gallia, staring at my wife's eyes. She saw me and nodded her head ever so slightly, her eyes full of fire.

Outside the temple, just beyond the steps along the sides of the building, were a host of market stalls selling ceramic, ivory and metal ornaments. Guards ambled around among the pilgrims who appeared to be spending drachmas freely at the stalls.

'These traders must have paid a hefty price to pitch their stalls here,' Domitus said to Lysander.

The latter shook his head. 'All these traders are employed by the office of the high priest, *lanista*, and all the profits go towards the upkeep of his position and the maintenance of the temple.'

We arrived at a stall staffed by silversmiths putting the finishing touches to solid silver replicas of the statue of Artemis that stood in the temple. Around six inches high they were exact reproductions and looked exquisite. They also commanded a high price that made Domitus baulk when he enquired the cost of one. He hastily put it down.

'Buy it,' said Gallia.

'They are beautiful pieces,' smiled Lysander. 'Worthy of the house of a rich *lanista*.'

Domitus turned to Gallia and then looked at me. Lysander's eyes darted between us but he said nothing. Domitus reached into the leather pouch hanging from his belt and took out a handful of money. He looked at the coins in the palm of his hand, shook his head and handed them to the silversmith, who handed him the statuette. He took it and passed it to Gallia. She was delighted by it.

Other stalls sold food and so Domitus purchased fruit, cured meat, bread and fruit juice and Lysander led us to benches positioned beneath shades where we could eat, drink and rest our legs. As we sat with hundreds of others who were partaking of refreshments I noticed dozens of tents of various sizes pitched around the temple, at least a hundred paces from the temple steps. I pointed them out to Domitus who asked Lysander if they belonged to pilgrims.

'Some do, *lanista*, but others are where those seeking sanctuary live. An ancient law of the temple welcomes all those seeking sanctuary. The city authorities are not allowed to touch anyone within the limits of the temple.'

Domitus stood and peered left and right. 'Where are the temple limits?'

'They are not marked, *lanista*,' answered Lysander. 'According to our ancient laws they are determined by the range of an arrow shot from the top of the temple steps.'

I saw a bare-footed man in his early twenties, dressed in a dirty beige tunic, talking to Hippo. The latter had appeared aloof and cold in the temple but was now smiling as she conversed with the swarthy individual.

'They look to be on friendly terms,' I said to Domitus.

'Who is the priestess talking to? Domitus asked Lysander.

He frowned. 'That is Cleon, *lanista*, a notorious criminal and rabble-rouser. He led an insurrection against the Romans and after it was crushed sought sanctuary here at the temple.'

'And the Romans let him live?' Domitus was astounded.

'They have little choice, *lanista*. To violate the sanctuary would incite a riot, if not a full-scale rebellion.' Lysander suddenly remembered to whom he was talking. 'I meant no offence, sir.'

Domitus shook a hand at him. 'No offence taken. The priestess seems to be on good terms with the rabble-rouser.'

Lysander looked at Hippo. 'The priestess' heart is filled with nothing but affection for the followers of the goddess, *lanista*. She pities Cleon.'

Hippo's face broke into a beautiful smile. 'I wouldn't mind her showering some of her pity over me,' said Domitus.

'Where's this High Priest Kallias, I wonder?' I mused to Domitus.

'Probably enjoying the affection of one of those young priestesses,' he joked. 'Lysander, where's the high priest?'

'After the early morning ritual he spends his time in the city dealing with administrative matters, *lanista*,' replied Lysander.

As we sat eating I continued to observe Cleon and Hippo talking. I noticed the presence of other men milling around her, most like him in their twenties, and all fit and strong. They did not look like pilgrims and I assumed they were Cleon's followers. I wondered how many of the thousands of people camped around the temple were criminals or rebels. It seemed a very strange state of affairs. Normally the Romans would have rounded them up and either crucified them or condemned them to the mines. It must have irked the governor enormously that so many enemies of Rome were camped just beyond the city walls and untouchable. As I finished my apricot Hippo gave Cleon a final smile and then walked back to the temple escorted by four guards.

When we had satisfied our appetites we walked back to the city, not an inch to spare on the road from the temple to the city gates so many pilgrims were there. The sun was now high in a clear sky and the temperature was rising rapidly, and the stench of sweating humans was quite pungent, made worse by the absence of any breeze. The heat must have made Alcaeus ill tempered because he began to berate Domitus.

'You really are a most disrespectful individual at times, Domitus. Anyone with an ounce of intelligence knows that high priestesses of Greek temples are virgins who are chosen for their piety and purity.'

'I never said they weren't,' shrugged Domitus.

'So to suggest that High Priestess Hippo has any amorous thoughts towards that young man in the temple grounds is not only insensitive but also sacrilege.'

Domitus rolled his eyes. 'Yes, Alcaeus, whatever you say.'

Lysander said nothing but he seemed surprised that Alcaeus should speak to his master thus. When we reached the city gates Alcaeus declared that he was going to visit the offices of the guild of physicians where he would make a sacrifice to Asklepios, the God of Healing, in the shrine behind the guild's offices. He looked at me as he stated this, his ill humour making him forget that I was but a lowly gladiator. Lysander was taken aback but I cast my head down and said nothing.

'If that is agreeable to you, *lanista*,' said Alcaeus hurriedly.

Domitus gave his consent and Alcaeus asked Lysander where the guild of physicians was located, being told that their offices were to the rear of the *agora*. After Lysander had given him directions he wandered off and we continued our journey back to our accommodation. When we arrived at the house, which was still guarded by Roman legionaries, Lysander took his leave, saying he had urgent business at the high priest's office. The head slave of the household reported to Domitus that a letter was waiting for him. We filed into the library as our *lanista* opened the scroll and read it.

We took off our black robes and relaxed in chairs as Domitus informed us of its contents. Slaves brought wine and fruit juice from the kitchens and served us drinks.

Domitus held up the scroll. 'Well, this is it. A note from the governor's office. The games begin tomorrow. Tonight, though, he invites all gladiators to the *cena libera*.'

'What's that?' asked Gallia as she admired her statuette of Artemis.

'A feast that is always held on the eve of the games,' Domitus told her.

'Where both gladiators and the condemned eat together,' added Drenis, 'though one could argue that all those eating are condemned in one way or another.'

'How macabre,' said Gallia.

'Everything about gladiatorial games is about spectacle, Gallia,' reflected Arminius. 'It is bloody theatre from beginning to end.'

'This is most excellent,' I said. 'At long last I can meet Burebista and tell him of our plans.'

'Which are?' enquired Domitus.

'That we intend to rescue him, Domitus.'

'And have you worked out the plan's specifics?' he asked.

I took a drink of wine. 'I will know that after I have talked to him.'

'So you are going to go through with it, then?' said Drenis.

'Of course,' I replied, 'did you expect me not to?'

He held out his cup to a slave holding a jug of wine. 'I thought we might get here and rescue Burebista before we marched onto the sand.'

The slave filled his cup and he stood, as did Arminius. They both held out their drinking vessels to me.

'Then, Pacorus, let us eat and drink, for tomorrow we die.'

I went in the company of Surena, Drenis and Arminius to the feast, all of us wearing simple tunics, sandals and leather belts. Domitus and Gallia remained at the house, the former checking our weapons and equipment that we would be using the next day. Gallia wanted to accompany me but Lysander, who had returned from his pressing business, informed her that adult women were banned from the *prytaneion* where the feast would take place.

The night was warm and the streets were full of people. Lysander was his usual talkative, informative self, telling us that the *prytaneion* was one of the most important civic structures in Ephesus. It was a temple-like building where religious ceremonies, official receptions and banquets were held. It was also the location of the city's sacred fire, which was kept continually alight to honour the gods who first bequeathed fire to humans.

When we arrived at the *prytaneion* we found it ringed by Roman soldiers, reinforced by a detachment of ten archers who stood to one side of the entrance. I was surprised to see many civilians, both men and women, milling around.

'They are encouraged to see and perhaps speak to the gladiators before they enter the hall,' Lysander said to me. 'In this way the governor hopes that word of the games will spread so there are no empty seats.'

'The games are popular?'

He looked disappointed. 'They are, though many of the Greek citizens in the city object to the spilling of blood in the Great Theatre.'

'And you?'

'I do as I am told,' he replied guardedly. 'You speak Greek very well for a slave who is not Greek.'

'I am not a slave,' I said. 'I am a free man.'

'Ah, yes, I forgot. My apologies.'

We reported to the duty centurion standing beside a clerk who carried a record of all the gladiator schools and their fighters. We were then checked for weapons, for dozens of potentially intoxicated gladiators could be an incendiary situation.

'I will wait for you here,' Lysander told us as we walked through the columns of the Doric courtyard that fronted the hall. The courtyard itself was surrounded on three sides by a colonnade and paved with a mosaic depicting the shields of Amazons against a floral background.

'Gallia would love this,' I remarked.

'As she will hate watching you in the arena,' said Drenis.

Surena rubbed his hands. 'It is very generous of the governor to lay on a feast for us.'

'Kallias is paying for the games,' I told him, 'not the governor.'

'More to the point,' Arminius said to Surena. 'Do not eat or drink excessively. You don't want a thick head.'

We neared the open doors of the hall and heard a great noise coming from its interior.

'It seems like many are enjoying themselves,' said Surena.

'The *noxi*,' said Drenis darkly.

'Who?' asked Surena.

'The *noxi ad gladium damnati*, those condemned to the games,' answered Arminius. 'Criminals, slaves and captured soldiers mostly, who will all die in the arena. If you are one you want to enjoy yourself as much as possible on what may be your last evening in this world.'

And enjoying themselves they were. The benches were filled with men stuffing their faces with food piled high on the tables before them. Slaves were ferrying huge quantities of wine to the thirsty, greedy throng, men already drunk shouting and cheering and fondling young slave girls who tried to place jugs on tables without being molested or having their clothes ripped off. Legionaries armed with swords stood around the walls of the hall and centurions paced up and down, occasionally striking one of the condemned with his vine cane.

But not all were drinking and eating to excess. At some tables groups of athletic, quiet men were either talking in hushed tones or keeping their own counsel, rarely looking up as they picked at their food. Drenis pointed to them.

'They are the gladiators.'

'Very well,' I said, 'let's find Burebista.'

Arminius looked around at the scene of riotous excess with its small islands of quiet sobriety.

'This takes me back. Never thought I would be at a *cena libera* again.'

'Feeling old, Arminius? Drenis teased him.

'Feeling hungry,' he answered.

'Me too,' said Surena, rubbing his hands. 'Let's find a bench.'

'You two go with him, ' I ordered, 'I will look for Burebista.'

Surena had already seated himself beside a group of drunken Greeks, who immediately filled a cup with wine and handed it him.

'And make sure he doesn't get drunk,' I told Drenis and Arminius.

I walked slowly between the benches where upwards of five hundred people were seated. The hall reeked of roast meat, wine and human odour, for many of these men had been rotting in jails prior to their 'performance' in the arena tomorrow and they stank. At least the gladiators presented a more tidy appearance, most dressed in loose-fitting tunics so their broad shoulders and thick, muscular arms would not be constrained. Looking at them I was taken back to Italy, to the army of many races that had fought under Spartacus. There were fair-skinned Gauls and Germans, olive-skinned Spaniards, swarthy Thracians and sinewy Armenians. There were also Egyptians and Nubians, their skin as dark as black marble and their heads shaved. All gathered in this great city to die for Roman entertainment.

There was a great roar as a female slave was dragged to the floor by a group of filthy criminals and stripped naked. She was held down, her legs forced apart, as one of the wretched convicts lifted his tunic and sank to his knees, ready to rape her. In an instant a centurion was behind him and knocked him unconscious with his cane, Outraged, his convict companions forgot about the naked girl and jumped to their feet. But the centurion drew his *gladius* and sliced open the guts of the nearest brigand, who looked surprised, and then horrified as he clutched at his belly that was pumping blood. He looked with pleading eyes at the centurion before sinking to the floor and lying there, his lifeblood oozing onto the sacred mosaic. The others looked at him, then at the centurion, and shuffled meekly back to their seats.

'Show's over,' barked the centurion as he wiped his sword on the tunic of the dying man and ordered other slaves to take him away.

'Where should we take him, *dominus*?' asked one of the slaves, quivering with fear.

'To the city rubbish dump,' came the reply.

Most of those enjoying the festivities did not even notice this little drama as the hall echoed to the sound of cheers and raised voices demanding more wine. Some guests, previously half-starved or badly beaten, had either passed out or were vomiting violently, their stomachs unable to cope with the great quantities of food and drink shoved into them. The fetid stench of piles of vomit added to the unique aroma that now filled the hall.

I continued on my way, occasionally catching the attention of a steely faced gladiator who held my gaze with pitiless eyes before returning to his meal. I walked towards the far end of the hall and my heart soared as I caught sight of him. He still looked fierce, a little older of course, his face clean shaven and his hair shoulder length in homage to his ancestry.

But he looked fit and well as he picked over slices of pomegranate. He was dressed in an immaculate red tunic with white stripes down either side. He sat apart from the other nine gladiators at his bench but all of them appeared sober and reflective, mentally apart from the debauchery around them.

I stood on the other side of the bench where Burebista sat with his head down, slowly picking up pieces of pomegranate to eat.

'Is this space free, friend?' I asked.

'I'm not your friend,' he said without looking up.

'There was a time when you regarded me as one, Burebista.'

He looked up, his visage wearing a countenance of annoyance. It changed in an instant when he recognised me. He jumped up.

'Lord, is it you? Are you a vision sent by Zalmoxis or are you real?'

Zalmoxis was the chief god that the Dacians worshipped.

I walked around the end of the bench and held out my arm.

'I am very real, my friend.'

He locked me in an embrace. When he released me there were tears in his eyes, and in truth in mine. I thanked Shamash that He had granted me this moment of pure joy.

'Sit, lord, sit.'

He laughed and held his head in his hands. 'I cannot believe that it is you and you are here. What divine intervention brings you to Ephesus?'

'To liberate you, Burebista. To free you as our lord would have desired, even though he died in Italy.'

Burebista waved over a slave and ordered her to bring a cup for me and fill it with wine.

'I have never forgotten Spartacus, lord. I have often thought that if I kept myself alive then his memory would still live. Until now I believed that I was the only member of the army of Spartacus still alive.'

'Not the only one, Burebista. There are others.'

The slave returned with a cup and another in tow with a jug of wine. As she poured it I began to tell Burebista about the flight of the Companions from Italy, my return to Parthia,

243

being given the crown of Dura and the subsequent civil war in Parthia. Of how Gallia was now Queen of Dura and Domitus the commander of its army and how a Cretan sea captain had travelled to my city to inform me that he would be fighting in the arena at Ephesus. He in turn told me how he had been captured after the breakout at Rhegium but had been expected to die from his wounds. However, Crassus had taken a personal interest in his welfare and assigned him expert medical care.

'I spent a year being nursed back to health, lord, during which time the Appian Way was decorated with the bodies of six thousand members of Spartacus' army nailed to crosses. They were left to rot as an example of what happens to those who challenge Rome's rule.

'I expected the same punishment but when I had fully recovered I was sold as a gladiator to the *Ludus* Capua.' He looked at the other nine men sat at the table. 'These men are from the same school, the best of our lanista's fighters, personally chosen by him to grace Ephesus' arena.'

He pushed another slice of pomegranate into his mouth and chewed slowly.

'And now I fight as a horseman in mockery of my time with Spartacus, a living reminder to spectators that Rome defeated its greatest threat.'

I laid a hand on his arm. 'Your time of torment is at an end, my friend.'

'What's this? Is this your Greek lover, Burebista?'

I heard the deep, mocking voice behind me and turned to see a large brute with a wild moustache, even wilder long hair and a round, pale face. I saw the swirling blue tattoos decorating his flesh, a gold torc around his neck and I was transported back to Italy. He was big, bold and had fire in his eyes and for a moment I thought that Crixus had returned from the dead.

'Watch your words, Acco,' hissed Burebista, 'I would not wish to spill your blood before we begin the games and send your soul to whatever black abyss the Gauls call hell.'

The Gaul roared with laughter. 'The day a Dacian can beat me is the day I will slit my own throat.'

I stood slowly as the Gaul turned his attention to me.

'What's your story?'

244

He spoke in Latin with an accent similar to Gallia's. He exuded confidence and disdain.

'None of your business, Gaul,' I answered.

'You should have a care, Acco,' said Burebista, 'this is Pac...'

'My name is Nikephorus,' I interrupted hurriedly, 'and I am a Parthian.'

He studied me for a few seconds, his eyes settling on the scar on my cheek.

'I've heard that the Parthians fight on horseback so they can run away quickly in battle. Real men fight on foot so they can get close to their enemies.'

I sighed. I had heard it all many times before from Crixus and his boorish companions. I was about to reply when Drenis, Arminius and Surena appeared behind Acco.

'Do we have a problem,' enquired Drenis calmly.

Acco spun round to face them as the gladiators at the table looked up and began to take an interest in what was happening. Acco looked at the Thracian with the short-cropped hair and facial scars.

'You're not a Parthian,' he said.

'Thracian,' growled Drenis.

'And I am Surena of the Ma'adan, barbarian,' announced my former squire, staring hatefully at Acco and folding his thick arms across his chest.

'Am I supposed to be impressed?' asked Acco.

'You will be,' sneered Surena.

'He's just a boy,' said one of the gladiators at the table, 'leave him alone. Acco.'

Surena switched his attention to the man who had spoken, glaring at him.

'Come here and say that to my face, *slave*, and I will cut out your tongue.'

The gladiator jumped up but I held out an arm.

'He meant no offence. Surena, be quiet.' I looked at Drenis and Arminius. 'Get him out of here. It's fine.'

Drenis nodded towards Burebista. 'Is that him?'

'It is,' I replied.

'Just a minute,' said Acco, pointing at Surena. 'I haven't finished with him.'

'Yes you have, Gaul,' I stated.

Two other gladiators at the table and Burebista stood as Drenis and Arminius squared up to Acco. The air was tingling with the threat of impending violence.

'You lot sit down,' ordered a centurion who appeared next to Burebista, 'save your fighting for the arena where you belong.'

Acco now had a new target to try his intimidation on. 'Why don't you go away before I shove that cane up your arse?'

The centurion tucked his cane in his belt and ordered over four legionaries before drawing his sword. Now all the gladiators at the table rose to their feet. Surena walked forward to stand beside me.

'We've beaten Romans before, lord.'

'Shut up!' I ordered as Acco squared up to the centurion, both unyielding in their stares. The legionaries also drew their swords as they closed behind their commander. The other gladiators slowly moved to stand on the flank of the legionaries, unconcerned that they were unarmed. A sudden blast of trumpets interrupted the stand-off, gladiators and Roman soldiers alike turning their attention to the source of the sound. I too looked round to see the obese figure of Timini Ceukianus flanked by two centurions and standing before six trumpeters and a small phalanx of legionaries. The din in the hall died down as all eyes turned to stare at the fat Roman. Ceukianus waited until there was silence, or at least a modicum of quiet interrupted only by men throwing up, belching and talking in inebriated gibberish.

'Tomorrow,' he began, 'the games begin and each of you have a part to play in ensuring that they are a success. As you partake of this lavish feast remember that it is Rome that has paid such hospitality, that it is Rome that allows you to live and that you are condemned men because you committed crimes against Rome.

'Though you are all from different parts of the world that world belongs to Rome. It has always been so and will always be so. No race can stand against Rome much less a group of condemned men. So eat and drink well and face your fate like men, not animals. In this way you will pay for your crimes in this life and save your souls for the next.'

He turned and signalled to the trumpeters, who sounded their instruments and shook the hall with their blasts. Then the magistrate with a large double chin and podgy, effeminate fingers waddled from the hall, followed by his escort. Within seconds of his departure the crowd's boisterousness returned as the banquet's attendees, taking Ceukianus' words to heart, indulged themselves even more.

Acco, bored, had wandered off, the gladiators had returned to their seats and the centurion and his men continued to patrol the crowd. Burebista grinned and indicated to Drenis and Arminius that they should sit with me. I grabbed Surena's tunic and pulled him down beside me.

'You carry on like that, boy,' Burebista said to him, 'and you will not see the morning.'

He nodded at the seated gladiators at the other end of the table.

'They are the finest gladiators in Capua whose swords have despatched many young fools like you.'

Surena looked unimpressed but remained quiet.

'So,' I said to Burebista, 'how do we get you out of here?'

He shook his head. 'You don't, lord. I am condemned to the games, which means I am either locked up or under guard at all times.'

'Why don't we create a diversion here?' suggested Arminius. 'Pacorus can get you out while the guards are distracted.'

'There is a ship waiting for us in the harbour,' I said.

Burebista's head dropped. 'If I escape then my wife will be executed.'

'Your wife?' I said.

'Her name is Anca and she is a slave in the *ludus*. We have been married for over a year.'

'She is in Italy?' asked Drenis.

Burebista shook his head. 'She was allowed to come to Ephesus with me, to ensure that I perform well in the arena and also as a reminder of the lanista's hold over me. So you see escape is quite impossible.'

'We can rescue you both,' stated Surena boldly.

Burebista leaned back and examined the long-haired young man with broad shoulders and clean-shaven face.

247

'You are either a fool or the bravest person in Ephesus,' he said.

'He's a fool,' offered Drenis.

I heard the sickening sound of a limb being broken and turned to see Acco shattering the arm of a poor unfortunate who had picked a fight with him. The man began screaming and thrashing around until Acco knocked him unconscious and roared with triumph.

'Acco is a famous gladiator from Rome,' said Burebista, 'who won his freedom and who has been tempted out of retirement by a large appearance fee.'

'He reminds me of Crixus,' I said. 'A tower of brute strength and aggression.'

'Who's Crixus?' asked Surena.

'Another beast from Gaul,' Arminius told him. 'He was a close friend of Pacorus.'

'Really?' said Surena.

'No, not really,' I answered.

'I have fought in the same arena as him,' continued Burebista. 'He's a man who lives, eats, breathes and sleeps combat. He fights with two swords.'

'A *Dimachaerus*,' said Drenis.

Burebista nodded. 'A very dangerous one.'

'I will work out how to get you and your wife out of here, Burebista,' I said. 'That I promise.'

'You did well to get in here,' he said to us all. 'Masquerading as gladiators was very clever.'

Drenis ran a hand over his scalp. 'We are not masquerading as gladiators, Burebista.' He pointed at me. 'Pacorus decided that it would be a good idea to infiltrate the games here as real gladiators. We will be appearing with you in the arena tomorrow.'

Burebista was wide-eyed with disbelief. 'Only fools or mad men volunteer to fight in the arena.'

Arminius held out a hand to me. 'Can I introduce you to King Pacorus of Dura, famous warlord, dreamer and regarded by many around this table as the biggest fool east of Ephesus.'

Chapter 9

None of us drank or ate to excess at the banquet, especially Surena who was under the watchful eyes of Drenis and Arminius, and so we left the festivities in a sober state. But I was feeling euphoric. Burebista was alive and I was convinced that we could save him and his wife. Admittedly the details had yet to be worked out but I believed that the gods were on our side and things would turn out to our advantage.

'Every man who enters the arena believes that the gods are on his side, Pacorus,' said Drenis as we relaxed after Lysander had shown us the way home. 'And most end up dead.'

I paced up and down the room, my body tingling with excitement. 'Ever since Athineos told me that Burebista was here I have believed that the gods wanted me to come here, Drenis, and nothing that has happened to date has convinced me otherwise.'

Gallia, her hair loose around her shoulders, was confused. 'How can a gladiator, a slave, be allowed to marry?'

'Top gladiators are too lucrative for their owner to be allowed to die needlessly as a result of too many fights,' Arminius told her. 'Burebista might only fight four or five times a year, perhaps less, so there's plenty of time for him to marry. Spartacus was married, if you remember. Besides the *lanista* will want to keep him happy, so allowing him to marry is a sensible policy.'

'Makes our task more difficult, though,' remarked Domitus.

Lysander appeared with a jug of wine from the kitchens. I turned to him.

'Lysander, where is the location of the accommodation holding the gladiators from the *Ludus* Capua?'

He looked in confusion at me and then at Domitus, the latter realising I had made a mistake.

'That's enough, Nikephorus,' snapped Domitus, 'you forget yourself.'

'My apologies, *dominus*,' I said meekly.

'Lysander,' said Domitus, 'I would like to know where the gladiators from Capua are accommodated so I can pay my compliments to my fellow *lanista*.'

'I shall find out for you, sir,' replied Lysander.

Domitus allowed the Greek slave to fill our silver cups and then waved him out of the room. He dismissed the other two slaves who had been standing immobile near the doors and closed it.

'You must be more careful, Pacorus,' Alcaeus admonished me, 'we are not at Dura.'

'He's just a slave,' sneered Surena.

Alcaeus turned on him. 'Don't be a fool. Slaves know everything that goes on in a household and they gossip more than old women in the market place.'

'Even if we know where Burebista and his wife are located,' said Drenis, 'we still have to get them out of their quarters, which are no doubt guarded as ours are.'

'I have heard that an especially brave gladiator can be awarded his freedom in the arena,' said Surena, 'by being given a wooden sword.'

Arminius nodded. 'It's called a *rudis*.'

'Perhaps Burebista can win his freedom, then,' suggested Surena, 'and leave Ephesus a free man.'

'Except that he is dangerous criminal condemned to the games,' said Drenis, 'which means that he can never be given his freedom. His fate is to be a gladiator until he is finally killed in the arena.'

Gallia curled her top lip. 'How typical of the Romans to think of such a cruel fate.'

Domitus shrugged. 'Burebista was one of the commanders of the Spartacus rebellion. Rome never forgets its enemies so Burebista will never be given his freedom. It would set a bad precedent.'

'It doesn't matter,' I said. 'If we know where he and his wife are being kept we can rescue them. We shoot down the guards and any gladiators that offer resistance and then escape on board Athineos' ship.'

'Or,' offered Domitus, 'we could infiltrate the *Ludus* Capua and smuggle them both out without alerting the guards, thus giving us a greater chance of getting to the harbour and aboard Athineos' vessel.'

I sat down beside Gallia. 'I will decide on the exact strategy tomorrow, after the games. But whatever happens we will make our move tomorrow evening.'

I felt very pleased with myself but Alcaeus suddenly stood, his cheeks flushed and his eyes bulging.

'Are you mad, Pacorus? Have you all taken leave of your senses?'

I looked at Gallia who merely shrugged, while Drenis and Arminius looked bemused. Now Alcaeus began pacing.

'This afternoon I made a sacrifice to Asklepios.'

'Who?' said Surena, who obviously had not been listening to the doctor earlier in the day.

Alcaeus glowered at him. 'The God of Healing, obviously. After prayers at the sanctuary the priest sacrificed a pair of hens that I had purchased. When he killed the second one blood spurted out in all directions, including on his robe. He told me that he had never seen such an effusion of blood and that it was an omen of bloody days.'

He pointed at me. 'It is a sign that Ephesus will see much blood in the coming days.'

'Hardly an omen, doctor,' remarked Domitus casually, 'seeing as the games are about to begin.'

Alcaeus regarded him coldly. 'I asked Asklepios to give me a sign regarding our group only, not the games in general. My blood ran cold when the priest interpreted the omens.

'So I ask you, Pacorus. I beg you,' his voice was loud and laced with emotion, 'abandon this insane project. Let us leave Ephesus tonight and return to Dura. Burebista is meant to be here, in the arena as a gladiator. It is his destiny; it is not yours.'

I stood and walked over to him, placing a hand on his shoulder.

'I cannot do that, my friend.'

Alcaeus went to bed in a bad mood but as I lay beside Gallia I was excited not only because I had spoken to Burebista but also about the prospect of fighting in the arena. I lay on my side and began stroking the soft skin of my wife. Gallia turned to face me.

'It will be hard for me to watch you on the sand,' she said.

I traced a finger along her cheek. 'Alcaeus was wrong. It is my destiny to follow in Spartacus' footsteps.'

I let my hand follow the contours of her lithe body, caressing her breast and continuing on down to her buttocks. I kissed her tenderly on the mouth and moved my hand towards her inner thigh. She grabbed my wrist.

'Not tonight, Thracian. You must conserve your strength.'

As per usual I awoke before dawn, thin shafts of sunlight lancing through the closed wooden shutters beyond which was the small balcony that overlooked the courtyard. Already slaves were sweeping it as I sat on the edge of the bed and pulled on my leggings and tunic. I looked under the bed and checked my *spatha* in its scabbard was still there. Of course it was, but old habits die hard. Mine and Gallia's bows were in their cases on the chairs by the table, Gallia's quiver of silver arrows beside our others carrying ordinary missiles underneath the chairs. Our bedroom was like a small armoury.

Gallia opened her eyes and began to pull on her clothes.

'I hate covering my head and face,' she complained.

'We don't want to draw attention to ourselves, you know that. In any case, you won't need to wear your Agraci robes after tonight. We will be sailing back to Cyprus and then Syria.'

She stood, her naked body framed in the light seeping through the shutters. She was so beautiful and I wanted to make love to her. She saw me making my way towards her.

'You have no time, Pacorus, and you will need your strength. Now go and eat some breakfast.'

My ardour disappeared. 'I sometimes think that the Gauls can be as cruel as the Romans when required.'

'Far crueller if need be.'

I wandered down to the banqueting room, slaves on their knees cleaning the stairs and hallway. The air was warm and fresh and the sound of the fountains in the courtyard created a calming effect. It was hard to believe that in a few hours the city would be witnessing large-scale organised bloodshed. The slaves did not stand when I passed them because they knew I was a gladiator, a Roman slave who shed blood for the amusement of the crowd. However, when Domitus appeared at the top of the stairs they stood as one and bowed their heads.

He followed me into the banqueting room and sat on the edge of a daybed, a slave rushing from the kitchens with a bowl of barley porridge for him.

He took the bowl and began shovelling the food into his mouth with his hand.

'You can take the Roman out of Rome but not Rome out of the Roman, it is true,' I chided him.

'Get some food in your belly, you're going to need it.'

More slaves arrived from the kitchens with barley cakes, eggs, grapes, myrtle berries, figs and bread. Jugs of watered-downed wine were placed on the table to be poured into bowls so we could dip our bread into it.

'This is going to be a strange day,' he said after he had finished his porridge. 'Myself and Gallia sitting in seats watching you and the others fighting for your lives on the sand below. Not sure I can hold with it.'

'It's too late for misgivings, old friend. Besides you know that highly prized gladiators stand a good chance of surviving a spectacle.'

He picked up a fig. 'In Italy, perhaps, but you have seen the fat oaf who is the *editor*. He reeks of sadistic perversion and has a few tricks up his sleeve, you mark my words.'

A slave handed me a bowl of porridge. 'I thought he just reeks. And what tricks?'

'I don't know,' replied Domitus. 'But *editors* like to make their mark on the games, which usually means devising new ways of spilling blood before a baying crowd.'

I took a mouthful of porridge and when I looked up Lysander was standing next to Domitus, as usual in a pristine tunic and wearing a broad grin. His ability to seemingly appear out of nowhere unnerved me.

'What is it?' queried Domitus.

'I have the information you requested, *dominus*, regarding the location of the *Ludus* Capua. It is next to a Roman barracks building.'

Domitus frowned. 'Next to a barracks, why?'

'Because the gladiators from Capua are all notorious criminals, *dominus*. All condemned to the games, so I was told.'

He looked at me. 'Not free men.'

Domitus waved him away.

253

'So much for your plan,' he whispered to me.

'It just makes our task more difficult,' I told him. 'Not impossible.'

I had no time to think about rescuing Burebista as the others came down for breakfast and a runner arrived from the *editor's* offices with orders that all gladiators were to assemble in the *agora* four hours before noon. We spoke little as we changed into our fighting attire. Though I had trained with it many times my bronze helmet still felt heavy, whereas my *sica* felt ridiculously light, almost like a feather. A deadly feather.

Drenis was attired in an identical manner to myself and Arminius wore the armour of a *Provocator*, his head protected by a heavy bronze helmet. Surena seemed naked by comparison with his bare torso, right arm and legs, the bronze *galerus* his only item of armour. Domitus threw pairs of sandals on the floor and instructed us to put them on. Ephesus may have had marble streets but none of us were used to walking around barefoot, except Surena. My former squire looked remarkably relaxed as he lazily manoeuvred his net and jabbed the air with his trident. His large red loincloth and wide leather belt with dagger attached gave him the appearance of the prince of an underwater kingdom, but then that was the idea.

Domitus went to Arminius, Drenis and myself and attached red and blue plumes to each of our helmets. Issued by the office of the *editor*, red was a colour associated with Mars, the God of War. Blue, on the other hand, was considered by Rome to be the colour of barbarians and thus a reminder to everyone that gladiators were foreign heathens. Our other symbols were of Dura: the griffin motif that I carried on my shield and helmet and the engravings of the same beast on the armour of the others.

Alcaeus, a large leather bag filled with medicines and bandages slung over his shoulder, stood with Gallia as Domitus faced us all.

'Time to go.'

The Romans called it the *pompa*, the march of the gladiators. It began in the *agora*, which was packed not only with fighters but also with jugglers, musicians, animal tamers, acrobats, young women with oiled arms and legs and obscenely short tunics and dwarves. I had to confess that the latter

254

fascinated me, with their short legs and arms, oversized heads and stubby bodies. They were dressed in brightly coloured tunics and scampered around between the gladiators, issuing challenges, bending over and breaking wind at large, broad-shouldered fighters and waving their wooden swords in the air threateningly. The crowd that the Roman guards had difficulty containing loved it and cheered and applauded the little monsters.

The *agora* had a carnival air as flautists played and drummers banged their instruments. Double-jointed young women danced in front of the gladiators seductively, most of the fighters ignoring them as they had seen it all before. I looked around for Burebista but could not see him as I stood with Drenis, Arminius and Surena. The latter was loving the entertainment and raised his trident in response when a part of the crowd cheered.

'They are not cheering at you, Surena,' said Arminius from within his helmet, 'half-naked young women are more attractive than you.'

I felt a jab on one of my buttocks.

'Fight me, you coward.'

I looked behind me to see a dwarf dressed in a perfect replica of a legionary's uniform, complete with tiny mail shirt, prodding a small wooden *gladius* at me.

'Be gone, you pesky fly,' I told him.

He jabbed the point of his toy sword into my other buttock.

'Tomorrow I will still be alive whereas you will be food for crows.'

He ran forward, kicked my left greave and then scuttled away, laughing as he did so. It was all part of the colourful pageant that I was a part of, a garish, indulgent display of Rome's power and the subjugation of its enemies. I prayed that Parthia would never be home to such spectacles.

Flustered, sweating officials rushed around checking the number of gladiators in each group, calling out names and nearly getting into fights when men wearing heavy bronze helmets that inhibited their hearing did not answer their names immediately. The officials began to berate the seemingly unhelpful gladiators, until the latter drew their swords and held

255

the points at the necks of the former. An overweight Greek middle-aged man, beads of sweat on his forehead, appeared before us.

'You are from the *Ludus* Palmyra?'

We nodded.

He consulted the tablet he was carrying, a stylus in his hand.

'I have four gladiators listed. Please acknowledge your presence when I call your name. Arminius, *Provocator*.'

'Present.'

'Drenis, Thracian.'

'Present.'

'Nikephorus, Thracian.'

'Here.'

'Surena, *Retiarius*.'

'Surena of the Ma'adan,' stated my former squire.

The Greek's forehead creased in confusion. 'What?'

'I am Surena of the Ma'adan,' reiterated our young fighter.

'He is Surena,' I said loudly so the official would hear. 'Thank you.'

'You have more things to worry about than the organisers not making a note of your origins,' I told him.

'I want them to know where I come from, lord,' he replied, 'so that when they come to record my victories they will know that I am a son of the Ma'adan.'

I saw the helmets of Drenis and Arminius shaking from side to side in response to Surena's words. He really did believe he was invincible. Perhaps that was the best way to approach the games. Ticket sellers and those taking bets went among the crowd to extract more money from the spectators, who were chewing on snacks purchased from stalls around the outside of the *agora*. Butchery appeared to be a most profitable business.

There was a loud blast of trumpets that made the crowd look towards the source of the noise. Small monkeys on the shoulders of animal trainers squealed in alarm and a frightened performing bear swiped an unfortunate women standing too close to it.

'Here we go,' said Drenis as legionaries made a path through the crowd so the procession could begin its journey from the *agora* to the Great Theatre of Ephesus where the games were to be held.

The crowd thickened as the column of entertainers, freaks, gladiators and animals made its way to Harbour Street and then headed north towards the theatre.

'How ironic that the arena should be called a theatre,' I said to Drenis above the tumult of the crowd.

'It is entirely apt,' he replied. He nudged me in the ribs.

'Now there's one who was born to stand on the sand of the arena.'

He was referring to Surena who had a wide grin on his face and was basking in the adulation of the people lining the street. The fact that they had never heard of him and were most probably not cheering him did not bother him in the slightest. He was here, at Ephesus, and determined to make his mark on the games. As was I, though not in the way the Romans expected.

Eventually we reached the theatre, which was cut into the slope of the city's Panayir Hill and was a magnificent piece of architecture. The semi-circular seating area had sixty rows of seats, divided by two walkways. The steepness of the rows increased slightly above each tier so those siting at the back of the theatre had a good view of the stage below. The steep-sided rows of seats also increased the enclosed feeling inside the theatre, making the atmosphere more intimate and intense. Facing the seating, on the other side of the arena, was the stage building to the rear of which the procession entered. The building was at least sixty feet high, with an ornamented façade facing the audience featuring reliefs, columns, niches, statues and windows.

We were ushered from the street into the large fenced-off area at the rear of the stage building, legionaries keeping the crowds back and creating a passage for the gladiators and entertainers. Many animals were held in cages in this area. Looking through the eye guards of my helmet it appeared that there were hundreds of them: wild boar, bears, wild dogs, wolves, hyenas, lions, Caspian tigers, leopards, panthers and crocodiles. I had never seen such a collection of exotic wildlife, all brought to this place to be slaughtered in the arena.

The ground floor of the stage building was pleasingly cool and the lighting subdued. It was really nothing more than a large open area with marble tiles on the floor and marble columns supporting the upper storeys. Only the gladiators were allowed into the building, the freaks and other entertainers being instructed to go back from whence they came or wait in the fenced-off area with the animal cages. Large awnings had been erected over them to keep the beasts in the shade, not out of concern for their welfare but to ensure they did not expire before they were killed in the arena. Roman logic was a wonderful thing.

As our eyes got accustomed to the subdued light I noticed that there were two fences arranged parallel to each other running from the open area in the rear to twin doors in the centre of the wall that faced the arena outside. Either side of these doors were two other doors – five entrances to the arena in all. All were closed.

Drenis took off his helmet and nudged me. 'The animals will go through those central doors after trainers have arranged fenced-off channels leading from their cages to this corridor. All very organised.'

Officials bellowed at slaves to fetch water for us to drink. It was hot outside and we were all covered in sweat. Young boys and girls offered us large cups and filled them with water. I drained one cupful and held it out to be refilled. Beyond the closed doors I could hear the rumble of an eager crowd.

'This place will stink of blood, piss and dung in an hour or two,' remarked Arminius who finished his cup, had it refilled and then poured the contents over his head.

'Why don't they open the doors?' asked Surena.

'Have patience,' Drenis told him, 'everything is done according to a strict timetable.'

I looked around at the assembled gladiators, most in a contemplative mood and staring at the floor or fiddling with a piece of armour or their weapon in a well-rehearsed superstitious routine. Others looked around, eager to catch the eye of a potential opponent and thereby hope to intimidate or unnerve him. But I detected no fear or apprehension in the air, just a grim determination laced with anticipation. I saw

Burebista at last as a man in a white tunic with red stripes removed his helmet to reveal his face.

'Wait here,' I told the others as I left them and made my way to Burebista's side.

The other gladiators from Capua recognised me from the previous night but none said anything as I nodded to Burebista.

'Tonight we get you and your wife out of here,' I told him.

He shook his head. 'It is too dangerous, lord. We are housed in a Roman barracks block. There are too many guards and locked gates. The *lanista* of my *ludus* is not stupid; he goes to great lengths to protect his investments.'

I thought for a moment. 'Would he be open to an offer for both of you?'

Burebista looked at me. 'He's a greedy toad, lord, so he might be. But he would demand a high price.'

I laid a hand on his arm. 'The gods smile on us, my friend, for Dura is rich. Leave it with me. And stay alive.'

I went to leave but he pulled me back. 'Have a care, lord. I have heard rumours that the *editor* of these games has been given free rein to his imagination. There may be some nasty surprises in the arena.'

I thanked him and walked back towards my companions. I had not gone twenty paces before the hulking figure of Acco barred my way. He was bare chested with ugly swirling blue tattoos adorning his broad chest, wide shoulders and thick neck. He and Crixus must have come out of the same mould in the underworld. His blue eyes were blazing with excitement, which, combined with his long fair hair and wild moustache, gave him a demonic appearance. The only armour he wore was leather *manicas* on his arms and legs.

'Looking forward to dying today, Parthian?'

'I am looking forward to shutting you up, Gaul.'

He chuckled. 'I will give you a quick, clean death.'

I sighed with boredom. 'I have heard it all before, Gaul.'

I walked past him.

'And tell that arrogant puppy of yours that he is next on my list,' said Acco loudly.

When I got back to the other three Drenis was grinning.

'Been making friends, Pacorus?'

There was a blast of whistles and officials shouted for us to replace our helmets as a great trumpet blare came from beyond the doors, the four flanking the central pair suddenly opening to let light flood into the ground floor. We were all momentarily blinded by sunlight as we donned our helmets and then filed out into the sun, into the arena of the Great Theatre of Ephesus.

The first thing that struck me as the crowd stood and roared its approval was the small size of the semi-circular area of sand. The diameter was no more than forty yards and the radius twenty yards. And the crowd that towered above us, numbering over twenty thousand, appeared very close. Because it had been designed for plays there was no wall surrounding the arena to protect spectators. Instead there was a row of posts positioned around the perimeter to which was fastened nets. In the first row of seats sat legionaries, no doubt to give added protection from wild animals that might be tempted to climb the nets.

The nearest seats were reserved for the city's élite: rich Romans, Greek aristocrats and foreign dignitaries. In the centre was a large crimson awning that protected the most important spectators from the sun. As we saluted the crowd and basked in its adulation I noticed that those under the awning remained seated. In the centre sat a stern-faced Roman with a long face, dressed in a black muscled cuirass similar to my own, a red cloak draped around his shoulders. He must have been Quintus Caecilius Metellus. On his left side sat another, younger Roman senior commander perhaps around thirty years of age. Handsome, he had a lighter complexion than his older superior. On Metellus' right side sat an imposing figure in a white robe that appeared to be edged in silver. He had a formidable visage, with a strong nose, a black beard and hair that was heavily streaked with grey. I assumed he was High Priest Kallias because on his right side sat the enticing Hippo, her hair oiled and adorned with a silver crown.

Behind Metellus I could see the obese Timini Ceukianus who was shovelling food into his mouth. He leaned forward and peered at the gladiators as there was another blast of trumpets. The crowd roared again and people sat down as a

260

figure dressed in a long white robe near the most important guests raised his arms and called for silence.

'High Priest Kallias welcomes you all to the annual games at Ephesus.' His voice was deep and the acoustics of the theatre ensured that it carried to every part of the stadium.

'High Priest Kallias has generously financed these games,' he continued, 'as a gift to his friend the governor, his Excellency Quintus Caecilius Metellus, the conquer of Crete.'

There was polite applause from the crowd as Metellus turned his head to Kallias and nodded his acknowledgement of the high priest's largesse.

'Before the festivities begin,' said the announcer, 'High Priest Kallias will ask the goddess for Her blessings to shine on these games and on Her city.'

I noticed the governor looked decidedly unhappy with the phrase 'Her city'. Ephesus was a Roman city and in the governor's eyes a Greek goddess had no authority over the People and Senate of Rome. As the announcer sat down Kallias rose to his feet, followed by over twenty thousand others who bowed their heads respectfully. Metellus begrudgingly rose to his feet and Ceukianus managed to lift his great bulk off his cushion-stuffed marble seat.

There was silence as the tall high priest raised his hands to the heavens.

'Great Artemis,' his voice thundered, 'the one who is the beauty of the earth, the green of growing things, the White Moon whose light is full and bright among the stars and soft upon the earth. From You all things are born and to You all things, in their season, return.

'Bless this Your city and these Your games, Divine One, and accept the souls of those who are to be sacrificed here, unworthy though they be, as tokens of our love for You.

'Hail Artemis.'

As one the crowd shouted 'hail Artemis' and Kallias returned to his seat. Metellus looked even more annoyed, his face a mask of stone. There had been no mention of Rome in the high priest's speech, even though the games were designed to be a display of the power of Rome and Roman ways. Kallias for his part looked immensely smug. I sensed a keen rivalry between the two.

261

The announcer stood again and held out a hand to the gladiators standing on the sand.

'From the four corners of the world have they come, men of iron and bronze to grace the holy sand of the arena with their courage and blood. They are the students of the finest gladiator schools in the world, those schools being Rome, Ravenna, Pompeii, Capua, Pergamon, Palestrina, Alexandria, Palmyra, Syracuse and Ephesus.'

The crowd rose to its feet and cheered the last name, chanting 'Ephesus, Ephesus' as the guards in the front and back rows looked at each other nervously. There must have been upwards of four hundred legionaries in the theatre but they were vastly outnumbered. Many among the crowd would have been Romans who were residents of Ephesus, but the vast majority of spectators were Greeks.

The referees who would adjudicate individual gladiator fights blew their whistles to indicate that we should leave the arena. As we turned and headed towards the doors Surena raised his trident and net and accepted the applause of a section of the crowd nearest to him.

'I am Surena of the Ma'adan,' he shouted.

'Surena,' I called to him, 'stop playing the fool.'

We were told to make our way to the second floor of the stage building as the beast hunters assembled on the ground floor. These men, armed with spears, knives and swords, were apparently trained to display their hunting prowess in the arena, being pitted against a variety of wild animals. Though looking at them with their fearful expressions and trembling limbs, I sensed that they were either slaves or petty criminals coerced into taking part in the games.

There were two pairs of stone steps at each end of the ground floor that gave access to the first floor, which contained rows of empty cots, and the second floor. Alcaeus informed me that the cots were for injured gladiators.

'If you get injured you will be pleased to know that the organisers of the games have spared no expense with regard to medicines,' he told me.

'Of course not,' said Drenis, 'gladiators are literally worth their weight in gold.'

We reach the second floor where gladiators took off their armour and relaxed at benches that had been positioned either side of tables. There were at least a dozen open windows that gave a view of the arena below but few seemed interested in watching the proceedings. Most had seen the spectacle many times before. They were more interested in sating their thirsts and picking at the snacks that were brought by slaves. These jumped when a high-pitched scream came from the arena as a man was mauled by a leopard or gored by a wild boar.

'Talking of weight in gold,' I said to my companions as we sat at the end of a table. 'I spoke to Burebista and he believes that his freedom and that of his wife could be bought, for the right price.'

The sounds of animals squealing and screeching and people shouting and screaming came from below.

'It will be a high price,' said Drenis.

'Then it is fortunate that Dura is a rich kingdom,' I retorted. 'I will ask Athineos to broker a deal.'

'He will want paying for his troubles as well,' said Alcaeus.

'It will be worth it,' I told him.

The animal hunts lasted about half an hour at most. Afterwards, as some of the one hundred and twenty gladiators dozed on couches that had been arrange around the walls, slaves wafting fans over them, the condemned were herded into the arena to be executed. There was a great roar from the crowd as leopards and panthers were released on to the sand, the animals immediately attacking the hapless captives whose tunics had been smeared with blood to make them more appetising to the animals. The cries and shrieks of the victims reached my ears and I shuddered.

'Not like you expected it to be, is it?' said Drenis.

I had seen criminals being executed but there was something bizarre bordering on the obscene at such wholesale slaughter.

'Roman justice is brutal,' I answered. 'I expected that.'

I declined an offer from Surena to observe the butchery from a window. After it was finished he returned and informed us that upwards of a hundred prisoners had met their deaths below.

263

'The sand is red,' he said.

It was now afternoon and many of the crowd had left their seats to either stretch their legs or purchase something to eat from the dozens of food stalls outside the theatre. I lifted an arm and saw that it was shaking a little. Pre-battle nerves, though I did not feel nervous but rather eager to get to grips with the enemy. I looked around. I would be fighting one of these men who appeared relaxed and even peaceful. Who would it be? I saw the wild hair of Acco. He and I would be a good match.

A small, white-haired Roman in a white tunic appeared, two referees flanking him. They blew their whistles to get everyone's attention.

The white-haired man spoke. 'The *editor* demands the presence of all gladiators in the arena in thirty minutes.'

There were murmurs among the fighters and Acco pushed his way to stand before the Roman.

'All gladiators? Hasn't the fat bastard arranged matched pairs yet? No doubt too busy filling his gut.'

'Or filling some a slave boy with his manhood,' called another gladiator to hoots from the others.

The referees blew their whistles again.

'Those are my orders,' said the Roman, 'so collect your weapons and armour.'

Drenis was frowning and Arminius was shaking his head.

'This is most odd,' he muttered.

Burebista came over as we began to file down the stairs.

'Watch yourself, lord, this *editor* is an oily beast and this stinks of his devious mind.'

But it was the arena that stank. Reeked of death, blood, urine and guts. I winced as my bare feet stepped on sand that was soft and wet, wet with blood of humans and animals. Slaves had been sent into the arena before we filed out of the stage building to sprinkle fresh sand but such had been the bloodletting that their attempts had been only partially successful. I was momentarily taken back to the Roman city of Nola, to its amphitheatre where Spartacus had been sitting on top of the wall that surrounded its arena after the city had fallen to him. He had told me that he had fought on the sand as a gladiator but his one abiding memory of such bouts had been

264

the smell of the arena. At the time I did not know what he meant. I did now.

I was brought back to the present by a mighty roar as members of the crowd jumped to their feet and whistled and cheered our entrance. A few of the gladiators raised their shields and weapons in acknowledgement, including Surena, but the majority just looked around in confusion. We had already been paraded around the arena. Something was wrong.

As we stood before the crowd, the governor and high priest talking to each other and the rotund Ceukianus whispering into the ear of the handsome Roman officer next to Metellus, the announcer waited for the din to die down before rising to his feet. Behind us the doors to the arena were closed.

'They are going to spring a surprise on us,' warned Drenis, nodding up at the announcer. 'When he stops talking turn round and expect the unexpected.'

'I thought the afternoon was given over to gladiator bouts,' said Surena, disappointment in his voice.

'Let me take you back to when a Roman army under Licinius Lucullus, half-starving and hundreds of miles from Rome,' the announcer's voice echoed around the theatre, 'was surrounded by over one hundred thousand heathen Armenians led by the tyrant Tigranes at a place called Tigranocerta.'

He looked down into the arena and held out an arm towards us. 'Behold the brave legionaries of Lucullus, men of bronze with iron discipline who do not fear long odds.'

'He sounds like Domitus,' said Arminius.

The announcer turned to the crowd, his voice like a clap of thunder.

'It was Roman discipline and Roman leadership pitted against Eastern fury. Who will triumph?'

'Turn,' shouted Drenis as I heard the doors open behind me.

'Surena, cover our backs,' ordered Arminius as he stood beside Drenis and I braced myself on the other side of the latter.

The crowd fell into silence as the other gladiators turned to see men pouring from the doors, shouting and screaming as they raced into the arena. They were mostly unshaven and filthy, wearing dirty, torn tunics with nothing on their grubby feet or their lice-ridden heads. They were either criminals or prisoners of war, emaciated and weak, but there were many of them.

Perhaps they had been told that if they killed us all their lives would be spared; more likely they knew that they were condemned men. But just a glimpse of freedom had intoxicated them and they came at us with a feral rage. Only a few had weapons – cheap swords, wooden clubs and knives – but desperate men are dangerous. A wild-eyed individual wielding a club swung it at my head. I ducked and let him run on to my sword, his eyes nearly popping out of their sockets as the blade sank deep into his belly. I used my shield to batter him aside as a man behind him threw himself at me, a knife in his hand. I caught his right arm on my shield so he could not stab down his knife and slashed at his belly with my sword. He screamed and fell to the ground, writhing in agony as more and more men ran out of the doors. There must have been hundreds of them.

The gladiators fought as individuals, sidestepping attackers to slice their calves and hamstrings as they passed. I saw Acco, a *gladius* in each hand, standing like a rock against which wave upon wave of assailants were crashing, being cut down by his scything blows. But the sheer number of attackers meant some gladiators either tripped and fell to the ground, allowing their opponents to stab and trample them to death, or were simply overwhelmed by sheer weight of numbers.

Drenis was also like a rock and Arminius and I stood with him, cutting down attackers as they came at us. Behind us Surena obeyed his orders and guarded our backs, thrusting his trident left and right at opponents who tried to get behind us. As the time passed there was a wall of dead and dying men in front of us, their bellies cut open and stab wounds in their torsos and faces.

A deranged, unarmed man hurled himself at me like a springing lion. When he landed on me I stabbed at his belly five or six times, blood sheeting over my chest and helmet. He groaned and blood frothed at his mouth but his dead weight collapsed on me and I fell to the ground, he on top of me. I heaved him aside just as a man armed with a spear appeared and stood over me, gripping the shaft with both his hands.

Grinning savagely as he prepared to thrust the point into my exposed chest, he died as Surena drove the prongs of his trident into his neck.

'Up lord,' he said, hauling me to my feet.

The members of the threadbare army swirled around groups of gladiators, trying to strike them with their weapons but invariably suffering horribly at the hands of the trained fighters. Only by isolating a gladiator, like a pack of hyenas circling a lone victim, could the prisoners hope to fell a student of a *ludus*. But even when isolated and surrounded it took upwards of ten prisoners to fell a lone gladiator, half of them dying before they cut him down.

The crowd was delirious with delight, shouting their encouragement to both prisoners and gladiators and revelling in the spectacle. I killed a man holding a sword who looked half-dead before I struck the fatal blow, severed the windpipe of another, reduced the groin of an opponent who tripped on a body in front of me to a bloody pulp then stooped to avoid a sideways blow with a sword before slicing open both calves of my opponent.

And still the prisoners kept coming.

The swords of Drenis and Arminius resembled silver flashes of light so fast were they being moved, cutting down, up and stabbing forward. They held their shields tight to their unarmoured torsos as opponents tried to strike them with their weapons, only cutting air or the surface of a shield before feeling the points or keen edges of their swords.

Surena was in his element, wrapping his net around the ankles of assailants and lunging forward to stab them with his trident, the deftness and speed of his strikes resembling those of a desert cobra. He ducked and dodged to avoid the weapons of opponents before attacking. He moved his net to catch an opponent's eye and then struck with his trident in the split-second when his enemy was distracted. And all the time the crowd cheered and roared.

Acco used one *gladius* to parry blows and the other to lacerate the bodies of opponents, applying enough force behind a blow to ensure that his victim would not rise once on the ground. For a big man he was remarkably light on his feet, darting forwards, backwards and sideways to avoid the clumsy attacks of the prisoners. Most of the latter were now dead, heaps of their slain littering the arena. Some, having dropped their weapons, attempted to flee back through the doors but they were now shut. They were hunted down and slaughtered by gladiators until there were no more prisoners left. The crowd gave a mighty cheer as the last one was hacked to pieces by two *Murmillos*. The re-enactment of the Battle of Tigranocerta was over.

I slapped Drenis and Arminius on the arm and thanked Surena for saving my life as the doors were opened once more and referees came from the gloom to order everyone back inside. Some gladiators, wounded in the contest, were hobbling and had to be assisted from the arena either by slaves who rushed from the stage building or their fellow gladiators. The announcer's words filled the theatre as we left the once more blood-soaked sand.

'Once again Roman discipline and courage has triumphed over barbarian numbers and tyranny.'

The crowd applauded as Surena turned and raised his bloody trident in a victory salute. Through the protective eyeholes of my helmet I just caught sight of Timini Ceukianus on his feet drooling over the cocky young man from the marshes.

Back inside the building we trouped to the top floor once more and removed our armour and helmets. The wounded were taken to the infirmary on the floor below and slaves brought food and towels so we could wipe the sweat from our bodies. Alcaeus fussed around us, examining us for wounds or bruises.

'The gods smile on you,' he said. 'This time anyway. And now you will have to excuse me. I am needed below.'

He disappeared with his medical bag as Drenis stretched out on a couch and Arminius inspected his helmet, which had a dent on its side.

'I'll have to get the armourer to fix this.'

'Surena of the *Ludus* Palmyra and Flamma of the *Ludus* Pompeii. The *editor* demands your presence in the arena.'

I heard the voice of one of editor's assistants and looked in alarm at Surena. I glanced at Drenis who shook his head. I went to remonstrate with the official but Drenis pulled me back.

'You are a gladiator, Pacorus, if you make a scene there will be severe ramifications. There is nothing you can do.'

Arminius was also shaking his head and I felt helpless. But Surena was busy wiping the shaft of his trident and ensuring his *galerus* was securely in place. He caught my eye and grinned triumphantly as a man I assumed was Flamma walked nonchalantly towards the stone steps.

'The gods be with you, Surena,' I said as he followed the Pompeian.

He turned and grinned. 'I do not need the gods, lord, only my skill and my weapons.'

Flamma was a *Secutor*, 'the chaser', who wore a smooth, full-face helmet, a *manica* on his sword arm and greave on his left leg. Additional protection was provided by his large, rectangular shield that had small tridents painted around its edge. His weapon was a *gladius*.

'What do those tridents on his shield signify?' I asked Drenis.

'The number of *Retiarius* fighters he has killed in the arena,' he answered.

My spirits sank. The sadistic lust of Timini Ceukianus that had been aroused when he and Surena had met aboard *The Cretan* had come back to haunt the latter and now he would die. With a heavy heart I walked to one of the windows to observe the proceedings below. I saw a small army of slaves pulling the bodies of the slain into the stage building to clear the arena for the coming bout. I looked at the crowd and heard the intense chatter that was taking place in anticipation of the fight that the announcer had just proclaimed. There was no attempt to cover the blood-covered surface with fresh sand as Surena walked out of the stage building in the company of Flamma and a referee who carried a short stick to administer the fight.

The crowd began clapping as the two fighters halted in front of the high priest and the governor and raised their weapons in salute.

Drenis appeared by my side. 'He's not dead yet. If he remembers his training the bout might end in a draw, which will mean both will leave the arena alive.'

I was not convinced. Surena believed himself to be invincible and though he was brave and strong his self-belief might work against him. I looked at the large figure of Ceukianus lounging in his chair and giggling like a small girl. How I would have liked to slit that blubber-covered throat. The referee held his stick between Flamma and Surena and looked up at the governor, who nodded. The referee removed his stick and stepped back and the duel began.

Gladiators crowded at the windows to see what most believed to be a formality: the death of this upstart from some unknown eastern place called Palmyra. The crowd cheered and roared as Surena crouched low, sweeping his net on the ground in front of him. He pulled it back and then tripped as it got tangled around his left ankle. My mouth opened in horror as he crumbled to the ground and Flamma raced forward to finish him off.

And stopped suddenly as Surena spun round and sprang forward to drive the prongs of his trident into Flamma's exposed belly. It happened so quickly that at first I thought I had imagined it. But as the crowd fell silent and Surena leaped back, Flamma's helmeted head flopped forward as blood began oozing from his guts on to his red loincloth. Everyone in the crowd seemed stunned, unsure of what had just happened.

Surena held his trident at the ready as Flamma fell to his knees and then collapsed face-first on the sand. Surena turned to face the crowd and raised his trident and net.

'I am Surena of the Ma'adan.'

There was a moment of silence and then the crowd saluted its newfound hero, clapping, cheering and shouting 'Surena, Surena' as the focus of their adulation walked around the arena, basking in the acclaim. He stopped in front of the dignitaries, pointed his trident at the *editor* and spat on the sand. Flamma's life ebbed away as Ceukianus, a face like thunder, signalled to the referee that Surena should leave the arena immediately. A slave carrying a large mallet came from the stage building as the referee pointed at Surena with his stick, then towards one of the doors to indicate he should depart the arena. The slave stood astride the body of Flamma, removed his helmet and then struck the corpse's head with a heavy blow of the mallet to ensure he was dead and not faking injury. I laughed and slapped Drenis on the arm as Surena gave the crowd one more salute with his trident before disappearing into the stage building. Behind him the theatre reverberated with the chant 'Surena, Surena'.

Burebista walked over to me, his hair matted to his skull after his exertions in the arena.

'The crowd has its hero, lord. Where did you get him from?'

'I first met him when I was a prisoner in a vast area of marshland. He saved my life. And now he is an officer in my army.'

'And a gladiator making a name for himself,' added Burebista.

I looked beyond him to ensure we were out of earshot.

'I will arrange for a representative to approach your *lanista* tonight with a view to purchasing both you and your wife.'

He looked embarrassed. 'It would have to be a generous offer, lord. Lentulus Vatia is above all avaricious.'

Surena returned to the second floor in an ebullient mood, accepting the grudging congratulations of many of the seasoned gladiators from the other schools. The crowd was still chanting his name when an official appeared to declare that the day's festivities were over and that we would be escorted back to our quarters. Alcaeus also returned to inform me that twenty-three gladiators had been killed in the mass bout that I had taken part in, with Flamma an additional fatality. There were ten fighters lying in cots on the floor below, none of whom would be taking any further part in the games. A quarter of the gladiators that had been brought to Ephesus were either dead or incapacitated.

We required an armed escort back our accommodation, not because we were in danger but because hundreds of people, mainly women of various ages, wanted to either touch or speak to Surena. The legionaries became increasingly short tempered as they tried to clear a path in front of us. The duty centurion also snapped at Surena not to dally and to ignore his fans.

'He's got no chance,' remarked Drenis as Surena kissed a pretty young woman on the cheek and then smiled as a legionary had to drag another women off him who had wrapped her arms and legs around him.

'What it is to be a god of the arena,' said Arminius.

271

When we finally reached the house we found a substantial crowd gathered around it, which broke into spontaneous applause when they spotted Surena. The centurion personally bundled him through the gates and then ordered the crowd to disperse and go back to their homes. Inside the entrance stood Lysander to welcome us back, the ever-present smile on his face. We went into the banqueting hall where Gallia and Domitus were waiting. My wife flung herself into my arms and clung to me tightly.

'That was the worst day of my life,' she whispered. 'I have never experienced such torture, watching you fighting and being unable to help.'

I cupped her face in my hands and kissed her on the lips. 'Shamash protected me, my love. He protected us all.'

We took off our armour and handed it and our weapons to slaves who took it to the storeroom where it was kept under lock and key, Lysander appearing and ordering them to be quick about it. Domitus clasped my forearm.

'Glad to see you're alive.'

Other slaves brought wine and water and Lysander told us that he had organised masseurs to visit the house

'Very sensible,' said Alcaeus.

'Get Lysander to go to the docks and bring Athineos here,' I told Domitus.

He called over our Greek guide and was explaining that he should go to the harbour and ask the captain of *The Cretan* to pay us a visit.

'I do not want you taking any further part in the games,' Gallia suddenly said to me. Lysander looked at her in confusion. Why would the wife of a *lanista* be interested in the life of a gladiator?

'Go now, Lysander,' Domitus ordered him.

Lysander bowed his head and hurried from the room.

'We must try harder to maintain the pretence that I am a gladiator and you are the wife of my master,' I said to her.

She was not interested. 'Domitus, you can report to the games' organisers tomorrow that Nikephorus will be taking no further part in the organised butchery on account of an injury.'

'You will do no such thing,' I said, looking at Gallia. 'I knew the risks when I came here and I will see the task through.'

'This is not like war, Pacorus,' she said, 'it is slaughter, pure and simple. What chance do you think you have of surviving another four days of this butchery?'

She looked at Drenis and Arminius. 'What chance for any of you?'

'It is easy enough, majesty,' said Surena, trying to be helpful.

Her blue eyes bored into him. 'Silence! You forget yourself. You may be a hero to the deluded fools outside but in here I am your queen.'

Surena blushed. 'Yes, majesty.'

'What would you have me do, Gallia?' I asked her. 'Do you wish me to flee this very night like a gutless coward and leave Burebista to face certain death? I will not do it. This is the pledge of the King of Dura. I will leave this city with Burebista and his wife or not at all.'

Gallia fumed but knew that I would not budge so she said nothing, her face a mask of anger. Domitus relaxed on a daybed and sipped at a cup of wine, indicating that Drenis and Arminius should do the same.

'Besides, if we depart now we will rob the city of seeing more of Surena in the arena,' said Domitus mischievously.

Gallia sighed. 'You are not helping, Domitus.'

I walked over to her and placed an arm round her waist. 'Shamash will protect me, my love. Come, let us not argue after such a day. Let us give thanks that we are all still alive.'

Her hard mask dissolved and she smiled, though her eyes were filled with sadness. We sat down on one of the couches and I beckoned over a slave holding a tray of figs. Another slave entered the room and bowed before Domitus, informing him that the masseurs had arrived.

A leathery middle-aged man called Argos used oils and his fingers to massage the tightness out of my muscles and relax my whole body. Other lithe, olive-skinned men worked their magic on Surena, Drenis and Arminius. I lay on the couch, the aroma of pine incense lulling me into semi-consciousness as Argos kneaded the muscles in my back and shoulders. Because he believed me to be a slave his conversation was quite informal.

'These are lash scars on your back.'

I grunted to signify he was correct.

'The life of a slave can be hard and short. But perhaps not as short as that of a gladiator.'

'We must use the skills the gods have given us.'

'Indeed,' he said. My body felt utterly calm and relaxed. 'The young one of your school, Surena, has made a name for himself.'

'He has talent, yes.'

'He might cost High Priest Kallias a great deal of money.'

Kallias was financing the games and as such would compensate any *lanista* whose gladiators were killed in the arena.

Argos was clearly in a talkative mood. 'I suspect the high priest would pay a huge sum if it meant embarrassing the governor and seeing his own gladiators triumphing over those who travelled from Italy.'

'The high priest and governor do not like each other?' I asked.

Argos laughed. 'The governor dislikes Kallias because he has great influence in the city and among the worshippers who flock to the Temple of Artemis, whereas Kallias believes that Ephesus is his city and therefore regards the governor as a foreign upstart.'

'They seemed tolerant of each other's company,' I said, thinking back to their behaviour at the games.

'Appearances can be deceptive. For example, the governor would like to seize the criminals seeking sanctuary at the temple and crucify them but if he violates the temple's rules he knows he may incite a riot. Kallias knows this and basks in the governor's helplessness.'

'I saw some of those criminals when I visited the temple.'

'Cleon and his band of freedom fighters,' said Argos derisively.

'You do not approve of a fellow Greek wanting to be free from Roman rule?'

He pressed his thumbs hard into the tight muscles at the base of my spine.

'Cleon believes he should rule in Ephesus. He has killed many Roman soldiers, or so he boasts, which has earned him the loyalty of a band of like-minded hotheads. Cleon's notion of freedom is very limited to him and his band of followers.'

'Then why doesn't Kallias evict them from the temple grounds?' I asked.

'Because it suits Kallias to keep Cleon at the temple as a visible reminder that the Roman governor of Ephesus is not all powerful. It is all very childlike.'

'I can imagine Cleon's presence at the temple irritates the Romans,' I remarked, 'especially if he has killed their soldiers. They are a very unforgiving race.'

'I have been a slave for a long time,' he reflected, 'and during that time I have had numerous masters, both Roman and Greek. I have found very little difference between them.'

He said nothing for a few moments as he picked up my left arm and began rubbing oil into it.

'Your body has seen much hard usage,' he said at length.

'Fighting takes a heavy toll on a person.'

'Massage, good eating habits, exercise, rest, fresh air and music will rejuvenate your body,' he told me.

'I will try to take your advice.'

Relaxed and refreshed, I sat with the others in the courtyard after we had eaten an evening meal of bread, cheese, figs and fish, all washed down with wine. A flustered legionary reported to Domitus that most of the crowd had dispersed but there were a still a few die-hard fans of Surena near the entrance.

'I can threaten to arrest them, *lanista*,' he said to Domitus, 'if you so wish.'

'Are they likely to cause any trouble?'

The legionary shook his head. 'They are mostly young women who want to get a look at your gladiator, *lanista*.'

He nodded at Surena who smiled back at him.

'Surena,' ordered Domitus. 'Go with this legionary and tell your adoring fans that they must return to their homes, otherwise they will be arrested for disturbing my sleep.'

For the first time that day Surena looked uncertain. 'They might mob me. Viper would not approve.'

Gallia rolled her eyes.

Domitus looked at the legionary. 'I'm sure this soldier and his fine companions will be able to hold back a gang of girls. Now go!'

'That fat bastard *editor* has the knives out for Surena,' I said after he and the legionary had departed. 'I worry for him.'

'Surena needs to learn when to keep his mouth shut and his eyes down,' said Arminius.

Gallia ate a wafer dipped in honey. 'Surena needs to be taught a lesson in humility. He is far too arrogant.'

'Don't you worry about Surena,' Domitus told us, 'the gods love him and won't let anything happen to him.'

I was not so sure but had no time to debate the matter further because Lysander arrived in the company of Athineos. The latter was dressed in a fine blue tunic, baggy white leggings and had small blue ribbons tied in his beard and gold earrings dangled from his ears. The editor had obviously paid him for his lions. Domitus thanked Lysander and said he could leave us, asking Athineos to take a seat. The big Cretan winked at Gallia and flopped onto a couch as a slave offered him wine, which he gladly accepted.

'Your Greek slave told me you wanted to see me,' he said to me. 'Are you ready to leave?'

'Not quite, Athineos,' I answered. 'I have a proposal for you.'

He drained the cup and placed it on the table beside him. 'Always open to a business proposition.'

'I want you to go the *Ludus* Capua this very evening,' I said, 'and say that you come with an anonymous offer to purchase the gladiator Burebista and his wife Anca.'

'What is the size of the offer?' enquired Athineos, looking at a slave and pointing to his empty cup.

'The *lanista* can name his price,' I said. 'Tell him that.'

Domitus looked bemused. 'Are you mad? He will demand an exorbitant price.'

I smiled at my general. 'I know that but his greed will make him unable to resist such an offer.'

I looked at Athineos. 'And tell the *lanista* that if he is interested then Burebista can take no further part in these games.'

A slave filled Athineos' cup. 'He will want proof that the offer is genuine. Hard currency, that is.'

'He will have it,' I said.

'There is also the question of my commission.'

'You will be paid well for your services, Athineos, but you must ensure that you make contact with the *lanista*, whose name escapes me.

'Lentulus Vatia,' sneered Gallia.

I thanked my wife. 'Yes, that's him. Ensure you speak to him tonight.'

I gave him a small gold bar with the emblem of a griffin carved on it, one of several I had brought with me from Dura. The advantage of having the house guarded at all times by Roman soldiers was that it was secure, and the money and gold we had brought from Dura was safe in a locked, windowless storeroom. Every slave in the house knew that if any of the money went missing they would forfeit their lives. I thought of Rsan and smiled. The trip to Ephesus was threatening to become more expensive than a military campaign.

Chapter 10

The next day the crowd of Surena's well-wishers re-assembled outside the house as we were escorted once more to the *agora*. It was going to be a beautiful sunny day, the blue sky containing only a few small white clouds. There was a slight breeze blowing off the sea that made the air fresh. Argos had certainly worked his magic on my body because I felt invigorated and my senses seemed heightened. Domitus and Gallia left us at the *agora* to take their seats in the arena, my wife wrapped in her *shemagh* and Agraci robe and looking distinctly unhappy. Her mood was made worse by not being able to embrace me before she left, though I had assured her earlier when we had been alone in our bedroom that I would take care of myself.

'Today will be harder,' said Arminius grimly as we walked to the Great Theatre, the acrobats and musicians in the vanguard of the procession of gladiators.

'Harder, how?'

'Yesterday's free-for-all might have been mildly alarming and a surprise, but we were fighting men who were ill armed and half dead. Today there will be matched pairs so watch yourself.'

'I think I can handle myself,' I told him.

He pointed at Surena a few paces ahead milking the applause of the crowd.

'Reckless, self-obsessed and believes himself invincible. He was born to fight in the arena. That said, it was stupid of him to insult the *editor* the way he did.' He turned to me.

'Whereas you are more thoughtful, more measured, as a king should be. But in the arena those traits put you at a disadvantage. So I say again, watch yourself because we will not be able to watch your back.'

'And you, Arminius?'

'I don't mind where I do my killing. Either in the area or on the battlefield, it makes no difference.'

There was a great throng around the theatre when the procession finally arrived at the rear of the stage building. Once more we walked through the area of cages filled with wild animals, though I noticed that some were now empty following the animal hunts of the previous day. I sniffed the air and

278

detected the aroma of blood. An aura of death now hung over the theatre.

Inside the stage building we filed up the stone steps on the ground floor as the beast hunters checked their weapons and equipment. In Parthia all kings, princes and lords hunted, learning to kill beasts from the saddle from an early age. But this was not hunting. Releasing wild animals into a fenced-off area from which they could not escape and then sending in men to butcher them was not sport. It was a slaughterhouse, nothing more, nothing less. I understood why gladiators had a low opinion of beast hunters.

The cots on the first floor were empty, the previous occupants having been taken to the accommodation of their respective *ludi*, either that or the nearby gladiators' cemetery that had been established by the Roman authorities. The room had been cleaned and washed and pine incense burned to mask the nauseous aroma of blood and guts. How many of those who were now ambling up the steps to the second floor would end up in the infirmary today? I asked Shamash silently that He would save my comrades from such a fate, or worse.

'You got lucky yesterday, boy. Today you will not be so lucky.'

I saw the imposing frame of Acco standing before Surena, trying to intimidate him with his wild eyes.

Surena looked at the big Gaul. 'Don't you want to rest after climbing the steps, old man, so you can get your breath back?'

Some of the other gladiators laughed at this retort, which made Acco angrier. He jabbed Surena in the chest.

'I'm going to order the organisers to arrange a fight between me and you today, boy, so I can shove that trident of yours up your arse.'

Surena stepped back. 'Why don't you try it now?'

There was a shrill blast of a whistle and an official was standing between the pair. Legionaries appeared at the doors to the room in answer to the whistle.

'No fighting here,' ordered the official. 'Any violence will incur the severest penalties.'

I pulled Surena away. 'Save it for the arena.'

279

'What's the matter?' Acco said to me. 'Have I threatened your lover? Perhaps you would like to fight me to defend your bed warmer.'

'Talk is cheap, Gaul,' was all I could think of as a reply.

Acco growled at the official, blew a kiss at the three legionaries who had their hands on the hilts of their swords and then drifted over to one of the windows overlooking the arena.

'Hopefully I will be matched against that oversized loud mouth,' said Surena loudly in an attempt to gain Acco's attention.

'Be quiet,' I ordered.

We went to sit with Drenis and Arminius, other gladiators taking their places with other members of their schools. Either that or wandering over to the windows to see the commencement of the animal hunts.

'While you two were indulging in idle gossip with the Gaul,' said Drenis, 'I was speaking to one of the lads from Capua. You may be interested to know that Burebista is not present today. Apparently his *lanista* has confined him to barracks for reasons unknown.'

I clenched a fist. 'Lentulus Vatia has taken the bait.'

'That pirate must have turned his head with promises of great wealth,' said Arminius. 'Let us hope that Dura has enough gold to satisfy his greed.'

There was a great cheer from those staring out of the windows, closely followed by a multitude of screams and cries.

'The lions are free,' shouted one of the gladiators.

I thought of Domitus and Gallia in the crowd and felt fear grip me. I jumped up and ran to the nearest window followed by the others. I looked down and horror embraced me. The theatre did not provide spectators with the same level of protection as amphitheatres because the first rows of seats were dangerously close to the arena. The organisers of the games had seemingly resolved this by seating legionaries in the first row of seats, the soldiers sitting behind a line of nets and posts to prevent the animals from escaping the arena. But they had underestimated the size and power of lions.

Too many of the beasts had been released into the arena, at least thirty, and though the hunters had killed ten the others, some wounded, pounced on their tormenters. There was a series of gut-wrenching screams as the animal hunters became the hunted, lions ripping out their throats and crushing their skulls in their jaws. The crowd would have been in ecstasy at seeing such a spectacle were it not for the fact that half a dozen other lions had jumped at and torn down the netting.

The gladiators were in fits of laughter as the crowd began fleeing their seats as one, two and more lions sprang from the arena into the seats. The legionaries in the front row were the first to flee, abandoning their shields before turning tail and clambering over seats and other spectators to save themselves. Many spectators were trampled underfoot as maddened lions sprang onto the backs of panicking civilians, clasping their jaws on the backs of their throats. It was chaos as soldiers hurriedly ushered the governor, the high priest and their entourages away. All attempted to escape from the danger.

All save two.

A line of lions were stalking their fleeing human prey, making their way upwards towards two solitary figures standing on a row of empty seats. One was casting off her black robes and tossing her *shemagh* to one side. Her blonde locks hung free around her shoulders as she plucked a silver arrow from the quiver slung on her back and nocked it in the bowstring. Beside my wife Domitus also threw off his cloak and drew his concealed *gladius*.

Gallia shot fast and accurately, her missiles striking each lion in turn. She had hit and felled three before she started to walk forward, stepping on seats in front methodically as she kept on shooting. Another lion was hit and wounded, another was killed and still Gallia kept on advancing, walking towards the snarling, angry collection of jaws, teeth and claws.

The gladiators were leaning out of the windows and cheering wildly now as Gallia put an arrow into a lion that was mauling a hunter, the missile going through its eye socket and killing it instantly. A large beast with a wild mane charged, leaping over seats to get at her. She shot an arrow that struck its chest but only momentarily halted its attack. It roared in pain and rage and leaped forward again and my heart was in my mouth. In a flash she had pulled an arrow from her quiver, nocked it and shot it into the lion's chest. It dropped but three feet in front of her but was not dead. With a supreme effort it lifted itself up to claw the blonde-haired devil that was so close. Domitus ran forward and stabbed the point of his sword under its jaws, stabbing again and again into its throat. Gallia stepped around it as she continued shooting at the lions in the arena. More hunters now came from the doors to finish off the remaining beasts and save their wounded comrades.

I was shouting and cheering as they killed the last lion and then looked at the woman with the bow who had now stopped shooting. They heard the cheers from the gladiators above and peered in amazement at the beauty that looked as though she had just finished a leisurely stroll and they too cheered. The theatre had never seen such a drama. Ephesus had never seen such a thing. Its citizens had been in danger and Artemis herself had sent them a deliverer. For what other explanation could there be for the sudden appearance of a fair-haired woman armed with a bow that shot silver arrows?

A hundred people had been killed in the crush as the crowd tried to flee the theatre and a further two hundred were injured. The governor and his younger subordinate returned to the theatre with two centuries of legionaries and a detachment of archers. To find Gallia and Domitus sitting calmly in seats near the red awning. Soon afterwards High Priest Kallias returned, also accompanied by soldiers, in his case a hundred temple guards. Already slaves were carrying the bodies of the dead from the theatre and others were desperately trying to wash those seats that had been splattered with blood. I noticed that the corpulent Timini Ceukianus was conspicuous by his absence.

As I watched the high priest and governor walk over to Gallia and Domitus and engage them in conversation I felt a surge of pride in my wife.

'Our situation just got a lot more complicated,' said Drenis as he saw the governor's handsome subordinate bow his head to Gallia.

I heard Surena's voice behind me. 'I know her and if you knew her you would know that what she just did is not out of the ordinary. I first met her when…'

'Surena,' I shouted. 'Get over here and shut your mouth.'

Surena threw up his arms to the group of gladiators gathered round him and ambled over.

'Watch what you say,' I told him.

He was undeterred. 'But did you see what the queen did, lord? Wait till I tell Viper.'

'We saw,' said Arminius, 'now calm yourself and think on that the crowd has a new hero and has forgotten you.'

Surena looked dejected. 'Surely not?'

'The crowd is fickle, Surena,' said Drenis, 'every gladiator knows that.'

It was two hours before the crowd was allowed to return, the lions and their victims having been cleared from the area and seating and the spectators receiving assurances that there would be no further beast hunts on the sand. Word soon quickly spread of the blonde-haired woman who had appeared in the theatre as if by magic to slay the beasts. An excited slave serving fruit juice told us that someone had told him that the woman was a servant of the Goddess Artemis in human form. He nearly covered my hand with juice as he filled my cup so animated was he.

Drenis was unhappy. 'You see, the news of Gallia's exploits spread through the city like ripples in a pond.'

I went back to the windows and saw people filing back into the theatre, a line of legionaries in the front row of seats as before and the seats under the awning surrounded by soldiers. I also saw Gallia and Domitus seated behind the governor and Kallias, the latter turning to them frequently to say something. The handsome Roman officer also glanced behind to catch sight of my wife, inciting a stab of jealousy within me.

'Gladiators will return to their quarters to await the *editor's* pleasure.'

There was a groan of disappointment as an official made this announcement, Acco making his feelings plain.

'I came here to kill people not to spend my time wandering around this city of effeminates.'

'He must be Crixus returned from the dead,' reflected Alcaeus.

'The dead must have got as sick of him as I did,' remarked Arminius, picking up his helmet.

'Will we be coming back?' queried Surena.

Drenis grinned evilly. 'Oh, yes, we'll be back.'

And so we were. In an attempt to calm the nerves of the audience the editor laid on a series of novelty events. A large cage was erected on the sand and four giant seesaws set up inside it. Eight condemned men were then thrown into the cage and told to sit on the seesaws. They were at first uncooperative until a pack of ravenous hyenas was released into the cage, whereupon the poor wretches sat on the ends of the seesaws. As the creatures snapped at human flesh, the men on the bottom ends of the seesaws, exposed to attack, desperately pushed themselves high into the air to escape the hyenas. But this meant that a man on the other end dropped to the ground, to be attacked by beasts. He instantly pushed himself up, leading to eight criminals desperately trying to 'out-seesaw' each other, much to the delight of the crowd.

Eventually the drama reached its inevitable, grisly end with the deaths of the criminals. Afterwards archers killed the hyenas. Gallia told me that the crocodile wrestlers from Egypt were brave and skilful but the crowd only became excited when hunters were ordered to kill the beasts after one badly mauled one of the wrestlers and hissed in the direction of the spectators.

We were ordered back to the arena just as the last of the 'humorous' acts of the day was being played out. This involved condemned criminals being made to walk across the arena on stilts, which was difficult enough for anyone not used to them. It was made worse because dozens of poisonous snakes were released onto the sand. The condemned inevitably fell off their stilts and were bitten by the snakes, enduring a slow and painful death as the crowd roared its approval. In this way upwards of a hundred men were executed.

Removing the snakes from the sand afterwards was a meticulous and time-consuming business, some of the snake handlers being bitten as the *editor*, who had at last returned to the arena, demanded that the process be speeded up.

Surena was pacing up and down with excitement as an official announced the first six matched pairs to enter the theatre. He was disappointed that his name was not called though mine was. I nodded to Drenis and Arminius and told Surena to save his strength as I followed the official with eleven others down the steps. I was pitted against a *Hoplomachus*, a 'hoplite fighter', a gladiator whose weapons and equipment were loosely based on the Greek warriors of old. He wore a bronze helmet with eye grilles, padded armour on his right arm and legs and protective greaves on the latter. He carried a small, round bronze shield.

We stood on the blood-soaked sand with the referees and raised our weapons in salute to the governor and high priest, though I raised my sword to my wife and Domitus seated behind them. The crowd fell silent as the announcer, after being given a list of our names, introduced each of us to the crowd. When our names were called we raised our weapons so the crowd would know us, though there was only slight polite applause when the name Nikephorus of the *Ludus* Palmyra was announced. I was slightly perturbed when the name of my opponent, Menedaius of the *Ludus* Ephesus, received rapturous acclaim.

Menedaius' main weapon was a thrusting spear, though he also carried a sword and dagger. When the bout began his first attack was against my torso, which I parried easily. He jabbed his spear forward to keep me focused on its iron head and attempted to smash his shield into my right arm to knock me over. I sidestepped his shield and tried to slice open the side of his chest with my sword but he too sprang out of the way. We danced around each other, jabbing and slashing with our weapons, our *manicas* being cut but not our flesh. I did not hear the groans as other gladiators were wounded or killed, or indeed hear the noise of the crowd as it begged for the life of a gladiator who had been knocked to the ground to be spared. I only heard my own breathing and saw only the figure of Menedaius through my eye grilles. I splintered the shaft of his spear as he tried to ram the point through my foot but missed, the hilt of my sword fracturing the grain with a downward blow followed by my right elbow being driven into his chest. He was winded but I was tiring as he drew his sword and came at me with a series of strikes. They were powerful but easy to block or avoid because Menedaius was also tiring. I had no idea how long we had been fighting but the *editor* clearly thought we had been on the sand for too long as the referee suddenly placed his stick between us to signal a halt in our duel. I stepped back, my heart thumping, as the *editor*, his bottom lip protruding in anger,

285

indicated with a terse wave of his hand that we should depart the arena. Thus ended the first bout of Nikephorus the gladiator.

No one cheered my exit.

When I returned, exhausted, to the stage building Alcaeus examined me after I had taken off my helmet, *manicas* and greaves.

'No cuts, just a few bruises,' he reported. 'This evening I will get Argos to massage you again so you will be fit for tomorrow's bout of butchery.'

I flopped down on a couch and Drenis passed me a cup of water.

'Well done, Pacorus, you acquitted yourself well.'

I nodded my thanks. I saw Menedaius taking off his equipment and one of his companions handing him water to quench his thirst. He saw me and raised his cup. I did the same. It was most odd. A few minute before we had been locked in a potentially lethal struggle, but now no animosity existed between us. Spartacus had once told me that a gladiator had no friends, only acquaintances, because you might be called on to kill any of the men you trained and lived with in the *ludus*. How solitary and tortuous must be the life of a gladiator.

The crowd erupted in clapping and cheering as the next set of pairs walked on to the sand. Some gladiators drifted towards the windows to watch the bouts. I drained my cup and suddenly realised someone was missing.

'Where is Surena?' I asked Drenis.

'In the arena,' he replied.

I stood and walked over to the nearest window where Arminius was looking down at the crowd. Thus far he and Drenis had avoided any fighting, for which I was grateful.

He nodded at the awning under which the dignitaries, Gallia and Domitus were seated.

'Gallia and Domitus have the best seats in the house.'

I saw Surena standing on the sand, along with the tiresome Acco, each of them surrounded by four gladiators. I felt a sense of dread.

'Why aren't they paired off?'

'Why?' said Arminius. 'Because that fat *editor* has not forgotten that Surena insulted him and is annoyed that he has become the crowd's hero. So he wants him dead, and if he dies a glorious death in the arena then the crowd will be delighted. He will still be their hero, of course, but a dead one. And Acco is fighting against the odds because he's a merciless killer who regards a one-on-one contest as an insult to his fighting prowess.'

'It's all my fault,' I said softly.

'All of us volunteered to be here, Pacorus. We all knew it was a suicide mission.'

I looked at him. 'You did?'

He grinned. 'Naturally. Only you believed it would end in success. The rest of us, Gallia included, have a more realistic view of life and the world.'

I now felt even worse as I stared down at Surena surrounded by two *Secutors* and two *Murmillos*. The latter were armed with a *gladius*, *scutum*, and full-face bronze helmet with a large crest, a padded *manica* on the sword arm and a protective greave on the left leg. Acco faced two 'Hoplite fighters' and two *Provocators* who wore the same armour and carried the same weapons as Arminius. Surena looked hopelessly outnumbered and under-armed and armoured and I felt a knot tighten in my stomach as the announcer warmed up the crowd.

'Beyond the civilised world live barbarians who know nothing of the rule of law and public morals. It is these peoples that Rome has made its divine mission to conquer to bring peace and prosperity to the dark corners of the world. Rome's mighty legions have fought these barbarians for decades, primitives such as Acco of the Gauls.'

He extended an arm towards the Gaul who raised his two swords and roared at the crowd, which responded in kind. The announcer held up his arms in an appeal for silence. The noise died down.

'And in the East,' he continued, 'live the barbarian Parthians, Armenians and Syrians, who sacrifice their own young and who have no knowledge of art or architecture. And in the Eastern wastelands live fearsome warriors such as Surena of the Ma'adan.'

The crowd jumped up, cheered and whooped with joy as Surena raised his net and trident and basked in the adulation of over twenty thousand followers. They began chanting 'Surena,

287

Surena' as the announcer sat down and the two referees looked at the governor. The fat head of Timini Ceukianus was bobbing up and down behind his uncle in excited anticipation of Surena's imminent death. He may have been fat and idle but he was just as Roman at heart as his more martial relative. He neither forgot nor forgave.

The crowd sat down and grew silent, a tingle of anticipation hanging in the air as people licked their lips at the prospect of two men fighting at odds of four to one. The referees stood in the circle of gladiators with their sticks levelled. The governor cut down with his hand and the bouts began.

In battle you keep a close grip on your weapon because it is your best friend. Legionaries throw their javelins and cataphracts spear enemies with the *kontus* because that is what those weapons are designed for. But a legionary never lets go of his *gladius* and a cataphract never releases the hold on his sword, axe or mace in the mêlée. Your close-quarter weapon is the only thing that prevents you being killed because no matter how thick your shield or armour, if you have no offensive weapon then eventually you will lose a fight.

But Surena broke the first rule of combat when he hurled his trident forward. He had been facing the governor, watching for his hand signal, and had launched his trident even before the referee had made his signal. The weapon flew through the air and struck the *Murmillo* he was facing in the chest, the three prongs embedding themselves in the exposed flesh. The 'fish man' collapsed instantly as Surena threw his net at the *Secutor* on his left side, the giant spider's web expanding as it flew at the gladiator. Surena pulled his dagger from its sheath and sprang at the *Secutor* like a panther. The *Secutor* caught the flying net on his shield and cast it aside easily enough, but the few seconds required to do so was all that Surena needed to thrust his dagger beneath the Secutor's helmet and into his throat. The crowd cheered wildly as the wounded gladiator collapsed on the sand.

Acco was dealing death with his two swords but all I was interested in was Surena, who now faced a *Murmillo* and *Secutor* who were standing beside each other, swords levelled and shields facing my former squire. The latter snatched his net from the sand and stood ready to face his two opponents, armed only with a dagger. The *Murmillo*, certain of victory against a man armed only with a dagger, raced forward. Surena threw his net once more, the material billowing in the air as the *Murmillo* cut it aside with his *gladius*. But Surena had picked up the dead *Secutor's* sword and performed a forward roll to the left, tucking the sword close to his body and then lashing out with it to slice open the *Murmillo's* right calf. There was a high-pitched yelp as Surena stood and raced over to the other *Murmillo* who lay flat on his back. He plucked the trident from the man's chest and turned to face the *Secutor* as the other *Murmillo* sank to his knees, blood spurting from his gashed calf. He was out of the fight.

Surena sheathed his dagger as he faced his last opponent still standing.

The *Secutor* circled Surena who gripped his trident with both hands, his left shoulder turned towards his enemy to maximise the protection afforded by his *galerus*. He suddenly fed the trident through his hands to jab the prongs in the *Secutor's* face. The latter slashed at the trident with his *gladius* but Surena feinted, snapped it back, leaped to the left and jabbed the trident forward again. He feinted right, jumped back and feigned an overhead attack with his weapon. The *Secutor* lifted his shield to deflect the blow but Surena was already thinking about his next move, leaning back as he crouched low to hurl the trident forward. In a second the three prongs had struck the *Secutor* in the torso, between his belt and rib cage.

The crowd uttered a collective sigh as the *Secutor* staggered, dropped his sword and pulled the trident from his body. He staggered a few steps more before falling to his knees as Surena lifted his arms to the crowd to milk their applause. He turned to the dignitaries and gave a clenched first salute, spitting on the sand once more when he caught the eye of Ceukianus. I saw Gallia smirk and Domitus rise to his feet to applaud the young man from the marshlands as the theatre was filled with the chant of 'Surena, Surena'.

He pulled his dagger from its sheath and walked over to the *Murmillo* who was lying on his side, holding his severed calf. The *Secutor* had meanwhile died of his throat wound, blood still oozing on to the sand. Common practice was for the wounded gladiator to kneel before his vanquisher, holding one of his legs and bending his head forward so the victor of the duel could deliver a fatal, merciful blow with his sword. But Surena merely tore off the man's helmet and slit his throat. The crowd gasped at this break from protocol and the referee rushed over to admonish him. Surena pushed him away and went to retrieve his net and trident, the former being ripped and now useless.

Acco had, meanwhile, also killed all four of his opponents, though his victory was marred by the crowd's worship of Surena, who was now walking around the edge of the arena with his arms raised, accepting the adulation. As he got near to Acco and his blood-covered swords he must have said something because the Gaul squared up to him and Surena prepared to fight once more. A referee blew a whistle and more assistants ran from the stage building to separate the two gladiators, leading each away to separate exit doors.

'You know,' Arminius said to me, 'you might have trouble getting Surena to come back to Dura with us. He has had a taste of the arena and he finds it to his liking.'

'He would never abandon Viper,' I assured him.

'He could always send for her.'

When he returned to us Surena allowed Alcaeus to give him a clean bill of health and then held out his arms so slaves could remove his belt and *galerus*. Fortunately Acco had decided to return to his quarters rather than spend any further time in the company of gladiators, so there would be no further friction between the two. At least not today.

'I will need a new net, lord,' he said to me as he sat down on a bench and snapped his fingers at a slave holding a jug of water. 'For tomorrow.'

'Hopefully you will be rested tomorrow after your heroics today.'

His face creased into a mask of disappointment. 'I cannot let down the crowd, lord. They will be expecting me.'

Drenis slapped him on the shoulder and looked at me. 'A crowd needs a hero and a hero needs a crowd.'

This day's crowd began to leave the theatre after a most interesting day that had seen a dozen more gladiators killed and many more fatalities as a result of the lions getting loose. As legionaries escorted us from the stage building a great crowd gathered round us as on the previous day. Our progress was very slow. I asked a legionary what the problem was as Surena accepted kisses and embraces from his ever-growing harem of young female admirers.

'Worshippers from the temple,' the legionary told me. 'They are blocking all the roads in the city. They want to see that woman who killed the lions with her bow. They believe she is a god, or something like that.'

When we got back to the house on the hill he discovered that the woman he was referring to was the 'wife' of my *lanista* because there were hundreds of people crowded round the building.

'The governor will need to send more guards,' he said as he and his fellow legionaries used their shields to create a path for us to the entrance.

As many of the crowd began to sing some sort of religious song and light candles, I walked into the courtyard to see Gallia seated with Domitus. I made sure Lysander was absent before taking her in my arms and kissing her.

'Hail to the queen of the Amazons,' I teased her.

'Hail to the king of the arena,' Domitus said as Surena entered the courtyard.

'A new king and queen,' remarked Drenis, 'the gods smile on us.'

'Indeed they do,' I said, 'because Burebista has been withdrawn from the games. Gallia's intervention today has convinced me that we have divine help in our venture. That crowd outside believes her to be Artemis herself.'

I gave no thought to Lysander's absence as Argos massaged the stress and aches from my body soon afterwards. After I had been refreshed I asked Domitus to send a slave to the harbour with a note for Athineos to ask him to come to the house and update me on the next step in our negotiations with Lentulus Vatia. But all thoughts of Athineos were put to the back of my mind when Lysander arrived with an invitation from High Priest Kallias himself.

'Kallias?' said Domitus. 'What does he want with us?'

Lysander stood with his hands behind his back, grinning as usual.

'The high priest requests the company of *Lanista* Lucius Domitus, his wife and the gladiator Nikephorus at his house this evening.'

Domitus looked at me. 'Why does the high priest want a lowly gladiator in his house?'

Lysander's smile continued to hold. 'I do not know, master, only that High Priest Kallias desires his company along with that of yourself and your wife.'

Domitus seemed uninterested, which made Lysander uncomfortable.

'It is a great honour, master, to receive such an invitation.'

I nodded at Domitus who sighed loudly.

'Very well. Tell the priest that we accept his invitation.'

Lysander bowed his head and scurried from the courtyard.

'You have certainly made an impression,' Alcaeus said to Gallia. 'Kallias is the most influential man in Ephesus, perhaps in this part of Asia, and to be asked to eat with him is an honour many of the most important citizens of this city would kill for. Strange that he should invite Pacorus, though.'

'Perhaps he was impressed by my performance in the arena,' I said.

'I doubt it,' scoffed Drenis.

Surena was most unhappy. 'Why wasn't I invited?'

'Because that fat *editor* wants to entertain you tonight, Surena,' said a grinning Arminius, 'in his bed.'

'That's disgusting,' remarked Gallia, 'but then you didn't have to sit near the odious fat Roman. He stinks and his breath is enough to sour milk.'

'You need to get your rest tonight, Surena,' I told him, 'so you are fresh for tomorrow's bouts.'

'You think I will be fighting tomorrow, lord?'

I thought about the *editor's* anger and disappointment when Surena had survived the fight against four adversaries earlier.

'I have no doubt.'

As we were not eating at the house we prepared ourselves for the meeting with Kallias. Domitus and I wore simple white tunics with leather belts and sandals on our feet. Gallia made more of an effort, donning a white silk dress that covered her legs but left her svelte arms bare. It was secured at the shoulder with silver brooches and around her waist she wore a thin silver belt. She let her locks hang loosely around her shoulders, wearing a silver tiara inlaid with lapis lazuli on her head and long silver earrings below. Her necklace was a solid silver torc-style ornament, the ends of which were griffins.

'Dobbai gave it to me as a present,' she told me. 'She said it combined my Gaul heritage with my position as Dura's queen.'

I touched one of the griffins. 'I like it.' I brushed her cheek with my fingers. 'Though not as much as the one who wears it.'

She smiled sheepishly. 'Remember who you are, Nikephorus.'

Lysander returned to the house with fifty palace guards to ensure our journey to the high priest's house was undisturbed. Most of Gallia's adherents had returned to either their lodgings in the city or their tents around the Temple of Artemis, the governor having ordered the city gates to be closed early to rid the streets of the worshippers of the goddess. I walked behind Domitus and Gallia, surrounded by a small phalanx of temple guards in their bronze helmets and bronze scale armour cuirasses as we made our way to the house of Kallias.

I say house but in reality it was a small palace located on the western side of a small square near the *prytaneion*. Those worshippers who had money to rent lodgings in the city called to Gallia and tried to touch her hair as we walked on the marble flagstones. But the guards kept them at a safe distance, occasionally using shields to knock individuals out of the way. They said nothing during the journey but I noticed that many cast glances at Gallia, especially her long blonde hair. I had seen that look before: when I had returned to Parthia after fighting in Italy and had brought Gallia back with me. People had been mesmerised by her fair skin, blue eyes and blonde locks. And here, at Ephesus, many believed her to be the reincarnation of Artemis herself.

The abode of Kallias was a magnificent two-storey structure with a façade that had Corinthian style columns on the ground floor, the columns being made of honey-coloured marble and the steps leading to the main entrance being white marble. There was a gated entrance to the square to ensure no undesirables entered, which meant the gaggle of worshippers who had followed us from our own accommodation were kept outside. The guards escorted us to the steps of the palace where a white-robed priest with oiled black hair and a black beard welcomed us and requested we follow him.

We walked up the steps and past the columns, in the recesses between which were white marble statues of Artemis, Zeus, Hera and Apollo. I detected the aroma of frankincense as we entered the reception hall that had white marble floor tiles, frescoes of Greek gods on the walls and more honey-coloured marble columns. Beside them stood guards armed with spears and shields. Slaves dressed in white *chitons* and bare feet tended to lamps and candles.

We were shown into the modestly sized banqueting hall that had even more marble than the reception hall, our guide bowing his head as he stood beside the open doors made of cypress. I notice that there were five daybeds arranged in a circle, each one having a table of the same height positioned in front of it. Normally at formal occasions Greek men and women ate separately but tonight was an exception for beside the imposing figure of Kallias stood the alluring Hippo, like Gallia wearing white and draped in silver jewellery.

Kallias walked forward, a smile on his large face.

'Welcome Lucius Domitus of the *Ludus* Palmyra,' his voice was deep and commanding. 'Please, take the weight off your feet.'

He led Domitus to a richly upholstered daybed next to his own as Hippo went to Gallia.

'Hail to you, lady, whose exploits this day have made you the talk of all Ephesus.'

Hippo clicked her fingers and a female slave came forward to escort Gallia to a daybed opposite Domitus. Hippo turned her big brown eyes to me.

'Welcome Nikephorus, valiant gladiator from the *Ludus* Palmyra.'

Unexpectedly she linked her arm in mine and led me to the daybed next to the one Domitus occupied and then she took her position beside Gallia and opposite Kallias. The high priest reclined on his side as slaves hurried from the kitchens with trays of food and jugs of wine.

I had spent many hours with Alcaeus, both on campaign and in the legionary camp, during which he had explained Greek eating habits. Royal feasts in Parthia tended to be lavish affairs to display a court's wealth and power to guests. It had been the same in Persian times and before them the Mesopotamians. But Greeks viewed such banquets as morally decadent and believed over-eating to be uncouth. Similarly drinking wine that had not been watered down was seen as barbaric. He was always telling me that Greeks approached both eating and drinking alcohol with frugality to highlight their idea of themselves as poor but free people. This was important more than ever now that Greece was under Roman rule because it was an expression not only of Greek manners but also of Greek freedom despite Rome's governance.

Tonight's feast was indeed frugal, though not unvaried. Slaves brought barley cakes, cold boiled dandelion, celery, melons, cucumber, pumpkins, onions, radishes and lettuce. A delicious treat was honeycombs served in their natural form. There was no meat, the Greeks believing that animals killed purely for consumption was frivolous. They preferred to eat meat from animals that had first been sacrificed to the gods. However, we were served with fish, mainly ray and skate, the latter's 'wings' being cooked in wine vinegar, olive oil and capers.

We sipped wine from shallow drinking cups made of ceramic and called a *kylix*. They had handles and bases and were decorated with images of nymphs and satyrs.

Kallias stared at Domitus over the rim of his *kylix*.

'The wine is to your liking, *lanista?*'

Domitus nodded. 'Most excellent, sir.'

'And you, Lady Gallia?' asked Kallias.

Gallia smiled at him. 'Your hospitality is impeccable, high priest.'

Kallias placed his *kylix* on the table before him and picked up a slice of melon.

'Nikephorus, the food is to your liking?'

I kept my head down to avoid his eyes. 'Yes, *dominus*.'

'It is a great honour to have you here with us,' said Hippo, 'especially you, lady, who displayed great courage in the theatre today. I am certain the goddess guided your hand when you shot those lions with your bow.'

'It must be so,' remarked Kallias, 'for how else could a woman shoot a man's weapon?'

Gallia momentarily bristled but remembered where she was. She smiled coyly.

'You are too kind.'

Kallias leaned back on his couch. 'You may be interested to know that before the Romans came the Great Theatre was the place where plays were performed. Indeed, when not the venue for Roman vulgarity actors still perform there.'

He looked at Domitus. 'I apologise for insulting your race.'

'No apology needed, sir,' said Domitus.

'Did you also know,' he said to Domitus, 'that actors in the theatre wear masks made of linen to hide their features, to disguise themselves?'

'No, sir.'

Kallias pointed at me. 'Just as gladiators disguise themselves in the arena by wearing bronze helmets. All except that young ram of yours; what is his name?'

'Surena,' answered Domitus.

'A modern-day Hector indeed. Where did you acquire him from, *lanista*?'

'From the East,' said Domitus evasively.

Kallias nibbled on his melon.

'The East, yes. Did you know that Ephesus is the destination of goods brought from the East along the so-called Silk Road?'

'I did not, sir, no,' replied Domitus.

'It is a most wondrous thing. Goods that are made in China travel thousands of miles across the Parthian Empire to arrive in Syria, Asia and Egypt. But perhaps more interesting are the stories that the caravans bring with them. Most of them are either made up or wildly exaggerated, of course, but not all. For example, we know that the ruler of the Parthian Empire is a tyrant named Mithridates, a man who reportedly murdered his own father. You have probably heard of him, *lanista*, Palmyra being so close to Parthia.'

Domitus looked disinterested. 'I have heard of him.'

'Parthia sounds a wild, lawless place,' continued Kallias, 'filled with warring factions. It certainly causes the Romans some disquiet, though sometimes that is no bad thing.'

He threw up an arm. 'There I go again, insulting you.'

'You do not insult me, sir,' replied Domitus.

'But you are Roman, are you not?' enquired Kallias.

Domitus nodded.

'But not your wife.'

Domitus shook his head.

'I am from Gaul,' said Gallia.

Kallias looked muddled. 'I am unfamiliar with Roman practices, *lanista*. You own the gladiators that fight for you, do you not?'

'I do, sir,' said Domitus.

'And yet unlike the other *lanistas* who are here in Ephesus your men are not kept under lock and key at night.'

Domitus smiled. 'I trust them not to escape, sir. After all, Palmyra is a long way from Ephesus.'

Kallias sipped at his wine. 'And Dura is even further away.'

To his credit Domitus did not blink. 'Dura?'

Kallias looked at Hippo. 'You see, high priestess, how good an actor he is.'

Domitus jumped off his couch. 'If you have something to say, priest, then say it.'

Kallias held up a hand. 'I meant no offence, general. For you are General Lucius Domitus, are you not? Commander of the army of the Kingdom of Dura and the steel fist of its king.'

He looked at me. 'Pacorus, son of King Varaz of Hatra and formerly Lord High General of the Parthian Empire.'

'The husband of Gallia, Queen of Dura and commander of a band of female warriors called the Amazons,' added Hippo.

I looked at Gallia as Kallias rose from his couch and dismissed all the slaves in the room, ordering the doors to be closed.

297

He turned to me. 'In your plans and deception you overlooked one important thing.'

'Which was?' I asked.

'Slaves,' he answered. 'There are two hundred thousand people in this city and at least a quarter of them are slaves. More importantly, all the ones who serve in the house you are currently living in are owned by the Temple of Artemis and its servants.'

'Including Lysander?' I asked.

'Lysander is a free man,' replied Kallias, 'but he too works for me.'

He pointed at me. 'Did you think that just because I am a priest I do not take an interest in what happens in the world? That I have not heard of King Pacorus and his blonde-haired queen, the man who destroyed a Roman army before Dura and turned back the army of Pompey? How easy it was, therefore, to make the link between a gladiator who wore a lock of blonde hair around his neck and who shared the bed of the wife of his *lanista* with the same individual.'

'What do you want?' snapped Gallia. 'I assume you did not bring us here just to enjoy our company.'

Kallias smiled and Hippo appeared delighted by Gallia's fierceness.

'I have heard that Queen Gallia is a warrior and your actions today have confirmed it.'

The high priest retook his seat. 'However, those actions have presented me with a problem.'

'The worshippers at the temple believe you to be the reincarnation of Artemis herself,' said Hippo.

Kallias' high forehead was wearing a frown. 'I do not know what reason brought you to Ephesus but I must ask you all to leave forthwith. Your presence may incite trouble with the Roman authorities.'

'You fear the Romans, High Priest Kallias?' I asked.

His nostrils flared. 'I do not fear the Romans, lord king, but I do not want to give them an excuse to unleash a bloodbath against the followers of the goddess.'

'I am not here to incite a rebellion,' stated Gallia.

'Then may I ask what are you here for, majesty?' Kallias retorted.

Gallia looked at me.

'We are here to free a friend from slavery,' I said, 'and cannot leave until the games are finished.'

'If you do not leave forthwith then I cannot guarantee your safety,' said Kallias.

'Meaning what?' I asked.

'Meaning that if I have discovered your identity then it is only a matter of time before the governor does.'

'Or you decide to tell him,' said Gallia.

Hippo's eyes opened wide in amazement that a woman, even a queen, would dare to speak to the high priest of the temple thus. But Kallias merely picked up a chunk of pumpkin with his hand and ate it.

'I have heard tales of the Queen of Dura,' he said after he had finished it. 'I believed the tales of how she shot down her enemies with her bow from the saddle were fantasies, that the band of women warriors called the Amazons was a lie invented to cower the enemies of the Kingdom of Dura. But I have seen with my own eyes your courage, your skill with a bow and your fearlessness.'

He rose from his couch and pointed at the doors.

'There are over twenty thousand visiting followers of the goddess camped around the temple or quartered in the city, plus thousands more who live in the city and pray to Her. By now every one of them will have heard of how a blonde-haired woman shooting silver arrows killed the lions that threatened to rip the theatre's crowd to pieces.

'Rightly or wrongly they believe that you, Queen Gallia, are at the very least one of the immortal Amazons sent by Artemis to show the people the goddesses' power. Others believe that you *are* Artemis Herself. It was not lost on those who witnessed your exploits that the Roman soldiers fled before the beasts whereas you not only stood your ground but advanced upon them.'

'The queen likes to get close to those she is slaughtering,' remarked Domitus jovially.

Kallias was not smiling. 'You may think it is a matter for mirth, general, but I am responsible for all the souls in this city and I will not place them in danger.'

'They are in no danger,' I said. 'As soon as we get what we came for we shall be gone from Ephesus.'

Kallias retook his couch and drank a mouthful of wine.

'I have no interest in revealing your identities to the Romans and nor will I do so. I just want you gone. And to expedite your leaving you might be interested to know that my esteemed friend and governor, Quintus Caecilius Metellus, is an enemy of Pompey, who slighted him in some way.'

'He has denied him a triumph, high priest,' said Hippo. 'It is some sort of parade through Rome that is accorded to returning victorious generals.'

Kallias nodded. 'That makes him an ally of Marcus Licinius Crassus, King Pacorus, a man I believe you are acquainted with.'

'Though not fondly,' I added.

Kallias picked up another piece of pumpkin. 'I am sure the governor would like nothing more than to ship you and your wife back to Rome as slaves to be paraded through the streets in chains, King Pacorus.'

'Dura and Rome are not at war, priest,' spat Domitus.

Kallias sighed. 'How little you know of politics, general. I heard that Pompey agreed a peace with King Pacorus because he did not want to be annihilated, or at least that is what vicious tongues say. The peace agreed between him and your king means nothing to Pompey's enemies, of which Metellus is one.'

He shook his head. 'What were you thinking of coming here?'

'I told you,' I said, 'we are here to rescue a friend.'

I explained to him about Burebista and my approach to the *lanista* of the *Ludus* Capua concerning purchasing his freedom and that of his wife. Of how I had believed that Burebista had been killed outside Rhegium during the fighting to rescue Spartacus' army, and how Athineos had travelled to Dura to inform me that he was a gladiator and would be taking part in the games at Ephesus.

'But what I do not understand, King Pacorus,' said Kallias, 'is why you came here pretending to be a lowborn gladiator to risk your life in the arena? Why not just send a representative to Ephesus to bargain with the owner of this Burebista? It makes no sense.'

300

Domitus laughed and gulped down some wine.

'There's no point in talking about sense to Pacorus, priest, he has none. He has a god-given gift for winning battles and wars but when it comes to common sense you will get more from one of those statues outside.'

Kallias was appalled by Domitus' intemperate words.

'You allow your subordinates to speak to you in such a manner, lord king?'

I told him about the Companions and how each man and woman of our close-knit band is allowed such familiarity, regardless of rank or race.

'That is why I have to secure the release of Burebista, high priest,' I told him, 'because he is a Companion and we leave no man behind.'

'Or woman,' added Gallia.

I saw Hippo smiling and staring with wonderment at Gallia. Perhaps she believed that my wife was one of the bronze statues in her temple given life by Artemis. But Kallias was at a loss to understand my reasoning.

'Tomorrow,' he said, 'the worshippers who have come to Ephesus will not be at the temple but around the theatre, hoping to catch a glimpse of Queen Gallia. It will be a volatile situation and will only take a tiny incident to spark a disturbance. If that happens the Romans will unleash great violence against any trouble makers.'

'I give you my word that I will not incite the crowd,' said Gallia solemnly.

Kallias stared into his *kylix*. 'I am afraid, Queen Gallia, that you will have no control over the mob's actions. Once seized by a collective madness no one individual can influence its mood. That is why it is imperative that you all leave and do not appear at the theatre tomorrow. I will not allow the Romans to butcher my people.'

'No,' I said, 'we cannot do that.'

Kallias fixed me with a hard stare. 'That is your final word on the matter?'

'It is.'

'Then our discussion is at an end.'

Kallias called for the doors to be opened and informed the captain of his guards that we were to be escorted back to

301

our quarters. He smiled politely as we took our leave and was surprised when Hippo stated that she would accompany us back to the house.

As before we were surrounded by a phalanx of temple guards, half a dozen carrying lighted torches to provide illumination. Beyond the gated square onlookers and well-wishers, all eager to catch a glimpse of or get close to Gallia once more surrounded us. The presence of Hippo beside Gallia only confirmed to them that my wife had indeed been sent by Artemis herself; for why else would the high priestess of the goddess' temple be accompanying her?

'When I heard the stories of Queen Gallia and the Amazons I did not believe them.' Hippo said to Gallia in Latin so the guards would not understand her. 'My apologies, majesty. You speak the language of the Romans?'

'Unfortunately, yes,' replied Gallia.

Hippo continued in Latin. 'When I saw you shooting your bow in the theatre it was a revelation. It was as though everything that I have held dear all my life had come to fruition. It is surely no coincidence that you have come to Ephesus, the city of Artemis.'

'We came to free one of our own,' replied Gallia, 'nothing more.'

'The gods may work through you, though you may not realise it, majesty.'

Gallia turned and looked at me. 'My husband worships Shamash, the Sun God.' She tilted her head at Domitus beside her. 'His general worships Mars, the Roman God of War. We have many gods in Dura. I like to think that the gods help those who help themselves. That they respect strength and determination but I ask no favours of any god.'

'Is it true that you have fought in battle?' enquired Hippo.

Gallia smiled. 'Many times.'

Hippo turned to look at me.

'It is true,' I said.

Hippo suddenly appeared sad. 'I envy you, majesty. To be a woman in this world is to be subservient but you have shown a glimpse of a different world where women are free to follow their desires.'

302

I had a feeling that she was not speaking of her role as a priestess but as a beautiful young woman with feelings for another. The captain of the temple guards called a halt as we reached our house, ordering the crowd that we had gathered to disperse back to their homes immediately. A few drifted away but the majority ignored his demand.

Gallia laid a hand on Hippo's arm. 'There is another life for you should you desire it, priestess. A gilded cage is still a cage.'

Hippo smiled politely and bowed her head to Gallia as the legionaries opened the gates to allow us to enter. When we were out of earshot Domitus turned to me.

'We should take that priest's advice, Pacorus, even though I don't trust him.'

But as we wandered into the entrance hall to the house, oil lamps burning on brackets on the walls and candles on stands by the doors, I realised that Kallias was the least of our problems. We walked into the *andron*, a salon that was usually reserved for men though Gallia had disregarded this formal rule as soon as she had arrived. We were stopped in our tracks when we saw the figure of Governor Metellus sitting in a chair.

He conformed to every notion I had of a senior Roman commander. Lean, severe and with an expression that was as hard as the blade of the *gladius* he wore at his left hip, he sneered at me as I stood in the entrance.

'King Pacorus of Dura. You will forgive me if I do not stand only I do not rise when slaves enter a room.'

Domitus made to throw himself at the man who resembled him in appearance if not in age, but I held out an arm to stop him. The handsome young tribune stood behind Metellus and there were six legionaries nearby, all with swords in their hands.

'Where are my men?'

'Under lock and key in the storerooms that were allocated for the quartering of gladiators when they are not at the Great Theatre.'

He looked at Domitus. 'You are a Roman and yet you ally yourself with these slaves. Why?'

303

'These *slaves*,' replied Domitus slowly and sternly, 'are my friends and are braver than any Romans I have ever encountered.'

The governor rose from his chair and walked over to me, our faces inches apart.

'I have heard much about King Pacorus, the Parthian who fought beside the outlaw Spartacus, who vanquished his foes in a civil war in Parthia, defeated a Roman army before the walls of Dura Europos and cowered the great Pompey.'

'Who betrayed us?' I asked flatly.

He smiled. 'Betrayed you? You seem to forget that you are in a Roman city, Parthian, under Roman jurisdiction. The *lanista* of the *Ludus* Capua sent a message that he had been approached by a Cretan captain who was negotiating on behalf of a person or persons unknown to purchase one of his gladiators. Does this sound familiar?'

I looked away from him without answering. He walked back to his chair and sat down.

'The *lanista*,' Metellus continued, 'a base individual common to his profession, would have been given short shrift had it not been for two other things he informed me of. First, there is no *Ludus* Palmyra. I know this because Palmyra is not under Roman rule, at least not yet.'

He looked at Gallia. 'Second, and perhaps more important, he informed me that the blonde-haired woman who had until today kept herself covered was none other than his wife. Or at least his former wife.'

'I am not the wife of that pig,' sneered Gallia.

'That is of no concern to me,' said Metellus, 'but I was interested in the story of how his wife had escaped from Capua, joined the band of Spartacus and subsequently became the scourge of Italy riding alongside the one they called "the Parthian".'

He pointed at me. 'You are he are you not?'

'If you know the answer then why are you asking?'

The strapping tribune walked forward and struck the side of my face with the back of his hand. The blow was heavy and made me smart. Domitus growled in anger but I shook my head at him as I tasted blood at the corner of my mouth.

'You will answer, slave,' ordered Metellus.

I said nothing as he nodded to the tribune who drew his *gladius* and held the point at Gallia's neck.

'If you refuse to answer Tribune Marcus Aristius will kill your queen.'

'I am Pacorus, king of Dura and husband to Queen Gallia of Dura,' I said loudly.

The governor waved Marcus Aristius back.

'According to Roman law you are an escaped slave and can expect to receive punishment commensurate with such an offence. However, as I do not wish to deprive those who have come to attend the games of their entertainment, I have decided that tomorrow you and your companions will fight in the arena. It would be callous to deprive you of the opportunity to fight in the arena since you have devoted so much time and effort to become gladiators. So gladiators is what you shall be.'

He pointed at Domitus. 'Tomorrow you will sit near me to maintain the fiction that you are the *lanista* of the *Ludus* Palmyra, and the day after the games you will be crucified outside the city so before you die you will have time to reflect on your betrayal of your race.'

He stood and looked at Gallia. 'And you will be returned to Lentulus Vatia, to be used as he sees fit. You will not be so pretty when you have been branded for being a runaway. Take them away.'

We were bundled out of the room into the courtyard and then into the storeroom next to the one where the others were incarcerated. After the door had been locked and guards posted Drenis shouted to us to enquire if were all right. I shouted back that we were, but our conversation was interrupted by a centurion informing us that if we did not remain silent he would order his soldiers to rape Gallia and break each of our left arms.

So we sat in silence, Gallia in my arms, as the guards laughed and joked outside. Dobbai was right. I was a hopeless dreamer and now my fanciful plan would result in the deaths of my friends and see my wife condemned to a life of slavery.

Chapter 11

The night passed slowly, but eventually the courtyard grew lighter as the first rays of the sun peaked above the hill to the east of the city to bathe Ephesus in glorious sunshine. Gallia opened her eyes and I kissed her forehead. I felt utterly helpless and forlorn and then I felt angry. Angry that I had allowed this situation to come to pass and even angrier in the knowledge that I was absolutely powerless. As my wife stretched out her tired limbs and stood up to peer through the grille in the thick door I realised that I was no longer a king but a Roman slave.

I had previously been captured by the Romans in Cappadocia and transported in harsh conditions to Italy where Spartacus had rescued me on the slopes of Vesuvius. During the journey I had been beaten and flogged and had often been bereft of hope. But my incarceration had ended in liberation followed by three glorious years fighting beside Spartacus against the Romans. But there was no slave army anywhere near Ephesus, no would-be liberators, only a docile population of a Roman city. I slammed the floor with my fist.

Domitus stirred. While I had been possessed of self-recriminations and regrets during the night he had slept like the dead. He was facing death on the cross and yet managed to sleep like a baby. He stretched out his muscled arms and looked at me.

'Did you get any sleep?'

I shook my head. 'No.'

He stood and stretched his back. 'Course not. Spent the whole night torturing yourself, no doubt. Why do it to yourself when the Romans will do it for you?'

I heard voices outside. I pulled Gallia back from the door as it was unlocked.

'Out slaves!' came the order as light flooded the storeroom. The door where the others were imprisoned was also unlocked and they too were ordered into the courtyard. Surena bowed his head to me while Alcaeus, Drenis and Arminius nodded.

'Are you all right?' I asked them.

I felt a sharp pain on the side of my face as a centurion struck me with his vine cane.

'No talking, slave.'

Surena began to move aggressively towards the centurion but I shook my head. There were ten legionaries in the courtyard, all of whom had swords in their hands in case of any trouble.

'You will all eat and change into your gladiator attire,' the centurion stated. 'Any trouble and I have orders to kill you on the spot.'

We were allowed to wash our faces, arms and legs in the fountains and relieve ourselves on the communal lavatories – a novel feature of these rich houses – that flushed out into the sewers beneath the street outside. The centurion must have been under orders to accord Gallia some respect because she was allowed back into the house to change and wash in private, female slaves attending her.

More slaves brought food for us to eat: eggs, barley porridge, grapes and figs. Lysander, no longer wearing a smile, poured water into our cups. He avoided our eyes as he did so, though when he filled my cup he whispered into my ear.

'This was not my doing, majesty. I work for High Priest Kallias, not the Romans.'

I looked up at him. 'I attach no blame to you, Lysander.'

'Many worshippers are flooding into the city to see Queen Gallia, majesty.'

He finished pouring water and withdrew from the courtyard. Domitus was wolfing down a bowl of porridge while Alcaeus was picking at a bunch of grapes more thoughtfully. Surena, Drenis and Arminius, like Domitus, were eating as though it was their last meal. I felt sick; it well might be.

'Get some food inside you,' whispered Domitus, 'you will need your strength today.'

'No talking!' bellowed the centurion as he circled the table like a ravenous wolf. We kept our heads down and I began to eat the bowl of porridge in front of me.

Gallia returned and was also served food and water. She was in a clean white dress and her hair had been brushed and her arms massaged with oil. She smiled sympathetically at me as she took her seat by my side. The slaves offered us more porridge and figs, which Domitus accepted, and then took away our empty bowls. The legionaries had sheathed their swords and the centurion had sat down on a stool and was eating a bowl of figs. Thrushes and plovers landed on the roof tiles and sang their songs and the occasional buzzard flew overhead. Despite the danger we were in the serenity of the courtyard and the sound of its fountains had a calming effect on me.

'I hope they give him the shits,' said Domitus slowly.

After we had eaten we were ordered to get into our gladiator clothing. Alcaeus requested and was allowed to reclaim his bag of medicines from inside the house but we were forbidden to carry our weapons to the arena. They would be taken to the theatre later by a detachment of legionaries. After we had dressed there was a blast of trumpets outside the house and the centurion ordered us all to stand in a line. His men drew their swords once more and stood behind us, the points of their weapons in our backs.

'You have an important visitor so stay silent and show respect. Remember that you are slaves. Any disrespect will incur the gravest penalties.'

There were footsteps in the house and the great bulk of Timini Ceukianus was I front of us, behind him a slave holding a parasol to keep the sun off his balding crown. The day was warm but not unpleasantly so but already the fat editor's forehead was beaded with sweat and his rancid body odour went before him.

His wore a leer on his bloated face as he viewed us.

'I've never had a king fight in the arena before. How marvellous.'

'He is a king no longer, sir,' said the centurion, tapping the cane against his right leg. 'He is a slave. They all are.'

'Thank you centurion,' snapped Ceukianus with annoyance, 'I am well aware of their status. I have been fully briefed by my uncle.'

Ceukianus waved him back and snapped his fingers. A young slave boy no more than ten years of age and dressed only in a loincloth came forward with a towel to dab the *editor's* sweaty forehead.

'I expect all of you to fulfil the roles allotted to you,' said Ceukianus. 'You are now the property of Rome and she will do with you as she sees fit. Most of you will soon be dead, so meet your end with dignity and be thankful that I have given you the opportunity to experience death on the sacred sand of the arena.'

His piggy eyes settled on the bare torso of Surena. He struck the boy slave with a flick of his hand to indicate he should withdraw and took a few steps so he was standing in front of Surena. He avoided the *editor's* gaze, his head cast down, as Ceukianus extended a hand and began to rub Surena's chest.

'The darling of the crowd,' he murmured. He licked his top lip with his tongue. 'Perhaps you will be my darling if I decide to let you live. Would you like that, *slave?*'

The tension was almost unbearable as Ceukianus waited for an answer. I prayed that Surena would keep his temper in check.

'I am unworthy, *dominus*,' he uttered.

Ceukianus began breathing heavily as he continued to fondle Surena.

'Nonsense. You are a magnificent specimen. I shall arrange for you to be brought to my villa tonight where I can get more intimately familiar with you.'

He traced a finger down the side of Surena's cheek. 'Don't use up all your strength in the arena.'

He sighed with satisfaction and turned to face the centurion.

'There is a large crowd outside, centurion, do not let them anywhere near the slave woman. In their childlike imagination they imagine her to be a demi-god.'

'Don't you worry about them, sir, my men will deal with any trouble.'

Ceukianus spun round, venom in his eyes. 'And if any of you cause trouble on the way to the arena I will feed you to the beasts.'

The walk to the theatre was a solemn affair, all of us with heads bowed on the centurion's orders and the crowd picking up on the air of threat. As we walked towards the *agora* to take part in the daily procession to the theatre the crowd's mood changed from confusion to anxiety and then anger as the legionaries pushed and struck any who tried to get near Gallia. Her face was a stone mask as she stared ahead with eyes full of resentment.

At the *agora* the mood became more light-hearted as musicians, jugglers and dwarves entertained the crowd. For a while. I noticed that there were many more people than on the previous two days and many of them were wearing clothing that indicated that they were followers of Artemis. Because the goddess was the protector of virgins and often portrayed in sculptures as a young girl, they wore their hair tied back and were attired in short tunics, both men and women. Those who could afford it had silver jewellery attached to their tunics because Artemis was known as the 'silver goddess'. Those too poor to afford jewellery wore sprigs of cypress, a tree sacred to the goddess.

As the procession got under way the worshippers surged forward to try to get near Gallia, only to be shoved back by a line of legionaries and two centurions who used their canes freely to crack heads and strike limbs. This did nothing to improve the humour of the crowd.

'I'm going to kill that fat bastard *editor*,' Surena hissed to me. 'He disgusts me.'

'Try to stay alive, Surena,' I answered, 'even if it means taking unpalatable decisions.'

My words fell on deaf ears as Surena seethed and thought only of vengeance. Domitus was walking next to Gallia, seemingly unconcerned, Alcaeus having the same demeanour. I looked behind at Drenis and Arminius who appeared remarkably relaxed. I put their sanguine attitude down to their having been gladiators before they had joined Spartacus. They had escaped from Italy to join me in Parthia and had built new lives for themselves at Dura. I had robbed them of those lives.

We reached the Great Theatre and filed into the stage building, past the animal cages. Many of them were now empty, their occupants having been slaughtered in the arena and their carcasses butchered and sold as meat to citizens. The Romans were efficient in all things. There were more guards inside the building than on previous days as we tramped up the steps to the second floor, Domitus and Gallia having been escorted to their seats in the theatre. I did not get a chance to say goodbye to them before they were bundled away.

Legionaries were posted at the entrance to the second floor chamber where the gladiators gathered before their bouts, much to the consternation of the fighters. They tolerated arena officials but objected to soldiers they viewed as inferior in terms of weapon skills and fighting prowess, and they made no attempt to disguise their contempt as they hurled insults at them. The centurion who had been our gaoler forced me up on my toes with the end of his cane under my chin.

'You cause any trouble and that blonde bitch will have her throat slit. You understand, *slave*?'

I nodded and avoided his gaze. I stared at the hilt of his sword and momentarily thought of making a lunge for it. But to do so would imperil Gallia so I played the listless slave. He grinned and walked away, ignoring the wolf whistles and jeers directed at him by the other gladiators.

The crowd was warmed up with beast hunts, the nets around the arena having been strengthened and heightened to ensure none of the animals could escape. I sat at a bench alone with my thoughts and saw Burebista being escorted into the room by legionaries. He immediately went to one of the windows. I looked at Drenis and Arminius and we went to stand before him. His face wore an expression of rage.

'Burebista?'

He managed a thin smile. 'Your plan nearly succeeded, lord, but you reckoned without the maliciousness of Lentulus Vatia.'

'I apologise,' I said.

'You have nothing to apologise for, lord, but these games will be my last. And to ensure I play my part the governor uses my wife as a hostage.'

He pointed down at the crowd, to the awning where the governor and the high priest were sitting. I saw Marcus Aristius sitting behind the governor, the fat *editor*, Gallia and Domitus and a woman with long black hair behind them.

'My wife, Anca,' he said, a note of distress in his voice.

As the beast hunters slaughtered a host of bears, leopards, dogs and panthers I looked at the row of legionaries sitting behind the nets and poles, more surrounding the dignitaries and two more lines at the outer edges of the audience. In addition, there were archers at the very back of the theatre's seats. Clearly the governor was not going to take any risks regarding security inside the theatre.

311

The crowd was muted in its applause of the beast hunters, many of the spectators more interested in trying to catch sight of Gallia or even get near her. As the last of the carcasses of the slaughtered animals were removed from the arena slaves ran from the stage building pushing small two-wheeled carts filled with sand, which they proceeded to scatter over the blood-drenched surface. After they had finished it was time for the *editor* to indulge his base instincts before the midday execution of criminals.

Ceukianus rose from his seat and clapped his hands. Moments later a score of young boys, the oldest no more than ten years of age, ran from the stage building on to the sand. There was a groan of disgust from the audience as the people realised that they were all naked, and obviously nervous. Then the central doors swung open and the same number of porcupines was ushered into the arena. A whistle was blown and the boys attempted to capture the animals, the spiny quills on their backs, sides and tails inflicting nasty cuts on the youths' naked flesh as they tried to pick them up or pounced on their backs. Ceukianus was in raptures as the boys' tender flesh was pierced and bled, members of the crowd hurling abuse at the *editor* for his depravity. I shook my head. The morality of the crowd was a curious thing. It was perfectly acceptable for animals and criminals to be ripped to pieces but the notion of innocent children being hurt for a fat Roman's amusement was viewed as being abhorrent.

The display was an exercise in futility as each boy was cut and bruised and gave up. Some started crying and the crowd began jeering and whistling. A hard-faced Metellus turned and uttered a few words to his nephew as Kallias shook his head. I saw that the seat next to him was empty and wondered where Hippo was. The *editor* stood and gestured to an official in the arena to bring the sordid spectacle to an end. Animal handlers came from the stage building to usher the porcupines back through the central doors into the fenced-off corridor and thence to their cages. The boys were led away to the other exits, several of the younger ones in tears and clearly distressed by the experience. But the *editor* called for one, a tall lad around eight years of age, to be brought to him.

312

The crowd nearest the dignitaries growled their disapproval as the boy was taken to the editor's side and Ceukianus began caressing his cut and bruised buttocks and legs. The governor turned for a second time and shouted at his nephew, the boy jumping at the outburst. Ceukianus ordered a guard to take the boy away.

The *editor*, now furious, nodded at the announcer whose deep voice resonated around the theatre. He told the spectators that fraudsters would not be tolerated in Roman Ephesus.

'But Roman corruption is,' shouted one man to great applause, who was quickly identified by the guards and manhandled from the arena.

The announcer maintained his professional composure and went on to inform the crowd that a local jeweller, Phormio, who was bundled into the arena by two legionaries, had been discovered using fake stones in his products. The legionaries left the hapless, portly middle-aged artisan on the sand and withdrew from the arena, the door being slammed shut behind them. He looked up at the crowd, clearly terrified, frantically rubbing his hands together as the announcer went on to tell the crowd that the jeweller had not only defrauded his customers but also Rome. As such he must be severely punished. The man jumped in terror as he heard a lion's roar coming from behind the central doors. Even from two storeys up I could see him trembling and then those occupying the front seats began to laugh and point as he pissed himself in terror.

'He shall face a beast and Jupiter will decide if he deserves to live,' shouted the announcer.

The jeweller shrieked in alarm and fainted, just as one of the side doors opened and a hen was thrown into the arena. The crowd fell about laughing as the legionaries re-entered the area and walked over to the unconscious Phormio. Many of the gladiators saw the funny side of the episode but I had no smiles in me this day. The legionaries kicked the jeweller awake and hauled him from the arena, leaving a circle of damp sand behind.

Ceukianus, sensing that the crowd's mood had lightened, rose to his feet and spread his arms.

'Am I not merciful?' he shouted.

'Are you not fat?' came the reply from a wit.

313

There was uproarious laughter as the incensed *editor* ordered the centurion standing near him to eject the individual. There was a scuffle as friends of the man who had made the comment objected to the Romans trying to evict him, the centurion being forced to use his cane on them as a detail of legionaries reinforced him. Once again the crowd became surly.

As I frantically racked my brain trying to think of a way to get out of our predicament, an official appeared in the doorway.

'The following gladiators are to enter the arena immediately. Surena, Arminius, Drenis and Nikephorus of the *Ludus* Palmyra. Acco the Gaul and Burebista of the *Ludus* Capua.'

Burebista turned to me. 'Zalmoxis calls, lord.'

He offered me his hand. I took it.

'Of all the men I have known and fought beside, lord, only you came back for me. For that I am in your debt and go to my death gladly, knowing that I will fall beside a great warrior.'

He went to a table and picked up his full-face bronze helmet and round shield. Legionaries filed into the room and began handing my companions and me our weapons. Surena snatched his net, trident and dagger from a soldier while Drenis and Arminius took their weapons in a more measured manner. Tears were running down Alcaeus' face as he stood before me. I laid a hand on his shoulder.

'My friend, we have come a long way together but now I have to leave you. Stay alive so the memory of Spartacus and what we created at Dura stays alive.'

He closed his eyes and nodded his head as I walked past him and out of the room. Our centurion gaoler led the way down the steps, past the first floor infirmary and down to the ground floor, which stank of animal guts and dung. The building was dark until one of the side doors was opened and brutal sunlight flooded in. The centurion barked an order for us to follow him and we walked out into the sun, and to our fate.

The crowd rose to its feet and began chanting 'Surena, Surena' when my former squire walked out into the sun. He raised his trident and net and basked in the adulation, totally unconcerned that this was his last day on earth. The legionaries

314

circled the others as the centurion pointed his sword at me and ordered me to walk forward to face the governor and high priest. He then pointed his weapon at Acco and ordered him to do the same.

'You point that weapon at me again and I will ram it down your throat,' said the Gaul loudly.

He stood beside me, a mass of muscles, hair and fury. I stood looking at Gallia, smiling at her and then nodding to Domitus. My wife appeared deathly white, my friend very angry. The announcer rose slowly, looking at the *editor* who, still resentful at the crowd's lack of deference towards him, nodded his ugly head. I put on my helmet.

The announcer stared at Acco and myself and extended an arm towards us.

'Behold the gladiators Nikephorus and Acco, who will now fight to the death for your entertainment in a contest to determine who will triumph in a battle between eastern and western barbarians. Will it be Acco, a fighter from Gaul, the land of savages that the gods have decreed will be civilised by Rome? Or will it be Nikephorus, a heathen born in the desert wastelands of Parthia where no culture exists?

'Let the gods decide.'

I saw Kallias staring at me, a look of what appeared to be sorrow on his face. The governor's top lip was fixed in a sneer and Marcus Aristius was looking contemptuously at my companions.

The announcer remained standing as more gladiators filed out of the stage building – 'hoplite fighters', 'net men', Thracians and *Murmillos* of the *ludi* Ephesus and Alexandria, at least thirty fighters. The crowd applauded the gladiators from Ephesus but were unsure what was going on. Usually the executions of the condemned took place after the beast hunts but there were now gladiators in the arena.

'The governor, his Excellency Quintus Caecilius Metellus, has no mercy for cowards, liars and enemies of Rome. Yesterday Roman soldiers fled before a few wild beasts, and their cowardice was made worse by their being shamed by a weak woman armed only with a bow. Therefore those soldiers will now face summary justice.

315

'But first they will witness the duel between Acco and Nikephorus so they can reflect on their disgusting behaviour and ask the gods to grant them good deaths.'

The doors opened behind us and Roman soldiers filed into the arena. They wore only their red tunics and had nothing on their feet and heads. As they shuffled onto the sand I noticed that they were chained together at the wrist in groups of five, one man in each group carrying a *gladius*. There were fifteen groups – seventy-five men.

The gladiators from Ephesus and Alexandria were grumbling among themselves. They did not mind killing each other but considered slaughtering criminals beneath them. They were, after all, skilled fighters not executioners. The former legionaries had tired, listless faces and appeared to be resigned to their fate. The gladiators would make short work of these shackled individuals. I thought that the scenario was a deliberate insult on the part of the governor towards Kallias and his gladiators and the other fighters from the East. Those gladiators now faced the condemned legionaries, who looked decidedly nervous, especially the ones carrying swords.

The announcer took his seat and a referee came forward to position his stick between Acco and myself. The Gaul stepped back and slashed the air with his swords. The referee removed his stick and the bout began. Acco came at me like a huge scything machine, his swords whirling in the air with the speed of dragonfly wings. I ducked and leaped to the left, attempting to slash his torso with my *sica*. But he brushed aside the blow and lashed out with the *gladius* in his left hand, which I deflected with my shield. But the blow splintered the wood and when I used it to parry two more blows it disintegrated in my hand.

The crowd was shouting and cheering now, urging us on and filling the theatre with a great din. I tried to dance around Acco, using nimble footwork to avoid his strikes. But he was amazingly light footed for such a brute and despite my movements dented the brim of my helmet with an overhead blow. My ears were ringing as I jumped back, ducked low and thrust forward with my own sword. I gashed his side and the crowd cheered but my success only made Acco more determined.

316

He pulled back the *gladius* in his right hand to give the impression he was going to strike with it but instead swung his other sword that lopped off my helmet's crest. He then lunged forward with the other *gladius* to strike me in the torso. I managed to step to the right to avoid the thrust before stabbing my *sica* at his face. But he slashed sideways with the sword he held in his left hand to parry the blow, stepped forward and smashed his left knee into my belly. Its force winded me and made me drop my sword. Acco swung his other sword into the side of my helmet, the metal protecting my skull but rendered me senseless. I collapsed to the ground and Acco kicked me onto my back. In a second he was straddling me with the point of a *gladius* at my neck.

The crowd fell into silence as all eyes turned to the *editor*, though only those in front and to the side of where the dignitaries were seated could see him due to the awning. I turned my head to peer up at Timini Ceukianus who wore a haughty expression on his podgy face. Through the helmet's eyelets I saw the portly magistrate draw a thumb across his throat and his mouth twist into a malevolent grin. I was finished. But before the crowd had a chance to respond to the editor's decision Gallia jumped to her feet and shouted at Acco.

'Gladiator. My name is Gallia of the Senones tribes, one of the ancient free tribes of Gaul. I am the daughter of the late King Ambiorix, the son of King Cavarinus, both rulers of the Senones.'

The crowd sat in absolute silence as this daughter of Artemis spoke in a language none had ever heard before. It was the tongue of the Gauls, though in truth I had some difficulty understanding what she was saying because although she had taught me her native language, she rarely spoke it.

'I see from the markings that you proudly carry on your body,' she continued, 'that you too are a member of my tribe. I say to you, Acco of the Senones, that the man at your feet is my husband, Pacorus of Dura, who years ago rescued me from a life of Roman slavery. I now ask you to spare his life, not because I, a mere woman, request it but because he has been a friend to the Gauls and to other peoples who have been subjected to Rome's tyranny.'

317

After she had finished speaking she remained on her feet and looked at Acco. But there was no pleading in her expression, just a fierce pride in her Gaul heritage, which was matched by Acco who now stood back from me.

'Kill him, you imbecile,' screamed Ceukianus.

Acco looked at the *editor* and spat in his direction, crossed his swords over his thick chest and bowed his head at Gallia.

'As you desire, princess,' he shouted in Gaul.

Why did he save me? He was a veteran of the arena who had killed many men on the sand. He was a living legend, a fighter who had won his freedom in the arena who had been lured out of retirement by an exorbitant sum promised him by Ceukianus. He was also a brute, a mountain of raw strength, courage and savagery who thought nothing of killing for profit or pleasure. Why then did he spare me? I do not think it was Gallia's words alone for he would surely have scoffed at a Roman woman pleading for the life of a man he had defeated. No, I believe that her speaking in Gaul and the mention of his tribe and kings he had perhaps fought under, made him think of a time before he had been a Roman puppet. A time when he was not like a trained animal released into the arena to amuse the Roman crowd, but a free man, a proud member of the Senones tribe with parents, siblings and perhaps even a wife and children.

A referee, a stocky man known as a *secunda rudis* on account of him being second-in-command to the chief referee, the *summa rudis*, hit Acco hard on the arm with his stick.

'Obey your orders, gladiator.'

Acco, perhaps still thinking about his Gaul past, remained stationary for a couple of seconds. But then in a flash rammed the sword in his right hand into the referee's mouth. He held the blade in place as his victim shuddered and blood sheeted out of his mouth. At the same time Marcus Aristius struck Gallia with the back of his hand, knocking her down.

And all hell broke loose.

The spectators nearest Gallia, enraged, threw themselves at the tribune as he drew his sword and threatened Domitus who had placed himself between the Roman and my wife. The tribune cut down two Greeks but more came at him as the crowd began to assault Roman soldiers. The legionaries nearest

318

to us were literally engulfed by a mob of angry Greeks, the latter wrestling and punching the soldiers and tearing off their helmets. I jumped to my feet and threw of my helmet as Acco whipped back his sword and the dead referee fell to the ground. I picked up my *sica* and ran to my companions as a religious frenzy took hold of the crowd.

Domitus lifted Gallia to her feet as dozens of her 'followers' grouped round her to protect her from Roman weapons. The latter were now raining death on spectators from the rear of the theatre as the archers began shooting indiscriminately at civilians. They easily cut down dozens of Greeks as they nocked arrow after arrow and shot them into the crowd. They gave no thought of what was happening behind them, which they soon had cause to regret when a horde of Greeks crested the hill. Like most Greek theatres the one at Ephesus had been built into the side of a hill, which meant that people could climb the other side of the slope to reach the rear seats where the archers were positioned. I looked up to see the bowmen literally disappear under a wave of Greeks and suddenly the crowd was in control of the arena.

'Time to get out of here,' I shouted to the others as the gladiators of the *Ludus* Ephesus ran forward and began hacking and slashing at the nets so they could get to grips with legionaries battling spectators. They too were followers of Artemis and they too took exception to Gallia being abused.

Behind us the condemned Roman prisoners stood in their chains, staring at the riot that was taking place in front of them, unsure what to do, as were the gladiators from Alexandria. I saw two referees making a dash for the doors.

'Stop them,' I shouted at Surena.

He sprinted towards the pair, hoisting his trident up and then launching it to hit one of the referees in the back. The man pitched forward as Surena ran past him, grabbed the second referee by the scruff of the neck and hurled him ahead. The man's momentum propelled him forward and his face smashed into the wall of the stage building. He crumpled to the ground, unconscious, as Surena bent down and slit his throat with his dagger. He turned to me and grinned.

'Shouldn't you be getting your wife?'

I turned to see Acco next to me, swords in hand.

319

'Seeing as she kept you alive you should rescue her from those filthy Greeks,' he said.

The 'filthy Greeks' were doing a splendid job, despite many being cut down by Roman swords as they battled the guards. I looked to where a great press of them was still shielding Gallia. I saw her blonde hair and Domitus' close-cropped skull. I nodded at Acco and ran forward.

'Keep that door open,' I shouted at Drenis and Arminius.

The nets had disappeared and the Ephesus gladiators were assisting members of the crowd in fighting legionaries. I jumped onto the front row of seats, stepped over a dead legionary and two Greeks and hopped on seats to get nearer my wife.

'Gallia,' I shouted but it was impossible to make myself heard above the racket.

I continued to tread on dead bodies and marble seats, taking me closer to the press of worshippers. They pointed at me and clenched their fists.

'Protect the daughter of Artemis,' someone screamed.

I stopped and gripped my *sica* as more anger-filled faces turned on me. They edged forward aggressively but then stopped in their tracks as Gallia spotted me.

'Leave him,' she shouted.

The mood changed instantly as she pushed through the throng and we embraced. They cheered and patted me on the back. I kissed her on the lips as Domitus also appeared.

'We need to get out of here,' he said, 'the governor will mobilise the garrison to deal with this lot.'

'A Roman with some common sense; most unusual.'

I turned to see Acco, much to my surprise. He bowed his head at Gallia.

'Princess.'

She stepped forward and kissed him on the cheek.

'I am in your debt, Acco.'

'We must leave, now,' insisted Domitus.

Guards were still battling spectators as the governor and his fellow dignitaries retreated from the theatre, protected by a phalanx of legionaries. Some had their shields raised to protect their superiors from the arrows that were being shot at them. A Greek in front of me screamed and collapsed, an arrow in his

320

back. Arrows were being shot in all directions as those who had overwhelmed the archers picked up the weapons and loosed missiles blindly. Domitus was right – it was time to leave.

Another arrow struck a man to my left, who pitched forward and collapsed over a seat.

'Protect the daughter of Artemis,' arose the cry as Gallia's supporters suddenly turned and raise their arms to shield her with their bodies. My wife was holding the hand of a clearly distraught woman with raven-black hair and dark brown eyes – Anca.

I smiled at her. 'I am delighted to meet you at last, lady, and hope...'

'Move!' shouted Domitus. 'All of you.'

We jumped over seats to reach the sand of the arena as fighting filled every part of the theatre. Greek gladiators were fighting Roman legionaries, Egyptian gladiators were battling enraged spectators filled with bloodlust who had jumped onto the sand to kill anyone who looked like a Roman, and the governor and high priest's entourage was still endeavouring to make their escape from the scene. I picked up a *gladius* and *scutum* beside a dead legionary and held the shield up to protect Gallia as we ran towards the open door being guarded by Surena, Drenis, Arminius and Burebista, who had discarded his helmet. He embraced Anca as Domitus began to shove everyone through the door. Arrows were now landing on the sand, or striking the unfortunate condemned legionaries.

'What about them?' I said to Domitus as Gallia and Anca were ushered into the stage building.

'What about them?' he answered. 'They are dead men either way.'

I saw the governor and Kallias among the press of high-ranking officials surrounded by soldiers, the latter trying to hack their way through the mass of Greeks trying to get at the Roman dignitaries. Some of the spectators had smashed the statues on the right side of the rows of seats and were pelting the Roman legionaries with chunks of marble. As with the arrows their aim was poor and many pieces of rock were falling in the arena.

'Get Alcaeus,' I ordered Drenis and Arminius, who nodded and ran to the steps leading to the first floor.

I was standing in the doorway to the arena and was about to shut it when Surena ran past me.

'Come back, you idiot,' I called after him, to no effect.

There were two main entrances to the theatre seats, both at the bottom of the seating rows, to the left and right near the arena. The governor's makeshift *testudo* was inching its way towards the exit on the left as viewed from the stage building doors. This brought it close to the arena and close to Surena who ran across the sand with his trident held at shoulder level. The nets and posts were all broken down now and he had an uninterrupted view of his target: the lumbering figure of Timini Ceukianus. I saw the *editor's* fat head and his white toga but only glimpses as *scuta* were raised in an effort to shield him and the other luminaries.

Surena ignored the rocks and arrows landing around him, slowed and hurled the trident forward. I watched its trajectory as it flew through the air straight as an arrow and struck Ceukianus in the side of the neck. I saw the *editor* fall and Surena yell his defiance.

'I am Surena of the Ma'adan and kneel to no man.'

He turned, clenched his fist and bounded back to the entrance.

Thus did Timini Ceukianus leave this life. He died as he had lived: overweight and repulsive.

'Give me a sword, warrior.'

I heard Gallia's voice and turned to see Acco hand her one of his weapons. She ran from the ground floor into the arena that was rapidly filling with people: rioters, Romans and Ephesian gladiators, the latter two groups engaged in their own private war. The Alexandrian gladiators, meanwhile, feeling left out of the violence, had decided to butcher the condemned legionaries and were going about their task with gusto.

'Gallia,' I shouted as she raced past me.

I ran after her, as did Acco. I saw her making for a portly, middle-aged Roman in a shabby toga who had left the rioting in the seats to seek sanctuary in the stage building via the arena, having spotted that the doors of the former were open.

'Dear husband,' she shouted as she ran up to the Roman and thrust the *gladius* into his stomach.

His eyes bulged wide and his mouth hung open as she extracted the blade and stabbed him again, and again and again, the front of his toga turning red. She pulled out the blade once more and he fell on his back, dead. But then she started to slash wildly at his corpse as I reached her.

'Gallia, we must leave this place.'

She spun round, her eyes filled with fury and her face contorted in anger. I thought she was going to stab me but then she recognised me and her anger was replaced by cold contentment. Acco stood looking at the butchered corpse.

'Behold Lentulus Vatia, *lanista* of the *Ludus* Capua,' she sneered, 'slave owner, degenerate and all-round Roman bastard.'

'That's my fee gone,' remarked Acco, who began to laugh uncontrollably.

Gallia handed him back the blood-smeared sword. 'My husband will reimburse you, Acco.'

I grabbed her dress. 'Time to go.'

We ran back towards the door, my shield held over Gallia as we did so. I heard Acco grunt and saw him stagger but he regained his footing and followed us through the door, which he slammed shut. I saw an arrow in the back of his shoulder. It took a few seconds for my eyes to get accustomed to the dim, stinking interior, but when they did I saw Alcaeus standing with Drenis and Arminius.

'We have to go,' I announced.

'To where?' queried Alcaeus.

'Back to the house to collect our bows and then to the harbour,' I said. 'The only way out of this city is by boat.'

Alcaeus saw the arrow in Acco's shoulder.

'Let me see that.'

Acco waved away his concern. 'I've suffered worse.'

There was banging on the doors as individuals were thrown against them.

'Move,' I ordered.

The ground floor was empty, slaves and animal handlers having fled in the confusion. I assumed that the remaining gladiators were still on the second floor but the absence of any guards was of more interest. We ran past the almost empty animal cages and through the gates to enter the street outside.

Already looters were at work, pillaging businesses and starting fires. The city was degenerating into lawlessness.

The ten of us moved speedily back to the house where we had been lodged and then imprisoned, skirting the *agora* where religious fanatics, looters, shopkeepers and frightened citizens battled for control over lives and property. Drenis and Arminius had discarded their helmets to lighten their loads but retained their shields and weapons. I had a *gladius* and *scutum* but Surena had only his dagger. Fortunately we only encountered either anxious slaves or the odd citizen disappearing into his home.

'We shall have to overcome the guards,' I told my companions as we came across the narrow road that led to the terrace houses.

But when we reached the house we found no guards, only open gates and a seemingly deserted residence.

'Have a care,' I warned as I led them through the gates, Domitus, Arminius and Drenis positioning themselves either side of me so we could lock our shields together.

We entered the building to see Lysander standing in the hallway, quaking with terror. His demeanour changed to utter relief when he saw us, but changed back to apprehension when he remembered our imprisonment and saw the weapons in our hands.

'Where are the guards?' I said.

'Gone, all gone, majesty.'

'Fetch us water and food,' said Domitus.

'And bandages,' added Alcaeus, staring at the blood oozing from Acco's shoulder.

Gallia pushed past us to go upstairs to our bedroom so she could change her clothes as Lysander relaxed a little and scurried away to find the kitchen slaves. Domitus ordered Arminius, Drenis and Surena to stand guard at the gates while the rest of us changed into more suitable attire as Alcaeus examined Acco's wound in the *andron*. I changed into my leggings, boots, silk vest and white shirt as Gallia donned the same attire.

'Thank you for saving me,' I said. 'How did you know Acco was one of your tribe?'

She shrugged. 'I recognised the tattoos on his neck and chest instantly. And you are welcome.'

I stood and cupped her face.

'Once again I owe you my life. To think, I always thought that the tattoos that decorate the bodies of Gaul warriors were meaningless swirls.'

She kissed me. 'That is because you are an uneducated barbarian.'

We went back downstairs to the storerooms to collect our weapons. In their haste to leave the Romans had ignored our swords, bows and quivers, though they had plundered all the gold that I had brought from Dura. I ordered Lysander to attend me as Gallia and I strapped on our sword belts and slung the quivers on our backs, positioning the feathered ends of the arrows at the top of our left shoulders for ease of retrieval.

'Why did the guards leave?' I snapped.

Gallia tucked her dagger into the top of her right boot.

'A messenger arrived at the house, majesty, reporting trouble at the theatre. We have heard nothing since, only the sounds of rioting, that and the plumes of smoke.'

We fitted the bowstrings to the ends of our bows and tested their strain.

'The followers of Artemis are rioting,' I told him, 'accompanied by the looters and arsonists who always appear when violence erupts inside cities. The Romans have their hands full.'

'What of High Priest Kallias?' asked Lysander.

'What about him?' I said. 'The last time I saw him he was skulking from the theatre in the company of the governor.'

I pulled back my bowstring. 'Unfortunately I did not have my bow with me so I could not kill him or the governor.'

He said nothing but I could see he was sweating.

'Go and attend to our refreshments,' I told him.

Gallia was holding something in her hand.

'What's that?'

She held up the silver statuette of Artemis. 'I hid it beneath our bed. The goddess smiles on us.'

'It was that old witch on Cyprus we have to thank. Who'd have thought a quiver filled with arrows painted silver would save our hides?'

325

I winked at her. 'And your blonde hair and blue eyes, of course.'

'We are not out of danger yet, Pacorus.'

It was now mid-afternoon and though the immediate area around the house was deceptively quiet I knew she was right. We had to get to the harbour fast to get on board Athineos' boat. We gobbled down fruit and barley cakes, washed down with water, as Alcaeus extracted the arrow from Acco's shoulder and irrigated the wound with watered-down wine. The Gaul did not flinch as he did so but merely stared at Gallia's martial appearance.

'You fight like a Senones, princess.' He glanced at me. 'So this one is your husband?'

'He is,' said Gallia. 'He is a king in Parthia and the victor of many battles.'

Acco seemed unimpressed. 'Where's Parthia?'

'East of Ephesus,' I answered, 'which is where we are heading.'

'You are coming with us, Acco,' said Gallia.

Acco winced as Alcaeus slapped honey and fat on the wound to staunch the flow of blood and assist the healing process. He then began wrapping a bandage around Acco's shoulder and under his left arm.

'Not too tight,' Acco told him, 'I don't want my sword arm restricted.'

'I don't suppose I could convince you not to use your left arm until the wound heals? You have lost a lot of blood.'

'You suppose right,' said Acco.

Alcaeus sighed. 'Of course not.'

Domitus and Burebista had relieved the three at the gates to allow them to change out of their gladiator gear, Surena having armed himself with his bow and the *gladius* and *scutum* I had taken in the arena. He now began chewing his way through a bunch of grapes.

'A pity we shall miss the last two days of the games,' he said to no one in particular.

Acco looked at him as Alcaeus finished tying off the bandage.

'Is he Parthian as well?'

326

Arminius laughed. 'Who? Surena? No he's a member of the Ma'adan.'

Acco looked at his bandage. 'What's that?'

'A tribe that inhabits a land of water in the arse end of nowhere,' said Drenis.

'The *editor* took a fancy to him,' said Arminius, tilting his head at Surena.

'I killed that fat degenerate,' hissed Surena.

'That's your career as a gladiator over,' said Drenis.

'We talk too much,' interrupted Gallia, 'we should leave this place.'

'She's right,' I agreed, 'we must go to the harbour.'

'What if the Romans have blocked the way already?' asked Acco, who was swinging a *gladius* in his left hand.

'Then we seek sanctuary at the temple,' replied Gallia.

'I'm not living like a woman, princess,' said Acco, 'I'd rather go down fighting.'

'You may get your wish,' I told him.

After we had finished filling our bellies we left the house, taking Lysander with us despite his protests. I wanted a guide to lead us through the city's back streets so we could avoid Roman patrols, but no sooner had we left the gates than we encountered a party of legionaries, around forty paces away. We were eleven, including Lysander, but they numbered at least half a century – forty men. Lysander tried to scuttle back into the house but I grabbed his tunic and shoved him into the centre of our little group as I nocked an arrow in my bowstring, as did Gallia and Surena.

'You will show us an alternative route to the harbour,' I told him as I drew back my bowstring and released it.

The arrow hissed through the air and struck a legionary in the neck. He groaned and fell to the ground. Two more hisses announced Surena and Gallia's flying arrows and another two Romans collapsed to the ground. Their centurion barked an order and the Romans locked their shields together to show us a row of red leather while those behind hoisted their shields above their heads. The mini *testudo* began to shuffle towards us.

'Shoot at their legs,' I said, 'try to hit as many as you can before they charge.'

Then there was the blast of a whistle and raised voices behind the *testudo*, which halted. There were more shouts and curses and suddenly the formation began to inch backwards.

'Don't shoot,' I said to Surena and Gallia.

'What's happening?' asked Acco.

'They are retreating,' Domitus told him.

My general was right, for after the *testudo* had fallen back twenty or so paces the formation suddenly broke up, the legionaries beating a hasty retreat back down the road, towards the northern part of the city. They left the three dead legionaries where they had fallen.

'Something must be serious for them to leave their dead behind,' remarked Domitus.

'The gods smile on us,' I said, looking up and down the empty street. 'Let us get to the harbour as quickly as possible.'

We began to walk towards the south when I heard shouting behind me. We turned to see a Greek man with a thick beard and bare feet running towards us, waving his arms. Surena raised his bow as he skirted the dead Romans.

'No, Surena,' I ordered, 'he is unarmed.'

'It is my brother-in-law,' said Lysander, stepping forward to greet his relative, who was in an agitated state.

'Hail, brother,' he panted, ignoring the rest of us as he smiled at Lysander. 'Glorious news. Cleon and his men have seized the *prytaneion* and now protect the sacred flame. Our liberation from the Romans is at hand.'

I looked at Domitus who shook his head. So Cleon had taken advantage of the disturbance in the city to make his grab for power. By the reaction of Lysander's brother-in-law there were some in the city that wanted to throw off the Roman yoke, but I doubted that they would succeed against the garrison.

'He obviously desires a glorious death,' said Domitus, 'but it isn't our concern. Let's move.'

'They are our concern.'

I heard Drenis' voice and turned to see a detachment of Roman legionaries approaching from the southern end of the street, marching quickly. At their head were a centurion and a standard bearer carrying a shaft that had a number of silver discs attached and topped with a silver human hand called a

Manus. The standard was a *signum* and was carried by a signifier that indicated that a full century – eighty men – was bearing down on us.

'We can take them,' boasted Acco but he was wrong. Our only alternative was to run as fast as we could in the opposite direction.

'Move!' I shouted and we ran for our lives.

The Romans had spotted us and the centurion spat orders at his men to increase their pace as they tried to catch up with us. We were unencumbered by armour and helmets and so our pace was faster, though Lysander and his brother-in-law had difficulty keeping up, the latter suddenly stopping as pain shot through his chest. Lysander also halted and went to help his relative. I slowed and turned to see the Romans about to engulf them when, out of a side alley, a group of Greek men suddenly appeared. A dozen, a score and more, launched themselves at the century with sticks, stones and a few swords that had been taken from dead Roman soldiers. We stopped and stared, open mouthed, as the Greeks fought like tigers. For a few moments the Romans were thrown back and disorganised, but after the initial surprise they closed ranks and there was a whistle blast, followed by a volley of javelins thrown by the rear ranks. What followed was like a drill on Dura's training fields. The centurion issued an order and the front rank raced forward to begin stabbing the Greeks with their swords. It took less than half a minute to reduce the Greeks to a pile of moaning, squirming offal, a few managing to flee back into the alley from where they had appeared. Lysander and his wife's husband were not so lucky, both meeting their ends on the points of Roman short swords.

We ran on, towards the *prytaneion* and into a sudden press of people trying to gain access to the hall. There were hundreds of citizens around the courtyard that fronted the temple-like building where the sacred flame burned.

'Those Romans will be here any minute,' warned Domitus.

'I wonder where the ones who retreated from us are?' queried Gallia as we pushed through the crowd and came across Greek men armed with spears and Roman swords and carrying Roman shields who were guarding the perimeter around the courtyard. Suddenly people began shouting and cheering as they spotted Gallia's blonde locks.

'The daughter of Artemis, the daughter of Artemis,' they shrieked and screamed as they closed in on us.

'You have to let us through,' I shouted to one of the guards, 'otherwise the daughter of Artemis will be crushed.'

He scowled at me, recognised Gallia and then beckoned to several of his fellow guards to assist him as he began pushing aside members of the crowd.

'Clear a path for the daughter of Artemis,' he bellowed as his companions joined him to create a makeshift corridor for us. He and they smiled when they saw Gallia as those nearest to her whipped themselves into a religious frenzy and began wailing and singing.

'This is bloody madness,' said Domitus disapprovingly.

'The Romans must have run away,' announced Surena.

'They're here, boy,' Domitus told him, 'don't you worry. They are waiting until everyone is nicely penned into this place and then they will attack.'

But all I could see around the colonnaded courtyard was a throng of men and women all desirous of entering the *prytaneion*. The guard I had shouted to, a man no older than twenty I estimated, led us to a slightly older individual who like him sported a thick beard and carried a Roman shield and a *gladius*. The helmet on his head perhaps marked him out as a leader of some sort.

He bowed his head to Gallia. 'Welcome, lady. Please follow me.'

He said nothing to the rest of us but his eyes lingered on Surena for a couple of seconds. Perhaps he recognised him from the arena. In the courtyard were men sitting in groups, most of them in their early twenties with stacks of spears near them and piles of shields, all Roman, next to the spears. Some looked up as we passed them, several standing when they saw Gallia and pointing at her.

Our silent guide led us into the ceremonial hall where the *cena libera* had taken place a few days before. Then the chamber had been filled with noise, drunken behaviour and condemned men. Now it was silent and reverential with Greeks guarding the sacred flame, not Romans. The guard ordered everyone apart from Gallia and myself to wait while he indicated that we two should go into a side room. Domitus looked alarmed but I held a hand up to him. We entered the room and saw Cleon sitting at a table, his torso covered by a bronze scale armour cuirass. I was surprised to also see Hippo standing by the door, who walked over and reached out to take Gallia's hands.

'Welcome, Queen Gallia.'

Cleon looked up, his face hard and determined. 'Greetings, King Pacorus. Zeus has guided you here to bear witness to the liberation of Ephesus. It is an auspicious omen that you have joined us.'

I was slightly alarmed that we had apparently been recruited to his cause.

'Auspicious, in what way?'

He stood and walked over to Hippo, slipping an arm around her waist and kissing her on the cheek. I suspected she was no longer the virgin high priestess of Artemis.

'Hippo informed me of your visit to the home of the traitor Kallias and the discovery of your true identity. Since then I have researched you and your history. You were the leader of the horsemen in the service of a slave general who fought the Romans, you returned to Parthia, became a king, destroyed a Roman army before the gates of your city and forced Pompey, called 'great' by some, to retreat from your kingdom.'

I had to admit he had done his research.

He looked at Gallia. 'And you, Queen Gallia, commander of the Amazons who displayed such courage in the Great Theatre and fired the imaginations of the citizens of this great city and the worshippers of the goddess. What explanation can there be other than you have been sent by the gods to light the flame of liberation?'

'You aim high, Cleon,' I said.

'The goddess smiles on him,' said Hippo, 'as she does on you, Queen Gallia.'

'What about the Roman garrison, Cleon?' I asked. 'For it certainly does not smile on you.'

'The disturbance in the theatre,' he bowed his head to Gallia, 'has resulted in many Roman casualties. The governor had too few soldiers to secure the gates of the city, which allowed me to make my move and seize the *prytaneion* and the sacred flame. Soon word of what we have done here will spread throughout Greece and Asia and will lead to the people overthrowing Roman rule.'

It would lead to a large army being sent from Italy, more like, but that was not my concern.

'Soon I will lead my *lochos* against the remnants of the garrison to secure the rest of the city.'

'Your what?'

'My men are organised according to the ancient hoplite custom, King Pacorus, and in honour of the gods.'

Apparently the smallest unit in his makeshift army was a file of eight men. Four files made up an *enomotia* commanded by an *enomotarchos*, and four *enomtiai* were combined to create what was called a *pentekostia*, a unit of one hundred and twenty-eight men. A *lochos* comprised four *pentekostiai*, which numbered just over five hundred men.

'Five hundred men is a small army to take and hold a city this size, Cleon.'

But he was supremely confident. 'More are joining us by the hour and soon the temple guards will be flocking to our side when they see that we have seized the sacred flame.'

He was also hopelessly naïve and I was about to tell him so when a man wearing a similar cuirass to Cleon appeared in the doorway.

'*Lochagos*, Roman soldiers are approaching the *prytaneion* from the south.'

Cleon picked up the Roman helmet on the table and smiled.

'The gods send us a sacrifice so that we may honour them, Nicias. Muster the men.'

I looked at Gallia and rolled my eyes. We had managed to escape death in the arena only to face our end among a deluded band of Greek freedom fighters.

Chapter 12

The screams and cries outside the hall heralded the arrival of the Romans as the crowd around the courtyard began to panic.

'You had better let them enter the hall,' I said to Cleon as we followed him outside, 'unless you want the Romans to kill them.'

He scowled at me. 'The Romans would not dare to kill innocent civilians.'

Domitus began laughing. 'Where did you get him from?'

The men who had been sitting in the courtyard were now forming into units as their commanders bellowed orders at them. They appeared to have a modicum of organisation and discipline, though their paucity of weapons and equipment made me fear for them.

The others crowded round as Cleon placed his helmet on his head and gave orders that the women and children were to be moved into the hall.

'Any capable of carrying weapons will stay and fight,' he said to his subordinate, who ran to the perimeter.

'Well,' said Domitus, 'we will leave you to be slaughtered while we take our leave.'

Cleon drew his *xiphos* and held the point at Domitus' neck. Drenis and Arminius moved towards the Greek, swords in their hands. I waved them back.

'Perhaps it is you who will be slaughtered, Roman,' hissed Cleon.

Hippo was looking decidedly nervous. The quiet protocol of the life of a high priestess was in stark contrast to the rapidly approaching outbreak of bloodshed she would be a part of.

'I would ask you to spare the commander of my army, Cleon,' I said. 'I need him.'

Cleon dropped his weapon. 'This man commands your army? A Roman?'

'It's a long story,' I told him as the sound of Roman trumpets and horns filled the air, 'one that I fear I do not have the time to tell.'

As women and children ran from the courtyard into the hall, Cleon's *lochos* had formed up, awaiting his orders.

'Stay or leave,' he said dismissively, 'it is of no concern to me.'

'Keep your eye on her,' I said to Gallia as Cleon marched off to place himself at the head of his army of liberators, leaving Hippo alone and even more nervous. Anca tried to comfort her. Acco moved to the side of Gallia, his swords resting on his shoulders.

I ordered Domitus, Surena, Drenis and Arminius to stay with me and asked Burebista to remain with the women.

'There are many women and children who are going to be butchered here today,' Alcaeus called after me as we ran to the marble columns opposite the hall's entrance. Behind us Cleon was giving a rousing speech to his men, telling them that the temple guards were on their way to reinforce them and in the meantime they would easily deal with the Romans who were filing into the square that surrounded the *prytaneion*. He reassured them that Artemis would not abandon them and finished by shouting 'freedom'. His men responded in kind.

'How many men have died in the name of that word?' said Domitus.

We crouched beside a column and watched the Romans deploy undisturbed. They had marched up the main street in column from the *agora* and were now deploying to attack.

'Four centuries,' said Domitus, counting the number of *signum* standards.

Surena turned to look back at the Greeks mustering in the courtyard.

'Just over three hundred against...'

He tried to count quickly in his head as he scanned the Greek ranks.

'Just over five hundred,' I told him.

'Good odds, lord.'

Drenis grabbed my arm. 'The odds just got longer.'

Between the centuries that were in close order eight ranks deep, two-man teams were siting scorpion ballistae. I had first encountered these deadly machines in Italy and we had them in Dura's army, having captured them from the enemy. I counted ten, each one capable of shooting iron-tipped bolts with deadly accuracy. The design was simple: two wooden arms inserted into two vertical and tightly wound skeins of leather, sinew or hemp or combinations of these materials contained in a rectangular wooden frame structure that formed the main part of the weapon. The arms were attached to a thick bowstring that was drawn rearwards to further twist the skeins and increase the torsion. The bolt was placed in the groove in the weapon's stock, the bowstring being pulled rearwards by means of a winch fitted to the weapon. It was held in place by a locking shaft at the back of the scorpion and released by a trigger. The bolt had a range of over three hundred paces and at short ranges could go through two men with ease.

We kept low, knowing what these murderous machines could do, though the Romans appeared to be quite prepared to let Cleon initiate proceedings. Domitus pointed to two individuals wearing black muscled cuirasses and plumed helmets accompanied by a group of centurions.

'The governor and his tribune.'

'I wonder where Kallias and his temple guards are?'

'Waiting to see which way the wind blows,' replied Domitus.

There was a great cheer behind us and we turned to see the Greeks march from the courtyard. The Romans were around fifty paces from the columns where we crouched. I saw Surena nock an arrow in his bowstring but Domitus tapped him on the arm.

'Save your ammunition, you will need it.'

'I have a clear shot of the governor,' he hissed.

'And those scorpions will have a clear shot of you,' replied Domitus. 'This is not our fight.'

Ever the realist, he was right. But it grieved me that we were mere bystanders to the drama and not active participants. But my thoughts were rendered irrelevant when Cleon led his men through the columns towards the waiting Romans. I noticed that many of them were bare foot as they broke into a charge at the moment the scorpions began shooting.

With a well-trained crew each machine could shoot up to four bolts a minute and these crews were very good. In thirty seconds they had unleashed a total of twenty bolts that cut down more than that number of Greeks. And then the legionaries charged. I had never been this close to combat without taking part and it was macabrely fascinating as each side fulfilled its role. The Greeks filled with passion and bloodlust against the iron discipline of the Romans.

There was a blast of trumpets and guttural war cries of Roman legionaries, followed by a volley of javelins and a series of groans and high-pitched screams as the iron heads hit flesh. The first two ranks in each century had already drawn their swords as they plunged into the Greeks, stabbing and using their shields to barge adversaries to the ground. Then the square was filled with the frantic clatter of swords striking swords as Cleon's fighters tried to stem the Roman flood. To no avail.

The volleys of scorpion bolts had taken the sting out of the Greek assault and the charge of the centuries had killed it stone dead. Now the Romans executed what they did best: grinding an enemy down in a remorseless close-quarter mêlée where their short swords could be used to maximum effect. To their credit the Greeks did not break, but their numbers were soon diminishing alarmingly as the swords of the legionaries found unprotected torsos, necks and faces. Cleon's men had no armour, only a few had helmets and a large percentage had only spears for weapons.

Within minutes the area in front of the columns was covered with dead and dying Greeks as centurions blew whistles to order those behind the front ranks to step forward and relieve their comrades. There was a brief lull and then the fighting began again, preceded by another volley of javelins thrown by the rear four ranks in each century.

'These Romans are good,' remarked Domitus admiringly. 'Almost as good as Dura's legionaries; almost.'

'Fall back,' I ordered.

The Romans were almost at the columns now, Cleon's men at last giving ground as their ranks were whittled down. I could not see him in the mêlée. He was already dead, most likely, cut down in the initial clash. The Romans were not in a hurry. They knew that they had won the battle and all that remained was to keep on killing until there were no rebels left.

We ran back to the hall and found Gallia and the others near the sacred flame, which was surrounded by women and children. I went over to the high priestess.

'Is there another way out of this building?'

She nodded. 'At the rear.'

'You have to get these people out now. Tell them to seek sanctuary at the temple outside the city. They will be safe there.'

'What of Cleon?' she asked as heads began to turn in response to the noise of battle outside growing louder.

'I do not know.'

Her eyes misted but I grabbed her arms.

'The Romans will kill everyone inside this building. Get them out now, Hippo.'

She raised her arms and, in a faltering voice, announced to the crowd that the goddess wanted them to worship Her at the temple outside the city and that they should depart immediately. I thought they might object but they eagerly rose to their feet and headed for the door at the rear of the hall. Mothers scooped up small children in their arms and departed as the screams of men dying outside filled their ears.

'I shall stay here,' Hippo said to me. 'I do not wish to live without my beloved.'

'The Romans are in the courtyard,' Surena shouted from the doors.

I ran over to him and saw that small groups of Greeks were frantically battling Roman soldiers in the courtyard, being forced to give ground as companions on either side were cut down. I was amazed to see Cleon, helmetless and bleeding but still alive, directly ahead, wielding his sword like a man possessed.

'Gallia,' I shouted.

She rushed over, bow in hand. I nocked an arrow in my bowstring and called to Cleon. Behind us the women and children were still fleeing the hall.

'Cleon, it is over,' I shouted, 'save yourself and your men.'

He did not hear me as the men either side of him died under a deluge of *gladius* strikes.

'We must leave, Pacorus,' said Domitus behind me.

'Cover him,' I said to Gallia and Surena as Cleon killed the legionary in front of him before stepping back as two more came at him. He tripped over a dead Greek and fell on his back as the Romans grinned to each other and raised their swords, to be shot dead by Surena and Gallia. Cleon jumped up and turned to see us in the doorway.

'Cover me,' I said as I raced forward to get near him.

'It's over, Cleon,' I repeated 'Get your men into the hall and out the back before you are all killed.'

I shot a centurion a few paces away in the face.

I grabbed Cleon's tunic but he wrenched his arm away.

'Stay, then,' I said. 'After they have killed you they will rape Hippo and nail her to a cross.'

Two more Romans came at me but were felled by arrows shot by Gallia and Surena.

'Pacorus,' shouted Domitus who ran forward and opened the belly of a Roman with his sword, 'get your arse in here.'

The Romans were nearly at the hall's entrance now, most of the Greeks being either dead or trapped in small pockets that were being systematically wiped out. I looked at Cleon and then ran back to the doors. Whether my mention of Hippo changed his mind or he saw with his own eyes how lost the situation was I do not know, but he suddenly called on those Greeks nearby to follow him.

The nearest century was closing on the doors as Cleon halted at the entrance and shouted at his men to get inside. A legionary lunged at him with his *gladius* and Cleon parried the blow with his shield, slashing his *xiphos* at the man's neck. The legionary caught the blow on his shield as the Roman beside him attacked Cleon from the side. Before the Greek had a chance to respond Acco rushed forward and stabbed the Roman in the neck, stooped low to slice open another legionary's kneecap and split the nose of a third with a flurry of sword strikes. He then leaped back, grabbed Cleon by the scruff of the neck and literally threw him inside the hall.

'Close the doors,' I ordered.

Domitus, Drenis, Arminius and Acco fetched benches, statues and a table and placed them against the doors.

'Move!' shouted Domitus.

Cleon grabbed Hippo's wrist as we flew to the door through which the women and children had escaped, to enter the square on the opposite side to the courtyard.

'This way,' shouted Cleon as he headed for a narrow side street.

'Our only hope is to get to the harbour,' I said.

It had gone ominously quiet, which indicated that the Romans had finished off the last of the Greeks. Soon they would be sending out search parties to hunt down any survivors. But Cleon knew Ephesus and led us east and then south through a maze of narrow streets and alleyways that resembled each other. I stayed in the rear of our small column, looking back at regular intervals to see if we were being followed. But the only thing I saw was the occasional curious face peering out from behind a shutter or half-open door.

After fifteen minutes of dodging through alleyways and skulking by the side of closed shops and houses we came to a sun-bleached building with cracked plaster and missing tiles on the roof. Cleon forced the door and led us inside, closing it when all had entered. He told his men to keep a watch at the windows but not to open the shutters as he walked into the small yard in the middle of the house. It was far removed from the grand building we had been accommodated in, being small and crumbling.

'Welcome to my home,' said Cleon dryly. 'I apologise that I do not have any slaves to attend to your needs.'

He pulled Hippo to him and embraced her.

'I have been living at the temple for many months and did not think to ever see these walls again.'

'They are crumbling,' said Domitus harshly as he looked at the chipped bricks and cobwebs hanging from the roof, 'like your rebellion.'

Cleon's eyes flashed with anger. 'Your tongue will get your head cut off, Roman.'

'He meant no offence, Cleon,' I said.

'He is just stating the truth, boy,' said Acco, blood showing on his bandage.

Alcaeus saw it too. 'Let me see that wound, Acco, it is bleeding again.'

But the Gaul held up a hand to him dismissively. 'I don't have time to bleed.'

'We cannot stay here, Cleon,' I said, 'we have to get to the harbour. Our only hope is to get aboard a ship.'

Cleon slammed a fist against a storeroom door, splintering the wood.

'No. We must get to the *agora* to link up with the temple guards.'

I looked at Domitus who rolled his eyes.

'The temple guards have abandoned you, boy. Kallias is a priest and a politician not a freedom fighter.'

'He's right, Cleon,' I said. 'I have met Kallias and above all he wants to safeguard this city.'

Cleon sneered. 'By abandoning it to the Romans?'

'Ephesus has been a Roman city for decades,' I said. 'There is no one in this city who remembers a time when the Romans were not in charge. Who wishes to be free of Rome? The fat merchants who have become rich because of Roman laws and armies that guarantee their goods are not stolen? The shopkeepers who reap the rewards of Roman ships bringing worshippers to Ephesus to pay homage at the Temple of Artemis? Or the priests at the temple who live like gods on the backs of the donations and gifts given to them by those same worshippers?'

He said nothing as he stared into Hippo's seductive brown eyes.

'If you want to sacrifice your life here, Cleon,' I told him, 'then that is your prerogative. But consider this. If you stay in Ephesus then you will also condemn Hippo and the men who escaped from the *prytaneion* to death.'

I signalled to Domitus and my other companions that we were leaving.

'For our part we are heading to the harbour.'

Hippo smiled softly at him and nodded.

'Wait,' he said, 'you will need a guide to avoid the main streets.'

He said nothing as he led us once more as we skirted the *agora* and then threaded our way through a number of side streets that ran parallel to Harbour Street to reach the harbour itself. During the journey I saw columns of smoke and shops that had been looted, their owners sifting through the debris but then throwing up their arms in terror when they spotted us. They ran away from us, as did men and women who had ventured from their homes once the rioters had passed.

'They will report our presence to the authorities,' said Domitus. 'Soon this area will be crawling with Romans.'

340

But it was not the Romans who barred our way but Greek temple guards when we approached the great warehouses to the rear of the docks. They defended every entrance to the harbour, not only on Harbour Street itself but also on every side street and alleyway. We hid in one of these, crouching beside a low wall and among the rotting refuse that had been thrown into the alley by the owners of the inns and brothels that served the multitude of dockers, sailors and travellers who worked in and visited Ephesus.

I went with Cleon to where the alley swung sharply left some twenty paces ahead. He peered round the wall and then crept back to allow me to do the same. I saw three temple guards in their bronze helmets, bronze cuirasses, white tunics and carrying shields and short spears. There were many tall buildings in this part of the city, mostly apartment blocks with storage spaces on the ground floor with living quarters where architects, surveyors, supervisors, foremen, sculptors, stonemasons, carpenters and brickworks' managers and their families lived on the upper floors. Beyond the apartment blocks were the great warehouses where grain and other goods were stored. Kallias had obviously sent his soldiers to guard the port area while the governor's troops dealt with Cleon's men, looters and arsonists. The Temple of Artemis and the docks were the city's two most valuable assets and the high priest was obviously determined to protect both, thus earning the gratitude of the governor and distancing himself from Cleon's uprising.

I crept back to the others. Hippo looked miserable, her formerly pristine white dress dirty and torn. Only ten of Cleon's fighters had escaped from the *prytaneion* and now they looked to their leader for directions. But the young Greek appeared at a loss as to how to proceed. The realisation that the temple guards were assisting the Romans must have been a bitter blow and now he just crouched with eyes cast down. It was time to take control of the situation. I waved over Surena and Gallia.

'There are three guards. We need to drop them all with one volley. Are you up to it?'

Gallia looked at me as though I had asked her if she knew her own name. Surena nodded gravely. We nocked arrows in our bowstrings and I told Domitus of my plan.

'Once we have shot them, we will calmly walk to the docks and to Athineos' vessel. Pass the word.'

He crept away to inform the others of the plan as I spoke to Gallia and Surena.

'They are temple guards so they are wearing armour over their chests and helmets on their heads. They are also carrying shields. Try to hit either their faces or necks. I will get them to turn to face us. Remember, one shot, one kill.'

'Are you going to talk them to death or are we shooting our bows?' asked Gallia impatiently.

Surena grinned but I frowned at him. I stood and walked around the corner to place myself in the centre of the alley, Gallia on my right, Surena on my left. I whistled to the guards. As one they turned and our arrows hissed through the air. There were three thuds and all three guards crumpled to the ground. I ran up to them to check there were no more guards close by. Gallia's arrow had struck a guard in the left eye, half the shaft lodged in the man's eye socket and brain. Surena had hit his man in the throat just below the jaw. My missile had also struck my target's neck, but in the side and not through the windpipe. My victim lay on his back, eyes wide open in terror as he tried to breathe while blood spurted from the wound like a small fountain.

'Losing your touch, Pacorus?' said Gallia looking down at the guard.

'I hit him, didn't I?' I replied irritably.

Domitus led the others round the corner and they ran past us as Acco relieved one of the men of his sandals and put them on. He looked at Gallia.

'In a different life you would have made a fortune in the arena.'

'In a different life I would have been queen of all the tribes of Gaul and led them to victory over the Romans,' she answered back.

We moved on and left the surviving guard to drown in his own blood. As we departed the alleyway and entered a narrow street that ran by the side of a huge mud-brick warehouse we began to encounter other pedestrians, a collection of sailors, whores, warehouse slaves, beggars and port officials.

'We stand out like a pile of camel dung on white marbles tiles,' complained Domitus.

'Let us quicken our pace,' I said, breaking into a low run as heads began to turn and stare at our strange, highly armed group. It was only a matter of time before the dead guards were discovered and the alarm raised.

But we reached the docks without incident. Cleon had regained some of his enthusiasm and pointed to one of the wharfs where *The Cretan* was moored, together with the other two of Athineos' vessels. Other boats were being loaded and unloaded along the wharf and at the dockside, the apparent chaos and noisy din masking our presence as we stood by the side of dozens of amphorae containing *garum*, the immensely popular fish sauce that the Romans could not get enough of.

A gaunt-looking port official in a tunic and sandals approached Domitus.

'These need to be loaded in the next hour if they are to be shipped today. I've got two thousand amphorae of olive oil arriving this afternoon, though they might have been stolen. We've heard of serious trouble in the city.'

Domitus raised an eyebrow. 'Trouble?'

'Some religious fanatics, so I've heard,' said the official. 'Anyway, are these goods yours?'

'No,' answered Domitus.

The official examined the rest of us standing with Domitus, all except two armed and looking decidedly out of place.

'Who are they?'

'Circus performers,' replied Domitus quickly, 'here for the games. They juggle with their weapons.'

The official wasn't interested as he looked at the amphorae, shook his head and wandered off. Our luck was holding. We walked past pallets loaded with marble from the quarries outside the city and others piled high with animal hides and came to the stone quay where Athineos' vessels were moored. Cleon held up a hand to halt us and pointed to figures standing guard over the gangplanks that led to *The Cretan*. Roman marines!

There were two of them, one at each gangplank, fully armed and equipped in bronze helmets, mail shirts, oval shields painted blue to match their tunics and helmet plumes. Two guards stood sentry over each of the other two vessels.

'Damn,' I whispered.

Domitus pointed at Gallia.

'Give your bow and other weapons to Pacorus.'

She looked most put out. 'Why?'

'You, Anca and Hippo are coming with me. I will be a brothel owner and you will be some of my girls. If we can entice the marines onto the boat we might be able to seize it.'

'A ridiculous plan,' scoffed Cleon.

'If you can think of anything better then let's hear it,' replied Domitus.

He could not, so as Gallia reluctantly handed her bow, quiver, sword and dagger to me he gave his shield and sword to Drenis and told Hippo and Anca to look seductive and stick their chests out. Gallia's nostrils flared with anger but any protest she was going to make was cut short by a loud sound behind us. A cart drawn by a mule had crashed into the amphorae, shattering many and spilling their contents on the stone flagstones. There was a furious argument between the official who had been speaking to Domitus and the cart driver that drew in more officials and dockers.

'The gods smile on us,' I said to Domitus, 'go!'

He and his three women sauntered along the wharf, past the first vessel, and halted at *The Cretan*. I watched pensively as Domitus tried to worm his way on to the vessel, but was distracted by arguments and then fighting that broke out behind us. It was just the cover we needed.

'Acco,' I said, 'change of plan. You kill the guards at the first ship and I will deal with the ones that Domitus is speaking to. Cleon, you and your men kill the ones at the other vessel. Move!'

I ran forward as the commotion behind us worsened, with fists flying and more *amphora* being shattered. Acco bounded in front of me and raised his swords, plunging one into the chest of a surprised marine and then brushing aside the *pilum* of the other guard before opening his throat with a side swing of his other sword. Surena shot the two marines speaking to Domitus before they had chance to react to the unfolding drama, his arrows hitting both in the chest. Cleon and his men raced past us as I bounded up the gangplank and jumped on deck. To find it empty. Domitus and the women followed.

'What the hell are you doing?' he fumed at me.

'Change of plan.'

I went over to the cabin and banged on the door.

'Athineos.'

'In here,' came the reply from inside.

I slid back the bolt on the door and opened it. A fuming Athineos burst out and was going to attack me, probably thinking that I was a Roman. His anger turned to confusion when he saw us standing on his deck.

'How in the name of Zeus did you manage to escape?'

I grinned. 'It's a long story and one I would be delighted to tell you. But right now we need to get out of Ephesus.'

He looked around. 'Where are the guards?'

'Dead,' replied Domitus, 'as will we be if we don't get moving.'

Athineos pointed at the locked hatches on the deck. 'My crew are in there.'

I ordered them to be opened. Drenis recoiled from the stench of rancid sweat as the hatches were opened and tired, dehydrated sailors were helped on deck. They were desperate for water and Domitus had to restrain them from knocking over the barrels filled with it near the cabin as they feverishly sated their thirsts. The ten-man crews were liberated from the other boats but half of them were in such a weakened state that they had to be assisted aboard *The Cretan.*

'Those bastard Romans had them flogged,' Athineos informed me. 'I told them that they had had nothing to do with bringing you here but they wouldn't listen. We were to be fed to the animals in the arena. Can you believe it, eaten by the very lions I had transported from Syria?'

'They are dead, Athineos. But more importantly we need to get out of this harbour,' I said as he began to pace up and down the deck, swearing vengeance on the Romans.

'How I would like to get my hands on that pretty boy tribune,' he seethed.

'You might get your wish,' said Domitus at the top of the gangplank and pointing towards the docks where a force of marines was mustering, led by an individual with a scarlet cloak and a magnificent red crest atop his helmet.

'How many?' I shouted to Domitus.

He screwed up his nose. 'Thirty or forty, and probably more on the way.'

'What about my other boats?' said an anguished Athineos.

'We must leave them behind,' I said. 'You have to get this boat under way.'

He had around fifteen sailors who were up to the task of casting off, unfurling the sails and rowing the small boats alongside that would pull *The Cretan* out of the harbour, which was bereft of any wind. He bellowed and cursed at his men as I ran to the gangplank to stand beside Domitus.

At the dockside end of the wharf marines were locking shields, ten across, while our esteemed tribune friend walked up and down the line, dressing the ranks and glancing at the three boats.

'They appear to be in no hurry,' I observed as Gallia and Surena, bows in hand, came to my side.

'They are waiting for slingers or archers, most likely,' mused Domitus. 'They will know we have our own archers and are taking no chances.'

Sailors were scrambling up the rigging to get to the sail that was furled under the topsail. Others were going over the side to man the two rowboats that would pull us out of the harbour.

'Archers,' announced Domitus as half a dozen bowmen trotted to the rear of the marines.

They were around fifty or sixty paces away, men in bronze helmets and some sort of armour over their white tunics. They were armed with Cretan cydonian bows made from bone, wood and animal sinew, capable of shooting arrows up to a range of one hundred paces. They were not recurve models like our own bows but were deadly enough.

'How many arrows do you have left?' I asked Gallia and Surena.

'Ten, lord.'

'A dozen.'

I slipped my own quiver off my back and counted the missiles. Eight.

'Athineos,' I called, 'do you have any arrows on board?'

'None,' he answered.

'We need more ammunition,' I said. 'We will take it from the enemy.'

Surena whooped with joy but Domitus was most unhappy.

'Having reached this boat it would be the height of idiocy to leave it.'

'We need to buy Athineos and his crew more time,' I said.

The last thing the enemy would be expecting was an attack, or so I hoped. So that is what I intended to spring. I called Cleon over and told him that I was going to assault the Romans so the crew could unfurl the sails and tow us out of the harbour. He immediately volunteered himself and his men, as did Acco, whose bandage was now soaked in blood around his wound. Burebista also volunteered his services, which meant there were seventeen men armed with shields and swords and three archers: myself, Gallia and Surena. Long odds but we had the element of surprise. I told Alcaeus to get Hippo and Anca into the safety of the cabin and Athineos to cast off as soon as he was ready.

'We will get back on board,' I told him.

He shook his head. 'You are mad, you know that?'

I grinned at him. 'The gods like mad people, my friend.'

There was a scream followed by a thud as one of the crew crashed to the deck, an arrow in his back. The Cretan archers were using their bows to kill the crew and stop us leaving. We ran down the gangplanks and headed for the marines. The three of us with bows halted on the wharf and began releasing arrows at the line of marines, stopping when our comrades ran past us and charged forward. We followed, pausing to shoot arrows through the gaps between our friends and allies. The Roman marines, taking casualties and totally surprised by our actions, momentarily lost their cohesion and their formation, just as Domitus led our makeshift force into their ranks. The marines and archers got hopelessly entangled as the Roman line fragmented. Acco was fighting like a man possessed by a demon, his two swords slashing left and right under and above shields to create a path of dead marines. I emptied my quiver shooting three archers who were exposed as the marines were cut down and cursed my luck when I had a clear shot of Marcus Aristius but no arrows with which to take it.

In the unfolding mêlée Domitus, Drenis and Arminius had an advantage over individual marines and within minutes all three had cut down at least two Romans each, while Acco had killed five or six on his own. Burebista's skills, honed in the arena, were just as deadly and soon nearly half the marines were either dead or dying. Cleon's men, not as skilled in the use of arms as the rest of us, suffered accordingly, five being killed in quick succession. But at least their leader accounted for three of the enemy as he fell back, Marcus Aristius screaming at them to hold their position, to no avail.

I slung my bow on my back, drew my sword and ran forward to assist Domitus as he grappled with a marine. I ducked to the right and rammed my *spatha* into the Roman's side, just behind the shield that was tucked tight into his left side. He yelped and fell as Domitus drove his *gladius* through his throat. I kept moving and crouched beside a dead archer, wresting the two quivers plus straps from his corpse. I slung them over my shoulder and went to another Cretan and relieved him of his arrows too. Surena and Gallia were doing the same when I heard a shout.

'Romans!'

I looked up to see another detachment of marines and archers running along the dockside, dockers and sailors who had been watching the scene scattering before them. I glanced behind to see *The Cretan* pulling away from the wharf.

'Fall back,' I shouted as an arrow hit one of Cleon's Greeks, pitching him forward over the side of the wharf and into the water.

Gallia stood up while Drenis, Domitus and Arminius locked their shields together and began to edge back as Marcus Aristius screamed at the newly arrived archers to shoot at us. Burebista ran over to me.

'Time to go, lord.'

But as he held up his shield to protect us I saw that Gallia was exposed. Marcus Aristius noticed it too.

'Kill that bitch,' he screamed.

Acco saw the danger too and ran over to her, grabbing her and turning his back to the enemy to make himself a human shield. Four arrows slammed into his back and he emitted a pitiful groan. I nocked an arrow and shot it, then a second, third and fourth, all finding their mark and forcing the Roman reinforcements to fall back, much to the disgust of the tribune. Surena also killed three of the Cretans, who retreated some more. I ran over to Gallia who was holding Acco in her arms.

'I'm done, princess,' he said quietly. His eyes turned to me.

'Get her out of here, that's an order, Parthian.'

He smiled at my wife and then grabbed the torc around his neck. He removed it and passed it to her.

'Go, princess, may Toutas be with you.'

She kissed him on the forehead and I pulled her back as Acco nodded and rose unsteadily to his feet. His back was painted red from the arrow wounds, his swords decorated with enemy blood. And as we ran back to the ship he was determined to spill more enemy blood as the marines raced forward. I was the last to leave the wharf as I heard a loud shout and turned to see Acco charge into the enemy, his swords glistening in the afternoon sun before he died a warrior's death. I turned and jumped aboard *The Cretan* as arrows hissed through the air, striking the hull and piercing the mainsail.

Drenis, Arminius and Domitus stood on the deck and cheered as the sailors in the two rowboats frantically pulled on their oars and Athineos steered his vessel away from the wharf and towards the open sea. Around us other merchant vessels were being towed to their berthing positions, their crews oblivious to the bloody drama that had just taken place. I dumped the quivers on the deck and went to stand beside Athineos while *The Cretan* moved silently through the water. He was in a sombre mood.

'That's me finished as a captain. Thirty years I have been sailing the Mediterranean and Aegean, hauling cargoes and making my fortune. All gone in the blink of an eye.'

'I am sorry.'

He brought up phlegm from his chest and spat it overboard.

'Don't blame yourself, young king. I got too cocky, too greedy. Plutus dangled the lure of wealth before me like a fisherman dangles a hook baited with a worm and I took it.'

'Plutus?'

He chuckled to himself. 'The God of Wealth. Now I have just this ship instead of two more and the Romans will declare me an outlaw and put a price on my head.'

'What will you do, Athineos?'

He did not reply, just shook his head forlornly and stared vacantly ahead at the gap between the two breakwaters where we were headed. I looked back at the diminishing wharf to see marines and a figure with a red-crested helmet standing between the two vessels of Athineos that we had left behind. I saw Marcus Aristius turn and walk back towards the docks and I suddenly remembered Julia's words.

'*Seek the lions at the island of Lemnos.*'

'We have to go to Lemnos, Athineos.'

'Mmm?'

'Lemnos, we have to go to Lemnos.'

He kept an eye on the ship's course. 'Lemnos, why? It's north of Ephesus and there's nothing there except more Romans.'

'I was told to seek the lions of Lemnos.'

He laughed. 'Lions? There are no lions on Lemnos but there are plenty of Romans. We must get back to Syria.'

'I will pay you whatever you desire, Athineos, just get us to Lemnos. You know the way?'

He said nothing for a few seconds as he weighed up my offer. He nodded. 'I know the way.'

Cleon was going among his four remaining men, laying hands on their shoulders and trying to raise their morale. How different things must have seemed to him just a few hours before when the whole of Ephesus had been gripped by madness, which he had hoped to take advantage of. Now he was but another criminal fleeing from Roman justice. But at least he had his beloved with him. I saw the figure of Hippo leave the cabin and run to him, the two embracing as the other Greeks flopped down on the deck to rest.

Athineos nodded at her. 'That's the high priestess from the temple. I remember seeing her when I visited the place.'

'You are correct.'

He was not happy. 'Her god will be angry that her high priestess has deserted Her and will curse us. You should send her back.'

'The authorities will either crucify her or burn her,' I said, 'depending on whether she falls into the hands of the Greek high priest of the temple or the Roman governor of the city.'

'Better her dying than the rest of us.'

I slapped him on the shoulder. 'Cheer up, my friend, we have escaped the city, Shamash be praised.'

He pointed ahead. 'Not yet, we haven't.'

I looked to where he was indicating to see soldiers on the end of one of the breakwaters, men in bronze helmets wearing white tunics – Cretan archers. And then I spied Roman legionaries manhandling two machines into place – scorpions. The gap between the two breakwaters was around two hundred and fifty yards, wide enough to allow two ships to pass each other easily. But not wide enough to allow *The Cretan* to dodge the enemy's missiles.

'Have a care,' Athineos shouted, 'enemy archers.'

'They will pick off the rowers first,' I said, 'leaving us dead in the water.'

Athineos began steering the ship away from the left-hand breakwater where the Romans and archers were positioned, but he had limited room for manoeuvre if he wanted to avoid a collision with the other breakwater.

'Get those men in the rowboats back to the ship,' I told him.

Athineos shouted to his second-in-command, a filthy wretch with a lice-infested beard, to get the rowers out of the water as he called to his men on the rigging to get down on deck.

'Everyone should get below deck,' he said. 'I can steer on the other side of the boat so the cabin will be a shield. What are you going to do?'

'Show these Romans what a Parthian can do with a bow.'

Actually there was only one Parthian – me – the others being a Gaul and a Ma'adan as I lined up with Gallia and

Surena near the prow and the rowers returned to the ship clambering up the sides. Everyone was despatched to the hold, including Hippo and Anca from the cabin, because scorpion bolts could go straight through the cabin's walls. Not that I intended to allow them to shoot.

Domitus, Drenis, Arminius and Cleon held Roman shields at the gunwale, with enough space between them to allow us to shoot our bows from the gaps between them.

'A choice bit of foresight on your part,' Domitus said to me, 'leading that charge to capture more arrows. I suppose you knew they would try to cut us off at the breakwater.'

In truth I did not. 'Of course, Domitus. That is why I am a king and you are a mere general.'

We had dumped the quivers on the deck behind us and now Gallia and Surena were nocking arrows in their bowstrings.

'Hit the crews of the scorpions first,' I said. 'Those weapons can cause us real damage. We can withstand their arrows.'

The Cretan was still drifting towards the open sea, though at an agonisingly slow pace now that it was no longer being towed. The scorpion crews were siting their weapons, which were around three hundred paces away. Well within range. They appeared to be more focused on ensuring deadly accuracy rather than a high rate of fire, for which I thanked Shamash. I nocked an arrow, raised my bow and pulled the bowstring back to full draw. Time slowed to almost nothing and I was taken back to my youth, to my first 'baby bow' that I was given at the age of eight. I remembered my tutors: frail, white-haired men who made shooting a bow seem like a sport of the immortals.

'You may be a pampered little prince,' I had been told, 'but only constant practice will make you a competent archer. In this you are no different from the poorest farmer.'

They had told my father that I was not an instinctive archer, though I had had no idea at the time what that meant. But they said that I could become a good bowman as long as I trained every day and listened closely to my tutors. And that is what I did. Hours spent honing hand/eye coordination, ensuring no more than four inches of arrow stuck out in front of my bow hand when the bowstring was at full draw. After my hand had been thwacked by a cane held by my instructor the old goat explained why.

'It produces inconsistent accuracy in the flight of your arrows and also adversely affects trajectory and penetration.'

'Concentration, that is the key,' another instructor had informed me during my teenage years. 'If an archer cannot concentrate on his shooting he will never be able to master the skill.'

Years spent on shooting ranges loosing arrows from the saddle when even riding at speed did not spare me their admonishments.

'Keep the shaft as close to your eye as possible without distorting your vision and breathe correctly.'

'How can you tell if I am breathing correctly when I am riding by you in the saddle?'

My impertinent questions were invariably answered by cane strikes on my knuckles. But for all their pettiness and sadistic indulgences they taught me the art of shooting a bow until it became second nature. As I pulled back the bowstring to full draw I took a deep breath, let out some air from my lungs to dispel any tension and then held my breath until I released the bowstring.

'A quiet mind cannot exist in a tense body.'

The arrow flew through the air, arching slightly upwards and then falling as it spun towards its target. I saw the iron tip strike one of the Roman soldiers, knocking him to the ground. The arrows of Gallia and Surena also found flesh as we stooped to retrieve more arrows.

How I would have liked Gafarn to be standing with me. My adopted brother was one of the finest archers in Hatra and probably among the best in the whole Parthian Empire. He was that rarest of things: an instinctive archer. When he shot a bow he used only his sight and instincts to hit the target. He practised, of course, but as my instructors informed my father after Gafarn had picked up a spare bow on a shooting range one day and proceeded to out-perform all the other boys, including myself, the gods had blessed him with a rare talent.

Some masters would have had Gafarn's hand cut off for his insolence but my father, perhaps thinking it would encourage me, indulged his abilities. The sons of Hatra's nobles hated Gafarn because despite his lowly status he was more skilled with a bow than they. And skill with a bow was one of the things that defined a Parthian lord; indeed, defined him as a man.

'A true instinctive archer can snuff out a candle with an arrow in total darkness,' my last instructor had told me when I had reached my twenty-first year, 'when he cannot see his arrow, his hand or anything else except the candle's flame.'

I had laughed aloud when he told me this. But my derision was silenced two days later when Gafarn did this in a blacked-out room in the palace.

We shot slowly, methodically, as the Cretans replied, their missiles slamming into the shields held up by our comrades. But the Romans and Cretans had no shields and as our arrows began to cut them down their volleys became less accurate and more irregular. We each selected our targets before releasing our bowstrings. It is better to shoot a dozen arrows well than a hundred poorly.

An arrow hissed over my head and slammed into the mast, another two struck the gunwale and five more sliced through the mainsail. But neither of the scorpions shot a bolt at us as *The Cretan* eased past the breakwaters and drifted into the blue waters of the Aegean. The wind caught the *artemon* and mainsail and propelled the vessel to the right. Athineos struggled with the steering oars to restore its course and prevent us from careering into the right-hand breakwater. The Cretans loosed a last volley that sent arrows skidding dangerously across the deck, two lodging in one of my quivers and splintering several shafts, but fortunately causing no casualties.

Athineos bellowed to us to get the hatches open to release the crew to retrieve the rowboats as the sails billowed and we began to pick up speed. The shield bearers placed their missile-peppered *scuta* against the gunwale and smiled boyishly at each other and us. I embraced Gallia as the others ran to the hatches and shouted to those below that we had escaped Ephesus.

Alcaeus stayed with the wounded sailors in the hold but the others came on deck and raised their heads to the heavens and thanked their gods for their delivery. Anca was crying tears of joy as she and Burebista embraced each other, both looking deliriously happy. Cleon, still clearly disappointed at having been forced to flee from Ephesus, at least managed a smile as the gorgeous Hippo dazzled him with the most beautiful smile and kissed him tenderly on the lips. I saw Surena go to work with his dagger on the main mast, carefully prising an enemy arrow from the wood and slipping it into a quiver. I soon was doing the same. We had shot off a good deal of the arrows we had captured on the wharf so it would be wise to retrieve as many as we could.

The sailors went back to their tasks after first hauling the two rowboats back on board and securing them to the deck. It was late afternoon now and the sea resembled a dazzling shimmering lake as the sun sank low on the western horizon. The breeze was pleasant, the day still warm and I raised my arms and thanked Shamash for His mercy in allowing us to escape from Ephesus. The Lord of the Sun had certainly smiled on this day.

Gallia was chatting to Hippo and Cleon, showing the former how to hold a bow and pull back the drawstring. The high priestess was delighted to be able to hold the bow of the Queen of the Amazons. Surena was slipping off the bowstring from his bow and counting the number of arrows in his quiver. Domitus sauntered over, holding his shield that resembled a pincushion.

'Let's hope that old witch we met on Cyprus was right,' he said.

'She is a seer,' I told him, 'someone who can see the future. Of course she is right.'

He placed the shield against the gunwale. 'I have just been talking to one of the sailors and he is mystified as to why we are sailing north instead of south.'

'We go to seek the lions of Lemnos,' I said.

He rolled his eyes. 'You sure you didn't get a knock on the head back in Ephesus? The sailor said that there is nothing north except trouble.'

'If we went back to Syria then we definitely would be asking for trouble,' I said.

'So where are we heading?'

I had no idea, only that we had to get to Lemnos. And after that? I shrugged vacantly.

'Very reassuring,' he muttered.

He looked around at those on deck, his eyes resting on Cleon and Hippo who resembled love-struck teenagers.

'What are you going to do with them?'

I gave him another shrug. 'I don't intend to do anything with them.'

He drew his *gladius* from its scabbard and began examining the blade for signs of any chips along the edges.

'Well, let us assume we get back to Dura, a big assumption. If the Romans find out you are harbouring a man wanted for inciting a riot at Ephesus they will either demand him back or march an army into your kingdom to take him back. Then there is the high priest.'

'Kallias? I think we can handle his army of over-dressed temple guards.'

He raised an eyebrow at me. 'He will want his high priestess back so he can burn her for her sacrilege and will be using all his influence to persuade the Romans to send an army to get her back.'

'And what would my general's advice be?' I asked.

He looked at the land on our starboard side. 'Dump them on the nearest island we come to.'

'I will think on the matter.'

He picked up the *scutum*. 'Meaning you will ignore it. I despair, Pacorus, I really do.'

He marched off to complain to Drenis and Arminius about me, shouting at Surena to stop playing with his dagger and do something useful. I smiled. It was good to see him happy. I walked over to where Burebista and Anca were both staring out to sea.

'A fine view,' I said.

They both turned, Anca sheepishly avoiding my eyes as she stared at the deck.

'In all the excitement of this day I have not had chance to speak to you, Anca. I apologise for my bad manners.'

She still averted my eyes. 'No apologies are needed, *dominus.*'

I smiled and reached out to hold her arm. 'I am not your *dominus* but would be your friend. Please, be at ease.'

She looked at me, her eyes brown and bright. She looked as though a great weight had been lifted from her shoulders.

'What part of Dacia do you come from, Anca?'

'I have never seen Dacia, lord,' she replied, her eyes filled with sadness. 'I am the daughter and granddaughter of slaves.'

'I promised to take her back to our homeland, lord,' said Burebista, 'though until today I had no idea how I would do so.'

'Parthia always has room for excellent commanders, Burebista,' I told him. 'I cannot promise you long life but I can guarantee prosperity and a life of freedom.'

Anca looked concerned. I smiled at her.

'The decision would rest with both of you, naturally.'

'Dacia calls us, lord,' replied Burebista. 'We go back to raise the standard of resistance against the Romans.'

Still the same old Burebista: reckless and headstrong. Just the type of leader Dacia would need if it was going to withstand the might of Rome. Anca looked alarmed. I turned to see Athineos' unkempt second-in-command whose eyes settled on Anca's ample bosom.

'Skipper wants to see you,' he uttered to me as the corner of his mouth curled up to form a leer as he continued to stare at Anca's chest.

Burebista placed himself between his woman and the lecherous sea dog.

'You have delivered your message.'

The sailor looked at the muscled Dacian before him, picked something out of his nostril and wandered off. I made my excuses and walked to where Athineos stood steering the vessel. Veins bulged on his thick forearms as he gripped the rudder to steer *The Cretan* north. He looked even fiercer than usual as the dipping sun turned the sky orange and the wind continued to drop.

'How good are your eyes?' he snapped.

'Good enough.'

'Then use them to take a look south.'

I did, and concern swept through me as I saw two small shapes on the horizon.

357

'Roman warships.'

I stared, open-mouthed, at the two vessels that seemed many miles away but also immediately threatening. I thought we had escaped from Ephesus but the Romans were apparently intent on tracking us down and either killing or capturing us so they could transport us back to Ephesus for exemplary punishment.

Chapter 13

'Are you sure?'

Athineos looked at me with a face full of wrath.

'An hour ago they were barely discernible dots on the horizon, now I can see square sails and ships sailing side by side. In another hour, when we will be pulling into shore to anchor for the night, I shall be able to see the eagles on the mainsails. Yes, I'm sure.'

'Can they catch us?'

He turned and squinted at our pursuers. 'Not today. They will also have to anchor soon.'

I looked up at the sky. 'But the wind will be blowing again tomorrow.'

He shook his head. 'It won't save us. They have sails too but what they also have, which we do not, are oars.'

They were triremes, warships that had three levels of oars, sixty-two on the upper level, fifty-four on the middle level and another fifty-four on the lower level. The upper-level oarsmen rowed through an outrigger and had a deck running the length of the ship above them, from which thick linen screens could be suspended to protect them from missiles or poor weather. The oarsmen on the middle level rowed through an open oar-hole, but those on the lower level, whose oar-holes were only eighteen inches above the waterline, had their ports enclosed by a leather sleeve.

'You remember me telling you about their rowers when we were on the way to Ephesus?' he said.

'That they are not slaves.'

'They are professionals. Each one sits on a cushion and they row to the beat of a drummer so they can get their rhythm,' he answered. 'And that rhythm is fast, Pacorus. The Romans may spout all this rubbish about Greeks being effeminate and boy lovers but they spend good money on Greek rowers because they know they are the best to be had. And like this ship each trireme has a mainmast and a small boat-mast forward.'

He told me that the sails were square-rigged and fitted with brailing ropes and could be removed before a battle.

'And triremes are fast,' he continued. 'No longer than forty yards and a beam just over six yards, their lightweight hulls are mortice-and-tenon construction in fir and oak and that means they can cut through the water at speed.'

'But surely they are carrying a lot of weight?' I said desperately.

He laughed. 'They carry a fair weight, yes. But they are slim, unlike this old lady, and they have a hundred and seventy rowers providing motive power. They don't fight, but the forty marines on each trireme do. So once we've been rammed they will either let us all drown or throw grappling hooks so they can board us to kill us with their weapons.'

He looked at me. 'Are you going to tell them?'

'Who?'

He nodded at the people on deck. 'Them?'

'Yes.'

As Athineos guided his ship into a small bay on the north coast of a small island called Psara, I gathered my companions on deck and informed them that two Roman warships were chasing us. The sailors furled the two sails and dropped a large stone anchor to secure our position in the shallow water and the cook began to prepare some of the meagre rations we had on board. None of us had much of an appetite as we sat in a circle on deck and picked at our cooked fish, rations that had been earmarked for the marines that had been guarding the sailors before we liberated them. Meanwhile the sun dipped in the west.

After we had finished eating Athineos called everyone together in front of the cabin for a briefing. He had forbidden the lighting of any torches as a precaution against the Romans spotting us.

'I thought you said they too would be forced to seek an anchorage,' I said.

'Never underestimated the Romans, Pacorus.'

He folded his thick arms in front of him.

'You all know that the Romans are after us and that tomorrow they might catch us.'

Some of the crew began to murmur among themselves.

'Silence!' barked Athineos. 'We have two options, as I see it. We can either sail to the mainland, fire the boat and try to evade our pursuers on foot, or we can sail for Lemnos in the morning and hope we get there before the Romans intercept us.'

'What's at Lemnos?' asked one of the sailors.

Athineos looked at me.

I turned to face the questioner. 'Salvation. I have arranged for reinforcements to be sent to the island and they will be able to deal with the Roman warships.'

The sailor seemed satisfied by my answer, though Athineos was taken by surprise.

'So, that being the case,' said the captain, 'I think it is best to push on to Lemnos.'

His crew was in agreement and went back to their stations in a satisfied mood. Cleon and his small band of men were similarly fortified by my announcement and Domitus smiled knowingly at me. Athineos took my elbow and led me into the cabin, shutting the door behind him. I could hardly see him in the dimness.

'Reinforcements?' he said quietly.

'Men perform better if they have hope, Athineos.'

'And when we get to Lemnos and there are no reinforcements?'

'I must ask you to have faith, Athineos, faith that things will turn out to our advantage. Besides, our luck has held thus far.'

'The thing about luck, Pacorus,' he replied, 'is that eventually it runs out.'

Alcaeus wanted Athineos to send men ashore to fetch fresh water, as our supplies were very low. The captain was at first reluctant but yielded after the doctor informed him that several of the crew that had been flogged by the Romans would be dead by morning if their raging thirsts were not satisfied. I offered to go along with the landing party to provide security, Surena and Domitus also volunteering their services. After a few minutes of prevarication Athineos finally relented and said he would lead the expedition. Cleon also wanted to come along but I asked him to watch over the ship.

Six sailors carried two empty water skins each and Athineos also carried a pair. Surena, Domitus and I shouldered one apiece. The crew lowered the rowboats into the calm black sea and we used ropes to clamber down the sides to get on board. The sailors were used to getting in and out the boats but Surena lost his footing and fell on one of the brawny sea dogs, who gave him a mouthful of abuse.

'Quiet,' hissed Athineos, 'the Romans might be in the next cove for all I know. No talking from now on.'

Because he had forbidden the lighting of any torches or candles on the ship our eyes soon got used to the darkness, the black craggy outlines of the island's rocky terrain discernible against the night sky. There was no moon but the sky was cloudless and it was possible to make out the shore, the beach and the sharply rising rocky hill beyond.

The only sound was the gentle splashes of the oars as they dipped in the water. After less than five minutes the boats ran aground on the soft sand, we stepped out and hauled them onto the beach. I looked back to see the black shape of *The Cretan*. It was so quiet I was aware of my breathing and the beat of my heart. Athineos gathered us in a circle and spoke in a whisper.

'There will be mountain streams inland from this beach. As soon as we find one we fill the skins and then leave. Keep your eyes peeled. The crews from those two triremes might be a stone's throw away or they might be a few miles away.'

He led the party off the beach, moving between dunes and clumps of grass to reach a wooded area with the mountain looming up on our left. We moved through a dense area of maple, beech and chestnut, the cracks of breaking twigs as we stepped on them echoing through the trees and causing Athineos to curse us. But after stumbling on for a few more minutes we heard the pleasing sound of running water. On hearing it I suddenly felt very thirsty and was glad when I could cup my hands in the small stream and drink the cool liquid.

'Hurry,' hissed Athineos as he pulled the water skins off his back and dipped them into the watercourse.

The others did the same and as soon as his men had filled their skins he tapped them on the shoulder to indicate they should depart for the boats. I had never seen him so nervous. Surena was grinning like an idiot as the captain urged his men to complete their tasks and retrace their steps.

'Fill that water skin,' I said to him, 'and be quick about it.'

'The island seems deserted, lord. Perhaps we could go hunting to fill our bellies with fresh meat.'

'Have you forgotten about the Romans?' I said.

He grinned, his white teeth flashing in the half-light by the stream.

'We won't have to worry about the Romans when we get to Lemnos and link up with our reinforcements, lord. Will Prince Orodes be commanding them?'

'What?'

Domitus kneeled and dipped his water skin in the stream.

'That's right, Surena, he will be leading the Durans and Exiles who have been transported to the island.'

Surena finished filling his skin and replaced the cork. The water containers were the hides of goats and calves sewn together with the hair on the inside to prevent evaporation of the water.

'Do you think we will hold any games at Dura, lord?'

'Games?'

'If we built an arena outside the city then we could invite gladiators from all over the Roman Empire.'

'Just what the king wants, Surena,' said Domitus, 'Romans flocking to Dura.'

'There will be no gladiatorial games at Dura, Surena,' I said, 'and no arena.'

He looked disappointed. 'That is a pity, lord, I would have liked Viper to have seen me in the arena.'

Domitus was shaking his head as Surena reflected on his lost opportunity for more glory in the arena. I hoped that one day he would become a great Parthian warlord as he had that crucial ingredient that all successful commanders must have: supreme faith in their own abilities. But at this precise moment he was nothing but an irritation.

I looked round to see we were alone; Athineos and his men had departed.

'Let's get back to the boats,' I said.

In front of us the cracking of twigs and occasional obscene word when a man tripped on a stone indicated the presence of Athineos and his men, some distance away. We quickened our pace but I stopped when I heard a rustling sound behind me. I turned and peered into the trees. I thought

363

I saw something but there was just gloom. I continued on, following Surena and Domitus who had increased their pace. I heard a twig snap and halted again. Domitus heard it too and also stopped and turned. The hairs on the back of my neck pricked up and my instincts told me something was wrong. I strained my eyes to try to see in the darkness. I saw what appeared to be the black shape of a giant lumbering towards me. But it had a head that was totally flat. It was a crest. I slipped my bow off my back and nocked an arrow in the bowstring as the figure got nearer. Behind it were more moving shapes – Romans!

I raised my bow and released the bowstring. I heard a hiss followed by a yelp that pierced the night air and did not stop to see if I had hit the man with the crest atop his helmet.

'Run,' I shouted.

Surena and Domitus bounded ahead of me as shouts erupted behind as the Romans gave chase. I heard a thwack and saw a javelin embed itself in a tree to my right. I ran on, stumbling into branches and bushes that impeded my progress but also that of my pursuers. Still gripping my bow, the water skin and quiver, branches flaying my torso, I at last reached the beach to see the two rowboats being pushed into the water. Domitus and Surena stopped and turned as I caught up with them and pulled another arrow from my quiver.

The enemy was fast on my heels but fewer than I had expected: I saw only five. I shot one who was about to hurl a javelin and Surena cut down another marine who was running at him. I nocked another arrow and shot a man who moved his *scutum* to reveal his torso as he ran at me. I estimated him to be twenty paces away, maybe less, so the arrowhead easily penetrated his mail shirt to pierce his belly. It didn't kill him but winded him and dropped him to his knees.

'Time to go, Pacorus,' shouted Domitus as Surena shot another arrow that struck the shield of the surviving marine.

I was about to turn and run to the boats when I saw the Roman with the crested helmet – Marcus Aristius, the man who had held a sword to Gallia's throat.

'Surena,' I called.

He came bounding back to me as Domitus screamed at me to get off the beach,

364

I handed my bow and water skin to him. 'Take these and go.'

He had no chance to reply as I pulled my sword and advanced on the tribune, thrusting the point of my *spatha* forward to skewer him. He deflected the blow and came at me with his own thrusts that I parried easily enough. I heard a low groan and out of the corner of my eye saw the surviving marine fall with an arrow in his throat. Surena just could not help himself.

Marcus Aristius knew how to use his sword, making a flurry of attacks directed at my head and torso. But I either avoided or parried them with relative ease. The fact that his men had been killed around him did not seem to perturb him in the slightest. And then I realised why as more marines ran on to the beach. I decided that discretion was the better part of valour and, after stepping back to avoid a side slash of his sword, turned and ran into the water. The boats were being rowed back to *The Cretan* and it took all my strength to swim in my clothing holding my sword to reach them. I threw my *spatha* in the first boat and Domitus and Surena hauled me aboard as Marcus Aristius stood at the water's edge and cursed me.

'That's why I did not want to go ashore,' said Athineos gruffly.

When we reached the ship he ordered that the boats remained in the water ready to pull *The Cretan* out of the cove when the dawn came. Drenis, Arminius, Cleon and his four Greeks had stood to arms when they had heard the tribune's curses and threats. But now they stacked their weapons when he stopped and silence returned to the night. A grateful Alcaeus came from the hold and took the water skins for the wounded, five of whom had already succumbed to their injuries.

'Thank you,' he said. 'Are you hurt?'

'Just wet,' I answered. 'I apologise for dragging you to Ephesus and for all the subsequent drama, Alcaeus.'

'Apologies not required, Pacorus. The truth is that I am grateful to you for giving me the opportunity to see Ephesus. It is truly a wonder of the modern world, and a Greek wonder at that.'

'Perhaps there will come a time when it is ruled by Greeks once again,' I offered.

'Not unless the Roman Empire crumbles into dust. It is too rich for the Romans to allow it to slip from their greedy paws.'

He sighed and looked at Cleon holding Hippo in his arms.

'What are you going to do with those two?'

'I have no idea,' I answered.

He slung a water skin over his shoulder. 'You should get her to say a prayer to Artemis in front of everyone. It will raise morale, and I have a feeling that we shall all need our spirits raised come the dawn.'

On Alcaeus' advice I asked Hippo if she would ask the goddess for Her protection and be our guide during the coming day. She turned away from me when I had finished.

'I broke my vows. The goddess has abandoned me.'

'I neither condemn nor condone your actions, lady, but what I would say is that had the goddess truly abandoned you then She would not have allowed you or the rest of us to escape Ephesus. That being the case I believe that your destiny lies elsewhere and in your quest you have the blessing of the goddess.'

She looked at me. 'When I first heard the name King Pacorus it meant nothing to me. Many kings and nobles have visited Ephesus seeking the favour of the goddess. But none have pretended to be a slave or risked their life fighting in the arena, much less risked their life to rescue a slave from Roman bondage. And then I met you and your queen at the high priest's house and I knew that your coming was a sign from Artemis Herself. And when word reached me that the audience in the arena was rioting and the disturbance had spread throughout Ephesus, I interpreted it as a signal that I should declare my love for Cleon who would free the goddess' city from Roman oppression.'

Her head dropped. 'But the rebellion failed and many Greeks died in vain.'

'And yet we lived,' said Cleon.

'Because the goddess willed it so,' I added.

She lifted her head. 'You really believe that, lord king?'

'With all my heart. And tomorrow shall be the day of our deliverance.'

She agreed to appeal to the goddess.

We gathered in front of the cabin as the dawn broke, the Aegean blue-grey and the sky shades of red and yellow as the sun rose slowly in the east. Hippo lit a simple white candle that she placed on the deck in front of her, raised her arms to the sky and called on Artemis to help and protect us. Her voice was strong and powerful as once again she became the High Priestess of Artemis.

'Artemis we praise You, sister of bright Apollo, first-born of blessed Leto, dear child of Zeus. Fairest among maidens, You roam the wilderness; the enchanting nymphs are Your friends and companions. You take joy in wood and meadow, swift-footed one, You who loves dances and games, You who wins every race. As the wild lands are Yours, so too are the wild beasts; huntress with a bow Your skill is unsurpassed, always do your arrows find their mark. Artemis, O kindly one, You ease the sharp pains of childbirth, and You are the fiercest protector of children. O luminous goddess, we praise and honour You.

'Under Your care are the creatures of the field and the forest, the sea and the sky. I pray to You, Artemis, keep safe these helpless ones who now stand before You, shield them from harm, defend them from those who would destroy them, guide them to flee and to hide from perils and foes. Goddess Artemis, I pray to You, shelter these Your servants.'

Hippo let her arms fall, picked up the candle and blew out the flame.

'It is done,' she said quietly.

'Get your arses into those boats,' Athineos bellowed to the sailors earmarked to pull *The Cretan* out of the cove. Two more hauled up the anchor as the others began scrambling up the rigging on the mainsail to unfurl it. He went to the stern, patting the swan head before he grabbed the steering oars. The sailors in the boats began frantically pulling on their oars as the wind began to pick up and fill the now unfurled sails. As the sky began to change from red to yellow and the sea became a lighter hue, those of us who were not attending to maritime duties leaned on the portside gunwale and stared south to where the Roman triremes would come from. I saw nothing but a calm, empty sea but knew that the enemy ships would

367

soon be snapping at our heels like angry wolves chasing a defenceless roe deer.

The rowboats returned to *The Cretan* and were hauled aboard as a brisk northerly wind picked up and filled the sails. It felt good to have the breeze on our faces and the mood of the crew and passengers picked up markedly as the sun appeared from behind Psara'a rocky crags to turn the sea a rich blue. Athineos steered the ship away from the island and towards the north where Lemnos lay, around a hundred and fifty miles away. Athineos told me that if the wind held it would take around thirteen hours to reach the island.

'That long?'

'It's a long way,' he said, holding the steering oar. 'But we are not carrying any cargo, which makes the old girl lighter, so we have a good chance of reaching our destination well before dark. You should get some sleep.'

'I'm not tired.'

But after an hour of the breeze in my face and the gentle rolling of the ship a great tiredness swept over me. The ship had a shift rota and several of the sailors were already lying on blankets on deck, fast asleep. Surena also had his head down, sleeping like a newborn. I stood looking down at him with Gallia beside me.

'Dobbai told me that he will be remembered by future generations,' she said. 'It is most strange.'

'I like to think that I found him in the southern marshlands, but perhaps the gods willed that I should go to the land of the Ma'adan so Surena could find me. Success seems to follow him like a loyal dog.'

I looked at her. 'What did Dobbai say about me?'

'That you ask too many questions. Come; let us find a place where we can rest. The excitement of the last few days is catching up with me.'

We found a quiet spot near the prow and slept on a makeshift mattress of empty sacks. It was hardly a bed fit for royalty but we slept like the dead and when we awoke several hours later I at least felt more human, albeit with aching limbs. I rose and stretched out my arms and inhaled the sea air, closing my eyes as the sun warmed my face. I looked around to see Domitus, Arminius, Drenis and Alcaeus wrapped in blankets fast asleep, and a new row of sailors taking their rest opposite them. I saw the two rowboats lashed to the deck, sailors going about their duties and Burebista chatting to Cleon. As Gallia was still sleeping I ambled over to them and enquired as to the whereabouts of Hippo and Anca.

'In the cabin,' Cleon told me, 'resting.'

I looked up at the billowing sails. 'If this wind holds Athineos believes we will reach Lemnos before nightfall.'

Burebista looked at Cleon who stared down at his boots.

'You disagree?' I said.

Burebista looked towards the stern. 'We might not make the island, lord.'

I saw the burly figure of Athineos holding a steering oar and then felt a sense of dread as I spotted, in the distance, two square sails. I left them and ran past the cabin to get a closer look at the triremes, which appeared a good way off.

'Made an appearance about two hours ago,' he said nonchalantly.

'Why didn't you wake me?'

'No point,' he sniffed. 'There is nothing you nor I can do. I got some shut-eye myself, telling my crew only to wake me if they got really close. As it is they are content to just keep us in sight. They are just using their sails, I would say.'

'Why?'

'Because even Greek rowers can't pull on their oars for twelve hours without expiring. No, they are using sail power to keep on our tail and when they get close enough they will make a sprint and catch up with us.'

'We can't outrun them?'

He shook his head. 'Their ships are sleeker than this old barrel and that means they cut through the water faster, even with the weight they are carrying.'

I looked at the triremes, the eagle insignia on their mainsails clearly visible.

'What would you advise?'

'Get something to eat,' he replied. 'You will need all your strength for the fight. I hope you have enough arrows left.'

'What tactics will they use?'

'When they get close enough they will employ their oarsmen to provide a burst of speed that will allow them to

369

swing out and then turn quickly to use the their bronze-covered rams to smash my hull. Then they will board us.'

He considered for a moment. 'Having said that, if both the triremes strike this boat at once they will probably cut her in half so we will all drown instead of being killed by the enemy's spears and swords.'

'A most heartening thought.'

When I returned to the deck I found Gallia awake and checking her bow, which like mine was without its bowstring. I told her about the trailing Roman triremes. She appeared unsurprised.

'You know the Romans as well as I do, Pacorus. They neither forgive nor forget. Did you think they would abandon their search and sail back to Ephesus?'

'Athineos says that they will catch up with us eventually.'

She pulled her dagger from her boot and examined its edges.

'But not before we have Lemnos in sight, I think. And then we will turn the tables on them.'

I looked around to ensure no one was within earshot.

'You know that there are no lions on Lemnos?'

'You should have more faith in Julia's words,' she reprimanded me. 'She was proved right with the quiver of silver arrows, was she not?'

I nodded.

'Well, then, pray that we reach Lemnos and then our faith will be rewarded.'

But there was a distinct absence of faith on board as the triremes got steadily closer and all on board *The Cretan* realised the danger we were in. We appeared to be in a trap that had no escape. If the wind dropped then the triremes could employ their oars to catch us. There was no land in sight so abandoning *The Cretan* was not an option. All we could do was watch the triremes get steadily larger and pray that the wind continued to blow to allow us to reach Lemnos.

A sparse meal of salted fish and rock-hard biscuits was eaten in silence and afterwards Athineos issued short swords and fishhooks to his sailors. The triremes were now perhaps two miles to the south, their oars out of the water and withdrawn about half their length into the hull. I called together my companions, minus Alcaeus who had returned to his medical duties in the hold. If anything the wind had increased in intensity, the mainsails causing the mast to creak as the air filled it. Cleon, his four remaining men, Hippo, Burebista and Anca also joined our group as I stood in the middle of it and explained our predicament. I told them that the triremes would attempt to ram us, after which *The Cretan* would probably break in two.

'We should shoot at them from the stern of this vessel, lord,' said Surena, 'pick off their soldiers before they get a chance to board us.'

'We would be shooting into the wind and have a limited supply of arrows,' I replied, 'but I agree that we should use them to kill their men before they board us.'

'Then wait until after they have rammed us,' offered Domitus. 'After the shock you will have time to use your bows. But if this boat breaks up then they won't board us because there won't be anything to board.'

'In which case we will need to get the rowboats in the water to save the women,' I said. 'Cleon and Burebista, I would ask you to get Hippo and Anca into one of those boats and ensure you and they get to Lemnos.'

Hippo looked at Gallia.

'What of your queen, King Pacorus?'

'She will be staying behind with her husband to kill as many Romans as she can,' stated Gallia flatly.

'Then I too will stay,' said Hippo, 'the goddess will protect us.'

'And neither will I abandon my husband's side,' said Anca defiantly.

'And he will not be abandoning his lord,' stated Burebista. 'We are staying.'

With nothing left to say, I descended into the hold where Alcaeus was attending his surviving patients. The compartment was hot, airless and rank with the smell of blood and sweat. Two of Athineos' men were assisting the doctor, whose tunic was soaked with sweat. He himself looked tired.

'You should get some air,' I told him. 'How are they doing?'

'The Romans did a typically thorough job on their bodies. I had hoped to save all seven when we reached Lemnos but I gather from the sailors that we have company.'

I nodded. 'We should get these men on deck.'

'Why?'

'If we are rammed this hold will flood in minutes and everyone in it will drown.'

He wiped his sweat-beaded forehead with a cloth. 'And if they are on deck they will be butchered by the Romans. Not much of a choice.'

'In here they will die for certain. On deck they have a chance, albeit a small one I grant you.'

So we spent the next half hour getting the wounded out of the foetid hold and into the fresh air. Even if they were all going to die at least they could feel the wind on their faces and the sun on their cheeks. Gallia laughed at me when I told her this.

The triremes were closer now – less than three hundred paces away I estimated – and Surena was straining at the leash to shoot at the figures standing on their decks: marines in mail shirts and blue tunics and Roman officers wearing burnished helmets topped with rich crests.

'At this range, shooting into the wind, your chances of hitting your target are slim,' I told him.

'There's Lemnos,' shouted Athineos.

We turned to see land in the distance, a slither of light purple on the horizon.

'How far away?' I asked.

Athineos looked at the horizon and then up at the billowing sails. 'About an hour I would say.'

He jerked a thumb behind him. 'They will have seen it as well.'

Everyone crowded at the prow of the ship, eager to see the island that I had promised would be our salvation but which in reality offered no more safety than the empty sea all around us. But they stood, pointed, congratulated each other and temporarily forgot about the two triremes closing on us.

Then the voice of Athineos boomed from the stern.

'They have dropped their oars.'

I turned to see the three banks of oars on each trireme dipping into the water in perfect unison.

'They will be on us in ten minutes or less,' shouted Athineos.

His foul-looking second-in-command began barking orders and the sailors grabbed their weapons and took up position along each side of the ship, ready to repel boarders. Domitus, Drenis and Arminius stood near the mast, ready with swords and shields to assist the sailors as and when required. Cleon and his Greeks did the same, Cleon escorting Hippo to the cabin first. Burebista also took Anca to the cabin and then went to join Domitus while Gallia rushed to the stern with her bow.

The honey coloured rock of the island was visible now, the mountains of Lemnos rising into the blue sky and an entrance to what appeared to be a huge bay flanked by sheer-sided cliffs directly ahead.

'I will take us along the east coast of the island,' said Athineos. 'I don't want to get caught in that deep inlet. There'll be no wind so we will be dead in the water.'

I was staring at the two triremes that had now taken up position either side of *The Cretan*, around a hundred and fifty paces to the rear and closing fast. They were actually moving away from us, which I found confusing. Athineos kept glancing back and must have read my thoughts.

'Remember what I told you. They are getting themselves into position, which means moving outwards so they can change direction and swing in to ram us. It won't be long now.'

'More Romans,' Surena suddenly shouted.

We all turned to the left, to the direction in which he was pointing, and saw two more vessels, triremes like our pursuers, approaching from the west. They were moving at speed and must have been sailing along the island's western coast. They had been moving against the wind and had had their sails furled. But now they had changed direction to swing round to approach us from the southwest. Their rows of oars were dipping in the sea but their motive power was suddenly increased as the mainsails of both ships were unfurled, momentarily hanging limply and then puffed out as the wind filled them. Four triremes were bearing down on us.

373

'Lions,' said Surena.

I looked ahead. 'What?'

He was frantically pointing his bow at the two new triremes that were bearing down on us from the west.

'They have lions painted on their sails, lord.'

I looked at the new arrivals and saw that he was right. Lions! The Roman triremes had eagles painted on their sails but these ships sported lions. We had found the lions of Lemnos but who owned these ships?

'They are getting ready to ram us,' shouted Athineos as the two triremes behind us suddenly headed right and left away from us, their rowers working frantically to power their vessels. I saw the one on our starboard side power ahead and momentarily forgot the two new arrivals as the Roman vessels continued to head away from *The Cretan*.

'They will swing in towards us soon,' said Athineos who appeared angry and despondent in equal measure.

The Roman trireme on our port side was also powering past us but was suddenly in the path of one of the new triremes that was bearing down on it.

'They are from Pontus,' said Gallia suddenly.

'Pontus?'

'Think, Pacorus. What is the sacred symbol of your own Exiles? It is the lion. Those ships are full of men from Pontus.'

I grabbed her and kissed her on the lips as the Roman ship on the port side tried to turn to face the oncoming duo of Pontic triremes but failed. There was a staccato sound as the right-hand trireme's ram sheared off the oars on the port side of the Roman vessel. Its own port-side oars had been swiftly withdrawn into the hull before it hit the Roman trireme and once it had passed the disabled vessel the oars were poked back out of the oar-holes.

'It's turning,' shouted Athineos and our eyes darted to the right to see that the other Roman trireme had swung left and was bearing down on *The Cretan*.

Athineos glanced left to see the damaged Roman ship falling behind and looked back to the other trireme aiming at our mid-ships.

'I'm going to change direction,' he said, 'so their rams hits my prow. Brace yourselves.'

I ran from the stern to shout at those on deck.

'Prepare for a collision at the prow,' I shouted, 'fall back to the mast.'

I ran back to Gallia, Surena and Athineos as the latter manoeuvred his ship into the path of the oncoming trireme. *The Cretan* was ninety feet in length and at least ten feet of that vanished when the trireme's bronze ram chewed into its timbers. The ship shuddered and groaned as its prow and *artemon* disappeared and the front of the trireme was towering over *The* Cretan's deck.

'Shoot at them before they board us,' I said as we stood on the cabin's roof as the first of the marines jumped from the trireme.

I had no time to think about the Pontic vessels as I nocked arrows and shot over the heads of my companions at the Roman soldiers boarding us. I hit at least three and two white-clothed archers who stood at the trireme's prow searching for targets. Gallia and Surena were releasing arrows at a faster rate than me, hitting Romans before they boarded *The Cretan*.

'I'm out of arrows,' shouted Gallia as another six marines came aboard, led by the tribune Marcus Aristius.

Surena shot one down. 'That was my last.'

I pulled back my bowstring and focused on the man who had dared to threaten my wife. Time to die, Roman. But he tripped over one of his dead men at the moment I released my arrow, which hissed through the air and struck the marine behind him in the chest. I put down my bow and drew my sword.

'Stay here,' I said to Gallia before jumping down from the cabin and running to support the others.

Domitus, Arminius, Drenis and Burebista were desperately trying to protect the wounded that had been brought from the hold, forming a line as Alcaeus tried to haul each patient back towards the cabin. Cleon had led a charge of his men as soon the first marine had jumped on board, but his ill-judged heroism had led to two of them being killed immediately. Archers on the trireme had picked off most of Athineos' sailors, who had no shields as a defence against their missiles. I picked up my *scutum* and kept it close to my body as I ran to attack Marcus Aristius.

He knocked Cleon to the ground and stood over him, his sword pulled back to deliver a fatal blow, when with my *spatha* held above my head I screamed a war cry. He stepped back, calmly raised his shield to block my overhead strike and flicked his wrist to thrust his *gladius* forward to stab me in the belly. I caught the point of his sword on my shield, my momentum forcing him back and away from Cleon, who sprang up and retrieved his sword.

Aristius' eyes flashed with scorn as he showed me the front of his *scutum* and drew back his sword arm prior to launching an attack. Then we both lost our footing as *The Cretan* shuddered again as one of the Pontic ships rammed the Roman trireme. It smashed into the latter just behind the prow, shearing off the front of the trireme and ripping out the ram embedded in Athineos' vessel. The latter immediately began to sink as seawater rushed into its smashed prow. The archers at the prow of the Roman trireme had disappeared and as the deck of *The Cretan* began to slowly fall towards the waterline I heard a creaking sound above me. I scrambled to my feet and looked up the see the mainmast falling. I leaped back just in time as the mast and furled sail attached to it crashed on to the deck, crushing two marines and three sailors as it did so. It also crushed the helmet of Marcus Aristius, reducing everything inside it to a bloody pulp. The tribune was no longer handsome as he had no face. I looked up at the sun and silently thanked Shamash for his divine intervention.

No one thought of fighting now as seawater flooded the deck and the stern of *The Cretan* began to rise out of the water. I heard shouts ahead, saw rowers throwing themselves from the deck of the crippled trireme and then heard a succession of thuds to my right. I turned to see grappling irons lodged in the gunwale with ropes attached. Soldiers on the deck of the Pontic trireme were pulling on the ropes to bring their vessel alongside *The Cretan* and prevent the latter, or what was left of it, sinking beneath the surface.

Domitus and the others came to my side. 'That was a stroke of luck. I thought we were going to drown.'

'Get the women out of the cabin,' I ordered.

'Help me,' shouted Alcaeus, still hauling wounded sailors towards the cabin.

I ran over to assist him but saw that the man he was dragging across the deck had glazed, lifeless eyes.

'He's dead, Alcaeus.'

His head dropped and he let go if the corpse. He looked around at the others he had been trying to save and I saw that at least three others had the hand of death upon them. Only two were still alive.

'What a waste,' he muttered.

'Prepare to be boarded,' shouted one of the soldiers on the Pontic trireme. 'We are not your enemies.'

That much was certain, though as Burebista escorted Hippo and Anca from the cabin I was concerned that our vessel might still sink at any time. The trireme's rowers had withdrawn their oars so the ship could be brought alongside, after which a dozen or more soldiers jumped aboard. We stood in a group in front of the two wounded sailors still alive and the women as Gallia and Surena came from the stern in the company of Athineos, who looked close to despair. There was a crashing sound and everyone turned to see the other Pontic ship ram the disabled Roman trireme, cutting it in half. The soldiers who had boarded us gave a cheer as an officer shouted at them to be quiet. His soldiers were attired in bronze helmets, and beige tunics with wide leather belts around their mid-rifts. They carried round shields faced with leather bearing a lion on all fours, matching the motif on the mainsail of their trireme. Like the temple guards at Ephesus they were armed with the curved *xiphos*, though a few had javelins. There were archers on the deck of the triremes keeping watch on our movements.

This commander stepped onto the leaning deck of *The Cretan* and stared at us. His appearance marked him out as a man of high rank, his burnished bronze helmet sporting two white feathers either side of its crown. His bronze scale armour cuirass shimmered in the sunlight, as did his bronze greaves. He was about my height, though when he removed his helmet I discovered that he was around twice my age, his neatly cropped beard and hair flecked with grey. Curiously for a native of Pontus, he had penetrating blue eyes. He had a dignified,

377

authoritative air, which was reinforced when he spoke in a firm, commanding manner.

'I am Admiral Arcathius of the navy of Pontus. Who is your captain?'

Athineos walked forward.

'I am Athineos, a trader from Crete and the captain of what's left of this vessel.'

Arcathius placed the helmet in the crook of his arm and examined our party.

'And what goods were you transporting that warranted the attention of two Roman warships, Captain Athineos?' asked Arcathius.

'Some people who wanted to leave Ephesus,' replied Athineos evasively, 'and who the Romans wanted to prevent from leaving.'

Arcathius remained impassive as he studied each of us in turn, his eyes eventually settling on Gallia beside me. My wife was holding her bow and had her sword strapped around her waist. I saw him noting the hilt of her dagger tucked in her boot.

I saw no advantage in disguising our identities.

'I am King Pacorus of the Kingdom of Dura and this,' I turned to Gallia, 'is my wife, Queen Gallia. I am the son of King Varaz of Hatra, friend of the lately deceased King Balas of Gordyene whom we also considered a friend.'

Arcathius' ears pricked up at this. 'King Balas? You are Parthian?'

'I am, admiral.'

There was a loud creaking sound and one of his men walked forward and whispered something in his ear.

'Agreed. Well, I am sorry to report, captain, that your vessel is about to slip beneath the waves. I offer you all sanctuary on my ship, which I suggest you take advantage of speedily.'

As we clambered aboard the Pontic trireme, several of the soldiers leered at the shapely figure of Hippo, but their eyes widened in surprise when they saw Gallia's blonde hair, blue eyes and martial accoutrements. The sailors cut the ropes, retrieved the grappling hooks and jumped back on the trireme. Athineos wore a sad expression as *The Cretan* drifted from the

378

ship for a few seconds and then silently slipped beneath the waves. I slipped an arm round Gallia's waist and kissed her on the cheek.

'That tribune sinks with her. The mast fell on him and killed him.'

'He deserved a longer death,' she said.

The other Pontic trireme was now slowly going among the rowers and sailors from the Roman vessels, throwing ropes into the water to pick them up. I estimated that we were around half a mile from Lemnos' shoreline and many rowers were swimming towards land.

'Surely they will drown?' said Gallia with alarm.

'Greeks are all good swimmers, lady,' said Arcathius behind us, 'they will make landfall as the wind and tide are with them.'

'What will you do with the ones your other vessel is picking up?' I asked.

'Those who do not wish to remain with us we will take closer to the island so they can swim ashore. They will be re-employed soon enough. Good rowers are highly sought after.'

'And what do you intend to do with us?' asked Gallia.

Arcathius smiled. 'Sharp and to the point, no doubt like your sword, Queen Gallia. Well, first I intend to sail us away from Lemnos so we can avoid any curious Roman vessels that the governor of the island may despatch. Then we will sail northwest to spend the night at one of our sheltered bays where we have hidden food and supplies. After a night's rest you will have the opportunity of either leaving us or accompanying us to our base.'

'Which is where?' I asked.

'The city Histria on the western coast of the Black Sea,' answered Arcathius.

I did not know where Histria was and had only the vaguest knowledge of the Black Sea, but I liked this straight-talking admiral and we badly needed rest.

'We would be appreciative of your hospitality, admiral,' I said.

The triremes picked up those in the water nearby and sailed close to the shore so they could swim to land. Arcathius informed me that they would probably be transported back to

Ephesus where they would be re-employed by the Roman squadron there. A handful decided to stay. As the sun dipped on the western horizon, the wind dropping and the sea turned into a shimmering carpet once more, I told the admiral our story. Of how I had grown up a Parthian prince and how fate had taken me to Italy. He had not heard of Spartacus but listened intently as I told him of his revolt against the Romans and my part in it, of my escape from Italy with the Companions and how I had travelled to Ephesus to rescue one of the latter.

'And did you succeed?' he asked as his crew furled the ship's two sails and the rowers pulled on their oars to power us through the almost flat sea.

I pointed to Burebista sitting on the deck with his arm around Anca.

'I found him lord, and now your ship carries him to freedom.'

He enquired about what happened after my return to Parthia and I told him about my marriage, which was attended by King Balas, my gaining the crown of Dura and the subsequent civil war in Parthia.

'I never met King Balas,' he said, 'but his memory is held in great esteem by many in Pontus. I am glad he did not live to see my country become a Roman whore.'

'Pontus is now ruled by the Romans?' I tried desperately to hide my disappointment.

'Worse than that,' he said bitterly, 'my lord, King Mithridates, the man who fought the Romans for thirty years, was killed by his own son Pharnaces, who has since become a Roman puppet. But there are many of us who carry on the late, great king's fight.'

'And not just in this part of the world, admiral.'

I told him about Dura's army, about the Exiles and how they had helped to destroy a Roman army before the walls of my city.

'The Exiles is an apt name, King Pacorus, for all true lovers of Pontus are now exiles from their own lands.'

'Is this place you travel to, this Histria, not in Pontus?'

He gave me a wry smile. 'No, in Thrace, though for how much longer I cannot say. The Romans circle it like wolves.'

The two vessels sailed into a small bay on a rocky, seemingly barren peninsula that Arcathius informed me was the gateway to the Hellespont, the narrow strait of water that gave access to the Black Sea. The ships were moored in the water close to a shingle beach that was surrounded by high, grass-covered hills. The rowers, sailors and soldiers left the triremes and went ashore to set fires, the firewood being stored in hidden caves above the beach. These small caves also contained grain that had been stored there a few days before by Arcathius' men. The fires were lit and the grain ground down and baked into unleavened cakes, which were eaten just before sunset. Everyone had an appetite aside from Athineos who sat staring at the flickering flames of the fire we sat around. I went over and sat beside him.

'I am sorry about your ship, Athineos.'

He shrugged. 'Like I said, I am paying for my greed. Strange how a life's work can disappear so quickly.'

'I want you to come back to Dura with us,' I said. 'It is the least I can do.'

He continued to stare at the fire. 'Dura is many miles from the sea, King Pacorus. What would an old sea dog do in your kingdom aside from spending his days getting drunk and whoring?'

'I did not say you should remain at Dura, I said that you should come back with us. I have an idea that you may be interested in.'

His interest perked up at this. 'What idea?'

'Let us concentrate on getting back to Dura first and then I will tell you. But I do not intend for you to end your days as a beggar in some nameless town in Asia.'

He stroked his beard. 'Well, as I haven't got a better offer, and since I am now wanted throughout the Roman world, I accept your offer.'

He turned to look at me. 'I can't abandon my men.'

He was talking about his grizzled second-in-command, two other sailors and the duo that were at death's door despite Alcaeus heroic efforts.

'I would not expect it of you,' I said, doubtful that the two injured men would survive the journey to Histria, wherever that was.

But they did survive, much to the surprise of everyone on board. But Alcaeus attended them closely and Hippo said prayers over them, the latter boosting their morale more than a crusty wiry-haired Greek whose temper seemed to shorten with every passing day.

Out of respect for Cleon and Hippo the next day Arcathius docked at the city of Elaeus, a settlement sited at the entrance to the Hellespont, on the left bank of the waterway. It was a beautiful place of white-walled buildings and endless olive groves positioned in a narrow plain between a range of rocky hills and the sea. Gallia and I walked with Arcathius through its clean streets and well-maintained buildings as we followed our Greek companions to the Tomb of Protesilaus.

'Was he a king?' asked Gallia.

Arcathius shook his head. 'No, lady, he was the first Greek killed in the Trojan War.'

'I have heard of that conflict,' I said. 'It was over a woman, I believe.'

Arcathius looked at Gallia. 'You are right. A Greek princess named Helen, supposedly the most beautiful woman in the world, and the wife of King Menelaus of Sparta, a Greek kingdom, was abducted by Prince Paris of Troy.'

'Where is Troy?' asked Gallia.

Arcathius stopped, turned and pointed towards the harbour. 'On the other side of the Hellespont, lady. It is now a small Roman settlement built on the remains of a once mighty city.'

He sighed and turned away from the harbour. 'Returning to the Trojan War, an enraged Menelaus mobilised all the other Greek kings to send an expedition to get his wife back. Legend has it that a thousand Greek ships sailed to retrieve his wife.'

'And did they succeed?' asked Gallia.

'Yes, majesty, they did,' answered Arcathius, 'but the war lasted ten years and thousands of Greeks and Trojans died.'

The shrine itself was an open precinct containing an altar and small temple, the whole surrounded by olive groves. Arcathius informed me that soil of the area was well suited to the cultivation of olives, so much so that Elaeus was called the 'The Olive City'. The nearby tomb was an impressive rectangular stone structure with carvings of the Trojan War on all its sides. Arcathius gave Cleon and Hippo money so they could purchase small cakes as offerings, the admiral telling me that the Greeks believed that continued remembrance of the dead by the living ensured immortality for the former. 'In Parthia we believe that the spirit lives on after death,' I said. 'But whether it goes to heaven or the underworld depends on the actions of the person in this life.'

While we talked Alcaeus also made an offering at the tomb. He and the two Greek lovers came away from the shrine in good humour and I was grateful to Arcathius for stopping off at the Elaeus, a Greek city a mere stone's throw away from Roman Asia.

The Hellespont was a most wondrous thing, a corridor of ocean flanked by cliffs that was filled with small fishing villages. The mood among the sailors and soldiers on board was relaxed, though the rowers strained at their oars to propel us through the Hellespont's forty-mile length.

'The current is against us,' Arcathius told me on the day after my conversation with Athineos. 'It flows southwest from the Sea of Marmara, which we will enter in about three hours.'

I saw numerous single-sail fishing vessels plying the waters and large cargo ships similar to *The Cretan*. As the soldiers relaxed on deck, their shields and javelins secured in racks, I enquired about the Romans.

'There are no Roman ships in the Hellespont,' the admiral informed me. 'I raid into the Aegean to show Rome that Pontus is still its enemy, notwithstanding the treachery of Pharnaces, but no enemy warships venture up this waterway.'

'Not yet,' I said glumly.

My spirits also rose the next day as we continued on our journey, Arcathius telling me that the shore on our port side was Thrace, the homeland of Spartacus and Claudia. The crew must have thought we were mad when I hugged Gallia and then Drenis, who sank to his knees and thanked the gods that he had been allowed to see his homeland again. A bemused Arcathius told him that we would be docking at the town of Heraclea Perinthus on the Thracian coast to take on water and food. Drenis thanked him and gazed at the shoreline of the land he thought he would never see again. It was the first and only time that I saw Drenis with tears in his eyes.

The port's harbour was filled with fishing and merchant vessels but did not compare to the great docks of Ephesus or Paphos, not that it bothered Drenis. We walked with him among his people in the crowded market behind the docks, the stalls and avenues between them filled with Greek and Thracian men, women and children.

The Thracian race was a collection of fair- and olive-skinned individuals, some having grey and blue eyes. Hair colours ranged from dark brown to blonde and even red. Many of the men had their long hair dressed in a topknot and most of the women and young girls had tattoos. Thracian dress included fawn-skin boots with tops turned down, woollen mantles and animal skin caps with their tails hanging down their owners' necks. The town was noisy and crowded and the Romans seemed a distant memory. But among the joy we felt to be among free peoples I wondered how we were going to get back to Dura. We might find sanctuary at Histria but would we ever get home?

Chapter 14

It took us three days to reach Histria, the last night before we docked a full moon filling the night sky and resembling a giant pale ball that the gods had thrown to earth. Histria was a city originally founded by Greek settlers over six hundred years ago and Arcathius, whom I found a most charming and interesting host, told us that many such settlements existed on the shores of the Black Sea. But recently all had suffered as a result of the Roman conquest of Greece and Asia Minor. The arrival of the legions had interrupted commerce and a lack of trade meant a creeping impoverishment that threatened the existence of the Greek colonies. He informed us that, unlike the Romans, the original Greek settlers had sought not to conquer the native tribes but to trade with them, to create mutually beneficial relationships in which all would prosper. In any case after a few generations settlers and natives intermarried, which meant that the blood of their offspring was a mixture of Greek and native.

'In Histria's case,' said Arcathius as his two triremes sailed into the harbour of the city, 'Greek blood was mixed with the Getea tribe who inhabit the hinterland. But these days it's difficult to tell the difference between the two so mixed up are they.'

'This city is like Dura,' said Gallia, 'where many different races mix freely and are all equal, men and women too.'

Arcathius looked at the sword hanging from her waist and the bow slung over her shoulder.

'From what you and your husband have told me about Dura, Queen Gallia, nowhere on this earth is like Dura.'

'You're right there, skipper,' said Athineos loudly as we all stood on the deck of the trireme as it inched towards the stone quay, 'the queen has a bodyguard of women who all wear swords and shoot bows and the king here lives in a palace that has no slaves.'

'It sounds a most interesting place,' said Arcathius.

Histria was also an interesting place: a port sited in a great open bay on a wide coastal plain with a citadel built on a hill to the immediate north of the city. The docks contained a variety of different-sized merchant vessels as well as a larger number of small fishing boats. But as the trireme was moored to the quay

385

and Arcathius led us ashore I noticed that, aside from the catches being unloaded from fishing vessels, the port was hardly a hive of activity.

Arcathius told us that he would take us straight to the citadel to meet the city's ruler, a king named Akrosas, who would arrange for a ship to take us to the eastern shore of the Black Sea where we could then travel south back to Parthia.

'I would do it myself,' he said to me, 'but my ships and soldiers are needed here to defend against Roman incursions into the Black Sea.'

'You expect a Roman invasion?' I asked.

He nodded. 'It is only a matter of time. Now that Pontus is a client kingdom of theirs the Romans will try to subdue all the Greek colonies in this part of the world.'

We walked from the docks into the city, which had the appearance and resonance of a place that had seen better days. The streets were paved with stone but were badly preserved, with weeds growing between the flagstones. Like Dura they were arranged in a grid pattern, though unlike Dura they were strewn with rubbish. Unwashed children in filthy clothes, with bare feet, ran around and stray dogs growled and bared their teeth at us as we passed. The citizens themselves were mostly fair-haired, many having locks as blonde as Gallia's and blue eyes to match. They wore light tunics and leggings and wore their hair long, some of the men sporting plaits.

The markets appeared busy enough, with ceramics, metals, honey, wax, fruit and linen being traded, presumably having been brought from the hinterland. The buildings showed their Greek lineage, being white-walled with red tiled roofs and all appeared to have been constructed from stone. But like the roads many were in a poor state of repair, with tiles missing from roofs and dilapidated, cracked walls. The people appeared hardy enough but many wore worried expressions and as we made our way towards the citadel a growing sense of foreboding enveloped us.

'Something is wrong,' Gallia said to me quietly as we reached the wall that surrounded the citadel. It was stout enough, being built of large stone blocks and interspersed with squat, square towers at regular intervals along its length. Guards standing at the entrance to the gatehouse giving access to the citadel on the hill waved us through when they saw the figure of Arcathius. They paid scant interest to the rest of us as they leaned on their hexagonal shields and stared vacantly ahead.

The buildings inside the citadel, which was originally called the acropolis in accordance with its Greek heritage, was tidier and more imposing than the rest of the city, its buildings well maintained. As well as the stone palace it housed armouries, stables, granaries, workshops and two magnificent temples, one dedicated to Apollo, the protector of the city, the other to Bendis, the Thracian Goddess of the Moon and Hunting. Hippo told us that Artemis and Bendis were considered by some to be one and the same deity, the Thracians having adopted the Moon Goddess and given her their own name.

White-robed priests and priestesses stood on the steps of the temples and watched us pass as we walked to the palace located on the north side of the paved square that the sanctuaries fronted. Hippo glanced at them with a whimsical look on her face. She could never go back to her life as a high priestess and I wondered if she was regretting the choice she had made at Ephesus.

At the entrance to the palace stood sentries with round hoplite-style shields adorned with a bow and arrow motif – the symbol of Apollo. These soldiers had bronze helmets, leather armour cuirasses and were armed with short spears and swords. We were delayed there while a steward was summoned to listen to our request to enter. A balding, flustered middle-aged man in a white tunic and soft sandals arrived after a few minutes. His consternation disappeared briefly when he saw the figure of Arcathius.

'Admiral, you are indeed a sight for sore eyes. I trust your sortie was successful? The king has been most eager for your return.'

'Two less Roman warships in the Mediterranean to worry about,' said Arcathius modestly.

The steward brought his small hands together. 'Most excellent news, admiral, and Apollo knows we need good tidings at the moment.'

Arcathius' eyes narrowed. 'What has happened?'

The steward shook his head. 'To Histria, nothing. But yesterday news arrived that the Romans had defeated a great army of Thracians to the west.'

'How far away are they?'

A veil of gloom descended over the steward's face. 'Three or four days, admiral. The king has sent riders to his allies requesting aid but...'

He showed the palms of his hands and let his head drop.

'Is the king here?' said Arcathius.

'Yes, admiral, and he will be delighted to see you and...'

The steward looked past the admiral to study the rest of us. His brow creased to create many worry lines.

'Allies against the Romans,' said Arcathius.

The steward's expression lightened. 'We need every ally in this time of trial. Please follow me.'

We walked into the palace and entered a place of white stone columns, floors with elaborate mosaics and walls adorned with beautiful murals depicting gods and hunting scenes. Images of Apollo and Bendis decorated the walls of the throne room, the ruler himself sitting in a chair carved from oak and decorated with copper embellishments. We were kept at the entrance while guards took our weapons and Arcathius, helmet in the crook of his arm, marched forward and bowed to Akrosas. The king was dressed in a simple loose-fitting white tunic, white leggings and a red cloak draped around his shoulders. He had neatly cropped fair hair encompassing a round, intelligent face. Seated next to him was a beautiful blonde-haired woman with a slender neck and high cheekbones. Indeed, she had more than a passing resemblance to Gallia. She too was attired in white, a flowing gown that covered her body and legs but left her arms bare. They both looked like celestial beings, insulated from the harsh world outside.

Arcathius engaged in polite conversation with them both and turned to look at us when the king pointed at our group. There followed more conversation between them before Arcathius returned and asked Gallia and me to accompany him. We walked to where the king and queen sat, who both stood to receive us.

'Welcome to Histria, King Pacorus and Queen Gallia,' said Akrosas, 'we are pleased to make your acquaintance.'

He held out a hand to his queen. 'This is my wife Rodica.'

'We are grateful for your hospitality King Akrosas and Queen Rodica,' I replied. 'May the gods smile on you and your kingdom, lord king.'

The exchanges were a mere formality but Akrosas seemed amiable enough, though his wife said nothing as he ordered wine to be brought and sent the flustered steward away to prepare rooms for us in the palace. When the wine had been served, which was excellent, the king sat back on his throne and continued to engage me in conversation, smiling politely at Gallia as he did so and examining my companions behind us.

'Admiral Arcathius informs me that you were being pursued by Roman warships when he came across you.'

'It is true, lord king, without the arrival of the admiral we would have surely died at the hands of the Romans.'

Akrosas ran a finger around the rim of his silver cup.

'You had been at Ephesus, I believe.'

I nodded. 'We had been attending the games there.'

'I see, and how may we assist you?'

'We seek passage back to Parthia, lord king,' I answered. 'I have accomplished what I set out to achieve but regrettably find myself still far from home.'

He smiled kindly. 'We will of course provide you with aid so that you may get back to Parthia, King Pacorus, though presently I have to deal with an urgent matter that requires all my attention. In the meantime I hope you, your queen and your party will avail yourselves of our hospitality.'

He engaged us in conversation until another steward appeared, the king ordering him to show us to our accommodation, after which he and Queen Rodica took their leave.

Our rooms were located in a wing of the palace and were both spacious and luxurious. Akrosas sent slave girls with fresh clothes and others with oils to massage the stress of the last few days away. I had to admit that I had not realised how tired and knotted my body was until a young woman with iron-hard fingers kneaded and massaged it. Gallia was also treated to a full-body massage, her naked body oiled and gleaming as she lay face-down, another slave girl massaging her lithe frame.

It was past noon by the time they had finished, both of us totally relaxed and content as they bowed and left. I would have liked to have made love to my beautiful wife but such was the state of blissful peace that I was in that I was happy just to let my eyes ravish her, and hers me. More slaves entered our room with water and fruit, oblivious to fact that this foreign king and queen were naked and totally helpless before them. An assassin could have slit both our throats without us raising a finger to stop him or her. But I felt no sense of threat in this palace, only a great sadness concerning an approaching darkness.

'Have you noticed that wherever we go, even to the extremes of the world, the Romans follow us?' said Gallia, pulling on a robe to cover her nakedness. 'Dobbai was right.'

'Dobbai?'

She left the bed to sit on a chair and began brushing her hair.

'When we were at Hatra and she sent you your griffin standard. Do you remember the letter that accompanied it?'

'Vaguely.'

'She said that your destiny was bound up with the Romans and so it has proved.'

'I don't think you can blame me for the Romans advancing against this city,' I protested. 'My initial impression is that Histria will fall like a piece of ripened fruit from the tree.'

Gallia stopped brushing her hair and stared out of the open doors that gave a view of a great plain beyond the city.

'And another piece of history will be eradicated by Rome.'

I sat up and pulled on a pair of linen leggings and a white tunic. I stood and went over to her, kissing the top of her head.

'While there are men still capable of wielding a sword then Rome will never triumph.'

She looked up at me, her eyes blue pools of desire.

'I feel like handling something of a more softer texture.'

I felt desire stir in my loins. 'Feel free.'

There was a knock at the door.

'King Pacorus, forgive the disturbance but King Akrosas requests your presence on the palace balcony.'

Gallia curled her lip towards the faceless voice behind the door.

'Tell him to go away.'

I desperately wanted to make love to her but was mindful that we were guests in Akrosas' household and also at his mercy.

'It would be politic not to offend our host,' I whispered.

'Go then,' she purred, 'but you had better make it up to me tonight.'

'I promise.'

She stood and shook her hair. 'I will hold you to that. A man should be a blend of aggression, passion, courage and honour. Too much of one unbalances the other elements and impairs his judgement. That is what I was told.'

'By whom?'

'Dobbai.'

I pulled on my boots and strapped on my sword belt. 'Dobbai? What does she know of affairs of the heart?'

'You would be surprised.'

I stood, pulled her towards me and kissed her lips. 'You're right. I would.'

Outside our room the steward who had met us at the palace's entrance waited with a worried expression. Clearly the approach of the Romans had filled him with dread, not least because he had probably heard what happens to cities that refuse a Roman summons to surrender. Perhaps he was thinking of ways to escape the palace before they arrived. But perhaps I was doing him a disservice in questioning his loyalty.

The balcony was actually a large terrace similar to the one we had at Dura, though this one was on the roof of the palace, giving uninterrupted views of the bay, the Black Sea beyond and the large plain that surrounded Histria. The steward escorted me into the king's presence, Akrosas leaning on the white stone balustrade that ran round the edge of the balcony. Guards stood at the entrance to the two doors that gave access to the balcony and others stood sentry near the king himself. He turned and held out an arm to welcome me as the steward bowed and left our presence.

'King Pacorus, may I offer you some refreshment?'

391

There was a large table filled with savouries, meats, bread and fruit and nearby it stood slaves holding jugs of wine.

'No, thank you,' I replied.

He continued to hold out his arm. 'Come, let me show you something.'

He turned back to the balustrade, resting his hands on its smooth white top. I stood beside him and looked towards the west where there was an ocean of green. I saw fields, what appeared to be vineyards and villages and farmsteads. Beyond the cultivated land appeared to be unending forest as far as the eye could see.

'When my ancestors arrived many generations ago,' Akrosas began, 'this land was a vast wilderness filled with even wilder people who lived in the forests and spent their time hunting and killing each other.

'Gradually, over time and after forging friendships with the locals, the land was tamed and civilisation was established. Learning and culture were planted along with crops.'

He held out an arm towards the vast area of cultivated land.

'Greeks and Getea worked in harmony to create this city and the land that feeds it. They cut down the forests to build the ships that allowed us to trade with other colonies in the Black Sea, as well as with Greece itself.'

His arm fell to his side.

'But then the Romans came. They conquered Greece and all the islands in the Aegean and our trading links were cut. And with the decline of trade came a decline in Histria's prosperity. And now a Roman army marches from the west to conquer us, to undo the work of generations and erase the memory of my forefathers from history.'

'You will fight, lord king?'

He looked at me with sad eyes.

'Admiral Arcathius informs me that you have spent many years fighting the Romans, King Pacorus, and that you have won many victories over them.'

'I have fought and beaten them, yes,' I answered. 'They are tenacious foes.'

'In the next few days I will lead my army against the Romans.'

The tone of his voice did not give me any belief that he would be able to defeat them.

'You are waiting for allies, lord king?' I said.

He nodded and looked back towards his lands. 'Fellow Thracians, though whether I can call myself a Thracian with Greek blood in my veins is a debatable point.'

He suddenly turned and looked at me intently. 'Would you fight, King Pacorus, or would you seek to evacuate as many of your people as possible before the Romans came?'

'I would fight,' I answered. 'Not to do so gives them an easy victory whereas if you engage them there is always a chance of victory.'

'And if I fail?'

I pointed at the stone wall that surrounded the city. 'Your walls are stout, lord king, and with the harbour you have the ability to bring in food and soldiers to withstand a siege.'

He too pointed, at the agricultural lands beyond the city walls. 'But the Romans would have my lands, King Pacorus, and what would I have? A starving city that would eventually fall to the enemy.'

He continued to stare at his lands, a look of resignation on his face. After a few seconds he sighed gently.

'But that does not concern you, King Pacorus. Admiral Arcathius has told me your remarkable tale and I asked you here to inform you that I have ordered a ship to be prepared to take you east to Pontus. Once there you can travel overland south to Parthia and your home. I will also provide you with money so you and your companions may purchase horses once you reach Pontus. I believe that you lost all your money during your flight from Ephesus. Kings should help each other in these trying times.'

'We did, lord king. You are generous indeed. But know that when I reach Dura all monies loaned will be repaid.'

He gave me a thin smile. 'It would be a poor show if I could not assist a man who has done so much to fight the power of Rome.'

Seemingly tired of looking at lush farmlands that would soon be in the possession of the enemy, the king asked me to accompany him to the Temple of Apollo a stone's throw from the palace. On the way I engaged in trivial conversation with him concerning palace architecture. But he was in the grip of a deep melancholy and I was glad to be out of his company when we reached the square and he informed me that he was going to pray to the god.

'Perhaps you would like to join me, in prayer I mean.'

'You are most kind,' I said, 'but my god is Shamash, the Lord of the Sun who has been my guide since childhood. It would be disrespectful to sacrifice to another god, I think.'

He nodded solemnly. 'Of course, you are right. Well, this is where we say goodbye. I have arranged for a banquet in your honour tonight before you and your queen leave us. I hope you will be able to attend.'

'We would be honoured, lord king.'

He smiled vacantly and departed for the temple, a man with the weight of a crumbling kingdom on his shoulders. I was immediately cheered when I spotted the delicious figure of Hippo gliding from the Temple of Bendis and was even happier when she gave me a dazzling smile and headed towards me. The pristine white robe she was wearing clung to her body and accentuated every curve of her frame. I could understand why Cleon had fallen in love with her.

'You have been praying, Hippo?'

'I have been begging the goddess for forgiveness, lord,' she replied.

'The king has arranged for a ship to take us to the East,' I told her. 'I would like you and Cleon to come with me. Unless you are thinking of staying here.'

She too now looked sad. 'I think that we would not be welcome here, lord. If the people found out that I used to be a high priestess of Artemis but broke my vows they would wish to be rid of us lest the gods became angry with them.'

I looked around the citadel. 'I think the gods became angry with these people long before you broke your vows, Hippo.'

I reached out and took her hand. 'Then come back to Parthia with us. There is a home for you both there, that I promise.'

She looked pensive.

'The thought of travelling to Parthia does not appeal to you?'

'It is not that, lord. I believe that the gods brought us here for a purpose but I do not know what it is. The goddess is still angry with me and has thrown a veil over Her plans.'

'It was good luck that brought us here, Hippo,' I said. 'How else do you explain the timely arrival of Admiral Arcathius? Surely Artemis herself sent him?'

'The gods may give mortals a reprieve so they can prepare for their next trial, lord,' she answered. 'Their divine minds are always many steps ahead of ours.'

I walked with her back to the palace and though her beauty and personality were most attractive I thought her analyses of what might or might not happen unnecessary. I escorted her back to her room and told her that she should not trouble herself unduly. We were free, uninjured and tomorrow would be taking ship back to Parthia. She rewarded me with a kiss on the cheek and another wonderful smile before she entered her quarters. Sometimes it was most excellent being a king.

I informed the others of the Akrosas' generosity and his invitation to the banquet that evening. On the way to the feasting hall Domitus pulled me to one side.

'Did he say how close the Romans were?'

'No. Why?'

'All they have to do is arrive and knock on the gates and this city will fall into their laps, that's why. If they make an appearance tomorrow there will be panic and chaos that we will be caught up in. You heard that steward. We should get on our ship tonight.'

I frowned at him. 'We will attend the banquet that is being given in our honour. It would be the height of impoliteness not to attend.'

He was unconvinced. 'As opposed to the height of stupidity not to see the warning signs.'

'What warning signs?'

'The rank stench of fear and defeat that hangs over this city.'

I sighed. 'Sometimes, Domitus, I fear we will never make a Parthian of you.'

He looked mortified. 'The day I grow my hair long is the day I open my veins.'

The palace's banqueting hall was a mixture of Greek style and local customs. The walls and low ceiling were decorated with frescoes depicting ancient myths and gods, especially Apollo, but there were no couches for reclining on. Rather, there was a top table raised on a dais where the king and queen sat and tables arranged at right angles before it. Those at the top table sat in chairs whereas the guests at the other tables sat on benches. A blast of trumpets heralded the arrival of King Akrosas and Queen Rodica, both of them again attired in pure white and wearing gold crowns on their heads. The queen was also wearing gold earrings and gold rings on all her fingers. They sat in the two richly adorned chairs in the centre of the top table, myself being invited to sit next to the king and Gallia next to Rodica.

When everyone was seated a white-haired man with a long beard of the same colour walked to stand before the dais and ordered everyone to rise. The king, queen and guests did so as the High Priest of Apollo called on the god to bless the feast and Histria. Everyone stood with heads bowed in silence as his thunderous voice filled the chamber.

'Sacred silence.

Let the sky, the earth, the sea and the winds sound.

Mountains fall silent.

Sounds and birds' warbles cease.

For Phoebus, the Light bearer King shall keep us company.

Apollo, King of the Sun and the Idea of light,

Send Your rays and light the sacred torch.

Apollo God of the Sun and the Idea of light,

Send Your rays and light the sacred torch,

for this Your city of Histria.

Send Your arrows to strike down the enemies of Your people.

And give victory to Your servant Akrosas in his coming trial.'

The king thanked his high priest and invited everyone to sit and eat the food that Apollo had provided, and in truth the god was most generous. A steady procession of slaves brought bread, cheese, a thick bean soup, cabbage, mushrooms and fresh peas. Others placed silver plates heaped with freshly cooked beef, goat and wild boar, all washed down with the delicious wine that Akrosas informed me with pride was the product of local vineyards. We were also served fish caught in the Black Sea, including mackerel, blue fish, mullet, sprat and turbot. I refrained from suggesting to the king that as long as the harbour remained open neither he nor his people would starve if the Romans laid siege to his city. But as the wine flowed and the guests relaxed the mood in the hall, previously polite but tense, became calm and even carefree. Rodica chatted to Gallia and Domitus was resting an elbow on a table deep in conversation with Arcathius opposite. Drenis, Arminius and Surena seemed happy enough, the latter laughing loudly as he shared stories of heroism with one of the admiral's officers. It was turning into a pleasant evening when it was suddenly interrupted by the arrival of an uninvited guest.

A guard entered the hall and walked to the dais, bowing and announcing to the king that Radu was outside. I had no idea who this person was but Akrosas certainly did, ordering the soldier to allow him to enter. I noticed Rodica rolled her eyes and said something to Gallia but what it was I could not hear. The king ordered the flute players to cease playing and waved away the jugglers who were throwing brightly coloured small balls in the air in front of the dais. The soldier exited the hall and seconds later a large, stocky man with a round face and white beard and hair stomped into the chamber. He was an imposing individual, his barrel chest enclosed by a thick leather cuirass and a long sword in a red scabbard strapped to his belt. He wore a short-sleeved white tunic and gold bracelets on his wrists. Akrosas rose and held out his hands to him.

'Welcome Radu, King of the Bastarnae and our most valued ally.'

Radu looked around at the assembled lords, priests and commanders of Histria. He winked at the queen and was surprised to see two other women present – Gallia and Hippo – before nodding at Akrosas.

'Hail, Akrosas.'

He looked at the slaves standing around the walls of the hall holding jugs of wine.

'Has Histria run out of wine?'

Akrosas gestured that Radu should be served. Two slaves rushed forward, one with a jug and the other with a tray of silver cups. Radu grabbed the jug and began drinking from it, wine spilling down his beard and cuirass. Many of those seated at tables were appalled by his behaviour. He threw the jug at the slave, who managed to catch it, and then belched loudly.

'I have come, Akrosas, in answer to your plea, but unless you can raise a great army then I say that Histria is doomed.'

There were murmurs around the hall at his impudence. I got the impression that the citizens of Histria viewed the other Thracian tribes as being inferior to themselves. Radu wiped a muscular forearm across his mouth.

'Ten days ago a great army of Bastarnae, Maedi and Dacians met the Romans in battle. All day long we fought them and at the end of it our dead covered the valley floor like fallen leaves in autumn.'

The murmurs in the hall died away as the guests took in this dire news.

'What is left of our army is falling back to Histria to be reinforced by the army of King Akrosas.'

'Where are the Romans now?' said Akrosas.

'Around fifty miles west of here, amusing themselves with pillaging local villages and taking slaves,' replied Radu. 'Those who have the means have fled into the forests, the rest are either dead or enslaved.'

Akrosas rose from his seat. 'I will be leading the army of Histria in person to give battle to the Romans.'

Polite applause greeted this declaration, which seemed to delight Akrosas but made little impression on Radu.

'How many men will march under your banner, Akrosas?'

'I think that is a matter for a council of war, Radu,' replied Akrosas irritably. 'But be assured that it will be enough to overpower the Romans.'

'I doubt that.'

I heard with surprise the voice of Domitus and looked up to see him standing beside his table. Several of the guests were whispering to each other, trying to identify this strange crop-haired individual who had dared to speak out of turn in the king's presence. Radu turned to look at him.

'Who are you?'

398

Domitus looked at Akrosas. 'With your permission, lord king, I would like to speak to King Radu.'

There were gasps and sharp intakes of breath from the other guests. This was unheard of and clearly marked out this clean-shaven man with the mean features as a barbarian. Akrosas, though, perhaps finding Radu's appearance and utterances irksome, nodded and retook his seat.

'My name is Lucius Domitus and I am the general of the army of Dura.' He pointed at me. 'That is my king, Pacorus of Dura, who has spent years fighting the Romans.'

'Dura?' spat Radu. 'Never heard of it.'

'And I have never heard of the Bastarnae,' said Domitus calmly, 'but let me tell everyone here how you fought your battle, lord king.'

'Ha,' bellowed Radu, 'I was there and you were not. What could you tell me that I don't already know?'

Domitus regarded him with his cold eyes. 'You outnumbered the Romans so you believed that victory would be easy. You and your fellow tribal leaders thought that storming the enemy camp would also be easy, until you discovered that the ditch that surrounded it was littered with spikes that inflicted terrible injuries on your warriors. But no matter, when the day of battle arrived you were confident that your numbers would simply overwhelm the invaders.

'So you mustered your army and the tribes gathered round their banners in a great mass that made the Roman force appear small and insignificant by comparison. Please feel free to interrupt me if what I am stating is incorrect.'

Radu said nothing so Domitus continued.

'And your warriors banged their spears against their shields and raised their war cries in an attempt to intimidate the enemy, which stood in silence in their ranks. But then you noticed that among the war cries and chanting there were high-pitched screams and you discovered that the Romans were shooting at your packed ranks with machines. They are called scorpions and they shoot iron-tipped spears that can impale three men at once. But then you already know this.

'After being goaded by the Roman machines your warriors could take no more of being cut down without reply and so you ordered a mass charge. Your men surged forward,

399

many still being cut down by the scorpions but also being killed and wounded by slingers and archers as they got nearer to the Roman ranks. And then, just before your warriors reached the front rank of the enemy, there was a volley of Roman javelins that cut down hundreds of your men. This broke up the momentum of your charge and then the Romans themselves charged, hacking into the ranks of your men with their short swords, forcing them back until they broke and retreated.'

Domitus stopped to pick up his cup and took a sip before continuing.

'And then the Roman horsemen charged into your disorganised and demoralised men, who ran for their lives and left the field to the enemy.'

Radu's green eyes narrowed and I could see that he was enraged by Domitus' words. But there was also a part of him that recognised that what my general had said was correct so he kept his emotions in check. The silence in the chamber was deafening as all eyes turned to Radu.

The king took a deep breath. 'How do you know of such things?'

'How, lord king?' answered Domitus, 'because I am a Roman and I have trained my men to fight and think like Romans.'

Radu drew his sword and walked towards Domitus, who stood his ground, unconcerned. I jumped to my feet, followed by Akrosas who shouted at Radu.

'Lucius Domitus is a guest in my palace, Radu, and may not be harmed.'

Radu pointed his sword at Domitus. 'You allow a Roman to drink your wine and eat your food? He and his kind are responsible for nearly four thousand Thracians that fell in battle. I can still hear their screams and see their shattered bodies.'

'And if you fight them again the result will be more Thracian dead,' said Domitus.

'I must ask you to put away your sword, Radu,' warned Akrosas as nervous guards approached the hulking brute.

The king of the Bastarnae looked contemptuously at the guards before slamming his sword back in its scabbard.

Akrosas, relieved, waved them back and sat down. I did the same as Radu folded his arms across his chest.

'You may think, Roman,' he sneered at Domitus, 'that your race is invincible but Thracians will never kneel to Rome. We may face defeat but we will die fighting.'

The guests applauded his words and some of Akrosas' commanders banged their fists on the table to show solidarity with their fellow Thracian. Domitus remained calm and waited for the hubbub to die down.

'The Romans are not gods, lord king. They can be defeated easily enough. It is just a matter of out-thinking them and not dancing to their tune.'

'You might want to listen to my general, lord king,' I said, 'he has never lost a battle.'

Radu turned his large head to peer at me, naked contempt in his eyes.

'I don't need any help to crush my foes.'

I smiled. 'As you wish, lord king.'

The arrival of Radu meant the feast was at an end as Akrosas announced that he would regrettably have to cancel the festivities to consult with his fellow king. He and Queen Rodica left the hall in the company of Radu and all the guests followed them, filing out of the chamber in haste so they could return either to their homes or their soldiers. Domitus was in a reflective mood as we wandered back to our quarters.

'This time next week that big king will be dead, most likely, along with our host and thousands of his men.'

'I thought he was going to kill you, Domitus,' said Gallia.

'You did take a chance speaking like that,' I agreed.

Domitus looked at Drenis. 'Yes, I forgot I was among wild Thracians who will slit your throat if you even look at them the wrong way.'

Drenis raised a thin smile but I could see that he was distracted.

'You are troubled, Drenis?' I probed.

'You heard that big king mention the Maedi?' he said to me. I nodded.

'They are my tribe, and the tribe of Spartacus and Claudia. Never thought I would even hear their name again.'

'I am sorry that they face defeat, Drenis,' said Domitus, 'but you can see what is going to happen. They will raise a great host and fling it against the Romans and thousands will be cut down and the legionaries will have another easy victory.'

He shrugged. 'We do the same against our enemies, do we not? In any case we will be leaving tomorrow so it's not our concern.'

When I wished the others goodnight I could see the pain on Drenis' face and the frustration etched on Cleon's visage. I could read their thoughts like they were written down on papyrus. Drenis wanted to stay and fight beside his fellow tribesmen, Cleon wanted to kill Romans and Surena just wanted to fight. Arminius for his part looked a little disappointed that we were departing Histria.

'I for one thank the gods that we are departing before any more fighting,' announced Alcaeus. 'We have been extremely lucky thus far but I don't want to tempt fate, or test the patience of the gods. This is not our fight.'

He was right of course. But as Gallia lay in my arms later that night after we had made love I stared at the ceiling, unable to sleep. Eventually I untangled myself from her limbs and left the bed to stand on the balcony of our bedroom. The night was fresh but not cool. Autumn had yet to arrive and so the days were warm and the evenings pleasant. The balcony faced west, the direction from where the Roman army would approach the city. The crops had yet to be harvested but there would be no one to work in the fields when Akrosas mustered all the young men to fight the invaders. I knew that many would not return to see their homes or their families. Perhaps none would. I looked into the moonlit sky and asked for directions from the gods.

'It is not our fight, Pacorus.'

I nearly jumped out of my skin when I heard the voice before recognising it. I turned to see Gallia wrapping a robe around her body. She looked like the Moon Goddess herself as its pale light highlighted her fair skin and blonde locks, turning them silver.

I turned back to look west. 'I don't know what you mean.'

She laughed mockingly. 'You think I did not see your face when we said goodnight to our companions? You think I did not see the anguish in your eyes when you looked at Drenis.'

'Drenis is a soldier,' I said sharply, 'he obeys orders.'

She glided to my side. 'Of course. He will take ship with the rest of us tomorrow, even though he desires more than anything else to stay and fight beside the members of his tribe. And we will leave this city, even though you think it is dishonourable not to offer King Akrosas your advice and your sword.'

I said nothing.

'When that savage of a king was enthralling us with the tale of his heroic defeat,' she continued, 'I was watching Burebista. I saw his face light up at the mention of Dacians arriving at Histria. He too does not want to leave, Pacorus, and neither do you.'

'Domitus wants to be away from this place,' I said.

'Lucius Domitus hates the Romans more than you do and would relish the opportunity to rub their noses in dung. But being Roman he maintains the air of a consummate professional. With Domitus you have to scratch the granite exterior to see what lies beneath.'

I turned face her. 'And you? What do you desire, my sweet?'

She took my hand. 'For you to come back to bed. As you are awake I can think of better things to do with your time than stare into the darkness.'

'But what of tomorrow?'

She led me from the balcony. 'It is already tomorrow.'

In the morning we dressed and were served breakfast in our rooms. Our nervous steward conveyed the apologies of the king but reported that Akrosas had weighty affairs of state to attend to and could not invite us to share breakfast with him. But the monarch would see us before we left to wish us a safe journey. Slaves brought our cleaned clothes and I strapped on my sword, picked up my bow in its case and walked to meet the others who had assembled outside the palace. Akrosas came to us there, dressed for war in a magnificent burnished bronze cuirass and a sword with a silver pommel in a scabbard decorated with silver strips. With him was Admiral Arcathius,

403

resplendent in his bronze scale armour, bronze greaves and feathered helmet.

The citadel was now bursting with activity as the king embraced me and wished us all a safe journey back to Parthia.

'The admiral will escort you to the docks,' he said.

At that moment I heard the clatter of horses' hooves on the square and turned to see a score or more riders attired in red tunics, beige leggings and equipped with javelins, round shields and bronze helmets. One carried a dragon windsock and on their shields they carried a serpent symbol.

'Maedi,' said Drenis.

The king smiled. 'That is correct. The man at the front is Draco, the leader of their tribe. And now I'm afraid I must bid you all farewell.'

He nodded to me, smiled at Gallia and then departed to speak to the newly arrived Maedi. We walked to the gates of the citadel that was now filling with soldiers, or rather civilians turned into warriors. I looked behind to see the blank faces of Arminius and Drenis, the disappointed expressions of Cleon and Surena and the resigned look of Domitus. Only Alcaeus appeared happy.

'You will stay in the city, admiral?' I asked.

'Yes. I have five hundred soldiers that came with me from Pontus. We thought we had found sanctuary here but it seems that wherever we go the Romans follow. But I shall not abandon Akrosas. He has been a friend and men need all the friends they can get in this world.'

I halted, the others behind me doing likewise.

'Fine words, admiral,' said Gallia, 'and ones that have decided my husband's course of action.'

Arcathius was confused but I looked at Domitus who smiled. I nodded at Drenis and he gave me a broad grin. Arminius laughed and slapped him on the back as Alcaeus looked around in confusion.

'I will not stop anyone taking ship for Parthia,' I said, 'but I cannot turn my back on this city and its people when it is in mortal danger. I am staying.'

Cleon embraced his remaining comrades. 'We are staying.'

Athineos looked at his crewmen and shook his head. 'We are not soldiers, King Pacorus, but I reckon that the gods watch out for you so it makes sense to stay put with you. We're in.'

'Sense?' Alcaeus was not amused. 'The king displays a total absence of sense.'

'I am not preventing you from leaving, Alcaeus,' I said.

'Don't be ridiculous,' he snapped, 'who else is going to patch you all up when the Romans have finished with you?'

So that was that. A bemused Arcathius left us to report to the king that we had decided to aid him in his fight against the Romans and after he had left we stood around, unsure what to do.

'I suppose we should go back to the palace,' I suggested.

'An excellent idea, Pacorus,' said Alcaeus. 'We can all write our farewell letters to our friends and family.'

But as we ambled back to the palace our resident flustered steward ran out to greet us with flapping arms. He appeared to be in a state that was halfway between despair and rapture as he conveyed his king's request to me.

'Majesty, his majesty requests your presence in his reception chamber where the other majesties will also gather.'

'A surfeit of majesties, it would appear,' remarked Alcaeus dryly.

The steward beckoned what appeared to be a younger version of himself to come forward.

'This man will show the rest of your party back to their quarters.'

He then smiled and clapped his hands together.

'The gods smile on Histria for changing your heart, majesty.'

'It was not the goods but foolish pride that did that,' said Alcaeus behind me.

I ignored his barb. The steward looked at Domitus.

'The king also requests that your general attend the meeting of kings.'

'He will be delighted to attend,' I answered for him.

'You obviously made a great impression with your speech last night,' I said to Domitus as we followed the steward back into the palace, the others of our party being escorted back to their rooms.

'Not as great as the Romans will make on this city if they reach it,' he snorted.

'That is what we have to prevent, Domitus.'

The reception chamber was a medium-sized room to the rear of the throne room, which contained well-upholstered chairs, a large rectangular oak table and a white-painted ceiling and walls that gave it a light, airy feel. The other kings were already present when a guard showed us into the room, the steward bowing and leaving as the guard shut the door behind us.

'Welcome, King Pacorus and General Domitus,' smiled Akrosas. 'Apollo sends a sign of our coming victory with your decision to stay at Histria.'

Radu, seated and holding a cup of wine, sneered but the others examined us thoughtfully. Akrosas introduced them, beginning with Draco, the leader of the Maedi. He was of average height with grey eyes and fair hair. Like his men he wore a red tunic but unlike them he sported a mail tunic that I guessed had been taken from a dead Roman. The leader of the Dacians, Burebista's people, had wild green eyes and long, unkempt hair. He wore a simple white tunic, red leggings and brown boots, with a sword at his hip. His fierce appearance reminded me of the Gauls I had met in Italy. His name was Decebal.

Akrosas fussed around like a sheepdog, getting us seated and ordering wine to be brought. He was more like a kindly philosopher than a king. Domitus asked for water instead.

'What's the matter, Roman,' said Radu, 'don't you have the stomach to drink like a man?'

'Wine dulls the senses,' replied Domitus nonchalantly, 'and if you are going to avoid another defeat you will need all your sense in the coming days.'

Radu flicked a hand dismissively at him but Draco focused his eyes on Domitus.

'You are a Roman?'

Domitus nodded. 'I am.'

'And yet you fight against your own kind?' queried Draco.

'I fight for my king,' replied Domitus, 'King Pacorus.'

'And Akrosas has told us, King Pacorus,' said Decebal, 'that your army has defeated the Romans.'

'It has,' I answered.

'How?' asked Draco. He appeared to be very thoughtful, cunning even.

'Our foot soldiers are armed, equipped and trained along Roman lines,' Domitus told him. 'Whereas the horse soldiers of King Pacorus are equipped and fight according to Parthian ways. But both horse and foot are trained to work together on the battlefield.'

Draco seemed impressed. 'That must have been a time-consuming process.'

'And a very expensive one,' I added.

'We are wasting time,' said Radu loudly. 'We need to stop the Romans otherwise they will be knocking on the gates of this city within the week.'

A concerned Akrosas looked at Domitus. 'General, what strategy would you advise us to adopt?'

'Simple,' responded Domitus, 'avoid battle.'

Radu guffawed loudly while Draco and Akrosas looked at each other in confusion.

'You advise retreat before the enemy?' said Decebal sharply.

Domitus sipped at the water that had been given him by a slave.

'Not at all. I advise fighting the enemy, only not on his terms. To that end, can you tell me about the terrain the Romans are currently marching through, King Akrosas?'

Akrosas looked confused. 'Terrain? What has that to do with anything?'

'It has everything to do with your current situation, sir,' said Domitus, trying to retain his patience.

Radu sighed rudely but Akrosas answered the question.

'Around the city much of the land has been tamed and cultivated, but further out the land is covered with thick forests interspersed with open areas of bogs, grassland and village settlements.'

Domitus looked at Radu and Draco. 'And you gave battle in one of these open areas?'

They both nodded.

Domitus stroked his chin thoughtfully. 'How many legions do the Romans have?'

Draco looked perplexed. 'Legions?'

'The Romans organise their armies around legions,' Akrosas told him. 'Each legion has as its emblem a silver eagle.'

'One eagle,' said Radu.

Domitus looked at me. 'Well, that is something at least.'

But though the Romans only possessed one legion the numbers that could be raised by the men present in the room did not amount to much. Radu had two thousand foot soldiers, Draco could muster two hundred horsemen and two thousand warriors on foot, while Decebal had a total of two thousand, three hundred men, two hundred of which were mounted. The largest contingent was King Akrosas' army of five hundred horsemen of his guard and three thousand foot soldiers. But the latter were mostly farmers and citizens that were ill armed and poorly trained. The only professional foot soldiers were the five hundred men from Pontus commanded by Admiral Arcathius. The kings could muster nine thousand foot and a thousand horsemen, but the great majority of the former would be swiftly defeated in an open battle with the Romans. Our problems were compounded when Radu revealed that the commander of the Roman army was a certain General Antonius Hybrida who had served under Sulla and had earned himself a reputation for brutality in Macedonia. That did not concern me but he was obviously a competent commander who would prove a resolute foe.

'Hybrida spends his time burning villages and rounding up slaves,' spat Radu. He looked at Akrosas. 'Soon he will be doing the same in your kingdom.'

'By doing so he gives us time to implement our plan,' I said.

Akrosas raised an eyebrow. 'Plan, King Pacorus?'

'I thought you said we weren't going to fight the Romans,' said Draco, 'or at least your general did.'

'I said that you should avoid battle,' Domitus corrected him, 'which is entirely different.'

'You talk in riddles, Roman,' said Draco in exasperation.

'Then let me put it plainly,' replied Domitus, who was beginning to lose patience. 'First of all you destroy the Roman horsemen so the enemy cannot scout the land they are marching through. Next, you use your warriors to set ambushes, mount flanking and harassing attacks and counterattacks. You attack and melt back into the forest before they can organise a response. You keep your forces scattered and in small groups so there is no main army for the Romans to attack. In this way you will wear them down and prohibit them from reaching this city.'

Akrosas seized on these words. 'That sounds like a most excellent plan.'

He looked at the others. 'What say the rest of you?'

Radu shrugged but acquiesced; Draco and Arcathius thought it a sound plan; but Decebal was against it.

'My men are warriors. It is not the Dacian way to skulk around in the undergrowth and kill an enemy like thieves.'

Domitus rolled his eyes but I smiled at Decebal. 'Then perhaps, lord king, you will join me when I ride out to deal with the Roman horsemen.'

'How many horsemen do you have?' he asked me.

'Four, including myself,' I replied.

There was an initial burst of laughter but this died away when they saw that I was serious, which in turn shamed them.

'I will ride with you,' said Decebal. 'It would be humiliating to let so few face so many.'

'It is my land that you will be riding through,' remarked Radu, 'so I will accompany you. Otherwise, Parthian, you will get lost.'

Draco also volunteered to go with me but Akrosas insisted that he should stay behind to be joint commander of the army of foot that would be following the horsemen. He probably realised that if Draco departed as well then he would be left to lead the rest of the army alone, something that no doubt filled him with trepidation. However, Draco did give his horsemen to Radu to command, the latter actually having no mounted troops of his own. Despite his protests Arcathius agreed to stay behind at Histria with his men to organise the defence of the city. Nevertheless, by the end of the meeting I had enlisted five hundred horsemen to be a part of the first stage of my plan.

'You stay with Akrosas,' I told Domitus afterwards. 'Take Drenis and Arminius with you for company but above all make sure the king does not yield to his commanders and fight the Romans in the open.'

'Why should he take any notice of me?'

I smiled. 'Why? Because although he is a good man; Akrosas is not a good commander. He will stick to your advice like a shipwrecked man clings to driftwood. You can also keep an eye on Draco to ensure that he does nothing rash.'

It was past noon when I went to the royal armouries with Gallia, Surena and Burebista, clutching a hastily written commission from Akrosas granting me licence to take anything that I desired. We each requisitioned four quivers filled with missiles with triangular bronze arrowheads and then headed off to find horses. Drenis had told me that Thracian horses made excellent mounts and when we arrived at the stables, the satisfying aroma of leather and horseflesh filling the air, we discovered that he had not exaggerated. The royal mounts were sturdy beasts with long, thick manes and short tails. I chose a brown mare with a white star on her forehead and the others also chose mares, which were more stable than stallions. Even though Remus was a stallion, I had ridden him for years and grown accustomed to his moods and idiosyncrasies. I did not have the time to learn those of a new stallion. The harnesses were red leather and comprised nose bands, chin straps, forehead straps and throat lashes, all decorated with bronze discs. The breast and girth straps and reins were also red leather. The large red saddlecloths were edged with yellow and the saddles resembled our own four-horned models. However, when we rode from the citadel, through the city and out of the gates to link up with our ad hoc flying column of horsemen, I was surprised to see that many of the Dacians were sitting only on padded saddlecloths.

We rode to the front of the horsemen where Decebal was conversing with Radu. Like many of their men we did not wear helmets – the armouries having none to spare – the two of them registering surprise at Gallia's presence. But Radu had been told of her arrival after the night of the full moon, which was interpreted as her being sent by Bendis to aid the city's cause, so he said nothing. Decebal was more forthcoming.

'You bring your queen along, King Pacorus?'

'She is a Gaul, lord king,' I said, 'a most warlike race.'

He saw the *spatha* at her hip, the dagger tucked into the top of her boot, the bow case and quivers hanging from her saddle and over her shoulder.

'So I see.'

'Let's be away,' said Radu impatiently, 'otherwise the Romans will be here before you can impress us with your tactics, King Pacorus.'

He shouted at his horse to move forward, the horsemen of the Maedi following. Decebal turned and gestured to his signallers to blow their horns, the mournful blasts of their instruments startling many of the horses. We turned our beasts and followed them, a great column of warriors armed with javelins, spears, axes, the deadly *xiphos*, a few long swords and even fewer bows, many men with their round or hexagonal shields slung on their backs. The Dacians carried dragon windsocks that fluttered above them, the red, white, green and brown tunics and leggings giving the column a very colourful appearance. But at that moment I would have swapped my whole kingdom for a dragon of Parthian horse archers and half as many cataphracts.

Chapter 15

We rode at speed, heading southwest, the direction from where the Romans were approaching. The immediate area around the city was largely flat and devoid of trees, but after an hour the fields and neatly arranged vineyards disappeared and we began to skirt copses, then woods and finally found ourselves riding through a strip of grassland in a forest of oak and ash. It was as though a god had laid his sword on the earth to create the sliver of open land we rode through, ahead of us the ears of hares popping up in the long grass before they bolted away. Overhead I saw the occasional magpie and crow but aside from wildlife the land was quiet.

Radu had brought along one of his scouts who rode ahead with a party of Dacian horsemen to provide prior warning of any Roman patrols. They reported back to their lords in the early evening that the enemy had not been spotted. After covering forty miles we made camp among the trees near a small stream where the horses could drink. The oaks were widely spaced and the ground was carpeted with wild grasses, mosses and fern. This was an ancient forest.

Guards were posted and horses unsaddled, though Radu and Decebal prohibited the lighting of any fires in case the Romans spotted them when darkness fell. Thus we drank cool water from the stream and ate fruit and cheese given to us by Histria's quartermasters. After we had eaten the tribal kings requested my presence at a council of war, which was held under an old oak with a broad and spreading crown and sturdy branches beneath. Radu sat with his back against the thick trunk while Decebal sat on a blanket opposite him, both of them devouring large chunks of cheese.

'So, Parthian,' said Radu stiffly, 'tomorrow most likely we will run into the Romans. How do you propose to put into action your plan?'

Decebal threw a spare blanket on the ground beside him. I unravelled it and sat cross-legged on it.

'First of all we have to draw their horsemen away from the main army so we can lure them into an ambush. That will slow down the main army, which will allow your own foot soldiers to catch us up.'

412

'So they can engage the enemy,' said Radu, a glint of excitement in his eyes.

'So we can set more ambushes for them, yes,' I replied. 'Above all we must avoid any pitched battle with the Romans.'

'Why do you fear the Romans?' asked Decebal.

'I do not fear them,' I riposted, 'but I respect their fighting abilities. You offer them battle and they will wipe you out.'

I looked at Radu. 'Just as they did with your army.'

Radu bristled. 'Careful, Parthian, your words may get your tongue cut out and your head stuck on the end of a spear.'

'That will not alter the facts, Radu,' I replied, 'which are that the Romans will easily beat anything you send against them in battle.'

Decebal appeared curious. 'What is it about these Romans that make them so formidable? Are they gods?'

'They are not gods,' I answered quietly, 'but their soldiers possess three things that give them supreme advantage on the battlefield.'

'Which are?' demanded Radu.

'Organisation, training and superior equipment,' I said. 'Your warriors fight in groups around their chiefs and village elders, their only thought being to close with the enemy as quickly as possible.'

'What's wrong with that?' sniffed Radu.

'Because it plays into the Romans' hands,' I answered. 'As my general explained at the feast, the Romans like nothing more than to be able to deploy their scorpions, archers and slingers against densely packed groups of warriors. Then, when the warriors are goaded into charging they run into a javelin storm that kills the momentum of their attack. So before the hand-to-hand fighting even begins your warriors have suffered heavy casualties. And in the mêlée they find that they cannot make any impression on the disciplined ranks of the Roman legionaries.'

Radu looked away, knowing that I was right but annoyed anyway. Decebal, though, appeared satisfied.

'When we encounter the Romans how do you propose to lure the enemy's horsemen into an ambush?'

'By dangling bait in front of them, lord king.'

413

Radu's ears pricked up. 'Bait?'

'Myself and my fellow horse archers,' I answered.

I returned to where my wife and companions were resting among the trees, our horses tethered to low-lying branches. Gallia was talking to Burebista, who was unstringing his bow, a model with straight limbs that was indigenous to these parts.

'It doesn't have the range of your Scythian models but in this terrain it performs well enough,' I heard him say.

I flopped down beside Gallia who passed me an apple.

'Our difficult allies have agreed to my plan,' I told them, 'though I fear that once they spot the Romans they will charge heroically to their deaths.'

'It is difficult, lord, for those whose customs demand bravery in battle to hold back when they see the enemy,' Burebista informed me.

'That's why the Romans always win,' I said bitterly.

'Not always, lord,' said Surena. 'We beat them at Dura.'

'I would have liked to have been there,' said Burebista.

'You and Anca will be at Dura soon enough,' I told him.

'Burebista is free now, Pacorus,' said Gallia. 'He might want to remain here, though not if the Romans prevail, perhaps.'

Surena stretched out on his blanket. 'Do you think we will be allowed to participate in the games at Ephesus next year, lord?'

Burebista laughed and Gallia frowned at him.

'Probably not, Surena,' I told him. 'The Romans don't take kindly to people who kill their *editors* and incite riots.'

Surena sat up. 'That fat *editor* was corrupt, lord. He wanted young men to perform unnatural acts with him. The Romans would probably thank me for ridding the world of such an individual.'

Burebista grinned. 'How little you know of the Romans.'

'One thing I meant to ask you?' I said. 'The arena at Ephesus is too small for horsemen. Why then did you attend the games, though I thank Shamash that you did?'

'Without wishing to be boastful, lord,' he replied, 'I was one of the lanista's most prized fighters. He told me that the Greek theatre at Ephesus was too small but it did not matter as horsemen always dismount to finish off their opponents in the arena. So I left my horse behind.'

'Was it very terrible, Burebista, being under the control of that brute Vatia?' enquired Gallia.

Burebista laughed again. 'You know what he was like, lady. As long as he was making money he was happy and I made him a lot of money. It wasn't so bad, aside from being a condemned slave, of course. These past few years I only fought a few times a year, and usually only at the large venues such as Rome and Pompeii.'

He looked at my wife. 'He was always aggrieved that you slipped through his fat fingers, though. He was also cursing Spartacus that he had led you astray, lady.'

Gallia threw her head back and laughed. 'Spartacus had nothing to do with it. I was sold by my father to be the whore of Lentulus Vatia and would have escaped his fat clutches with or without Spartacus.'

'Rome will not mourn the death of a *lanista*,' mused Burebista. 'It is ironic that for all his money Lentulus Vatia never achieved his dearest wish.'

'Which was what?' I asked.

'To be considered respectable and not a lowly, despised *lanista*.'

'Alas for Lentulus Vatia,' said Gallia with a mocking voice.

The new day dawned warm and sunny, rays of light lancing through the trees to illuminate the verdant terrain all around us. We were in the saddle as the sun was still creeping above the eastern treeline, though our pace was slower than the day before. Once more scouts were despatched to discover the whereabouts of the Romans and they returned two hours before midday with news that they had spotted the enemy less than five miles away. Radu, as I feared, was all for intercepting them as quickly as possible, but Decebal had thankfully reflected on my words the evening before and asked for my advice.

'We should find a good ambush position along their line of march and then take cover in the trees,' I told him. 'I will ride ahead to lure them into our trap.'

'What if they don't take your bait?' snapped Radu.

'Then we will try your strategy, King Radu,' I answered.

He seemed satisfied by this as he wheeled away and conveyed the plan to the commanders of the Maedi. Decebal turned to speak to his second-in-command who rode back to his men.

'Well, King Pacorus, the time of trial approaches. Let us hope the gods favour your plan.'

'If they don't,' I replied, 'then the Romans will be dining in Akrosas' palace in three days.'

We rode forward for another mile, following the scouts as they retraced their steps. We halted when we reached an area of open grassland bordered on one side by a large bog beside a river and forest on the other. The latter was an expanse of beech trees, the forest floor a mass of moss and fallen, decaying branches. But it was possible for five hundred horsemen to become invisible just back from the treeline. I rode to Radu and Decebal as my companions pulled their bows from leather cases and strung their bowstrings. Among the trees men gripped their spears and took the shields off their backs. They were enthusiastic enough but I wondered how they would fare in a fight with Roman horsemen? Hopefully the element of surprise would tilt the balance in their favour.

'Resist the temptation to charge if there are only a few of them,' I told them. 'The Romans may anticipate our stratagem and send only a token force ahead.'

Decebal nodded to indicate he would heed my advice but Radu turned his head away from me.

'It will be your foot soldiers and those of King Akrosas that will give you victory, remember that.'

I cantered back to where Gallia and the others waited, along with a scout who would show us the way back to the Romans. As we trotted through the meadow I probed him about the enemy horsemen.

'How many did you see?'

'Thirty or more, excellency,' his accent was thick and I had difficulty making sense of his bastardised Greek.

'They were well equipped?'

He nodded. 'Armour, helmets, spears and shields, excellency.'

416

We left the meadow and rode through a gully in a beech copse, skirted a forest pool and came into another area of open ground where the long grass brushed the bellies of our horses.

The scout slowed his horse to a walking pace. 'Have a care for potholes and rabbit warrens,' he shouted.

We followed his lead and studied the ground around us. We concentrated so much on where our horses were treading that we failed to notice the group of horsemen around two hundred paces ahead.

'Romans,' Surena hissed.

I looked up to see what appeared to be a score of riders – two *decuriae* – all showing red tunics, mail shirts, helmets and green-faced shields. I heard the distinctive sound of a *bucina*, a shell horn, and as one the enemy horsemen levelled their spears and advanced towards us.

'You can go,' I said to the scout as I pulled an arrow from the quiver slung on my back. Gallia, Surena and Burebista did the same.

The latter grinned at me. 'Just like the old days in Italy, lord.'

I nocked the arrow in my bowstring, reins wrapped around my left wrist, and raised my bow. There was a sharp crack as Gallia loosed her arrow, Surena and Burebista following. I saw the missiles arching into the air as I let the bowstring slip out of my fingers to launch my arrow. I wheeled my mare to the left and dug my knees into her flanks. I looked over my shoulder as I followed the others back into the trees, the Romans closing on us. I heard a shriek as a horse stumbled and fell into an unseen depression.

'Halt,' I shouted.

The others turned their mounts and came to my side.

'Rapid volleys,' I ordered, 'drop as many as you can.'

We rode forward a few paces to position ourselves just back from the treeline, the Romans still cantering towards us. I pulled an arrow, nocked it and shot it at the oncoming enemy, the others doing likewise. Within seconds we had loosed three volleys, the bronze arrowheads striking the leading horses and throwing their riders. The horses behind reared up on their hind legs as the Roman advance degenerated into chaos. We kept shooting, loosing up to seven arrows a minute and felling

417

at least another six riders. They were less than a hundred paces from us and, having halted their advance, we could now pick our targets. A thrown rider, winded and helmetless, picked himself up, clutched his bleeding head and then collapsed as Gallia put an arrow in his back. Horses bolted as the signaller blew his horn and those Romans still in the saddle turned and withdrew. Surena put an arrow in the back of the rearmost rider but the Roman managed to stay in the saddle, slumping over the neck of his horse. Surena urged his horse forward.

'Stay here,' I snapped at him.

'They're getting away, lord.'

I smiled with satisfaction. 'That's the idea. With any luck they will be back with the rest of the Roman horsemen. Now all we have to do is wait.'

We dismounted, checked our mounts for any wounds and counted our arrows. Beyond the trees wounded horses and men cried and groaned as they lay in the sun. Some of the horses tried to rise but their wounds were too severe and so they flopped back down on the ground. I handed Gallia my bow and pulled my dagger.

'Surena, you are with me,' I said. 'We must put those poor creatures out of their misery.'

He handed his bow to Burebista and followed me into the meadow.

'Let the Romans have a slow death,' Gallia called after me.

Surena laughed but I told him to slit the throats of the wounded men as well as the horses. It pained my heart to slit the throats of injured horses but the only veterinaries that could treat them were in the Roman army, and in any case the arrows had pierced their bodies deeply and they were losing much blood. But as a Parthian I took no pleasure in kneeling beside them, holding their heads my arms and staring into their terror-filled eyes as I swiftly drew my blade across their throats. I tried to make their end as swift as possible but I still asked Shamash for forgiveness for my actions. Surena slit the throats of the two injured Romans, both pierced by arrows and both having broken bones when they had fallen. When he was walking beside me back to the trees his face was creased by worry lines.

'Will the queen be angry with me, lord, for disobeying her orders not to kill the enemy wounded?'

'She will forgive you, I'm sure.'

'She really hates the Romans.'

'She does,' I agreed.

'Do you hate them, lord?'

'No.'

He was surprised. 'Even though they treated you harshly?'

I laughed. 'I have received worse treatment at the hands of Parthians. You remember Chosroes?'

'I do,' he spat.

'When you let hate rule your emotions, Surena, your judgement becomes clouded and a commander cannot allow that to happen.'

'Romans!'

I heard Gallia's voice and saw her pointing. I turned to see dozens of enemy horsemen flooding the far end of the meadow. I ran back to the trees, Surena bounding past me. I vaulted into the saddle and my wife handed me my bow. I shoved it into its case and grabbed my reins.

'Time to flee,' I said.

We retraced our steps through the trees and into the long grass beyond, the enemy horsemen closing on us. I kept glancing behind and saw a tide of horseflesh pouring out of the trees. There were scores of them, which suggested that the main army was very close. We kept ahead of the Romans as we passed by the trees where the horsemen of Radu and Decebal lay in wait. When the Romans appeared they charged from the vegetation, shrieking their war cries as they did so. They burst from the shade to attack both flanks of the Romans, who immediately slowed as their officers frantically tried to reorganise their commands. There was a flurry of horn calls as the Thracians and Dacians closed the last stretch of ground between them and the Romans.

I halted and wheeled my horse about as I called to the others to stop. The clatter of clashing weapons and shouts of men fighting filled the air as hundreds of horsemen battled each other. But though the Romans had been surprised they were not overwhelmed and within minutes a grim mêlée began to develop. Saddles began to empty and horses crumpled to the ground but the Romans did not break.

'Pick your targets,' I shouted.

My mare was skittish, probably unused to the sights and sounds of battle, so I stroked her neck and resisted the urge to ride into the battle. I had already emptied half a quiver and in the next minute or so used up the remaining missiles as I shot at Roman horsemen. Surena, Burebista and Gallia reaped a rich harvest of Roman dead, shooting from a stationary position on the edge of the fighting. But though it was satisfactory to empty enemy saddles I also saw many Thracians and Dacians fall, expertly speared by a Roman rider or cut down by a swing of a *spatha*. The enemy were better equipped and no doubt trained and they proved hardy opponents.

I learned afterwards that it was Decebal who won the fight. He kept his men under tight control and split the Roman formation in two, first surrounding and destroying one part before turning his attention to the other section. But it cost him half his men – a hundred and fifty warriors – to do so. For our part we must have killed over fifty Romans, using up half our arrows in the process. When it was over the Dacians and Thracians went among the dead to pillage the Roman corpses, taking their mail shirts, helmets, weapons and anything else of use. The stench of death was tangible in the summer heat, the buzz of flies that came to feast on dead flesh discernible over the moans of wounded humans and animals.

The vast majority of the Dacians and Thracians had now dismounted and were either looting the dead or congratulating themselves on a hard-won victory.

'They have no discipline,' uttered Surena contemptuously.

'Stay here,' I said to him and the others as I spotted a group of horsemen among the debris of battle. 'I need to speak to Radu and Decebal.'

I nudged my horse forward towards the treeline and away from the dead men and horses that littered the ground. The mare was still jumpy but I continued to pat her neck as she trotted to where the air smelt sweeter and there were no flies. I rode along the edge of the forest and then wheeled her right to take me to where Radu was roaring with laughter in his saddle. Decebal sat on his horse opposite and as I got closer I could see that his tunic was splattered with blood and his hair was even wilder than usual. He turned when Radu pointed to me.

'So, Parthian,' he said loudly, 'your plan worked. We have destroyed the Romans' horsemen.'

'*Part* of my plan has worked,' I cautioned. 'The difficult part is still to come.'

Radu waved away my prudence. 'This is just the beginning of our triumphs. I will admit, though, that your Roman was right.'

'He will be arriving soon with King Akrosas, King Draco and the foot soldiers,' said Decebal.

Radu raised his arms. 'And then we will slaughter every Roman and rid them from our land.'

The men behind him cheered and Decebal smiled. I heard a thud and saw a warrior behind Radu topple from his saddle, then heard a succession of screams around us. My horse became skittish again and began to move sideways as more warriors were hit. Out of the corner of my eye, to my left, I glimpsed a line of red shields and in front of them individuals in white tunics with whirling arms.

'Slingers,' I shouted. 'Fall back.'

Radu roared in anger as another of his men was hit but Decebal kept his head and ordered a signaller to sound retreat as men forgot about plundering the dead and raced to their horses. The main Roman army had been closer than I had realised as centuries and cohorts marched into view, slingers clearing a path for the legionaries as they moved as though they were on the parade ground. I urged my mare on as Decebal and Radu galloped beside me, their men following. Gallia and the others waited for me before they too retreated, dozens of warriors in Roman helmets and mail shirts racing past them. We rode hard for at least half an hour to put as much distance between the Romans and ourselves as possible. Eventually the pace slackened with the realisation that we were not being pursued. The kings gave the command to dismount and walk the horses so they could catch their breath. We had ridden at the rear of the column so we could shoot at any Roman horsemen that pursued us. But luck was with us and we had an undisturbed flight. I checked my arrows and found I had only one full quiver left. The others had a similar amount of missiles.

421

'Well,' I said, 'at least we know where the Roman army is. Let's hope that King Akrosas arrives soon.'

Dura's foot soldiers could march up to thirty miles a day but I doubted that the Thracians and Dacian warriors could match them. Still, they had had a day and a half of marching and must be relatively close to our position, wherever that was. I was mulling over these thoughts when a messenger arrived from Decebal informing me that he and Radu would be making camp. Once more we melted into the forest, only this time we moved deeper into the trees to put as much distance between the Romans and ourselves as possible.

Once again the lighting of any fires was forbidden and so warriors sat on the ground in sullen silence after they had unsaddled and tethered their horses. Guards were posted and parties despatched to find water desperately needed by both men and beasts. With their captured arms and armour the warriors looked much more martial, but as I walked to converse with the two kings who stood beneath an ancient oak once more I could see that our numbers were sadly depleted. Both of them were in a sombre mood when I arrived.

'My few surviving chiefs report that we have lost a hundred and sixty dead,' muttered Decebal.

'Maedi losses are eighty killed,' reported Radu, though his concern was less as they were not his people.

I tried to cheer them. 'But at least we have dealt the enemy horsemen a crippling blow and we know where the main Roman army is.'

'Your strategy commands a high price, King Pacorus,' retorted Decebal. 'Perhaps too high.'

'We must hold our nerve, my lords,' I said. 'When King Akrosas arrives we will be able to grind down the enemy.'

'Perhaps it is us who will be ground down,' said Radu bitterly, his bravado having seemingly disappeared.

'When King Akrosas arrives,' I said firmly, 'he will bring with him nine thousand foot soldiers and five hundred horsemen, more than enough to destroy the Romans.'

Decebal leaned against the massive trunk of the tree. As far as I could see none of the blood that had been splashed on his tunic and leggings was his own.

'You think so?'

'I know so,' I replied.

'It's true that my warriors are itching to exact revenge for their recent reverse,' said Radu reflectively as he took off his armour and threw it on the ground.

'With all my experience of fighting the Romans I tell you that they are in a very precarious position,' I told them. 'Imagine a house built of wood that is riddled with woodworm. You only have to kick in the door and the whole rotten structure will come crashing to the ground.'

I looked at them both with as much determination as I could muster and they appeared to respond positively to my words. I left them in a steadfast mood, which was just as well because I doubted that even with the addition of Akrosas' men would they be able to defeat five thousand highly trained legionaries.

'I am apt to agree with you.'

Domitus placed his hands behind his head and reclined on the blanket, his weapons and armour by his side. King Akrosas had issued him with a magnificent burnished bronze cuirass that gleamed even in the dimness of the forest as the light began to fade fast as evening approached. He and the king had ridden ahead of the main body of foot to catch up with us, the rest of the army being left under the command of Draco. The latter was only around five miles away but Akrosas had been impatient to find out how we had fared.

'It will be difficult but as you have eradicated their horsemen it will at least slow them down, which in turn will give these barbarians time to organise themselves.'

'Organisation is not a word that is readily understood by Thracians and Dacians,' I complained. 'No offence,' I said to Burebista.

'None taken, lord.'

Gallia looked at Domitus who had his eyes closed.

'Is he asleep?'

'He is not,' replied Domitus.

'Where is Akrosas?' I asked him.

'Talking to his fellow kings,' replied Domitus. 'He does a lot of that. Drove me to distraction with his constant questions on the way here. He seems to think that the gods sent me to be his personal military adviser.'

'That's good, Domitus,' I said, 'if he is listening to you then at least he is getting good advice.'

He grunted. 'Easy for you to say, you don't have to listen to him.'

The temperature among the trees stayed warm enough when night finally came, though I still woke aching and feeling grimy as the camp stirred and men went about preparing their meagre breakfasts. Most of the fruit and cheese they had been issued with had gone and so they were reduced to chewing on salted fish washed down by water from the nearest rivulet. As we checked over our horses a messenger arrived from Akrosas along with a sack full of bread, cheese, apples and another with fodder for our four horses.

'The king requests your presence at his headquarters after you have eaten breakfast, majesty,' said the man, one of Akrosas' bodyguards judging by his leather armour, helmet and shield with its bow and arrow motif. 'Along with General Domitus.'

I looked at him. 'Headquarters?'

'A temporary awning in the forest, majesty,' he replied.

After he and his companion had left their bounty we fed the horses and then sat in a circle to eat the food. It was fortunate that there was ample sustenance as Surena ate like a man who had not tasted food for a month.

'Most important meal of the day, breakfast,' he informed us. 'It is important to have a full stomach at the start of the day.'

'So it would seem,' I said.

He continued to treat us to his knowledge of diet and hygiene.

'Bad idea those drinking from the forest ponds, though. Stagnant water can play havoc with even the strongest stomach.'

'Perhaps you should be King Akrosas' adviser, Surena,' suggested Domitus. 'You two would get on well.'

Surena looked at me expectantly but I shook my head.

'I think not, Domitus. It is you whose advice he trusts.'

'Yes, but will he take it?' he replied.

The 'headquarters' was nothing more than a large piece of linen strung between two oaks but Akrosas looked very martial in a gleaming bronze scale armour cuirass and a sword in a scabbard adorned with silver decoration. He also looked remarkably fresh for a person that had been lying out all night.

'He brought a few slaves with him to ensure his stay in the open was not too stressful,' Domitus whispered to me as we walked to where the king stood with the other leaders.

'Ah, greetings, King Pacorus and General Domitus,' he said, smiling, 'it is going to be another fine day. A day worthy of our victory over the Romans.'

I looked up at the forest canopy and saw beams of sunlight lancing through the foliage. It did indeed appear that the day would be dry and warm. He and Draco were dressed smartly and appeared refreshed, in stark contrast to Decebal's blood-stained clothing and Radu's damaged armour and red-rimmed green eyes. I probably looked as shabby and tired as they did. I also noticed that Draco was giving Radu hateful stares, though why I did not know.

'Today we crush the Romans,' said Radu sharply.

Akrosas looked intently at Domitus 'What is your opinion, general?'

'My king informs me that the Roman horsemen were dealt a cruel blow yesterday.'

'So were my horsemen,' said Draco bitterly, his eyes on Radu.

Radu shrugged. 'Men die in battle.'

'But not your men,' Draco spat back at him.

The big man's anger was now stirred. 'If you have something to say, Draco, then say it instead of whining like a virgin maid.'

'My friends,' interrupted Akrosas, 'if we quarrel among ourselves then the only beneficiaries will be the Romans. General Domitus, please enlighten us with your advice.'

Domitus drew his sword and cleared a piece of earth of leaves and twigs with his foot. He made six marks in the soil, one behind the other.

'This is how a Roman army marches,' he began, pointing his sword point at the first mark, 'at the tip of the marching column are horsemen, lightly armed foot soldiers and archers. Behind them is the vanguard made up of auxiliaries, more horsemen, a party of legionaries, standard bearers and the colour party that guards the eagle, the legion's most precious possession.'

I glanced at the others who appeared engrossed by what Domitus was saying. He pointed at the third mark in the soil.

'Next comes the command group containing the army's leader and his senior officers, plus mules carrying the army's machines.'

'Machines?' said Draco.

'The scorpions and larger engines that are used to besiege cities.'

Akrosas looked very pensive at the mention of siege engines. Domitus continued.

'After them come the legionaries marching six abreast, followed by the carts, wagons and mules carrying food, spare weapons, ammunition and replacement armour and shields.'

He pointed at the last mark. 'Finally there is the rear guard made up of auxiliaries and horsemen. They usually post horsemen to act as flank guards, though after yesterday's mauling they may not have enough.'

'Fascinating,' said Akrosas in admiration. 'And every Roman army marches in the same fashion?'

Domitus nodded. 'Yes, sir.'

He pointed his *gladius* at the kings. 'Now, sirs, your task is to hit this army at several places while it is strung out along its line of march, which is easier said than done.

'The Romans are not stupid but they do not know that there are nine thousand enemy foot soldiers in these trees and that is to your advantage.'

He let his sword drop to his side. 'Your only advantage so use it wisely.'

Radu looked with excited eyes at the simple gashes in the soil. I knew what he was thinking: nine thousand foot soldiers plus over seven hundred horsemen against a weakened enemy, an enemy that was strung out in line.

'Rome's soldiers are trained to respond quickly to crises that may develop, both on the march and on the battlefield,' I said. 'We must stick to the initial strategy.'

'Hit and run,' added Domitus. He pointed at each of the marks he had made in the soil. 'Hit them all along the line and from all sides. Then you may save your kingdoms.'

426

'We do not have the luxury of time to grind down the enemy,' I told them. 'Therefore we must speed up the process, which means that I must have command of all the horsemen we can muster.'

'Why?' said Radu.

'I intend to use them to attack the Roman carts and wagons.'

Radu looked disgusted. 'Is this how the Parthians wage war, plundering carts while others do the fighting?'

Domitus shook his head as he wiped the point of his sword and slid it back in its scabbard. Akrosas maintained his polite demeanour but was also confused, while Draco and Decebal regarded me with suspicion.

'It is quite simple,' I said. 'The wagons carry the enemy's supplies. Destroy them and the Romans will be forced to withdrew, either that or die.'

'Each Roman soldiers carries a few days' supplies on his person while on the march,' added Domitus, 'but if their supplies are destroyed then they will face some hard choices, as King Pacorus says.'

Akrosas, who was mindful that it was his city that was in the greatest danger, added his support for the plan.

'I believe it is a most prudent scheme.'

The others agreed, Radu begrudgingly. All that remained was to work out the specifics. As the foot soldiers were some miles to the east of our position it gave us time to set the trap that the Romans would hopefully walk into. There was only one route to Histria unless the enemy wanted to hack their way through thick forest, which made choosing our ground easier. But I still worried that as soon as the Romans were spotted the Thracians would charge out of the forest to fight them.

We broke camp and retraced our steps, riding through the trees to stay away from meadows and plains where enemy scouts would already be operating. The moss and soft undergrowth muffled the sound of the horses' hooves as we trotted through the verdant forest, the occasional magpie taking flight above us as we passed underneath.

Domitus was in an ill temper, either due to his having to ride a horse or the thought of the coming clash I did not know.

'You disapprove of my plan, Domitus?'

427

'You haven't seen the calibre of the foot soldiers of our allies,' he said. 'As for the plan, well, even Dura's army would have difficulty in coordinating a simultaneous assault against an enemy that is strung out over several miles. But this lot? There is no hope.'

'There is always hope, Domitus. Besides, if we can destroy their supplies then that might tip the balance in our favour.'

'*Our* favour? This is not our fight. We should be sailing back to Parthia by now.'

'King Akrosas extended the hand of hospitality to us,' I said. 'What sort of guests would we be if we turned our backs on him in his hour of need?'

'Living ones.'

It took the rest of the morning to organise the Thracians and Dacians into their ambush positions. The actual site was spread over five miles, the width of the open ground in the area varying between a hundred and four hundred paces in extent. In an effort to simplify things as much as possible, each of the kings was assigned a sector of the ambush site. King Akrosas and his three thousand Getea foot would attack the Roman vanguard and command group; the rash and boisterous Radu and his two thousand Bastarnae would assault the right flank of the Roman army, while Draco and his fifteen hundred Maedi would attack its left flank. With the addition of Akrosas' five hundred horsemen I was able to muster seven hundred and sixty riders for the assault on the enemy baggage train, while King Decebal would command his two thousand Dacians in the assault on the Roman rear guard.

I liked the wild-haired Dacian leader. Beyond his intimidating appearance and unrefined manners he was a thoughtful and intelligent king. Actually he was very similar to Burebista who came to me when the horsemen and Dacian foot had been withdrawn back from the treeline and were resting among the trees. Even out of the sun it was very warm, thousands of midges tormenting men and horses alike. I was counting my remaining arrows when he walked over to me.

'I would like to fight among my fellow Dacians, lord, with your permission.'

Gallia smiled as she examined the white flight feathers of her arrows.

'You do not need my permission, Burebista,' I told him. 'You are a free man.'

'That is something I am still getting used to, lord.'

I stood and placed a hand on his shoulder. 'You are free to forge your own destiny, Burebista, you and Anca. That was always the purpose of our journey to Ephesus.'

'Thank you, lord.'

The warriors he desired to fight amongst were called falxmen and they were a fierce lot. They wore leggings and tunics but no helmets, armour or shields. Their main weapon was a two-handed instrument called a falx, which was a wicked curved, scythe-like blade on the end of a long handle that was sharpened on its inner curve. In this way the damage from a blow was done with a pulling motion, the force capable of hacking off a limb.

'He will probably get himself killed,' remarked Domitus as he hoisted himself into the saddle of his patient mare, 'then what will you do?'

'At least he will die a free man. Where are you going?'

'King Akrosas has requested my presence,' he replied. 'He can't wipe his arse without my advice, it would appear.'

'You should be flattered,' I said.

He settled himself on the horse's back. 'I should but I'm not.'

He reached down and offered me his hand. 'Mars be with you.'

I took his hand. 'Shamash protect you, my friend.'

Gallia came over, pulled him down and kissed him on the cheek.

'I order you not to get killed,' she said severely.

He cracked a smile. 'Yes, majesty.'

He raised a hand, turned his horse and trotted away, two of Akrosas' royal guards escorting him back to the king, who was about three miles to the northeast. As he left Decebal arrived on his horse with a brace of his scouts.

'The Romans approach, King Pacorus.'

I mounted my trusty mare and walked her through the trees, preceded by the scouts, leaving behind the hundreds of

429

horsemen and falxmen who thirsted for battle. When we got nearer to the treeline we dismounted and left the horses with the scouts as I crept forward with Decebal towards the edge of the forest. We crouched low against a lime and looked out into the meadow of long grass to see the sun glinting off javelins and helmets and horsemen equipped with large green-faced shields.

'Looks like the vanguard,' I said quietly. 'They are the target of King Akrosas. It will be another two hours before the baggage train arrives.'

'That long?' said Decebal.

'Roman armies can move fast over well-maintained roads, but dirt tracks and open ground slows wagons and carts. Besides, they are in no hurry. They will be cautious after what happened yesterday.'

'They will also be on the lookout for us,' he warned.

'That too. I just hope Radu can restrain himself and allow the vanguard to pass him by before he attacks.'

'Radu wants to avenge the humiliation of his defeat,' he said, 'but he is not a fool. He will curtail his recklessness.'

I doubted that but there was nothing I could do to influence the events that were going to unfold. We made our way back to where the horsemen and falxmen waited, most of the latter laying on the ground beside their fearsome weapons, seemingly unconcerned about the approaching battle they would fight in. I called together the leaders of the Maedi, Dacian and Getea horsemen, the latter the best equipped in their helmets and leather armour. I tried to impress on them all that their task was to destroy what was in the carts rather than loot them.

'Remember,' I said to them, 'that you will have superiority in numbers so make it count. Kill any guards quickly and then destroy the wagons.'

I sensed that they listened to my words concerning killing but ignored the rest. Capturing slaves and taking plunder were integral to the Thracian and Dacian way of war and all of them were probably thinking of returning home loaded down with Roman loot. But their morale appeared to be high, notwithstanding the losses they had suffered yesterday.

Decebal posted a number of scouts at the treeline to keep him updated as to the progress of the Roman army. After the briefing I had taken the opportunity to rest my eyes and must have fallen into a deep slumber, from which I was awoken from by Gallia's boot.

'It is time,' she said curtly.

Around us there was great activity as riders slung saddlecloths and saddles on their horses' backs and secured harnesses. There was an ominous rumble as Dacians grouped around their chiefs in their war bands and headed toward the edge of the forest. Decebal came over to me and proffered his hand.

'Zalmoxis be with you, King Pacorus.'

I shook his hand. 'And with you, King Decebal.'

He turned to order over his bodyguard that was holding his horse, hoisted himself into the saddle and trotted away. Surena and Gallia were already in the saddle as I walked over to my mare and untethered her. I adjusted the strap of the quiver that was slung on my back and vaulted into my saddle. Behind us a mass of horsemen were gathering, which I led forward with a wave of my arm. I had forty arrows left, slightly less than Gallia and slightly more than Surena. But in the coming clash it would be the men behind me who would decide the outcome of the battle not a few paltry missiles.

'Keep close,' I said to Gallia and Surena. 'When the fighting begins any semblance of order will disappear.'

'I wonder if we shall see Burebista again?' mused Surena.

I wondered the same thing.

There was bright sunlight and no breeze as we broke cover and advanced towards the line of wagons and mules that covered the grassland in either direction as far as the eye could see. The 'plan' had been for the various contingents to launch their attacks as soon as they heard the sounds of fighting that signalled that the Getea had locked horns with the Roman vanguard. In this way the Bastarnae and Maedi would hear the sounds of battle and join the mêlée, which in turn would alert us at the rear of the enemy that the time had come to reveal ourselves. I thought I heard the faint sounds of battle to my right as I left the treeline but that noise was soon drowned out by seven hundred and sixty riders screaming their war cries as

431

they bore down on the enemy. We charged in one long line, though it was more a ragged collection of groups because the men stuck to their tribal chiefs as they cantered through the long grass.

Ahead were Roman horsemen, a thinly spread line acting as flank guards for what appeared to be auxiliaries standing nearer the wagons. A few charged our line but were simply brushed aside by the Thracians and Dacians. The wagons were now less than two hundred paces away as I nocked an arrow and shot it at a slinger who had just released his stone. He disappeared into the grass as my arrow hit him but the hisses in the air indicated that his fellow slingers were still a threat as riders were struck and dislodged from their saddles.

We reached the wagons and slowed our mounts, or at least myself, my wife and Surena did. Many of the Thracians and Dacians, possessed by bloodlust, galloped straight at them and either became entangled with the mules that were pulling them or were thrown as their horses reared up in alarm at the obstacles immediately in their path. Those who were thrown and had not been badly injured immediately sprang to their feet and attacked the unarmed drivers, hacking at them with axes.

Within minutes the wagons had been captured, the few enemy archers and slingers being hunted down and killed, though not before they had emptied a sizeable number of saddles. Then, just as I had feared, the horsemen began to loot the waggons. I became the commander of thieves as they acted like excited children while ransacking the transports. I rode up and down the line, shouting at them to stop what they were doing, or at least unhitch the wagons and carts. Their responses varied from ignoring me to outright abuse. In the end I found half a dozen signallers and with a mixture of threats and pleading got them to blow their horns to signal recall.

Gradually a semblance of order was restored as the commanders, now attired in captured Roman helmets, cloaks, mail shirts and carrying entrenching tools, cooking pots and javelins precariously perched on their saddles, mustered to me.

'Unhitch the mules,' I shouted to them, pointing left and right at the long column of transports. 'The mules.'

I gave a huge sighed of relief as they appeared to understand and rode away, then sat in stunned silence as their men began to slaughter the mules. My orders misunderstood, I just watched as they killed every mule within reach, then set about smashing up the carts and wagons.

'Well,' said Gallia as she studied the outbreak of destruction, 'at least the Romans have been denied their baggage train.'

We had achieved a decisive victory but I had no idea what was happening further up the line or with regards to the rear guard. So once more I ordered the signallers to blow their horns and keep on blowing them until the Dacians and Thracians had desisted from their slaughterhouse activities and reformed in their ranks. It took around half an hour for them to do so, by which time the signallers were exhausted and the riders were splashed with blood. The smell of gore soon permeated the air and entered our nostrils, spooking our horses.

'We will assist King Decebal against the Roman rear guard,' I said to the leaders. 'Follow me.'

I turned my mare left and cantered along the right flank of the smashed Roman baggage train, the delighted booty laden warriors following. We rode for half a mile before coming across Decebal and his men, all of whom were either leaning on their falxes or sitting on the ground among piles of dead. I saw no Romans still standing.

I rode over to where the king was riding among his men, reaching down to shake the hands of those he knew and shouting encouragement to others. My robber horsemen dismounted, being careful not to disturb their ill-gotten gains, and took off their stolen helmets to wipe their sweaty brows. The sun was high in the almost cloudless sky now and the temperature was climbing. When I reached Decebal I saw that his tunic was even more blood stained and there were splashes of gore on his saddlecloth.

'A hard fight, lord king?' I asked him.

He looked at me with tired eyes. 'Hard enough. The enemy rear guard comprised slingers, archers, horsemen and legionaries. I have lost a quarter of my men at least. And you?'

I was almost ashamed to give him my report. 'The enemy baggage train had been destroyed with little loss.'

I did not tell him about the looting, but then as a Dacian he would think it remiss if booty had not been taken.

'My men can do no more fighting this day,' he said flatly.

'We should leave this place of dead flesh,' I said, 'and get the men and horses to water and into shade.'

He wiped his sweat-beaded forehead with a dirty rag. 'Agreed.'

He pointed at a knot of wild-looking men stripped to the waist, their long hair matted to their necks, and ordered them over.

'Get the men back into the forest,' Decebal commanded.

In the next few minutes fifteen hundred men, some of them hobbling from wounds, slowly began to make their way back to the forest where we had lain in wait for the Romans. I was about to return to the horsemen when I saw that one of them was Burebista, looking tired but appearing to have no visible wounds. I jumped down from my horse and rushed over to him, embracing him and giving thanks to Shamash that he was unharmed.

'It took us a while to break them, lord,' he said. 'They had stiffened the rear guard with three centuries of legionaries that proved tenacious foes.'

'It is ever so.'

He looked in the direction that the Roman army had marched. 'And the other tribes, have you heard how they have fared, lord?'

I shook my head. 'No word as yet.'

But as we stood among the sweet-smelling long grass we heard a noise that we both recognised. A barely discernible noise of tramping feet marching in unison, interspersed with the sharp sounds of trumpet blasts. We had both heard those sounds many times and said nothing as we stared at each other. There was no wind and so the noise was not being carried on the breeze, which meant that it would not be long until we saw the source of the sounds that had sent a shiver down our spines.

'Get into the forest,' I told him before vaulting back into the saddle.

'Romans,' I shouted, 'Romans approaching.'

434

The Dacians turned to stare at me with disbelief, looking around at the dead auxiliaries and legionaries, thinking that some were still alive. But then they too heard the noise, craning their heads to hear more clearly. Decebal heard it too and began riding up and down with sword in hand, shouting for them to make haste.

'We will cover you, lord king,' I shouted to him.

He raised his sword in acknowledgement as I told Burebista to stay alive and then headed back to where the horsemen were regaining their saddles.

Gallia's face was a mask of concern. 'Surely they can't have destroyed all the other tribes?'

'We shall know soon enough.'

Amid much complaining my recalcitrant horsemen followed their leaders as we headed back towards the smashed wagons and dead mules that were now crawling with flies. We cantered along the line of wrecked, stationary transports and their slaughtered drivers, mostly unfortunate slaves that might have expected liberation but instead found death at the hands of undisciplined barbarians. The latter, having reaped a great bounty, were now less willing to re-engage the enemy. Their surliness increased when we came upon the main body of the Roman army and even my spirits sank when I saw a long line of red shields marching slowly towards us.

I called a halt as I watched what appeared to be a giant square of legionaries advancing towards us. I sent riders ahead to discover if the Romans were being assaulted on the flanks, but warned the horsemen to be wary of getting too close to the enemy. There might still be archers and slingers within their ranks who could pick off lone horsemen with ease. They galloped away but I knew the answer when the Romans came nearer, marching in perfect step and at a pace that suggested that their army was not being assaulted from the flanks.

'Have a care,' I shouted to commanders grouped behind me, 'their ranks may part so horsemen can sally out against us.'

They were around half a mile away now, and I gave the order for the majority of our horsemen to withdraw into the forest and ride to link up with King Decebal. I remained with Gallia, Surena and a score of Dacians and waited for the scouts to return. When they did my fears were confirmed: there was no sign of the Maedi, Bastarnae or Getea.

'They are all dead?' said Gallia, dumfounded.

'I do not know,' I replied before giving the order to retire, the din of Roman trumpets in our ears as we did so.

The Dacian foot reached the sanctuary of the forest before the Romans arrived. I sat on my horse in the trees with Gallia and Surena and watched them pass, a great mass of red shields and tunics retreating crab-like towards the site of their previous night's campsite. They halted to relieve the wagons and carts of anything useful, which meant they tarried only briefly. I saw few horsemen among their ranks, though the legate and his senior officers were surrounded by upwards of fifty riders. I also saw a glimpse of the legion's eagle, the sun catching its wings as it passed.

'So, your plan has failed,' said Gallia, staring with contempt at her mortal enemies. 'They must have destroyed the foot soldiers of Akrosas, Radu and Draco.'

I said nothing as I tortured myself with thoughts of Domitus, Arminius and Drenis lying butchered somewhere. Surely they could not have perished having survived all the travails at Ephesus and afterwards? I heard the mocking laughter of Dobbai in my head and her sharp words.

'The gods are above all cruel, son of Hatra, and delight in the miseries of men.'

'Then why have they protected us thus far?'

Gallia turned to look at me. 'What?'

'Nothing. We must return to what's left of our army.'

With a heavy heart I wheeled my mare around and headed into the forest. It was now late afternoon and the temperature in the trees was stifling. Sweat was pouring off my face and my tunic was drenched. Gallia had tied her hair into a long ponytail that hung down her back but was sweating nevertheless, her cheeks pink as she perspired. Only Surena, who had been born and raised in the heat-ravaged marshlands south of Mesene, seemed unaffected by the high temperature.

Decebal had retreated at least a mile into the forest's interior, having posted sentries on foot at regular intervals to ensure he was not surprised by a Roman incursion. Small groups of falxmen eyed us warily as we approached them, waving us through when they recognised our attire and our horses' saddlery, if not ourselves. Eventually we came across a great lake in the middle of the forest where the Dacians and horsemen were camped. Hundreds of naked men were splashing around in the water and others were leading horses to the lake's edge to drink. Saddles and saddlecloths littered the ground along with sleeping warriors lying under trees and others, wounded, propped up against their trunks. Some had horrific injuries, half their faces torn away or their bellies sliced open, but they did not cry or moan; they just stared with vacant eyes at the waters of the lake. Many would be dead before nightfall.

We slid off our horses and led them with our heads down to the water so they too could drink. Afterwards we took off their saddlery beneath a huge oak tree and I was about to take the weight off my feet when Decebal himself arrived with his mounted bodyguard. Both he and his horse looked tired.

'A rider has come from King Akrosas,' he said. 'He asks that he joins us to discuss the recent battle.'

I felt relief sweep through me. 'It is good to learn that he is well.'

'What of General Domitus?' asked Gallia.

'I have heard no news concerning the general,' said Decebal.

So I saddled my weary mare once more and accompanied Decebal and his men to Akrosas' 'headquarters', which turned out to be a round tent that had been sent from the city, together with carts carrying food and fodder. Fortunately the king and his army were only a mile to the east of our lakeside position, which meant that my horse was saved an arduous journey.

The campsite among the trees was filled with warriors sitting around campfires that filled the early evening air with smoke. I took the fires as a sign that the kings were no longer concerned about the Romans knowing of their whereabouts. When I entered the tent with Decebal my belief was proved right.

'Hail, King Decebal and King Pacorus,' said Akrosas, rising from a chair and holding up his silver cup to us. 'To victory.'

437

I smiled and then beamed when I saw a mail shirt-attired Domitus seated next to the king. He nodded to me and sipped at his drink.

'Wine for the kings,' ordered Akrosas.

Slaves rushed forward proffering cups that were filled. I drank the delicious liquid greedily. Draco and Radu also held cups but seemed less enthusiastic than the king of the Getea.

'Sit, please sit,' Akrosas pleaded, slaves positioning two chairs near the entrance to the tent, a single pole in the middle supporting its sagging roof.

Akrosas sat down and spread his arms. 'I praise Apollo that you both live. I trust the god blessed you with victory?'

Decebal drained his cup and held it out to be refilled. 'We destroyed the Romans' rear guard but had to retreat when the rest of their army appeared.'

'My horsemen captured their baggage train,' I added, 'and relieved it of anything valuable.'

Domitus cracked a smile but my inference was lost on the others. I doubted that Akrosas was even listening as he jumped up once more.

'Myself and my fellow kings this day defeated the Roman army, which now limps back to the foul abyss whence it crawled from.'

I could see that he was already thinking of the heroic poem that he would write to celebrate his triumph.

'Among the sacred oaks of Histria,' continued the king, 'the barbarian invaders were put to the sword. I shall build a shrine to Apollo in this forest as a lasting monument to the martial superiority of the Thracians and Dacians.'

Radu, Draco and Decebal appeared bemused by these words but I did not deflate Akrosas' childlike enthusiasm.

'A most worthy intention, lord king,' I said.

Domitus rolled his eyes but Akrosas was delighted and tipped his head to me.

'And now, sir,' said Domitus, 'we must address the strategy for tomorrow.'

Akrosas frowned. 'Strategy, general?'

'He means wiping out the Romans instead of letting them crawl back to Macedonia,' spat Radu.

'A mere trifle,' said Akrosas dismissively. 'They will surrender anyway.'

'We must attack them,' insisted Radu, 'and wipe them out.'

'I agree,' said Draco. 'We have lost too many men to let them escape.'

'I would advise against it,' argued Domitus. 'An animal is at its most dangerous when it is cornered.'

Radu stood. 'No! You have no say here, Roman. Tomorrow I will attack with my men. That is the only strategy the Bastarnae will tolerate.'

Draco nodded. 'The Maedi will stand beside you.'

'And the Dacians,' added Decebal.

Their eyes settled on Akrosas.

'Well, naturally the Getea will be present to complete the victory.'

The 'victory' of which Akrosas boasted was only half-complete and had been bought at a high price, as Domitus informed me afterwards.

'As I thought, Radu and Draco hurled their men against the legionaries' flanks, which at least got their attention while I dealt with the vanguard. I managed to persuade Akrosas to keep his men on a tight leash, hit-and-run attacks spread over a wide area. He was deliriously happy when the Romans fell back.'

'I can imagine.'

'More importantly,' he continued, 'the Getea lost only two hundred men, whereas Radu suffered six hundred slain.'

'Six hundred?'

'Like I said, he threw all his men against the legion.'

I shook my head. 'And the Maedi?'

'Draco told us that four hundred of his men are dead or wounded. Still, we have destroyed the enemy's vanguard, rear guard and baggage train, which means they will abandon the advance on Histria.'

'*We*, Domitus,' I grinned, 'are you warming to these people?'

'Yes, like a wolf warms to a bleating lamb.'

'What about Drenis and Arminius?'

439

'They are safe,' he said. 'I have enlisted them as Akrosas' personal advisers.'

'And Cleon?'

He thought for a moment. 'Still alive, I think.'

'Make sure he takes no further part in the fighting,' I ordered. 'I have plans for him.'

'What plans?'

I tapped my nose with a finger. 'You will find out soon enough.'

'The immediate questions that need answering, of course, are how many men did the Romans lose today and what will they do tomorrow?'

I left him and the other kings to ride back to Gallia and Surena before night fell, the smell of wood smoke filling the air as I slid off my horse near the lake that the Dacians besieged. Decebal had sent my queen a gift of a young deer that one of his men had shot, which Surena had gutted and skinned and was now roasting over a fire. I was delighted to find Burebista seated on the ground chatting to Gallia, showing her his fearsome falx. I told them all what had happened on the other sectors of the battlefield and the plan to recommence hostilities tomorrow. Gallia was delighted that Domitus, Drenis and Arminius were well and Burebista appeared in high spirits. But I worried that he and his fellow tribesmen would suffer more heavy casualties tomorrow.

When the new day dawned, like the ones before it hot and airless, the two armies gathered their strength once more for a renewal of hostilities. Both were like wounded animals that, although they had a lot of fight left in them, had suffered grievously. The army of the kings had suffered nearly eighteen hundred dead and wounded, a high proportion of its total strength. We had no idea how many men the Romans had lost but the fact that they remained in their camp, positioned three miles to the west in a wide expanse of open ground, indicated that they too had suffered significant losses.

'They are waiting to see what we do,' said Domitus as we assembled once more in the tent of King Akrosas, 'which tells me that they have abandoned the advance on Histria.'

Akrosas brought his hands together and grinned like an idiot.

'Praise Apollo.'

'So all that remains is to destroy the Romans,' said Radu, who had regained his verve after appearing deflated after yesterday's losses.

'We tried storming their camp before,' said Decebal, 'and achieved nothing except the loss of many comrades.'

Draco, still smarting from the previous day's bruising, was in agreement.

'I am unwilling to see any more Maedi sacrificed needlessly.'

'So force them to fight on your terms,' said Domitus, who was now standing and pacing up and down in front of the kings. I smiled when I saw that he had found a vine cane, taken from a dead centurion no doubt. Just like at Dura he began to tap it against his thigh as he spoke.

'Forget about assaulting their camp. Instead, wait until the Romans retreat for that most likely is what they will do. Yesterday they lost their rear guard, all their transports and most of their auxiliaries and horsemen, in addition to at least a cohort of legionaries.'

Radu looked around confused. 'What's a cohort?'

'Nearly five hundred men,' I told him.

'Ten percent of their best soldiers,' added Domitus. 'I would advise the same tactics that were used yesterday.'

'We lost many men yesterday,' growled Draco.

Domitus stopped pacing. 'The difference is that today the Romans will be retreating instead of advancing.'

He was right. It was two hours after dawn when the enemy struck camp and headed towards the southwest, to Macedonia. The legionaries dismantled the camp and assembled in close order to begin the journey back to Roman territory. They posted few horsemen on the flanks and ahead of their formation, testament to our success during the preceding two days. The spirits of the kings were raised when a scout returned with news that several dozen Romans had been left behind in the camp. At first they suspected it was a trick to lure them into the enemy's base until Domitus told them that the Romans had left behind their wounded so they would not be slowed down on the march.

Radu, revenge on his eyes, demanded that he and his men be allowed to kill them and Akrosas agreed, shaking his head at the barbarousness of the enemy in abandoning their wounded.

'I would have done the same if I had been the Roman commander,' Domitus told me as Radu left to muster his men. 'Shows that they are in a desperate state, though.'

'If the kings can hold their nerve,' I said, 'then they might just take an eagle.'

'The only eagle this lot is going to take is one that you shoot out of the sky with that bow of yours.'

But as the army left its camp I was optimistic that the kings had learned their lesson and were content to shadow the Romans, waiting for opportunities to launch fast attacks against them to gradually wear them down. Radu took his Bastarnae and slaughtered the Roman wounded. The main weapon of his warriors was the *rhomphaia*, a curved blade sharpened on the inner edge like a sickle. Unlike the falx it was a one-handed weapon, the Bastarnae carrying a small shield for protection and also sporting helmets, though no body armour. Many were bare-chested, their bodies adorned with tattoos and their hair dyed blue.

For most of the morning the two sides were content to watch each other from a safe distance, myself and Decebal leading the horsemen who rode in the rear of the Roman column, the foot soldiers of the Dacians following us and the warriors of the Maedi and Getea moving through the forest on the flanks of the Romans. Occasionally a party of Thracians would race from the trees to attack the legionaries, who invariably responded with javelins, any auxiliaries near them adding their arrows and slingshots to the missiles. At first the Thracians launched many such assaults, which slowed the Romans as they halted and adopted an all-round defensive posture, but a sizeable number of Maedi and Getea were killed or wounded in these forays for few Roman casualties and so they stopped.

After a while we dismounted and walked our horses in the wake of the enemy, which was around four hundred paces ahead, moving at a slow pace, weighed down as they were with the heavy load each legionary was carrying. As the time passed it was almost sleep inducing trudging along in the summer heat, everyone left alone with his thoughts. A vision of Claudia came to me, laughing and playing on the palace terrace at Dura under the watchful eye of Dobbai. I saw Rsan's serious face, the fatherly figure of Godarz and the valiant Orodes, listening intently to a petitioner in the throne room. I suddenly longed to be back in Parthia, to be among my people at Dura and not wading through high grass following a beaten enemy.

'King Akrosas requests your presence, majesty.'

I looked up to see one of the king's bodyguards sitting on his horse. I raised my hand to him and squinted up at the sun. It was getting hotter. The guard saluted and rode away to speak to Decebal, no doubt informing him that Akrosas also wanted to see him. I hoisted myself into the saddle, my mare turning her head and shaking her mane.

'Hopefully he is going to inform me that he and the army are returning to Histria,' I said to Gallia.

'That would make sense,' she replied, 'so I suspect it will not be what he wishes to talk to you about.'

My wife knew the nature of men well enough, for when I arrived at the phalanx of Getea horsemen that surrounded the king I found him in an excitable state. Domitus, by contrast, looked very sombre and shook his head when he saw me approach. Decebal was hot on my heels as I rode up to Akrosas.

'Congratulate me, King Pacorus, I have had a vision sent by Apollo.'

This sounded ominous. 'I congratulate you, lord king.'

'One of my commanders, who was raised in one of the villages that litter this area, remembered an ancient trail that threads through the forest near here. This trail will allow us to take a shortcut to intercept the enemy.'

'To what end, lord king?'

He looked nonplussed. 'To what end? So we can destroy the Romans, of course. If we overtake the enemy and place ourselves in their path then the Romans will be left with two choices: to attempt to seek an alternative route or surrender.'

'Or go through you,' said Domitus on his other side.

'Nonsense,' stated Akrosas firmly, 'you yourself said that the Romans are at the end of their strength, general.'

Akrosas smiled at me. 'I would like you and King Decebal to take the horse and follow this trail to halt the Romans and give me time to arrive with the foot soldiers.'

He turned and waved forward one of his men, a soldier in a brown leather cuirass, gilded helmet and armed with a sword.

'Leon will be your guide.'

'Are you certain of this, lord king?' I asked.

'Quite certain,' replied Akrosas firmly. 'Not only has Apollo sent this divine message it is well known that in war an attacker needs numerical superiority to overcome a defensive position, and we will have both a numerical superiority and a strong defensive position.'

'Perhaps you should tell the Romans that,' said Domitus.

Akrosas ignored his barb as I turned my horse and rode back to the mounted warriors in the company of Decebal and Leon. I glanced back and raised a hand to Domitus who nodded in acknowledgement. As Akrosas issued his orders to the officers of his foot soldiers and sent messengers to the Maedi and Bastarnae who were shadowing the Romans, we rode to the horsemen and called together their commanders. Decebal told them in a flat voice of the journey to head off the Romans, which was greeted with universal approval. Afterwards seven hundred riders mounted their horses and followed Leon as he led us towards the thick forest situated on our left flank. One forest looked much the same as another to me but it was good to be out of the sun as we rode two abreast along a barely discernible path that snaked its way between oaks, lime and hornbeam. The forest was lush and verdant, at times dark as the canopy blotted out the light, horses slipping on the greasy ground that never saw the sun. Such stretches brought a welcome relief from the heat as cool air blew in our faces. We splashed through shallow streams filled with mossy boulders and came upon peaceful ash groves that looked as though they had been created at the dawn of time.

After an hour of riding through a lush wilderness we entered an area of open grassland that narrowed at its midpoint to almost touch the forest opposite. Upon closer inspection the gap was actually around a hundred and fifty paces wide. I could see why Akrosas had been so tempted by this place: deploy

444

soldiers in the gap so they formed a wall of leather and iron to face the Romans. What a pity that he had no soldiers, only ill-armed and poorly disciplined warriors.

The horsemen dismounted on the orders of Decebal and stood facing the northeast in a line, shields locked together and spears facing towards where the enemy would come from. Men were detailed to take the horses back into the trees so they could enjoy the shade. I called Surena to me and pointed at the warriors filling the narrow gap.

'The kings have decided to destroy the Romans here, Surena. We are the vanguard and hold this place until the foot soldiers arrive. The enemy will have to pass through this gap if they are to continue on their retreat. What is your appraisal of this position?'

He looked around and at the warriors standing in a ragged line.

'It is a good defensive position, lord, but it will take great determination to hold it against the Romans.'

'I agree, Surena, and it is therefore regrettable that the warriors available to King Akrosas and his fellow kings are no match for the Romans. I fear that the legionaries will break through this position, weakened though they undoubtedly are.'

'Why then do the Thracians and Dacians offer battle, lord?'

'A mixture of pride and vanity,' I replied. 'Akrosas believes that this place was revealed to him by Apollo himself, and thus guarantees him victory. But Akrosas has also achieved what no other Greek commander has done in a long time. He has forced a Roman army to flee with its tail between its legs. That is a fine achievement. Now he seeks to destroy that army, which is pure vanity.'

'Did you tell him that?' enquired Gallia.

'Not in so many words.'

'Which means no,' she said disapprovingly.

'This is his kingdom, my sweet, not mine.'

An hour later the rest of the army arrived, Getea warriors wearing woollen leggings tied at the ankles and belted at the waist, their linen tunics drenched in sweat. None wore helmets though a good majority were wearing leather caps, though they would not stop a *gladius* blow. Their weapons comprised short spears, axes and daggers, their shields a mixture of round and hexagonal shapes. They cheered the soldiers of the king's bodyguard as their commanders herded them into position. Akrosas insisted that his soldiers should stand in the centre of the battle line as he rode with Domitus to behind the rapidly forming mass. We nudged our horses forward as the Thracian and Dacian horsemen walked back to the trees to collect their mounts. There was a tangible feeling of tension in the air as the Bastarnae, Maedi and Dacian foot arrived and shuffled into position.

It took a surprisingly little amount of time to fill the gap with the foot. In the middle stood the Getea, two thousand eight hundred of them. On their left stood Radu's fourteen hundred Bastarnae and on their immediate right were deployed Decebal's fearsome falxmen, now numbering fifteen hundred men. Next to them, on the army's right flank, were grouped Draco's eleven hundred Maedi, all attired in red tunics. The Maedi were also equipped with javelins that comprised the army's only missile troops.

When the foot had been deployed Akrosas called the kings together to explain to them the tactics that would be employed.

'The Romans will attack, and like a wave will lap against our breakwater of warriors,' he declared. 'All the horsemen will deploy immediately behind the foot, ready to charge the retreating Romans after they have been rudely handled by our foot.'

Seven and a half thousand men stood in close order in seven or eight ramshackle ranks, the horsemen grouped according to their tribal allegiances. Domitus had ordered Drenis and Arminius to attend him on horseback and now they both sat awkwardly on their mounts behind him as Radu, Draco and Decebal returned to their men, all of them walking to stand in the front rank of their warriors.

'I am glad to see you two,' I said to Drenis and Arminius.

'I would prefer to be on my own two feet,' complained Drenis.

'You will obey orders,' growled Domitus. 'This has the making of a bloody mess and the king doesn't want you two among it.'

446

Akrosas, sitting on his horse a few paces in front, turned. 'Did you say something, General Domitus?'

'No, sir.'

Akrosas turned his grey stallion. 'I would consider it an honour, King Pacorus, if you would share joint command of the horsemen with me so that we may enjoy the fruits of victory together.'

I bowed my head to him. 'It would be an honour, lord king.'

There was a sudden ripple of excited chatter among the foot and the clatter of shields and spears being picked up. I looked beyond the battle line to see the sun reflecting off hundreds of helmets and javelin points that spread from left to right to fill the horizon between the trees. Akrosas drew his sword as the warriors on foot began to bang the shafts of their spears against their shields and sing their war songs as they girded themselves for the coming clash. And in the distance the Romans continued their remorseless advance.

Chapter 16

The Romans called it *cuneus*, meaning 'wedge', a tactic that employed triangular-shaped legionary formations to create or exploit gaps in an enemy battle line. But in the oppressive heat in this verdant part of the Kingdom of the Getea there was no wedge. Instead, Antonius Hybrida launched two cohorts in column formation at converging angles against Akrosas' men, so that they would both hit his warriors at the same time. The Romans had changed formation with a tremendous thunder of trumpets that spooked our horses and caused a few to bolt from the ranks. To their credit the Thracians and Dacians responded in kind, hollering at the enemy at the tops of their voices as the two great columns, legionaries trotting towards them six abreast, advanced like two hideous giant serpents.

'This is going to end badly,' I heard Domitus say as the enemy closed to within two hundred paces of the Getea.

Then, with horror, I saw individuals between the converging columns manhandling scorpions forward, frantically positioning the machines and loading them with ammunition. Hybrida had managed to salvage his scorpions but had abandoned his siege engines in the retreat. There was a succession of sharp cracks followed by ear-piercing screams as bolts skewered the densely packed Getea. Some bolts went through one man and lodged in a warrior standing behind him, and within seconds the Thracian line was wavering as at least a score of scorpions unleashed two volleys against the Getea. And then the *cuneus* hit them.

Discipline and organisation.

For some strange reason those two words appeared in my mind as the Roman columns converged on the Getea and pushed straight through them. There was the customary volley of javelins from the first three ranks of legionaries in each column, followed by another volley as their comrades behind them also hurled their missiles at the Thracians, but there was no vicious close-quarter battle when the front ranks of each side clashed. The Thracians, having been raked by scorpion missiles, buckled under the hail of javelins and then crumpled when assaulted by the short swords of the legionaries. The Romans were better organised and disciplined than the

Thracians but they were also desperate to get back to Macedonia and so they fought with a controlled frenzy as they stabbed at unarmoured Thracian torsos and heads.

Within minutes our battle line had been split in two as the two Roman columns converged into a great blunt instrument of iron, wood and leather that pushed on remorselessly. Then it suddenly stopped, a blast of trumpets piercing the air.

'The Romans have been halted,' announced Akrosas triumphantly as what was left of the Getea, Dacians, Maedi and Bastarnae began a furious battle against the flanks of the two Roman columns that now slowly began to push outward towards the trees on either flank.

'They are attempting to form a corridor through which their mules and remaining supplies can escape,' shouted Domitus as the air resounded with another succession of trumpet commands and volleys of javelins were hurled at the warriors battling the Roman flanks.

The Bastarnae were fighting magnificently, their fearsome *rhomphaia* hacking into the front ranks of the Romans and inflicting many casualties as they severed calves, hamstrings and even lopped a few Roman heads clean off. But Radu's warriors had only small shields and no body armour, and even though they sported helmets they were terribly vulnerable to the javelins that arched over the battling front ranks to land among those behind. Almost every missile found its mark and within minutes scores of Bastarnae lay in heaps on the ground.

A vicious mêlée has also erupted on the right wing where the remnants of the Getea plus the Dacians and Maedi assaulted the Roman left flank. The Maedi warriors had javelins that they threw at the packed ranks of legionaries, the latter adopting *testudo* formation as soon as their centurions realised that the enemy also possessed javelins. This not only negated the Romans' own missiles but allowed the Dacians and Thracians to engaged in a close-quarter fight with the legionaries without the threat of being decimated by enemy spears. Soon the falxmen were slowly whittling down the Romans, though not without suffering casualties themselves in a battle of attrition.

449

Akrosas, his eyes bulging in excitement and trepidation, looked left and right as the battle unfolded in front of him. The Romans had smashed through his Getea to divide the army's foot warriors. On the left the Bastarnae were suffering heavy casualties and being forced back towards the trees. On the right the Dacians and Thracians were more than holding their own; perhaps they were winning. Directly ahead was a slowly expanding line of red shields as the width of the Roman corridor increased, though there appeared to be no movement on its right side as we looked at it. A few Getea had reformed and attacked the Roman centuries that faced us but were speedily dealt with. Soon groups of bedraggled and wounded warriors were falling back towards where the horsemen were deployed, their heads down, tunics shredded and arms and bodies showing *gladius* cuts. I saw Akrosas' head stop turning and stare directly ahead. I knew what he was thinking: behind him were seven hundred horsemen; in front of him what must have seemed a thin Roman line, a very tempting line.

He drew his sword. 'King Pacorus, will you join me in delivering the blow that destroys the enemy?'

Domitus looked at him and me in alarm. 'You will not break them, sir, they are disciplined soldiers...'

'No, general,' said Akrosas sharply, 'this is the moment when I finally rid Thrace of these barbarian invaders.'

He turned and ordered his officers to signal the attack.

'Domitus, Drenis and Arminius,' I shouted as behind us horns were blown and hundreds of spears were levelled, 'you will all retire to the trees as none of you can ride a horse with any skill.'

I pulled an arrow from my quiver. 'Protect Akrosas,' I said to Gallia and Surena.

The horsemen never reached the Roman line. They began trotting towards the enemy, dragon windsocks barely stirring in the still air as groups of horsemen brandished their spears and urged their beasts on. They broke into a canter around two hundred paces from the locked shields of the Romans that suddenly parted to reveal a row of scorpions. Perhaps two score of the infernal machines unleashed volley after volley of deadly metal balls. They were only small but they slammed into horses to inflict horrific injuries, two, three score of animals collapsing to the ground and throwing their riders. The scorpion crews worked like men possessed to load and shoot their machines, which discharged their iron balls of death and mayhem like a cobra spits poison. Riders went down to my left, right and behind me as I shot my bow at the scorpion crews, feverishly pulling arrows from my quiver and shooting them until it was empty. Akrosas, visibly shaken by the death being meted out by the scorpions, sat stationary in his saddle as he stared in horror at the face of one his officers, which was turned into an awful circle of gore when an iron shot struck it. I pulled on my reins, grabbed his reins and yanked viciously on my mare's bit to turn her quickly.

'Fall back,' I shouted at Gallia and Surena as other horsemen retreated rapidly.

Akrosas made no protest as I screamed at my horse and dug my knees into her flanks to make her gallop faster. Gallia and Surena were beside me as we raced away from the scorpions.

'Into the trees,' I shouted at them and anyone within earshot.

We diverted our horses left to take them, and us, into the trees where we pulled up our mounts. I released Akrosas' reins and apologised to him. But he was in a daze and barely acknowledged me. Other horsemen flooded into the forest, including Domitus, Drenis and Arminius. Domitus had a thunderous look on his face and nudged his horse forward when he spotted Akrosas surrounded by the surviving officers of his bodyguard. He was obviously going to give the king a piece of his mind but I called him back.

'He has learned his lesson.'

And so had the other leaders. The short, bloody battle with the Romans had resulted in hundreds of Thracian and Dacian dead. With the defeat of the horsemen the other leaders had ordered their men to seek the sanctuary of the forests, the warriors melting into the trees, leaving the Romans free to recommence their march back to Macedonia. I rode back to the treeline with Domitus to watch them pass, the legionaries adopting a ragged square formation, in the centre the legionary eagle, the commanders on horses and mules pulling carts loaded with wounded I assumed. The Romans left no injured on the battlefield.

'We inflicted substantial losses on them,' said Domitus. 'I see no horsemen, no auxiliaries and no scouts. Their pace is also slow. They are tired and thirsty, I'll warrant.'

'So are we, my friend, so are we.'

After the Roman column had departed only the moaning of the injured and the pitiful cries of wounded horses disturbed the quiet. Akrosas, plunged into deep despair, sat on the ground with his head in his hands; the soldiers of his bodyguard stood around, uncertain what to do. I examined my mare to ensure she had no wounds and rode her back into the grass. Gallia and the others accompanied me. Other groups were walking from the trees to search for lost comrades, kill those too grievously wounded and retrieve those still alive who were capable of walking.

'All this was unnecessary,' grumbled Domitus, looking around at the scene of carnage.

'The most important thing is that we are all unhurt,' said Gallia harshly.

'What do you think the odds of that happening after all that we have been through?' asked Drenis.

'As Dobbai said,' Gallia answered, 'as long as we are seven then we will all return to Dura.'

But there were hundreds of others who would never return to their homes. As the hours passed it emerged that over fifteen hundred warriors had been killed. Draco had lost two hundred killed, Radu three hundred slain. Decebal's foot soldiers had lost three hundred dead but the heaviest losses were among the Getea that had borne the brunt of the Roman assault. Akrosas had fancied himself as a new Alexander of Macedon but his men had been woefully deficient in weapons, armour and training and had suffered accordingly: no less than seven hundred of them had perished. Surprisingly our horsemen had lost only seventy killed, though the enemy's scorpions had slaughtered and wounded three times that number of horses. I was deliriously happy when I discovered that Cleon and Burebista had survived the carnage, though the last of Cleon's followers were dead.

452

That night men sat in stunned, silent groups round fires as they mourned their dead comrades and thanked the gods for their deliverance. But there was little food and even less fodder so everyone endured a miserable night, their heads full of morbid thoughts and their bellies empty. The next day the march back to Histria began. During the night my mare had gone lame so I walked beside her for the duration of the journey. The kings kept to their respective tribal warriors and avoided each other, while Akrosas avoided everyone. I comforted myself with the knowledge that nearly five hundred dead legionaries had been counted on the battlefield.

By the time we clapped eyes on the walls of Histria we were filthy, stank, our clothes were torn and dirty and there were black circles round our eyes. But as the gates of the city opened the residents, no doubt filled with dread at the prospect of being either killed or enslaved by the Romans, rushed out to greet their returning heroes. Men who had been hobbling along with the aid of makeshift crutches, and who had appeared to be at death's door, suddenly underwent a miraculous recovery as vivacious young girls embraced them. Hand-drawn carts heaped with food, water and wine were soon among the warriors, their drivers demanding that their cargoes be consumed post haste. What semblance of order that had existed vanished as hardened warriors wept as they were cradled in the arms of grateful old maids.

A dazzlingly attractive woman no more than twenty years old offered Surena a full water skin. He smiled, took it and drank most of the contents, wine pouring down his neck. He wiped his mouth and promptly threw up, his stomach unused to the rich liquid after days of eating hardly anything. He looked shamefaced at the woman as we fell about laughing. But I wasn't laughing when I went to visit Alcaeus who had volunteered to assist in the treatment of the wounded. A large warehouse inside the walls of the citadel had been designated a temporary hospital, the patients lying in rows on the dirt floor. Physicians, slaves and priestesses from the Tempe of Bendis attended to the wounded, their low groans unnerving me as I found my Greek doctor ordering two slaves to take away a dead man.

'You look like I feel,' I told him.

He cracked a weary smile. 'Thank the gods you are alive. How are the others?'

'All in one piece,' I said. I saw the figure of Hippo kneeling beside a patient.

'What is she doing here?'

He looked at the former high priestess. 'She has been here since the hospital was established, working without complaint and undertaking the filthiest of tasks. I think she sees it as penance for her sins.'

'The gods must have accepted her penance,' I said. 'Cleon survived the battle.'

'She will be pleased. One thing you should attend to before the feast that will invariably be held tonight. Athineos got himself arrested while you were away. He currently languishes in jail.'

Alcaeus was wrong about the feast. So exhausted were the returning 'heroes' that they immediately fell asleep when they reached the square inside the citadel, servants arriving to take the equally exhausted horses to the royal stables to be watered and treated. Akrosas took himself to the Temple of Apollo to pray for forgiveness for letting the Romans escape, even Rodica being forbidden to enter the shrine. The king stayed there all night, the other kings returning to the palace to bathe and acquire clean clothing. I let Athineos languish for a further night in jail, being too exhausted to care about his welfare. One man I did make time for was Admiral Arcathius whose Pontic soldiers had garrisoned the city in the king's absence.

He was dressed in his magnificent scale armour cuirass when I visited him on the palace balcony later that afternoon. We sat under a white linen sunshade as slaves served us wine, fruit and delicious honey cakes. I was careful not to indulge, as I did not want to empty my stomach as Surena had done earlier.

'My congratulations, King Pacorus,' he said. 'You have saved this city from a terrible fate.'

'I fear the Romans may be back, admiral, though at least we gave them a bloody nose.'

'You have given King Akrosas time in which to muster an alliance of Thracian and Dacian tribes,' he said, 'and I will ensure that he does not waste it. The news of the Roman

454

reverse will spread like wildfire through the kingdoms and I will make sure that the king fans those flames.'

He put his cup down on the small side table in front of us. 'And you, King Pacorus, what will the hero of Histria do now?'

'He will return home, admiral.'

Akrosas, wearing fresh clothes and now more at ease with himself following his night of penance in the Temple of Apollo, proclaimed two days of celebrations for the city's residents. The royal stores were opened so that food could be distributed to the population. The royal treasury purchased all the fish that had been landed during those two days and also gave them to the residents. The priests of Apollo and Bendis gave thanks in their temples and the king and queen gave a magnificent feast for the kings who had accompanied him on his expedition against the Romans.

There had been a touching scene when Cleon had been reunited with Hippo, the two of them sobbing as they held each other in their arms. A less inspiring sight had been the appearance of an irritable and drunk Athineos who had been released as part of a general amnesty decree issued by Akrosas for minor offenders. I found the captain in his room in the palace, slumped in a chair with his head in his hands and feeling very sorry for himself.

'I am a captain without a ship or a crew,' he muttered. 'The last of my shipmates have deserted me and taken service aboard some Greek merchant vessel.'

He reeked of self-pity as well as wine.

'First of all stop drinking so much. You smell like an alehouse. Second, stop feeling sorry for yourself. You still have your health and your wits.'

He regarded me with bloodshot eyes. 'If you came here just to lecture me then you have my permission to leave.'

He took another large gulp of wine from the *kylix* that he drained and refilled.

'I came here to inform you that good fortune lies just around the corner for you, Athineos, though you might not know it. Because of you I have been able to fulfil what I regarded as a sacred quest. That being the case, I am in your debt and I always pay my debts. Therefore I desire you to

455

accompany me back to Parthia so that you may be rewarded. I know the loss of your ships was a cruel blow so I wish to recompense you for your misfortune. So what do you say, Athineos?'

I heard a snore and saw his head slumped forward, the *kylix* dangling from his limp hand. He had fallen asleep!

'The gods give me strength.'

A more attentive audience was Cleon and Hippo. The day after the banquet, when Radu and Draco were preparing to leave Histria with their men, I visited the makeshift hospital where Hippo had continued with her duties. Despite the smell of blood and guts and her gore-covered apron she still looked alluring, her dark brown eyes full of enticement. Alcaeus was very flustered and barely acknowledged me as I walked between the rows of lacerated and broken bodies. Cleon was loading soiled straw into a wheelbarrow, Hippo beside him.

'This is no place for you, majesty,' she said when I approached.

'When you have seen as many battlefields as I have, lady,' I replied, 'this place appears mild by comparison.'

Cleon stopped shovelling blood-soaked straw.

'You will be leaving soon, majesty?'

I nodded. 'That is why I came.'

'To say goodbye?' there was sadness in Hippo's eyes.

'To say that I desire both of you to come back to Parthia with me.'

Cleon was surprised. 'Parthia? What is there for two Greek exiles, majesty?'

'A new and fulfilling life for you both,' I told them. 'You are free to make your own choices, but if you come back to Parthia with me I promise that you will no longer be exiles.'

Hippo looked at her beloved. 'I do not understand, majesty.'

I placed a hand on both their shoulders. 'All I ask is that you trust me. At the very least in Parthia you will not have to look over your shoulders out of fear that a Roman arrest warrant will be served on you.'

I looked around at the dozens of groaning, mutilated men lying on the ground.

'A high priestess should not have to toil in such a place as this.'

She smiled sardonically. 'Artemis is still angry with me, I think.'

'If that was true, Hippo, then she would not have permitted you to leave Ephesus. She has a plan for you, for you both, and I am the agent of that plan.'

After the celebrations the city returned to normal. Akrosas invited Gallia and me to take refreshment with him and Rodica on the palace balcony. As we sat beneath sunshades to be served by bare-footed slaves in pristine white *chitons* Akrosas waved forward a thin, middle-aged man who had been loitering in the corner of the balcony.

'This is Captain Hestiodorus, King Pacorus, who will take you and your people to Pontus. I have commissioned him and his ship and will allocate funds from the treasury so that you may purchase horses for your journey back to Parthia after you have landed in Pontus.'

'You are most generous, lord king,' I said.

He waved Hestiodorus away, the latter bowing deeply as he retreated from our presence.

'I don't suppose I could persuade General Domitus to remain at Histria?' enquired the king mischievously. 'He would be well rewarded and I would make him my high general.'

I laughed. 'I fear he misses his children too much, majesty.'

'His children?'

'The soldiers of the army he has raised for me,' I told him. 'He oversees them like a jealous mother hen tends to its chicks.'

Akrosas smiled at his wife.

'A great pity. I could use the advice of such a man. I fear the Romans may return.'

'They may, lord king, but your victory has given you time to organise the defences of this kingdom and form an alliance between Thracians and Dacians. There is strength in unity.'

The rest of the afternoon was spent in polite conversation, Rodica questioning Gallia about Claudia and our quest to find and free Burebista.

457

'And he will return to Parthia with you, King Pacorus?' asked Akrosas.

'He will. I intend to make him a senior commander in my army,' I said with satisfaction.

The next day we took our leave of Akrosas in the palace before being escorted by Arcathius from the citadel to the docks. The streets were filled with traders and citizens going about their business, small children marching alongside us and even one or two stray dogs. There was a slight easterly breeze that freshened the air, which became decidedly salty as we approached the harbour. The fish market was already bustling, baskets of fresh catch being purchased from the boats that had landed them. Merchants were overseeing bulk purchases for salting and smoking and tax collectors haggled with irate captains who pleaded poverty. By the amount of baskets of fish that filled the quay I doubted that poverty was a threat to any of the captains of Histria's fishing vessels.

As well as the original seven of us that had travelled from Dura our number included the grumbling, irritable Athineos who was at least sober and who had made a partial effort to tidy himself up. We reached Captain Hestiodorus' ship, a merchant vessel with two masts, one amidships, the other at the prow. It was also equipped with oars.

'It is a merchant galley,' Arcathius told me. 'The king chose it especially because its combination of sails and oars will get you across the Black Sea more speedily.'

'The king is most generous,' I said.

We had few belongings, having lost our possessions in Ephesus, and we carried our swords strapped to out belts and our bows slung over our backs. Akrosas had provided us with fresh clothes and spare footwear, and had even given us full quivers for our journey, though I hoped that we would not have need of them. As the others filed up the gangplank I waited on the quay for the rest of our party. Minutes later Cleon and Hippo appeared, both of them looking cleaner and happier than they had appeared in the hospital.

'If your offer is still open then we would like to accept passage to Parthia,' said Cleon.

'We have no home and our only friends are departing on this ship,' stated Hippo pitifully.

458

'When you walk up that gangplank,' I told them both, 'your new lives begin.'

Hippo dazzled me with a smile and Cleon looked relieved and grateful as he followed his high priestess up the wooden platform. There were only two left. I began pacing up and down on the flagstones as slaves began to load the ship with food and water. Towards the stern of the vessel Arcathius chatted to Hestiodorus, both of them leaning on the gunwale as they watched the supplies being brought aboard. Then I saw them – Burebista and Anca – and joy gripped me. I walked up to them, grinning like a child.

'We are not coming, lord.'

Burebista's words struck me like arrows.

'Not coming? Why?'

'I, that is we, wish to return to Dacia, lord,' he said softly. 'I never thought that I would see freedom again, let alone Dacia, but I wish to return to my homeland. King Decebal has promised me a position in his army.'

Disappointment enveloped me like a thick fog.

He looked uncomfortable, even ashamed. 'I hope you do not think ill of me.'

Part of me wanted to berate him for his ingratitude and to order him aboard the ship. Did he not know that I offered him power, position and riches if he so desired? But then I was ashamed. Ashamed that I could think such thoughts. What were riches and position compared to the greatest prize of all – freedom? Had I freed him from the Romans only to make him my slave? I placed a hand on his shoulder.

'How could I think ill of my finest dragon commander? You must follow your heart, Burebista.'

The anger and disappointment melted away and were replaced by great sorrow because I knew that I would never see him again. But he was a Dacian and his homeland was but a few days' ride from Histria.

'During my years of slavery,' he said, 'the thought of freedom and seeing Dacia again kept me alive. Then they were dreams but now they are reality, thanks to you, lord.'

I insisted that they both went on board to say their farewells to the others. I remembered a time, in Italy, when Gallia had been scathing about Burebista but now she

459

embraced him fondly and wished him well, Anca too. When they had finished saying their goodbyes I kissed Anca on the cheek and embraced Burebista like a brother. He was my brother, a brother-in-arms. As Arcathius said his farewells and the ship was pushed away from its moorings and the rowers dipped their oars in the harbour's water to take us out to sea, I stood on the stern and raised my hand to Burebista and Anca as they stood on the dockside. I kept my eyes on them until they were barely discernible shapes in the distance and then vanished altogether.

'The gods be with you both.'

'That's the thing about freedom. Those who have it often do what you do not want them to do.'

I caught site of Domitus' short, thick fingers being placed on the gunwale beside me.

'Are you disappointed, Pacorus?'

'A little. But Burebista must follow his heart. At least we gave him the opportunity to do so.'

I looked at him. 'By the way, King Akrosas asked me if you would be prepared to stay on at Histria as his high general, a task for which you would be handsomely rewarded.'

'What did you tell him?'

'I lied and told him that you were far too valuable to lose.'

He spat over the side. 'Is there any chance of turning this boat around?'

The combination of oars, sails and no cargo except for us meant that the ship achieved a good speed as it headed east towards Pontus. It looked like a trireme but the captain explained that its pointed prow made cutting through the water easier and was not for ramming. As we got under way Athineos rediscovered some of his old enthusiasm. No doubt being back at sea reinvigorated him as he lectured us on the ins and outs of shipbuilding. Apparently the ship's hull was caulked, which meant that it was covered with a mixture of pitch and beeswax so it was waterproof. In addition, the underwater surface of the hull was sheathed in lead as a protection against sea worms.

'The thin lead plates are nailed over a layer of tarred fabric using lead-dipped copper nails,' he informed us as we sat on the deck in the sunshine. 'You see cargo ships are normally always kept afloat rather being hauled ashore like warships, so without the lead sheathing the worms would eat away the hull.

Gallia and Hippo had been given the small cabin at the stern of the ship, the rest of us and the crew sleeping on deck in tent-like structures that were erected at night when we pulled into shore. There were twenty oars on each side of the hull, each one powered by a rower. Though they were free men the conditions inside the hold were very cramped and because it was also very hot the rowers sat at their oars in only their loincloths.

The summer was nearing its end but the winds were fair, the sea calm and so we made good progress, hugging the southern Black Sea coastline as we journeyed east towards our destination: the port of Trapezus. Hestiodorus was a talkative fellow and each day, as the linen sails billowed and the oars dipped in the blue sea, I visited him at the stern as he steered his ship. After being happy that we were finally travelling back to Parthia I became concerned that we were heading for a Roman port, Pontus having submitted to the Romans following the death of Mithridates.

'There is no need to worry, majesty,' he said, gripping the steering oar as seagulls glided on the wind overhead, 'Pontus is now a Roman client. There aren't any Roman soldiers in the country, at least not yet.'

'Are you sure?'

'Only Roman merchants in Trapezus, majesty, welcomed by King Pharnaces, their new friend.'

It took us ten days to reach Trapezus, a fortified city nestling at the base of the foothills of the Pontic Mountains. Greek settlers had established the city over six hundred years before but now it was wholly Pontic, lion banners hanging from port offices and from the towers of the fort. In the airless humidity they hung limply from their flagpoles, a poignant symbol of how a once great kingdom had been emasculated by the Romans. With the money provided by Akrosas we were able to purchase horses, tents, food and fodder for our onward journey south. Once more we donned flowing robes and headdresses to disguise our faces, not that I expected our identities to be discovered.

461

We left Trapezus the day after we had landed in the city. I thanked Captain Hestiodorus and wished him fair winds on his voyage back to Histria. I wondered how long it would be before Roman merchants and officials would be resident in that city. The power of Rome seemed like a great shadow that was spreading remorselessly over the known world. It was the first time that Hippo had ridden a horse and she was distinctly nervous as she tried to wrap her shapely thighs around the saddle's horns, having exchanged her dress for a pair of leggings that clung to her legs in the humidity and raised the morale of the male members of our party. Not that we needed cheering. We were going home and as soon as Hippo, flanked by Cleon and Gallia, had become accustomed to sitting on the back of her mature grey mare, we commenced our journey south through the great passes of the Pontic Mountains. Our destination was Zeugma, the former Parthian kingdom that was now also a client of Rome, ruled by the decrepit King Darius, who I had once met when I had been a headstrong prince of Hatra.

We rode through dense hazelnut forests, the trees extending up into the mist-wreathed mountains. At night we camped by the side of gushing rivers, streams and crystal-clear lakes. The mournful howling of wolves could be heard outside our tents every night and occasionally a brown bear would approach our camp in search of food, to be driven off by whoever was standing guard. There were many travellers on the road as we headed south, like us making camp on the outskirts of the cities we journeyed through – Satala, Melitene and Samosata – before reaching Zeugma.

The humidity had disappeared when we reached Darius' capital but it was still hot, the lush landscape of Pontus being replaced by arid desert as we crossed into Roman Syria and headed southeast towards Dura. We were going home.

Chapter 17

Four months to the day after leaving my kingdom we trotted by the spot where Pompey and I had agreed the boundaries of Dura and Syria, a *kontus* and *gladius* arranged side by side on top of a stone obelisk. Surena, Drenis and Arminius gave a cheer as we passed the marker, Domitus reaching over and shaking my hand as we rode past it. There were no other riders on the road as we continued on into the Kingdom of Dura, the blue waters of the mighty Euphrates on our left flank. I began to think of Claudia and seeing my old friends when I heard Domitus' voice.

'A reception party.'

His eyes were keener than mine as I stared into the shimmering heat haze. But then I spotted them: riders approaching at some speed.

I turned to the others behind me. 'Some of my horse archers.'

There were nine of them, all dressed in white tunics and riding well-groomed horses that shone in the sun. My chest filled with pride as I watched them approach, three flanking left, three flanking right as the others slowed their horses in front of us. Our party of ten must have appeared suspicious to the young, confident junior officer who commanded the horse archers, our robes caked in dust and our faces and heads covered.

He raised his hand to us. 'Halt!'

The two riders behind him rode their mounts up to his side as those on our flanks nocked arrows in their bowstrings and turned their horses to face us.

'No sudden movements,' I said to the others.

The officer looked at me and then at my companions.

'Wise words. State your business.'

'We are travelling to the city of Dura.'

He leaned forward in his saddle. 'I asked what was your business, not your destination.'

'Are not travellers welcome in the Kingdom of Dura?'

'I have my orders to intercept any suspicious-looking parties,' he said curtly, 'especially those coming from Syria. Very few traders come from Syria, much less parties of armed horsemen with no goods.'

'Are we at war with the Romans?' I asked, concerned.

The officer looked at his subordinates and laughed. 'We? What would a shabby looking individual like you know of the affairs of the Kingdom of Dura?'

His smile disappeared as his tone became menacing.

'Remove your headdresses and identify yourselves.'

The two either side of him nocked arrows and held the bowstrings in their fingers. I was very aware that they could shoot their bows with deadly accuracy in the blink of an eye. I held up my hands and slowly moved them to my *shemagh* to remove it, announcing after I had done so.

'I am Pacorus, King of Dura and son of Varaz, King of Hatra.'

I heard Gallia's voice behind me. 'And I am Gallia, Queen of Dura.'

The others likewise removed their headdresses, the officer's eyes widening in alarm as he beheld his king, queen and commander of Dura's army.

'Put away your bows,' he ordered his men before leaping from his horse and going down on one knee before me. His men followed his lead.

'Forgive me, majesty, I had no idea that you would be visiting these parts.'

'Get up,' I told him. 'What news of Dura?'

He sheepishly regained his saddle as his men put away their bows.

'Dura, majesty?'

'What the king means, boy,' said Domitus gruffly, 'is the city still standing?'

He looked confused. 'Dura still stands, general, of course. As long as the griffin guards the city it will never fall.'

He invited us to break our journey at the fort nearest to the border where he was based, but I told him to send a courier pigeon to the city to inform Governor Godarz of our approach and then bade him farewell. Domitus complimented him on his professionalism before he and his men left us. It was a hundred miles from the northern border of my kingdom to Dura so it took us two more days to reach the city, its honey coloured walls glowing in the sun as we approached it on the afternoon of the third day. A permanent dust haze hung over the caravan park to the north of the city walls where dozens of camels, mules and horses of the trade caravans congregated. Other caravans were winding their way slowly west, towards Palmyra, or east, taking them over the pontoon bridge built by an Egyptian engineer. From the square, mud-brick towers of the wall that surrounded the city flew red griffin banners. Gallia came to my side and I reached over to take her hand.

'It's good to be home,' she said, her eyes moist with emotion.

The pungent aroma of the caravan park entered our nostrils before we reached it, the odour of camel and horse dung and men who had not washed for weeks producing a unique smell. Godarz organised a small army of workers to clean the park every day, heaping the dung into wheelbarrows that were taken to the fields to fertilise crops. But such a concentration of animals and filthy men meant that you could always smell the park before you reached it.

As usual there was a great press of people, carts, horses and draught animals around the Palmyrene Gate, but they suddenly parted as a column of riders came from the city.

'Another reception party,' observed Domitus. 'Let's hope it's friendlier than the last one.'

They rode two abreast, a hundred cataphracts in full scale armour and wearing full-face helmets, their horses also encased in thick hide and overlapping steel plates. From every *kontus* flew a pennant with a griffin motif and from every saddle hung an axe and mace. At their head rode a man also attired in gleaming scale armour though his helmet was open faced. And that face was that of my friend Prince Orodes. The horses and their iron-shod hooves kicked up a great cloud of dust as they galloped towards us, civilians scattering out of their way as they approached. No one had taken any notice of our ragged group but they paid attention to the steel-clad soldiers whose approach made the earth shake. They looked magnificent, the sun glinting off whetted *kontus* points and burnished armour and helmets.

Orodes was wearing a broad smile when he slowed his horse a few paces from mine and drew parallel to me.

465

'Hail, King Pacorus, welcome back to your kingdom.'

I extended my arm and we clasped forearms. 'Greetings, my friend, it is good to see you.'

Gallia drew near him, leaned over and kissed him on the cheek, causing him to blush.

'Welcome back, majesty.'

Gallia sighed. 'Oh, Orodes, you are so formal.'

He exchanged greetings with Domitus and then began scanning the others in our group.

'We have all returned, thank Shamash,' I said, 'plus others we have collected along the way.'

Under the escort of the cataphracts we rode into the city, all of us drawing our swords and saluting the stone griffin atop the Palmyrene Gate as we passed under it, much to the amusement of Cleon and Hippo. The main street leading to the Citadel was lined with legionaries, Durans on one side and Exiles on the other as we trotted across the flagstones and rode to the gates of the Citadel. There was a sharp blast of trumpets when we rode through the gates, a century of legionaries in front of the headquarters building snapping to attention as we rode into the courtyard. The cataphracts took up position in front of the barracks to the left of the palace. On the other side of the courtyard, near the palace, were arrayed a hundred Amazons in mail armour and helmets. And at the top of the palace steps stood Godarz, Rsan, Dobbai and our beautiful daughter.

Gallia had no time for honour parties or protocol as she vaulted from her saddle and bounded up the steps to scoop up Claudia into her arms, my daughter throwing her arms around her mother and bursting into tears of joy. Waiting stable hands walked forward to take our horses, bowing their heads to me as I dismounted and walked up the steps. I placed my arms around Gallia and Claudia and kissed them both. Domitus slid off his horse's back and walked over to the legionaries to inspect them.

'Viper,' called Gallia, 'dismount and greet your husband.'

A slim figure in the front rank of the Amazons jumped from a horse and ran over to hurl herself into the arms of her husband, wrapping her arms and legs around him. Her helmet clattered on the flagstones as they kissed each other and the

Amazons cheered. I tore myself away from my wife and daughter to face Godarz, who bowed his head.

'I was getting worried,' he said.

'I always return, my old friend,' I replied.

'All is well, Lord Rsan?' I asked.

The treasurer bowed to me. 'Your kingdom prospers, majesty.'

The stable hands took away our tired mounts as I ordered a palace steward to take Cleon, Hippo and Athineos to rooms in the palace.

'Which one is the slave that you risked your life, your wife and your kingdom to rescue, son of Hatra?'

I turned to face her. 'No welcome for me, Dobbai, not even a smile?'

She scowled. 'Did it turn into a vain mission, son of Hatra, an exercise in vanity like I warned you?'

'On the contrary,' I corrected her, 'I not only found Burebista but freed him.'

She looked at Cleon, Hippo and Athineos being escorted into the palace.

'I recognise the pirate and the young enchantress is obviously not him, so that leaves the angry looking young man beside her.'

'We left Burebista in his homeland,' said Gallia as she lowered Claudia to the ground and walked over to embrace and kiss Dobbai on the cheek. 'He goes to fight beside his own people against the Romans.'

'So you rescued him from death in the arena so he could be killed in battle. How thoughtful of you, son of Hatra.'

I was too tired to engage in her word games so ignored her as Orodes dismissed the cataphracts and Gallia gave the orders for the Amazons to stand down. I was about to follow her and Claudia into the palace when I noticed that Domitus was still inspecting the legionaries. I descended the steps and strode across the courtyard.

'Here you are, general.'

The centurion handed Domitus a vine cane as he walked slowly among the mailed soldiers, each one holding a white-faced shield sporting red griffin wings and white plumes in their helmets. I stood to one side and watched as he inspected the

467

soldiers he had created. Afterwards, cane in his right hand, he came over to me and watched them file back to the barracks.

'I had forgotten how fine the soldiers of this army are, Pacorus.'

'It is good to be back, I agree.'

I left him conversing with the duty centurion and walked to the stables to see the one who had not been in the courtyard. My steps quickened as I neared the white-walled buildings that held Dura's finest horseflesh. Stable hands bowed as I passed them and went into the bright and airy building where Remus had his stall. The old hand whom I had left him in charge of smiled and bowed as I approached.

'Welcome back, majesty.'

I did not reply but Remus must have recognised either my steps or what the stable hand said as he began to buck with excitement, kicking the door of his stall.

'Hey, calm down,' I said as the man opened the door and I went inside.

Remus had his ears forward and his tail raised high to show his excited state as he pushed his head into my chest and snorted contentedly. I stroked his head and neck and told him how happy I was to see him, and to my surprise felt emotion welling up inside me. I had not realised how much he meant to me until this moment. His eyes were bright and alert and his coat and tail shimmered in the light. He looked in perfect health.

'He did not pine for me, then?' I joked.

'For a few days he did, majesty, but he knows we love him and Prince Orodes took him out every day so he could get his exercise.'

'He let Orodes ride him? I am surprised.'

'Oh no, majesty, the prince rode his own horse when he took Remus out. Prince Orodes said that only you should ride him.'

I smiled. Same old Orodes: a stickler for protocol.

It was amazing how quickly things returned to normal. Hippo and Cleon were given a room in the palace, Domitus went back to commanding the army, Alcaeus back to leading the corps of physicians and Drenis and Arminius returned to their duties. Athineos was also quartered in the palace where he

468

spent most of his days drinking wine and arguing with Dobbai about the existence of sea monsters and mermaids; he telling her that he had slept with one of the latter but she insisting that only one of the former would tolerate carnal relations with him. They seemed to like each other's company and for that I was glad as it stopped him slipping into a drunken gloom.

Normality also involved the weekly council meeting held in the headquarters building, which could be immensely tedious though on this occasion I was eager to hear news about the situation in the empire.

'Fortunately neither Mithridates nor Narses got wind of your extended leave of absence, Pacorus,' said Orodes who decided he should stand while giving me his briefing, which Domitus and Gallia found most amusing.

'There are no reports of any incursions into King Nergal's kingdom, nor indeed any activity concerning Ctesiphon or Persepolis at all.'

'No doubt the bloody nose that we gave Narses' agents at Uruk has convinced him and his false high king that we are not to be trifled with,' I said contentedly.

'I doubt that,' said Dobbai, 'Mithridates and Narses will strike at you directly, son of Hatra, when they judge it right to do so.'

'Though King Tiraios has paid with his life for his failure,' reported Orodes. 'He and his family were executed and replaced by one of Narses' satraps. His name is Sporaces, so Nergal informs me.'

I nodded. 'Excellent. That makes it a lot easier.'

Dobbai eyed me suspiciously. 'Easier for what?'

'Nothing. Thank you, Orodes.'

I looked at Rsan, 'Lord Rsan, perhaps you could give us a summary of the state of the kingdom's finances.'

Rsan stood up but I indicated that he should remain seated. He turned to one of his scribes who handed him a scroll.

'Before I begin, majesty, this arrived a few days ago, addressed to you. The courier who brought it said that it should be delivered to your majesty's treasurer. Rsan handed me the scroll. I broke the wax seal and read it. It was a bill of sale. I handed it back to Rsan.

469

'See that this is paid immediately.'

Rsan read the scroll and went ashen faced.

'Surely this is a misunderstanding?'

I shook my head.

He continued to look bewildered. 'But, majesty, this is a bill to pay a woman on the island of Cyprus five thousand drachmas, plus a supplementary amount of two hundred drachmas for expenses incurred pertaining to a one-armed slave named Adad.'

I nodded.

'Five thousand, two hundred drachmas?' he said again, thinking perhaps that the sum might diminish the more he uttered it.

'The advice of Julia saved our lives,' said Gallia, 'it is a small price to pay, I think.'

'The queen is right, lord treasurer,' added Domitus, 'even though the old witch is an extortionist.'

'You cannot put a price on the help of the gods, Roman,' snapped Dobbai. 'You should be thankful that Julia assisted you.'

'We are,' I said. 'So please arrange payment forthwith, Rsan.'

He grumbled some more and shook his head but seeing the futility of any argument moved on to give a long and dreary rundown of the revenues enjoyed by the kingdom. His summary being that trade was healthy, crops were in abundance and tax revenues were growing.

'Though the army is a heavy drain on finances,' he concluded.

Godarz had nothing to report concerning affairs within the city itself.

'Day-to-day business continues as normal, the trade caravans provide the city's brothels with a healthy trade and we regularly hang thieves, rapists and murderers, impaling the latter along the roads as a warning to others.'

Dobbai stood and brushed down her black robes. 'So there you have it, son of Hatra. The kingdom functioned very well in your absence; indeed, perhaps we should make Prince Orodes king and then you would be free to spend your time travelling the world freeing slaves, which you then let go.'

470

'We freed Burebista,' I told her as she shuffled from the room, 'so he could follow his own destiny.'

'I call it ingratitude,' was her parting shot.

The next day, after I had spent what seemed like an eternity listening to petitioners in the throne room, most concerning trivial bickerings that another, less tolerant ruler would have had settled with a flogging, I rode Remus down to the Palmyrene Gate so I could stand beside the stone griffin and be alone with my thoughts. That morning I had ridden him for the first time since I had returned from my travels and he had proved a handful, nearly throwing me twice in a fit of pique. It was his way of reminding me that I had been absent for too long.

'I have to be away one more time, my old friend,' I said as I stood before the griffin. 'But this time you will be coming with me.'

'They say that people who mumble to themselves are beloved of the gods.'

I recognised the voice of Dobbai behind me.

'Though I have never put much stock in that belief. Why would the gods speak to the demented, who are invariably shunned by polite society?'

She stopped beside me and sat on the stone plinth on which the griffin sat. The afternoon sun was dipping low in the west, casting the vast legionary camp in a golden glow. To the south were the royal estates, an unending strip of fields and date palms adjacent to the Euphrates disappearing into the distance. To the north was the bustling, dusty caravan park and beyond that more fields next to the mighty river.

'Do you pine to be back in the arena at Ephesus, son of Hatra?'

I turned and laughed. 'My exploits on the sand are already forgotten, I think.'

She nodded. 'While you were listening to the gibbering idiots in the throne room Gallia was amusing us on the terrace with tales of your heroics in the arena. Lucky for you that she had not forgotten her mother tongue.'

'Yes, once again she saved my hide. Looking back, it is amazing that we all escaped in one piece.'

471

She sighed. 'I told you that seven was an auspicious number. You had the favour of the gods, even if you did your best to get yourself killed.'

She ran a finger along the griffin's body. 'And you returned with some interesting individuals.'

'Athineos lost his ships and his living. The least I can do is recompense him for his loss.'

Her head snapped towards me. 'I was not talking of the pirate. You should have him flogged and banish him from the kingdom. I was speaking of the high priestess and her firebrand lover. Why are you so interested in two Greeks who should have been burnt side by side at Ephesus?'

'I see that you are in a compassionate mood today.'

'Do not try to be clever, son of Hatra, it does not suit you. Courtiers and politicians are masters at deception but you are neither so do not insult my intelligence.'

She stood and stepped closer, her black eyes examining me.

'I see vengeance in your eyes, but aside from Mithridates and Narses who else has stirred your wrath?'

I shrugged in silence.

Her haggard face twisted into a leer. 'Shall I tell you?'

I shrugged again.

'You are like that horse of yours, you never forget. Indeed, you have a tendency to bear grudges. It must have irked you enormously when Narses convinced King Tiraios to attack Uruk, and perhaps annoyed you further when Orodes informed you that Tiraios had been killed on the orders of Narses, thus denying you of the opportunity to kill him yourself.'

'Is there any point to this?'

'Do you want to know what I think?'

'Not really,' I replied.

'I think,' she said forcefully, 'that you are intent on seizing Charax for yourself and, after you have killed this Sporaces, you will install the priestess and her lover as rulers. And in so doing you will send a message to Narses that the King of Dura is not to be trifled with. Perhaps you will send the head of Sporaces to Narses to reinforce your message.'

I turned away from her to look at the red fireball that was the sun slowly disappearing in the west and said nothing.

472

'Your silence speaks volumes,' she continued.

'Narses must be shown that his actions have consequences,' I said at last. 'That force will always be met with force. He and Mithridates made a mistake in not attacking Dura while I was away, but now I am back and they will know of it.'

She chuckled. 'They never thought that you had left Parthia.'

I turned away from the west. 'Any spy worth his salt would have known that the king and queen of Dura were not in residence.'

She pointed at me. 'A veil of concealment enveloped this kingdom while you were away.'

'You did that?'

'That is what you pay me for, is it not?'

I was surprised. 'I pay you?'

'Even though I live modestly I still require monies to facilitate the safety of the empire and your kingdom, son of Hatra.'

'I thought the army did that.'

She shuffled away. 'How little you know, son of Hatra. Perhaps you should inform your two Greek playthings of the fate you have engineered for them.'

'They are free to follow their own will,' I called after her.

'Nonsense. Their fate was determined on the day they were born, as was yours.'

As I pulled on the oar in the fetid hold of the ship I wondered if I had made the right decision.

'Pull on those oars, your miserable bilge rats.

The booming voice of Athineos filled the hold and was met by dozens of groans.

'Any complaining and you will feel the lash on your backs,' he hollered.

But extra effort was almost impossible in the airless, rank hold that was filled with the sweating bodies of hundreds of men.

It was a lumbering, top-heavy warship that in its glory days might have presented an awe-inspiring sight. But now it was old and its timbers creaked alarmingly, though that was not the worst aspect of this ancient tub. It stank to high heaven. Its

473

captain and crew had been hired in Gerrha; the trading port that was a centre for shipping, slaves, incense and silk.

I had gathered Athineos, Cleon and Hippo on the palace terrace and told them of my intention to attack and seize Charax and install the young lovers as its rulers. I told Athineos that after the port was taken I would buy him a ship and a crew so he could resume his career of maritime trade.

'You cannot sail in the Mediterranean,' I said, 'the Romans will catch up with you eventually and nail you to a cross. But there are no Roman ships in the Persian Gulf or in the waters of the great Indus Ocean.'

He thought for a moment, stroked his ragged beard and then grinned mischievously. He spat in his right palm and offered me his hand.

'Done.'

I shook his hand.

Cleon was beside himself with excitement as Dobbai snoozed in her chair nearby but Hippo seemed more concerned than delighted.

'Your offer is most generous, majesty,' she said.

'You have reservations?' I enquired.

'Of course not,' Cleon answered for her. 'Charax is an ancient Greek city, I have been told. We will be among our own people and free from the Romans. What else could a man wish for?'

'I am unworthy.' Hippo whispered.

Cleon rolled his eyes and Dobbai opened hers.

'Only the gods decide who is worthy or not, child,' she said. 'You must ask yourself why you were brought here. Your goddess has not abandoned you, child, she watches over you still.'

Cleon put an arm around her waist.

'You see, the gods are with us. Dobbai speaks to them so she knows.'

Dobbai glared at him. 'I do not speak to the gods, foolish boy. They reveal certain things to me, that is all.'

'But you can work magic?' he asked.

She gave him a malicious smile. 'I have not used the old magic in an age but I can attempt to cast a spell that will

474

permanently shrivel your manhood if you would like a demonstration.'

Cleon looked uncomfortable as Hippo shook her head at him.

'Actually,' said Dobbai in a matter-of-fact fashion, 'I think the son of Hatra's scheme has merit, which is a marvel in itself.'

'You are too kind,' I said.

Dobbai settled back in her chair and closed her eyes. 'A Greek city filled with Greek temples should be ruled by Greeks. It is the natural order of things.'

So here we were, crammed into a stinking hold of a former warship, pulling on oars in the unbearable heat. The ship, a hundred and thirty feet long and with a beam of twenty-three feet, had three banks of oars on each side. Two hundred and seventy rowers pulled on lengths of wood, those on the lowest level being operated by a single rower, the middle- and top-level oars manned by two rowers each.

It was my misfortune that I was seated on a stained, sticky bench on the lowest level, seawater sloshing beneath my feet from the leaking hull. Iron rings fastened to the old timbers were mute testimonies to the slaves who had rowed the ship until only a few days ago: chains fixed to those rings and threaded through other rings attached to the ankles of the poor wretches condemned to this stinking hulk.

Athineos had hired the vessel on my behalf and had sailed it north from the 'white walled' city of Gerrha with a crew of fifteen sailors and two hundred and seventy slave rowers. The ship had a mainsail and an *artemon* in addition to its oars so propulsion was not a problem, the more so with a keen northerly wind. Malik had told me that a man could purchase anything in Gerrha, no questions asked. As long as a buyer had gold the city's authorities were not interested in what the purchase was for, which suited me fine. Athineos steered the ship north along the west coast of the Persian Gulf until he arrived at a spot in Agraci territory where a great signal fire had been lit on the beach. I was also waiting on the sand, along with four cohorts of Durans, two hundred horse archers and Gallia's Amazons. As before, when we had marched to save Uruk, the men, women and horses had been loaded on rafts and floated

475

down the Euphrates and then south to the rendezvous point on the Persian Gulf's shoreline.

Because they had missed out on the trip to Ephesus Orodes and Malik insisted on joining my mission to Charax, as did Yasser who sent a message informing me that it was considered bad manners among the Agraci to exclude friends from impending shedding of enemy blood. Drenis and Arminius behaved like spoilt children and pestered me to be included in the party of Durans going south. I submitted to their adolescent pleas just to shut them up.

Out of courtesy I informed Nergal and Praxima of my plan and they immediately wrote back informing me that they too wished to be included in the ever-increasing force that I was assembling. It was ridiculous. However, once Gallia read their missive she declared that she too would be travelling south with me, along with the Amazons who had been most upset that their queen had travelled to Ephesus without her. With the additional two hundred horse archers that I added to the force over seven hundred men and women made the journey down the Euphrates.

I had sent Surena, still flushed with his exploits at Ephesus, ahead to make contact with his Ma'adan concerning collecting intelligence regarding the defences and layout of Charax. I had asked Nergal but it seemed there was no one in the whole of Mesene who knew anything of worth about the Greek city on the Persian Gulf. I had also asked Malik to ride with Athineos south through Agraci territory all the way to Gerrha to hire a large vessel that could accommodate all our forces.

'There ain't a ship existing that can carry six hundred soldiers,' he told me as he counted out the gold pieces on the eve of his departure.

'How may men can a warship carry?' I asked.

He picked up a gold coin and bit on it. 'Two hundred, two hundred and fifty at a push.'

We were sitting in the headquarters building with Malik and Domitus, the latter with a face like thunder because I had told him that he should stay at Dura and command the army, which was his official role.

'The answer's simple,' he growled.

It wasn't to me. He sighed and rolled his eyes.

'How many rowers on a large warship.'

Athineos carefully replaced the many coins in the large leather saddlebag he had been given.

'Two hundred and seventy, give or take.'

'Then use the Durans as rowers,' said Domitus sharply. 'They are stronger and have more stamina than any half-dead galley slave.'

Athineos nodded. 'Makes sense. What shall we do with the galley slaves, though, kill them?'

'Certainly not,' I said. 'We will deal with them when you arrive at the rendezvous point with the ship.'

So he had set off with Malik and an Agraci escort, and a great deal of gold in his saddlebag. I asked Malik to stick close to our Cretan friend who might be tempted to abscond with my gold before he reached Gerrha. But he did not and when he and the ship arrived at the point two hundred miles north of the city after three days at sea, I decided to have the slaves taken back to Dura. They would stay with the hundred horse archers detailed to guard the horses while we were at Charax, either that or take their chances fleeing west into the desert. Weak, emaciated and half-starved, they decided to await our return.

Nergal and Praxima joined us at Uruk along with a bodyguard of fifty horse archers. They also brought an abundance of food and fodder from the city's warehouses to supplement our own rations.

I now had Nergal's long legs above me as I pulled on my oar as Athineos steered us towards Charax. Sitting next to him was Malik, with Orodes and Yasser above them.

'This is most bracing,' said Orodes as he heaved at his oar.

'I tell you what, prince,' shouted Drenis directly behind him, 'to make you feel at home we'll shave your head, shackle your leg to the hull so you have to relieve yourself where you sit, feed you watery slop twice a day and lash your back at regular intervals.'

Orodes ignored his sarcastic comment but those soldiers around him burst into laughter. A few of them, now highly trained soldiers in my army, had been former galley slaves and bore lash marks on their backs. But those backs were now broad and strong as they pulled on the oars that propelled our aged ship towards Charax.

It was the beginning of autumn now but still fiercely hot and though on deck there was a welcome wind, in the hold it was airless. So we sat in our loincloths only, our weapons and armour stacked on deck where the archers kept watch for enemy vessels.

Surena had returned from his reconnaissance mission with news that a mud-brick wall that had round towers at regular intervals along its length encompassed Charax, but reported no defences on the seaward side. That was because in all its history it had never been assaulted from the Persian Gulf. That was about to change.

Athineos steered our top-heavy and leaking ship into a shallow bay a few miles from Charax on the evening before our assault, the rowers taking the opportunity to escape the foetid hold and sleep beneath the palm trees beyond the sandy beach. I forbade the lighting of fires lest the garrison or any fishing vessels observed their glow, not that there was any need for warmth. The temperature decreased slightly during the night but it was still very mild. Guards were posted but Surena assured me that the only people who inhabited this area were either mad or fleeing from justice. It was too close to Charax for the Ma'adan to establish settlements, the Greek inhabitants of the city having a hostile attitude to the people of the marshlands.

I sat with Gallia, Nergal and Praxima on the beach as the sun disappeared in the west and a pale grey moon appeared in a starlit sky. Durans sat around sharpening their swords and horse archers checked their quivers and bowstrings. Praxima and Gallia were chatting away like a pair of young girls, remembering their exploits in Italy and their subsequent time together in Parthia before Praxima had become the Queen of Mesene. Nergal, though, appeared withdrawn.

'Something troubles you, my friend?' I said.

His gangly legs were drawn up so his chin was resting on his knees.

'Narses can send soldiers to attack Charax at any time, Pacorus.'

478

He turned and tilted his head to where Surena, Viper, Cleon and Hippo sat in a group on the sand, engaging in jovial conversation.

'They will be in danger.'

'Cleon raised a small army in Ephesus,' I told him, 'right under the noses of the Romans. Narses made a mistake killing Tiraios and his family and installing one of his men as ruler of Charax. That will have alienated the people, or so I hope.'

'You took a great risk going to Ephesus, Pacorus.'

'You are right,' I agreed, 'but I had to go to see if Burebista still lived.'

He nodded. 'And the gods smiled on your curiosity. What was it like being back in a Roman city?'

I thought for a moment. 'Like I did not belong. They are still as cruel and pompous as when we were fighting in Italy. Nothing changes as far as Rome is concerned.'

'Nothing except the extent of the territory they control,' he said grimly. 'Burebista should have returned with you to Parthia.'

'He wanted to be among his own race. He had a Dacian wife and his countrymen were preparing for another war with Rome, together with their Thracian allies. At the end of the day we all must choose our own destiny.'

'And those we wish to die among,' he remarked sombrely.

'Do not worry about what Narses might or not do regarding Charax,' I said. 'When civil war resumes in the empire his hands will be full dealing with events elsewhere.'

'When will that be, Pacorus?' asked Praxima, who had been listening to our conversation.

'Soon, I hope,' I said. 'My army is itching to get to Ctesiphon.'

'Mesene will stand with you,' said Nergal.

I placed a hand on his shoulder. 'I know that, my friend.'

We all turned on hearing raucous laughter behind us.

Praxima tilted her head towards Surena. 'Gallia told me he covered himself in glory at Ephesus.'

'He did,' I agreed. 'Dobbai says that he is destined for great things.'

479

'If he manages to stay alive,' said Gallia. 'His recklessness is breath-taking at times.'

'The gods favour the bold,' I said.

At least I hoped they did for I was relying on their help to assist me in the assault on Charax. I had learned that to succeed war plans needed to be as simple as possible because when implemented they had an alarming tendency to fall to pieces within the first few minutes. So the idea was to sail into Charax's harbour, destroy the soldiers sent by Narses and install Cleon and Hippo as the city's new rulers. Simple.

We would be assaulting a city that I knew nothing about but fortunately Athineos, in his sober moments, had thought of this and had purchased a papyrus map of the layout of Charax. He now laid it out on the small table in the cabin, which in truth smelt almost as bad as the hold. I stood with Gallia, Nergal and Praxima plus the four centurions, including Drenis and Arminius, and the commanders of the horse archers crowded round the table. It was just after dawn and the temperature was rising rapidly.

Athineos picked his nose and pointed at the map.

'Straightforward layout, as you all can see. The harbour leads to all the public buildings that are in the centre of the city, surrounded by streets and side streets crossing each other at right angles.'

I pointed at the area containing the public buildings. 'So what is here?'

Athineos screwed up his face. 'Temples, squares, shops and the theatre, like the one at Ephesus.'

'Where is the citadel, the fort that houses the garrison?' asked Nergal.

'There isn't one,' replied Athineos. 'I heard there is a palace of some sort near the temples but most of the garrison are housed in the towers along the wall.'

'And what size is the garrison?' I probed.

He shrugged. 'No idea.'

'Once ashore we will seize the *agora*,' I told them all. 'Tell your men not to damage any buildings or harm any civilians.'

'If they get in the way that might not be possible, majesty,' remarked a tall, athletic centurion.

'Once the fighting starts the civilians will scatter like frightened sheep,' I told them. 'All we will have to do is wait for the enemy to show their faces.'

They showed no concern, and with good reason. They knew, as did I, that many Parthian kings regarded foot soldiers as little more than expendable slaves. Palace guards protected a ruler and his family in his capital and when he went to war he did so accompanied by cataphracts and horse archers, the latter raised from among the kingdom's farmers and city dwellers. The aristocracy and their sons provided a kingdom's cataphracts, but only a few kingdoms, the wealthiest, could afford to have large numbers of full-time cataphracts and horse archers. Hatra was one and Dura was another. But I knew that Narses would have sent only foot soldiers to garrison Charax, poorly trained and equipped troops who were expendable, more suited to terrorising civilians than fighting the foot soldiers of Dura.

We sat at our oars in the cloying heat and rowed slowly. Today we wore our uniforms: every legionary in his tunic, mail shirt, sword belt, sandals and helmet. The leather vests had been left at Dura. The shields were stacked in the passageway next to the rowing stations ready to be used once the journey was over. There was no jovial banter today, no well-intentioned ribbing or raucous laughter. Every man was focused on his task. But it was hot, so mercilessly hot as we sat, sweated and pulled on the oars. Fortunately there was a fair wind that filled the sails and hastened us towards our destination, though we did not feel the benefit of it below deck. The Amazons and dismounted horse archers above checked their quivers and bowstrings. They had three of the former and two of the latter, each quiver holding thirty arrows. The missiles had three-winged bronze heads and three flight feathers – eighteen thousand arrows in total. Nergal's fifty archers were also equipped with three full quivers, Praxima informing me that they had been chosen because they were the best bowmen in the whole of Mesene.

'Not as good as me, of course,' their queen had told me, 'but above average shots.'

The spirits of the Amazons were very high now that their former commander was back with them, Gallia also filled with a

481

steely determination to get the task done. All I wanted to do was get out of this infernal hull as rivulets of sweat ran down the side of my face onto my neck. Orodes, dressed in his magnificent silver scale cuirass, must have been close to passing out as the first hour at the oars passed. At least my black leather cuirass was relatively light. I slipped into a sort of semi-conscious daze as I pulled on my oar, everyone around me similarly immersed in befuddlement. This is what it must be like for galley slaves: worked like dogs day in, day out, rowing for hours at a time with no hope of relief or rescue. The others must have felt the same as me: battle would be welcome compared to this living hell.

'Charax in sight.'

The deep voice of Athineos shook us out of our semi-consciousness. Suddenly the air crackled with a palpable sense of anticipation laced with excitement. At once the oar strokes were crisper as men gripped the wood more firmly. I heard shuffling on deck and the patter of boots coming down steps as archers carrying ladles of water sated the thirst of those on the benches. Today the legionaries would be carrying no *furca*, no water bottle and no javelins. They would be going into Charax light, as would the archers. The *gladius* and the bow were our weapons but speed and surprise would be our allies.

I drank from the ladle held at my mouth by Gallia, whose hair was tied in a long plait hanging down the back of her neck beneath her helmet, the cheek guards of the latter hiding her features. Other Amazons stood behind me to give succour to Orodes, Malik and the others. Malik was wrapped in his black Agraci robes, as was Yasser, the latter relishing the coming fight. This was immediately imminent as a sailor descended the steps and shouted the captain's orders.

'Captain says we will dock in a quarter of an hour. So gentle strokes only.'

The pace maker at the stern, a pot-bellied jowly man with a cruel leer, reduced the number of strokes per minute on the hide surface of his kettledrum. Our instinct was to quicken our strokes to get to the target more speedily, but he gave us evil stares as he banged his drum with what seemed like very long intervals between each strike. The archers disappeared back on

482

deck as the minutes passed and then another order reached our ears.

'Stop rowing. Pull in the oars.'

We shipped the oars, the pace maker stopped banging his drum and we all stood as the ship glided towards the wharf. Because it was a warship and as we were not unloading anything, or at least that is what the port authorities believed, we approached the docks prow first. We carried no markings aside from the two eyes painted on the sides of the hull at the prow. The garrison, alerted that an unidentified warship was docking, would send soldiers to assemble on the wharf before we had docked but that was fine: the more we killed at the docks the less to fight later.

Men wished each other good luck and clutched their lucky talismans before securing their helmet straps, drawing their swords and gripping the handles of their shields. Drenis, Arminius and the other two centurions had whistles around their necks.

'You all know your orders,' said Drenis, the senior centurion present, 'so listen for the commands and keep formation. You've fought the soldiers of Mithridates and Narses before and know how soft they are. But resist the temptation to chase after them when they flee.'

Confident laughter filled the hold as the ship came to a halt. I slapped Arminius on the arm and walked to the steps, Orodes, Nergal, Malik and Yasser following. Stepping on deck was most refreshing, a gentle wind blowing in from the sea and the air, though warm, markedly better than the stench of the hold. I turned to nod at Athineos manning the rudders at the stern and walked towards the prow where two sailors had thrown ropes to waiting dockers who secured them to wooden posts. Other sailors pushed two gangplanks from either side of the prow towards the wooden wharf.

'State your business,' shouted the man I assumed to be the commander of ten of Narses' men, the soldiers behind him wearing baggy yellow leggings and red tunics, leather caps and armed with thrusting spears. Our old enemies from Sakastan. The commander had a sword at his hip and wore a leather scale cuirass and helmet. The ox hide shields of his men were painted with the bird-god, symbol of their master. How I hated that motif.

'I'm waiting,' the commander called as the gangplanks were fixed in place and I walked to the top of one of them.

'I think that is your signal, ladies,' I said loudly.

The Sakastani commander looked at me quizzically as two arrows thudded into his chest. He collapsed as Gallia, Praxima and several Amazons stood at the prow and shot down the other soldiers as I calmly walked down the gangplank in the company of Orodes, Nergal, Malik and Yasser, the latter two armed with curved swords and carrying small round, black shields.

As soon as the last enemy soldiers had either been shot or had fled for their lives there were whistle blasts and the ship's occupants began to pour down the gangplanks. Gallia, Praxima and the Amazons ran forward to provide a defensive screen as Drenis, Arminius and the other centurions marshalled their centuries. Those enemy soldiers wounded but still living were finished off by Yasser who went among them with a satisfied grin, lopping off their heads with expert swings of his sword. The other hundred horse archers ran down the gangplanks and formed up behind the Durans as I led the charge into the city.

We ran along the wharf, sailors and dockers scattering before us, some throwing themselves into the muddy brown water of the harbour to avoid the phalanx of soldiers racing towards them. The harbour itself was large but not packed with shipping, testament to Charax's fading fortunes as a port. We reached the main storehouses – mud-brick structures painted white with tiled roofs – and then headed into the city itself. It was difficult to estimate its size as we trotted long a dirt road that led towards the centre of the sprawl of mud-brick buildings, but it appeared to be smaller than Dura.

Nergal's fifty archers were left on the ship to guard it and secure Hippo who had been left in the care of Athineos. When I had told him of my plan to assault Charax he was unimpressed but as he had been paid a king's ransom for his services went along with it.

'Don't worry,' I had told him, 'if anything goes wrong you will be able to make your escape on the ship.'

'And who is going to row it out of the harbour, great king,' he remarked sarcastically, 'fifty archers and a high priestess?'

I had smiled at him. 'Then you had better pray that my plan works, Athineos.'

Our target was the *agora*, the ancient place where all freeborn Greek citizens gathered to hear civic announcements, muster for war or debate politics. It was also the place where traders and craftsmen conducted their business, though today when over three hundred mailed soldiers and two hundred archers appeared in their midst they ran for their lives. Most had already packed up their wares before we had arrived, our presence having been announced by the screams of alarmed women and the wailing of their children. The *agora* itself was a large square patch of hard-packed dirt, its northern and western sides enclosed by a peristyle. We had entered the Greek square on its open, eastern side that led to the temple complex housing the sanctuaries of Apollo Delphinios, the patron of sailors and ships, and Nike. On the southern side of the *agora* was the *prytaneion*, which many people fled to on our arrival.

There were more whistle blasts and the centuries deployed into square formation: each century taking a side of the square and deploying into four ranks, each one of twenty men. Behind each century stood fifty archers. Around the *agora* stood abandoned stalls, and on the iron-hard dirt smashed pots and a handful of sandals. A stray dog peered around one of the stone columns of the peristyle, cocked its leg, barked and then scampered off. The doors of the *prytaneion* were slammed shut and an eerie silence hung over the *agora*. I stood in the centre of the square with Nergal, Orodes, Malik and Yasser, the latter looking around at the seemingly empty city.

'Perhaps they have fled, Pacorus.'

'I think not,' I answered, 'beyond the walls of this city there is nothing save a patchwork of fields and beyond them marshlands. There is nowhere to flee to.'

The legionaries rested their shields on the ground as they stared ahead, swords in hand, ready for the coming fight. Behind them the archers sat on the dirt, out of sight.

'Perhaps we should find the palace,' suggested Orodes, his scale armour cuirass looking like polished silver in the bright sunlight, his helmet also shining.

I shook my head. 'This is the spiritual heart of the city, is that not correct, Cleon?'

Our young Greek firebrand, attired in a mail shirt and carrying a Duran shield sporting red griffin wings, nodded curtly. His love had wanted to accompany us but I had said no; I only wanted those who could fight to be standing with me this day. I smiled when I caught site of Praxima's red hair poking out from beneath her helmet, sitting next to Gallia. Now there was a woman who could fight.

'We should fire some of these buildings,' said an impatient Yasser, 'to smoke them out.'

Patience was never a virtue rated highly among the Agraci.

'It will not be long now, have patience,' I said.

The sound of distant shouts and chanting resulted in a ripple of tension shooting through the legionaries and archers. The former immediately lifted their shields without being commanded while the latter pulled arrows from the quivers they had placed on the ground and casually nocked them in their bowstrings. But they remained seated.

Then the enemy appeared at last.

They poured into the *agora* from the northeast corner, a great mass of Sakastani warriors brightly dressed in yellow leggings and red tunics. Some carried great two-handed axes that could cleave a man in two with a single mighty swing; others were armed with curved swords similar to those carried by Yasser and Malik. But the majority were spearmen armed with a thrusting weapon that had a large, leaf-shaped blade and hoisting a wicker shield covered with ox hide. The latter offered good protection, with several layers of bull's hide being glued to the wicker inner side. Many had leather caps for head protection that might deflect a glancing blow but would not stop an arrow or determined sword thrust.

There were hundreds of them, flanking left and right to fill the northern and western sides of the *agora* and then the southern side in front of the *prytaneion*. More and more came from the northeast to fill the eastern side of the square and

486

completely surround us, the distance between the horde of red and yellow and each side of our square being less than fifty paces. As the Durans stood silent in their ranks there was some frantic shuffling among our opponents as the axe men were shoved to the fore to face the legionaries, ready to attack and hack us to pieces.

'Now!' I shouted.

The four centurions blew their whistles and as one the legionaries kneeled, at the same time the archers rising to their feet to shoot at the closely packed ranks of the enemy. The Amazons and horse archers aimed at the faces of the enemy, all maintaining a steady shooting rate of five arrows a minute – fifty arrows every twelve seconds being loosed from each side of our defensive square and over the heads of the legionaries. Two hundred and fifty arrows each minute striking eyes, noses, teeth and necks. A thousand bronze-tipped missiles every sixty seconds in total. The result was a continuous and horrifying high-pitched squealing sound that reverberated around the *agora* as hundreds of men were struck by arrows.

The lucky ones died.

Arrowheads sliced through eyes and necks to pierce brains and windpipes, other missiles went through men's mouths, the points emerging from the back of their throats. In two minutes the archers had loosed two thousand arrows and the Sakastanis had had enough. The first to break were those on the open, eastern side of the *agora* who promptly turned tail and ran. Those on the southern side, in front of the *prytaneion*, promptly fell back into the courtyard of the latter, their commanders frantically trying to erect a shield wall between the columns of the portico. They succeeded, though not before arrows had felled dozens more. The Sakastanis that filled the western and northern sides of the *agora* made their way towards the eastern side, those with shields being shoved by irate commanders into the front to form a shield wall to protect the rest. But they tripped over dead and dying men as they inched their way towards safety, the archers taking their time to find targets. Their rate of shooting decreased markedly but their aim was still accurate and almost every arrow found flesh.

After four minutes the enemy had departed the *agora* and I ordered the archers to cease shooting. All that was left was the miserable sounds of men whimpering and groaning and the sight of bodies twitching and jerking among those that were absolutely still.

'Scan the rooftops,' I shouted, pointing at the tiles of the peristyle, 'look out for enemy archers.'

There was no movement on the roof but there was a loud smashing noise coming from the *prytaneion*. Between the columns the row of shields was still in place but behind it troops were desperately trying to smash down the doors to the city's main function hall.

'What now?' asked Yasser, staring admiringly at the dead that carpeted the ground around our square.

'Now we finish what we came for,' I said. 'Prepare to march.'

The centurions blew their whistles and the legionaries snapped shields to their sides. At the *prytaneion* the row of enemy shields melted away as the desperate soldiers behind them finally forced the doors and gained entry to the hall.

'You let them go, Pacorus?' asked Orodes.

'If we get to the palace and kill or capture Sporaces then they will lay down their weapons readily enough, my friend.'

'It would be preferable to kill him,' remarked Yasser.

We moved out of the square at speed, the archers deployed outside the square on all sides to shoot any enemy stragglers or enemy bowmen lying in wait. There were none. We marched through the temple quarter, through the Sanctuary of Apollo Delphinios, a marvellous open-air enclosure with an altar in the centre and surrounded on three sides by a portico. The sanctuary was empty but the enclosure was littered with discarded shields that showed the path the Sakastanis had taken. We followed the trail, passing the Temple of Nike, a colonnaded structure constructed on an artificial terrace and accessible via two rows of steps on its north and south sides.

Beyond the Temple of Nike, on a stretch of brown dirt in front of the squat and rather austere palace, stood a phalanx of soldiers. Most were from Sakastan but in the centre was a small block of soldiers wearing bronze scale armour, bronze helmets with yellow plumes and carrying rectangular wicker shields, on which had been painted Simurgel motifs. Obviously from Persis, they were armed with thrusting spears and attired in black tunics and leggings. They presented a most professional appearance but there were few of them, perhaps a hundred at most.

I did not have to issue any orders as Arminius, Drenis and the two other centurions barked their commands and the centuries deployed into attack formation. Each one formed into eight ranks, each one of ten legionaries. A hundred archers moved to stand behind the centuries while the Amazons split into two groups to cover our flanks. Gallia commanded one flank, Praxima the other. The latter was having the time of her life back among those she had commanded.

I wandered to stand in front of my men, Nergal, Orodes, Malik and Yasser accompanying me. Across no-man's land a figure also pushed his way through the enemy ranks, a man mountain with a wild beard and thick black hair. His head appeared too small perched on his over-sized shoulders, as did the sword with a curved blade that he held in his bear-like paw.

'I would speak with your commander,' he bellowed in a deep voice.

'Tell your archers to kill him first,' advised Yasser, licking his lips at the prospect of more slaughter.

I walked forward a few paces. 'Who dares to address the conquerors of Charax?'

Behind me the legionaries rapped their *gladius* hilts on the inside of their shields.

Narses' human mountain took several steps forward, his huge boot-encased feet kicking up dust as he did so.

'I am Sporaces, lord of Charax and loyal servant of High King Narses.'

He too was dressed in black, indicating that like the soldiers similarly attired behind him he was also from Persis.

I walked closer to him, my sword in its scabbard while he brandished his weapon.

'*High King* Narses? Has he murdered Mithridates just as Mithridates murdered his own father?'

He looked at me with callous brown eyes. 'Do you have a name?'

'It is customary,' I said casually, 'that when two commanders meet neither unsheathe their swords, which not only could be interpreted as a threat but is also most impolite.'

He sniffed contemptuously but did slide his sword back in its scabbard.

I smiled at him and removed my helmet. 'I am Pacorus, King of Dura, son of King Varaz of Hatra and sworn enemy of Mithridates and Narses.'

'King Pacorus,' he growled. 'So, you are the king killer I have heard so much about. I had been told that you had the biggest balls in all Parthia but you are smaller and thinner than I thought you would be.'

'That is because you are taller and fatter than you should be,' I replied. 'What do you want?'

He stepped back a couple of paces and spread his arms.

'What do I want, king killer?' he shouted loudly so everyone could hear. 'I wish to challenge you to single combat so we can fight man to man, as in the old days, to decide which of us will rule this miserable collection of mud huts.'

His men cheered and raised their weapons as the Durans and archers opposite remained silent.

Sporaces pointed at me. 'So what is to be, Pacorus of Dura, will you show the world that you are a man or will you hide among your warriors with your sword sleeping in its scabbard?'

He was perhaps nine inches taller than me, probably weighed twice as much and his long arms would give him a greater sword reach. But I was fast and agile and big men carrying too much bulk always tired quickly in a fight. Besides, I was Pacorus of Dura, former Lord High General of the Empire, and had never lost a battle. I did not intend to do so now.

'I accept your challenge,' I said quietly.

He moved towards me, a gesture interpreted as a threat by Gallia and Praxima who had walked forward from their respective wings to stand less than twenty paces behind me. They pulled back their bowstrings and aimed their arrows at Sporaces.

The big man was outraged. 'What's this? Has Pacorus of Dura no control over his soldiers?'

I turned and angrily gestured for my wife and her friend to lower their bows. Sporaces grunted and removed his massive scale armour cuirass, a thick coat of hide on which had been

490

stitched overlapping rectangles of iron. He shouted at one of his men who sprinted forward and caught the armour as Sporaces threw it to him. Narses' pet looked at me.

'I will give you five minutes to say your goodbyes to your men.'

He walked back to his troops who began shouting and cheering once more. I ambled back to Orodes and gave him my helmet. Gallia and Praxima ran to join me.

'This is a bad idea, Pacorus,' said the prince.

'We can shoot them to pieces,' urged Gallia. 'He knows his position is a weak one, that's why he challenged you.'

'Gallia is right, Pacorus,' said Nergal. 'The archers can win this battle on their own.'

I beckoned Surena forward and handed him my leather cuirass when he arrived.

'Let me fight him, lord,' he grinned. 'I fought bigger men than him in the arena.'

Gallia rolled her eyes as Praxima pointed at Sporaces.

'I can put an arrow through his eye from here. Just give me the command.'

Suddenly Drenis and Arminius had joined us, both shaking their heads.

'He's even bigger than Acco,' observed Drenis, 'and you know how that ended.'

'You are a great king and warlord, Pacorus,' said Arminius, 'but you're no brawler.'

'Enough!' I commanded. 'I would remind you that I am your king, not your slave. It is reassuring that you think so little of me that you believe I cannot defeat that big barrel of blubber. Just because he is fat bastard you think he has supernatural powers. But he will tire quickly in this heat and big men are slow and unwieldy.'

I looked at Drenis. 'He's bigger than Acco, you are right. But Acco was trained for the arena and this idiot only knows how to butcher and torture unarmed civilians. The fight will be over in the blink of an eye.'

I unbuckled my belt and handed it to Surena, all of them cowered into a sullen silence. Even Gallia was, for once, lost for words. She knew, as did the others, that we stood before our soldiers and it was unseemly for leaders to bicker in front of those they led. I pulled off my sweat drenched tunic and handed it to Surena, pulled my sword from its scabbard and cut the air with it. Orodes stepped forward and offered me his hand.

'Shamash be with you, my friend.'

Nergal and Praxima embraced me while Malik and Yasser slapped me on the back. Drenis and Arminius wished me good luck, trying to be optimistic as they did so. Gallia pulled off her helmet so I could kiss her on the lips.

'Come back to me,' she whispered.

I looked into her blue eyes. 'I always come back.'

Then I went to rid the world of Sporaces.

The two sets of soldiers focused their attention on us as Sporaces cut the air with his sword. His black tunic was like a tent so vast was his frame but I comforted myself with knowing that I was quicker than him. He stopped slashing the air with his weapon and gazed down at me.

'When I butcher you, king killer, I will allow your soldiers to depart Charax. I am a man of mercy. I will give you a quick, merciful death and I will allow your men their lives, so merciful am I. You agree to these terms?'

I laughed. 'You know that my archers can cut down your men where they stand, just as they did in the *agora*. And my swordsmen can slice up what is left. But I tell you this, Sporaces, when you are lying dead on this parched earth I too will show mercy and allow your miserable soldiers to crawl back to Persis.'

The boasting and insults were all part of a dreary, pre-battle ritual that many men took delight in but I found tiresome. I gripped my *spatha* tightly and looked up at the burning sun in a cloudless sky, asking for Shamash's protection in the coming duel. Out of the corner of my eye I caught sight of small groups of civilians, curious men and women a few hundred paces away that had ventured from their homes or temples to see what was happening. They would have seen two groups of soldiers standing motionless a hundred paces apart, with two individuals at the centre point of no-man's land also not moving.

'The time for talking is over,' growled Sporaces who stepped forward and swung his sword at my head.

I jumped back and then leaped to the left as he came at me with a whirl of sword strikes. Alarm coursed through me as I realised that not only was he very fast with his sword strokes but also amazingly light on his feet. I ducked, feinted left and right and tried to dance around him in an effort to avoid the scything sword strikes, but every time I thought I had out-manoeuvred him he deftly pounced to reposition himself to face me. I thrust my *spatha* forward but he nimbly jumped back before aiming an overhead blow at my head that I avoided with difficulty, ducking down and to the left and feeling the rush of air against my right ear as his blade missed me by a hair's breadth.

I slashed at his mid-rift but his blade parried mine and brushed it aside. In an instant he flicked his wrist to deliver a wicked back-slash that cut my silk vest and drew blood. There was a groan from the ranks of the Durans and archers as I retreated a few steps and the Sakastanis cheered at their leader having drawn first blood. I ignored the noise and comforted myself with the fact that Sporaces, for all his aplomb with a sword, would soon tire.

Except that he didn't. In order to gain an advantage I launched my own series of attacks, delivering a succession of controlled strikes aimed at inflicting a debilitating wound on Sporaces that would slow him down. But he parried each strike with his sword, either that or moved his great bulk aside or backwards so that I struck only air. The result was that I ended up panting with sweat running down my face. It ran into my eyes, stinging them, as Sporaces screamed and came at me again, trying to slice open my legs with downward strikes or cut deep into my head and shoulders with overhead blows. I caught one of the latter on the flat of my blade and held his weapon momentarily, before he punched me in the face with his left fist.

I staggered back, pain like red-hot needles shooting through my brain as blood began to pour from my broken nose. I shook my head to regain my sight as Sporaces turned to his men and roared. The soldiers roared back at him in triumph, while from the Durans there was only stunned silence. I felt sick and weak and knew that my life would be over unless I could extricate myself from this dire predicament.

493

Sporaces was more confident now, circling me like a lion hunts a wounded prey. His face and neck were smeared with sweat but his breathing was not as laboured as mine and he had no blood on his clothes. He suddenly sprang forward, his sword point aimed at my belly. I leaped back, brushed aside his blade with my *spatha* and flicked the latter back to cut Sporaces' chest. But like a cat he sprang back so my blade missed and then ran forward, raised his knee and smashed it into the side of my ribcage. The blow sent me sprawling to the ground and caused me to let go of my sword. A sharp pain went through my left side and I grimaced as I attempted to haul myself up. I was momentarily blinded as the sun glinted off something bright and shone into my eyes.

I blinked, spat dirt from my mouth and saw that Sporaces was standing over my sword. The sun glinted off something again. It was Orodes' silver scale cuirass.

Sporaces smiled, placed a boot under my *spatha* and flicked it up towards me. I reached out to catch the grip and winced as pain tortured my left side.

'*Strike when the silver man glitters.*'

I heard Julia's words as clearly as though she was standing beside me. I laughed because it was laughable. My pride had led me to this point. I had thought to emulate Spartacus and been found wanting and now I faced my just punishment. The sun caught Orodes' armour once again.

'How many signs do you want, Pacorus?'

It was his voice behind me. The man I had followed and loved like a brother. I spun round to see him but there was no one. I gripped my sword and understood. I turned to face Sporaces, who in his conviction that he had defeated me was more measured in his movements. He casually stepped forward as I ducked left and slashed at his hamstring. He avoided the blow with ease but it turned him. And I turned him again when I sprang forward and once more tried to slash at the back of his legs, the swing weak as strength drained from me. I was unsteady on my feet. He began laughing at my miserable attempts to wound him, turning once more as the sun reflected off Orodes' cuirass and into Sporaces' eyes. He squinted and was, for a second, blinded. But a second was all I needed as I summoned my last reserves of strength and hurled myself

494

forward, grasping my *spatha* with both hands, putting all my weight behind the thrust. The point smashed a rib as the blade entered Sporaces' chest to move down into his lung and guts.

I moaned with pain as I fell to the ground, Sporaces standing over me. But he did not move. Like a statue he was perfectly still, most of my sword embedded in his body. I staggered to my feet as the Durans, Amazons and horse archers gave a mighty cheer and the Sakastanis fell silent.

I collapsed at the same time that Sporaces hit the ground, catching sight of a figure attired as a Thracian gladiator standing on the dirt as I lapsed into semi-consciousness. I tried to speak as he clasped his *sica* to his chest in salute. The bronze helmet hid his face but I swore I recognised the frame and the stance.

'Lord,' I whispered as Orodes rushed to my side as a debilitating weakness and nausea embraced me. I looked up at him as I felt myself sinking into unconsciousness.

'The enemy are to be spared their lives and sent back to Persis,' I mumbled before all was dark.

I awoke in a spacious, airy room that had white painted walls and ceiling. Gallia was holding my hand and seated beside the bed as feeling began to return to my body.

She smiled, leaned over and kissed me on the cheek.

'How are you feeling?'

'Like I have been trampled on by a herd of bulls.'

My chest and belly were bandaged and a dressing had been applied to my nose, which felt very sore.

'The doctors say that you will make a full recovery,' she told me, 'though you will be sore for a few weeks.'

She shook her head. 'You should have let us shoot the enemy to pieces. Ephesus should have taught you that you are not a gladiator. You are lucky to be alive. The gods must have been watching over you.'

'Someone was watching over me,' I smiled, grimacing as I disturbed my broken rib.

We stayed a week in Charax, during which time the enemy soldiers were repatriated back to Persis, minus their weapons and armour. As I recovered in the palace I received a delegation from members of the city council, or what was left of them following the rule of Sporaces. A lean, severe man named Patreus had been elected by them to be city leader. After

495

he had conveyed the people's gratitude for rescuing them from the despotism of Sporaces, he informed me that Charax would no longer be ruled by kings, either home-grown or sent from abroad.

'We will revert to the ancient Greek system of *demokratia*,' he told me.

We were both seated in a rather splendid reception room in the north of the palace, overlooking a well-tended garden of miniature date palms arranged in rows. I sipped at a cup of wine.

'What is *demokratia*?' I enquired.

'An ancient system whereby the city's citizens meet to elect their leaders.'

I laughed, causing a sharp pain in my ribs. 'What a strange idea.'

'It is one of our most cherished ideals,' he said, 'the idea that free Greeks shall choose their leaders and their destiny.'

I had no knowledge of this *demokratia* but I knew what it was to be free and enslaved and in all conscience I could not deny the people of Charax that which I held most dear. So my plan regarding Cleon and Hippo was in tatters and the people of the city would elect their own supreme commander, which turned out to be Patreus. I also discovered that the ancient Greek notion of freedom was very qualified, only freemen being allowed to choose their leaders; women, foreigners and slaves being forbidden to vote. After his election I visited Patreus and managed to convince him to make Cleon and Hippo citizens of the city. I had told them that they were welcome to return with me to Dura but they were both besotted with Charax, a city of free Greeks far from the Romans, and so they stayed.

As did Athineos. Like the pirate he was he managed to sell the warship he had purchased, with my money at Gerrha, to the city authorities, assuring them that with minor repairs it could be the flagship of the Charaxian navy. With the profit he made he purchased a merchant vessel and named her *The Cretan*. I went to see him on the day we left. He stood on the deck of his new ship and wore a mischievous grin as he shook my hand.

'The last time we said farewell to each other,' he said, 'you were a fugitive and I was a successful captain. Now you are a king and I am living on my wits.'

I looked around at the splendid vessel and its pristine mainsail. 'I'm sure you will survive, Athineos.'

He smiled, a glint in his eye. 'So am I.'

Patreus provided ships to transport us to the west to collect our horses and other horse archers. Athineos waved to us as he stood on the gunwale of his ship the day we departed, Cleon and Hippo beside him. Charax was bathed in brilliant sunshine as we left, a city seemingly from another era that had done away with kingship forever. As it became smaller on the horizon Orodes joined me at the gunwale.

'Are you disappointed, Pacorus?'

'Disappointed?'

'About Cleon and Hippo not being the rulers of Charax?'

'They are both happy,' I said, 'deliriously so. Who am I to deny them their desires? It was my wish that they should rule Charax, not theirs. Some battles cannot be won.'

I turned away from the sea. 'By the way, my thanks for saving my skin.'

He looked at me blankly.

'Your cuirass, Orodes, it shone in the sun and blinded my adversary to allow me to strike with my last reserves of strength.'

He smiled but looked back towards Charax. 'Do you think the city will survive, Pacorus, with no king to rule over it?'

'I hope so, my friend, but I have to say that this system they have, this democracy, is most strange.'

'They allow the people to choose their leaders.'

I shook my head. 'Imagine that, the people of a kingdom electing their rulers. It will never catch on, of course.'

Yasser wanted to kill the slaves that had been consuming our rations as they awaited our return, but I told him that I would offer them sanctuary at Dura as free men. They accepted but it made our journey north a long one. When we reached Uruk we stayed in the city for a week so the former rowers could rebuild their strength. It was decided to utilise their skills and let them row their way up the Euphrates in boats while we resumed our journey on horseback. Yasser was still complaining that they would abscond without any guards and overseers as we bid him farewell by the blue waters of the river. But none did and so they either joined Dura's army or became farmers. Gallia and Praxima had a tearful farewell, the latter embracing every Amazon before we crossed the Euphrates to ride north along the western riverbank back to Dura.

Cleon kept in contact with me for years. He immediately offered his services to the city as a soldier, his enthusiasm ensuring he rapidly ascended through the ranks. He eventually rose to command the army he had been instrumental in creating. He and Hippo had three children, a daughter and two sons. They called the daughter Ephesia.

He also kept me informed of what Athineos was up to. True to form the Cretan found the waters of the Persian Gulf much to his liking: full of business opportunities and devoid of Romans. Cleon wrote me that Athineos ended up owning a small flotilla of merchant vessels and had told him and Hippo that he had purchased a map from an old sorcerer in Gerrha that showed the location of an island overflowing with gold. Located off the coast of Africa, he had set out in *The Cretan* intent on discovering this fabled isle and bringing back a ship filled with riches.

No one ever saw him again.

Epilogue

Claudia put the last scroll of papyrus down on the table and leaned back in the wicker chair. It was perhaps two hours before dawn and very still. The flames of oil lamps did not flicker on their stands around the terrace or on the table that had provided the illumination to allow her to read her father's tale. Even though he had died only recently the events of his life seemed like a distant age to her, a more violent age. And yet her parents had been happy in each other's company and in her childhood Dura had always been a place of safety and reassuring strength. She smiled when she thought of Haytham and his son Malik, the Agraci leaders who had struck terror in the minds of Parthians who lived east of the Euphrates but who had been like a father and uncle to her.

She picked up the silver statuette of the Goddess Artemis that her mother had purchased in Ephesus all those years ago. Intricately wrought, it was one of the few possessions of Queen Gallia that she possessed, aside from her sword, bow and a torc that had been given to her by a dying Gaul. Her mother had never been one for riches or property and did not even possess a crown when she and her father had ruled Dura.

Still clutching the statuette she stood and walked to the door that led to the throne room, the guards that had stood sentry on the terrace escorting her as she walked through her palace. In the silent throne room she halted and stared at the griffin standard that hung on the wall. Vagharsh, the first standard bearer to have carried it, now long dead, had once told her when she was a young girl that the banner had been created by the gods and had been carried to Dobbai by a real griffin before it came to Dura. He also told her that it was only on loan and that one day the gods would send a griffin to take it back to the land of the immortals.

She walked across the stone tiles of the throne room and into the reception hall, the guards following. Claudia halted at the top of the steps and looked around the courtyard. She could see the glow of oil lamps coming from behind the shutters of the headquarters building where the sacred standards of the Durans and Exiles – the golden griffin and silver lion – were housed under constant guard. Even at this hour the palace never slept: stable hands on night duty were checking stalls and cleaning saddlery, guards patrolled the walls and slaves were preparing the ovens in the bakery. She walked down the steps, sentries beside the columns snapping to attention as she did so. She crossed the courtyard, her escort following, and headed towards the closed gates, stopping when she reached the granite plaque set in the wall near the entrance to the Citadel. The duty centurion came from the guardroom beside the gates and saluted.

'Is everything all right, your majesty?'

Claudia turned away from the plaque. 'Have a torch brought here.'

'Torch for the queen,' the centurion shouted at the guardroom, his deep voice shattering the pre-dawn quiet.

A legionary in a white tunic, mail shirt and helmet rushed from the guardroom with a lighted torch in his hand. He saluted the centurion and passed it to his superior. The centurion slipped his vine cane into his belt and took the torch.

'Hold it near the plaque,' Claudia told him.

The granite slab was cast in a red glow as the centurion moved the flame nearer the stone so Claudia could read the names.

'You know the story of the Companions, centurion?'

He nodded. 'Yes, majesty. The one hundred and twenty followers of your parents, the king and queen, who came from over the seas to fight beside King Pacorus and Queen Gallia.'

Claudia studied the columns of names carved into the stone.

'One hundred and twenty men and women,' she said. The centurion nodded.

'Which would make one hundred and twenty-two in total, including my father and mother.'

'Yes, majesty.'

'But there are one hundred and twenty-three names carved on this stone.'

'Majesty?'

Claudia ran her fingers over the names of her mother and father, the latter having been recently carved.

'One hundred and twenty-three,' she said to herself as her eyes settled on one name: Burebista. She smiled. Even though

500

he had never set foot in Dura her father had not forgotten that the Dacian was also a Companion, the band of brothers and sisters who had helped to make this city among the strongest in the Parthian Empire.

'Thank you, centurion,' she said.

The torch bearer bowed his head and retreated back to the guardroom. Soon the Citadel would be stirring, soldiers assembling in front of the barracks for roll call prior to another day of duties, clerks arriving from the city to work in the treasury, palace and headquarters' building and a long line of petitioners outside the palace who would attempt to bribe, flatter and impress her chief advisers. Perhaps today she would take a break from royal duties and accompany the Amazons on their daily training exercises. It had been a while since she had felt the wind in her hair while shooting a bow from the saddle. Too long. She would take her mother's bow and wear her mother's sword at her hip.

Claudia turned and headed back to the palace, her escort close behind. The duty centurion stood outside the guardroom, gently tapping his cane against his thigh. He watched the queen and her small party ascend the steps and disappear into the palace. The courtyard was empty, the Citadel was quiet and all was as it should be in the city of Dura.

Historical notes

Following their liberation from Roman captivity Burebista and Anca returned to Dacia. But their hopes of a simple, happy life were dashed as he was drawn into Dacian politics. His military expertise meant his services were in great demand and he was soon successfully leading Dacian armies against the Celts that threatened his country from the northwest. He defeated them in 60–59BC, after which he was offered the leadership of all the Dacian tribes.

After 55BC Burebista conquered all the Greek cities on the west coast of the Black Sea, including Histria, thereby increasing the economic strength of Dacia as a whole. Records of the time allude to him leading Dacian armies up to 200,000 strong. Whatever the truth it is a fact that Burebista crushed the Celtic tribes to the northwest and southwest of Dacia after 48BC. While Burebista ruled no Roman army dared threaten Dacia. Soon after 44BC however, jealous nobles assassinated Burebista and the Dacian confederacy quickly fell apart.

Ephesus continued to prosper under Roman rule, entering a 'golden era' following the accession to power of the Emperor Augustus in 27BC. Augustus made it the capital of the Roman province of Asia and it received the title 'First and Greatest Metropolis of Asia'. During his reign Ephesus became the third largest city in the Roman Empire after Rome and Alexandria. It reportedly had a population of over 200,000 people and prospered as a centre of commerce, learning and religious devotion.

The city went into relative decline in the second and third centuries AD as the Roman Empire was assaulted by external foes. However, it was earthquakes and malarial mosquitoes that finally finished Ephesus as a population centre, sometime between the sixth and tenth century. Today Ephesus is a magnificent ruin in western Turkey but only a single stone column of the once mighty Temple of Artemis is extant.

And what of Dura Europos? Long after the reign of King Pacorus had ended, in 165AD the Roman Emperor Lucius Verus captured the city. Thereafter it became a garrison of the empire, though the Romans allowed the locals to retain their customs as long as they paid their taxes. Dura fell to the

Sassanid Persians in 256AD, the city subsequently being looted and abandoned. In the following centuries the name Dura Europos was completely forgotten.

But in April 1920 Indian troops under British command, battling local Arab tribesmen in the aftermath of the disintegration of the Ottoman Empire following World War I, dug in on a piece of high ground beside the River Euphrates. As they dug their trenches they came across ancient paintings showing Middle Eastern faces and uniforms alongside Roman priests and soldiers. Within two years the site had been extensively excavated, and there were subsequently ten major archaeological digs between 1928 and 1937. In the early 1980s a major Franco-Syrian project at Dura unearthed some significant finds. Excavations were resumed in 1986 and continued until recently.

True to Pacorus' wishes the city became a melting pot of different races and religions. During the many excavations inscriptions have been found in Greek, Latin, Aramaic, Hebrew, Syrian, Palmyrenean, Safaitic, Pahlavi and Persian.

Many artifacts were also unearthed as Dura slowly revealed its secrets. Among them was a damaged granite plaque that had been inscribed with many different names, the purpose and significance of which left archaeologists baffled. They identified Greek, Gallic, Spanish, Thracian and Dacian names, we well as Parthian monikers. Above the names was a single word in larger, bolder letters:

COMPANIONS

DISCARD

DISCARD

44686436R00279

Made in the USA
Lexington, KY
06 September 2015